BY THE SAME AUTHOR

Dark Glasses
The Ballad of the Yorkshire Ripper
The Yellow House
And When Did You Last See Your Father?
As If
The Cracked Pot
Too True
Selected Poems
The Justification of Johann Gutenberg
Things My Mother Never Told Me
Oedipus/Antigone

# SOUTH OF THE RIVER

# SOUTH OF THE RIVER

Blake Morrison

Chatto & Windus
LONDON

Published by Chatto & Windus 2007

4 6 8 10 9 7 5 3

Copyright © Blake Morrison 2007

First published in Great Britain in 2007 by
Chatto & Windus
Random House, 20 Vauxhall Bridge Road,
London SW1V 2SA

www.randomhouse.co.uk

Addresses for companies within The Random House Group Limited can be
found at: www.randomhouse.co.uk/offices.htm

The Random House Group Limited Reg. No. 954009

A CIP catalogue record for this book
is available from the British Library

ISBN 9780701180461

The Random House Group Limited makes every effort to
ensure that the papers used in its books are made
from trees that have been legally sourced from
well-managed and credibly certified forests. Our
paper procurement policy can be found at:
www.randomhouse.co.uk/paper.htm

Typeset by Palimpsest Book Production Limited,
Grangemouth, Stirlingshire
Printed and bound in Great Britain by
Clays Ltd, St Ives plc

For Gabriel

'There are many, and also the most part, that creep after his way and his hole . . . Though they have no red beards, yet there are found more foxes now than ever were heretofore. The righteous people are all lost . . . I wot not what end shall come to us hereof . . .'

*History of Reynard the Fox*, translated and printed
by William Caxton, 1481

# CONTENTS

# Part 1

## *New Dawn*

2 May 1997

## *LIBBY*

HALF A decade later, as she stood by a high window ready to throw herself out, what Libby would remember of that day wasn't the dinner-table conversation with her husband, or the footage of Tony Blair waving to the crowds, or even the interview with the man who would become her lover. It was the fox she saw at first light, leaving its tracks across the dew-white grass.

The fox was large, brassy and, despite a slight limp, horribly robust. She shivered as she watched from the bedroom window. A male, probably: too big for a vixen; too big, really, for a fox. There were more of them every year, more and larger. They already had the run of the garden – digging up plants, shitting on the patio, stealing any item (toys, gloves, trainers) accidentally left out. 'If they catch us, will we be eaten, Mummy?' Hannah and Rose sometimes asked. 'Don't be silly,' she told them, without conviction. It wasn't rational to be afraid of foxes. But what was rational about foxes living in a city? Not just living in but occupying, controlling, taking over. She shivered again, then banged on the window. The fox turned its head and stared back: Fuck you, lady, I'll do as I please. She banged again, to no effect. Then something next door caught its attention and off it went, up and over the garden fence with practised ease. A pigeon croo-crooed from the roof, soothing as cough medicine. But there were prints on Libby's small back lawn. Today was going to be difficult. And the fox seemed a bad omen.

Behind her, under the duvet, Hannah and Rose lay sleeping either side of Nat. They had appeared an hour ago, complaining of sore throats; Nat, staying late at Deborah's election party, had crawled in not long before them. What if the girls were too ill to go to school? Once dosed with Calpol they had nodded off, but soon it would be time to wake them. Millie, the live-out nanny, was 'marvellous', everybody said. Any nanny who stuck the job for a month without committing infanticide was likely to earn the adjective, but in Millie's case it was true. Still, Millie had a hospital appointment and wouldn't be around till after three. And though Libby herself sometimes worked from home on Fridays, today was the SaxonAir meeting, which she couldn't afford to miss. There were no friends she could turn to, either, at such short notice. Which left only Nat – and the prospect of eight hours' mayhem.

If only I'd skipped Deborah's party, she thought, slipping into the shower, I wouldn't feel so tired. That American woman annoyed me, too, across the buffet table: 'Don't you feel conflicted,' she said, 'working full-time and having young kids?' It was an aside, unmalicious, a conversation-filler between the exit polls and the first results. Libby was used to worse. Cold, people called her. Hard as nails. A ball-breaker. Not to her face, naturally. But she knew – from sly jokes and overheard remarks. But when the American woman implied, between forkfuls of roast peppers, that because she worked long hours she couldn't love her children, Libby came close to losing her cool.

She had moved away rather than reply. The love she felt for Hannah and Rose needed no defence. She would not have expected it. Might not even have chosen it. But couldn't help it. She had been intrigued, during her first pregnancy, when a brown line appeared down the middle of her stomach, like longitude, and could remember thinking: I'm a globe, a planet; in my keeping lies a vast population of one. Men didn't understand. They saw that line running from breasts to vagina and it confirmed what they thought already: that this was a woman's only roadmap, her $A-Z$ or (since there was nothing between those two poles to interest them) her $A-B$. For women, the line marked the discovery of new hemispheres; the world took on a different shape. Whether you worked or not was irrelevant. Once you were a mother, nothing was the same.

One towel round her head, another knotted at her breast, she tiptoed from the fogged-up bathroom and stood in front of the bedroom mirror. Only a couple of stretch marks, no visible cellulite, crow's feet barely apparent in the curtained light. No grey hairs in the auburn, either. And she was slim, thanks to the exercise bike and her genes: Thin Libby. But she had lost the bloom that made men lust for her through her twenties. Nat, luster-in-chief, had aged, too, of course. But there was still something unlived-in about him. Whereas she, or so she feared, was wearing less well.

'Time to get up, everyone,' she said, to the three-headed monster in the bed. A groan from Nat was the only response. He had come back from Deborah's silly-drunk, blabbering stuff about history being made. Sod history – when your children are ill, your hair's wet, you're stressed about work and you've a headache, history doesn't amount to a bean. I've more important things to think about than a change of government, she thought. More important, that is, to me.

'Come on, *up*,' she said, and coaxed her two children – three children – down to breakfast. The day hung in the balance over Weetabix and scrambled egg: were Hannah and Rose really ill? Or merely disoriented by spending yesterday at home, the school having been requisitioned as a polling station? Nat, hungover, unshaven, in pyjamas, felt as desperate as she did – Fridays were his writing day, he had a lunch with Harry to go to, and if forced to play nanny for a few hours he would pay Libby back tonight with mournful sermons on the incompatibility of parenting and artistic creation, 'the damp dishcloths of household duty snuffing out the flame of inspiration', etc. Household duty? Nat? He might vaguely offer to help sometimes ('help', see: as if his role was purely voluntary), but tidying up mess didn't come naturally to him; creating it did. How someone who spent so much time at home could be so undomesticated was one of life's mysteries.

'No daughter of mine is going to school if she feels sick,' Libby said, pouring out more orange juice. The trick was to insist they stay at home while implying how brave and clever it would be if they didn't. At 8.20, Hannah announced she was feeling better and went off to get dressed; Rose, with a little prodding, followed. By 8.40, with cheese sandwiches, crisps and apple juice in their lunch boxes, Libby was heading out the door with them, leaving Nat to not get on with his writing.

Bankside Primary was less than half a mile away and unless the weather was freakishly bad Libby liked to go on foot, the last mother in London to walk her kids to school. Today the sky was clear, the heat unseasonal, the air unnervingly bright. Even the sun over the roofs looked freshly minted. Not a day to rush, but the meeting with SaxonAir was scheduled for ten and she wanted to brief her colleagues beforehand. The account was large and the client unhappy. No wonder she had slept so badly, even before the girls climbed into bed. If Nat had a proper job it wouldn't matter, but the family depended on her earnings.

'Will you spend a day with us soon?' Hannah asked.

'I'll be home all weekend.'

'I mean at school.'

'Of course, sweetie. When things have settled down a bit.'

Other mothers put in time as classroom volunteers. Hannah and Rose kept pressing her to do the same. And she would have liked to, if only to see how the school worked. Because it wasn't working, for Hannah and Rose, that was the thing. Oh, they weren't unhappy – consented to attend most days, had acquired friends who invited them to parties and sleepovers, knew more about the Chinese New Year and Indian deities than she did. Which was great. She just wished that they could read. They were seven and five now, and surely ought to be reading. She blamed herself: if only she had more time, if only when she did have time she wasn't so exhausted. But reading was part of the curriculum – surely the school had responsibilities too. When she raised the subject with Mrs Swayne, the head teacher, at the last parents' evening, she had been made to feel pushy. But was it pushy to think a child of seven should be reading? In her day, hadn't it been more or less expected? What Libby remembered from school in Ballymena was symmetry: desks in neat rows, hair tied in bunches, a rectangular blackboard dominating each classroom. Whereas the ethos at Bankside was chaos by any other name. 'Unconfining', Mrs Swayne called it: in the informal, progressive, *unconfining* atmosphere of Bankside, children could thrive. To Libby, Ballymena was the better model. But to find it these days you had to go private, which she lacked the money for and, even if she had it, would have resisted. Look what private school had done to Nat.

Still, at least Nat could read.

At the school gates she secured her escape through counter-suggestion.

'You look a bit pale, Hannah. Shall I take you home to Daddy?'

'I'm fine,' Hannah said.

'And I'm even finer,' Rose said.

'Well, OK, then. But you must go to Mrs Swayne if you're unwell.'

She kissed them both, then turned guiltily away and headed down the hill towards the station, wondering, as she always did at this point of the day, why she chose to live south of the river when from Islington or Hackney she could be at her desk in twenty minutes. In a year or two, the Docklands Light Railway would be extended to Lewisham but till then she had to go overground to London Bridge then on the tube via Bank, a cumbersome journey at the best of times and there were few of those.

On the train she took out her mobile and called Angie. According to the rules of middle-class commuting, mothers used mobiles to fix piano lessons or remind Ingrid to take the puréed carrot out of the freezer, not to call their PA. But Libby's life ran counter to the rules. This morning, like most mornings, was a crisis. She couldn't not work on the way to work.

'I'm running late,' she said.

'You stayed up, then?' Angie said.

'Why, do I *sound* tired?'

'For the election.'

'Oh, that.'

Libby knew she ought to take more interest, but elections were a boy thing, like football.

'No messages?' Libby said.

'Nothing that won't keep.'

In advertising, nothing kept. If you had a thought you had to act on it, before your rival thought it. Even instantaneity was too slow.

'Tell me.'

'Annie Cleeve called. I said you'd phone her once you were in.'

Angie was protecting her. She didn't want to be protected.

'Because?'

'The ChildPlanet ad came out smudged.'

'Just that?'

'It was in the Arts Section and they asked for News. She was a bit upset.'

'She didn't shout, did she?'

'Just put the phone down on me.'

'Bitch. I'd better call her.'

Saying sorry always strengthened the client relationship. The pie principle, Libby called it: eat humble and they would be nice as.

'Oh, and if the SaxonAir people get there before me,' she told Angie, 'give them coffee in the conference room. With croissants and stuff. Make a fuss.'

She hung up, suddenly conscious of other passengers listening in while pretending to read their newspapers.

Disembarking at London Bridge, she noticed, with a pang, that the outbound train at the next platform would be calling at the station she had just come from. For a moment she considered catching it and journeying back to a life she'd never known, as a stay-at-home, unconflicted mother. Then she headed for the Underground as fast as she could.

2

## JACK

THE FAMILY of Raven had been long settled in East Anglia. For centuries they raised cattle in the meadows by the Waveney, the sluggish river which divides the counties of Suffolk and Norfolk. But then great-great grandfather set up a sideline in agricultural machinery, and as it grew so the cattle, the land and finally the farmhouse were sold off. For the past eighty years the family business had been light engineering. The works stood where one of the outlying barns used to be, next to the B-road between Harchope and Frixley. Parking his Jaguar in the usual space, Jack snuffed the air as if he owned it. On a morning like this – blue skies, wide horizons, the barometer settled on Sunny – he liked to forget he was the MD of a small company, and to imagine himself ploughing and tilling his loamy acres: a gentleman farmer of the old breed.

The fax was waiting for him on his desk. One skim was enough: '. . . enjoyed our recent meeting and hope your flight back . . . highly competitive market . . . more attractive rival bids . . . regret to say . . . no reflection on the quality of your . . . feel sure that as the economic climate changes . . . hope that it won't jeopardise our personal friendship . . . trust that if you and Nancy are passing through Toulouse this summer you will . . . yours ever, Luc.'

Jack's instinct was to tear it up, but Hook would have to see it, and then it would need to be filed. He left it on his desk and walked to the window. In the yard below, two men in oily blue overalls were wheeling welding equipment into one of the sheds. Horace Sanders and the young Kinder boy, it looked like. Good lads, anyway. They were all good lads. But spirits were hard to keep up when the orders weren't coming in, and when word got round of the non-emergence of the SGS contract morale would suffer. Four hundred thousand quid down the pan. With the loss of that Belgian contract last week, and two smaller ones in Germany, that made Raven & Son nearly one million under-budget. What a start to the financial year. Four long-standing customers gone in a month. Last year's turnover had sunk from £2.1 million to £1.4, which was bad enough. But at least they were in profit, just. Whereas 1997–8, at this rate . . . it didn't bear thinking of. Eight rows of green machines sat in the far corner of the yard, alarmed and chained to discourage the local hoodlums. Eight rows of fifty. Four hundred machines at a RRP of £749.99–£300,000 worth, of which Raven & Son might see a third and, after wages and overheads, make a profit of £20,000. That was supposing someone bought them. Those four hundred had been meant for Belgium, but the bastards had pulled out a week before delivery. Luc had been less insultingly last-minute, which was to be expected when they had known each other for fifteen years. 'Personal friendship' came a bit rich all the same. A personal friend would have had the guts to telephone. A personal friend would have stood firm during difficulties which weren't the fault of the supplier. A personal friend wouldn't go running off to one's rivals. But it was true SGS had been muttering about the 'expense' of Jack's machines for at least two years. The problem wasn't Luc but his board. Business moved fast these days, and even the French were in a hurry. The rivals undercutting Raven & Son were almost certainly those Dutch arseholes, Luffnest or whatever they were called, the ones who used plastic covers rather than metal. Duff workmanship, anyone could see. When their machines fell apart six months from now and the customers began screaming at local agents and SGS lost its reputation for quality, then Luc would come crawling back, beret in hand. But in the meantime Jack was in the shit.

He peered miserably at the rest of the post – flyers and invoices, not a single new order, let alone a cheque. Was his mistake to have narrowed the business to mowers? And not just any old mowers, but traditional petrol-driven cylinder mowers with two- or four-stroke engines? Hapgood, Proctor & Raven (later Raven & Son) had originally made all manner of products – steam engines, threshing machines, circular saws, road rollers, power pumps, and corn-grinding mills – but then John-Joseph Junior, aka grandfather, an amateur driving enthusiast who competed at Thruxton and Brooklands, began to specialise in car engines, and launched the Viking Warrior in 1920. The only buyers were family friends and fellow enthusiasts – barely half a dozen cars came out of the factory in a year. Yet Raven & Son retained its good name as a maker of quality engines. And a government contract to develop 'a motorised cycle sturdy enough to flourish in adverse conditions' kept it going through the war. Convinced the future lay in motorbikes – that it would be decades before British working men were able to afford family cars – Jack's father launched the Viking Arrow (Mark I) in 1949, on Jack's twelfth birthday, with the slogan 'Quality Bikes for Family Types'. Hopes were high that the Arrow would catch on. But the only buyers were 500cc enthusiasts. A wife, two children and dog couldn't be accommodated in a sidecar. And by the end of the 1950s, the small family car became affordable after all.

'Here's your tea,' Karen said, scurrying out almost before she'd put the mug down. To have a secretary so finely attuned to one's mood was consoling. In thirty years, there'd been only three of them: Irene, whom he'd inherited from the old man; Michelle, who'd succeeded her in 1980; and for the past decade and more Karen. It was Michelle who'd seen the best years. Newly appointed, she'd gone with him on a recce to the Paris Show, when he first saw the potential of selling to Europe. By then mowers, originally a sideline, were Raven & Son's sole product. From cars to motorbikes to mowers: the bathos of it broke the old man's heart. But Jack could read a balance sheet and knew he had no option. The Paris Show was his breakthrough. No other British mower company bothered to attend. You were lucky to *see* a lawn in France or Germany, so what was the point? Cheap plastic Flymos or lumbering sit-ons were all they used. That was the common wisdom. Defying it, Jack took a stand in 1982 and brought his new model – the Greensleeves Three – and sat it on a bed of real turf. There was a long wrangle with French customs about importing the turf, but thanks to Michelle's persistence they eventually gave him the go-ahead, 'for trade exhibition purposes only'. The turf, rather than the mower, was what did it: its stripes were manicured, watered and spotlit, to emphasise the symmetry and sheen. The classic English mower for the classic English lawn: that was the pitch. The French and Germans loved it; the Dutch, Spanish, Italians and Scandinavians, too. A word-of-mouth thing happens at every trade fair, and the word in Paris in 1982 was Greensleeves. Michelle – mid-thirties, strawberry blonde, freckles, cornflower eyes, snub nose – was the perfect accompaniment; chaps from Malmö to Milan queued up to inhale her Englishness. They had appointments back to back from breakfast till close of play. Three major new contracts followed, Jack's first in Europe, one of them with Luc.

Exciting times. What had gone wrong? The strengthening pound was part of it. But other British exporters seemed to get by, and the exchange rate didn't explain Raven & Son's dwindling share of the home market. He blamed himself for taking his eye off the ball. Michelle's sudden departure was a turning point. She was only a secretary, and yet . . .

Karen, buzzing through, broke his train of thought: your wife for you, sir. Nancy had been under the weather lately, and when this morning he carried a tray up to her in bed – tea and toast, on her favourite blue china (Real Old Willow, Swinnerton, Staffs.) – she had slept on, lost in white, till he kissed her goodbye. Hard to say what the trouble was. But since her back began playing up a year ago, she had stopped taking the dog for walks and put on weight. Poor Nancy: the handspan waist was gone; the hourglass had become a pear; her flesh wobbled like a bouncy castle. Her only exercise was gardening and even that (to use her word) left her 'shattered'.

'How you feeling?' he asked, down the line.

'Not bad. Bit stiff.'

'You've been overdoing the weeding again.'

'Who else is there to do it?'

'I could find you someone,' he said, ignoring the dig and running some names through his head, young chaps in need of extra cash who wouldn't mind doing the heavy stuff – leaving Nancy the fun bits, whatever they were. For himself, gardening held no attraction. He would not go as far as Sammy, his ten-year-old Labrador, who saw the garden as a place for pissing on. But a space one-tenth the size – patio, fishpond, sundial, trellis thick with honeysuckle and clematis, lawn that could be mown in five minutes – would suit him fine.

'No other symptoms?' he said, back on her health.

'The odd shooting pain in my arm,' she said. 'Nothing serious.'

'Shall I call the surgery for you?'

'No. I wasn't ringing to whinge. I forgot to tell you earlier – the girls from the tennis club are coming for lunch.'

'So I've to stay away.'

'Don't be silly, I thought you might come and join us. I expect you need cheering up.'

For a second he thought she meant the SGS contract. But how would she know about that?

'I just heard on the radio,' she added. 'Everyone predicted they'd win, but–'

'Oh, that.'

'I didn't expect a landslide.'

'No.'

'Did Freddy Finch get in?'

'Don't know. But it's Friday,' he said, changing the subject, 'and on Fridays I go to the George.'

'Skip it for once. I'm sure the girls would love to see you. Oh, and the other thing is . . .'

In the old days, the other thing was that she loved him and sometimes rang to say so and to urge him to 'Come home early for a change', so that (this she didn't say) they could go to bed. Now all that was past, which made them gentle with each other, as though the loss of sex was a shared grief, like the death of a good friend. No one's fault and no hard feelings: that was understood.

'. . . the light bulb in the living room: you've still not changed it.'

The sodding light bulb. Had she nothing better to do than nag him?

'Damn. Sorry. I'll do it tonight. Tomorrow anyway. This weekend for sure.'

Why couldn't she do it? But Nancy was shaky on stepladders. Or stepladders were shaky under her.

'So you'll come for lunch?'

'I'll try.'

'And if not, when will I see you?'

'Oh, the usual.'

The usual was six but seven on Fridays.

'OK, love, see you later.'

'Love' was her current mode of endearment. When love had been there in all its intensity, she had called him 'dear'.

Ten-fifteen. Time to get on. He must find a buyer for those machines in the yard. Offer a hefty discount. Cold-call some potential clients. He had already put out some feelers, after the loss of the Belgian order last week. But the positive responses were few, and all 'positive' meant was *not actually being told to fuck off*. If he felt stronger after lunch, he would make some calls. In the meantime he had better see Hook, the foreman, and let him know the score. Jack had a soft spot for Hook, bolshie though he was: better a foreman who stuck up for the workforce than one who sucked up to the boss. But he wasn't in the mood for conflict.

He stood at the window again, above the yard. It was the tea break and the lads – all thirty-four of them by the look of it – had gathered outside, sitting on oil drums and wooden crates. Lots of laughter down there: because the weekend was coming, and the day was warm, and for some of them (though surely no more than a handful) the election of a Labour government was good news. The laughter would stop, once they heard the worst from Hook. Who'd work for a family business, in the nineties? Who'd *run* a family business? Maybe the time had come to step down. But he had no son to take over, and neither Sasha (with her art history) nor Ischia (with her IT skills) had the makings of an entrepreneur. Nor did Nathaniel, his nephew, the only other living male Raven, who did some half-cock teaching job in London.

One day he would sell the business. But not till he had exhausted all the options. He owed it to his workers. And to his ancestors. And to himself.

## 3

## ANTHEA

SOMEONE MUST have complained about Anthea Hurt because without having done anything wrong she now faced the sack. It must be the slob whose application she'd turned down the other day, the one who'd muttered 'bureaucratic lesbian bitch' as she left and to whom, in return, she'd given the finger. It had occurred to her to report him to Personnel. The public weren't allowed to abuse council staff, any more than they were railway guards or traffic wardens. But he had said it quickly and under his breath and, if challenged, would doubtless deny it. He was a fat, grease-haired car dealer with a hundred-year holm oak in his garden, which he wanted to supplant with a swimming pool. His manner, as they roamed the plot, had been a mixture of sycophantic and combative, with a bit of flirtation thrown in. He had only become angry when she warned him of the unlikelihood of his application succeeding: conservation area, need to protect character of local environment, longevity of the tree in question, which appeared to be in good health, etc. Even when he began to rant about the injustice – the bloke next door who'd put a swimming pool in his garden: how come *he*'d been allowed, etc. – the anger wasn't directed at her. Till she took out her keys and got in the car, at which point he hissed, or possibly hissed, 'bureaucratic lesbian bitch', and she, driving off, not thinking he would see, gave him the finger.

Lesbian? As she'd joked to Rachel, recounting the story, how did *he* know? Was it the trousers, nose rings, short hair or indifference to his flirting? Part of her had felt pleased rather than insulted: as though all that were open to her again, if she chose. All? It had only been a phase. Every half-alive woman at Plymouth Uni circa 1990 had experimented with same-sex sex, either from curiosity or despair with men or both. In her case, it had been just twice. Al was a one-night stand. But the relationship with Sam drifted from one term to the next. Not that she'd not slept with a boy or two, on the sly. And there was always Jake in the background, whom she'd known since the sixth form and half believed she was still in love with, useless though he was. By Christmas of her second year, she'd done lesbianism. She hadn't much missed it or thought about it since. Still, in the right circumstances, with the right woman . . . The slob was wiser than he knew. But that was no reason to abuse her. She ought to have lodged a complaint against him, before he lodged one against her. Because Mr Norland had now asked her to come to his office, and no one went to Mr Norland's office unless they were about to be sacked.

She slipped downstairs to the front of her building, to call Rachel on her new mobile. She'd have phoned from the office, but some fascist in Accounts was rumoured to be tracking personal calls. There was a No Smoking rule, too, which was why the council's front steps were always crowded. She walked a few steps away, not wanting to suffocate or be overheard.

'Hi, Rach: how's the head?'

'Fine. How's yours?'

'Absolutely wonderful, except that I'm about to be sacked. Old Nod wants to see me.'

'Maybe he wants to promote you.'

'They don't promote Tree Officers. There's nowhere to promote us to.'

'Or give you a pay rise.'

'They don't do pay rises, either. We're on a fixed scale. Chickenfeed increasing to peanuts after thirty years' service.'

'Maybe he wants to ask you out, then.'

'It's not funny, Rach. You should see him. I'd *rather* be sacked.'

It was rumoured that Mr Norland had a penchant for parading round his living room in a wetsuit and flippers. Anthea didn't believe it. Even so.

'When are you due to see him?'

'In ten minutes.'

'Well, call me back after – I'm sure you'll be fine.'

She wished there was someone she could talk to at work. But, as she'd explained to Rachel, when you share an office with a corpse, a serial killer and a Stasi agent, conversation doesn't come easy. Maria, who 'headed up' Burials, came to life only when showing off her holiday snaps, mostly of churchyards. Gerald was clearly working in Sewage in order to dispose of his victims. And Helga, whose patch was Leisure, divided her time between listening in on others' phone calls and bullying child-sports organisers to raise a master race of athletes. True, there was a portion of the day – lunchtime – when Anthea merely disliked her colleagues rather than loathing them. But that was only because they weren't around, and she could read in peace. It would be a relief to escape them permanently. If it weren't for the loss of a salary. And her pride.

At eleven fifteen, she presented herself on the seventh floor. As Head of Planning, Old Nod was grand enough to have a secretary, Rilda, who asked Anthea to sit down 'till Mr Norland becomes available', though what prevented him being available at once wasn't apparent: she could see him sitting at his desk, seemingly (which would make a change) with both eyes open. Rilda went on with her typing, the clickety-click of it helping to conceal her boss's inactivity. After five more minutes of intense unavail-ability, Old Nod finally roused himself, glanced up, spotted Anthea and beckoned her in with his left hand: to get out of his chair and come through to greet her would have been a civility too far. As she entered, the left hand moved again, to indicate a chair, and the eyebrows shifted upwards. How did people in power – most of whom were stupid, lazy, insensitive and discourteous – get to be in power in the first place, she wondered, preparing herself for the worst.

'Good of you to come,' he said. 'A phone call would have done it, really, but there's nothing to beat seeing people in person.'

Anthea could think of several things that beat seeing Nod in person, and resolved to list them for his benefit once he'd sacked her.

'I get so little chance to meet the team,' he added, before the phone went and he picked it up. Anthea took this as a hopeful sign. If Rilda knew that Nod was about to sack her, wouldn't she be screening calls? Soon find out – though at the rate things were moving (with Nod asking after whoever-it-was-on-the-line's wife and children and second cousins on the in-law side) she'd be lucky to know by next week. But the caller must have become impatient, too, because Nod was soon reduced to listening, his patter a mere 'No . . . no . . . no, of course . . . I can see that . . . no, yes, well, I do understand' until with a flourish of 'a great disappointment – we'll have to make other plans' the call was over. 'Sorry about that,' he said, looking as crestfallen as expressionlessness allowed. Whether a dinner party had fallen through, or the council's favourite building contractor had gone bankrupt, she couldn't tell.

'As I was saying, I meant to send you a memo,' he went on. (Had he been saying that? Or anything remotely like it?) 'There's a meeting this afternoon about the Hardhill Estate. Ways to regenerate it, how to make use of the central funding we've secured, and so on. I'd like you to come along. Give us the tree angle.'

'There are no trees at Hardhill.'

'Just my point: should we have 'em?'

'I usually brief Mrs Loss for meetings.'

'She's on holiday this week, see. No one to look after Environment. Which is why I'm asking you. Two thirty in the Council Chamber. Good. I'll let you get on.'

Meaning that she must now let him get on, which he wouldn't but she did. At the door, suddenly grateful to him for having spared her, she turned back to give him a smile, but he was once again engrossed in inertia. Nod was certainly efficient at getting rid of people. Though not in the way she'd anticipated, thank God. And not in a way that could disguise his lack of efficiency in other respects: he must have known Mrs Loss was away but had left it till now to ask Anthea to stand in. It must be a test, she realised. He'd invited her along because a new job was being created and he wanted to assess her talents. Or because an existing job was being axed, ditto. More likely the latter. By the end of today, she could still be jobless after all.

Outside the lift, before returning to her desk, she gazed through the windows at the car park below. There was her car, snug in its space, a Fiat Punto – 58,000 miles on the clock, two owners only, a snip – which she'd bought to facilitate her visits assessing tree applications, council policy being to refund all expenses incurred during work hours, provided that these were for 'legitimate and authorised purposes only' and were claimed within twenty-eight days by submission of the appropriate form, 'which must include receipts, mileage details, address of locations travelled to and from, brief description of duties undertaken, precise time of arrival and departure, and the signature of the relevant department head'. Anthea Hurt, Tree Officer (Assistant Grade). How did she get into this? Beyond the car park, outside the nursery school, a group of heavy-weary mothers were crossing over with their young towards McDonald's, like a herd of bison heading for a waterhole. The mothers must be, what, thirty at most. At their age, what would Anthea be doing? Not bringing up kids, that was for sure. Nor working for the council, or *any* council. What then? A director of nature documentaries had been the original plan, which was why she took Media Studies and Ecology as joint honours. But to work in film or television you had to be confident and the shyness that had afflicted her at school didn't evaporate at university. She imagined herself as a park ranger in the Scottish Highlands or forests of Wales, far from human habitation. But after Plymouth she'd ended up following Jake to London and, till the relationship broke up, studying to be a teacher. Then the Tree Officer job came up. She hadn't much wanted it but she was offered it and in a spirit of let's-try-and-see she took it. Here she was two years later, with a rented flat in Carshalton and a Fiat Punto. A checkout girl could earn more. And after this afternoon's meeting, a checkout girl was what she might have to become.

She rushed to her desk. There was only one file to clear and then she could mug up on Hardhill. The file lay open where she left it. Case 17958B: the unauthorised pruning of a tree in Marshmoor Gardens. She had visited last week and taken photos. Acacia. False acacia, in fact, *Robinia pseudoacacia*. Spring-flowering, with fragrant white flowers and pinnate leaves, then those bristly grey-green peapods in late summer. American originally. Hard to establish. Subject to wind damage. This one must have stood forty feet high, dominating the house (twigs in the gutters, shadows in the room), till the owners, without permission, had it lopped. She'd never seen one with so large a girth. But everything above the trunk had gone, apart from a handful of smaller branches whimsically left behind as though to hide the evidence. It looked like a toddler's drawing of the human body – a torso sprouting spindly arms. Some hardline environmentalists argued that trees had the same rights as humans. Didn't they have arms, hands, veins, skin, a body? If you wounded them, did they not bleed? If you choked them, did they not die? For a time – when she first came to London to live with Jake – Anthea had thought the same. There was a demo one weekend, in Wanstead, to save a 250-year-old sweet chestnut on George Green from being felled to make way for the M11. The day was warm and bright, and she and Jake stayed past midnight, roosting in the branches. Her tree-hugging phase, Rachel called it, and even Anthea had been careful not to mention it when she went for the job, fearing the council would see it as a disqualification. She was over it now, just as she was over Jake. But the massacre of a tree made her furious. And she'd never seen a tree as brutalised as that acacia last week.

She ought to take the couple to court and teach them a lesson. They were old, though, and distraught at what had happened. The cowboys who cut the acacia had taken their money and scarpered, without trace. What was the point in hounding a sad old couple? The shame of a fine would probably kill them and couldn't restore the beauty of that tree.

Soft touch, Anthea. Nod *ought* to sack her. But she hadn't the heart or the leisure to be punitive. '26 April 1997,' she wrote on the file. '45 Marshmoor Gardens. Report of excessive pruning. Tree officer AH investigated. Conversation with owners re employment of qualified tree surgeons in future. Follow-up letter sent out, 2 May. No further action required.'

4

*NAT*

IN NAT'S younger, more vulnerable years, his father Ronnie had given him some wise advice. 'Make the most of your advantages,' he said. 'There's more to life than work.' Ronnie had certainly made the most of *his* advantages, leaving his marriage and clearing off to Spain before Nat became a teenager. With his departure, many of Nat's advantages departed, too:

not money so much (his mother was the rich one and enough survived, even after Ronnie had fleeced her, for Nat to go to boarding school). But security, optimism, family life, the friendships he'd made at the local school – these disappeared, and Nat, an only but previously happy child, became a solipsistic adolescent. His one consolation lay in books. And as childhood passed to adulthood, he graduated from reading books to trying to write one.

Some people are Sunday painters. Nat was a Friday writer. Mondays to Thursdays he gave to his students, and weekends to his family, but Fridays were for him. Attic time, he called it, since that's where he sat, at home, under the eaves, in his own headspace, struggling to preserve something of himself for posterity (unlike his father, gone without a trace even before he died). Less gifted colleagues used their free days for academic research. Nat was a creator.

On his door hung a notice pinched from his old school: SILENCE: EXAMINATION IN PROGRESS. The notice had a dual function: to deter members of his family from entering, and to keep himself focused and alert. On a good Friday, his speed of thought and ear for dialogue were amazing, at least to him. Today, though, he was suffering from a headache, and his ears whirred with the tinnitus of a pop song. 'Things Can Only Get Better.' Too right.

If only Deborah had been less generous a hostess. The pain behind his eyes reminded him of the last vodka she'd poured him, though there were surely other, unremembered vodkas after that. He felt like curling up in the basement. That's where he had planned to put his desk when they first moved in, in the dark alcove next to the wood burner. But Libby had grabbed the basement for her kitchen, leaving him an attic study with a view over south London. The sense of omniscience should have been inspiring. But the light through the dormer was too bright and the birdsong from the maple too noisy. He was tired, nauseous and still drunk.

The whole electorate must be the same, he thought, a people at one in alcoholic stupor. He felt like shit.

As a rule, politics didn't interest him. 'That's why you're so keen on Blair,' Harry had taunted him last night. 'He's not interested in politics, either.' Stuff Harry. This was history being made. After eighteen years the old blue blood blister had finally burst. As Nat's glass kept filling up, the announcements from draughty sports halls began to merge – 'I the returning officer for Heartland hereby give notice that . . .' – and the country turned red before his eyes. Even Marcus Fox went, diehard Tory, Chairman of the 1922 Committee, driven out by a fresh-faced local. Out with the old Foxes. In with the new. For the rest of his life, Nat would remember exactly what he was doing last night – at any rate, when his current amnesia wore off he would remember some of it. He'd tried to explain this to Libby, when he climbed into bed. 'Go to sleep,' she said, 'you're drunk.' True. But it was the sense of occasion that had kept him drinking – the map of Britain changing colour, a vast bloodstain leaking down from north.

He had also stayed up for Rufus Huish, whom he knew from school and Oxford and who was standing somewhere in the Midlands. In the event, there'd been no shot of Rufus but when his result flashed up round 2 a.m. – 4,973 maj, LABOUR GAIN – Nat insisted that everyone toast him. Libby had left by then. He ought to have left, too, but Deborah and Travis were still going strong. He could remember the ice in his vodka and thinking what wonderful friends he had. The young MPs with their victory waves might have been in the room, *really* in the room, partying along. And so many identical twins! Only when Deborah, Deborah and Deborah stood in front of him, offering to call a cab, did he realise it was time to go. How he made it home he wasn't sure but the walk must have sobered him up. He could remember getting out of bed for a piss and seeing the sun rise through the bathroom's frosted glass and thinking 'New dawn'. Later, going downstairs for a glass of water and two Nurofen, he turned on the television to double-check he hadn't imagined the landslide, and there was Blair, borne down by private jet from the north-east to greet the faithful on the South Bank with the same words: 'A new dawn has broken, has it not?' It was past five by then and Nat went back to bed. But after Hannah and Rose climbed in beside him, complaining of sore throats, he hadn't really slept. And now he was paying for it.

He stared at the blank screen, reviewing his morning. In the two hours since having the house to himself, he'd done . . . what exactly? Stick the breakfast bowls in the dishwasher (though not the non-stick pan in which Libby had made scrambled eggs, with the yellow layer stuck to the bottom – leave that to Millie). Make himself a mug of tea. Take it upstairs. Turn on his PC. Answer the phone (wrong number). Go down again when the milk float went by at 9.20, to bring in the bottles. Swallow more Nurofen. Make himself more tea. Go back up to his desk. Come down again at 9.55 for the post, and sift through it several times in disbelief that it contained only two items addressed to him (the first an invitation to renew his subscription to a magazine whose last eight issues lay unread, indeed unopened, on his attic floor; the other an electricity bill for £243.39, a figure which, despite its seeming precision, was based on a wild estimate of units consumed, just as the previous two bills had been). Make himself coffee, since he was near the kettle. Answer the phone (another wrong number). Call the agency to whom he intended to send his new play (answering machine only). Call Harry, to check what time he'd booked the restaurant for (no reply at home, and the mobile was switched off, so he'd assume it was one o'clock, but what was the name of the place again – Die Kantine? La Cantonade? Il Contino? – his brain really wasn't in gear today). Sit at his desk. Go for a pee. Make coffee. Swallow more Nurofen . . . In one respect, the list was reassuring: the word 'desk' appeared several times, which was evidence he'd been making an effort. On the other hand, the word 'write' didn't appear once. He refused to feel downcast. Not to work after a night like last night was unsurprising. The main thing was to put yourself there, in readiness. It would come.

*Wilderness Avenue* the new play was called. New-ish: he'd been working on it since his agent, now his former agent, Stefan, had read it in draft and told him to 'make it more sexy'. Sex wasn't Nat's strong point. In his view, sex should happen offstage. Or with the lights down. Or between the lines. He'd tried to be responsive, nevertheless, making particular efforts with the scene in which the hero visits the eponymous road with the intention of buying a house, no. 69 ('You could use that,' Stefan had said), and finds himself in the company of a beautiful widow.

| | |
|---|---|
| YOUNG MAN | If I wanted to get in before anyone else . . . |
| WIDOW | And . . . ? |
| YOUNG MAN | Made an offer, you'd . . . |
| WIDOW | Yes, I'd certainly . . . |
| YOUNG MAN | You'd entertain . . . |
| WIDOW | Entertain an offer, from you, yes. |
| YOUNG MAN | And if I wasn't close enough . . . |
| WIDOW | We'd try to get closer . . . |
| *Pause.* | |
| YOUNG MAN | So. Can we sleep . . . ? |
| WIDOW | Oh yes. |
| YOUNG MAN | Good. Let's sleep on it then. |

'Sexy enough for you now?' Nat asked Stefan, after reading it to him over the phone. Stefan said he hadn't meant sexy-suggestive but sexy-commercial, and ceased to be his agent shortly afterwards, pleading 'overcommitment' to more lucrative authors. Fuck Stefan. When Nat read the house-buying scene aloud to his students, they were enthusiastic, particularly Claire, the most insightful of them. But since he'd not yet found a director, producer, company, venue or agent willing to take on *Wilderness Avenue*, he continued to tinker with the typescript. Tinkering was his speciality. The predecessors to *Wilderness Avenue* were *Terrace of Unhope*, *Desperation Way* and *Lonely Crescent*. Nat was nothing if not consistent. He had been tinkering with the same play – composing, recomposing and decomposing it – for eleven years.

Despite acting in and directing several school plays, he'd begun writing for the theatre comparatively late. Fresh out of Oxford, he published poems in little magazines (minuscule magazines, if the truth be told), before writing a novel about a fat man who falls in love with a very thin woman. He found an agent, sat back and waited for the offers to pour in. When they didn't, he experimented in other forms – stories, screenplays, novellas, even libretti – before eventually turning to plays. Some dramatists get the bug for drama from sitting in theatres. Nat got it from not sitting in theatres – by ostentatiously walking out of West End productions and embarking on a one-man mission to rescue British theatre. His greatest success so far had been *Suicide Alley*, a production of which was mounted by some of his students in a disused warehouse in Deptford. There weren't many takers among the general public. But a couple of agents came along, including Stefan, who believed Nat could make a go of it as a playwright, so long as his plays bore more relation to 'the real world'. Several producers had spoken vaguely of future slots, if Nat could get a script to them, but each time he had missed the deadline. Now Stefan had dumped him, too, for failing to pander to the braying idiots of the West End. More fool Stefan. 'You have to laugh,' Libby liked to say. The comedy of *Wilderness Avenue* wasn't meant to be laugh-out-loud, but subtle, quiet, more or less inaudible. Still, on days like this, when little got written (and most days, these days, were like this), Nat worried that he might be too subtle for his own good.

'How can you expect to write plays when you're such a narcissist?' Libby had shouted the other night, during a row about childcare (she'd had the ridiculous idea that *he* might collect the girls from school on Fridays, thereby saving the expense of Millie doing it). 'Plays need dialogue, and the only voice you listen to is your own.' She had only said it because he was so clearly winning the argument. Besides, in his view Narcissus was an unfairly maligned figure. As he patiently explained to Libby, a writer must protect his headspace, not let it be invaded by piddling distractions such as taking the girls to dance lessons or putting out the rubbish for the binmen. An obvious point, but Libby – whose horizons were horribly narrow these days – couldn't see it. Like Harry, churning out copy for the local newspaper, she had sold her soul to Mammon. Not that Nat would ever rub their noses in it: Libby was his wife, Harry his best friend, and it wasn't their fault that they lacked creativity. But both were morally the worse for *ware*.

I could use that in *Wilderness Avenue*, he thought, before realising no theatre audience would get the pun.

How was a man supposed to create a masterpiece when he was free to write only on Fridays? Giving up teaching would allow Nat all the time he needed. But giving up teaching would also deprive him of what little he earned. Libby claimed not to see what he was 'fussing about': 'Six measly contact hours a week, Nat: what difference would dropping your classes make? At least going to college now and then gets you out of the house.' She was being unfair – a class might last only an hour, but the preparation took twice that, and then there were the phone calls, the assessments, the photocopying, the admin, the sessions down the pub, all of it eating into his free time, his headspace. And of course Libby never understood about creativity – how draining it is on body and mind.

A breakthrough was certain to come sooner or later. But there was no doubt his self-esteem had taken some knocks lately. He was overweight, to start with – the roly-polyism of a sedentary life – and had begun looking for shoes with long pointy ends, like clown's shoes, so that when he looked down he could see his feet again. He had also turned forty, which was unnerving and, he couldn't help feeling, a mistake. At Oxford he had boasted to friends that he would be famous by thirty, notorious by thirty-five and dead by forty: where had it all gone wrong? By the standards of his peers, he was a failure. How was success to be quantified, though? Nat had always defined it inversely: if a book was a best-seller, it couldn't be worth reading; if a record was a hit, it couldn't be worth listening to; if a film made millions at the box office, it couldn't be worth watching. This aesthetic allowed him a happy coexistence with failure.

The challenge would come when he was accepted. For the past two decades, there had been as much likelihood of that as Labour winning a general election. But after last night, he felt hopeful that things would change. It was no coincidence that the dawn celebrations had taken place south of the river, at the Royal Festival Hall. Lambeth, Southwark, Lewisham: the boroughs of south London were famously depressed, but under a new government the whole area would come up and Nat would come up with it. He didn't personally know Blair, who had been three years ahead of him at Oxford. But they would probably find they had friends in common. Invitations would come for soirees at Downing Street. Grants and prizes would go to struggling men of genius. And Nat would be recognised and acclaimed.

Consoled, he let his fingers hover over the keyboard. Time to make the most of his advantages. Things could only get better for Nat Raven.


## 5

## *LIBBY*


LIBBY'S OFFICE at Arran & Arran faced east, downriver to City Airport and the Thames Barrier. There were few more panoramic views in London, and she felt lucky to work where she did. But given that she spent most days on a round of phone calls, meetings and emails, she didn't consider her job particularly exciting. 'Oh, you're in *advertising*,' people enthused, as though advertising had the glamour of the fashion industry. Glamour? When Libby started out, advertising was regarded as squalid. All the Creatives were there by default, killing time until their novel was finished or their screenplay went into production. (Had Nat but known, he would have fitted in perfectly.) And even account handlers like her could feel faintly sordid. It was Mrs Thatcher who made commerce acceptable and advertising sexy. These days people would kill to be sitting where Libby was, on the twenty-eighth floor of a glass tower in Docklands. If only they knew how tedious the work could be! But it did not seem tedious this morning, as she arrived to chair a meeting that had always promised to be awkward and which now, because she was late, threatened far worse. You have to laugh, Libby was fond of saying, but today was no laughing matter.

Simon Mirtle-Thorne from SaxonAir had asked to meet the Creative team working on the new campaign: he hadn't said what he thought of the roughs Libby had sent him last week, but his request for a ten o'clock didn't sound promising. Arran & Arran liked its clients to feel valued, and no client was more valued than SaxonAir – which was why Libby had done her best to oblige him. But in her experience, bringing Suits and Creatives together was unhelpful. As Account Director, she preferred to talk to each side separately. Otherwise, you got scenarios like the one she saw now, walking into Conference Room 2. No five people could ever have looked more uncomfortable with each other. Greg Drosz, Arran & Arran's new Creative guru, was squatting on a windowsill with his back to the room, as though prepared for defenestration should the mobile phone call he was engaged in turn out badly. Stan Humbel and Tarquin Clove, the copywriter-and-artist duo who had produced the roughs, were struggling to extract coffee from a black-handled silver Thermos. (Were you meant to depress the top, loosen it, or remove the thing altogether? Libby didn't get it either.) And Simon and his assistant Tanya Something were sitting stony-faced at the table, both in pinstripes. An array of croissants, short-bread biscuits, strawberries and grapes had failed to sweeten relations. Even on good days Simon could be fractious before his first Campari. And to judge by his expression, today wasn't one of those.

Five people? Actually, she realised, there were six. Meetings required a minute-taker, and the person taking minutes wasn't Angie, her PA, but the intern, whose last day this was and who had asked could he sit in to 'get an impression'. Libby felt vaguely guilty about the intern: though he had been at Arran & Arran for six weeks, she had barely spoken to him and couldn't even remember his name. But she nodded to him now as though she did.

'Lovely to see you,' she said, taking a seat next to Simon. 'All well?'

'Ish,' Simon said. 'Shall we get on?' Pink-striped shirt, green tie with giraffes, gold cufflinks engraved SMT. No kiss for Libby. Not a good sign.

Libby called for the others to join them at the table. Stan and Tarquin brought their coffees over but Greg remained on the windowsill, whether in suicidal despair or as a power play it wasn't clear. He had joined Arran & Arran six months ago, from a firm in Sydney. Heading the list of achievements on his CV was a jingle he had written for a US food manufacturer ('You must remember this / A quiche is just a quiche / Stir-fry is just stir-fry / But now there's something new to try / Home Ranch Steak Pie'). Greg was a genius, everyone said, and lived up to the image by dressing entirely in black – not just the clothes, but wristband, signet ring and eyeshadow as well. An imposing figure. But he and Simon had never met before, and Greg's predecessor as Creative Director, Larry Pound, was a hard act to follow, his campaign for the new shuttle service to New York and Los Angeles having helped double SaxonAir's revenues. Besides, Larry and Simon were close friends.

Libby chinked a spoon against her water glass: 'Greg?'

'OK, guys,' Greg said, dropping down from the window, 'SaxonAir. Well-respected company trying to shed its fusty image: that was the brief.'

'More specifically, the rebranding of business class,' Libby said, not daring to look at Simon, and wondering which was worse, Greg's assumption that he'd be the one chairing the meeting or his thumbnail sketch of SaxonAir, whose pre-tax profits the previous year had been £54.2 million, 18 million up on the year before.

'Yeh, yeh, how to make business class sexy. But we've the bigger image problem to consider too. Image disaster, let's say. Image catastrophe. How can we drag SaxonAir towards the twenty-first century?'

No one spoke. Simon's ears had turned red. Greg, oblivious, cantered on.

'As I saw it,' he said, 'there were three ways to go with the campaign. One, emphasise the cheapness of SaxonAir business class compared to Virgin, British Airways, et cetera. Two, mention the perks: use of executive lounges at Heathrow, gourmet meals on board, Gucci toiletries on Atlantic routes, twelve-inch TV screen for inflight entertainment, et cetera. Three, talk about legroom – thirty inches rather than the standard business twenty-seven. Well, option one is tacky – and what's to stop your rivals cutting their fares? Two's also a no-no: we need a single idea, and perks only work as a package. So we went with three, legroom. Personal space, let's call it. The world's over-crowded these days. People will pay a premium not to feel hemmed in. And what's the best way to escape your neighbours? By flying business class.

'So Stan and Tarquin came up with some great roughs. And I passed them on to our Account Director. And she had them biked them to our client. Who asked for this meeting. Presumably to congratulate us, Mr Thome?'

'Mirtle-Thome. And no. We think they're crap.'

Libby's training said she must leap in quickly but she felt too miffed to play peacemaker. It wasn't just Greg's failure to use her name, but the sneer when he pronounced her job title – Account Director, aka Money-grubbing Birdbrain. (She got the same kind of snootiness at home, from Nat.) Simon, too, had treated her badly – normal procedure would have been to tell *her* what he thought of the roughs, ahead of the meeting, not land her in it like this in front of her colleagues.

'*We?*' Greg said.

'Tanya, myself, the whole SaxonAir marketing department – I dare say the board, too, if I'd shown them.'

'Can we remind ourselves what the roughs were?' Libby said, belatedly. 'In case there's been some misunderstanding.'

Simon shrugged. Greg nodded at Tarquin (gold earring, white cotton shirt, spiky blond hair), who brought a whiteboard easel over. Someone from Research must have used it last: a black felt-tip line rose smoothly across it from left to right – a graph of profits in the e-industries, maybe. Tarquin tacked up a series of sketches.

'Rough One,' Greg said, resuming control, as though Libby weren't there. 'Man in suit performs Cossack folk dance between his seat and the seat in front of him. Outstretched legs, you notice. Dionysian hilarity. The man's having a great time.

'Two: Family of three in Row 36 – man, woman, child – spread out a picnic on the floor in front of them. Tartan rug. Wicker hamper. Cosy yet bucolic.

'Three: Man in shirtsleeves finds himself sitting next to hated figure – Hitler, Stalin, Saddam Hussein – but he's so cocooned that the hated figure doesn't impinge on his space.

'Four, a variation on the previous. Woman in suit is next to passenger with nasty personal habits. A nose-picker, say –'

'Why not go the whole hog?' Simon said. 'She could be next to someone wanking . . .'

Greg shook his head and spread his palms out, in an image of wounded pride – a Creative genius impugned by a tasteless Suit.

'You're unhappy with our ideas?' he said. 'You have better ideas?'

'It's not our job to have the ideas,' Simon said. 'That's what we pay you for.'

'We found the message confusing,' Tanya said, more mollifying.

'Business-class passengers are meant to be sophisticated,' Greg said.

'They'd have to be masterminds to get the point of these,' Simon said.

'I don't see the problem,' Greg said.

'The problem is the negative subtext,' Simon said. 'Fly SaxonAir, where the food's so bad you're better off bringing your own picnic. Fly SaxonAir, where your fellow passengers are rowdy Cossack dancers. Or evil tyrants. Or snot-nosed nerds.'

Greg folded his hands in prayer under his chin, like a monk withdrawing from the world.

'We've done other roughs,' he said, with his eyes closed.

Tarquin pinned up more sketches.

'A woman swinging a cat by its tail.'

'Ever heard of the RSPCA?'

'A man with his leg full out in a plaster cast.'

'Fly SaxonAir and you'll end up in traction.'

'There's no point going on with this,' Greg said.

'Agreed,' Simon said. 'We might as well all go home.'

Simon and Greg were moody bears with grizzling egos. Her job was to act as go-between – to smooth out the roughs. But once again she was lost for words.

Then the intern spoke.

'Aren't there more roughs?' he said. 'I'm sure I saw one earlier.'

Stay out of this, you're only here to take notes, Libby felt like screaming. But he was trying to help.

'There is *one*, I suppose,' Tarquin said, after a nervous pause. 'It was Stan who gave me the idea.'

'It's a bit different,' said Stan, who as the copywriting half of the partnership rarely wasted his words on speech.

Tarquin pinned up the sketch. The woman at its centre was lying naked in a tipped-back armchair; only the seat belt round her waist told you this was business class not a boudoir. She wore a choker round her neck (it was fastened by a buckle at the middle, in mimicry of the seat belt), and a flower of some kind – rose? jasmine? orchid? – was tucked behind her left ear. Behind her, in the aisle, stood a young male flight attendant in uniform: striped trousers, white shirt, peaked cap. He was carrying a tray on which were placed, to the left, an ice bucket with champagne (the bottle angled suggestively towards her), and, to the right, an overflowing bowl of cherries. The flight attendant was bending down towards the woman, desperate for her to accept his offerings, while she gazed straight ahead, oblivious to his entreaties, her eyes playfully enigmatic, her lips slightly parted in sensuous pleasure. Her right arm lay on the seat rest; her left was draped across her crotch. She was white, young and naked. The flight attendant was black.

'I feel I've seen it before,' Simon said, after a long silence.

'Manet's *Olympia*,' Stan said.

'I played on the original,' Tarquin said.

'Are there any words?' Tanya said.

'Do we need words?' Libby said.

'In the Lap of Luxury,' Stan said.

'Too naughty,' Libby said, 'given her crotch.'

'Is it exploitative?' Tanya said.

'All ads are exploitative,' Tarquin said.

'But is it *too* exploitative?'

'Well, obviously she's wearing no clothes.'

'I meant racially exploitative,' Tanya said. 'Of *him*. The black as servant, or stud.'

'It's not saying he's a stud.'

'No, but . . .'

The room fell silent again.

'I don't know,' Simon said.

Libby sensed he did know – to express even the faintest interest in the sketch when he'd come here angry and implacable must mean he liked it. But that still left Greg, who might be offended by Tarquin producing the sketch without his permission. It would be just like Greg to play dog in the manger.

'Greg?' she said.

Greg stood by the easel, examining the sketch, then turned to face his audience, back in charge.

'We batted the idea around when we first discussed the campaign, remember – airborne erotica, mile-high fucking, the Big O in the Sky. My only reason for not going with it was the client. Would SaxonAir have the courage? I thought not.'

The original idea, Greg was saying, was Greg's. Libby had more sense than to interrupt him.

'Personally, I love the sketch. OK, it's raw still, the details are fuzzy, the shoot will be a nightmare, but when it's a billboard the drive-by impact will be terrific. A good ad grabs you by the balls but a great ad gives you a blow-job as well, and this is a great ad, I promise you. This ad's going to get talked about by *everyone*. This ad will be remembered when we're all dead.'

'And sell some business-class seats?' Simon said.

'Yeh, yeh,' Greg said. 'That too.'

'I'm wondering if she should be *totally* naked,' Tanya said, still pondering the sketch.

'I thought of draping her,' Tarquin said.

'With a fur stole, say,' Greg said.

'Across her left arm,' Tarquin said.

'To cover her pudenda,' Libby said.

'It will need some fine-tuning,' Simon said.

'But you do like it?' Libby asked him.

'It's more the kind of thing I had in mind.'

God, these male egos. Simon, too, wanted the credit.

It was agreed they fine-tune, after which, if all was well, Simon would get his board onside and then green-light the shoot.

The handshakes were stiff but it was amazing there were handshakes at all.

'Thanks, you're a genius,' Libby whispered to Tarquin, before escorting Simon and Tanya downstairs. 'You, too, well done, let's speak later,' she said to the intern.

And I still don't remember his name, she thought.

'Difficult chap, your Greg,' Simon said to her, in the lobby. '"The idea came up when we first discussed it": bollocks.'

'What's he called again? Simon Arsehole-Wanker?' Greg said to her back, on the sixteenth floor. '"The kind of thing I had in mind"? He'd never have thought of it in a million years.'

'I know,' Libby said. 'But that's the trick. Let your man think he's the creative one and you can't go wrong.'

6

*JACK*

JACK SAT in the George, with a pint of Best. After the morning he'd had he felt consoled here, under the horse brasses and hunting horns and prints of whiskered squires engaged in fisticuffs. The silver tankard he drank from was one he'd been given on his twenty-first birthday: Bruno, the landlord, kept it for him high up, next to the Scottish malts, and instructed his bar staff that it was Mr Jack's tankard and Mr Jack's alone (he'd once come in on a hot July night during the carnival, when the pub ran short of glasses, and was gratified to see it safe on its hook). Behind him a log was burning in the inglenook fireplace – a real log, the kind that charred and turned to ash.

A fire seemed superfluous, on a day like this. But the bigger nuisance was the jukebox, which stopped a chap hearing other chaps, though currently that wasn't a problem, with Jack the only customer apart from two young scruffs in the corner, the two who must be responsible for the music, if you could call it that. *And all the roads we have to walk are winding, And all the lights that lead us there are blinding* – strewth, what whiny, miserabilist piffle was that? Why did no one write cheerful tunes any more, with a good beat, the sort the Beatles sang before they went druggy? Nancy preferred classical. He would come home from work and there she'd be, in the greenhouse, watering the tomatoes, with a Bach Passion belting out from the CD player: *Ruht wohl, und bringt auch mich zur Ruh.* Talking helped plants to grow, she said, just as listening to good music helped people grow. She teased him for his tastes, which he had formed late and never moved on from: the Beatles, the Beach Boys, the Bee Gees, the Kinks and (well, yes, this was shameful) the Monkees. But this was the stuff he and Nancy used to dance to in their early thirties. There was a kind of loyalty to her there, little though she liked pop music now.

'Another, Jack?'

'Don't mind if I do.'

There were four of them who met on Friday lunchtimes: him, Harris, Tony Griffin and Dom Askew. But Tony was sitting in the magistrates' court in Ipswich. And Dom, who ran the garden centre, had gone to Norfolk with a delivery of ballerina roses. Harris, the local bank manager, would be here regardless, which given this morning's fax from SGS was rather handy – with only the two of them there, Jack could sound him out about a loan. Five past one: where was Harris? Had some kerfuffle to do with the election delayed him? Some urgent message from HQ in London? Labour getting in was a worry for anyone in finance; Jack was old enough to remember the last time. But surely there would not be a full-scale panic yet.

'Did you watch last night?' Bruno asked, nodding at the television stationed above them. Till last month there'd been a tank of tropical fish there. The telly was meant to bring in extra customers.

'Not for long,' Jack said, glancing up.

A reporter with a hand mike stood in Downing Street, then they cut to some earlier footage: *Blair triumphant, blah, landslide victory, blah, youngest prime minister this century, blah, blah, blah.* Seeing which way the wind was blowing, Jack had been in bed before midnight. The one time he had voted Labour was in 1959 and then only to piss off the old man. Wilson, Foot, Kinnock – he trusted none of them. Only Callaghan had seemed half decent, but he was up against Thatcher, and Jack couldn't not vote for Thatcher. He'd once met her in the VIP tent at an agricultural fair. Wonderful woman – said what she thought, looked you in the eye, stood for what was best about England, not least the right to say no to the bloody unions. Still, Thatcher had gone half bats by the end, and Jack had never warmed to Major. He'd voted Conservative yesterday because the local MP, Freddy Finch, had once bought one of his mowers. He'd voted Conservative yesterday because the Conservative Party was the natural party of small businesses. He'd voted

Conservative yesterday because, at sixty, he couldn't imagine voting anything else. But his heart had not been it. The buggers deserved to lose.

Above, where the fish tank had been, Blair swam into Downing Street like a gaudy koi. The volume was low because of the jukebox, but Jack could hear the chanting of the crowds (party workers, no doubt, bussed in to play Joe Public): *Toe-knee, Toe-knee, Toe-knee*. How could other countries be expected to take Britain seriously, now a grinning boy was in charge? Clinton wasn't old, either, and behaved like an adolescent, screwing everything in sight. But Clinton had gravitas, whereas Blair was as brash as a callisthenics instructor, *Toe-knee, Toe-knee, Toe-knee*. Thirty years back, he'd have had to be Anthony to enter politics, and the full works, Anthony Charles Lynton Blair, would have been to his advantage. In Jack's first job, the one his father had pushed him into as 'useful experience' (how a canning factory was meant to prepare him for Raven & Son he never explained), people at managerial level called each other by their surnames, saving Christian names for the workers: 'Have a word with Bill about overtime, will you, Johnson?' 'If Sid's on holiday, you'd better get Jeff to do it, Wilkins.' In a family business, the formalities of the old class system made no sense: these days everyone at Raven & Son called him Jack. But to have a whole nation *Toe-knee* you was carrying informality too far.

'Not eating today?' Bruno said.

'I thought you'd never ask.'

'Roast beef on brown bread, with watercress, cucumber and English mustard, but no tomato?'

'That's it.'

His usual bar snack. (Bar snack, he thought: a meal not eaten in a snack bar.) Today's hot special was John Bull beefsteak, with Heritage green beans and Olde English mash, but Jack always stuck to cold.

At home Nancy would be serving quiche to whichever of the ladies had joined her after tennis. Nancy herself no longer played: since the onset of her back problems, she sat out even Friday-morning doubles. But she was still Hon Sec and liked to keep an eye on the club. It was mean of him not to have joined them. Meeting new people made him feel self-conscious, because of that birthmark on his forehead, which – so Nancy said – made him look like Gorbachev. But these were old friends. There'd be Elise, for example, Harris's wife, the little Frenchwoman with green eyes. He could have exchanged pleasantries, grabbed a plateful and changed that damn light bulb. But here he was waiting for Harris.

'What I promise, I will deliver,' Blair was saying into a fantail of microphones. *Deliver.* Everything was delivered these days – health, profits, education. Everything but the mail and milk, which came late or not at all.

'Jack! I was worried I'd miss you. Have another.'

Harris, not before time, looking his usual jaunty self. No six-foot-six man in his late forties deserved to look as lean and unstooped, not even one who jogged, played squash and golf, and (by all accounts) enjoyed a strenuous extramarital sex life.

'Bad morning?' Jack asked.

'The New York office phoned at ten to one, for God's sake. Think they're doing you a great favour with a breakfast conference. Forgetting their breakfast is our lunch.'

'I'm surprised they bother. A small branch in England – what's the point?'

'We all have to be global these days.'

'Wish I was.'

'You're strong in Europe, aren't you?'

'We are. Were. In France especially. Now the Dutch are undercutting us, it's tough.'

He must try not to be negative – not to sound, to use his daughters' expression, 'like a loser'. The potential for expansion was the thing to stress.

'Of course, with investment we'd soon see them off.'

'Those look good: can I have the same?' Harris said, as Bruno handed Jack his sandwiches, then added: 'Classy lot, the Dutch.'

What was he thinking of? Dutch engineers? Dutch painters? The Dutch football team? Talking football was a good way to engage Harris but Jack knew too little to attempt it. The only sport he actively pursued was hunting (as joint MFH, Master of the Foxhounds, for the Harchope & Nelles) and the only one he vaguely followed was motor racing – Formula One, the Isle of Man TT races, stock cars, speedway, powerboats: anything with engines. If he had sons, they would have kept him up to the mark, but as it was . . . Cruyff – now *he* was a famous Dutch player. Long retired though, leaving who: Bergkamp, was it, and the one who wore sunglasses, Edgar Something? That was three more names than Nancy would know. But not enough to keep his end up with Harris.

Come the next pint, he would steer the talk back to Raven & Son. All in good time.

'Elise thriving?' he asked.

'In very good form,' said Harris. 'Enjoying getting through the money. It's what they're for, isn't it?'

'What is?'

'Wives – to shop away our hard-earned dosh. Nancy's the same, I bet.'

'Absolutely.'

Absolutely not. Nancy was always careful with money, and since the recent sticky patch at work had become positively parsimonious, as though saving on home expenses would keep Raven & Son in the black. No wife could be more supportive, and though their marriage had its longueurs he felt a flush of self-hatred at misrepresenting her in order to cosy up to Harris.

'I see Freddy Finch lost,' Harris said.

'No! Did he?'

'Probably would have anyway. Only had a five thousand majority. But bonking his secretary can't have helped.'

Pot calling the kettle black, Jack thought.

'How's the City reacting?' he said, as Harris's sandwiches came.

'They're upbeat. They like Gordon Brown.'

'God knows why. He can do what he likes, with that majority. Nationalise the banks. Cream off profits. Tax us all to ruin.'

'He and Blair are young. Which makes Britain attractive to foreign investors.'

'What about the export trade, though? What'll Brown do there?' He had landed where he wanted, light as a parachute. 'Take me and my problems in France.'

'You were saying – the Dutch.'

'At eight francs to the pound, buying British makes sense; at ten francs to the pound, it doesn't. Our machines are 25 per cent more expensive than they were last year, without us having raised prices. The exchange rate is killing me. Others are having it worse,' he added, reminding himself not to sound like a loser, 'but I could do with some injection of capital. In fact . . .'

Harris wasn't listening. His eyes were on the set, where *Toe-Knee* was winding up his speech. 'Enough of talking,' the tinny voice said. 'It is time now to do.'

'Wish I could believe the hype,' Jack said, seeing a panel of studio pundits loom up. 'Another?'

'Better not,' Harris said. 'I have to get back.'

'Hard at it, eh?'

'I want to finish early. Slip a round of golf in while the weather's good.'

More likely he'd be slipping something into his teller, Jane or Deirdre or whatever she was called. The town was awash with rumours, the teller having told everyone except, it seemed, Harris's wife Elise. But it wasn't a subject for discussion, let alone a joke.

'Before you shoot off,' said Jack. 'Been meaning to ask you. This investment business . . .'

'Investment?'

'For the company. Developing our machines. Moving into new markets. I've been thinking of coming to you.'

'Me?'

'The bank. About a loan.'

'By all means. I'll get our Client Manager to send you an application form.'

'Is that necessary? We've been with you for ever – since my great-grandfather, I think.'

'Or you could come in – one of our Relationship Team will help you complete it. Nothing too onerous.'

'And then?'

'Your application would go forward for appraisal.'

'But you'd be the one making the decision.'

'If only. We're like everywhere else these days – head office will take an overview.'

'You knowing me personally won't help?'

'Your application will get fair consideration, Jack. Like every other application. And your history with us is bound to count for something.'

'I couldn't be certain, though.'

'So long as your business plan stands up . . . Look, call me at the office. Better place to talk than here. Mustn't mix pleasure and business, et cetera.' Harris nudged his arm. 'All right?' he added and, all right or not, was gone.

Jack ordered a last half of Best, with a whisky chaser, not a combination he usually allowed himself at lunchtime but this didn't feel like a usual lunchtime. What was the point of friends if you couldn't turn to them in a fix? Not that he was in a fix. And not that Harris was all that close a friend. But he might have been less heavy on protocol. 'Relationship Team', 'overview': the pompous prick. A local bank worth its name should be getting behind local businesses, not making them feel small. 'Mustn't mix pleasure and business'? Hah! Harris had been mixing it with his teller for months, by all accounts: what would head office think, if an anonymous letter arrived, with photos of them screwing on his desk or in the vault or wherever it was they did it . . .

Ashamed at the thought, Jack knocked back the whisky. Perhaps he had expected too much. Nothing Harris had said was discouraging. Had he not invited him to drop in to discuss it further? What more could he have done? A man in his position, manager of a small-town bank, had to be wary of showing favouritism. In his office, Harris would be less inhibited – and advise Jack how to ensure the application's success. It was not a large loan Jack had in mind: £100K should do it, though if Harris encouraged him to go for twice that, why not? A shaft of sun fell between his stool and the log fire. A less mournful tune struck up from the jukebox. *Don't look back in anger, I heard you say*. Another half-pint could do no harm. He would draft a business plan tonight, while the iron was hot. Enough of talking. It was time now to do.


7

*HARRY*


IN THE doorway, as he stepped from the sunny pavement into Cantata's candlelit gloom, Harry had a premonition not of food or pleasure but of something sinister, malign and even (a word he wouldn't use lightly) evil. The smell of burning fat from the kitchen set it off. The sudden silence from the nearby tables made it worse. And, to clinch it, there was the skinhead young waiter, who coolly – wilfully – looked right through him. Harry told himself he was being paranoid. He and Nat had met here before and it had been fine. But even the civilities of the maître d' (Creed, ah yes, would he like to go straight through?) failed to banish the sensation. First the man he had gone to see two hours ago, and now this. He ordered a tomato juice and tried to calm down. As Nat would be the first to tell him: this is London, you're imagining it, stop being so paranoid. The offending waiter, with his oil-grey skin, was laying out cutlery three tables away. How old was he – eighteen? twenty? Just a boy, in his first job. But when he walked past Harry's table he blanked him again, as though Harry didn't exist or, if he did, had no place in a place like this.

Restaurant guides called Cantata 'small and friendly'. Unlike Le Pont de la Tour or the Chop House, it didn't overlook the river but sat back a street, in an alley between tall warehouses smelling of spice. He and Nat had been drawn to it by the cheapish menu, which for Nat, even on Libby's income, was a consideration: the two of them lunched together every few months, and for the last couple of times it had been here. Most of the customers seemed to be middle-tier businessmen. Harry sipped the bitters in his tomato juice (pepper, Lea & Perrins, Angostura), feeling out of place. Feeling *in* place was a matter of money, age, education, dress, accent, colour. How enviable to feel confident that Cantata was for the likes of you. But maybe no one felt it. Even the man at the next table doing *The Times* crossword might secretly imagine himself to be an outsider. Did Nat feel in place here? To rephrase that: *would* he feel in place if ever he got here? It was now past one twenty and the arrangement had been to meet at one.

Nat had been running late ever since they first met, back in 1980. In his last year at school, as preparation for a degree in film and journalism, Harry had signed up for an evening class at the local college. 'Getting Started' the course was called. He didn't know what to expect – certainly not Nat, who puffed in ten minutes late, just as everyone was about to give up on him. He looked too young to be a teacher. There was a clownish innocence, even in his clothes – blue jeans, white jacket, turquoise shirt, red neckscarf, black hat, and a pair of clogs, shaped like Cornish pasties, with a crust down the middle, which he wore to this day. And he was handsome, in a blond-curled, David Gowerish sort of way. Clearly a prodigy, a fraud or a pushy Oxbridge sort – whichever, someone your average evening-class student in South Norley might choose to resent. And they did resent him. When Nat asked about their previous experience of writing, one man snarled, 'The course is called "Getting Started". We're not meant to be writers already, are we?' while another said he'd signed up for the wrong class and walked out. Harry began to feel sorry for Nat. He readied himself to be won over. And was.

The class was open to all kinds of writing – poetry, fiction, revue sketches, screenplays, memoirs, travel writing, drama – in part because (so Harry came to realise) the teacher himself was actively experimenting in several different genres; to put it less flatteringly, Nat had yet to find a form in which he could succeed. As a tutor, he was too pontifical, too sure he had all the answers. But what he lacked in technique he made up for in enthu-siasm. And he was quick to take Harry under his wing. Harry had often asked himself why. Because he seemed so eager? Because he was young and male, when the other students were mostly middle-aged women (whom Nat treated with gallant condescension)? Or was it the liberal thing, Harry being what he was and Nat wanting to display his tolerance? Whichever, Harry felt supported and enfranchised – the boy from Peckham overcoming his 'disadvantaged background' through the endorsement of a mentor. Soon they were meeting up outside the class, at weekends. Nat invited Harry to films, exhibitions, poetry readings, anything cultural except West End plays. Harry took Nat to south London clubs that he would not have known were there, let alone dared to enter – the student teaching the teacher. Nat hadn't yet met Libby, and neither he nor Harry had a steady girlfriend. Some in the class suspected they were gay.

Two tomato juices under his belt, Harry looked to the door: one thirty, and still no sign. Nat's lateness had got worse over the years, but even by Nat standards this was going it some. Anyone else would have called to apologise. But Nat being Nat didn't own a mobile ('I refuse to be at other people's beck and call,' he explained, when Harry once made the mistake of suggesting he get one. 'Every man is an island, Harry. Every creative artist, anyway.') Maybe Nat had forgotten their lunch date. His mentioning it last night was no guarantee he had remembered it today. Should Harry call him at home? Or pay for the drinks and clear off? There were things he ought to be doing at the *Gazette* – not least following up this morning's visit to the fox man. He wasn't paid to sit around waiting for unreliable friends.

On cue, like one of the Revd Awdry's trains, Nat puffed in. He looked more haggard than usual, baggier under the eyes, but his suffering wouldn't be real suffering – just a hangover or an unproductive morning's work.

'Sorry,' Nat said, after a hug. 'I walked right past the place, then couldn't remember what it was called.'

'Hair of the dog?' Harry asked.

'Better not,' Nat said. 'Bad idea to drink at lunchtime.'

It was a ritual between them: Harry would suggest ordering wine, Nat would decline at length ('Friday's my writing day. If my characters don't have my undivided sober attention they'll refuse to speak, the law of Bacchic inspiration has never worked for me', etc.), Harry would pretend to take offence ('Sorry for asking'), then Nat would back down and order something, 'just this once'. Perhaps Nat's other lunchtimes *were* teetotal. But all his abstinence for art's sake had produced little or nothing – not a publishable story or a stageable play in years.

'Oh, go on then,' Nat said. 'I suppose we could toast the new government. Just this once.'

'The Orvieto?'

'Fine.'

The Orvieto was what they always had after Nat had refused to have anything.

'I didn't notice when you left Deborah's,' Harry said.

'Fourish. How about you?'

'After Portillo.'

'Amazing night,' Nat said. 'The right party got in at last.'

'Only by modelling itself on the wrong party. I wish I knew what Blair believed in. At least with Foot and Kinnock, we knew where we were.'

'Yes, in the wilderness. Blair has made Labour electable. Here's to him.'

They chinked glasses. After the morning Harry had had – the fox man, the pee-smelling flat, the skinhead waiter – the Orvieto tasted good.

'Did you watch the celebrations?' Nat said. 'The train drivers were tooting their horns as they came in over Hungerford Bridge. It'll be great for our bit of London, you know – when Tate Modern and the Dome are finished and so on.'

'It'll take more than Blair to regenerate south of the river.'

'And all those new young MPs!' Nat said, ignoring him. 'No more sad old gits, just people like us.'

'People like you, Nat. Not people like me.'

'What's the difference?'

'How many of them come from the working class? Or the ethnic minorities? Take your friend, who won that seat.'

'Rufus Huish.'

'You were at school together, right?'

'Yes.'

'At *boarding* school. As Blair was. Same old system.'

'It's not which school you go to that matters, it's what you believe in.'

'It's not what you believe in, it's what you do.'

Harry hadn't intended to argue about politics. But he was irritated by Nat's cosy euphoria. For a brief moment in the early 1980s, the two of them had gone on marches together, screaming abuse against the evils of capitalism, racism, Thatcherism, the police, the media, anyone over forty. Let's carve it out for ourselves, fight for freedom, open it up – in those days they'd had conviction. Now Nat was an old badger dozing in his sett.

'So you don't mind Blair saying he's a fan of Mrs Thatcher?' Harry said, still needling.

'That was only to get the tabloids on his side. Now he's in power, he can do as he likes.'

'He hasn't the guts. Did you notice how he didn't even kiss Cherie last night? Terrified it might be construed as sleazy, even though she's his wife.'

'You should write a column about it, Harry.'

'I don't write columns, Nat. I'm a reporter.'

'How's that going?'

'Fine. My probation ends next month. Then they won't have to treat me as a cub any more. What are you going to have?'

'The scorched tuna with lentils sounds good.'

'No starter?'

'Have we time?'

'There's always time for a starter.'

'The rocket salad with shaved Parmesan, then.'

'Dieting?'

'You're right. I'll have risotto. Then the lamb.'

Lamb, Harry thought, the perfect choice for a woolly liberal. Where had the old conviction gone, the old bite? Nat was a sheep. Britain was a nation of sheep.

'How's the teaching?' Harry asked.

'Nearly over. It's exams.'

'And the writing?'

'Coming along.'

It had been coming along for as long as Harry could remember, and he knew not to ask more. Nat still wore a mask of quiet confidence, an air of all-will-come-good-eventually, but Harry could see signs of doubt; the peeling forehead, the bitten nails, the fraying hair. There was also a new tic, the twirling of the ring on his wedding finger until it bumped across the ridge of the knuckle and eased upwards, free to slip the bonds. If only the plays would come off as easily. It was years since Nat had finished a new one, and it wasn't as if the old ones were much cop. Poor Libby, having to subsidise it all. Nat's teaching brought in less than they paid the nanny.

A waiter was carrying a bread basket round and Nat called him over. It was the boy from earlier, the one who wouldn't look. Harry watched him closely as Nat dithered over the choice: ciabatta, pumpernickel, cheese-and-olive, rye. He had a shaving nick on his chin and an accent Harry found hard to place, but the eye contact with Nat was good. Once he turned to Harry, though, his eyes remained fixed on the platter. Harry made him run through the names of the bread again. Ciabatta, pumpernickel, cheese-and-olive, rye. 'Rye,' Harry said. But when the boy tonged the bread on to the side plate, he kept his arm at full stretch and refused to meet Harry's gaze.

'Did you see that?' he asked Nat, once the waiter had moved away.

'Did I see what?'

'He refused to look at me.'

'Probably just shy.'

'Come on – it was blatant.'

'He had a foreign accent. Scandinavian, maybe.'

'East European. Which makes sense.'

'Does it?'

'You think I'm being paranoid.'

'I don't know. I didn't see.'

Perhaps he *had* imagined it. There was no getting it over to Nat, anyway. He had become a woolly lamb or dozy badger, a Whateverist, an Anythingarian. Once there'd been passion. Now he was complacent – and fat.

The starters came. The Orvieto was almost empty, though Harry had hardly touched a drop.

He ought to talk about the fox man, get it off his chest. No doubt Nat would have an opinion.

'Funny thing happened this morning,' he said.

'Another bottle?' Nat said.

'Why not?'

'Orvieto again?'

'Sure.'

'You were saying. Go on.'

To have a stranger turn up on your doorstep can be intimidating, of course. But it was the man himself who had phoned the office and asked for a journalist to come round. ('He sounds off the wall,' Deborah said. 'But it might make a fun piece.') So Harry was expecting to be welcomed. And for the door to open when he rang the bell. Instead of which he was made to wait while the ghost inside monitored his face through a peephole.

'Mr Lavell?'

'Yeh?'

'I've come about the fox.'

Harry wore a suit and tie, and shiny black shoes, the image of honest professionalism. He did his best to look solid and trustworthy, not like a novice feeling his way. But when the door opened it was only by a fraction, and the chain stayed on. All Harry could see was half a face – and one brown eye fixing him with suspicion, as though he were a mugger or worse.

'Harry Creed,' said Harry, handing over a business card. 'I've been with the *Gazette* for eight years.'

This was true, more or less. For seven of those years he had worked shifts as a freelance subeditor, cutting overmatter, changing commas, thinking up headlines. But now he was a (probationary) staff reporter.

'Oh, the *Gazette*,' the half-man said. 'We wasn't expecting a . . .' The sentence remained incomplete but the chain was unhooked, the half-face became a full face, and Harry was allowed to enter. No shake of the hand, no greeting or apology, but he was in.

He followed Mr Lavell down a dingy passage into the kitchen, where two narrow glazed doors gave on to a small yard. Inside the doors stood a Maclaren buggy, with a small child asleep in it.

'Daniel,' Mr Lavell explained. 'Before it happened, I used to put him outside for his naps.'

Harry took his notebook out and wrote down details of the family: Terry Lavell, thirty-two, an unemployed construction worker; partner, Ellen Robertson, twenty-nine, a part-time dental receptionist (currently at work); Daniel, their only child, fourteen months. At the same time, he surreptitiously noted the items on the kitchen table (father and son had just returned from Safeway): one sliced white loaf, four tins of baked beans, one Smirnoff vodka bottle, three Lutomer Riesling wine boxes and twelve cans of John Smith's bitter. Did alcohol explain the outlandishness of Mr Lavell's story? There was no knowing, till Harry heard it in full.

'So what exactly happened, Mr Lavell?'

'Terry. Tel to all my mates.'

'What happened, Terry?' said, Harry, Hal to none of his.

'You wanna sit down?'

'Don't go to any trouble.'

'It's no trouble. Let's sit outside.'

Terry fetched two white stacking chairs from the corner of the yard, brushing leaves and winter dust from their seats. Harry's use of a notebook seemed to have eased his suspicions. That happened, he found: once people trusted you were taking them seriously, they relaxed. But Harry didn't forget the doorstep unwelcome: 'We wasn't expecting a . . .'

It was a Tuesday, Terry said. Since losing his job, he took care of Daniel three days a week, while Ellen was at work. It had been a usual sort of morning (television, benefits office, Safeway, ducks in the park) but surprisingly warm, which encouraged him, when they got home, to wheel Daniel outside and leave him sleeping in his buggy. Terry was talking on the phone ('to a mate, couldn't have been more than a minute, like') when he heard Daniel crying and, looking out, saw the buggy 'sort of jolt from side to side'.

That will be Daniel waking up, he thought, but then the cries grew louder, 'more like a tantrum', and when he looked again he saw a 'large brown creature' beside the buggy, 'a giant fox thing', its teeth 'snarling' and its long tail 'waving angrily about'. He dropped the phone and ran out. The creature turned, bolted, and made off over the garden wall. Daniel, unclipped, was badly distressed, his all-in-one suit ripped open at the neck.

'What were the injuries like?' Harry asked, glancing in at the smooth-faced, sleeping child.

'Once he was cleaned up, not too bad, just cuts and grazes. It's made him all jumpy, though. Wakes up screaming in the night.'

'And the animal . . . ?'

'Was huge. Big as me nearly. Size of a wolf.'

'It looked like a fox, you said?'

'Yeh, I ain't ever seen one that big before, but we're plagued by foxes. I told the council. Have a read of these letters while I make us some tea.'

Terry fetched a file from the top of the television. There were twenty or so letters in it, copies of ones sent to the council by Terry, and then the replies, across which Terry, in yellow marker pen, had scrawled disbelieving expletives and exclamation marks. It seemed Terry wanted the council to move him to a three-bedroom house elsewhere in the borough. Failing that, he wanted all foxes in the area to be put down: they weren't merely a pest but 'posed a serious danger to small children'. Terry had used that phrase in a letter sent to the council back in March. The reply from the council's Environmental Health Officer, received the day before the attack on Daniel, stated that it was not council policy to exterminate foxes, and that Mr Lavell's request to be rehoused had been passed on to the appropriate department, where it would be considered through the normal channels.

Harry asked if he could transcribe a letter or two. 'Be my guest,' said Terry. They drank tea and chatted some more while he made notes. Then Daniel woke up and Terry unclipped him from the buggy, raising Daniel to his face and cuddling him. 'Like a vixen tenderly nursing a wounded cub,' Harry wrote in his notebook, but no wounds were visible and the image was too fanciful for the *Gazette*. Besides, the paternal solicitude might be just a show: who could say what kind of father Terry was? Not Harry, anyway, for whom the issue of fatherhood was a troubling one and not to be thought about in the middle of a job.

In the hallway, showing Harry out, Terry asked when the article would appear. Harry said it wasn't for him to decide but he was hopeful it would be next week. Which he was, since (this he didn't say) stories about animals were always a good bet: loyal dogs, cheeky budgies, foul-mouthed parrots, ancient tortoises, death-defying cats.

'I look forward to it,' Terry said, trusting, hopeful, offering his hand.

Harry avoided Terry's eyes. He'd no idea yet what he would write. But how credible was a killer fox?

'So what do you make of it?' Harry asked Nat. For once Nat seemed to have been listening. For once Harry felt respected for his storytelling, not guilty of cliché or caricature or agitprop or one of the other crimes which Nat used to denounce at the Getting Started class. Nat looked disturbed.

'There was no sign of injuries, you say?'

'Not a mark on him. But the attack happened three weeks ago. The cuts could have healed.'

'Did his dad take him to hospital?'

'Yes. Guy's. That afternoon. So he says.'

'No photos of the injuries?'

'None I saw.'

'So it's probably just a con.'

'To get himself rehoused, you mean?'

'Or to save his own skin. If there *were* injuries, it could have been him who caused them.'

'I hadn't thought of that.'

'It's obvious: the kid was whingeing, the dad was drunk and knocked him about, then the partner came home and went ballistic; so he made up the fox.'

'I could ring social services – to see if there's a history of parental violence.'

'Rather you than me, Harry,' Nat said, pouring himself the last of the wine and signalling a change of topic. 'I'm not cut out for real-life dramas. I prefer inventing them.'

'It was you who got me into journalism, Nat.'

'Was it?'

'Yes, first the writing class, then the Claudia Moule connection.'

'Well, I suppose that's right,' Nat said, blushing. 'There's a sort of Claudia figure in my new play, actually. A scene where she and this . . .'

As he listened, Harry sipped his second glass of Orvieto – two glasses out of two bottles, his usual allocation when lunching with Nat, who never noticed how much more he had, or if he did notice, considered 5:1 in his favour a more or less equal share. It was the same with their conversation, which was always weighted in favour of Nat and the subject closest to Nat's heart, namely Nat. Greater love hath no man than love of self – Nat was the kind of man who would take himself on romantic holidays for one. Still, they had just spent twenty minutes on Harry, and if the rest of lunch belonged to Nat that was fine. Had Nat's blush just now been a blush of pride that his protégé had done well? Or a blush of shame that he had prostituted his talent? You never knew with Nat. All you knew was that you'd end up listening to him. And that if he proposed ordering more wine you'd agree to it, not because you wanted more or expected a fair share of it but because Nat, for all his faults, was your friend.

'So you think the fox is worth pursuing?' Harry said, interrupting. 'If you saw the story in the paper, you'd be interested?'

'Absolutely,' Nat said, without conviction. 'This bottle's empty, by the way. Do you fancy a Calvados to finish?'

<br>

## 8

## *ANTHEA*

A LESS suitable venue was hard to imagine, but Mr Norland held all his Planning meetings in the Council Chamber, on a dais which looked down into a vast gilt abyss with row on row of empty seats. The chamber gave committee meetings a sense of occasion, he said. It also reminded council employees of their responsibility towards the people they served, 'the citizens who look up to us, in hope and trust, from those empty seats'. Anthea found the logic hard to follow but nodded. The other heads around the table nodded, too.

A dozen of them had been assembled, along with two water jugs, a sludge-green tea service, a plate of biscuits and a heap of stapled handouts: official bulletins, budget statements, draft proposals, minutes from the previous, etc. The tea smelled like unwashed leotard, and dunking shortbread in it did nothing to improve the taste. Each speaker sat behind a nameplate (Health, Housing, etc.) but the nameplates were only shorthand for their real titles, which were so long that you could doze off while saying them. Environmental Sustainability and Community Regeneration Manager. Prohibited Substance Misuse Criminal Justice Worker. Mentoring, Integration and Employability Trainer with Special Responsibility for Ethnic Minorities. A proposal to retitle Anthea as a Quality Vegetation Management and Arboricultural

Planning Applications Officer had luckily been dropped. She remained a Tree Officer. At least for now. There was still time to be jobless by five o'clock.

The regeneration of the Hardhill Estate raised some vital questions, Mr Norland was saying. Anthea tried to give them her full attention but other questions intruded. For instance: did Mrs Merivale (Kerbside Recycling and Domestic Waste Operations Coordinator) really imagine that the long red hair sprouting from the mole on her left cheek was a thing of beauty? Anthea knew she ought to concentrate on issues, not personalities. But trees were her only reason for being here. And trees were item 15, the last on the agenda.

The last time she had sat in a council chamber was in Deptford, for an all-party open forum during the 1992 election campaign. That was during her year living with Jake: Arboretum, the squat in Plaistow, teacher training at Goldsmiths College, the writing class in Norley on Thursday evenings, Free Palestine marches, the struggle to save the planet from global warming. Among the demos she and Jake had gone to was one to protect an area of ancient forest – Oxleas Wood – from the developers. It was Jake's idea to go to the meeting together and heckle. But then a jam session with Arboretum intervened and he asked her to heckle for him. She took her seat. The hall was crowded. She had planned to start heckling the moment the Tory stood up to speak, but in the event she lacked the guts. Half an hour remained for questions, a chance to redeem herself. But she had always been nervous in public – not just afraid of being noticed, but afraid of being noticed trying not to be noticed – and for all her eagerness to please Jake she felt too scared. Luckily someone else raised the issue: where did the parties stand on Oxleas Wood? The local Labour candidate, playing to the crowd, said that any forest the Conservatives wanted to destroy was surely a forest worth preserving. She left in sullen despair, angry with Labour for not having an eco-policy, angry with herself for not having spoken up, and angry with Jake for not having come. On election day, she voted Green. As she had again yesterday evening, on her way home from work.

A wasp buzzed back and forth in the tall windows, desperate to escape. Mr Norland had moved on to Drains. Anthea looked up from her agenda to find Mrs Merivale staring. Had her failure to pay attention been observed? Or was it the nose rings, three to the left and two to the right, a full Olympiad, which friends said were cool and Anthea barely noticed any more but which older people – her mother, for instance – thought disfiguring? She ought to participate in the discussion. Drains were a vital environmental issue. But opening her mouth in a roomful of strangers took more courage than she possessed.

The long hand of the clock passed VIII, while the shorter one crawled towards IV. Did she dare take the last Bourbon, or should a debutante restrict herself to pink wafers? Security, Nod was saying, had become a major problem on Hardhill. The question was where the money should go – into surveillance cameras, bobbies on the beat, neighbourhood watch schemes, state-of-the-art burglar alarms, anti-vandal paint, fences with iron spikes, entryphones or electronic gates. It was an open discussion. Recreation had as much to contribute as Housing. She could see Nod smiling at her encouragingly. But when he winked to bring her in, she buried herself in the agenda. What had Mrs Crabbe said all those years ago, on her school report? 'Anthea's written ability isn't in doubt – if only she could contribute to class discussion!' Same old Anthea. Same sidling eyes and lowered head.

The Other Anthea – the one locked up inside her – would be less fearful. She'd raise a hand.

'Yes, Anthea?'

'Improving security means transforming how tenants feel about themselves and where they live. If we want a safer Hardhill, we should spend our money on trees and flowers. Change the environment and you change the people.'

It was what she thought, so why not say it? Her mother used to be an actress. And her father had believed in 'putting your oar in' – he would hate to see her oar lying unused. The people round the table weren't ogres. She shouldn't feel scared of them just because they were old.

Nod moved the discussion to the next item, while Rilda dutifully took minutes. What would the minutes record of Anthea, except that she had been present? If only the Other Anthea could speak.

'Item 8: Health and Sanitation Issues. The Tree Officer, Anthea Hurt, asked whether consideration could be given to the creation of a herb garden containing plants with medicinal properties.

'Item 9: Incidence of Suicide on the Estate. The Tree Officer suggested that the creation of all-encircling ponds, or "moats", round the three residential tower blocks, would have a benign effect on the occupants as well as providing those who did leap with some chance of survival.

'Item 10: Truancy Rates. The Tree Officer argued that pupils would be less likely to "bunk off" if the footpaths linking Hardhill Comprehensive to the estate were replaced with a rhododendron maze.

'Item 11: Graffiti. The Tree Officer said that the erect phallus spanning floors 13 to 18 of Ararat Tower was surely intended as a homage to Pan or Dionysus, and that the offender – or "artist", as she called him – be commis-

46

sioned to complete a series of wall paintings in celebration of Roman, Buddhist and Hindu deities.'

If only. The agenda moved on.

'Item 14,' said Nod. 'Environmental Health. Mr Hapgood, over to you.'

How had she ended up working in a dead-end job? Anthea wondered. More to the point: how had she ended up as her? She felt like a leaf, blown by every passing wind, one minute a kooky hippie chick studying star signs, the next a hardline Trotskyist. No one knew the real Anthea, not even Anthea. The outer self was dull and dutiful, with only those nose rings to hint at something braver. The inner self was noisy and passionate, but the noise came out as a stammer and the passions varied from day to day. She blamed the Terrible Thing that had happened for arresting her development. She blamed Jake, for screwing her up. But mostly she blamed herself.

'Item 15,' Nod said. 'Hardhill and Trees. Anthea?'

Her *raison d'être* at last. She must make a mission statement. A love song to trees. She cleared her throat to speak.

But as she did the clock struck V, the clang of it drowning her opening – 'I'd l-l-l-like to b-b-b-begin b-b-by . . .' – and reminding everyone present that the meeting was now due to end, it being a Friday, with a pleasant evening in prospect (the outside temperature warm enough to prompt thoughts of barbecues), and council employees having no financial inducement to work extra hours. Nod raised his hand like a traffic policeman. 'We're about to overrun,' he said. 'But I'm sure Anthea can be trusted to keep it short.' The Other Anthea would have told him to stuff it. Even this Anthea felt a twinge of frustration as well as a surge of relief. She had planned a soul-stirring homage to an ancient oak she knew, 'one of the last living English giants' – a hundred feet tall, thirty tons in weight, ten miles of twigs – whose inner waterways were more complex than England's canal networks, and whose domes and vaults were more dramatic than any mosque. She would go on to rhapsodise about gingko biloba and other immigrants that had made good in Britain – Lebanese cedar, Japanese maple, Himalayan magnolia, Moroccan broom. And she would conclude with a word or two about trees that wept – weeping willow, weeping ash, wisteria, laburnum – the image of their tears being the cue for a polemic on the tragic rape of the environment by multinationals, agribusinesses and *poor local planning*. But all she had time for was three bullet points: 1) there were no trees at Hardhill, 2) there ought to be trees at Hardhill, 3) funds must be set aside for planting trees at Hardhill.

Half a minute was all it took. She succeeded in stammering and repeating herself, all the same. And even half a minute was too long for Mrs Merivale, who ostentatiously tidied her papers and adopted an upright, point-of-departure posture in her chair.

'Thank you, Anthea,' Old Nod said. 'Most interesting.'

It had not been interesting. To make it interesting, she would have to be someone else. She stood up and followed the others down from the dais, glancing at the empty chairs, which would, she was sure, be grateful for the council's diligence. She was a washout. If Nod had any judgement, he would sack her. If she had any courage, she would resign before he did.

9

*NAT*

NAT SAT on the train, feeling sorry for himself. The drink had worn off, to be replaced by a sense of waste. *Post vinum omne animal triste.* What had he done with the past two hours? Or previous twenty years? What would he do with the life to come? The thought of *Wilderness Avenue* sitting on his desk waiting to be worked on made him will the train to go slower, or speed straight past his stop, or fetch up in a siding in remotest Kent, anything to delay the moment of engagement, though engagement was hardly the word given the disconnectedness he felt from his creation. No wonder people didn't bother with lunch these days. Lunch squandered time and money. Lunch wrenched you from routine. Lunch never used to be this bad. In his early days in London, Nat would get together with his Oxford cronies, Mike Tindicott, Rufus Huish and Wilberforce Jackson. Mike was freelancing as a publisher's reader, Rufus stalled on the lower rungs of the civil service, and Wilberforce trying to make it in the art world. Ambitious and underpaid though they all were, they were never so poor or busy as to miss their Friday lunches. There was a trattoria in Red Lion Street which offered spaghetti carbonara for £1.95 and a passable house red for even less. The food didn't compare with the food at Cantata, but nor did the prices, and the conversation seemed to go somewhere, if only because the four of them were going somewhere, or thought they were. To recall those times filled Nat with despair.

When his stop came, on impulse, he stayed in the carriage. He could go on to South Norley, and drop by his room at college, where there were essays to mark. It would be less painful than not working on *Wilderness Avenue*.

Harry had depressed him too. Was he cracking up? That paranoid stuff about the waiter avoiding his eye. The boy had been shy, that was all. And the shyness came from being a foreigner, ill at ease speaking English, which Harry had failed to notice till Nat pointed it out. As a teenager, Harry had showed such promise. But now he was thirty-something and finding it hard to move on. Maybe the pressure of gathering stories was too much for him and he should go back to being a sub. What Nat valued, as an artist, was inherence – *in-here-ness* – whereas Harry, like all journalists, was a skimmer, unable to penetrate the depths. Disconsolate though the lunch had left him, Nat felt braced by contempt for his old mate.

From the station, it was a ten-minute stroll to his workplace – not the place where the *real* work went on, but the one that paid the mortgage, or the small portion of it not paid by Libby. The day was still warm. He was glad of the walk. *Solvitur ambulando* – he could work out his ideas on the hoof. It was quiet here, too, apart from one woman, up ahead, talking into a mobile. He caught the inconsequential drift as he passed her – someone else with nothing to say but saying it. Nat had no desire to own a mobile. A mobile would stop him thinking. And his thoughts were valuable, if only to him. Sometimes when he walked he talked aloud to himself. And why not? He had yet to find a better listener.

Beyond the common, the familiar yellow-brick building came into view. When Nat began there, the place had been SORCE, the South of the River College of Education. Then the merger which gave it polytechnic status made it SORP. Now it was a fully-fledged university, USOR as it appeared in all the literature ('Looking for a USOR-friendly degree course?'), or, as Nat mournfully thought of it on days like this (and most days, these days, were days like this), SORU. Adult Studies, the department for which he worked on a part-time (0.3) basis, had also undergone a name change: after a spate of enquiries from men in dirty macs, it was now called ICE, Initiatives in Continuing Education. He was an ICE-man, full of SORU, but he didn't complain. ICE gave him a sense of purpose. ICE, unlike the theatre world, made him feel wanted. And ICE gave him somewhere to escape to whenever, as now, he felt depressed.

At Mandela (formerly Galileo) Tower, he swung the door open, nodded at the security man behind the desk, and – seeing the lift was, as usual, out of order – climbed the concrete stairs to the ninth. His room was a ten-foot-by-six yellowing cell with a view of the car park. The drawback of being a 0.3 was that the room had to be shared. But Lucinda Vurt, his co-habitee, whose home was in Aberdeen, appeared so infrequently that they'd only once ever met. The barrenness of his cell made Nat feel virtuous. And so did coming in on Friday afternoons, when all his fellow lecturers were 'working from home' and the only human presence was Lisia, the twenty-something departmental secretary, whose favourite reading matter was *Good Housekeeping* but whose intelligence he valued, since on good days, when she had time to spare, she would make them both tea and bring it to his room and regale him with scurrilous stories of his colleagues, 'tossers' she called them, an opinion he shared, since none of them seemed to appreciate the major talent (his) gracing their department. Nat felt especially unloved by his Literature colleagues. You'd think – well, he thought – they would be begging him to give talks and readings, and that a permanent sinecure, a 0.7 on top of his 0.3, was the least he deserved. But not only had this not happened, the Head of Literature, blue-eyed, yellow-haired Brik Pedersson, that drybones of Norse mythology 450–900, had lodged a formal complaint when one of Nat's famously animated classes overran by a pathetic three minutes, leaving him, Brik, the next occupant of the lecture theatre, 'severely inconvenienced by Mr Raven's amateurish and uncollegiate approach', and provoking the Dean's office to write to Nat with a reminder of 'the need for responsible timekeeping'. So much for creativity in higher education. Still, Literature's loss was ICE's gain. Nat's students might not be honours students (ICE's courses were offered as 'preparation for or relaxation from the rigours of a formal degree'), but they were, he felt certain, honoured to have him in their midst.

Today Lisia merely waved when Nat collected his mail, a signal that she was too busy to play tea lady. Never mind, Nat thought, I've more important things to do than gossip. He stared through his window at the air conditioning on the gymnasium roof, wondering what these more important things were.

The typescript in the brown envelope made no impression on him at first. He barely glanced at the covering letter, knowing it would be like the others – abject in its apology for submitting something that was late, over-long, mistyped, ill-punctuated, unsourced, coffee-stained, composed in the shadow of bereavement, retrieved from the maw of the family dog, etc. The other Shakespeare assignments had come in a week ago, and he sighed as he added this one to the pile. It was only by accident that the title page caught his eye. *The Book of Foxes*, it said, which didn't sound like an essay on the Problem Plays. He examined the covering letter. The writer called herself Anthea Hurt: 'Remember me from Getting Started? Probably not. I spent two terms going nowhere in your class back in 1992. My fault, not yours.' Anthea Hurt: was she the social worker who'd planned a musical about Dr Barnardo? Or the accountant with the limp who'd written that monologue about a gay broker coming out on the floor of the Stock Exchange? Her letter said she was working in Croydon, but didn't specify what the work was. Nat's students down the years seemed to end up in every profession except the writing profession, which despite the start his classes gave them had proved strangely resistant to their talents. In this they were model protégés; the writing profession didn't recognise Nat, either. He had always said it was a long, hard struggle. And if it was longer and harder than any student of his could afford financially or survive emotionally, no matter. His only task was to lay the foundations.

'Please don't feel under any obligation,' the letter said, 'but I'd be interested to know what you think. And if you *do* write back (you could email – do you have email?), be honest and tell me if I'm wasting my time.' Nat felt more flattered than put upon: that a student from five years ago should seek his opinion was the most *affirmed* he'd felt all day, and never mind if he couldn't remember who she was.

He turned to the first story. It was short. All the stories were short. They were reminiscent of someone – Ted Hughes, was it? – and before he knew it he'd reached page 30 and a tale called 'The Birth of Sex'. It was while he was reading this that something strange happened. At 16.53 – he could time it exactly, because his digital clock was the first thing he saw – he jerked upright, convinced he was the victim of some trick. He had been dreaming Anthea Hurt's typescript – not dreaming *of* it, as an object, but dreaming the images inside. At one level, it was simply explained: last night's lateness or the lunchtime wine must have made him nod off. But what was odd, and made him get up and pace the room (insofar as a tiny room can be paced), was the sense *he'd written the stories himself.* The writing was less polished than his own, of course, but it was as though his imagination had been tapped into; as though Anthea Hurt had seen into his head.

He sat down again, and took a cigarette from the drawer – Lucinda's drawer, Lucinda's Silk Cut – to stop his hand shaking. It was mad to react like this. Nothing he had written resembled *The Book of Foxes*, even in embryo. A search through his notebooks at home, a scroll through his disks and files, would settle the matter. But the stories were sexy, violent and deeply disturbing. It wasn't just that they had spooked him, he felt as though he owned them.

By the time he finished a second cigarette, he felt calmer. There were perfectly logical reasons why the stories had touched a nerve. Harry had told him that story at lunchtime, about a fox attacking a toddler, and then Anthea Hurt's stories brought back memories from his own childhood, such as the time he had wandered into a wood with pheasant coops and seen dozens of dead foxes strung up by the tail. As for the strange passage where she described two foxes being knotted – well, he'd seen something like that only a week ago, on the way to work, when a male dog, trying to dismount after mating, seemed to find itself clamped. He had mentally recorded the image, intending to put it in his notebook, but had then forgotten about it, until *The Book of Foxes* turned up and described it for him. How weird was that?

Above all, though, he was haunted by the images of fox blood. It was Uncle Jack's fault. The summer his father left, Nat had been sent to Frixley for a week, with instructions to be 'brave'. And because Uncle Jack had a passion for hunting, Nat was taught to ride. Till then the closest he had come to riding a horse was playing cowboys and Indians in the playground, when (whichever side you were on) you whipped yourself on the rump as you ran. The reality of riding was less fun: the helmet strap cutting into your chin; the dust and horsehair pricking your eyes; the ponies puffing out their stomachs out as you saddled them, so that a mile down the road the girth strap came loose and you toppled to one side. He stuck it out, though, if only to please Uncle Jack, and on the last day, after a week of spills first on, then off the leading rein, he was taken cubbing, 'as a treat'. He didn't know what cubbing was; nor the reason for stopping by a brambly hollow; nor the purpose of the pups brought by the kennelman. The pups themselves looked bewildered – even more so when an adult hound, snuffling through the hollow, surprised a large brown fox. 'Let him go,' Jack shouted, 'it's his cubs we want.' The cubs appeared almost as he said it, six of them, blundering about in a daze of bracken and yellow gorse, as another fox, their mother, tried to lead them away. The hounds piled on top of her. 'Let the pups have a taste,' Uncle Jack shouted. The cubs were driven towards the pups. The pups bit the cubs and were bitten back. It was an even contest, until the pups got the hang. Nat sat frozen in his stirrups while the hounds joined in. Soon nothing was left, only blood-splats in the bracken and the vixen's tail. Uncle Jack picked the tail up and brought it across. 'Chin up,' he said, and swished it over Nat's face. He had imagined a fox's tail as soft, like the stoles and muffs in his mother's wardrobe, but the tail was harsh, bristly and left a smear of wetness on his cheek. 'There, you've been blooded,' Uncle Jack said. The kennelman and his sons applauded – it was like being awarded school colours. But he could not forget the shrieks of that vixen.

As they rode home, the blood stiffened on his face. A bead of your own blood didn't taste bad, but he had a horror of tasting fox blood. In the downstairs toilet at Jack's house, he Luxed away the stain on his cheek, denying his mother the chance to see his warpaint when she came to collect him. But an after-reek remained. It remained there to this day, and now *The Book of Foxes* had unstoppered it – the smell of fox blood trickling through his mind.

A knock on the door made him jump. He half expected to find Anthea Hurt.

'You all right?' Claire said, stepping through. 'You look as though you've seen a ghost.'

Claire was his oldest student – not in terms of age (she couldn't be more than thirty) but in longevity of attendance. It had become a joke between them: that her poor little brain absorbed so little, she had to Get Started again every academic year. It wasn't true; she too worked at SORU, as part of some cross-disciplinary research project in neuroscience and biochemistry. Nat's class was her escape from the lab. She had no great opinion of the poetry she wrote, and nor had he, but she was adept at encouraging others. The two of them had become a kind of double act, good cop and bad: her being there to offer balm left him free to be brutal.

'I've brought my suggestions for the anthology,' she said.

'Ah yes, good, thanks.'

The 'Getting Started Anthology' – in reality a cheaply produced pamphlet – appeared at the end of each academic year. Nat thought it good for morale, not least his own: the quality might not be great but the range of work coming through (stories, poems, novel extracts, plays, satirical sketches, even – once – a libretto) was evidence that his class deserved SORU's support. It was Claire who did most of the editing and proofreading. He had quite forgotten they were due to meet today, to agree whose pieces would feature and in which order. That was the thing with Claire – however sweet and friendly, she was, to him at least, wholly forgettable. If asked to describe her, he would not have known where to start, though as she sat down next to him now – round glasses, short brown hair, no hint of the lab in her small pale hands – she seemed too distinctive to be called plain. Some men might find her attractive. He assumed there was a man, in the background, but she had never said and he had never asked.

As she passed the different typescripts for his approval, his mind kept wandering back to *The Book of Foxes*. Their conversation was mostly a monologue, hers, with distracted *mmms* and *yes*es from him.

'That all seems fine,' he said, at last.

'If you really think so,' she said.

'Absolutely.'

'I'll take this over to Repro then,' she said, closing the folder.

'By the way,' he said, though there was nothing by the way about it, 'do you remember an Anthea Hurt?'

'Should I?'

'She was in the class for a while. A few years back.'

'Doesn't ring a bell. What about her?'

'She sent me some stuff, that's all.'

'Stuff?'

'Stories. Folk tales. All about foxes.'

'There was someone who brought along a poem about foxes once. A woman with long skirts and knotty hair. Total nutcase. You'd better be careful.'

She laughed as she said it, teasing, halfway out the door. But suppose Anthea Hurt *was* a nutcase. In his worst moments – and there'd been several of these lately – writing no longer struck him as a profession, the skills of which could be taught, but as a form of hysteria: something the mad did, or which the sane could do only *in extremis*. Worse, he wondered if there was something in him that attracted madness. One student had stalked him after he said her work lacked irony. Another left prophecies of ruin on his answering machine because Nat had told him his dialogue sounded archaic. Ideologically, on the matter of loonies, Nat was a liberal, preferring them not to be stuck in bins. But as for the oddball ingrates who hated him for not acclaiming the immensity of their talent, he would be happy to see them all locked up.

'See you next week, then,' Lisia called, passing his door. Five thirty – he ought to be getting home. But there were fourteen *Measure for Measure* essays to mark. And *The Book of Foxes* lay open at page 31, commanding him to read on, if he dared.

*10*

## HARRY

'MERCATOR GROVE: that's off the Eye Street, innit?'

'We're on the corner,' Harry said. 'Where the bakery used to be.'

The car was a rust-flaked Toyota, with a driver who wore shades and a baseball cap. Most minicab drivers knew less about London's geography than about Lusaka's – and nothing at all about the principles of the internal combustion engine. But the Toyota seemed to have petrol in its tank and (at the last count) all four wheels. And, however circuitous, at least the journey back to Lewisham would be cheap – that had already been agreed outside Cantata, when the driver sidled up soliciting a fare. Journalists on the *Gazette* were supposed to stick to buses and trains; if Harry tried claiming expenses for a cab, Mills would query it. But public transport from Tower Bridge was tricky, and Harry had pieces to get on with. Hence, at his own expense, the cab. He was a driven man, in more ways than one.

'Yo friend Nat want to come with you?'

'No,' Harry said, 'he had a train to catch.'

In truth, he hadn't offered Nat the choice. It was bad enough him arriving so late, and then Harry had to pay the bill for them both, because Nat, not for the first time, had forgotten his credit card. A New Dawn, Blair kept telling the reporters. It didn't seem that way to Harry, morose, beleaguered and a hundred pounds worse off.

If Harry had been driving (and for a time he had owned a car, till he tired of the police pulling him over), he would have chosen a quieter route. South of the river was tough at the best of times – the air more acrid, the concrete bleaker, the buildings dirtier, the street vibe more menacing than to the north. And today, under the high blue sky, the Old Kent Road seemed more than usually cluttered with gruesome memorabilia: bunches of flowers strung to lamp posts, yellow police signs appealing for witnesses to such-and-such a crime. Arse-end of London, people said. Arse-end of Europe, even. But it was the end Harry belonged to, the hole from which he had crawled. He could remember, as a child, seeing rag-and-bone men on horse-drawn carts – an image of Victorian London, in the 1970s. Pawnbrokers, too, still did a brisk trade. Later came porn shops. Now most of the shops on the Old Kent Road were phone shops, selling cheap international calls. They were passing one now: a woman in a burkha stood inside, cradling a handset, on the line to Mombasa or Tehran. The image encapsulated south of the river: you lived here but your heart lived somewhere else.

'You watch the fight last night?' the driver asked – grey-fuzzed neck, eyes in the mirror, and that baseball cap.

'The fight?' Harry said.

'The election, man.'

'Ah, right.'

Harry followed the train of thought. They were at the lights by the Thomas à Becket, an old pub with a boxing ring upstairs. If you were passing on the top deck of a 36 bus, you could look in and see young men learning to fight. A useful outlet, people said. It kept aggression off the streets. And yet every half-mile came those yellow police signs with their appeals for witnesses to rapes, muggings, aggravated assaults, racial attacks.

'When Portillo got floored,' the driver said, catching Harry's eye in the mirror, 'it was beautiful, man. Like Lennox Lewis socked him in the jaw.'

Harry had still been at Deborah's when the result came through: a senior minister in John Major's government losing his seat to a boyish no-hoper called Stephen Twigg; Portillo standing centre stage, thick-necked and with a glazed stare, like a Spanish bull after the sword has gone in; while behind, over his shoulder, Twigg sheepishly grinned and rolled his eyes – gosh, dearie me, who'd have believed it? The crowd at Deborah's had guffawed. But there had been fear on their faces as well as pleasure. They had grown used to the idea that no political party they voted for would ever come to power. What scary new world was this?

'Jesus, man,' the driver shouted, braking, as a black Golf swung out from Asylum Road. 'See that?' he said in the mirror to Harry, for corroboration.

'Crazy,' said Harry.

'Dese niggas ain't got a clue.'

The patois must have been meant as a joke they could share, a multi-layered allusion to demography, ethnicity, prejudice, south London road behaviour, etc., through which the formal contract of driver and customer could be discarded and a new intimacy take its place. Either that or the guy was a wind-up merchant. Or a self-hating bigot. Or a loon. None of these could be discounted. Once, on the M23 to Gatwick, a cab driver confided to Harry that he had just been diagnosed with lung cancer and felt ready to do himself in – not a thing you want to hear when you're being driven at eighty miles an hour.

'So what you do, man? Yo livin, like?'

'I'm a journalist. Local newspaper.'

'Hey, how you get into that? Cousin o' mine at school, he interest doin' the same.'

'Well, I trained. At uni. But you also need luck, I guess.'

And contacts – it was true about Nat getting him in. 1984–90: the Lean Years of Harry Creed. Eager, clever and highly presentable, with a 2:1 in Film and Journalism from East London Poly, and references glowing enough to light a small town. A coming man whose moment refused to come. Doomed to waste half a decade on the dole. Several times he was shortlisted for jobs on provincial newspapers. He would meet the other candidates over coffee, and go in feeling confident, then depart twenty minutes later knowing he would be offered jackshit. Habit dulled the pain of rejection. For a year he worked part-time in a Holborn wine bar. But why should someone with a good degree squander his life serving drunks in suits?

Then a friend of Nat's cousin Sasha joined the *Gazette* as features editor. Claudia Moule: twenty-two, straight off a journalism course in Glasgow, blonde, pushy and on the lookout for freelancers. When Nat arranged for them to meet, and Claudia promised to put some work his way, Harry didn't hold his breath. But one week the *Gazette* lost half its staff to flu, and Harry, called on spec, was offered a subbing shift. Left to Claudia, a single shift was probably all it would have been. But Reg, the chief sub, an ex-comp in his fifties, took a shine to Harry. The *Gazette*, like every other paper, had just been through the print revolution, and Reg – the only comp to make the switch upstairs – needed allies. Being Peckham-born and working class 'and so forth' was in Harry's favour. He could also spell, which, as Reg said and Harry soon found out, 'most of the toffs and young Turks around here can't'. Soon the shifts at the *Gazette* became regular; at last he could call himself a journalist. But the problem of working as a sub – *OED*: beneath, inferior, subordinate; a stand-in or substitute – was that no one thought you capable of writing. The breakthrough came when Claudia left to join the *Telegraph* and the new features editor arrived, Deborah, who let him file the occasional piece on sport or jazz. When Deborah became editor-in-chief last year, the *Gazette* was revamped, with a commitment to cover 'community issues', and Harry was made a (probationary) staff reporter. From sub to cub in seven years: it wasn't lightning progress. But he was doing what he wanted at last. And once his probation was over, his place on the paper would be secure.

'Here you are, innit,' the driver said, off Mercator Grove.

'Nine pounds, did you say?'

'Right enough.'

'Keep the change.'

As Harry said, the offices of the *Gazette* had once been a bakery: the shopfront was now Reception, the back room for the ovens Editorial, and the upper floor where the family had lived Classified and Display. On hot days you could smell dough – a century of it rising through the bricks. This afternoon, Editorial was almost deserted – the paper came out midweek, so Fridays were always slack, and with the fine weather people had bunked off early. He could spot only Deborah, behind her glass screen, and Mills, the deputy editor, half asleep over a paperback (he wasn't *still* reading *Captain Corelli's Mandolin?*). Not that the place was exactly frantic even on press day. The *Gazette* – the *South-East London Weekly News Gazette*, to give it its full title – boasted sales of 80,000 and a readership of a quarter of a million. But there were only a dozen journalists on the staff.

On his desk Harry found three pictures taken by Malcolm, the *Gazette* staff photographer, who must have arrived at this morning's assignment just after Harry had left. 'This one's the best,' he had scrawled on the yellow Post-it. Evidently the mother, Terry's wife, had turned up too. The three of them were posing by the steps to the garden, as though for *Hello!* – angry dad to the left, devoted mum to the right, cheeky toddler who nearly became a tragic victim in the middle. Harry could see the story now, on a top right-hand page, five hundred words, with a photo of the family (plus an inset of a fox's head) across three columns, and a head-line in 48-point Bodoni: FOX TRIED TO KILL OUR BABY. Or would that be too heavy? Mr Lavell, Terry, Tel to all his friends, was depending on the *Gazette* to change his luck. Harry remembered the look in his eyes as he said goodbye, on the front step; the scowling half-face of earlier had become full, open, even matey; the eyes were plaintive and sincere – 'Help us,' they pleaded. 'Tell the world the story I told you.' But how could Harry tell the story when he didn't believe it – and felt anxious about his ability to write at all?

He pushed the photos aside and looked at his notes again. Surely foxes were harmless – a normal part of modern city life. You saw them trot-ting along pavements or scurrying under hedges or sunning themselves on the roofs of garden sheds. It sometimes seemed there were more foxes in London than there were people. And that half the people were foxes, too: sneaky, mean-eyed, nocturnal. But as to the threat which foxes posed to children – neither a trawl through the cuttings, nor a search online, revealed a shred of evidence.

He did his best to check out the story, nonetheless, calling Guy's Hospital to ask if a Daniel Lavell had been treated for injuries three Tuesdays ago. 'We can't give out information about individual patients,' the girl in Admin said, but then she softened slightly ('A fox? How weird is that?') and put him through to her friend in A & E, who promised to check the rota and get whichever medic had been on duty that Tuesday to call him. He also rang social services, and was passed from Family Services to Crisis Management to Child Protection, with long pauses in between, only to be told, as he should have guessed, that all their files were 'strictly confidential. Have you tried the police?' He did try the police. But the duty officer sounded harassed and more or less accused him of wasting police time. London Zoo were dismissive, too: no, sir, no escaped wolves or giant foxes to report. He felt ridiculous – a raw cub or wacko scribbler chasing tall tales.

'So did you have fun last night?' Deborah asked, emerging from her glass cubicle, lipstick-fringed styrofoam coffee in one hand, cigarette in the other.

'Great party, thanks.'

Harry approved of Deborah, quite aside from her being his boss. House prices, restaurants, council-refuse policy, sex traffic, the difficulties Somali children experience in south London schools, the source of the River Quaggy: anything and everything seemed to fascinate her. 'Tell me about it,' she'd say, but not cynically, as most people said it, but in a spirit of 'I'd like to know more'.

'Travis and I didn't get to bed till five,' she said. 'Nat wouldn't leave. We had to kick him out in the end.'

'I just had lunch with him. He was still drunk, I think.'

'And you?'

'It's been a quiet day.'

'How's that fox story?'

'Coming along.'

He would have said the same even if the piece were finished. Show Deborah a piece too early and by press day she would be bored and pull it – whereas stories produced at the last minute excited her news sense.

'Is the dad as flaky as he sounded on the phone?' she said.

'Hard to say.'

'Could be a fun piece, though?' she persisted. 'Unless you think it's something for D & G.'

D & G was shorthand for the David and Goliath column, a weekly slot Deborah had invented to emphasise the *Gazette*'s credentials as a people's paper, by 'giving you the ordinary honest unsung heroes of south London a voice in your battle against the big-shot bureaucrats and thugs'. (Harry itched to insert a comma or two in the standfirst, but he was a reporter now, not a sub, and to Deborah the unpunctuatedness was punchier.)

'No, it's not a D & G,' Harry said.

'Ah well. What else are you working on?'

He ran through his list with her. Commuters protest at the new rail timetable, Eltham couple celebrate their eightieth wedding anniversary ('Wow! Is that possible?', 'They're ninety-nine and ninety-seven'), council workers threaten strike, marathon runner raises money for disabled kids – the usual stuff. Each issue of the *Gazette* carried thirty news stories, and as a cub reporter Harry was given those which nobody else wanted. There had been a week when twelve items in the paper were his, though the fact was hidden by pseudonyms: 'By Harold Faith', 'By Harriet Crudd', 'By a staff reporter', etc. He didn't mind being denied the credit – seeing your name in print was exciting the first time, but after that it was narcissism. And he didn't mind the slog of daily hackwork. But once his probation was over he would like to be given some serious assignments.

'Let's see where we've got to on Monday,' Deborah said. 'Doing anything at the weekend?'

'Not much. You know me.'

She raised her eyebrow ironically, to imply she knew him all too well – that he'd be out clubbing, or flying to Barcelona, or shagging someone stupid, or whatever else a single man in his early thirties did at the weekend. But 'not much' was the truth. He would go to the launderette, and visit his mum, and watch *Match of the Day*, and work out at the gym, and play computer games, and pray for Monday morning. Leisure didn't suit Harry: it made him worry about having no life beyond work, a worry he didn't have when he was working.

'What about you?' he asked.

'Birthday party for my youngest. A sleepover – God knows why they call it that. I'm going to take off now. Why don't you do the same?'

He said he would. But after she'd gone he created a file called FOXDOC and tried to rough out a piece. Just keep it simple, he told himself. A catchy first para and the rest will follow. Yes, there was more to the story, but there was more to every story and a jobbing journalist could only go so deep. 'We wasn't expecting a . . .' That too was a story. But not a story he was able to write.

The sun crept lower through the blinds. But the piece didn't come easily. By the time he quit his keyboard, with only a couple of hundred words to show for his efforts, it was evening.

# *JACK*

BRACKENED HEATHLAND, open pasture, pine forest, reedbeds, shingle beach – this was England at its best. Jack always followed the same route: through the fields behind the Hawk & Handsaw, across the wide marshes to the dunes, up the beach, past the hides of the bird reserve, then left back inland at the National Trust place, winding down by the river into the woods, crossing over by the little wooden bridge and striking deeper into the forest, then left again at the top of the hill along the bridleway and circling back to where he'd parked the car: six miles at least and with infinite breeds of birdlife along the way. You didn't need to be a twitcher to enjoy it. He and Nancy used to come most Sundays. Today being a weekday was quieter, almost deserted in fact. His one regret was not bringing Sammy. Still, there'd be time to take Sammy out later. Perhaps they'd walk up to his local, the Fox & Feathers. He had the taste now, after the session at lunch.

A bird wept overhead, *wee-lee-lee-laa-wirrit-wirrit*. Curlew? Lapwing? Gull of some kind? The beach was more shingly than last time. It changed from month to month.

He felt guilty, he had to admit, but there was bugger all to do at work and Karen could always call him on his mobile. He'd had the damn thing only a month, and there were features that still baffled him, such as the current blankness of the screen – did that mean no reception? Hook had been on at him to provide 'senior employees' with mobiles, for ease of liaison round the factory. But he was damned if he'd waste the money even as a tax dodge: why couldn't a chap walk the fifty yards to another chap and address him in person? Still, he might buy Hook a mobile to keep him sweet, or make him less bitter than he'd been this morning when told the news about SGS – 'Slimy Gallic Shits', as he christened them twelve years ago, the only previous occasion there had been trouble, and as he called them again this morning in Jack's office, adding: 'Trust the bleeding French to let us down. We should have stuck with Blighty.' Not sticking with Blighty had given Raven & Son twelve highly profitable years, when otherwise they would have gone bankrupt. But there was no point reasoning with Hook; best buy that mobile and shut him up.

Beyond the National Trust entrance, breaking custom, Jack walked on rather than circling back. It meant angling off right past fairy-tale cottages hidden deep in bluebell woods, then following a narrow path above the crumbling sand cliffs. Nancy would be gardening or sleeping off lunch now – having failed to show up for lunch, he was not expected till seven at least. No one at work seemed to be missing him, either. If he kept going, he'd reach the tea rooms and buy a scone. It was twice the usual distance, but he felt better than he'd been feeling all day.

Going home late on Friday was a ritual he had developed with Michelle, back in the eighties. The end-of-week review, they called it: no phone or personnel to interrupt them. In theory, they met to bring the figures up to date and plan his diary for the following week. In practice, as they got to know each other, the sessions became a discussion of anything and every-thing, accompanied by a bottle of claret. Michelle was adept at hearing rumbles from the factory floor, and several likely disputes were averted through her forewarning him. Work as well as pleasure, then: they made a good team, though he would not have used the word 'intimate' of their meet-ings, as she did later. It was true they sometimes spoke of their respective families, and that he once complained of Nancy's lack of interest in the business or indeed in him. He was not unhappy, he said – he could remember using exactly those words: 'I'm not unhappy' – but in some respects life could be better. Michelle, whose two daughters were much younger than his two, said she knew what he meant: her husband, Marcus, was an airline pilot and often away; it could get lonely. This exchange of mild gripes was as intimate as it got – until one Friday night Michelle announced that she was thinking of leaving Marcus: she had found a woman's eyeliner in his jacket pocket, 'no doubt some air-hostess tart's', and was 'sick of feeling ugly and humiliated'. Jack patted her hand consolingly – 'stroked and fondled' would not have been his description – and, with reassurances that he thought highly of her work and did not consider her ugly in the least, cheered her up as best he could. Nothing more was said. He assumed her marital trou-bles must have passed. Then one Friday some weeks later – it was rash of him, in retrospect, to have launched into a moan about Nancy getting fat and 'losing interest in the physical side of marriage' – Michelle burst into tears, and told him she could no longer keep her feelings 'bottled up': her marriage to Marcus was an empty shell, and meanwhile she had fallen in love with him, Jack. He must forgive her for her boldness, she said, but she knew he felt the same; he was a gentleman, a perfect gentleman, but she had seen how he looked at her: surely it, them, love, was meant to be. Jack gulped his claret, appalled. He tried not to show *how* appalled, and said um, yes, well, er, he was of course flattered that a woman of Michelle's age and attractiveness should be drawn to a chap like him (which he was – that birthmark had always made him feel ugly), and he hoped she knew how much he valued her, both as a colleague and a friend, but – he saw her flinch at the 'but' – had she considered the practical difficulties, the awkwardness at work and the cruelty to loved ones? She put her face in her hands. So, she sobbed, she was wrong then, he had no feelings for her at all. No, not wrong, of course he had feelings, but he had not allowed himself to think of her 'in that way'. She cried behind her hands. He passed her a handkerchief. 'There, there,' he said. 'I don't want your pity,' she hissed. He was handling it badly, he knew, but how could he handle it well? She left with fresh make-up and a brave red smile and an apology for having 'misunderstood the situation' – she felt a fool, she said, the love was clearly all on one side. On the Saturday night, still shell-shocked, several numbing whiskies inside him, he lay next to Nancy and thought how much nicer it would be to lie next to Michelle: she was right, he had always wanted her – those cornflower eyes, the slim brown legs, that black silk blouse with the top three buttons undone. Any other man would have made a move by now, why not him? If they were careful, perhaps a clandestine extension of their Friday nights need not wreak havoc. He would put it to her.

On Monday Michelle phoned in sick. That day, and the next, he reached only her answering machine – and did not dare leave a message for fear of causing her trouble at home. On Wednesday she was back in the office, pink-eyed and heavily made up, and handed him her letter of resignation – she was on a month's notice, but 'all things considered' she trusted he would let her leave right away: 'In fact, you'll obviously be glad to see the back of me.'

He said of course not, she must stay, this was unnecessary. The necessity or otherwise of it was a matter for her, she said.

He said he had been thinking over the weekend. He should have thought earlier, she said, when they were having their 'intimate' talks and he was 'stroking and fondling' her.

He said he was very fond of her, they had always been friends, perhaps she was right and they could be more than friends. No friend would have toyed with her as he had, she said.

He said she had misunderstood. She understood perfectly well, she said, and the shame she now felt for having allowed herself to be trampled on and treated like a tart was unendurable and even if she and Marcus were to separate, which looked increasingly likely, she would *never never never* ask anything of him, Jack, again.

Her cornflower eyes were flint. She spoke with the rage of a rejected lover, but they had not been lovers – none of the fruits yet all this gall. She was too angry, too quick for him, too far ahead. Her closing down on him was as much a shock as her opening up had been. The chance was there to change his life, but before he could react she whisked it away.

'Breathe a word about me and I'll tell everyone, including your precious Nancy,' she said as she left. The lunacy of the threat – tell everyone what? – was cathartic. She was unstable, a loose cannon; he should steer clear.

He typed the formal letter himself, accepting her resignation 'with regret' and offering her one month's extra salary 'in recognition of your invaluable service to this company' ('hush money', he imagined her thinking as she read it, 'blood money'). He promised her a 'marvellous' reference. But no employer wrote to ask for one, and he did not speak to Michelle again. She later moved away from the area, he gathered, whether with or without Marcus was unclear. He thought of her with regret, yearning and cold terror. As far as he could tell, no one at Raven & Son had known a thing – what was there to know? But he had been scalded. Here he was, years later, scalded still. She had discovered some part of him he didn't know was there, and long after she'd gone the sense of a life lived more intensely remained – a sense of Jack behaving less like himself so as to become more truly Jack.

Ach, he thought, as the waves broke far below, I drank too much at lunchtime, this is nonsense. I'm a sixty-year-old man with a wife, two daughters, a mower business, and a birthmark on my forehead. I should stick to what I have and what I know.

A quarter-mile further on, the cliff path descended to the beach. Finding the tea rooms already closed, he wandered across to where the boats sat on the shingle – old fishing boats smelling of tar and cod. For a moment he felt lost, overawed by the grey immensity of the sea and the yellow cliffs they ate into year by year. Then he remembered the pub, just up the road, and left the beach and headed that way, picturing himself on a bar stool with a slow, second pint of Best (the first having been a thirst-quencher). Should he call Nancy on the mobile, and tell her where he was? No need. If he was back at the car in half an hour, say, he would be home be eightish. And if it was later, so what?

## 12

# *LIBBY*

LATER, THINKING back, she blamed a chain of random events. If she had not been so impressed by him at the SaxonAir meeting. If the advert for the job had already gone out. If she had slept better the night before. If he had been a fraction less charming, if he had omitted the story of the builder, if his shirt tail had not been hanging out when he stood up to go . . . There was some theory whereby the flap of a butterfly's wings in China could set off a hurricane in Kansas; Nat often banged on about it. Now she understood what it meant.

Her usual lunch was a baguette and *café au lait* from Pret A Manger, eaten *très vite* and *à seule*. Today was the same, except for the last bit: she had company. The intern, Damian – she'd had to ask Angie to remind her of his name – with his white shirt, blue suit, red tie, fuzzy blond-streaked hair, high voice, attentive gaze, upright posture. Any number of young men in the building looked like this; no wonder she had failed to notice him. But few of them would have dared speak up.

'That was smart work this morning,' she said.

'I spent a day with the Creatives last week,' he said, 'and saw the sketches. Plus Tarquin and I had a drink together after work.'

Was Damian gay, then? Certainly Tarquin was.

'Well, however you did it,' she said, 'you saved our bacon. I owe you one.'

'Don't mention it, Mrs Raven.'

'Libby.'

'Don't mention it, Libby.'

'So tell me about yourself. What work have you done before? How have you liked it here? What are you planning to do next?'

Questions came easy to her. She was used to interviewing. Every few weeks or so her latest Account Assistant would be headhunted and she'd have to find a new one: Amanda, the current incumbent, had just handed in her notice. Libby found the process trying. The girls who applied (it was always girls) were all so bright, nerveless, fluent, *finished* – and bland. They hadn't just been coached, they'd been cloned. Susanna, Marina, Perdita and Amanda became one indistinguishable Sumapanda: Surrey private school . . . Gap year . . . Oxbridge . . . Upper second . . . Keen to do good in the world while also (laugh) earning good money, blah, blah, blah. Ten minutes was all she gave to each candidate. Two was enough for most of them. In fact, if they failed to make an impression on entering the room, they could forget it. But whichever one she appointed, none lasted the course. Libby would leave the office on Friday and on Monday morning a new Sumapanda would be sitting there: blonde hair, black jacket, flash of cleavage, silver bangle, just like the last. Safe and serene, every one of them. But she wasn't looking for a millpond.

Damian was different. A man, obviously. But slightly older, too, four years out of university and with a career so spotty that he'd been willing to come to Arran & Arran as an unpaid intern. That was worrying, or perhaps to his credit, she wasn't yet sure. The vacant post, Amanda's, wasn't on her mind when she began asking questions, but as he talked she glanced over his CV. Comprehensive school in Ealing, Economics degree at Warwick, gap year in South-East Asia, two-year spell with Andersen, then it all went hazy circa 1996.

'So you left Andersen,' she asked him. 'Why?'

'I didn't feel challenged.'

'More challenge to work than do nothing.'

'I've never done nothing.'

'There's a year unaccounted for here. What happened?'

'I was hoping you wouldn't ask.'

'I *am* asking.'

She watched his Adam's apple as he spoke. It was a story about starting up a dotcom and going bust – familiar stuff, and she found herself looking at her watch. But then he moved up a gear.

'I'd taken out a loan and bought part of warehouse in Bermondsey, with room for an office on the ground floor and one-bedroom flat above. To convert it is going to cost me 150 grand, but the builder comes with lots of recommendations and he makes good progress and we get on really well. So one Wednesday, a lorry rolls up with the materials for the upstairs flat. He says do I want to check everything's there, but I'm busy, and wouldn't know what to look for anyway, and by now the guy's my friend. Then he asks could he have his seventy-five grand – that's in the contract, half the payment due on delivery. He says he knows I've better things to spend my dosh on, nudge-wink, and not to worry, but the money I've

66

borrowed is in the bank, so I write him the cheque, and he takes it and folds it in three and puts it in the left breast pocket of his check shirt, and starts telling me about the wooden floor he plans to fit and the specially imported Norwegian pine it's made from, "so when you take the chicks up you can hear their heels go clickety-click up the stairs". I remember that because it's the last sentence I ever heard him speak. To cut a long story short, he disappeared and declared himself bankrupt, after pocketing three large cheques in one day. By the time I gave up pursuing him, I'd gone bankrupt, too. All in all, I don't feel too good about what happened. And I didn't think it would look good on my CV.'

'Well, you score points for honesty,' she said. 'Belated honesty,' she added, trying to sound severe.

'OK, I was gullible,' he said, meeting her eye. 'But I learned my lesson. If you gave me a job, you'd not be disappointed.'

'Who's talking about a job?'

'I heard your assistant's leaving.'

'You think you could do her job?'

'I think I could learn from you. You're highly experienced.'

*Highly experienced?* Was that his way of saying she seemed old to him? She bristled but let it go.

'Anything you'd like to know about the post, if I *were* to consider you for it? The salary and so on?'

'No, I trust you to be fair.'

'Nothing else you want to ask?'

'Well, I am interested in how *you* first got into advertising. And how much it's changed over the years.'

Touch of smarminess. But with that sting in the tail: how old did he think she was?

'That would take too long,' she said. 'I've a meeting to get to.'

'I understand,' he said. 'Maybe we could go for a drink sometime instead.'

When he stood up to leave, his shirt was hanging out, like the tail of some animal. She found it oddly attractive. She found him oddly attractive. There was an energy about him. He reminded her – almost – of Nat, who had once had energy too.

('He probably invented the whole builder story,' Nat said, when she recounted the episode over supper that night. 'To show himself in a bad light, knowing it would really show him in a good.' 'I hadn't thought of that.' 'Yes, he's probably much more cunning than he looks.')

(Later still, much, much later, Damian would tell Libby that he had indeed invented the whole story. It was true a builder had once ripped him off but that was over some roof tiles and only for a couple of grand. Oh, and he hadn't left Andersen of his own volition, he was pushed out, after a female colleague he had slept with bombarded senior staff with emails about his allegedly sadistic sexual tastes – 'I had to go, but they gave me a golden handshake of fifty grand.')

(She didn't believe that story, either. Damian's stories weren't the sort to invite *belief*. 'I never know what's true with you and what's not,' she once said to him. 'Well, I can tell you why I wanted the job,' he replied. 'Because I wanted *you*. You can trust me on that one.')

*Experienced?* Was that how she struck people? she wondered, as she climbed into a cab below Canada Tower five hours later. Amid the euphoria she'd felt when Mark Arran announced his plans, there was the bruise of one of the phrases he used – 'as you would appreciate with all your experience, Libby'. He meant it as praise; he'd been lauding her for saving the SaxonAir account that morning, word having reached him in his eyrie. But the praise and the champagne and the promised rewards of a restructured company couldn't obliterate the hurt in *experience*, the same word Damian had used earlier. She had taken most of the steps a woman could take to stop herself looking old or becoming invisible – not least by retaining her slimness. But however hard you worked at eating salads and chain-smoking, you couldn't hide the truth. In most professions, thirty-five was considered young. But in advertising you were past it by forty. The wisdom of age? Forget it. The only wise they wanted was streetwise and you had that at twenty-one.

How did she first get into advertising? By getting a job at Copy & Co, in the early eighties, with her current boss, Mark Arran. (Mark later joined forces with Arran Petrie, making a virtue of the coincidence of their names by creating a new – now well-established – company called Arran & Arran.) Where did she begin? At the bottom, coffee-making and sandwich-buying for the Creatives, before she slipped her way up. Slipped, not slept: there was the once with Herbie Root, in the days before Nat, but by then she had risen from junior clerk to secretary to receptionist to deputy assistant (Research) to assistant deputy (Media). In those days women were hired on strictly decorative grounds, with a willingness to file or fuck considered an asset. Libby avoided the first and drew the line, with one exception, at the second. Sleeping with Herbie had been his reward for not pestering her to sleep with him, unlike every other Creative. She was young and single then, and unused to eulogy. All the *Hey, gorgeous*es and *You're beautiful*s might have gone to her head but for wise old Angie, all of twenty-eight then, who advised her, over a bacon roll and coffee, that the way to verify a wooing Creative's sincerity was to ring him at home, at the weekend, and offer to meet him, at which point you found that he was engaged, married, gay, impotent or agoraphobic. 'They're all bullshitters,' Angie said. 'Take it from me.' So Libby did. And Angie was later rewarded, not sexually like Herbie (whom Libby had got so drunk that he would remember nothing of the episode), but hierarchically: the day Libby became Account Director, she appointed Angie as her PA.

'You should push yourself more,' Angie used to tell her. Back in those days Libby's only concern lay in pushing her husband – pushing publishers to consider his poems and stories, pushing directors to read his plays and screenplays, pushing Nat himself to get out of bed. Once he was famous, the plan went, she could stay at home and have his children. In the meantime, she would support him as best she could. The work was menial and badly paid; she got more fun from studying French at night school. But then Mark Arran handed her the file for Strays, an animal welfare charity run by two sisters in Peterborough. Strays was a hopeless project, or learning curve, that was understood: the sisters, everyone assumed, were two cat-obsessed old biddies with no budget. But when Libby turned up at their home, she found two serious-looking businesswomen in their forties – and a commitment to spend at least £50,000 on an ad campaign. Donations to Strays from the general public averaged £1.5 million annually: Libby had found a little gold mine. It was more luck than judgement, but she never looked back. Rather Strays than selling Nat's screenplays.

Ah, Nat. His various defects invariably came to mind at this point of the day – among them, insensitivity, indolence, fecklessness, self-absorption and the assumption that she would be the one cooking supper and putting the girls to bed. The list was long, and treating herself to a cab home from Canary Wharf did little to compensate. But Nat had two saving graces: he a) loved her and b) seemed not to notice that she was getting older. He even called her Beth sometimes, a name she did not care for and considered laughably unsuitable, suggesting as it did someone earth-mothery, big-breasted and with shoulder-length blonde hair, but which took her back ten years whenever he said it.

They had met at a private view – an exhibition of woodcuts by Wilberforce Jackson. Nat knew Wilberforce from Oxford, and Libby knew him because Mark Arran had commissioned him to redesign the logo of a cereal – a once-famous cereal, since defunct, in part because of the awfulness of that logo, or so it was generally agreed in the trade. On the back of the cereal packet, as it were, Wilberforce conned some gallery into exhibiting his 'powerfully sensuous' woodcuts. Half the staff at the agency were invited, but most had better things to do, which was how Libby, then a minion, came to be there. She arrived in black and under the illusion that artists were interesting. Wilberforce Jackson's chief interest, she soon discovered, was in putting his hand up skirts, or at any rate up hers. She moved to a safe distance, and stood in front of the one woodcut in the room which did not show a woman in some humiliatingly contorted sexual posture. Not that the woman in it was not being penetrated but at least she seemed to understand what was going on, unlike her dumbly enraptured sisters, all of whom lay open in wonderment at being pronged by some bearded twit. On another day, with another artist, she might have been curious about the huge endowment of these men, who in their beards at least bore a disturbing resemblance to their creator. As it was, she found the work ugly and pathetic, and resolved to tell Mark Arran, even if it should cost her job as chief errand-girl and tea-maker at Copy & Co, that he must under no circumstances employ Wilberforce Jackson again. Then Nat spoke.

'But is it art?'

'Um.'

'Go on, be honest, what do you think?'

'I think it's self-aggrandising crap?'

'Interesting. The artist's a friend of mine. We used to share digs.'

'That's mean – you should have said.'

'It's all right. I don't go for it either.' He leaned towards her, conspiratorially. 'UIOA.'

'UIOA?'

'Up Its Own Arse.'

'And every other orifice.'

'My name's Nat, by the way.'

'Mine's Elizabeth.'

They toured the walls with their wine glasses, whispering disparagements. He was tall, blue-eyed and curly-haired, and intrigued by her accent.

'Where's it from?'

'Ballymena?'

'Is that the North?'

'Yes.'

'So you've . . . growing up where you did . . . given the situation . . .'

She was used to this. It went with the territory.

'Have I witnessed bombs going off? Watched British soldiers being stoned? Lost friends in sectarian attacks?'

'Yes.'

'No.'

'Oh.'

In Ballymena, the Troubles had seemed remote, something on television – Belfast might as well have been Hanoi. But people in London were always reluctant to believe it. Angie had a similar problem, coming from the North-East ('You mean your father didn't go down t'pit?'). The two of them were a constant disappointment.

'And you're . . . ?'

'From Sussex originally. But I met Wilberforce at Oxford.'

His aversion to Wilberforce's woodcuts turned out to be less comprehensive than hers. Over a pizza in the Italian restaurant round the corner (Luigi's, their sentimental favourite ever since), he admitted to having bought three of Wilberforce's etchings the previous year. 'I was helping him out,' he said, embarrassed. 'Anyway, they were cheap.' A glass or two later he admitted to finding the woodcuts 'disarmingly candid'. Candid? Was that a posh word for pornographic? He blushed. 'Not pornographic. Erotic.' Erotic? He had to be joking. But it was too late by then. She liked Nat. She even loved him a little. He had done this strange thing, mid-conversation – reached over as if without noticing and taken the cuff of her black silk blouse and rolled it between his forefinger and thumb. Much sexier, somehow, than touching her.

In the street, he invited her back to his flat. On one condition, she said – that he did not insist on showing her his etchings.

He didn't. So she did.

In bed he called her Beth.

She was in too good a mood to correct him. And too distracted, till next morning, to notice the Wilberforce Jackson hanging over his bed.

They moved in together two months later. She was twenty-three, empty, eager, ready to be impressed. He was older, nearly thirty. It didn't seem *too* old. In many respects she was more worldly. His naivety, lack of a salary and unhistory of girlfriends might have rung warning bells. But he was serious, enthusiastic, ambitious and in love with her. For now he ran an evening class. But he was going to be a famous writer and then he would give up the night job. Teaching stopped the creative juices flowing, he said. When he said it, his juices would usually be flowing through her. She loved the pump and sweat of him. And she loved living with a man who was *creative*. Back in those days, no one in advertising would have dared to use the word of themselves – not even the Creatives. Creativity was reserved for art, and advertising was in a different league, everyone knew that. If ever she was in danger of forgetting it – when she came home excited by the brilliance of some slogan or brand name or choice of music or clinchingly apt visual design – there was Nat to put her in her place.

His mother Eunice was against the marriage. Until a month before, when she came up from Sussex for the weekend, she remained unaware of Libby's existence. Most of Sussex came with her: among the contents of two large suitcases were four dresses, three hats, two pairs of boots, two umbrellas, a fur stole, a pair of binoculars and a shooting stick. (Where she planned to use the shooting stick in Lewisham was unclear.) Before she showed up, on the Saturday morning, all traces of Libby were removed from the flat: 'Mummy can be neurotic,' Nat said. 'Let me break it to her gently.' It was agreed that Libby would go out for the day. When she came back, at teatime, Nat introduced her as his girlfriend – actually, which annoyed her, as 'a girlfriend'. To skirt the issue of living arrangements, the plan was that Libby 'miss the last train' to wherever, so that Nat could offer her a camp bed (while he slept on the sofa and Eunice in their double bed). Tea was formal and Sussexy, with the silver teapot Eunice had given her son on his twenty-first birthday. All went well until Nat failed to find a knife to cut the fruit cake Libby had bought. 'Top left-hand drawer, Nat,' she said, not thinking. 'How clever of you to guess,' said Eunice. 'But it's Nathaniel, dear, four syllables, Nath-an-ee-el.' For Eunice, getting people to say Nathaniel was a full-time occupation – a redirection of the energy she would have put into her own marriage had not Nat's father Ronnie run off. Even at the wedding, she could not let go. The best man's speech, the toast, the telegrams – all were interrupted by her plaintive 'Not Nat, not Nate, not Nathan, Nath-an-ee-el, four syllables, please'.

The flat they then shared had two rooms: a bedroom (with a tiny bathroom L-ed off) and living room (with a tiny kitchen, ditto). When Libby pictured it now, she saw herself standing at the oven making lasagne (or chicken korma, or boeuf bourguignon, or pork cassoulet), while Nat sat with his back to her at a small wooden table by the window. He was writing. So she assumed. In truth, as she now knew, he wasn't writing but hovering, pen above paper. She missed the innocence of it, nonetheless: Nat at his table, composing his unwritten masterpiece; Beth (as she tried to think of herself) gazing proudly-fondly from the kitchen, her wooden spoon deep in plum tomatoes and kidney beans. What did she think of herself then, now? What did Libby think of Beth? Nothing! Nothing, because she had made herself nothing in order to be something to this man, this Creator. Of course, she called herself a feminist. She might have missed out on university but she had read the books (Greer, French, de Beauvoir, Dworkin, Millet) and knew all there was to know about Wilberforce Jackson's objectifying male gaze. But six months of being in love with a would-be writer and her mind was mulch. There she stood, red-faced, overweight, up to her eyes in steam. When Libby thought of it now, in the taxi home, it wasn't Nat she resented, the male exploiter, the man who thought hoovering would compromise his artistic integrity (the man who when he did once hoover caused the girls to exclaim, in a panic, 'What's wrong, Daddy, is Mummy dead?'). No, the person Libby resented was Beth. She wanted to whip her silly apron off, clap her oven gloves over her ears and stuff her in to bake. She felt humiliated even thinking of her. She would like to burn her.

She had burned her. Out of the cinders, crisply dressed, brittle-hard and twenty pounds lighter, stepped Thin Libby. But it took years. It took two babies and three promotions. It took the death of love. No, not the death, not even the waning, the transformation – she still loved Nat, but not with the anything-is-possible passion of then. She did not dismiss that passion as a silly Beth thing. Whenever she thought of Nat sitting there at the table, his curly hair, the nape of his neck sweetly exposed, his blue eyes smiling at her (as she too would be smiling, if someone drudged like that for her), she could feel again the hope she had felt for them both and the promise of the greatness they would accomplish together. That passion, those dreams and longings, were still inside her somewhere, like a tiny offshore island which appeared whenever the tide was low – when *she* was low – the water falling away from the rocks to expose the vulnerable bits, the old purple hurts with their squishy centres, the soft anemone secrets and frail, enduring hopes.

Enough of fancy metaphors, she thought, as the cab came out of the Blackwall Tunnel under the Thames: I'm not supposed to be the creative one.

But she was creative. She had good ideas. Last year she worked with two of the best young film directors around – they were now making their first feature films and when asked, in media interviews, would probably say they had done the adverts for the money, 'to stay afloat for the projects that really count'. They could say what they liked. She had caught them at the right moment, at the height of their powers. They would make ninety-minute movies weaker in plot and thinner on character than their twenty-second ads for Arran & Arran. And it was Libby who had first suggested using them.

Mark Arran understood that. He had let her come up through the ranks. And finally, after ten years, he was about to give Libby her due. This has been a good day, she thought, as she paid the driver, the cab rocking and shaking outside her front door. I've saved the SaxonAir account, hired a good-looking young assistant and drunk champagne in the penthouse with Mark. Now I'm slighty squiffy and desperate to eat something. And later, when the girls are asleep, I would like my husband to make love to me. However *experienced*, I'm still young enough for that.


## 13

## *ANTHEA*


'DON'T LAUGH,' Anthea said to people when they asked her what she did, 'I'm a Tree Officer.' Usually they did laugh, or at any rate smirk, at which point she would change the subject. The only people who didn't seem to find it funny were her colleagues at the council. But then nothing seemed to amuse them at all. She'd had hopes, before she started the job, that Friday evenings might be a chance to socialise. But on Friday at five o'clock everyone went straight home, taking their briefcases and laptops with them, and none of the pubs or wine bars near the office, or further away, included a single person she recognised. She knew. She had checked. Not that anyone from the council seemed likely to become a soulmate. But even a drink with her immediate colleagues (the corpse, the serial killer and the Stasi agent) would have been preferable to ending up back at her place, alone.

'Her place' was a high-ceilinged, two-bedroom rented conversion in Carshalton. The building had originally been a hospital, and Anthea's flat was part of the ward for Tropical Diseases. The next block, Maternity, now housed a gym, sauna, swimming pool and bar, for exclusive use of residents. Despite the rent, which amounted to more than half her salary, it was a flat she felt happy coming home to: the apple-white walls, the mock-marble uplighters, the indigo rug she had brought back from Tunisia. But to come home straight from work on Friday evenings seemed like a confession of failure, especially tonight, after her humiliating performance earlier.

'I *deserve* to be sacked,' she told Rachel from the bathtub. 'Two hours of sitting there too afraid to speak; then half a minute of saying the obvious.

When Nod came down to my office, which he *never* does, I thought, Oh-oh, this is it.'

'And?' Rachel said.

'He came to *thank* me. Can you believe it? I thought he was taking the piss. But according to him, everyone else at the meeting was bitching and squabbling. Very diplomatic of me to stay out of it, he said. In fact, I'd not even noticed.'

'So instead of being fired you were patted on the back.'

'Yes.'

'There's a lesson in that. About *valuing* yourself more.'

'Shut up, Rach, you sound like my therapist.'

'I didn't know you had a therapist.'

'I don't. But if I did he'd sound like you.'

'*He?* All the therapists I know are women.'

'That's true,' Anthea said, thinking of Bryony, the Council's Equal Rights, Social Entitlements and Civic Opportunities Counsellor with Special Responsibility for Ethnic and Gender Disprivilege, a post so multiply un-rewarding that she offered private therapy on the side. 'But the shrink my mum sent me to as a teenager was a man. Dr B. Fisher. He said my prob-lems were due to post-traumatic stress brought on by seeing my father's corpse.' Anthea put on an accent that she hoped would sound Viennese, though Dr Fisher had grown up in Warrington (the one fact about his personal life he had ever volunteered). '"And zees in turn compounded zee trauma you have untergone in infantzy on zeeing his penis." Anyway . . .'

'Anyway what?' Rachel said.

'Anyway, what are you doing tonight?'

'Gerard rang.'

'Oh.'

Gerard was Rachel's new boyfriend and, like her, a solicitor. When they went out, they talked contract law and repugnant wills.

'He invited me to Libra.' The wine bar round the corner from court. 'Want to come?'

'Mmm, better pass.' It was bad enough feeling a spare part without being reminded that their jobs paid twice as much as hers did.

'I could ask him to bring a friend.'

'The Rachel and Gerard Dating Agency. For sad sacks like Anthea.'

'I didn't mean it like that.'

'I know. But I think I'll stay in. I'm just not in the mood.'

'Is it Jake?'

'Is what Jake?'

'Has seeing him again upset you?'

'Not really.'

Not really, meaning yes of course. It was so like Jake to have turned up out of the blue like that last weekend. And then after a takeaway, and several drinks, and a spliff or two, to tell her how much he missed her. And so like him to get her into bed. And then to leave next morning, reassured she still loved him. So like him – and so like her.

'He can't bear you escaping his clutches,' Rachel said.

'He's between girlfriends.'

'You should tell him where to get off. Like I did Fletcher.'

'I know. I will.'

Fletcher had got Rachel pregnant a year ago, despite telling her he'd had the snip. After the abortion, Anthea sat with her every night for a week, soothing, counselling, holding her when she cried. 'You're a good listener,' Rachel sobbed. A better listener than a Tree Officer, perhaps. She had an ear for the music of human misery and never tired of hearing its track.

'Don't sit moping,' Rachel said. 'Come to Libra.'

'No, really,' Anthea said. 'There's a film on telly I want to see. I'll be fine.'

She put the phone back in its cradle on the floor, dripping water over the lino. It was this time last week the bell rang and there had been Jake – jeans holed at the knees, beads on his wrist, hair in shock. How could she not let him in? They went back a long way. She had been a schoolgirl the first time. Then they'd lived together in London, while she was teacher training and he jamming with Arboretum. Arboretum folded through a lack of gigs. The relationship folded too – even without a band Jake always had some groupie on the go. An alternative lifestyle, he called it, and for Anthea, ever since, life had been a quest for alternatives to Jake, a quest which made her take up, and drop, in rapid succession, yoga, quilt-making, the piano, judo, self-defence, sculpture, bungee-jumping, astrology, windsurfing and writing. 'Try anything once,' her father used to say. And so she had.

Her father. That was the *real* reason she clung to Jake – The Terrible Thing that happened at fourteen. There she was, secure and happy, living in Malvern, when all of a sudden, out of nowhere . . . The Fall. Literally. Six foot three of Daddy crumpling to the ground, on Speech Day, outside the refreshments marquee. She had been standing with friends, five yards away. 'Anthea, your dad, look,' someone said, with a giggle. She felt embarrassed. He must be drunk. But then the men running across from the St John's Ambulance tent. And a doctor in green kneeling over him, mouth to mouth. And then the ambulance, and the maths teacher driving them in its blue wake. DOA, it said on the form. Just forty-six. In her grief, she blamed herself: he had dropped dead from disappointment in her; if she had been cleverer, sportier, more accomplished, he would still be here. Slowly sorrow turned to rage. Better to rage than maunder, said her mother, who on a would-be-consoling Greek holiday hurled her wedding ring into the Aegean. She was drunk at the time. And continued drinking when they got home. Mummy, aka Bella, stage name Hilly Field, had once played titled young ladies at the Bristol Old Vic. Now, bingeing, she was slapstick – smeared rouge and sodden knickers. Anthea waited for the show to be over. But on it ran. She became used to fending for them both – to mothering her mother. There were collapses downstairs, spells of catatonia, trips to A & E for gashes and suspected fractures. After one particularly noisy gin-sluiced harangue (Mummy, in a nightdress, yelling 'You heartless cunts' to the midnight stars), a neighbour called the social services and Anthea was taken into care. There was a case conference, and an assessment of suit-able friends and family – 'suitable to look after you', the social worker explained, 'while your mother works through her bereavement issues'. The best option would have been Granny, her paternal grandmother in Swansea, who phoned every day throughout the crisis. But Swansea was judged too far away, which was how she came to live with the Heals. A Hurt fostered by Heals: the perfect match. It was intended as a short-term placement, until her mother (by then in a local rehab centre called the Grange) could convince the local authority of her capacity for consistent parenting. But Anthea's world had collapsed. Her father was dead and her mother marooned on Planet Inebria. She had lost both parents, not just the one.

At school, she was recast as a tragic heroine. New friends queued up to share her pain. She refused the part. She didn't want their pity. The pity was all her own. Under the eaves of her bedroom at the Heals', she refined her prelapsarian myth. Till her father died, the story went, she had been Anthea 1, secure and relatively happy. Now Anthea 1 was dead and Anthea 2 had taken over, pale, nervy, sullen, stammering, a shadow of her old self. The school made allowances for Anthea. It understood. Until she came out of her shell and started truanting. Further 'episodes' followed: rudeness in class, violations of dress code, a bottle of Teacher's – Teacher's! – smug-gled into school and passed round Year Sevens. The Heals tried to talk to her; her social worker and moral tutor, too. Anthea 1 listened and was peni-tent; Anthea 2 smouldered in rebellion. In the end, the latter won the battle. First she screwed up her mocks. Then she fell in with Jake. Two months before her GCSEs, she was caught having sex with him behind the chemistry lab. And though the school allowed her to sit her exams, they refused to have her back in the sixth form.

The notoriety of exclusion did as little for her as the celebrity of orphanhood. She lay low at the Heals', banned from seeing Jake, cut off from all friends, while her stammer grew worse and the local authority pondered her future. She had not intended expulsion as a cry for help, but that was how her mother heard it. Roused from grief and stupor, she discharged herself from the Grange and took her daughter in hand. A sixth-form college was found to rescue Anthea's education and a psychiatrist, Dr Fisher, to restore her sanity. The crammer, the shrink and the widow: between them they got her through. But the effects of the Terrible Thing were still there – in the voice that dared not speak, the eye that would not meet another's. Something had died and wasn't coming back.

In other words, she thought – bathed, dried, in a bathrobe, settling down at the kitchen table with a bowl of noodles and a glass of Pinot Grigio – I'm totally fucked up.

Was that why she had taken up writing? And – unlike all the other things – stuck with it for over a year? Because to sit in the pearly light of her laptop made her feel like someone else, someone bolder, brighter and less damaged? 'By writing you can own your past and shape your future,' Dr Fisher said, who also saw it as a way to cure her stammer. The stammer didn't go away but she found that writing poems and stories helped her feel better about herself. At uni the habit stopped, but then she had taken that course in London, on the rebound from Jake. In those days her writing had been rubbish. But the tutor had encouraged her and lately her writing had improved, so she liked to think. What would others think? Rachel was too close a friend to be honest and Jake didn't read books. In the end the only choice seemed to be what's-his-face, her tutor at USOR, Dr Raven. He was too academic to be a writer himself but he would know if her stories were any good and, if so, how to go about getting them published. After a lot of dare-I-daren't-I, she had printed them out, along with a covering letter, just last week. The moment the Jiffy bag left her hand she regretted it. But she could hardly write a second letter telling him to ignore the first. So far there had been no word from him. He might at least have acknowledged receiving the package. Maybe he had left the college. He had the air of a man who would be teaching his Getting Started class for ever, but he could have been sacked or gone mad or even died – you never knew.

In her heart of hearts, she did know: he had read her collection of stories – running title, *The Book of Foxes* – and hated it. Rereading it now on her laptop, half drunk, as night fell, Anthea hated it, too. What had been good enough to post off ten days ago seemed trite, repetitive, in need of binning. Dr Raven's failure to reply was due to embarrassment. The stories were naive. She was naive, to have sent them off so full of hope.

Dispirited, she shut her laptop and sat in front of Channel 4. If I were serious, she thought, I'd get up early tomorrow, and spend all weekend working on my stories; if I were serious, I'd write on the office computer during my lunch hour instead of reading. But I've no belief in myself. Whatever the necessary qualifications for authorship – ambition, arrogance, obsession, hunger, perseverance – I seem to lack them. What does the world care whether my stories get written or not?

<br>

## *14*

## *HARRY*

<br>

HE WAS running down Paradise Street towards Jamaica Road when the Astra went by. Two heads and eight fingers appeared from its rear window, and it was the larger of these heads – young, male, Caucasian – that hurled the words. Harry didn't react, just kept going, a man in shorts and a running vest on his evening jog. The words were tossed from the window, like an apple core or greasy bag of chips, then swallowed by traffic. Three words in all: verb, adverb, noun (*offens*); an injunction and an insult. If he had been wearing his headset, as he often did, he would not have heard. But having heard, he could not pretend. Trouble always comes in threes, his mother said, and she was right. First the fox man; then that waiter in Cantata; and now abuse from a passing car.

*Go* . . . He was going, at a modest pace, along the river near the Rotherhithe Tunnel, off Salter Road. His route was a six-mile circuit to Southwark Park and back, past wharfs, docks, locks, a Holiday Inn, an urban farm and bright new blocks of waterside housing. On a good day he could do it in forty-five minutes (his record was 43:12). This evening, the Cantata lunch heavy on his stomach, he was taking it slowly. It was a warm evening in a new country, and whole families had come out – babies, toddlers, parents, grandmas – to test the air. Some of them smiled as he passed: good on yer, guv. The sun lay low behind him. A lovely dusk. And him in his vest, panting. But he had not forgotten the shout from the Astra, wishing him elsewhere.

*Go home . . .* Home is what you know, and all he knew was south London. His mother had lived in Peckham since she was twelve. Her father did have an elsewhere: he came to England as an adult, in 1948. By the time he died he was part of immigrant legend – PhD students queued up to interview him, and he once featured (a soundbite eighteen seconds long) in a documentary on Channel 4. A good man, Harry's grandfather. Came off the boat at Tilbury, expecting the high life, and could not find it. Could not find digs either (No Irish, No Coloureds) or a job to fit his skills. But he found a wife, and found religion, and settled for clerking at the post office, and, thankful for small mercies, did not complain for the rest of his days. Why complain? There was always rum and calypso ('My baby just cain't stop blowing ma saxophone'). Harry knew those stoic genes, that *Windrush* amenability. He had them, too. No complaints! Even today, pushed to the limit, he had kept his mouth shut. But that did not make him immune.

*Go home, nigger.* It wasn't the first time but it still shocked him – not just to hear the word, but to think it defined him. That's what *prejudice* meant – prejudging a person; making assumptions on the basis of skin. He preferred to be invisible. Black journalists were as rare as black skiers, and as Harry Creed he could hide behind his byline. H. Creed, or H. J. (for Jerome) Creed would be more anonymous still; no one would even know his sex. But at least Harry did not scream black, and never mind that he was named after the singer Harry Belafonte (his dear old mum had put Harry, not Harold, on the birth certificate). Those who knew, knew – and locally, after several years on the *Gazette*, that meant quite a number. But why make it an issue? Why mug people with it? Or let them mug you? Newspapers taught you to be up front – to get the nub of the story in the first para. But the colour of the author wasn't the story. It was Harry's privilege to say nothing. His temperament too. He was a quiet person, and didn't want people to feel *swamped*.

The Thames ran high and swollen to his left. Sugar boats from Kingston used to come this way, delivering to the Tate & Lyle refinery in Woolwich. There had been blacks in south London since the sixteenth century: Ignatius Sancho, Olaudah Equiano and all the rest. And yet Negritude still surprised the natives: 'We wasn't expecting a . . . *nigger.*' After Stephen Lawrence was murdered by racists in Eltham, the *Gazette* had tried to increase its coverage of the black community. Harry was a sub at the time but when Deborah announced that she was looking for someone to write a weekly rap column, in a voice that would speak for young black men, he was tempted to give it a go. In fact, he did give it a go, in secret, at home. But one paragraph of brudda-demotic was enough to dissuade him: 'Las week at wuk mi sit at mi desk tinking ow di world as ird nuff fran di White Receeved Inglish dat disses and belikkles wi, and how wi muss tek it pon wi to brek outta tradishan and leggo in ginuwine bad man talk like dis bout ivry blasted ting under di sun . . .' Blackness in pores, yes. Blackness in prose, no. He'd spent years mastering the language of his masters and had no wish to chain himself up again, in patois.

There were people who found Harry's attitude annoying (who found it an Attitude), and thought he was betraying his race. Be proud, brother, they said. Be out there. What is it you're trying to hide? He had never understood the pride thing. Pride was to do with achievement – success in your work, behaviour, judgement, areas you had some choice in. But skin? Skin was a throw of the dice. You were born that way. It was wrong that it be held against you, but you could take no credit for it, either. As it happened, Harry preferred black skin. Black meant sheen and beauty. Whereas white meant . . . semolina pudding, toadstools, lard, dirty laundry. But he didn't want to have to think about it. Forget skin. Whites were allowed to forget theirs. Why not him?

He ran on, hugging the river path. Behind him, in west London, the sun was setting: its blood-orange double was sinking through the glass towers across the river, at Canary Wharf. If he were less shaken up, he might stop and enjoy the view. Best to keep moving, though. You never knew who was behind you. Nat would say he had imagined it. But there was no doubt. The speeding Astra. The two heads and the eight fingers. Then the words, tossed from the window like an apple core or greasy bag of chips.

*Go home.* He was there now, turning inland at Evelyn Street then cutting left through council blocks to his flat. He checked his time – 49:23, slow but respectable – then fished two keys from the sewn-in pocket of his running shorts to let himself in. 'On the cusp of Greenwich,' the estate agent blurb had said when he bought the place, but Harry wasn't fooled. Deptford was Deptford – had been since Christopher Marlowe was stabbed in a brawl here four hundred years ago and always would be. The communal hallway smelled of fresh paint yet retained its authenticating dinginess; in earlier times it had been a tea warehouse. He was relieved to reach his own flat on the top floor – wide oak floorboards, exposed brick, a distant view of

Canary Wharf. The living room was bare, except for a sofa and television. You could sit a dozen in it comfortably, but Harry felt more comfortable sitting alone. There were schoolmates – not really mates – who would diss him for having bought a flat here, indeed for buying a flat at all: gentrified Harry, the sell-out, in his Uncle Tom cabin by the Thames – is Peckham not good enough for you, brother? They were the same mates – not really mates – who had called him a coconut for getting O levels. But he liked it here. And liked the job which had made it affordable. He had no desire to move back to the ghetto.

In the bathroom, before he showered, he examined himself in the mirror. Black though he looked to the abusers in the Astra, he saw himself as pale – paler, anyway, than his two sisters, with their inky glow. Family legend had it that his great-great-grandfather was the product of a plantation rape, and the Saxon genes had later come out in Harry. He was the sludge in the pigmentocracy, the less-than-black sheep of the family. Dirty Harry.

Outside a car horn was yowling like a wounded animal.

He cooked as he wrote, slowly, with an eye for presentation: scrambled eggs, celery, tomato, brown toast, bottle of Beck's. Pride in one's work: that was the secret. Believing in what you did and striving to do it better. Local newspapers mattered; even cock-and-bull stories about foxes attacking children mattered. *That* business had been niggling all evening: having stalled over a draft for two hours, he realised he didn't know how to handle the story. Suppose Terry – Tel to his friends – was telling the truth. Suppose there *had* been a fox, not as big as Terry claimed, but wrong in the head in some way, so that when it saw the child in the buggy it thought, mm, food, or, aah, danger. Hence the bite marks. If there were bite marks. But how to find out? Those with information had refused to speak or failed to call him back.

He opened his laptop and downloaded the attachment, FOXDOC, he had sent himself from work. Outside he could hear music floating from the river. Sudden flashes lit the Velux windows in the eaves: fireworks, he decided – you didn't get shooting stars till summer, and the neon underglow of an urban sky made them impossible to see even then. Maybe the fireworks were Blair fireworks. Was the victory party still going on? Deborah and Travis were probably down at Millbank, joining in. But he was Harry Creed, on probation, with a story to write.

A bit of fun for page 7 – that was how Deborah wanted him to play it, and surely she was right. He would tell the story as Terry had told it to him – but with ironic quote marks and sceptical asides and you'd-be-mad-to-take-this-seriously exclamation marks. 'Leave it to the subs,' Mills liked to say, 'they'll tidy it up for you.' Comments like that made him nervous (was his copy so bad?), though even worse was the time when Mills asked, *Could we have more colour, Harry?* Mills had blushed, realising, as the word came out, but the affront was professional, not racial. So Harry Creed, a man of colour, was a colourless writer, was he? Fuck Mills – he would give him colour with this fox piece. Terry Lavell would feel betrayed. But Terry was a liar and a racist. Terry deserved all he got.


## *15*


## *LIBBY*


THE TAKEAWAY was Libby's idea, and though Nat was reluctant to collect it, the effort of lunching with Harry having exhausted him, her offer to put the girls to bed won him round. 'Putting to bed' meant nagging, tidying up after, bathing, drying, dressing and reading aloud to, but she found the process strangely therapeutic. During the story they snuggled up in bed – her and Nat's bed, which these days seemed less marital than familial, a place where children were entertained, not conceived. By the time she heard the front door bang and caught a whiff of marjoram and okra, the girls were asleep.

'So how was Harry?' she asked, scooping korma from a silver tray.

'All right.'

'Nothing happening in his life?'

'Not that he said.'

'And you?'

'Me?'

'You were going to call that agent.'

'I did call.'

'And?'

'She was out.'

'So?'

'I'll call her next week.'

'And will your play be ready to show her by then?'

'Not sure.'

'It's coming along OK?'

'So-so.'

It was like interrogating a truant. Very occasionally on a Friday, Nat would have written something. Those were the jolly poly-syllabic Fridays. This was a glum mono-. On average, in a year of Fridays, the monos outscored the polys by ten to one. Despairing at his lack of progress, Libby had once suggested he see a therapist, 'to take you out of yourself'. But that wasn't somewhere Nat wished to be taken.

He poured the last of the Shiraz, taking pains to give himself the larger share. 'And how was *your* day?' she would have liked him to ask in return. The fax from ChildPlanet, the SaxonAir meeting, Damian's intervention, the builder story he had told at lunch, what people at work were saying about Blair: there was no shortage of stuff to talk about. Above all, the conversation with Mark Arran, of course.

'And how was my day, you're probably wondering,' she said. 'Well, it looks like I'm getting a new job.'

'What,' he said, mildly intrigued, 'you're leaving Arran & Arran?'

'Mark is restructing the company. Or thinking about it. If he does I'll be offered a senior position – and join the board. It'll mean working more hours. But also more money. In the autumn this would be. He asked me to think it over.'

It hadn't required much thought.

'So are you pleased for me?'

He ought to be pleased for her – and for himself, further relieved of the need to contribute to the household budget.

'It sounds good,' he said.

'Is that all?'

'Well, they could do with a woman on the board,' he said, like the prophet Tiresias summoned to interpret an inexplicable phenomenon. 'Good for their image as a forward-looking company. Helps the balance of the power, too – someone from Northern Ireland, when they're all men from the Home Counties. And I dare say you'll brighten up their meetings.'

'You think I should get my tits out for them, Nat?'

If the man who loved her thought she'd been promoted only by virtue of her gender and nationality, what would men who didn't love her think? She was tempted to chuck the Shiraz in his face. Or to pass up the job in order to spite him.

'Did I say something wrong?' he said.

'Do you ever say anything right?'

She knew he thought adverts a waste of space – dead matter on arts pages which could more profitably be filled by an article on neglected British playwrights, or one particular neglected British playwright – but he shouldn't treat her as a waste of space, too.

'Trivial pursuit, trivial person,' she said. 'That's how you make me feel.'

'You're not,' he said, contrite. 'Those bastards are lucky to have you.' He laid his hand on hers. 'We should celebrate.'

He kissed her and fetched a bottle.

'Cheers,' he said, chinking glasses. 'To my beautiful, untrivial, deservedly elevated wife.'

That was better. After several more minutes of him toasting her beauty and talent, she was just about ready to forgive him.

'So what are we doing at the weekend?' she said.

'You're going to teach me how to use email,' he said.

'Really? Why the change of heart?'

'All my students use it. Maybe email would help me cope with the flood.'

She hadn't noticed the flood but she was pleased that he had seen sense at last. How could anyone, even a teacher (though she was careful never to call him that), function without email? Two years ago, for his birthday, she had bought him a state-of-the-art Pentium, with scanner, CD-ROM drive, modem, Internet access, Windows '95, the works. For months he was too scared to touch it. He still only used it as a glorified typewriter. He had a similar resistance to mobile phones. There was no one more technophobic than Nat. She had had to drag him kicking and screaming into the twentieth century. Now the century was almost over, he had finally arrived.

'For instance, this student from years ago has sent me some stories. It'd be easier emailing her my response than sending a letter.'

'If you're not her tutor any more why send a response at all?'

'She wants to know if she's any good.'

'Tell her to join a writing group.'

'They're interesting stories.'

'Whatever. You're not paid to give her feedback.'

'She says she picked up a lot from my class.'

'Men, probably.'

'I don't even remember what she looks like.'

'Good. Keep it that way. You need to spend more time on your own work, not waste it on the girlies.'

Her jealousy of his female students was a joke routine they had. But she meant the bit about him protecting his time. He was too soft a touch.

'You're right,' he said, 'I shouldn't waste time having lunch out, either.

I sometimes think Harry has a screw loose. He kept moaning on about New Labour being no better than the Tories. How many black MPs had been elected. How many ethnics would be in the Cabinet. Blah blah. He can't get excited about Blair at all.'

'I don't blame him,' Libby said. 'I can't, either.'

'Then he claimed the waiter was being racist.'

'Racist how?'

'Kept ignoring him, supposedly. Nothing in it, as far as I could see. It was just like the time in the car.'

The time in the car was a decade ago, when Harry drove them home after a meal and was flagged down by a squad car – typical harassment, he claimed, and if Nat and Libby hadn't been with him the police would have found some excuse to charge him. Probably true, Libby decided, but Nat had disagreed and called Harry paranoid.

'If society's so racist,' Nat said, topping up her glass, 'how did Harry get where he is – a good job, his own flat, et cetera?'

'It's not been easy for him,' Libby said. 'You've no idea what it's like.'

'And you have, I suppose.'

'Some idea, yes.'

She meant her Irishness. Some accents were as hard to lose as skin colour. There were still people who assumed she was a nurse.

'But he's so fucked up about it,' Nat said. 'If anyone reminds him he's black, even in a neutral way, he feels insulted. I think he wants to delude himself he's white.'

'He just wants to be treated as an equal,' Libby said, 'to be judged on his own merits.'

'Have you read his pieces in the *Gazette*? They're so vacuous. His personality goes missing the moment he puts pen to paper.'

'He's insecure, that's all. And shy.'

'He's not shy. He's ashamed. Ashamed of who he is. The whole business with Marcia and Stephen, for instance. Does it really have to stay a secret after all this time? He won't even let us tell Deborah.'

'It's stupid, I agree. All the same . . .'

'I know, he's our friend. But that doesn't mean we can't be critical.'

Enough of Harry; she would like to talk about her day. But the phone went before she could – her mother calling from Ballymena, with the usual half-hour litany: the loneliness since Dad passed away, the deteriorating bus service, the litter in the streets, the rudeness of teenagers, and now these pains in her gut which she ought to see the GP about, only it was impossible to get an appointment. Libby's guilt as a working mother had nothing on her guilt as an absent daughter. The weekly call from Ballymena – more like three times a week, actually – was punishment for having left home at nineteen, and she never finished talking to her mother without feeling worse than when she started. Dad had died three years ago, a few weeks into retirement, God's reward to him for stopping work. He had been Libby's rock, whereas Mum was a scold. Now her rock was Nat who, despite his ineptness, was a loyal partner and, despite his career frustrations, seemed happy being married to her. As well he might. Few husbands had it so easy. But she felt a soft spot for him now as he cleared away the Indian, spilling pilau rice on the carpet, letting the grease-bottomed brown paper bags stain the tablecloth, but at least (as he would put it) *showing willing*. Tidying up while she sat with the phone was his way of empathising – he had a mother, too, and knew how it felt to be mummed-out. He set a last glass of champagne in front of her and kissed the top of her head. So this is what it means to be loved, she thought, as her mother ran on. Some women might long for a worthier recipient of their affection. But if there are other men I could love more deeply than Nat, I haven't yet found them and I'm not going to start looking now. It isn't just the history we share, and the children, and the chattels (those Chinese lamps, that onyx elephant, the bit of driftwood, shaped like a snake, I can see in the fireplace). It's the knowledge he loves me as he will never love anyone else.

In the bedroom, she watched him watching her undress. The attentiveness was comic as well as touching, as if he had no idea what might emerge when she unclipped her bra – each time a different miracle, though always the same 34B. In frolicsome moments, she lingered over the moment of unclasping; in spiteful ones, she undressed in the bathroom to deprive him. Tonight he pretended to be reading but as the bra fell to the floor his eyes lifted from the page. You have to laugh, she thought. But to be desired like this after a decade together seemed faintly miraculous and was half the reason she desired him back. Maybe the wine and the champagne were making her soppy. But a thirty-five-year-old working mother of two was allowed to be soppy, sometimes. She slipped beside him, under the duvet, and kissed his neck. He put his book down – no greater compliment – and stretched across her. He had put on weight. His chest hair felt rough against her nipples. But no one else held her like this. And as long as she was married no one would.

There might be better husbands in the world. But as long as Nat loved her, she would be held.

# JACK

A JAY cackled from a distant copse. No question: Jack was lost. After leaving the pub, he had passed the church, then turned left beyond the graveyard along the remains of a Roman road leading back to the heath. Or so he thought, until he came to a crossroads, a meeting of four paths, and when the track he chose petered out in ferns he had to retrace his steps and choose another route, a bridleway, which led him to the forest clearing – 'dell', Nancy would have called it – where he now stood, only to find it unringed by hoofmarks and therefore not a bridleway at all, unless he had missed a turning somewhere, which was always possible, just as it was possible that the glade – 'dell' – whose pinewood silence he now inhaled was the same one he had passed through just after the church, which would mean he was walking in a circle, or semicircle, or figure of eight, and must now be more or less back where he started, though he could see no signs of a spire and was surely facing west, towards the sun. The mocking call of that jay again. No panic. It wasn't yet eight o'clock. He would soon be (hah!) out of the woods. He could feel the mobile in his pocket, smooth as a beach stone. Once back on track, he might phone Nancy, to tell her to drive over. They could meet halfway for a meal at the Golden Goose. Evenings like this – warm with the tang of pine in them – were as rare as new governments and far worthier of celebration. His head was fuzzy after the Adnams, and there was a blister coming on his left heel, but the little sun shafts through the firs were like microsurgery. He felt fine.

From the clearing, he took the least unlikely-looking trail. If the orange glow on the skyline was to be trusted, he was on course. And if he meandered south towards the marshes, taking longer, well, the light would be good for another two hours. What was the rush?

It had been a day for hard truths and now he faced another: *he did not want to rush home to Nancy.* Life without her was unimaginable. But only because the stupor of marriage had stopped him imagining. He was bored. She was bored. Their marriage had given up on them. That must be why he felt happy to linger here, and why, almost every night, the short drive home was drawn out by him stopping for a quick half, or not-so-quick couple of pints. Other husbands did the same; he knew – he drank with them; it didn't mean they were disloyal. But when a marriage grew musty from unuse . . .

The path bent left and descended towards the river. There was a bridge down there and after that he would be home and dry. He had come to resent Nancy, that was the truth: her stolidity, her gardening, her indifference to him. At their silver wedding party, in the speech to assembled friends (champagne flutes, marquee, a balmy night like this), he had called her 'the finest little homemaker a man could hope for'. But all that home seemed to amount to these days was Nancy asleep in bed or on the sofa. She would be sleeping now, curled up in front of the Young Musician of the Year contest or some such improving television, the sort she used to force the girls to watch, though it was not so improving as to keep her awake even back then. When he pictured her it was as someone with her eyes closed, possibly dead. Was this a death wish, or death fear? He had no fantasies of strangling or poisoning her, but she was comatose in all his dreams, an undrunk cup of lapsang beside her. Sleep was forgivable, at their age. He nodded off most evenings, too: nodding off was all most television was good for. But surely marriage should be less somnolent, even after thirty-five years. Marriage, he used to think, would bring him to a place like this – high skimming clouds, a buttery sun, the dusk call of warblers, somewhere bright and expansive, not a low-beamed room with a shrinking screen.

A heron rose from the reeds in front of him, leggy as a new-born foal. His heart lifted, then sank again. There was no one to share this with. He had come here – by choice – alone.

The river was less a river than a stream, but marshes lay beyond. He could swear there was a wooden bridge here. But ten minutes of toing and froing failed to locate it. He was stuck south of the river, in marshland. The pub, his car and home lay to the north.

No panic. It was only eight thirty.

Nancy had seemed a wise investment once. Now all she did was eat or sleep or ache – a poor return. Dear Nancy. It wasn't her fault. But her failure to keep pace with him was resentable all the same. He ought to have taken what Michelle offered, a body with some life in it still. Where was Michelle now? Odds were, if he went looking, she would be holed up in a village not far from here, a semi-recluse with a cottage garden full of lavender and a gnarled front door that would open even before he knocked: 'What took you so long, Jack?' That smile, those cornflower eyes, a new start.

But these were thoughts he ought not to be having. It wasn't as if he hated his life.

There was no bridge, so he turned back, and where the stream narrowed he took a chance and stepped across. How did the song go? *Green grow the rushes-o*. These rushes were brown, and higher than his head, and he couldn't see what lay beyond. Up the coast, there were wooden walkways through the reeds, with wire netting stretched across the sleepers – a pity there were none of them here. He picked his way along a grassy path raised above the bog. The path came to a halt by a hawthorn tree. He eased himself round and placed his right foot in the ground beyond. It disappeared up to the ankle. He grabbed a hawthorn branch to steady himself, but it was prickly and he had to let go, and in letting go his left foot slipped in the mud and he went down on one knee, so he was splayed like a dancer, one leg in the water, the other perilous on the slimy bank. He imagined himself being sucked down, deeper and deeper into the swamp, till his chest went under, then his shoulders, then his head, with nothing to show the passing search parties, not even a hat floating on the brackish surface. A banal way to die. A slipping away. But his left foot held firm, and by grabbing the hawthorn trunk (less prickly than the branch), he levered himself upright and his right leg came out of the water with a slurp, a belch of redemption. He was soaked up to the knee. But safe.

He retraced his steps and crossed back, south of the river again, and leaned down to wash his hands in the brackish water before walking on. One hundred yards downstream he found the bridge. If only he had walked this far earlier instead of giving up. Impatience was an old failing of his. Yet he had been in no rush. (He had been in no rush and nearly drowned in the rushes.) Now his trouser leg was sodden and his boot squelchy. He wrung his sock out and walked on.

It was warm still. His clothes would dry out in no time. In half an hour he would laugh about this. He could laugh about it now, if he called Nancy.

After the bridge, the path became a cart track and curved upward. He had his bearings now, more or less. The cart track would join the road through the bird reserve. His limbs – the dry ones anyway – felt pleasantly weary. What an adventure. Nancy would tease him, when he told her. Still, he didn't call her. Stubbornness prevented it; let her call him.

Around nine, on the ridge path to the Hawk & Handsaw, he finally took out his mobile. The screen was showing blank, as it had been at the National Trust place. Still no reception, he thought, then realised the bugger had turned itself off. It had a habit of doing that. No wonder the walk had been peaceful. He pushed the button at the top. A pair of spectacles appeared, indicating a message had been left, but the screen went dead again before he could access it. Damn thing: he was always forgetting to charge it, as if in protest against having to use it at all. 'Can't think how we ever coped without mobiles,' people said. They coped as he had for the past four hours, that's how. It would be Karen who had left a message, or Hook, or a guilt-struck Luc, and he didn't want to hear from any of them. As for Nancy, he would ring from the call box at the pub and hope not to disturb her televisual slumbers.

Ahead of him, to the right, at the edge of the wood, a dozen or more red deer were grazing. The largest of them lifted its head, catching a whiff of him, then resumed: no danger. Marvellous that deer could be so trusting: their liquid eyes and velvet nostrils caught the slightest hint of danger, but these ones, in a reserve, had learned to ignore the alarm signals – were going against their own nature. Jack had never hunted deer; never intended to, either. Fox-hunting was different, a form of pest control – he had seen what foxes do to lambs, not to mention chickens in coops.

His trouser leg was dry and he wiped his shoes clean with dock leaves.

After the bird reserve, the last quarter-mile to the pub ran between irrigation ditches. Was this the same river he had crossed already? He ought to know, after years of coming here. In the fading light, coots and moorhens skittered between the reeds. He had seen a kingfisher here once, a flash of blue like someone throwing a sapphire.

Almost dusk. A bat zigzagged overhead. Nightlife was about to begin. He could hear an owl calling in the distance, and pictured it as a woman in fancy clothes – sequins and feathers, frills and lace, a huge white breast. Or like Nancy in her wedding dress. Where was the wedding dress now? Dangling in the wardrobe probably, like a corpse.

Music rolled backed to him from the pub. Here finally. People were sitting at the wooden tables in the garden. Glorious evening to be out, but Jack headed inside – enough of dusk and midges. Some yappy teenager was using the call box, so he bought himself a pint of Adnams, very necessary after a walk of such distance, replacement of essential fluids and so forth. There was a television on in the corner, with Blair, all teeth and smiles, taking up residence. The ten o'clock news: he was really quite late. After standing discouragingly close and eyeballing the lad, he finally had the phone to himself.

It could take as many as twenty rings to stir Nancy, but this time she answered after two.

'Hello,' a voice said.

'Nancy?'

'Jack, thank God.'

'Who's that?'

'It's Elise. I'm at the house. We've been trying to reach you for hours.'

# Extract from *The Book of Foxes*

by Anthea Hurt

## The Solitude of Vixen

Vixen had the run of the place. The waters bowed down before her. The hills were in her keeping.

But vixen felt lonely. The rocks wouldn't eat with her. The wind wouldn't sleep with her. The moon was cold and distant.

She strolled around, a one and only. There were fruit, fish and insects, but no one to keep her company. 'Oh, I'm so alone,' she thought.

God, waking, took pity on vixen. When He'd made her from a nostril hair, He had also made her double, to patrol the far corners of the Earth. The two weren't meant to live together. But since vixen seemed to be pining, why not let them?

So God brought fox to vixen. They stared, as though into a mirror, then bared their teeth and rushed at each other's throats.


## Vixen and Fox

God was angry. But for Him, fox and vixen would be nothing. He took them by the scruff of the neck, and told them to bury their differences.

It wasn't easy. When vixen saw a forest of saplings, fox saw an army of spears. When vixen heard bees, fox heard an enemy password. When vixen smelled salmon leaping the falls, fox smelled his next meal. They might be doubles but they couldn't agree.

God decided fox had better go back. But before He could arrange it, He fell asleep. In a flash they were at each other's throats again.

Fox pinned vixen to the forest floor. She'd thought her brain would save her in a fix. Now she knew fox was the stronger. Some light had dawned in him too. He grinned, then let her go.

Soon, they had another fight. Again fox pinned vixen to the floor. This time he nipped her ear, enough to draw blood.

After that, she avoided him. But when he tracked her down a third time, he showed no mercy. The claws of his right foot were sharper than a carving knife. Vixen's neck was slashed open and her blood leaked out.

Fox dragged her body down to the sea. Wading in up to his knees, he pushed her under and watched her sink. He was Lord of the Earth now. Or so he thought.

Behind him, as he walked away, something happened in the water. Vixen's blood, mixing with mud, bubbled and frothed. The sea became a crucible. A whole new world of not-vixen came to life.

And in time, out of the mud, came llama, dingo, warthog, antelope and bison, and all the other animals, including vixen herself, reborn and pledged to be fox's eternal enemy.


## How Speech Began

At first, nobody spoke. There was no need. The creatures understood each other and were happy to do without words.

All except vixen. Why should we be silent? she wondered. Every creature looks different. Why can't we have our own voices too?

Vixen went to the pinewoods, where no one could hear. She tried to make sounds. Her throat felt tight and for aeons she got nowhere, but at last she uttered a small, strangled cry.

With practice, she began to make other sounds: yelps, yaps, barks, growls, howls, grunts, shrieks. Returning from the pinewoods, she showed off to the other animals. They'd never heard the like.

Vixen went one better. She began to utter words. Really it was only the one word but she gave it different inflexions. I, she went, and eye and aye and aiieee.

God was perplexed. He'd made an Eden of silence, in which the creatures obeyed His rules and swallowed His story. Now vixen had ruined everything.

I I I I I I, she went. So God ceased to be the only voice. And a cacophony could be heard through the land.


## The Birth of Sex

Vixen and fox got on no better than before. Now they had voices to scream with, their fights were even worse. Rabbits trembled in burrows and birds in nests. Even God could get no sleep.

In His rage, God roped fox and vixen together by the tail. He planned to force them to be friends. But they ran off in opposite directions – rump to rump not shoulder to shoulder, tail to tail not eye to eye.

As they struggled and chafed at the rope, the flesh below their tails was terribly damaged. Vixen suffered a wound that wouldn't close up. Fox developed a long, thin tumour.

Finally in desperation, they turned to face the same way. Fox climbed on vixen's back. Vixen howled to the moon. The wound grew deeper, the tumour more swollen, till they flopped, growling and panting, to the floor.

God, exasperated, cut the rope. If fox and vixen wouldn't rub along together, let them go. There was no point trying to teach them friendship.

But the rope had been on too long. There was no escaping each other now. Each night they itched to join up again, wound to tumour.

## How Vixen Made Man

First the moon existed, then God, then vixen, then all the other creatures. Each made the next one down. The moon made God from nail clippings. God made vixen from a nostril hair. And so on, in turn, one after another. But it was vixen who made man.

Creation was supposed to have stopped. But the animals felt tired and needed a servant, someone to cook and tidy. Vixen called a council, to decide what form this servant – man, as they came to call him – should take.

Lion said man should be fierce and covered in golden fur. Stag said man would look foolish without a magnificent pair of antlers on his head. Beaver thought that man should have a paddle tail, owl that he have wings, mole that he be blind and live underground.

Vixen was impatient. She suggested they each take away a lump of earth and mould a model. At dawn they would meet again and choose a winner. A good idea, everyone said, but it had been a long day, and before they could work at their models many fell asleep.

In the small hours, vixen went round in secret looking. Only three models had been started. Chameleon wanted man to come in several colours, dolphin gave him a large brain, and bear made him stand on his feet. Before destroying the models, vixen stole these three ideas.

When they met at dawn, only vixen came with a model. So her version of man was chosen.

Vixen made us. We are in her power.

## The Boneless Babies

It wasn't just men and women who had babies. A woman and a woman could conceive one too.

It worked like this. One woman lay on top, rubbing herself against the woman beneath, like a spoon scraping a dish. In time, one of the two women would give birth – sometimes both of them. But woman-woman babies were different from man-woman babies. They were boneless, like water.

The babies grew, despite their lack of bone. In fact, they flourished. Not having bones, they had strong muscles and sinews instead. They were more flexible than ordinary babies – more intelligent, too.

Soon boneless babies were as common a sight as ordinary babies. Some said bonelessness was the way of the future. But a group of hairy men objected. They hated women mating with women. And they hated boneless babies.

This group of hairy men was very powerful. They voted to move boneless people to ghettos. They voted to jail any woman found mating with another woman. They voted to kill boneless babies at birth.

Their votes became law. Whoever protested was executed. A few boneless babies were born in secret but in time there were no more. The hairy men had won.


## The Lost Child

Fox developed a taste for children. Babies and toddlers were juiciest. But he wasn't too fussed. Any child, even the scrawniest, would do.

Vixen told fox to pack it in, before there was trouble. Look what man did to lions and tigers, when *they* killed children. Did fox want to end up as a pelt on a wall? If not, he should stick to hens.

Fox wouldn't listen. Children were easy pickings, he said. If their parents couldn't bother to look after them, tough. Vixen should stop nagging and join him. Why not tonight? They'd go out and have a slap-up meal.

So vixen went along. But when fox snatched a child outside its house, she was straight on to him, snapping and snarling till his jaw opened and the child fell out. Then vixen growled so fiercely at fox that he backed away, hair on end, and left her to it.

Left her, he thought, to fill her belly. But the child was only scratched. And when vixen licked his wounds, which tickled and made him laugh, she fell in love with the child and decided to keep him.

She felt bad. His parents would be upset. But once his wounds healed she would return him. Honest.

It was the same with the next kid she took, a girl, found wandering alone in the dark. The parents must be taught a lesson. Only then would the girl go back.

Fox no longer eats kids. Nor does vixen, of course. But when a child goes missing, you can be sure she's the one behind it.

## The Invention of Death

No one died at first. When creatures suffered death, they shed their skin, as a snake does. A new skin grew beneath and, under the skin, new organs. You could come back from the dead for ever, good as new.

Soon, the world became crowded. The creatures tried burying their dead, before they grew new skins. But it was no good. 'Where've you been?' the dead would ask, as their relatives returned from the graveyard.

'We've been burying you.'

'But why? I'm good as new, see.'

The world grew more crowded. Was it time to abolish immortality? Vixen called a meeting.

Wolf spoke first. 'Let's vote to change the rules,' he said. 'When creatures die, let them stay dead. There's not the space for all of us.'

'I disagree,' said walrus. 'Flowers come back, and leaves. Why should it be different for us?'

'I've had enough,' said elephant. 'I can't move without stepping on people. I wouldn't mind dying tomorrow.'

'Me, too,' groaned mouse, from under elephant's feet. 'What's so great about eternal life?'

'All right,' said vixen, 'but shouldn't death be only for the old?'

'No, for everyone,' said wolf.

The animals put it to the vote. Wolf won and looked smug. Next week, his daughter fell sick and died. Vixen met him weeping: if only, wolf wailed, they had voted differently.

There was no going back. But vixen, out of pity, suggested a compromise. Let creatures die – but be reborn aeons later as other creatures.

Fish would come back as snails, and snails as fish. Hawks would come back as leopards, and leopards as hawks.

'And wolves?' asked wolf.

'Wolves will come back as gazelles,' said vixen.

'And foxes?'

'Foxes will come back as men.'

They shook hands on it.

Those are still the rules. Every man was once a fox. Every woman was once a vixen.

# Part 2

## *God Save Our Team*

30 June 1998

## *JACK*

'FIVE JOBS should do it,' Jack said, with an I-dare-you stare at young Marcus, who had budgeted for nine or ten. Six was what they agreed yesterday. But now Hook was with them, Jack couldn't go that high. A job meant respect, self-worth, a place in the community – notions which Marcus, with his balance sheets, didn't understand. He got the point of Jack's stare, at least, lowering his head and adjusting his sums.

'Five!' Hook said, wiping the back of his hand across his nose, the indoor equivalent of spitting. 'Five!'

Beneath the silver snot-smear on Hook's wrist there were liver spots, just like Jack's. They were supposed to be class enemies – foreman versus boss, shop steward versus managing director – but they had more in common than Jack would ever have with Marcus.

'There's no choice,' Jack said.

'That'll be twenty-four men left. I can remember when we were fifty.'

'It's a necessary rationalisation?' Marcus said. 'Many companies in the export sector are having to downsize? But a modest restructuring will reduce overheads and secure long-term investment?'

Hook looked bemused by Marcus's interrogatives. They had intrigued Jack, too, at the interview. In reality, Marcus was a cocky little bastard. But he ended each sentence with a question, as though unsure of himself. Jack had appointed him on that basis – because his hanging sentence-ends suggested amenability and a willingness to learn. It had been a mistake. The interrogative hesitancy, Jack later realised, came from Australian soaps – some of the younger lads in the yard spoke the same way. Marcus didn't listen to Jack. Marcus listened only to money. And money said Raven & Son must lose jobs.

'You said the bank loan would tide us over,' Hook said.

'I did. It has. But we aren't getting the orders,' Jack said.

'Intervention at the human resource level will hopefully ward off a negative equity situation?' Marcus said.

'Without redundancies,' Jack translated, 'we'll be bankrupt by the end of the year.'

Over half the £200,000 had gone since January. Twenty-five men on an average of £20,000 meant a wage bill of half a million a year. The loan was officially ring-fenced for development. But with reserves unable to cover running costs, the ring fence had been scrapped. Jack could fudge the minutiae with the bank. But he couldn't hide the bigger picture. They were a quality engineering firm, when quality engines weren't in demand; a family business, when the family was dysfunctional; a country enterprise, when the countryside was going to the dogs.

'We're here to talk names not numbers,' Jack said.

He was known as an equitable employer. But men would have to go.

'You make suggestions, and I'll discuss them, but I'm not volunteering anyone,' Hook said.

'Fair enough.'

If it were up to Jack, Marcus would be the first. But the loan had come with strings. When Harris and his faceless crew agreed, 'in principle', to lend the full amount (twice what he'd originally been thinking of), Jack was quietly astonished, and suspected it must be Harris feeling sorry for him, because of Nancy. A meeting was arranged: 'in principle' meant certain safeguards were being sought, and they wanted to discuss them. It was early July, the wisteria in bloom by the gate, just a couple of months after the fateful day. He left home with the usual sick feeling – anxiety at leaving the house. At the bank Harris was gentle; so were his cronies (including one from head office), who sat there playing with figures and avoiding his eyes. Appointing a deputy manager would inject some young blood, create an extra pair of hands, allow someone with a background in finance to oversee the business plan, leaving Jack free to develop the new machine, etc. – i.e., they thought him too old and broken to cope alone. 'It'll mean an adjustment,' Harris said, seeing Jack's uneagerness. 'You're used to running the show. But it's your interests we're protecting as well as ours.' His interests? Which were those? Harris's cohorts sat there gravely suited, with their balance sheets. Jack asked if could he think it over. Of course, said Harris – but he let it be known that their 'proposal' was a condition of the loan. So Jack had agreed. And advertised. And hired Marcus – button-down collar, red tie, Armani suit – thereby squandering part of the loan on a deputy manager he didn't need. If the new Greensleeves had been ready, there would be no panic. But it was still being tested, and orders for the previous model were non-existent. He had to lose jobs.

'Let's start with the easy bit,' Jack said. 'Two early retirements.'

'Sanders, H., and Wilmott, R.?' Marcus said.

'Horace is fifty-eight and Bunny's fifty-six,' Jack said. 'They might be glad of it.'

'They're sick of working,' Hook said, 'but they can't afford to retire.'

'We'll be as generous as we can.'

'Just as well their wives have jobs.'

'Now to the younger lads,' Jack said. 'Who was the last one in?'

'Kinder, J.? Appointed January 1997?'

'Josh.'

'He's been expecting it,' Hook said. 'Said his brother-in-law might have a job for him. I told him to take it.'

'An inexpensive settlement – he's on two weeks' notice?' said Marcus.

'You miserable bastards.'

'A month's wages,' Jack said, 'plus two weeks' redundancy.'

'Kett, S.? Appointed July 1996?'

'Steve! Over my dead body. He's one of the best.'

Eleven fifteen, the clock said, and struck, once, with a solid tung. Henry Mayer, Tunstall, 1802. Nearly two centuries old and still going. Those clockmakers knew a thing or two. Family businesses run from barns or back rooms, and handed down from father to son. Generations of apprentices slowly maturing to master craftsmen. Hard not to be nostalgic. Skilled men lost jobs in those days, too, but there was always farm labour, whereas now . . .

'How far back do we have to go after Steve?' Jack said.

'Milder, K., and Milder, P.? February 1995?' Marcus said.

'The brothers. Keith's the older one, isn't he?'

'The older. But the better worker,' Hook said.

'Pat, then?'

'Rather him than Steve.'

'How'll you explain it to Pat?'

'I've had some problems with him. Keeps turning up late. Trouble at home. I'll feel a sod, but if there's no choice . . .'

'They'll all get two more weeks than they're entitled to.'

'Henscrats. Rabbit droppings.'

'That's Pat, Josh, Horace and Bunny. What about the fifth?'

They ran through some names. Hook rejected them. They ran through the rest of the names. Hook rejected them too. Jack sat with his elbow on the table, head in hand, surreptitiously feeling the mole on his forehead next to his birthmark – couldn't be right, something new growing at his age, best see the GP. Cancer: horrible to live with, horrible to die from. Bad as having a stroke. Since last May he had thought a lot about death. Hourly occupation, almost. At least work took his mind off it – off Nancy. Whatever the stresses, it was best to be here. Or in the George. Or on horseback. Anywhere but the hollow of home. He was becoming addicted: to drink, to hunting, to balance sheets, to forms of oblivion. The little oblivions hiding the big.

They had reached deadlock. Hook swiped his hand across his nose: weren't there other ways to save money? Jack proposed a few, knowing Hook would reject them. A pay cut across the board: 'Doesn't seem right, to penalise everyone.' The abandonment of holiday pay: 'Not on – there's legislation against it.' Pruning of overheads – tools, tea, overalls, stationery: 'It wouldn't come to a bean.' Jack mentioned the other options, selling up or closing down. They went back to the names, and after some wrangling came down to two. Arleigh, R., and Lustig, K.: Robin and Ken. Robin was the more skilled but had no family; Ken was forty-three with four kids. A classic dilemma.

'Shall I ask Karen to bring some tea in?' Marcus said. It was a real question for once, and the first sensible thing he had said all morning.

Hook drank noisily. Marcus said that the orderly roll-out of appropriate manning levels in relation to trading viability was necessarily disputatious but that a helicopter view of market prospects revealed no commodifiable alternative? Jack recalled being roped in to judge the village horticultural fair and agonising over whose leeks to choose; it was like that now, but with the prize – or booby prize – a redundancy cheque. The clock above the desk ticked on. How much would it fetch? Jack wondered. A present to Grandfather. But that was no reason to keep it. He should get it valued. Even £1,000 would come in useful. The other office heirlooms – oak desk, beechwood filing cabinet, walnut calendar-and-blotter set – might fetch the same. £2,000 would let him pay a basic worker for six weeks. Not to be sniffed at. Hook finished his tea. The room fell silent, aside from the clock.

'We should set sentiment aside?' Marcus said. 'The company comes first?'

'How would you know?' Hook said.

'The financial position is plain, Mr Hook?'

'In my book, it's men who come first.'

'In mine, too,' Jack said. 'But one of them has to go.'

'And Lustig K., by your own admission, is the weaker asset?' Marcus said.

'Cheaper for you to get rid of, you mean.'

'The less meaningful resource?'

Hook put his mug down with a bang.

'Robin then.'

'Arleigh, R.? It's agreed?'

'If Mr Hook says Robin, then it's Robin,' Jack said. 'We'll give him a glowing reference. A man like him won't find it hard to get work.'

'A man like him is impossible to replace,' Hook said.

Hook shoved his chair back and stood up. Some upbeat homily was called for. But Jack was at loss for one. Even Marcus had more sense than to speak.

'That it, then? There's nothing more you want?' Hook said, gripping the chair back.

'How should we handle telling them?' Jack said.

'I'm not doing your dirty work.'

'I'll see them this afternoon, then. One by one.'

Hook nodded, as though to say do what you like, but when he reached the door he turned.

'It's not my doing, mind,' he said. 'You make that clear.'

'They know it,' Jack said. 'They know you.'

'And make sure to see them all before five. Big game on tonight. They'll want to get off on time.'

The door thudded behind him. Marcus sat opposite, busy with figures. He would expect a cosy hour with Jack 'reviewing the human resources situation in the light of the agreed restructuring.'

'I have some phone calls to make,' Jack said.

'Of course,' Marcus said. 'Call me when you're through?'

*Call me when you're through?* Who do you think you are, you little shit. You come in, strut around, dispose of workers like refuse, and now you're telling me what to do. I give the orders round here, sonny. Me, Jack Raven, your boss. You think you could do the job these men do? You wouldn't know where to start. And yet I'm paying you four times what I pay them, arsehole.

That was telling him.

But what he said to Marcus was, 'Fine.'

'Shall I inform the bank?' Marcus said, gathering up his paperwork. Another genuine question, it seemed.

'Leave that to me,' Jack said.

If he called the redundancies 'streamlining', Harris would welcome them as a 'move in the right direction'. But why inform him at all? It wasn't his job to keep the bank happy. So long as they had their money back, with interest, they'd no right to interfere. The only point to be made to Harris – and the George, over a lunchtime pint, was the place to make it – was about leadership. No London upstart was going to boss Jack Raven around.

'You'll need to draft official letters to all five men,' he said.

'Yeh, yeh,' Marcus said, on his way out.

*Yeh, yeh.* Yeh, yeh, meaning that's obvious, you boring old fart. Yeah, yeah. Like the Georgie Fame song. Jack had once heard Georgie Fame, with the Blue Flames, at the Hippodrome. 'And when she asks me if everything is OK / I give my answer, the only thing I can say, / I say yeh yeh.' Great stuff. There'd been a decent B-side, too. Jack's vinyl singles and LPs were somewhere in the attic. Yeh yeh, meaning pleasure and affirmation, not the know-all cynicism of a Marcus. Happy times, the 1960s, and Georgie Fame had looked a happy man. But hadn't his wife, Lady Someone, recently killed herself? Jumped off the Clifton Suspension Bridge, so the *Telegraph* said. Tragedy can happen to anyone, the Georgie Fames as well as the Jack Ravens. A woman's body falling through space. Like that recurrent Lockerbie nightmare he had, the passengers, still strapped in their seats, hitting the ground alive. Best think of something else.

He buzzed Karen, asking her to schedule five ten-minute meetings for mid-afternoon. Above him the clock struck one. He unwrapped his sand-wiches – ham and egg – and ate them at the desk, with the portraits of his forebears staring down at him: John-Joseph, John-Joseph Junior, Joseph-James. What a family of clowns and no-hopers. It was a miracle he had a business to run – or ruin – at all. First Grandfather, parpety-parping time and money away in open-top cars. Then Father, with his costly flutters on the horses. Then Ronnie, dead at fifty-six and disgraced long before that – my brother the pornographer. Jack had done his best to keep the business afloat. But he had sired no son to take over. Which was as well, perhaps, given the feckless family gene, but still left him feeling a failure.

While he ate he skimmed the *Telegraph*. Sensation as murder suspects appear at Stephen Lawrence Inquiry. Masked youths throw petrol bombs at security forces in Co. Armagh. *Penthouse* to publish nude photos of intern who alleges affair with President Clinton. Just the one cheering item – 'Huntsman cleared of charges of rearing fox cubs in captivity': excellent, a defeat for the Antis, for once.

The bread was stale and stuck in his throat – he threw the crusts into the waste bin. First Nancy, now this. And bloody Marcus hovering next door, desperate to discuss ongoing income streams and the paramountcy of front-end loading. Anyone else would call it quits. He could take his pension, the with-profits Equitable Life policy, and cash in his various investments while the FTSE was up near the 6,000 mark. Sell now and he could become a man of leisure. But where was the comfort in living comfortably? He rose from the desk, to make his own coffee.

2

## ANTHEA

'HOW MUCH are these?' Anthea asked, pointing to the mangoes.

'To you, darling, 50p the pair,' the man said. A gust lifted her dress, and she dropped both hands to hold it down, like Marilyn in *The Seven Year Itch*. The pears and apples lay piled on lurid artificial turf, as though this was a Kentish orchard, not Woolwich.

'I'll take that melon, too,' she said.

The man's skin was the colour of aubergines. He handed over the blue plastic bag.

'Respect, respect.'

Was it respect he was offering? Or a leer? She couldn't tell; she didn't care. The sense of euphoria was general. It was the sunshine. And the World Cup. St George's flags draped from windowsills, like tongues hanging out, or fluttered on the aerials of transit vans. She wished a breeze could pass through her. The plastic bag cut into her hands. She had fifteen minutes to be back at her desk.

The mangoes and melon were an impulse buy. Never mind. She'd make a sorbet. Or serve them fresh, in slices, with Greek yogurt (he would not want cream). The Greek yogurt she could get from Sainsbury's. Unless they sold it at the cheese stall, along with Emmental and Brie. Would he want cheese, after paella and dessert? In the old days she'd not been interested in cooking. She used to live on rocket salads and chocolate. Now she was trying to learn.

At the fish stall, she bought prawns, mussels, haddock and squid. They had samphire, too. The people's asparagus. From the Kent marshes. Lorried up only that morning. 'Cook it till it's soft and you can suck it off the stalk,' the fish man said. Samphire and saffron. It didn't matter if she found no arborio rice. Let him eat pilau. As if he'd notice. It was her he was coming for, not the food.

In Sainsbury's, she picked up the saffron, along with matches, candles and paper napkins. Could the girl at the checkout tell she was cooking for her lover? Could the old lady behind her tell, the one who'd put the divider between her cat food and Anthea's love food? She liked the feeling they might guess. If this were a musical, she'd be singing her love to the rooftops. But the relationship was one she couldn't acknowledge. She might be cooking for her lover, but her lover was married to someone else.

At the office, seeing the shopping bags, the man on Reception gave a knowing wink: having a party, eh? Winks, leers – it would be wolf whistles next. Must be the sun. Or pheromones. Or the lightness of her summer dress. In the lift to the fourth, she watched herself in all the mirrors. The new Anthea. That dress (thin shoulder straps, V-neck, bare legs), where she used to wear jeans. Single diamond stud in her nose instead of rings. And the hair, blonde, not long or peroxide enough to be brazen but less modest – less mousy – than before. The new Anthea seemed less her than the old Anthea; she wasn't sure she could condone her. But it was nice to be noticed for a change. So long as the men doing the noticing didn't think she was dressing for them.

The office was empty. She kicked her sandals off and ate a yogurt. The fan blew the silver top across the desk, where it stuck to the side of Mr Fell's terminal, like a Post-it. Mr Fell had two grown-up daughters and spent his weekends walking in Kent. Obviously he would disapprove of her private life. As, in principle, did Anthea. It had been several months now. What if it all came out? Even her grandmother seemed to have intuited it, when she called that morning.

'Happy birthday, love.'

'I don't feel twenty-five.'

'You sound in a good mood, anyway.'

'I am.'

'Must be a new man.'

'Is that the only way to be in a good mood?'

'I'm only teasing, pet.'

She *was* only teasing, and they had gone on to talk about Anthea's work, in which Granny, having worked for the council in Swansea, took a genuine interest – far more interest, in fact, than Anthea took. Granny was lovely. Without Granny she would not have survived the Terrible Thing. But if a partially sighted eighty-year-old living two hundred miles away could rumble her secret, what hope was there of fooling everyone else?

She yawned. Two thirty and still no sign of Mr Fell. His diary was empty till three fifteen but he never took more than an hour for lunch. It was strange he had left no note.

The phone rang. Mr Fell's phone. He had no answering machine – only her.

'Is that Domestic Violence?' a voice said.

'No. [But I'll happily organise some for you, madam.] This is Environmental Health.'

'What?'

'It's Anthea Hurt speaking.'

'Hurt?'

'[You will be.] Domestic Violence, was it? Just putting you back to the switchboard.'

Moving into London hadn't been the plan. But when she called Jake from her mother's house, in the Lakes, explaining what had happened, he pushed her: 'You can crash at my place. I really miss you, angel.' She brought two suitcases and clothes to last a month. But he was not there to meet her at Euston nor – seemingly – at the Stratford flat. Typical Jake. Or perhaps a new dynamic Jake, working long hours: he had a proper job now, as a Community Relations Officer in East Ham. She sat in a nearby pub with her suitcase, unpicking beer mats and brooding on Old Nod, who had been as nice about it as he could be – awfully sorry, unable to renew her contract, no reflection on her abilities, needs must, last one in first one out, happy to provide a good reference, doubtless employers would be queuing up to have her, etc. Despite Nod's kindness, she felt rejected and vaguely ashamed and unmistakably in need of loving comfort, which was why, when Jake invited her she came. I wonder how the lime trees are doing in Marshmoor Gardens, she thought, as she left the pub. It took a while but this time Jake answered when she knocked: 'Hey.' He was wrapped in a bedsheet and seemed surprised to see her; no surprises there. His embrace was nervous and lukewarm. Ten seconds in and it was how it had always been – her asking to be loved, him backing away. As he closed the door, a female voice sang down: 'Jehovah's Witnesses, was it?' Miranda, he explained, 'a colleague from work'. The colleague from work appeared at the top of the stairs, an assemblage of white curves and a glossy black triangle. 'Christ, Jake, you could have warned me.' That was Miranda speaking but it might have been Anthea. Jake excused himself: 'Sorry about the mess. I'll just get dressed.

Make yourself at home.' Three weeks' crockery sat in the washing-up bowl. There were whispers from upstairs and some fairy tale when he came down again – Miranda was crashing in the spare room, she'd been asleep, both of them had, they had worked through the night on a regeneration project in Stepney which Anthea must come and see. Miranda appeared with her clothes on and a 'Hey'. She had to be going, she said. 'Smoke?' Jake said, rolling up as the front door slammed. Anthea shook her head. Was there time to catch the last train back to Oxenholme? she wondered. 'I'd offer you a drink,' he said, 'but . . .' She imagined his bedroom: spermy sheets and empty wine glasses. 'It's OK,' she said. 'Present for you.' He took the whisky bottle and kissed her on the cheek. 'Angel.' Idiot, she thought, as she took her first sip, still making the same mistakes. The real idiocy was sleeping with him later. Without protection, too. She was drunk. Even so. You never knew where Jake had been. Or rather you did.

Next day, she went looking for alternative accommodation, and took the first thing she saw, a flatshare across the water in Thamesmead. Jake, relieved, said he was sorry she couldn't stay longer and promised to take her out to dinner 'very soon'. She hadn't heard from him since. *Sorry about the mess.* With Jake, mess was the order of existence.

To tide her over, she took a waitressing job, in a restaurant called Millennium, where the customers were rude ('Millennium? Is that how long it takes to get served, love?') and the manager a sadistic cheapskate. Then she saw the ad: no previous experience required, but an interest in environmental issues would be an advantage. The interview was perfunctory: none of the other candidates had her local authority background, let alone a reference from Nod. Environmental health meant everything from noise pollution to pest control, but once inducted she became part of the hygiene team, visiting shops, takeaways, factory canteens and restaurants in the company of Mr Fell, who wore a blue tie and button-down collar and had a talent for spotting little-known offences – they would go to investigate a breach against regulation 13a, and find 4b, 11c, 18d, 26e and 39f being breached as well. Her role, as underling, was to take notes, fill report sheets, and send out letters on council notepaper. Her office was a yellow-painted cubbyhole, with a computer that froze six times a day and a window too high to see out of. As for her colleagues – she had known livelier trees. But there were bright spots, like the trip they paid to Millennium, where she took pleasure in directing Mr Fell to the waste-disposal system, which he found to have 'serious flaws', worthy of a large fine – a revenge on the manager for having cheated her of her last week's wages. Three months in, Mr Fell still referred to her as Annabel. But it was a job. It paid the rent. One day she would change the world. Meanwhile, she was working for Greenwich Council.

And she was writing. With a cubbyhole of her own, and minimal duties to perform, she often sneaked an hour in on her stories. But for the distraction of tonight's meal, and that yogurt smear on Mr Fell's terminal, she could be writing now.

Where *was* Mr Fell? Why no message? It disturbed her not to know his whereabouts.

It was Dr Raven – Nat – who got her writing again. They first met up at a coffee shop called Inca, in St Martin's Lane. Her mornings were free – she was waitressing at Millennium then – and though the venue (his suggestion) seemed a little cramped, she managed to find a table in the corner. She felt nervous – email was one thing, meeting in the flesh altogether different. Would she even recognise him? She did, the moment he walked in: the curly hair, the glasses, the bulging stomach, the Cornish-pasty shoes. They sat at the tiny metal table trying not to touch knees. She had a stye coming in one eye; he had cut himself shaving; neither was at their best. Conversation was awkward. Under the whoosh of the cappuccino machine, she found it hard to make herself heard. Or was it just him being obtuse?

Eventually they got on to the stories. They showed promise, he said, but she must take her writing more seriously. She doubted they did; she doubted she could. But so much had gone wrong in recent months she needed to hear it. Her use of tone and imagery was impressive, he said. She smiled. Whenever she came across words like tone and imagery, she felt like locking herself in a cupboard – the review pages were her least favourite part of newspapers. Why the smile? he asked. Oh, it's nothing, she said. *The Book of Foxes* is a good title, he said. I've been thinking of changing it to *The Book of Vixen*, she said, sipping her camomile. Not a wise move, he said. She felt faintly patronised, like a nerdy wannabe being patted on the head by a lofty sage. But he was trying to be helpful. She drained her cup. I'm really grateful to you for seeing me, she said.

And she was. Her flatmate, Emma, who was studying architecture at Greenwich University and with whom she had shared a bottle of Southern Comfort the previous night, thought it was *really weird if not perverted* for a tutor to see a student, let alone an ex-student, off campus and one-to-one: 'He must fancy you.' No, he just feels sorry for me, Anthea said – I'm jobless, rootless and boyfriendless, after all. How the boyfriend thing slipped out with Nat she wasn't sure, but it did, in the doorway of Inca. At least she wasn't self-pitying about it. A relationship I was in broke up, she told him, but I'm fine, I've come to London to start again, all my old ties are bad for me. Won't I be bad for you then? Nat said. That's different, she laughed. It isn't *personal*.

They shook hands on leaving. Across the road, she bought some postcards she liked – lush paintings of flowers by some woman artist. She sent him one the next week, thanking him for his help and attaching a new story.

They met again: it became a ritual. She posted drafts to him, at college, with chatty postcards attached; he brought the drafts, heavily blue-pencilled, to Inca. Guilty at taking up his time, she offered to rejoin his class – no point, he said, she was too advanced. Well, they could always email each other, she suggested – true, he said, but face-to-face was more productive. She felt no qualms about his attentiveness. It was her work, not her body, which interested him. But she was pleased her stye had gone. She was sleeping better, too. The colour (so her mother would have told her) had come back to her cheeks.

Three o'clock. Still no sign. Had Mr Fell had a heart attack? She logged on to check her emails. HAPPY BIRTHDAY, she saw. Her first thought was Jake. But Jake would never remember her birthday. Only her mother remembered. And Granny. And him, of course. Since she was seeing him tonight, she hadn't expected him to bother, but there was his username. And HAPPY BIRTHDAY over and over. She had warned him not to email at work. Office passwords weren't secure. Council PCs were strictly for council business. She could lose her job.

Working for the council had put an end to mornings in Inca. But the stories were coming along. Nat was still arguing with her about the title. *The Book of Foxes* was good, he said, because it alerted readers to her tricksiness. But I'm not tricksy, she said. A book of foxes, like Chinese boxes, and fiction as a game – that's what the title will say to people, he said. But it isn't a game, she said. You mean your stories have some personal significance? he said. Not personal so much, she said, *political*. In what way political? he said. There's stuff about gender and environmentalism, she said. Fair enough, he said, but let's not make the politics too explicit. OK, she said, you're the boss.

He wasn't her boss. Her boss – team leader, now missing person – was Mr Fell, who expected better of her than to sit around reading personal emails. But if Mr Fell could not be bothered to tell her his whereabouts and just swanned off to . . .

Christ, she thought, on her feet and halfway out the door, the Swan, I'm supposed to be at the Swan in Bexley, alleged breach of regulation 24a, he said he'd go straight on from the other job and I was meant to meet him, Jesus, where's that lift, stuck in the basement probably, it'll be quicker using the stairs, I'll probably get the sack for this, be 'let go of' again, Hi, Kirtley, yeh, but I'm in a bit of a rush, stupid cow, does she think I normally run down the stairs, last flight, ground floor, exit to street, how do I get to Bexley, not by bus that's for sure, I'll have to get a cab and pay for it out of my own pocket, serve me right, *if* I can find a cab, but there is one, look, God must be on my side.

'Taxi, taxi.'

It's love that's doing this to me, she thought, without regret.

It was a postcard that changed everything. 'Sorry to have been out of touch,' she wrote. 'The new job's keeping me very busy. But here are two new stories, squeezed out during quieter spells. Do call one evening, if you've time – I'd love to hear your comments.' He rang next day: 'When shall I come? Is tomorrow OK?' By 'call' she had meant phone, but he read visit. Embarrassed, she backtracked: wasn't Thamesmead inconvenient for him? Not at all, he said. She regretted giving him the address. She would be on her own. Emma had moved out, to live with her boyfriend, and she had not yet found a new flatmate. But when he arrived, out of breath, half an hour late, and sat at the kitchen table, it was literary-critical business as usual. She was surprised how comfortable it felt to have him there. But also, when he suggested they meet again the following week, a little embarrassed: he had young children, evenings must be awkward for him, he already had enough students without her. No problem, he said. But what did his wife think? It was no big deal, he said, blushing; his wife was used to him being out and about, they both had independent lives. *No big deal?* she thought, closing the door behind him. She felt both offended and relieved. Confused, too: there had been that blush. Obviously his wife, his *independent* wife, knew nothing about her. She remembered what Emma had said: 'He must fancy you.'

There was no excuse for not being on her guard. But weeks went by with nothing to arouse suspicion. She wrote; he criticised; she rewrote; he edited; they met, he went away. One night they had a glass of wine before he left. 'I do understand, you know,' she said, pouring it out. 'You're married, you have young children, it's not like I expect this to go anywhere.' 'What?' he said. She already regretted opening her mouth. 'Us meeting up and stuff.' He seemed puzzled. 'But we want your writing to go some-where, don't we?' he said. 'Yes,' she said, 'yes, of course.' More weeks went by; he was away (school holidays) and she had less time for writing; the sessions dwindled. One night he phoned. How about she came to him for a change? See where he lived. Let him play host. Next Saturday morning, for instance? If she had nothing better to do. Would it not be disruptive for his family? she asked. No, he said, they were away for the weekend, he'd be at a loose end. He paused, waiting for an answer. She might be busy, she said, she had vaguely planned to visit her mother in the Lake District. Well, never mind, he said, it was just a thought. But if she happened to be around, why not drop in for an hour? Saturday morning felt safe and neutral. Nat was safe and neutral. What did she have to worry about? All right, she said, but inside she was thinking forget it, too weird, no way will I turn up. 'My wife and children' he called them, distancingly, compartmentalisingly, as if he couldn't bear to say their names, or couldn't bear to say them to her. During the week she had flu, and missed two days at work. On the Friday night, she emailed to say OK, she would drop round, but only for half an hour, at most. Next morning she felt wobbly again and nearly cancelled. She had these fantasies of fighting him off – there she was, in his arms, struggling not to be over-powered, and him with his desire, his strong arms, his hardness pressed against her. She felt ashamed of her mooniness – her Mills & Booniness. At 11.40 a.m. she rang his bell. God knows why I've come, she thought, and was turning away, down the path, when the door opened. He smiled benignly from his spectacles – safe as houses. The basement kitchen was cosily familial. Every scatter-rug, every framed black-and-white print, every dinner plate on the dresser confirmed how settled in his life he was. He made her coffee and they sat by the French windows, looking out into the long thin garden. That mug she was holding had been bought at Hemingway's house in Key West, he said, then invited her to see his other artefacts, as though this were a National Trust property and he a guide. She must be curious where he did his writing, he said. Not really, but she went along with the tour, out of politeness. On the way upstairs ('my study's in the attic'), she glanced in at his bedroom, his and his wife's bedroom, and quickly looked away again, unsettled not so much by its rumpled intimacy – strewn duvet, scattered pillows – but by the perfume on the dressing table: her mother's brand, Estée Lauder.

'Don't miss this,' he said, halting on the attic stairs and opening the door to a smaller bedroom, 'we just redecorated it.' One of the girls' rooms. 'Hannah's,' he said, risking the name.

She gazed at the blue wallpaper. 'What shade is it?' she asked.

'Azure,' he said.

Azure. She could remember him denouncing the word in a story of hers: 'sub-poetic,' he said. Perhaps domesticity robbed you of your critical faculties. Or his wife had bought the paint. What was his wife called? He still hadn't said her name. On the wall was a photo of his two girls, with matching school sweaters and missing teeth.

'Sweet,' she said. 'How old are they?'

'Hannah's eight and Rose is six.'

She smiled and calculated. He'd had his fortieth last year. So if he was now forty-one, and she was twenty-four, and Hannah was eight, that made her closer in age to his eldest daughter than to him. Only just, by a year, but still . . . She felt like a child suddenly, disoriented, out of her depth and faint with flu, and sat down on the little pine bed, Hannah's bed, as though to relearn the spring and bounce of childhood – the confidence all would turn out well, a confidence she had lost in her teens and which, sitting in the house of this married, middle-aged man, she saw, with *azure* clarity, would never come back. He looked bemused, expecting her to joke and get up, so his tour could continue. Out of nowhere, she began to sob, weeping for her childhood and for Hannah's. 'What's wrong?' he said, worried, and sat down next to her. 'Sorry, this is stupid,' she said, sniffing and composing herself but staying put. 'Tell me what's wrong,' he said, and put his arm round her. 'It's nothing,' she said, angry at making an exhibition of herself and angry with him for not pretending not to see. 'Tell me anyway,' he said, his arm still round her shoulder. 'I'm fine, leave me alone,' she said, yanking herself free, like an adolescent rowing with her father, as she had with hers, bitterly, the week before he died, remembering which made her weep afresh. Nat encircled her more closely this time, took her into him, under his wing. 'What's wrong?' he said again, but she was too tearful and too confused. She could feel his bristles on the back of her neck (his wife away, he hadn't shaved), which reminded her of her father again, with his thick moustache. So much about Nat was like her father. No, nothing about Nat was like her father – he was fatter, sweatier, redder in the face, less neat. But the comfort of being in his arms, hugged, held, enfolded, anchored: that was the same. It felt as if he could keep her from the demons that pursued her, even though the demons were him. *I should stand up*, she thought, in case he gets the wrong idea. But when he stroked her head and shoulders, he did it like a father, not a man on heat. *Even if he were on heat, he wouldn't ask me to have sex with him*, she thought. *Not asking is a way of protecting us both – me from having to refuse and himself from the guilt of infidelity. For all his pompousness, I'm really very fond of him.* She nuzzled against his neck, not from fondness, but because his shirt front, damp with her tears, was uncomfortable. She was feeling better now, breathing on his neck, no more grief. She nuzzled closer. His hand moved from her shoulder towards her breast. He's misunderstood, she thought, but she could handle it, could handle him handling her – her crying had upset him, she owed him this in return, if it made him feel better, and her feel better, why not? Now his lips were on her cheeks, her eyelids, her lips. His tongue was there, too – and politeness, equivalence, required a response. This wasn't sex, sex would be wrong, but their tongues were locked, his fingers undid her blouse, her hand was inside his shirt, her nipple hardened in his palm. It was comfort not sex, but sex was comfort, or this sex was, all this undoing of each other (zips and buttons) till both of them were undone, and, though something somewhere was vaguely uncomfortable, to feel him feeling her felt good, she deserved this after Jake, they both deserved it, they had worked so hard together at her writing and behaved so well and this, the licence to behave badly, was their reward – though there was nothing bad as such about lying on the bed together half undressed, and him now sliding on top of her, she hadn't planned this, she had planned the opposite of this, but he might as well come inside her, there, God.

Afterwards, they lay a long time before she felt the weight: his body on her, the guilt, the significance of the transgression. Something was digging into her back, reinserting her in reality. 'Could you just . . . ?' she said, rolling Nat off. She sat up. Six plastic beads fell away, from where they had been sticking to her skin. A seventh remained in the small of her back, till she brushed it off. Nat, half asleep, hadn't noticed. But when she scooped the seven beads in her hand and shook them, he propped himself on one elbow. She held her palm open for him, like a child offering M&Ms. The beads were red, yellow, green and blue. A little girl's jewellery starter kit. She'd had a set herself once. You strung the beads together then bedecked yourself. She could remember mimicking Mum with her twinset. Or wearing beads like a hippie on her ankles. Nat smiled, bemused, at her open palm. Did his daughter play such games? Had she taken the beads away with her for the weekend, missing these few? To Anthea, it was as though the beads had been left intentionally, to dissuade her from the offence she had just committed. The bed was a bed of nails now; her back had seven holes in it – stabs of conscience, stigmata of sin.

She stood up and began to dress, without a word. He lay there on the bed, his elbow propping his face, his cock limp on the sheet. He'll have more sense than to ask me to stay, she thought, the best thing now is to pretend it never happened. But he began to pressurise her, nonetheless: what's wrong, where are you going? She pulled her tights on, sealing her crotch. All she wanted was to leave the crime scene. He grabbed her arm. She snatched it back. He leapt from bed. She rushed downstairs. He ran behind her, naked, to the front door. She flung it open, knowing he'd shrink back. He watched, hands over balls. She unlatched the garden gate and was through.

She wandered the streets in the rain, mascara-streaked, berating herself. It was a Saturday lunchtime, families going about their shopping, and here was she, wicked and adrift. She should never have sat on that bed. Never have gone round. Never have met him at Inca. Never have sent him her stories. Never have attended his Getting Started class in the first place. Bad enough to sleep with him anywhere, but at his home was infinitely worse. It was all her fault. Though partly his fault, too: what was he up to, asking her round, making her coffee, inviting her upstairs? In fact, mostly his fault: if she were twenty years older than someone, and a mentor to them, she would be kind, protective, beyond self-interest. Indeed, *completely* his fault: for him to make love to her on his daughter's bed – how sick was that? All she had wanted was to be comforted, as anyone normal could have seen. She would never talk to him again. She would tear up his letters, stop sending him her work, refuse to answer his calls and emails. Fraud. Child-snatcher. Pervert.

She wandered the streets for half an hour then rang his bell to say she had nothing more to say to him. It was evening before she left.

Since then they had been meeting at her flat. As before, but not as before. Each time she told herself there would be no next time. Her emails said the same: it was an erotic movie that should never have been made, a cyber-space fantasy, falling in love like this would end in disaster, too many other people stood to be hurt, why couldn't he see how unhappy it was making her. Let's talk about it on Tuesday, he would email back. Then on Tuesday they would go to bed. On other evenings, too, if he could slip away. So much lovemaking. But was it mere – mere! – sensation? She knew what Emma would say, if she knew. And what Rachel would say, and anyone else who cared for her interests. That he had sucked her in. Taken advantage. Abused his position of trust. She had these thoughts herself. But in all her computations (of moves made and initiatives taken), she appeared to be equally active. Perhaps *more* active. Always that image: her sitting down on his daughter's bed; her leading him on.

So here she was, at twenty-five, spending her days with one middle-aged man and her evenings (some of them) with another. If the cab wasn't at the Swan in the next two minutes, Mr Fell would probably sack her. But as for Nat, it was up to her to sack him. Could she? Of course: the new confidence she had gained from being with him would empower her to do without him. Then again: why should she sack him? She was happy. He was happy. And so far their happiness had done no harm to anyone else.

*You worry too much*, he had written in that last email. Till recently she'd been a scaredy-cat and ugly duckling. Now she was stronger – like the Anthea she'd been until her father died, or perhaps a new person, Anthea 3. She might not entirely believe in this Anthea, let alone approve of her. But she intended to enjoy herself, and what the hell.

'The Swan, love? There you go.'


*3*

*LIBBY*


IT WAS good manners to use your clients' products. Prudent housekeeping, too, since some of them came as freebies, and in a household that survived on one income – yours – you couldn't afford to look gift horses in the mouth. So . . . Libby's skirts were from Mandalay, her shoes from Boot Chic. Her car was a Sonnet, and when she drove – weekends only – she filled its tank with Eco-Econ. At breakfast she drank Haiko herbal tea, with half a Homebacke scone; at night she drank Koala County Sauvignon Blanc. She washed her skin with Fragranz, shampooed her hair with Candour, brushed her teeth with Brio and deodorised with Zest. When she wrote by hand, she did so with a Flourish. And when she smoked (to keep her weight down), she chose Oregon. Her pillows were made by Duskdown, and her kitchen units by Cumbrian Oaks. Her girls were kitted out at Hoity-Tots, and she flew with SaxonAir. She had gone downmarket once, with the Indie Spice account, back in the eighties (the jars of chicken tikka masala, years-past-their-sell-by, were still sitting in her larder). The rest of her products were top of the range. She kept a selection of them at the office, both to display to visiting clients and to add to her workplace comforts. But she had never handled a coffee account, and just now – a Tuesday, mid-afternoon – the omission was a matter of keen regret. It wouldn't have to be Kenyan Ochre. Any caffeine would do. Oh, for a shot of Naff Cafetière. Or a dose of Cheap-and-Nasty Filter. Even a swig of Instant Bilge. She had been in since seven this morning and would be here past seven tonight.

Long hours were part of the business, but now she was setting up her own business they had become even longer. It wasn't just panic about the launch. There was also the impending loss of Millie, who was leaving to train as a psychiatric nurse – as Nat had joked through gritted teeth, seven years in the company of small children made psychiatric nursing the obvious career move. A new nanny would not be hard to find but to the girls Millie was irreplaceable. Nat favoured telling them now, so they could get used to the idea, but Libby was keeping it secret till after the launch. She couldn't claim that Millie was letting her down – no nanny had ever been more loyal. But she could have done without having to do without her just now. First Nat, fucking things up with Rikky Falcon, then Millie – you could never rely on people. And the launch less than a week away. Sod's Law.

She ran down her three columns of clients: On Board, Wavering, Outside Chance. The first column was short, the second not much longer, the third had a hundred names. How many calls had she put in today? Thirty? Forty? And not one of them returned. Next time she set up her own agency, she would avoid the World Cup. Men allegedly thought about sex every fifteen seconds. At present, they were thinking football 60/60/24/7. There was nothing like football to remind Libby she was a woman. And nothing like an England football game to remind her she was Northern Irish.

'Wasn't the Savernake guy due in at three?' she asked Angie.

'Sorry, I should have said. He rang at lunchtime to rearrange. Had to leave early today, he said.'

'Because of the football.'

'Probably. He sounded that sort.'

'They're all that sort.'

'I know. And it's not just the men. Carly's come back from lunch with her face painted. Some guy in Leicester Square. The Union Jack, one-inch square, on her right cheek.'

'Christ.'

Libby wondered if she had been right to recruit Carly. But her work so far had been terrific – any snippets in the trade press were down to her. Maybe face-painting was fashionable among young PRs. Maybe Carly would agree to be painted with the agency logo, for the launch next week.

'Is that it for meetings?' Libby said.

'You have a four thirty. Mr Michaels. He won't cancel.'

'He's not interested in football, you mean.'

'He's over from Amsterdam – runs some sort of agribusiness.'

'Oh, him.'

'And Zach called. His artwork's ready.'

'Let's get him in before the Dutch guy.'

'The brainstorming group come at five.'

'I thought we said six.'

'They asked to bring it forward. Just this once. Because of the . . .'

'I should have known. Whose turn is it to sit in with them?'

'I'm not sure. Leave it with me.'

Most things were left with Angie, since she was Admin. The only other full-timers were Carly (Publicity), Gavin (Finance), Charmaine (Brands), Josh (Research) and Sasha (Legal). A skeleton staff. For the foreseeable future, they'd have to answer their own phones. And type their own letters. And each do the work of three people. She'd explained all this when head-hunting. Those who left good jobs – and everyone except Carly had left a good job – decided it was a risk worth taking. Libby's reputation preceded her. She had made a name for herself. And now she was the name of an agency, twice over.

Raven McCready. Her married name and her maiden, joined together. Or as Carly put in press handouts, 'Raven McCready: a New Agency for a New Age'.

'It's your funeral,' friends said, when she first told them. They were worried, naturally. A new venture is always a risk. And as they saw it, she had left Arran & Arran on a whim. But it wasn't a whim. The thought had been there for several years. And the SaxonAir debacle had been the last straw. She had worked so hard to bring Greg Drosz and Simon Mirtle-Thome together, and the business-class advert was a triumph, winning the Creatives two awards. But there had also been some bad publicity. A letter to the *Guardian* used the E-word, exploitation, and pickets appeared outside the offices of SaxonAir. What people objected to in the ad wasn't female nudity, but the use of a fur stole to conceal it. END THE SKIN TRADE! the placards of animal rights activists screamed, UNFAIR TO FUR! Then came a further scandal: a couple on a night flight from New York were caught having sex beneath their business-class blankets and charged with public indecency; though the carrier was Virgin, the media speculated, only half jokingly, that the suggestiveness of the SaxonAir ad had been an incite-ment. With a bit of goodwill, the damage might have been repaired. But

Greg's ego was too big for goodwill and Simon took his next campaign else-where. His phone call to Libby exempted her from blame: 'New manage-ment team here, different priorities, fundamental reappraisal of our image, etc.' There was an inquest: not even Arran & Arran could afford to lose a £20 million account. No one blamed Libby but Libby felt blamed. It wasn't paranoia. First the job that Mark had semi-promised her was slow to mat-erialise. Then he gave it to a prat called Julius Kite.

That was January. By March she had lined up the staff, premises, funds and potential clients to start her own company – and handed in her notice. Mark thought it a ploy.

'If money's the problem,' he said.

'It's not.'

'I accept you're due a rise.'

'It's a bit late for largesse, Mark.'

'Haven't I always encouraged you?'

'On and off. Now I want to do my own thing.'

'I trust you won't be taking any of your clients with you – that's to say, our clients.'

'It depends on them.'

'I'd hate for there to be anything' – he searched the ceiling for the right word – 'unethical.' An-iffy-girl was how it came out. Mark's pronunciation went haywire when he was tense.

'I'm sure most of my clients will stay with you,' she said. 'But if any approach me, I can hardly refuse to talk to them.'

So several approached her, and she didn't. There were a few others she invited to a lavish farewell lunch – they, too, were fair game. She didn't want clients so big that she couldn't afford to lose them. But it was crucial to have a blue chip or two – British Gas, Harrods, Schweppes, the Royal Academy, Barnardo's and so on. Meanwhile, the smaller clients already signed up would keep her busy till the autumn. So much for being an-iffy-girl.

Her one regret was not bringing Damian. Within three months of her hiring him, he'd risen from Account Assistant to Account Handler. And in the reshuffle since her departure, he'd been promoted again. With a bit more nerve, she could have poached him. But she didn't want a major falling-out with Mark, who could still, if he chose, make life difficult for her (Angie was her only staff theft). Then there was the other factor. Damian's way of looking at her. Not sexual appraisal exactly. But not as neutral as a young employee should be with his (female) boss. In this busi-ness everyone flirted. But she felt uneasy in Damian's presence, aware of herself physically – skin, breasts, legs, lips – to a degree that seemed improper with a colleague. Her regret at leaving him behind was tinged with relief.

The launch would be extravagant: Moët & Chandon, Thai food, lilies, balloons, goody bags for three hundred guests – all this at the Seaman's Hall, in Somerset House, part of the Courtauld Institute, overlooking the Thames. She had been shameless in calling in old favours. Even the venue had come cheap thanks to, of all people, Annie Cleeve of ChildPlanet, who happened to be a Courtauld trustee. The party would show that Libby meant business – that Raven McCready wasn't some brash upstart but an agency with clout. The established agencies could sit back – they had won their laurels and gone flabby, whereas she had everything to prove. When prospective clients asked the obvious question – why entrust themselves to an untested outfit? – that was her answer: because she *needed to succeed*.

'Zach's here,' Angie said, ushering him over.

'That was quick.'

Twenty-two years old, shaved head, a friend of Tarquin (who had suggested him) and no less gay. He had come to show his artwork for the Tikko ad. Tikko had been Libby's first signing. They were tiny compared with Sony but the Tikko MD-256 had been voted last year's top minidisc player and the MD-257 was selling even better. Now the MD-258 was in the wings. The ad for it, twenty seconds long, would be shown in selected cinemas and on cable. The agreed parameters were *youthful, urban, cheeky, clever, postmodern.*

'To me urban says shopping mall,' Zach said, talking Libby through his sketches. 'And clever says fox. So fox in a shopping mall is how I start.'

'God, I hate foxes,' Libby said. 'I can smell them all over my garden.'

'They're the Brits' favourite animal now.'

'Says who?'

'Some survey I read. It's an anti-hunting thing. People identify with foxes. Bushy tail, bright eyes, smart brain, born survivor, would win any reality-TV show. Kids love them. Adults too.'

'So in the ad . . .'

'So in the ad,' said Zach, who like most Creatives became animated only when showing off his work, 'the fox enters the mall, passes two old ladies drinking tea in an outdoor-indoor café, takes an escalator to the Underground (trotting down the left while people stand to the right, see), hops on the tube as the doors are closing (there's the tip of his tail just avoiding being trapped), occupies a seat, exits at the next stop, takes the up escalator, comes out in the street, crosses at the lights, between the stalled traffic, and heads towards the park. All this in eleven seconds. The fox always on the move. With its eyes staring and its ears pricked. Which gives the viewer the idea the fox must be looking for something, that it's hunting rather than being hunted – here it is running past a pond (completely ignores the ducks), weaving through a maze of box hedging, then leaping over a crossbar. Still in the park, you notice. And all the while there'll be background music getting louder. Fifteen seconds gone. Now the climax. The fox reaches a park bench and stops. There's a teenage kid on the bench, listening to music (so that's where the music's been coming from). The kid stares at the fox. The fox stares at the kid. The kid takes off his headphones, lays them on the bench and walks away. The fox moves in, as the rightful owner. Advert over.'

'Then the words come up?'

'The word. Tikko.'

'With a voiceover of some kind.'

'Just the logo.'

'No slogan?'

'No.'

'Not even the model number? Or the price?'

'The minimalism is the point.'

'But people won't know what they're buying.'

'Sure they will. They'll get the logo.'

'For a nanosecond.'

'It's interactive. The punters have to do some of the work.'

'All of the work, as far as I can see.'

'You're being unfair, Mrs Raven.'

'Libby.'

'You're being unfair, Libby.'

'That's what I'm paid for. Someone has to anticipate Tikko's objections.'

'You don't like the ad, then?'

'I didn't say that.'

She made him take her through the roughs again and suggested some changes and mentioned a couple of other projects he might find interesting.

'So you do like it?'

'I will like it,' she said, 'if it's on my desk by Friday morning.'

Till she found the right person, she was acting as Creative Director. And whatever happened, any Creatives she used would be employed on a freelance basis, rather than slouching round the office on salaries. At Arran & Arran, there'd been a Creativity Zone, with a jukebox, a fruit machine, a pool table, a red telephone box, a trampoline, an orange bouncy rabbit, three scooters, a galvanised dustbin, a chess set and a Monopoly board, such objects being provided for the purposes of play, stress relief and, most important, inspiration, the principle having been enshrined even before Greg Drosz's arrival that no Creative could possibly achieve greatness without the freedom to spend the day behaving like a three-year-old. Libby was having none of it. Any Creatives she used could come in when they had something to show and receive no payment till the work was finished. Then if they burned out at thirty, as most seemed to, she would not have to subsidise them for life.

Before Angie could bring in Mr Michaels, she slipped to the Ladies. It was the mirror she needed more than the loo. If Raven McCready was going to succeed, she had to look presentable. Damian had suggested she join a gym called Tones. Half the members came from Adland, he claimed, and many deals were struck on the treadmill. But working up a sweat with clients was a male thing. She preferred the solitariness of her exercise bike in the bedroom at home. Her legs remained her best feature and she was careful to show them off. (Her mother's comment, after the ravages of the first labour, was 'Well, you still have your legs', as though amputation below the hip was a common consequence of childbirth.) Today's skirt was short and tight, whereas the blouse was loose. She ought to change her shade of lipstick. But it would have to do.

'Ah, Mr Michaels,' she said.

'I am talking with Mrs Raven McCready in person?' he said.

'Kind of. So what can we do for you?'

He was tall – why are the Dutch always so tall? – and extremely dull. Twenty minutes would be enough. After that, she would call Nat and ask him to take over from Millie – so she could sit in with the brainstormers and remind them who was boss.

4

HARRY

'WILL YOU help?'

Not this, Harry thought, not now. It was stifling. He had a story to finish. It wasn't fair.

Reception knew the rules: admission by prior appointment only. Kylie, the current receptionist, was fearless with nutters and time-wasters. The Firewall, they called her: no virus got through. But this time Kylie had let her guard down. There were two women – sisters – asking for him in Reception. Please, Harry. *Please*. It won't take long.

'Will you help?'

Help? Help how? Journalists weren't good samaritans. You couldn't be a *behalfer*, writing to indulge people. There was enough pressure on you as it was – from the editor, and the subs, and the advertising department – without strangers turning up to bend your ear. He'd been easy-going in the past, as a cub reporter, but now he was learning to be tough.

'Will you help?'

Fuck off, he ought to be saying, tell them I'm away from my desk.

'Go on, then, bring them up.'

By rights he should have been down the Elephant, at Hannibal House. In conference yesterday morning, Mills, as acting editor, had toyed with sending him there, for the inquiry into Stephen Lawrence's murder – the five suspects had finally been summoned to appear. Deborah would have insisted on it. But Deborah had flown to France for England's game with Argentina – her husband Travis had been given two tickets through some corporate scam – and despite Harry's eagerness to go, Mills, the bastard, had decided against it: Stephen Lawrence, yeh, yeh, the inquiry had been running for weeks, *Gazette* readers were bored with it, nothing of interest ever happened there. Harry might have pushed it more but Mills was intractable and he ended up going to Chislehurst instead, to interview an estate agent about the boom in the housing market. And of course, Sod's Law, the inquiry turned out to be eventful. Two dozen members of the Nation of Islam had stormed the public gallery, dressed like a gospel choir, and disrupted proceedings. The chair had been forced to call a two-hour recess. And afterwards, when the infamous five left the building, one of them, Neil Acourt, wearing sunshades, provocatively waggled his fingers – come-and-get-me – at the heckling crowd. 'Wonderful colour,' Mills himself admitted in conference this morning. But though the suspects were at the Elephant again today, and this time Harry *had* pushed very hard to go, Mills refused to let him, because it was press day and he couldn't be spared and anyway (so Mills claimed) they had 'missed the boat'.

Now, on top of that, two women were stalking him.

Joy and Charity were their names. He asked did they want coffee, and

Kylie was dispatched to make it – not her job, but she owed him. They moved to Deborah's office, behind glass, where no one would disturb them. There was a television in the corner, with Sky News showing shots from the Elephant of trouble – fisticuffs – outside the courtroom. Fucking Mills! Knowing the footage would stop him listening, Harry turned it off.

The two women – unlikely-looking sisters – sat down. Charity reminded Harry of his mother: the floral dress, the sweat-beads on the brow, the mass, the gravity, the silver crucifix nesting in her bosom. Joy looked much younger: tan leather cap, wrap-around shades, leather zip-up jacket, gold bangles, long purple fingernails with squared-off ends.

*Will you help?*

Charity launched in. She was head honcho, the voluble one, while Joy played dumb behind her shades. They had a story for him about the New Cross fire. He did know about the New Cross fire?

Everyone knew about the New Cross fire. Even Kylie, bringing the coffee, knew about it, though at the time she would have been a toddler. 18 January 1981. A party for teenagers at 439 New Cross Road, just down the road from Goldsmiths College. An all-night party – the fire had broken out round 6 a.m. At that point there were forty or so kids in the house, many of them asleep. Consumed by heat or overcome by smoke, thirteen died, all of them black. How the fire started was a matter of dispute. There had been a fight. Maybe. A gatecrasher dropped a burning cigarette on the foam-filled sofa. Perhaps. Some nutcase set a chair alight then climbed to the top floor to burn on his own pyre. Possibly. The police said it looked like an accident – but if it was arson it must be black on black, in-house, not a race issue. The word on the street was different. There were stories of a white youth seen getting out of an Austin Princess and hurling a petrol bomb. And of a young PC finding a Molotov cocktail in the house – and a bottle with a wick in it in the garden. It would all come out, people said. But then the witnesses who had seen the arsonist faded away, the incendiary devices went missing, the young PC stayed silent, the coroner returned an open verdict.

In our hearts, Charity said, laying a hand on her bosom, that fire is burning still. We lost a nephew in it. Just thirteen. Our sister's child. Our sister is still too distressed to say his name.

Harry lowered his eyes and drank his coffee. There were things he could tell them about that night. But you don't go blabbing to a deputation of the bereaved.

*Will you help?*

The family needed justice to escape from limbo, Charity said. A new report was due to be published, reassessing the evidence with state-of-the-art forensic science. But a friend of theirs who had seen a draft said a race attack was still being denied. The original investigation had been a cover-up. The open verdict had been a cover-up. And now this report was, too. What could they do? Write letters to their MP, chain themselves to railings, organise marches – they had tried all that already. Their nephew was a good kid, a sensible kid, they were all good kids, murdered in a racist arson attack. The police were covering their own backs. Word had come down. The report was (excuse her) a whitewash.

'To a young man like you the fire is ancient history,' Charity said. 'But perhaps you understand our feelings.'

'Of course,' Harry said.

He understood better than he could admit. *He'd been at that party*. Only briefly, as a gatecrasher, with his friend Winston, hours before the blaze broke out, on their way to another party, but still. Owning up to that would create expectations – that he might remember their nephew; that he might have noticed something; that his personal involvement would make him write the story. It wouldn't. He didn't want to get into this. It would be I-journalism – I was there, I felt this, I thought that – and the only I-journalism Harry believed in was Impartial and Impersonal. Being there wasn't a reason to write the story. Being there was a reason not to.

A phone was ringing in the distance. Like a mother sheep with a crying lamb, he recognised it as his.

'Excuse me,' he said. 'Call of nature. I'll be straight back.'

The answering machine clicked in before he got there. He listened but didn't pick up. It was Nat, to say he would be coming round to watch the England match, but that he might be late, so if by any chance Libby rang could Harry tell her he would be definitely be there, and apologies if this seemed convoluted but he would explain when he arrived, that's if it was still OK for him to come as planned and if . . . The message cut out. 'As planned'? Harry had no memory of a plan. His plan was to watch the football in the pub over the way, the Lord Nelson, which had a giant screen. Of course, if Nat was coming, or eventually coming, he would stay in and watch the game with him, but this was not the moment to call him back, with Joy and Charity awaiting his help.

On his way to Deborah's office, he passed another television. More live footage from the Elephant. Fucking Mills!

He sat down again. Kylie's coffee tasted bitter.

Joy had spread out a scrapbook. There were pictures of firemen with hoses; pictures of the dead as gleaming schoolkids; pictures of mourners filing past graves. Here was a page of their nephew, with his football team, by a swimming pool, in a steel band. Then the protest march. Twenty thousand people walking past the Courts of Justice on the Strand. 'That's me,' Joy said, pointing to a woman marching under a banner, 'and that's Charity.' Harry didn't tell them he had marched. That his friend Nat had marched. That the fire and the march had made him, for a time, a political activist. It wasn't relevant. And it would raise false hopes.

Joy, blubbing, removed her shades, to use a tissue. If he were writing the story, he'd mention that, for colour ('Joy's eyes fill with tears as she recalls the last hours of the tragic teenager . . . etc.'). He remembered the fox man's eyes, Terry Lavell's, a year ago. The same look in them. The same appeal. The same hope that a newspaper could change his luck.

'We've read some of your pieces,' Charity said. 'That's why we came to you.'

'Sure,' Harry said, flinching. He ought to be flattered. But he didn't like the pigeonhole Black Journalist. 'Have you tried the *Voice*?' he said. 'Or the *Nation*?'

'We'd rather the *Gazette*.'

The right answer. He felt ashamed for asking. The *Voice* and the *Nation* might be black newspapers but the New Cross fire wasn't a story just for blacks.

But what *was* the story? That the relatives were still grieving? Of course they were. That the report might decide the fire was an accident? Well, maybe it was. In the heat of youth, he had been certain it was an arson attack and racist murder. Now he suspected he was wrong.

*Will you help?* No, he couldn't help. It wasn't only his having been there which disqualified him. The night of the fire was also the night that he had met Marcia. The night that led to Stephen. It was something he preferred not to think about. He had stashed it away for seventeen years.

They realised how busy he must be, Charity said. But as a concerned citizen, a responsible journalist, a . . . ('a brother,' Joy said), surely he could do something. There must be people who'd seen things who'd never come forward. A new investigative piece would stir huge interest.

A television set flickered in the distance. More footage from the Elephant. Harry's memory was running footage, too. First the party – he and Winston meeting Marcia and Paulette, and heading off with them down the steps of 439. Then the scorch-smell from the burned brickwork next morning. Then the march from south of the river to Westminster a month later: the banners and placards, the shouts bouncing off the office-fronts as they passed down Fleet Street ('Thirteen dead and nothing said!'), he and Nat walking with their arms linked somewhere near the back, Nat – in a beret rather than his usual hat – clearly fancying himself as the new Blair Peach. Who remembered *him* now, the white schoolteacher from the East End batoned to death by police at an anti-racist rally? There was that story, and the Lawrence story, and the New Cross fire story, and they were all part of the same story, which was Harry's story. But Harry couldn't write it. This wasn't the time or place.

'Will you help?' Charity said, again. 'Could you do something?'

The *Gazette* had taken on an intern. Suppose he offered them her? Suzie wasn't black. But nor was she too close to the material.

'To be honest with you,' he said, not being honest with them, 'I'm not the right person. But I know who is.'

Passing the buck, it was called. But what else could he do? Joy and Charity waited mournfully in Deborah's office while he went in search of Suzie.


5

*NAT*


MEMO TO self, Nat scribbled: get a letter knife. Opening post with a nit comb was nonsensical but the nit comb was the first thing to hand. A registered letter: how mysterious. Perhaps the National wants to commission a play from me, he thought, till he spotted the college postmark. He held the nit comb by the tooth end, using the long steel handle to slit the envelope. It was a form letter, with 'Dear Mr Raven' filled in by hand. Every tutor working for ICE must have been sent one. Still, if he were not feeling so robust, the letter would have offended him. Contemptuous hilarity was his first reaction. But as he sat marking exam papers, that changed to injured pride.

'USOR' it said at the top. The incoming Principal, Keighley Steel, was grateful to him for his long-standing commitment to the college and sincerely hoped she would be able to extend his part-time contract with ICE. She must point out, however, that once she was fully 'on board' she would be reappraising the college's role as a service provider to the local community, and though there was no intention to cut back on the range or quality of courses on offer, a number of overdue reforms would be implemented during the next academic year and, regrettably, certain 'long-standing, more traditionally based units' might have to be sacrificed to make room for units more consonant with the college's commitment to 'an innovative, multi-ethnic, equal-opportunity, value-added, access-prioritised approach to adult learning'. No specific decisions had yet been made, and most part-time tutors could expect to be re-engaged; all of them, it went without saying, were greatly valued. But these were challenging times, and certain evening classes – ones lacking popular assent or with a negative fiscal impact – might have to be shelved.

She was sending this to his home address, rather than internally, since many tutors were currently away from college marking exam papers and it was vital they receive her letter, and understand the situation, as soon as possible. Might she take this opportunity to wish him a pleasant and fruitful summer vacation?

Nat shoved the letter back in the in-tray. 'It goes without saying': why say it then? 'Long-standing': Getting Started had been running since 1981, but seventeen years wasn't especially long-standing in academe (one Oxford tutor he knew of had given the same lecture course for half a century). 'Popular assent': enrolment figures for Getting Started had never been high, but the number of students who came back each year, to start afresh, was surely proof of its popularity. 'Access-prioritised': for God's sake. If Getting Started got the chop, through petty-bureaucratic dumbing-down, where else could imaginative, aspirant writers in south London hope to be nurtured? He thought of Claire, his longest-standing student: the class was the highlight of her week, otherwise confined to tedious lab work. For himself, it didn't matter. He would still have his other teaching, the daytime courses on Shakespeare and Chekhov. And even if they went, it might be no bad thing – he had always dreamed of throwing off the shackles of paid employment in order to write full-time. But he had his students to think of – and, beneath the prospect of being liberated, his injured pride.

He clicked his email: it had been an hour since he last checked, and even spam was preferable to marking exam papers. Libby thought him a novice in cyberspace; if only she knew. Emails had changed his life. Or falling in love had. Hard to tell which came first. The technology was part of the romance: tapping in his password (like punching numbers on an entryphone), hearing the be-de-de-de-be-beep-deep and hiss as he got through, seeing the YOU'VE GOT EMAIL welcome mat, then finding the longed-for username inside. The instantaneity was so erotic. No need to talk sexy; the medium was sexy in itself. As a child he loved the sound of letters falling through the letter box. And now this neo-Victorian postal system brought him umpteen deliveries a day. Most of the mail might be junk mail (how to lose weight by sleeping, how to get rich sitting at home, how to enlarge your penis through positive thinking), but a sentence or two from Anthea was worth the wait.

This time he drew a blank. He would be seeing her in a few hours. It was hard not to feel disappointed, all the same. He called up her last email, sent last night, which she had asked him to delete, along with all her others. For Anthea's sake, if not for his, he had been diligent about deleting, but not before copying her emails into a separate file, called ANT. Every word she wrote was precious, even when, like last night, what she conveyed was doubt and unhappiness ('not sure how much longer . . . pain of bottling it inside me . . . feel I'm being short-changed'). He tried to reassure her by emailing several times a day – so he was with her even when not. There was so much to say, and he wanted to say it as best he could. The right words in the right order. If only the same energy could be directed towards his plays. But there was no time. And he lacked the motivation. Theatre was dead – whereas emails were life and art rolled into one, the soul in spate, the heart at high tide, the mind streaming to articulate itself. He was in love.

It was astonishing. Nat Raven didn't have affairs. Least of all did he have affairs with students. There had been a couple of lapses in his first year of teaching, before he met Libby, when he was more or less a student himself: that American divorcee after a drunken end-of-term party, and the single mother in the New Cross tower block who wrote that note on the bottom of an essay ('Come round any night after nine,' it said, and he had, more than once, until a large man with a ponytail answered the door and he had to pretend to be looking for a lost cat). Once married, he became a home-body, cosseted and neutered. It was uncool. He would have preferred to be a libertine, like Byron or Rochester. 'Monogamy,' he told his students, 'is the last refuge of the fearful.' But libertinism required a purposefulness he lacked. And a neurosis about betraying his muse kept him faithful. Work was his wife and mistress: 'To be tied to apron strings is the writer's dread; to be tied to a bedstead his fantasy and ruin; to be tied to a desk his true vocation.' Pursuing women meant leaving home. Home was where the work got done. Ergo no pursuing women.

Going to bed with Anthea had changed all that. They had been taken by surprise. She came to his house and he put his arm round her and the heat of their bodies did the rest. The strangest morning of his life. He was in shock. They both were. She left and walked the streets. What had he done? And what would the punishment be? When the doorbell rang, he half expected an avenging angel with a sword. But it was Anthea come back again, a web of drizzle in her hair. He sat her in the kitchen, next to the Rayburn, her heavy coat still on, and made her tea. She cupped her hands round the mug and held it under her chin, to get the warmth. She felt so confused, she said. He stroked her hair, wiping the drizzle away. Why confused? He was happily married, she said, she should never have done what she did. He didn't know about happily, he said, but any fault was also his. What's going to happen next? she asked. What did she want to happen? he replied. We should go back to being friends, she said. They would always be friends, he said, but now their relationship had deepened into something else. Into what? she asked. Into love. That's what he felt for her, love? Yes. He didn't think her a slut? Christ no, she was adorable. He didn't make a habit of it, then? A habit of what? A habit of fucking his students. Of course not, and she wasn't his student, and he would prefer to call it making love. So when he said he loved her, he wasn't just saying that? No. All this in the kitchen, as she held the mug with Hemingway's face on it. She stood up to be hugged. He was up against the Rayburn, and could feel warmth seeping through him front and back. They moved to the living room. She let him take her coat and hang it up next door (a relief, because the rain had made it damp and the smell was faintly unpleasant). Then she sat him on the sofa, undid his zip, and pushed him back. When he'd said that about love, he was saying it to reassure her. But I do love her, he came to realise, as he came.

Outside, beyond the glass, clouds rushed in, like latecomers to a play. The stage was theirs. Had there ever been theatre of such quality? In all the history of those streets? To his mind, never. It was as if all the houses had been built, all the gardens laid, every brick pointed, as a backdrop for that moment.

His emails tried to explain it – to explain how she had given him his life back. 'That first time at my house, and then again last week when you . . .' When she what? Finding a language for such acts embarrassed him. Sex should happen offstage, he always told his students, like war in Greek tragedy. Knowing looks across a room were more erotic than writhing bodies in bed. Now he wondered. Had he shied away from writing about sex through lack of inspiration – because sex with Libby had been bad? Bad wasn't the word.

But it had been unenterprising, domesticated, routine. Marital sex was like living in London – after a time you took it for granted. He had been bored, that was all. Bored round the house and bored in bed. It wasn't her fault. After a decade together, love had been subsumed by children, gas bills, mortgage repayments and empty bottles left out for the milkman. With Anthea it was purer – no shared possessions, just two bodies in a room. And the purity intensified the physical sensations. 'When I'm inside you, I feel . . .' What? What did he feel? Bliss is an anaesthetist. He would come round, after orgasm, with no memory. It was the particulars he wanted to record but he could record them only by detaching himself, and if he detached himself there wasn't the same intensity. What could he write that wouldn't diminish or brutalise those sweet intimacies? Her nipples were . . . um, ripe figs, oily nubs, turreted hill forts, perching black butterflies. No words could do justice. Yet the urge was to write it down.

'We should be as open as we dare . . .' He had no instinct for deception. Till now there had been nothing to hide. The little that happened to him he shared with Libby at the end of each day. It was non-news or bad news mostly – work-in-regress, jealousy and dejection, student obtuseness. Now he burned with news he couldn't tell. His mind was sharp. His body felt restored. He loved his life. These were things Libby might have rejoiced in, had the source of his happiness been her. He was tempted to tell her anyway. Several times he was on the verge. If he explained he had no plans to leave her, that this other relationship needn't threaten theirs, would she begrudge it? If she were the one feeling happy and renewed, would *he*? But perhaps women were less understanding, more possessive. Anthea thought so. Last week, in bed, as evening sun came through the blinds, tigering her flesh, she had pleaded with him to say nothing. If your wife knew you were here, she said, it would destroy her. Nonsense, he said, how can the happiness of someone you love destroy you? But this is *our* happiness, she said, stroking the back of her hand down his cheek, it isn't for sharing. Perhaps she was right. Duplicity, he used to think, was wrong. Now he felt in two minds about it. He had acquired an exciting second life – why give it up for the sake of moral scruple? He agreed to say nothing. The fiction of the Tuesday masterclass would continue. And he would destroy the emails. This wasn't for sharing.

He felt guilty at how unguilty he felt. When they made love, he had a sense of entitlement. Anthea was what he deserved. Surely nothing that felt so good could turn out badly. At home, instead of withdrawing, he became more engaged – a better husband, a better father, eager to prove himself. Most nights he bathed the girls, read them stories, tidied the toys away, made Libby supper. She could see he had been energised. So it's going well, she said. Yes, he said. Enjoying the students for a change? Yes. And the play's coming along? Kind of, he said, and cleared the table and made her herb tea. It wasn't guilt. It was euphoria.

He only wished Anthea felt as good about it as he did. Sometimes when they made love, she seemed to disappear. Was this was what love did, in removing you from the quotidian – remove you even from your lover? Or was she so frustrated with the limits of their relationship that she had to block out the reality? He knew she couldn't be taken for granted. She was young and would wait only so long. Not that she was pushing him to leave Libby. Or complained at their lack of time together. It was too early and she was too considerate. But the time would come for him to choose.

'Let's follow where love leads,' he tapped out. '*Carpe diem*. One day we're a blob of semen; the next embalming fluid. We should love each other while we can.' It was a portentous patchwork of stolen quotes, but he hit the Send key all the same, then copied it into his ANT file. It was important to keep his own words as well as hers. They formed a dialogue. In time they might make a play. He had already begun to edit them – to make the dialogue less stilted and to suppress sentiments (mostly Anthea's) that didn't accord with his sense of truth or aesthetic propriety. There was nothing wrong with this. The motive was to celebrate their relationship, not exploit it. One day he would tell her and present her with the finished text – the play of their own life.

He felt raised, like Lazarus – born-again. As though the spirit of a new nation was blowing through him. That Jiffy bag from Anthea had arrived the day after the election. New Labour, new Britain, new Nat.

Why did he love her? Because her eyes shone. Because of the blue dolphin on her left buttock. And how she never sat but perched, cross-legged and precarious, on a chair arm or sofa back. Her strange, unearthly cry when she came. The musky scent on her clothes and skin. Her hair – blonde on top, tawny below. How she listened to him intently, as Libby hadn't for years and Hannah and Rose had stopped doing since starting school. The jewel in her navel, the stud in her nose. The little dent or inverted beauty spot in her forehead, perhaps a chickenpox scar. Her misspellings – seperate, dedecate, dissapear. Her love of oranges – she sometimes ate the peel. The breathiness of her voice. That habit she had of putting his hand in her pocket when they were outdoors. (It had been a dread of his, a writer's dread, or a chafing husband's, *to live in someone's pocket*. But he was happy in hers.) Her walk: whereas Libby had a busy, trip-trotting, tip-tupping-on-her-heels walk, straight from A to B, Anthea glided and loped, and snuffed the air, and listened, and let her eyes graze, and wouldn't be rushed lest she miss some morsel of pleasure – a basket of geraniums hanging from a terrace balcony, a black cat, a neon sign with vital letters missing. Why did he love her? Because of her appetite for life. Because at forty, with life closing down, she had given him a second chance.

She was mysterious: that too. His daughters loved Kinder eggs – hollow chocolate eggs with a plastic puzzle inside. The eggs had two matching halves, and he thought of Anthea as his perfect fit, his exact match, his anagram – the Ant to his Nat. She was a puzzle as well, and he liked the intrigue. Libby had always been so present, so lively, so *there*. There was nothing about her he didn't know. That was the trouble with marriage: you began as separate beings but became a double-headed monster, socialising with similar monsters. With Anthea, there was something discreet and withdrawn. She was his double, the lost half he had been searching for all his life. But also impenetrable. Sometimes it felt as though he had hatched her from his own mind. When he lay on her breast, his ear cupped to her shell, was it the beat of his own pulse he heard? Or the roar of her ocean?

These were strange thoughts to have. He would like to talk to someone. But who? Not Libby, obviously. And no colleague at work could be trusted. It would have to be Harry, then. Harry lacked the depth, and Harry lacked the experience. Still, for practical reasons, if no other, Harry must know. Twice already, he had used Harry as an alibi. Which was a rash thing to do without telling him. Perhaps the three of them could go out together. Once he saw Anthea, Harry would get the point. Any man would. She was wonderful. Yes, Harry might feel envy, or discomfort at the change, or upset on behalf of Libby, but he was a friend, and we all want the best for our friends.

The phone rang, its tone muted by the exam papers which were burying it, but sharp enough to dislodge him from his reverie. It was Libby. It usually was Libby these days. Since starting her company and working long hours, she liked to phone through instructions – make the girls this, buy the girls that, get them to practise their instruments, etc., etc. No wonder he had fallen in love elsewhere. Libby was bossy and manipulative – a control freak, though the phrase had lost its usefulness now that everyone else was a control freak, too (the freaks were people like him, who went with the flow). She seemed to think his only role in life was to be at her beck and call.

Now she was asking him to take over from Millie so that she, Libby, could work late.

'But it's my masterclass,' he said.

'Not again.'

'It's every week at present.'

'The odd informal session with a handful of students, you said.'

He had thought it unwise to tell her the masterclass was for one student, beautiful and female.

'It's a bit late to cancel now.'

'Put it back an hour. Tell them you'll be late.'

'I arranged to watch the football round at Harry's afterwards.'

'Come on – you're not even interested in football.'

'This time I am – it's a big match.'

'Bigger than me launching my company?'

'Of course not. But . . .'

There was no but. She was right. He would have to call and cry off. Anthea would understand. Or would she? 'Yes, I understand that you're married and I come second' – that's what her reaction would be. It was her birthday. He couldn't not see her.

'What kind of client wants to meet you tonight?' he said. 'The whole country will be watching the match.'

'I'm not seeing clients. But I've masses of work to do. Writing my speech, for instance.'

'I'll help you with it over the weekend.'

'And I've hundreds of emails to deal with.'

'Deal with them here.'

'With the girls around?'

'I'll make sure they're in bed before I go out.'

'You can't leave them on their own.'

'I'll ask Millie if she can stay late. She doesn't usually mind.'

'It's not fair – she has her own life.'

'She can always say no.'

Hannah and Rose pushed the door open. They must have been listening outside.

'Is that Mummy?'

He passed the phone over, knowing Libby would feel better for talking to them, and sat there playing with the nit comb while they spoke. When Millie came in, wondering where her charges had got to, she too spoke to Libby, and told her it was really no problem staying on – then gave him the phone and took his daughters back downstairs.

He had Libby to himself again. It was safe for him to be generous.

'Look,' he said, 'if you really want me around tonight, just say.'

'You go and watch the football,' she said. 'It sounds as if Harry needs your support.'

'That's true.'

It wasn't, but last week when he came home late he said he'd been discussing Harry's depression – though she mustn't allude to the depression if they met, because Harry would be too ashamed to admit it.

'There's my masterclass before I see Harry,' he said. 'Unless you want me to cancel it.'

'It's all money, I suppose. We might be glad of the extra if my business bombs. In fact, you might have to teach full-time.'

'I'm not sure if I –'

'Joke, Nat.'

'Ah. So all's OK?'

'Yes, I shouldn't be that late. As long as every train, bus and taxi driver isn't watching the match, too.'

She hung up, in the same wry spirit – *You have to laugh* – that had made him love her, once. But the marriage had been dead for years – and he trapped in its coffin. Libby exploited his good nature. When he wasn't babysitting, she expected him to play the artist. He was her bit of culture, to show off to friends. Hey, look, I'm not as shallow as a career in advertising would suggest, my husband is an intellectual, a writer, teacher and thinker – that's what his presence allowed her to say. Natural enough, of course. He *was* cultured, and had been vaguely surprised, reading this morning's paper, not to find himself among the 'senior figures from the world of culture whom Tony Blair met with yesterday'. Wasn't Rufus Huish working on some arts subcommittee? If so, why hadn't he thought to invite Nat? Still, being cultured didn't mean acting like someone's poodle. Last Saturday, for instance, at the dinner arranged for that sleaze merchant Rikky Falcon, he had to perform for the whole table. And how they lapped it up – apart from Libby, who, for once, suffered a serious humour failure. *You have to laugh.* Why hadn't she then? Everyone else got the point of the cutlery joke. She needn't have made such a meal of being offended. Where had the old ironic distance gone, the sense of separation between who she was and what she did? She had become over-involved in her own life.

Of course, our lives are important to us because they're ours, he thought. But one mustn't lose sight of the eternal verities.

He put down the nit comb and tried to concentrate on marking exam papers, though the letter from SORU was a distraction. How ironic that his contract should be threatened, just when his teaching had hit new heights. The other week more than twenty students had come to hear him talk about Shakespeare – a record. Doubtless the letter had been drafted by some dolt in Finance, and the Principal hadn't checked the recipients. Once she realised the error, she would be pleading with him to take on more work. But they ought to be more careful. A man could be offended. A man could take his talent elsewhere.

Another half-hour of exam papers, then five minutes chatting to the girls, and he would be gone. He had bought Anthea's birthday present already, but there were some more items to pick up en route. He checked his wallet: empty. But Libby kept a mug on the kitchen dresser with money for emergency use – and he was sure he had seen a couple of twenties. A bunch of roses, a bottle of Moët, and a packet of Mates. Infidelity was surprisingly expensive. But £40 ought to be enough.

6

*JACK*

FOR YEARS Jack had left the shopping to Nancy. His only purchases, at the post office-cum-general stores in Frixley (pint of milk, local paper, Mars bar), were made from a sense of civic duty. Shopping bored him. He hadn't the time. And it felt unmanly. The food he ate, the chairs he sat in, the ornaments, the colour schemes, even his clothes – all were determined by Nancy. Then two or three years ago, when she first developed back problems, he began going with her to the local Sainsbury's, she with a limp and list, and he, the henpecked husband, trolleying alongside. In time he stopped resenting the imposition. Most of their week was spent apart. Shopping brought them together – if only to argue which cheese to buy or which jar of pesto. Now, shopping alone, he felt bereft. 'What's the worst thing?' This was. Not lack of sex or conversation or blaming himself for what had happened, but having to shop on his own.

These days he shopped midweek, on his way home from work – less risk of running into neighbours then, less likelihood of having to field their solicitude. But today, before he could take evasive action, Elise, Harris's wife, spotted him in Fruit and Vegetables. She was wearing leather boots, bright red lipstick and a green ribbed sweater – a woman who dressed up, even in supermarkets. How nice to see him, she said, and what a lovely day – this morning she had driven to the coast for a walk, then risked a swim, no one around, lovely and bracing, freezing cold in fact but worth the plunge. She was testing the bark of a pineapple as she spoke. Light hair, grey-green eyes, tiny nose and ears – and that busy mouth. The ice mouse, someone had called her. But she wasn't cold, only petite, five foot two at most. How odd for her to be married to Harris, who was over six foot. Did looking up to him give her a crick in the neck? Did she heap her chair with cushions at the supper table? Only lying down with him in bed would she . . . Jack moved off towards the freezer section to stop himself thinking about Elise in bed. Something stirred in him every time he saw her. Strange sensations. Or maybe not so strange – it was Elise who had answered the phone that terrible night.

Her trolley followed his basket. She had done the small talk and was on to the big. How was he coping? 'I'm fine,' he told her, and reached for a bag of garden peas. The freezer breath made his eyes water. People said it was good to talk but you couldn't get personal in Sainsbury's. She must have seen his reluctance but stood looking into his eyes, then rested her hand – her tiny right hand – on his. 'Ooh, cold hands,' she said. Warm heart, he thought, but mine isn't any more, which is why she's trying to spark it back to life. It was only for a second but he felt the charge. 'I know how lonely it can get,' she smiled. 'If ever you need company, Jack . . .'

She wheeled her trolley towards the checkout. The green ribbed sweater was long, but not so long as to cover her bottom. He tried putting a name to the smile she had given him: tender? pitying? dutiful? 'If ever you need company': a chat on the phone, a walk with the dogs, supper with her and Harris – that was all she meant. She had no reason to be nice to him, other than having been so close to Nancy. 'I know how lonely it can get.' Perhaps she did. When Harris wasn't out playing golf, he was screwing one of his minions at the bank. Rumour had it that she knew and had gone to see the latest one, Sheila, while Harris was up in Leeds at a seminar on staff-management relations (hah!), and that, having explained she wasn't there to exact revenge, she laid down her conditions for the pursuance of the affair, namely that Sheila a) behave discreetly, b) put Harris under no pressure to leave home, and c) make him use a condom, since, despite what he might have told her, she, Elise, still enjoyed an active sex life with her husband and had no wish to pick up some nasty infection, as she had during one of his other flings, with a previous teller (Oh, did Sheila not realise she was the latest in a long line?). Jack had heard the story third-hand. Apocryphal or not, it was one which showed Elise in a new light, no longer the duped provincial housewife about whom people use words like 'mousy' but a spirited and independent exotic who would certainly have been worth trying to get into bed if she didn't stir something strange in you and if you weren't, as Jack had been, more or less loyal to your wife. Did Elise take lovers? A woman like her could have her pick. Harris was a fool. Those grey-green eyes, the touch of her hand.

He checked his list: yogurt, bananas, granary loaf, kidney beans, bacon. However few the items, he needed a list to jog his memory – at his age, holding more than three things in your head at once was almost impossible. He noticed it at the pub, getting a round in; at work, too, when the name of someone he'd employed for years momentarily escaped him. He ought to go down the pharmacy aisle and find those vitamins Nancy used to swear by. Gingko something. Supposed to keep the brain in tip-top shape. Fat lot of good they did hers, but still. Gingko malabar, gingko vellova, some such name: if he were taking them, he would remember. Kippers, lettuce, tomatoes, asparagus, ice cream: all had been crossed off but for the ice cream. He preferred a choc ice himself, not those plastic tubs that went crispy and hard. Apart from the odd steak, only soft foodstuff came into the house now. Nothing to trouble a narrow gullet. Nothing on which you could choke.

A line of girls sat making music on their checkout tills – blonde, bosomy, seductive as Rhine maidens. As the shopping flowed by they fished for bar codes. Bloop. Each item had a different note. Bleep. How was a man to steer himself through? Jack chose the least attractive face, the shortest queue. Nina, it said, on her lapel, which tilted upwards because of the ample breast it rested on; the rest of her, below the waist, was hidden, like a mermaid. She scanned his carrots, innocent of his appraising stare. Blup. Oh, to rest on a bosom like that. Someone's dog was howling from the car park. Down, boy. Three aisles along from him, Elise signed her receipt and moved off through the doors, her jumper still not covering her bottom. The juddering belt carried his sirloin into Nina's hand. Bleep. He clocked her breasts again, under the uniform. She was young, no more than a schoolgirl. Didn't Hook have a granddaughter called Nina? She took his card. 'Cashback?' 'No thanks.' Fancy lusting after the granddaughters of your peers. Men had been arrested for less. He stuffed two bags full, averting his eyes. 'Have a nice day,' she said, handing him the receipt.

At his car he saw Elise again. 'Look after yourself,' she shouted through her rolled-down window. 'Go carefully.'

'You too,' he said, slamming his boot.

*Go carefully.* A thing his daughters said, too. Commonplace pleasantry, but in their case perhaps intended as a warning. If he were planning to do something, the car would be an obvious place. Not in the garage, immobilised, with a tube from the exhaust pipe, but like this, pulling out of Sainsbury's in front of a ten-ton truck, or at speed, on the road back to Frixley, overtaking on double white lines. He enjoyed the odd risk. Last Sunday night, he'd driven the three miles home from the Bull without lights. Why not? He knew every curve, a moon shone down to guide him, you never met cars at that late hour, even if you did their headlights would be visible half a mile off (unless of course they were doing the same as you). OK, it wasn't going carefully but he felt better for it – as he did now, accelerating to ninety (and leaving a Lotus in his wake) on the dual carriageway. Adolescent? Maybe. Thrill-seeking? Certainly. Suicidal? No.

*Look after yourself.* That was another one. Till recently, he had thought that's what women did – look after the children, the house and you. Nancy, no feminist, had been good at all that. He was having to learn fast. Look after myself? Don't you worry, he'd say next time, I am doing.

He was depressed, though, he couldn't deny it. Who wouldn't be? As the vicar said, he had suffered a 'grievous blow'. The worst was thinking he might have averted it. For weeks before, Nancy had been under the weather. And the morning it happened she had mentioned shooting pains in her arm. Why hadn't he made her see the GP? The standard tests – pulse, blood pressure, cholesterol – would have rung warning bells, and she'd have been told to take it easy: more gentle exercise, less strenuous gardening, a course of warfarin. The friends who were with her that day said she looked tired. If only he'd come home for lunch or cut his walk short. According to the specialist, it would have made no difference: the stroke was massive; he couldn't have helped. But doctors were paid to be consoling. 'You mustn't blame yourself,' friends said. Who else could he blame? It wasn't just the thought of her lying there undiscovered for hours, but what had brought it on – her climbing on a chair, to change a light bulb, a job she'd been asking him to do for weeks. Did the act of stretching upwards cause the clot? The dizziness? Had the blow as she fell contributed? Elise was the one who found her: she was driving past, on the way to collect Harris from the golf club, when she realised she had left her tennis racket behind at lunch. No reply when she rang the bell. She was going to drive off but some instinct made her walk round, and when she reached the French windows, still wide open from lunch, there was Nancy lying on the parquet, an upended chair beside her and light-bulb shards all round. Pure chance, everyone said; they didn't use the word luck. Luck might have been for her to lie there till Jack came home.

Thirteen months and three weeks too late, he turned into the drive, noting the lawn needed a mow and the beech-pruning wouldn't wait till autumn. In front of the house, the drive fanned out round a circle of rose bushes. His usual parking space was to the right, in front of the garage, but the red Fiat was there, so he parked, slightly disgruntled, on the left. The red Fiat was the Irish girl's car. Aileen. Nice manner. She gave the impression of enjoying her work. A sense of vocation was hard to find these days. Aileen came with Shirley, who was older and less chatty. They alternated with other pairs, usually Jill and Betty, though you never quite knew – the agency would make no guarantees about 'specific personnel', only that all employees were 'trained and qualified'. £6.50 an hour they were paid (he knew, Aileen had told him), though the cost to him was £11.50, which meant the agency took 40 per cent. Most of the day only one of them was here. But during 'labour-intensive periods', namely breakfast and bedtime, they worked in pairs – not to make it more sociable for the client but because agency policy said one person couldn't do the lifting. He found that hard to believe. *He'd* done it on his own. But you couldn't argue. Nor begrudge the expense. Fate had chosen this. You were – hah – paralysed.

As he turned the key, he brushed against the honeysuckle framing the door. Its whiff followed him in – the sweetness of the sickroom.

'It's only me,' he called.

'Hello, Mr Raven.'

That was Shirley, from the living room. Aileen would have called him Jack – she'd be upstairs, running the bath. A houseful of women: it was like this when the girls were growing up yet utterly different – then Nancy had been around, *really* around. 'You mustn't blame yourself,' people kept saying. Oh yeh? Who else to blame?

Finding Nancy on the parquet, Elise had done all the right things – dialled 999, loosened her clothing, wrapped her in a blanket, swept up the broken light-bulb shards. The GP, Dr Bruin, was there even before the ambulance. They had her in intensive care thirty minutes later. Learning the news from Elise, Jack drove straight to the hospital from the pub. He prayed to God, *Do not let her die* – literally prayed, for the first time in fifty years – saying the same five words over and over through the dark lanes. His prayers were answered. And yet . . .

'And how's himself today?' Aileen asked, from the stairs. Dark eyes, pink

cheeks, warm country smile: a mystery she wasn't married, though she did
have a boyfriend – had had for six years. 'Now if *I* was your boyfriend,' he
sometimes teased her when he came home for lunch. 'Oh, you're a one.'
How he'd love to stroke that hair of hers. What if he did, right there, in
the kitchen, as she carried out her spoonfeeding? Would Nancy see? If she
saw would she understand? There were times he felt so angry, he didn't
care.

'She's had her tea,' Aileen said. 'We're going to give her a little bath
now.'

At the hospital he had clung to her, like a drowning man. The doctor
put the odds at one in three: another stroke, even a small one, would finish
her off; as it was, with her system traumatised, she might not pull through.
Holding her hand seemed the only chance – a link to the world they shared,
when all the rest was strangeness and machines. He stroked her palm and
spanned the sapling of her wrist. He hummed the few classical tunes he
could remember – if music could nurture tomato plants, why not humans?
There were scratches on her face, where she had rubbed against the light-
bulb shards on the parquet – though comatose, she hadn't been still. A cerebral vascular accident, the specialist, Dr Hunter, said. A transient ischaemic
attack resulting in occlusion of the left carotid artery, ostensible destruction
in the vascular territory of the left hemisphere, and major damage to the
corpus callosum. In plain English, half her brain was shot to pieces and
she was paralysed down one side. Jack stood with Hunter examining the
CT and MRI scans. They meant nothing to him and (said Hunter) proved
little about Nancy's prospects – two patients with similiar-looking strokes
might have totally different outcomes. 'So what are you saying exactly?' Jack
asked. Hunter looked away, then enquired what line of work Jack was in.
Lawnmowers, he told him. Well then, Hunter said, he should think of brain
tissue as a patch of lawn scorched by a summer heatwave. In time some of
grass would grow back, but no one could say how much – science hadn't
yet found a way to reseed nerve cells. 'So . . . ?' So nothing. 'With infarcts,
one simply can't tell.'

Nancy's no longer my wife, he thought, she's an infarct.

After a week they moved her from intensive care. There were reflex-
ology tests, and games of matching words and objects, and a few encouraging signs. Later she was transferred to the Harchope Rest and
Recuperation Centre, aka the local nursing home, and Jack went back to
work, mornings only, returning to sit with her afternoon and evening. The
sense of reprieve was immense, until, after three months, Hunter's team

gave their considered prognosis. Would she be able to walk unaided? Possibly not. Feed herself? Hard to say. Speak? A few simple words maybe. Sit upright in a chair? Eventually, yes – for limited periods. They were putting the worst case, he told himself; knowing Nancy, she'd be herself again in no time. But it took two more months of physio before she came home. And still she wasn't Nancy.

He followed Aileen into the living room.

'Hello, love,' he said, kissing the top of the head, then each cheek. 'Had a good day?'

No answer. She sat in her armchair, wobbly as a new baby, eyes lofting into space. The nurses said the same as the doctors: keep touching her, keep talking, it will come. Would it? Sometimes she made a racking noise in the back of her throat that could pass for 'Jack'. Sometimes her eyes seemed to be following him. Even now, as he knelt by the chair and squeezed her hand, he could almost persuade himself she was returning the pressure. But of the Nancy she used to be there was no sign. He stood up and stepped clear, to let the nurses move in. They took an arm each, and hauled her upright, tightening her hands on the frame. Shirley walked backwards at the front, easing the Zimmer over the carpet; Aileen, behind, held the harness, to stop her falling. Shush, shush, the carpet went, under her feet. At the bottom of the stairs, the electric chair, the Stannah, sat waiting, and they backed and hoisted her in, no easy job given what a year of drugs and inertia had done to her weight. Aileen climbed ahead, ready to unload her at the top. Shirley pressed the red button to dispatch her upwards, then walked behind. The Stannah's mechanism reminded him of a chainsaw: the higher the chair climbed, the more it whined. Chairlifts at ski resorts worked the same way. That week in Innsbruck, their first and last skiing holiday, when the girls were small. Nancy hated it, saying the boots hurt her ankles, though she had taken the chairlift happily enough. What sensation did she have, in the Stannah? He used it himself, back in February, after hurting his knee while out hunting – just for a week, till it healed. Odd sensation, riding upward on cogs and chains. Whenever the vicar spoke of Christ 'ascending to heaven', it came to mind. £5,000: hell of an outlay. Most improvements to a house added to its value. Not this one, unless the buyer was a cripple. They had begun to talk of selling, before last May. At a stroke – hah – those plans had gone. But if it helped to move into town, closer to the hospital, then he would.

He sat on the patio with a gin and tonic. Mild sun, haze, midges dancing like champagne bubbles: glorious. Or would be glorious, if he could share it with someone. Getting Nancy to bed took the nurses forty minutes, after which it was up to him. For the first few weeks, he tried sleeping next to her, in their old room, his right hand resting on her right breast as it had each night for thirty-five years. It didn't work. Dr Hunter had warned him stroke victims could be noisy and restless. But it wasn't lack of sleep which moved him to the spare bedroom, but the sensation of lying next to a corpse. Incontinence pads were easy; it was the vacancy he couldn't endure. His wife still lived with him, but where was his wife? Fading sunlight, gin and tonic, honeysuckle, the sound of a tractor in a nearby field. Around now, she'd be out her with her scissors, in the herb garden, snipping mint or rosemary. Around now, as was.

During the winter, he had thrown himself back into hunting. 'Because Mrs Raven's like this doesn't mean you can't have fun,' Aileen said. It wasn't fun he wanted but forgetfulness. A good gallop took you out of yourself. The vicar, calling on spec, had suggested bereavement counselling: 'I know she's still alive, Jack, but the emotional impact is similar.' Meddling bastard. Dom Askew agreed: 'Damn vicars – they should stick to God.' For a week or two Jack had gone to church, finding solace in its whitewashed hush. But the hush was only proof of God's indifference. Hunting was better therapy. Once a week, sometimes twice, and lasting hours, not the fifty minutes you spent at evensong or on a psychiatrist's couch. He should find a summer hobby, too, though hobby wasn't the word – hunting was a passion, not a pastime. Townie Labour MPs didn't understand that. This Foster chap was trying to outlaw the practice. Over Jack's dead body. If hunting went, so would England. 'To be born English is like winning first prize in the lottery of life.' Who said that? Cecil Rhodes, was it? You couldn't say it now. Same with fox-hunting: you were meant to feel bad for doing it. Jack only felt bad when not doing it. He still attended most meets of the Harchope & Nelles, but Otto Leddel, as joint MFH, had taken over all the fund-raising and admin. Nice chap: was said to be Austrian but he spoke with a Manchester accent and his restoration of Stormbrooke Hall (Stonybroke Hell, as the locals used to call it, after a succession of previous owners went bankrupt) was done with impeccable taste. As a favour to Jack, Otto was also stabling Maiden, his nine-year-old mare, more cheaply than they charged for livery at Easthorpe. Some mornings, on his way to work, Jack dropped in to feed her a carrot or two. The stablegirl, Lolly, whose bosom jiggled under her check shirt, was a bit of a carrot herself.

Six twenty – time for another before the nurses went. He topped himself up, then ambled down to the silence of the greenhouse. No Classic FM, no whining Labrador. Sammy. Another casualty of the past year. If he hadn't been so immersed in Nancy, might he have noticed the tumour on Sammy's neck? As the vet said, putting on his plastic glove, eleven was a good age. Sammy lay there without a whimper as the needle went in. Good boy: the doleful eyes, the quiver through the moulting coat, then peace. Damn nuisance while alive. But to hear his bark would be a comfort now. An evening tear ran down the glass. It was hot and musky, under the panes. The twelve tomato plants Dom Askew had brought round the other week were already wilting. Jack filled the watering can from the tap, and tipped its rose, till the compost in the pots slurped and darkened. Further away, brown stalks poked from terracotta troughs. Apart from a couple of geraniums, everything of Nancy's had died. She would be furious but what could he do? He hadn't the foggiest what she was growing. From time to time he watered her musty seed trays, in hope of a miracle. Useless. Unrevivable. Same as her.

'We're on our way now, Mr Raven,' Shirley hallooed from the kitchen door. 'Just coming,' he shouted back. Disrespectful not to show them out. And a chance to catch a word about Nancy. He overtook them in the hallway and lifted the latch.

'How's she been today?' he said.

'Fine,' Aileen said. 'Same as usual.'

'She's nice and comfy now,' Shirley said.

Nice and comfy would be for Nancy to be dead, but no one was allowed to say that.

He stood in the doorway as Aileen's Fiat scrunched across the gravel and down the drive. That sweet-sick smell again. Over his head, the honeysuckle clambered to Nancy's window. Six feet above him, when she should be six feet under. He imagined picking up a pebble and tossing it against the panes, as he had that summer in 1961, the year before they married. More pebbles, a handful, till the window opened, and her head and shoulders appeared, framed like a portrait. Nancy restored: bare arms, a lacy nightdress, and him below serenading her. What was it he'd sung? Something corny from that year. 'O solo mio', maybe, or 'Magic Moments (Filled with Love)'? He'd meant it as a parody, mock-heroic, but it worked. Was it that night or a different one they'd slipped down the garden, her parents' garden, and made love in the toolshed? The old man kept her under lock and key (only child and all that), but she outwitted him. Easy to forget how bold she'd been. A miracle she didn't get pregnant before the wedding. Her litheness in that bridal dress. Swimming in Bermuda on their honeymoon. Dancing the twist. Two births within fifteen months taken in her stride. Always so fit. What had gone wrong? Nothing had gone wrong. Life took its course, that was all. He stood on his front step, the sun fading behind the elms, ready to toss the pebble and begin again.

# 7

## *HARRY*

THE FIVE men were leaving court, in single file, stepping out into the flash-bulb brightness, hurried but trying not to run. They began high above the crowd but the ramp took them steeply down and soon they were level, within spitting distance. A van stood waiting, twenty yards away. You could see they wouldn't reach it unscathed. An arm flew out from the ranks. Then plastic bottles, oranges, eggs, flour, glass. The five pressed on, trying to shield themselves from flying debris. The crowd surged against the barriers, shouting *scum, scum, scum, scum*. A man in grey fought free and leapt over, throwing punches. At the foot of the ramp the police had formed a cordon, but the mob was pushing in, narrowing the channel, and some of the officers, weak or complicit, let them. A fist came through the ruck, a boot, a hand grabbing at hair. Someone's nose was bleeding, someone else fell to the ground. For a moment, it seemed the five would stay to fight their ground, to kill or be killed, but then a space cleared, they were up through the doors and into the van, and the van sped off, and the screen cut to the newsreader back in the studio.

Harry stood watching, beneath the high screen. Mills stood next to him, no less entranced. I should have been there, Harry kept thinking, but there was no point saying it to Mills. By the time *Gazette* comes out the story will be dead, he'd say. Or: I assume your property piece is ready – you've no business to be watching television if not.

Behind them, in Deborah's office, Suzie was still talking to Joy and Charity. He felt guilty at letting them down, but their pleas had only made him more implacable: those eyes, that passivity, the will-you-helps.

A lawyer explained to the anchorman why the five suspects had never been brought to court – why the inquiry at the Elephant was not the murder trial which the Lawrence family had been pushing for. Lack of hard evidence was the reason: no knife had been found, no DNA or bloodstains, no witness to put the suspects at the scene. But the police had bugged the house where one of them lived, and tape recordings of their conversations had been leaked to the press and quoted back at them during the inquiry: *I reckon every nigger should be chopped up, mate, and left with nothing but stumps . . . I would go down to Catford, places like that, with two sub-machine guns and skin some black cunt alive, torture him and set him alight . . . I'd blow his two legs and arms off and say, 'Go on, you can swim home now.'* Vile stuff. Harry wished he'd been there to watch the five men try to disclaim it. I should have forced Mills to let me go, he thought, just as I should have asked to cover the story five years ago, when I was working as a sub, but I lack the gumption, I do what I'm asked to do rather than initiating, good old Harry, colourless but dependable. If the business with Terry Lavell last year hadn't undermined me, I would be calling the shots by now.

'Watching the match tonight?' Mills said, friendly for once.

'You bet,' Harry said.

'Play yourself?'

'Not any more.'

At school he had been good at football, but came to resent the assumption that naturally he would be. Black footballers are legion. Black journalists you can count on one hand.

'Should be a good game,' he said, heading back to his desk. Another reason for not succumbing to Joy and Charity: he wanted to be gone by seven and had a piece to finish first.

'According to Stan Leigh, assistant manager of Matthews & Co, property prices look set to . . .'

Though the Terry Lavell piece hadn't stopped him passing his probation, it was an unprofessional piece, no question. He had written it in a rage – against Terry, against Mills, against Nat, against New Labour, against a lonely, wasted weekend spent failing to get the tone right. He could remember the headline he wrote, studded with disbelieving quote marks: 'FOX' 'ATTACK' ON 'BABY', CLAIMS 'FATHER'. Though the subs rewrote it, the mocking scepticism remained. 'Nice piece,' Mills said. Within two hours of the *Gazette* coming out, Terry called. He was shocked, bitter, outraged: Harry hadn't checked the facts, Harry had made him look like a liar, he would go to the ombudsman, the High Court, the House of Lords, whatever it took to clear his name, and if the authorities didn't help him he would settle with Harry in his own way. 'Are you threatening me, Mr Lavell?' 'Not threatening, just letting you know.' There were several more calls over the next few days, each an octave more hysterical than the previous. And when Harry stopped answering the phone,

Terry took to phoning Deborah, to demand apologies, retractions, that Harry be disciplined, that Harry be sacked. 'Sorry for getting you into this,' she told Harry, 'I should have seen the guy was a basketcase.' To her credit, she held firm and finally instructed the paper's lawyer to write to Terry – any more harassment of *Gazette* employees and the police would be called. After that Terry fell silent, though whenever Harry left the office late at night he imagined him waiting in the shadows – with a knife, a gun, a Ku Klux noose.

Life would have been easier for him had he believed, as Deborah did, that Terry was just a nutter. But he regretted the piece even before it appeared. Two phone calls knocked him back. First the doctor from Guy's: sorry to be slow returning Harry's, he had been off duty for two days, but yes he remembered the child with wounds to its face, odd sort of injury, odd sort of claim by the father, too, but certainly the line of the scratches suggested the claw of an animal, a dog probably, which would be consistent with similar injuries he had seen in A & E, though an urban fox couldn't be ruled out. At this point the piece was with the subs, but there would have been time to call it back and tone it down – why didn't he act? Next day a geneticist rang, Professor Dove. A friend of his at London Zoo had mentioned Harry's phone call the previous week. It might sound outlandish, he said, but giant foxes – which he gathered Harry had been making enquiries about – weren't mere science fiction. Three hundred and fifty thousand genetically modified or 'transgenic' animals were used in British laboratories every year. Some of these were refined (often larger) versions of existing species. More radically, some were amalgams of different species, combining (say) a dog and a coyote, or a wolf and a fox. So within the confines of a lab, giant carnivores certainly existed, and for experimental purposes some of them were doubtless injected with drugs to exacerbate their aggression. Of course, the labs were rigidly controlled, with little chance of animals escaping or being smuggled out. Still, Professor Dove said, such creatures were no mere figment of the imagination.

By then the paper had been put to bed. There would have been no reason to change the story even if it hadn't been put to bed. And yet.

Perhaps if Terry had waged a less vitriolic campaign, Harry would have forgotten the whole thing. But the idea that the story might be true now obsessed him. It wasn't that he was fanatically high-minded: in journalism, betrayal is a professional necessity – every time you write a piece, someone feels aggrieved. The obsession was the animal – the idea of a creature at large, furtive, malign, half glimpsed but never detected; a creature out of the night, or swamps, or concrete sewers; not even a creature

– a supernatural force, a resurgence of the primitive at the heart of modern London. It wasn't a notion he could share with anyone. Even calling it a notion was going too far – it was a hunch, a sensation of evil, a shiver down the spine. But he couldn't dislodge the image it provoked – of an unknown creature running free and preying on children.

He became an addict of 'Wild at Heart' documentaries; of amateur footage showing people being attacked by crocodiles, tigers, bulls, rhinos, hippos; of the yeti, the Beast of Bodmin, the Loch Ness Monster. More practically, he gathered evidence from cuttings and websites – evidence against himself, as it were, and the injustice he had done to Terry. There had been another alleged fox attack on a child, in Croydon, less than ten miles away, in 1996. The year before that the body of a tramp was found, near Waterloo Bridge, with the presence of fox faeces and urine nearby – the man was said to have died after choking on his own vomit but his face and body had also been 'posthumously mauled by an unknown animal'. And only last year a nine-year-old boy, playing with two friends next to a warehouse fence in Wapping, was nearly scalped through the wire by an Alsatian-like dog – the oddity being that the owners of the warehouse, EuroKay Software, denied keeping guard dogs. Killer foxes? It sounded bonkers. But sometimes you could be too sceptical. There were stories of children going missing in south London. Not all of them made the news but he picked up rumours. Sometimes, late at night, returning to his flat, he sensed strange movements behind him, the pad of retracted claws, fur brushing against a lamp post, or strange predatory cries from the waste lots.

Was he losing it? He had no friends at work to confide in. Deborah, Suzie, Mills – none was close enough for him to share his fears with. He had always been private – a man with a secret – and now his privacy deepened. Most Wednesdays, after work, the other journalists drank together in Yates's Wine Lodge. Occasionally Harry joined them, but if ever the talk became too prying he made his excuses and left. He could imagine the comments once he'd gone. *That Harry's a dark one. What's the score with him, do you reckon? I thought he was shagging Kylie. Bollocks, mate – he's gay. Nah, he doesn't do sex, he's a churchgoer. And a fitness freak.* Stud, pooftah, Christian, long-distance runner – they weren't sure and never would be. He wasn't sure himself.

It was all tied up with Marcia, of course. And Stephen. But Stephen was a secret – a six-foot-one, size-thirteen-shoe, thirty-eight-inch-chest secret, but a secret nonetheless.

This was why he couldn't write the story of the New Cross fire. Because of Marcia. And Stephen. Because of a girl he slept with. And a boy. He *had* tried to write about it shortly after the event, by turning it into a screenplay. He was a student at East London Poly by then but he still went to Nat's Getting Started class whenever he could, and it was Nat, shown the screenplay in confidence, who confirmed the worst: 'I'd shove it in a drawer and forget about it.' So Harry had: it was buried in his desk at home, inside a pink folder he sometimes took out, and hovered over, but didn't dare open. That whole period of his life was best forgotten. Joy and Charity had invited him to remember it. 'Will you help?' I'm more sorry than I can tell you, ladies, but no.

They seemed to think he had helped, nevertheless. When Suzie brought them over to say goodbye, Charity smiled and crossed herself, as though offering up a prayer for him. Churchgoers – he had worked that out already. Living where they did, they probably attended the same church as his mum.

I should dig out that screenplay, he thought, if only to destroy it. I wouldn't want anyone to come across it. Not even Nat.

' . . . as Stan Leigh says: "The way house prices are rising, by 2010 half the population of London will be millionaires." ENDS.'

He sent the property piece to the NEWSFILE and copied it to Mills. His nth article this week, some of them no more than fillers, but still. He'd been overworking. His mind wasn't right. Tonight, for a few hours, he would watch football and chill out. The fire, Marcia, Stephen, the other Stephen, the giant fox, those five young men swaggering down the ramp outside the Elephant, all the ghosts and monsters: let it go, man. Make those damn cogs in your head stop whirring for once. Lighten up.

'All OK with the ladies?' he asked Suzie on his way out.

'Yes, they were fascinating.'

'Think there's a piece in it?'

'Absolutely. Thanks for putting me on to it. Such a tragic story.'

*8*

*ANTHEA*

HOW CAN something so small be so strongly flavoured? she wondered. The orange threads of saffron in the spice jar looked like hair fibres under a microscope. She tipped the contents into a teacup, where a splash of boiling

153

water unleashed their scent – crocus flowers, it said in the cookery book, but the crocuses she had known as a child, under the apple tree, smelled quite different. She pushed the cup away for later, and washed the mussels. Crocuses had been her father's favourite flower and mussels were the only seafood he could tolerate. Wisps of black beard clung to the shells. Tiny barnacles too – shells growing on shells, parasitically, like tics on cattle. She thought of Nat leeching on her body while she, in return, picked his brain. He fed off her, she fed off him. Love was like that.

Most recipes for paella included chicken, but she preferred a slice or two of aubergine. She chopped it up, along with onion, garlic, red pepper and tomato. The paella pan was round with a looped handle on each side – like a shiny face with big ears. She had bought it only last week, in a junk shop. When the vegetables softened to gold, she turned the heat down and added the rice, then the saffron and stock. The fish needn't go in till Nat arrived. Twenty minutes in a high oven would be enough.

A meal had been his idea: a birthday treat. He had proposed eating out. But even in town, there was the risk of bumping into someone. We'll get a takeaway then, he said. But every takeaway in the area was dire. Which was why she had offered to cook for him. It's not fair, he said, I'm the one who should be cooking. Maybe so, she said, but I'm not letting you near my hotplate. I'll bring the fizz then, he said. Just bring yourself, she said. I insist, he said. All right, she said, fizz it is.

In the end, she had bought her own fizz, just in case. Tonight fizz, not lit crit, would be the prelude to bed.

She peeled the mango and the melon, and arranged the cubes in a glass dish – a sorbet had been beyond her. Then after laying the table (white tablecloth, paper napkins, red rose, scented candle), she dumped her fish-smelling clothes on the bathroom floor, and stepped behind the glass screen. What would a stranger see, walking in? A young woman in her prime? Or just confusion – a body in a mist? How strange to spend her birthday this way. *The older man* sounded sophisticated but the man in question was over forty – almost geriatric. Rachel had told her to stop worrying: having lovers, geriatric or otherwise, was good experience, she said, a way of learning what to look for in a partner. Anthea felt less sure. The rushing water couldn't shift a sense of grubbiness. She didn't want this, she didn't not. It would be wrong for Nat to leave his wife. But how long did he expect her to play the mistress? It was time they discussed it. Any birthday was a turning point, and a twenty-fifth, a quarter-century, was momentous. Over dessert, without getting heavy, she should ask him what his intentions were. Or maybe ask him in bed, after they had made love, when he would be better placed, detumescent, to listen.

She scanned the clothes rail in the bedroom for something suitable. There was a strapless red frock she had bought for special occasions, but why dress up to eat supper in your own flat? The black trousers and embroidered sleeveless silk blouse were less flagrant. She compromised with the earrings. And the bangles. She wanted to look serious, but there was no call to be dowdy. Were these the dilemmas any mistress went through? Archaic though the word sounded, that's what she was. It was Jake's fault. He had messed her around and now she was another man's paramour. The scaredy-cat as vamp. The ant turned temptress. It was the age of the makeover and Anthea, blonde, svelte and unrecognisable from a year ago, was its archetype.

By seven she was ready and opened a bottle of Chardonnay; the fizz could keep till he arrived. They never drank when they were working, but this was different – and if she was going to ask him awkward questions she needed fortifying. She turned the television on: any noise would do to drown the noise of the next-door neighbours; any noise but football, which was the noise coming from their set and the only noise she could get on hers. A pity she hated football. An interest in it granted entry to the human race. Even Mr Fell had said he planned to watch the game tonight. She switched on the CD player instead. Something old, from Nat's era maybe. She compromised with Tracy Chapman, and sat listening at the kitchen table, straight-backed in trousers and blouse. 'Fast Car', 'Talkin' Bout a Revolution', 'She's Got Her Ticket': the songs were about running away and being with a man and fighting for justice, as though love and belief might go together. For a time, with Jake, she had believed they could. That was the basis of their relationship, he said, the personal as political, loving each other and loving the world. But global warming hadn't abated, oil companies continued poisoning the earth, trees were still felled by developers – and Jake (for whom loving the world meant loving every woman in it) had proved a lost cause. As for Nat, he had little interest in politics beyond Westminster. Famine, disease, global capitalism, Palestine: she had tried to engage him but, to her dismay and secret pleasure, his only engagement was with her.

Ten minutes passed. He had a habit of being late, but surely tonight he might have made an effort. She poured another glass and began to feel vaguely drunk. 'Baby, can I hold you tonight?' the song went. That a clever middle-aged man like Nat was willing to imperil all he had (a wife, a home, two lovely children) seemed impressive and rather frightening. Not that she considered herself worth the effort. If ever he *did* leave home, he would be disappointed. Nor did her writing merit the praise he heaped on it. When he called it 'organic', she thought of vegetables sitting forlorn on a shelf in Asda, scabby and overpriced. Maybe his encouragement was just a con to get inside her cunt. Well, he was there now. Not this minute – God knows *where* he was this minute – but his ploy, if ploy it was, had worked. In which case, now that he was home and dry, though dry was hardly the word, why keep up the flattery? And why the desperate sadness every time he left? She could only conclude that he loved her. Or thought he loved her. Same thing.

But if he loves me, she thought, why is he late? He knows it's my birthday. He knows how much this means. So where is he?

The CD fell silent. The playing time was 35.51. That's how long she had been waiting.

Finally she decided he wasn't coming – that he had lost his nerve or his wife had found out. All this agonising (so unlike her) about what to cook and what to wear and what to say to him. And now look, he hadn't even turned up. Fuck him, fuck all men, she would open the fizz and drink it herself. A waft of arctic smoked from the freezer shelf where the bottle was cooling. Moët & Chandon. She unfastened the little metal helmet. Daddy used to do this on Christmas Day. Once he showed her how. *Don't shake the bottle or you'll lose half the contents. Just ease the cork up between your thumbs without twisting and it will come.* It came. The pop had a pleasing dignity. But still a rush of froth poured forth over the rim. No glass to hand. She put her lips to the bottle top, to stop it spilling, and swallowed bubbles. Then the bell rang. She spluttered and coughed. Her heart leapt up, and she leapt up, and she opened the door with froth on her lips and saw that he too was carrying a bottle of Moët. They stood in the dingy hall, speechless, with matching bottles, one open and one not, and stared in each other's eyes, not knowing what to do next, then laughed – together, at the same moment – and kissed and moved in unison down the hallway, her hand pulling his.

*The same as the first time*, she thought, *me leading him on.*

She didn't stop on her way to the bedroom, not even to pick up the glasses for the champagne.

Much later, in the ruins of the paella (mussel shells, pink-black prawn heads, sticky clumps of rice), this was the image that came back to her. Her right hand holding the Moët, her left hand leading him on.

## 9

## *LIBBY*

THE GIRLS had brought a note home. Mrs Swayne regretted to inform parents of a further infestation of head lice at school – would they please take the appropriate remedial steps?

Remedial: a word for teachers, not advertisers. What people wanted these days was an instant cure, and 'remedial' implied too slow a process. Most of the naming session Libby had just come from had been devoted to thinking up names for a prototype saloon car that would be 'sportily male, elegantly female and sturdy with family values'. A client wanting it all ways, as usual: the group had obliged as best they could, swigging wine, snacking on cashew nuts and tossing out suggestions. Nebula, they went, Torque, Pzazz, Opera, Marco, Gemini, Gamma, Pheon, Leda ('You could have "Follow my Leda" as a bumper sticker'), Dallas, Pila, Circuit, Chequer, on and on. There'd been ten there tonight, mostly men, four of them unpublished writers (perhaps she should rope in Nat). She had sat in for twenty minutes, to remind them who was boss, while Gavin led the discussion and jotted down suggestions. The rule was to give only the brief, not identify the client. 'What about the speed aspect?' Gavin would prompt, and so it would continue: Gazelle, Cheetah, Javelin, Rabbit ('Oh, come on'), Peregrine. The recruits had come through friends and word of mouth. Libby wondered what was in it for them, apart from the wine and travel expenses: the banter, the company, the mental stimulation? It was like Scrabble. They joshed around but at the end there would be fifty words. Tomorrow she would tick the best half-dozen, and Sasha would run a copyright search. Then back to the client.

What name could they invent for a nit shampoo? NoLice, KleenScalp, Nits 'Яn't Us? Next week, for a joke, she would ask them.

The girls were in bed but still awake.

'Has your head been itchy, Hannah?'

'No, Mummy.'

'What about you, Rose?'

'No, Mummy.'

'We'd better do it, anyway.'

'We already had a wash with Millie.'

'Not the yukky shampoo.'

'It's so stinky, Mummy.'

'I know, sweetie. But we have to.'

When was the last delousing? Two months ago? The childcare manuals said nits were nothing to do with dirt; in fact, the cleaner the hair, the more vulnerable to invasion. But she hated the Dickensian associations. The texture of the things, too – their crunch between her fingers and the squishiness of those nestling white eggs. She could remember them from her own childhood. Her mother said she must have picked them up from the 'other children' in her class, meaning the Catholics. 'You don't want them breeding,' she said. There was a drawing of Medusa in her Ancient History book, and she pictured lice as little hissing snakes. Forcing them out was like a torture ritual. First the wash with acrid shampoo. Then interrogation under a spotlight. Then the violence of the nit comb – the teeth biting your scalp, the hair-yanking, the humiliation of having to sit there, yesterday's newspaper spread beneath your feet. Her eyes watered even now. Her mother had felt accused – 'bad parent, bad parent' – and that was what made her so brutal. A bit of Libby felt the same, that nits were socially shameful: to hold your head high, your children's heads had to be free of them. Nitpicking: strange that the expression should be pejorative. Who wouldn't be a nit-picker? Only a sluttish, no-good (working?) mother.

'Come on,' she said, 'into the bathroom.'

'Oh, Mummy.'

'*Now.*'

Once in the bath they sat facing each other, under berets of foam. This was the fun bit – laughing at each other's silly white hats. It was less fun clawing her nails through their scalps. Then the rinse, as they lay back, little Ophelias in the river weed, puffy clouds melting round their heads. When they sat up, she examined them for eggs, trying to be gentle, plucking at the strands like a harpist.

'Can we watch *The Lion King*?' they pleaded, from the cooling water. This was their routine after a picking – to sit together on the sofa, watching television, while she ran the nit comb through, and never mind that it was way past their bedtime.

'Jamas back on first,' she said, and they ran off squealing to their room. Where was the nit comb? In the bathroom cabinet, usually, next to the eyedrops and bars of soap. But it wasn't there – nor next to her brushes in the bedroom.

'Have you seen the nit comb?' she shouted, as the girls raced past towards the stairs.

'No, Mummy.'

'Has Millie been using it?'

'I think Daddy had it.'

'Daddy?'

'He did, didn't he, Rose.'

The nit comb was no ordinary comb but an antique, steel-toothed and long-handled, courtesy of Lady Bountiful, Nat's mother, who had made a great to-do of bequeathing it ('Finest Sheffield steel, dear – I picked it up at a fair at Harewood House, probably used to be *royal*'). Whatever its lineage, it wasn't to be found in the bathroom. Libby went downstairs and searched the less obvious spots – kitchen dresser, dining-room drawer, sideboard – and then, climbing to the attic, the least obvious spot of all, Nat's study. The usual squalor. Little chance of unearthing the comb even if it were there. Did Nat think he had nits? It wasn't like him to notice anything about his own body. If she didn't remind him to shave, or take showers, or go to the barber, he would never think to bother. To the right of his desk were empty notebooks and folders optimistically marked 'WORK IN PROGRESS'; to the left student essays; in the centre, heaped round the keyboard, a muddle of books, envelopes, yellowing faxes and postcards (one of them, she noticed, a Georgia O'Keeffe). It wouldn't be beyond him to use a nit comb as a bookmark. But there was no sign.

She joined the girls again, with Simba, in the circle of life. At this rate their hair would be dry before she found that bloody comb. Even if he had used it, Nat wouldn't remember where he'd left it. Always forgetful, he had become more distracted in recent weeks, because of her working late, and Millie announcing her departure, and the girls starting to grow up – all these changes, and he so hopeless at coping with change. He tried his best. He even cooked for her some nights. And put the girls to bed. But the effort had worn him out. Twice, poor lamb, he had fallen asleep at the supper table. Maybe exhaustion also explained his behaviour last Saturday. Or maybe it was drink. Either way, she still hadn't forgiven him. She recalled it now in horrible detail, as she sat between the girls and *The Lion King*. The Rikky Falcon disaster. The Night of the Wrong Knives.

It wasn't her habit to entertain clients at home. Most of them lived north of the river, which meant coming over Tower Bridge or through the Blackwall Tunnel, a journey they found impossibly arduous and sinister, as though Brockley were as distant as Bhutan. Then there was the Nat problem. It had taken her years to accept it was a problem. In her early, junior shots at entertaining, his lapses seemed amusing foibles. He would spill wine over the notoriously fastidious key accounts manager. Or rant on to an equities broker about the 'the greed-sickness – the me-ism – of Thatcherism'. Or enumerate the joys of small children to a woman who (as Libby had studiously forewarned him) had spent ten years failing to get pregnant. In those days her job wasn't important enough for her to care about him fucking up. If people wondered why she was married to an idiot, let them. Then she was promoted, acquired a decent portfolio, and they moved to Brockley, into a house that, once converted (the basement becoming a kitchen-diner), was perfect for dinner parties. She was selective. With stuffier clients, she stuck to lunch in town. Dinner *chez eux* was on offer only to those who could embrace what Nat called 'the raffish-bohemian pleasure principle, that sod-you opposition to cap-doffers and time-servers which has given this nation its few creative geniuses' (translation: it was all right for everyone to join Nat in becoming argumentative and drunk). Her *place-ments* always put him at the far end of the table, where she didn't have to hear his faux pas. Few of her clients went so far as to *like* Nat, but some took him to be a househusband (which made her look a high-flyer) and others had heard he was a playwright (which explained those interminable dramatic monologues). Either way, it was bearable. Until last weekend. When Rikky Falcon came round.

The Night of the Wrong Knives.

The day had started badly, with a shopping expedition (squeezed into the hour when the girls were at ballet class) to buy a new nightdress. Since Nat allegedly appreciated her nighties, or what they contained, she dragged him along. Drag was the word. Even before they reached Lingerie he was grumbling – about the crowds, the prices and the 'commodification of liber-tarian notions of free will and self-improvement to squalid bargain-hunting in M&S'. Come on, she said, even intellectuals are in favour of shopping these days. It shut him up for a while, till she stepped out of the cubicle in a blue silk nightdress. 'Be honest,' she said, 'what do you think?' 'Er, it's all right, I guess,' he said, looking round to see if anyone else was looking. 'It doesn't suit me, does it?' 'Um.' 'They have it in black as well – should I try that?' 'Don't bother.' 'Maybe you're right. I'll look at those cotton ones over there.' 'No, get that one.' 'But you don't like it.' 'It's fine.' 'Look, I'm not fishing for compliments, just tell me what you think.' 'The essential you is present whatever you wear,' he said. 'Yes, Nat, but people look better in some things than in others.' 'Outwardly, the forms might change. But the inner self remains unaltered. The fallacy is to suppose that if we exchange the objects surrounding us, or the clothes we dress in, we too will be made new, or be granted the means to perceive ourselves as new, whereas –' '*Christ, Nat, I just want to buy a bloody nightdress.*'

In the remaining twenty minutes he became less unhelpful, and she bought one, and they got through the day, till dusk and the wrong knives.

Libby hadn't grown up with high-table etiquette. Knife, fork, spoon, cork table mat, side plate with two slices of buttered white bread, cup and saucer for tea: that was how her mum had laid out for supper, which was 'tea' in the family parlance and served at 6 p.m. precisely (Big Ben tolling from the radio to prove it). She'd moved on a bit since then, into the English middle class – water glasses instead of teacups, separate meals for children, ETA of adult food on the table anything from 8 to 10 p.m. But no one would describe her as a stickler. So when she asked Nat to lay fish knives, it wasn't affectation. The fish knives, rarely brought out, had been a wedding present from his mother, who had been given two cases for her own wedding and was grateful to offload one at last. Normally Libby laid the table herself. But since she had done everything else that day, chopping and peeling while Nat entertained the girls by watching videos with them, she left him instructions and took a bath. Rikky Falcon was Head of Marketing at FizzCo, the second largest drinks firm in the country. She had worked with him once at Arran & Arran but he wasn't a signed-up client of theirs – and FizzCo, it was rumoured, had a new drink in the can. It had been hard, reeling him in. Lunches had given way to dinners and twice they'd ended up in flashy nightclubs. Rikky, though barely forty, was one of the old school: to do business, in his definition, was to eat, drink, smoke, gossip and make any woman with him feel adored. In his louche way (pink silk tie, gold cufflinks, black hair on the back of his hands), he was good company – but a bit too fond of playing the roué. 'I'm a married woman,' Libby would say, whenever he flirted, just as she used to tell boys in Ballymena 'I'm a virgin'. He understood it was a game – that she would never fall for him. But could FizzCo be made to fall for Raven McCready? Something different was needed, to tip the balance. It took courage to invite him to her house. Dinner on a Saturday would mean him driving over from Essex with his wife. But he was a sport and accepted.

The wife – Annabel – proved to be blonde, equine and supernaturally silent, and Rikky spent the evening ignoring her. The other guests were Josh (from the office) and his partner Yeadon, and Deborah and her husband

Travis. She had been panicking beforehand: what if the cream curdled? what if the guests had nothing to say to each other? But the talk was noisy, and everyone asked for seconds of artichoke soup. It was then she noticed that Nat had laid ordinary knives. She whispered to him to sort it out while she fetched the main course: sea bass, petits pois, roast peppers and pomme dauphinoise. 'Smells wonderful,' Rikky said. Nat was holding forth to Annabel ('Of course the trouble with Stoppard is . . .'). The Chardonnay bottle beaded with cold sweat, the candles flickering like fireflies, the gleam of the Sheesham Wood table: it was almost perfect. Except.

'Could you get the fish knives, Nat?' she said, going public as sweetly as she could. 'They're just behind you, darling. In a case.' There were fish forks in the case as well, but she would leave him to work that one out.

'For God's sake, Beth,' he said, refilling his glass, 'don't be such a fusspot.'

The 'Beth' was provocative. To everyone else here, she was Libby. She should have noticed he was drunk.

'Second drawer down in the dresser. The silver ones. Your mother gave them to us, remember?'

'You don't seriously expect me to disinter a family heirloom in order to impress our guests? They're only silver anyway. Unless you've gold bars on the table these days, no one gives you a second look.'

Perhaps if she had laughed, he would have backed down. But she felt too tense. And irritated. They (unlike the knives) were on display.

'I'm serving sea bass, Nat. Hence fish knives.'

'It's the end of the millennium, Beth. Do our guests really care?'

Even he ought to have seen it was unwise to ask. She was on the point of going to the dresser, with a pretend-forgiving look of 'Well, if you won't, my sweet . . .' undercut by an 'I'll speak to you later', when Rikky spoke.

'When the lovely lady of the house, having prepared a wonderful meal for us, issues a none-too-demanding request as regards cutlery, I think it's pretty damn ungracious to refuse her, old chap. Middle drawer was it, Libby?'

Silence. Rikky fetched the fish knives (and forks). Nat poured himself more wine.

For a second, passing round the vegetables, Libby's abyss-dread returned. But somehow they pulled back from the brink. Rikky and Yeadon found they had friends in common. Deborah gave a knowing wink: *Husbands!* And Nat, after a minute's chastened silence, described his work-in-progress to Rikky's wife, who listened with mute incomprehension. Everyone pretended nothing had happened. The difference with Nat was: *he thought nothing had.*

Afterwards Rikky insisted on carrying the plates through to the kitchen, on the grounds he needed a smoke.

'Wonderful food, Libby,' he said, brushing against her as he set them down. 'Hope I wasn't out of order back there.'

'Not at all. Nat doesn't mean any harm. He –'

'The drink, I know. Annabel gets the same. On her best behaviour tonight, mind. Strict instructions from yours truly to keep it shut. Can't be trusted not to make a fool of herself otherwise.'

'Really? She seems lovely.'

'Believe me. A cross to bear. Another thing you and I have in common, precious.'

He looked her in the eye, as he said it – the same you're-a-bit-of-all-right look he had given her many times before, but without the throwaway smile. Asking him to dinner was supposed to make him take her more seriously. She would confront him with what she had – a devoted husband, two sweet daughters, domestic bliss – and he, disempowered, would start to do business with her. It hadn't worked. He assumed the opposite of what she intended – that things were bad at home and she was available. Now the flirting would get flirtier and the FizzCo contract more elusive. All this she grasped as she rescued the crèmes brûlées from the grill. Rikky stood on the kitchen doorstep, and lit a huge cigar. Like a photo of Churchill on VE Day. All that was missing was the V-sign.

Nat had let her down before, from a bumbling unworldliness. But the business with the knives bordered on the malicious. And now Rikky was playing footsie with her under the table.

Worse might have followed, but she was saved by Rose, who appeared during dessert, saying she had been woken by a vampire in her wardrobe (neurotic kids on display, too – Rikky was being given the works). Nat departed meekly to settle Rose down and didn't reappear till the guests were putting their coats on; doubtless he had fallen asleep. While his wife managed 'Lovely, you must come to us', practically her first words all evening, Rikky chastely kissed Libby on both cheeks – furtively running a hand down her hip as he did so. There goes FizzCo, she thought, as he drove off, before turning on Nat. What on earth? Her tirade washed over him. Had he forgotten how to behave when they had guests? Did he think it reflected well on him to insult his wife? He stacked the dishwasher in silent penance. How many times had she explained the importance of hitting it off with Rikky? He took the bottles into the yard and shook out the tablecloth. Did he positively want her new company to fail? He swept the floor, neither defending himself nor apologising. It was as if he'd entered a trance, where fate would take its course whatever.

That was last weekend: the Night of the Wrong Knives. In itself, it didn't much matter – Libby had plenty of other potential clients. But Nat worried her. Was he losing the plot? Were her long days and nights in the office driving him nuts? He looked well these days, younger and slimmer, and claimed the writing was 'going great guns'. But when the new play ran out of steam and his spirits sank, as they would, then what? Since Stefan dropped him, he had failed to find a new agent. Rejection of his work used to demoralise him – it certainly demoralised her – but now he floated on a crest of unconcern. She feared the day when reality hit home. In the old days she had believed in his talent as much as he did. But too many people whose judgement she trusted had told him to stick with the day job. Too many agents – thirty-five at the last count – had turned him down. One of these days he might have to accept that teaching was his real vocation. Perhaps he had already begun to accept it, and this new masterclass on Tuesday evenings was part of a sea change. But none of this excused him messing up like that last Saturday night.

Her daughters squealed as King Mufasa went under the buffalo herd.

'Time for bed,' she said.

'Oh, Mummy. This is the best part.'

'And our hair's still wet.'

'Just ten minutes, then. While I find that comb.'

10

## HARRY

THERE WAS a queue in the off-licence – too many other men with the same idea – and by the time Harry reached home and turned on his set the teams were already in the tunnel. Even he, abstemious, couldn't watch the game without a drink. After the day he'd had, he needed the solace of semi-oblivion.

Defeat was the likely prospect. Argentina had Batistuta; England had Batty; that summed it up – all the skill and finesse were with the opposition. But Harry was English. And England had Sol Campbell and Paul

Ince. There was Ince now, in the tunnel, with his shirt off. In 1966, when Harry was three, England had won the World Cup without a single black player in the squad. The kids of the *Windrush* generation were at school then, or yet to be conceived. But in the 1980s and 90s they had come through: Cyrille Regis, Luther Blissett, Garth Crooks, the Fashanu brothers, Carlton Palmer, John Barnes and Ian Wright. If there were any justice, Wright – flash, lippy and aggressive – would be playing tonight. He was over thirty now and past his best. Still, every black kid in London wanted to be him.

The teams were lining up for their national anthems, England in white, Argentina dark blue. Harry turned up the volume.

> *God save our gracious team,*
> *Long live our noble team,*
> *God save our team.*

'Our' team? His team? Yes. But in the team there was also a sub-team; every race was about race; if you were black you wanted blacks to win. Frank Bruno. Linford Christie. John Regis. Lennox Lewis. The same tonight, with Sol Campbell and Paul Ince (and Rio and Les Ferdinand on the bench): he would pray for them to be the match-winners, or not to make the key mistake. '*Happy and glorious*,' Sol and Paul sang, half a beat out of step, like all their teammates.

As Harry watched, one of his earliest memories came back. Summer of '68. The low ceiling, the tatty sofa, and him and his father watching the Mexico Olympics. In the 200 metres, black sprinters from the US finish first and third, Tommie Smith taking gold, John Carlos bronze. Medals round their necks, the two of them stand on the rostrum, then raise their black-gloved hands in joint salute. Harry's too young to understand the gesture, but the electricity in it skizzes all the way from Mexico. His dad, one of whose last appearances at home this will be, tuts at the television: 'It ain't good, it ain't good, I can feel trouble coming.' He's right, in more ways than one. For making their gesture, Smith and Carlos are sent home in disgrace. And a week later Harry's father slinks off with his suitcase, leaving three kids and six months' rent arrears. Black power, black weakness. And the image of two gloved fists.

Seven forty-five. Kick-off time and still no Nat. Obviously the match didn't matter that much to him. Nothing mattered that much to Nat. Privilege was demotivating. Privilege made you careless. Whereas Harry had had to fight to belong. He sometimes thought of showing Nat the shithole where his childhood passed: the Peckham flat they'd moved to after Papa left; his mother sleeping on the sofa while he and his sisters shared a bed; the smell of damp and rot. But threnodies of self-pity weren't Harry's thing. Never to yield or doubt yourself. Seeing the captains shaking hands, he thought of those two gloved fists, rock-steady in the blue.

*Come on, England. Come on, England.*

From the first, Argentina looked the better team – dangerous forwards, quick-thinking midfielders, a solid defence. England seemed to be suffering in the heat. The red-haired Paul Scholes was typical, running and puffing to no purpose, outwitted by deft Latinos. Five minutes in, the Argentine captain, Simeone, chased a ball into the area and Seaman, England's keeper, brought him down. Harry, already on his second beer, groaned at the recklessness – the ball had been drifting away; the lunge was unnecessary. Seaman got a hand to Batistuta's penalty but couldn't keep it out. One–nil and the game had barely begun. It would end up a cricket score at this rate. Little Ortega was pulling every trick: nutmegs, dummies, cushioned headers, backheel flicks. And Simeone, shaven-headed, was working with him, ready to receive and spread the play. The Argies were running the show. Twice Beckham gave the ball away. Harry felt dismayed at the mismatch. Superstitious, too: if he were watching the game with Nat, or at the pub, surely England would be better than this. Why was Nat always so late? The other Tuesday, at Davey's wine bar, they had been due to meet for a drink at eight thirty, and he hadn't shown up till after ten. It was true he phoned a message through; the bar manager passed it on – something about the car breaking down. But the story he told when he finally arrived – involving the AA, and a faulty solenoid, and him being out in Thamesmead seeing a student – hadn't hung together. In fact, Harry realised, in the portion of his brain not consumed by the sight of Ortega running deep into England's half, the story had been total crap. And now Nat was late again.

At the back Sol Campbell was working overtime. Did those England fans with St George's flags consider him one of them? If the team played well, maybe. But if it lost, he and Ince would be the scapegoats, you could be sure. Racism was always there, waiting to explode, and when it did, as with Stephen Lawrence, you were supposed to turn the other cheek – to behave, as Doreen and Neville did, with quiet dignity. *Dignity*: a synonym for passive suffering and restraint. Sol Campbell didn't look dignified (look at him chasing and sweating), but reporters sometimes used the word about him. Fuck dignity. Stand up for yourself, man. We need to win.

The ball was back with Beckham. For once England were pushing upfield. The phone went. Harry picked it up, thinking it must be Nat.

'Harry?'

A header on from Scholes, and Owen, chasing it, sandwiched between two defenders and careful to brush against them, went down in the box. Penalty! If theirs was a penalty, that's a penalty too, ref. The referee, the tall Dane, Kim Nielsen, wearing red, blew his whistle. Players from both sides surrounded him. Penalty, it has to be a penalty, ref.

'Harry?'

'Oh, it's you. How you doing?'


## II

## *LIBBY*


'I'M FINE. Is Nat with you?'

'YES.'

A pause. Distant crowd noise, like a roar of surf. And that yes, more emphatic than seemed called for.

In their bedroom, unable to locate the nit comb, she remembered: after the masterclass, he was going round to Harry's, for the match. If he knew where the nit comb was, he could tell her. And if he had taken it in his jacket by mistake, he could bring it back. Harry's flat was only five minutes' drive away. It wasn't much to ask.

'Could you put him on then?' she said.

'What?'

'You are watching the match?'

Daft question. She could hear the commentary in the background.

'Nat's not here.'

'Oh. I thought you –'

'He left a message, to say he'd be late.'

'Still teaching, I guess.'

Another pause. She wasn't getting Harry's attention.

'Don't worry about it,' she said, knowing he wasn't worrying. 'It's not important. But tell him to call me when he arrives. Good match?'

'One–nil to them. But we have a penalty.'

167

'I'll leave you in peace. Come over sometime. Fix it with Nat.'

'Will do.'

As she was putting the phone down, she heard a roar, a triumphal YES, even louder than the first. She was glad of that. Harry had seemed odd – a little down, as Nat said. But surely no one with clinical depression roared his head off like that.

'Time for bed, girls,' she said, again. But they begged ten more minutes of *The Lion King* – and she, a guiltily absent working mother, felt powerless to deny them. Where had Nat put that comb? Their hair was drying so fast she would have to wet it again. It was fine hair just like hers but blonde. To be expected, of course, since Nat was fair. Even so. She had to fight to overcome her prejudice, since *she didn't like blondes*. She didn't like them (adult blondes, that is) because they didn't like what they were. The odd freak Nordic aside, blondes were brunettes in denial. Research showed that men were more attracted to blondes. But since no woman wants to admit that her allure lies in a bottle of hair dye, blondes always fibbed about their motives: I went blonde because it looks better (to men); because it feels nicer (with male hands running through it); because every woman has the right to choose (to look like a slapper). Was there such a thing as an un-vain blonde? Or one who didn't lap up the compliment when some man too dumb to recognise dark roots when he saw them told her what lovely natural blonde hair she had? And had anyone noticed (Libby had noticed) how blondes always spoke in lispy little kids' voices, like Petronella Pans? Libby's one experiment with her hair had been to perm it, back in the eighties: Frizzy Libby. Since that lapse in taste, she had kept it short – and brunette.

God, I'm crotchety, she thought, and kissed the tops of her daughters' heads. Not their fault. She really didn't mind them being blonde.

The phone rang. Must be Nat.

'Libby? Hi.'

'Oh, Damian.'

'You sound disappointed.'

'No, sorry, I was just . . . How are you?'

'I'll call back if it's not a good time.'

'It's fine. But why aren't you watching the match?'

'Not my thing, football.'

Point in his favour, she thought. Despite the way he used to look at her, he was probably gay.

'I wanted to tell you before you heard,' he said.

'What?'

'I've been promoted.'

'Again?'

'There's been a reorganisation. Julius got the chop. Mark said he wanted someone younger.'

'I told you Julius was crap. So you've –'

'Been asked to do his job. I don't have his experience, obviously. Nor yours of course. But in effect I'm the new Julius.'

'Congratulations.'

A year in advertising and he was doing the job she had failed to get after ten. Not that she would take it now, even if they asked her. Still, it made you think.

'I'm planning a dinner to celebrate. Will you come?'

'That's nice. But it's still awkward for me, with Mark and everything.'

'Not that kind of dinner. The two of us. On me. As a thank-you. You don't realise how many interviews I had before you gave me that job. And now, look.'

'Maybe lunch rather than dinner. Once I've got the launch over with. Did you get an invite by the way?'

'Yes, I'm coming.'

'Good. Just don't bring Mark.'

'I'll email you some dates then.'

'For lunch.'

'Dinner would be better.'

'I'm a working wife and mother, remember.'

'I know. You don't let me forget.'

I'm right not to, she thought, hanging up. Damian was like one of those dogs that jump up and lick you all over. More a gun dog than a lapdog, though perhaps her lap was where he wanted to be. Or thought he did. Like most men, he would probably run a mile if she responded. Not that she ever would respond – but if she were less busy, less married, less consumed by the girls might she feel different? He was a good-looking young man – the fair skin, the clean fingernails, that cute little mole on his chin. And full of drive and machination – a busy fox, where Nat, dozing at his desk, was a flopsy bunny. When she was his boss, Damian's attempts to impress her had been easy to explain. Now the attention was more personal. Which was flattering. But also why she had to keep him at a distance.

She sat down between Rose and Hannah again.

'Last two minutes,' she said. 'Then bed.'

## 12

## NAT

IN THE shower, under the rose, Nat watched the blood circling the drain. He felt wasteful, as though he had poured away a bottle of claret. But it was evidence, and all evidence must be destroyed. Not easily done. There seemed to be gallons. The water ran clear for a second but when he rubbed another part of himself the water turned red. He felt like the anti-hero of a Chabrol film. If he parted the shower curtain and peered through the steam, he could see her blood-smeared body on the bed: white pillows, fine blonde hair, and the deep scarlet stain she lay drowned in. The rose-fall swathed him in mist. Within the stream running from his balls were pinkish strands, like frayed cotton, and specks of black, like tea leaves. This was love and yet it looked like murder. It must be his guilt – towards his lover, whom he desired but didn't live with; towards his wife, whom he lived with but didn't desire. Guilt hadn't been part of the contract. But guilt had sneaked up on him in the shower.

Had the blood taken the edge off the sex? Not for him. He wasn't squeamish. It was she who seemed discomfited, when he came up with his face painted, like an Apache. There'd been no blood when he began; it was as though he'd drawn it from her, like a wellhead. Sorry, she said, she'd forgotten she was due to start – maybe he'd prefer to stop. No, he said, putting his penis where his mouth had been. Later, lying in the carnage, she said the bleeding might be a problem with her coil. Unkeen on condoms, disinclined to go back on the Pill, she'd had it fitted only last week. Was what he felt earlier, a wire brushing the tip of his penis? Maybe the device had become dislodged, she said. Or mortally shuffled off, he said. What? she said, dozing. Never mind, he said. Mortal was spot on. The bed was like an abattoir.

Marriage tries to sanitise sex, he thought, and to pretend its purpose is procreation. But sex is messy and brutal.

He soaped himself afresh, and watched the last pink rinse-tints disappear. He was clean, a new man, ready for any challenge. Beyond him her shoulders rose and fell. He was struck by the little-girliness of her bedroom

– the teddy by the pillow, the rag doll on the rocking chair, the Save the Whale poster.

He sat on the bed, in her towel, and touched her cheek.

Oh my God, she said, the paella, what time is it?

Not late, he said, eight-something.

I must have dropped off. God, I feel hungry, don't you feel hungry? I'll get us supper.

That'd be lovely, he said.

For a second, when I woke, I thought you'd gone.

I don't ever want to go, he said, kissing her.

Let's check your eyes to see whether you're lying, she said, looking into him. Mmm, big pupils. Like pools of ink. That means you like me.

Yours are big too, he said. And very black.

He could find no trace of himself. She was a bottomless well he had fallen down.

It must be love then, he said.

Shhh, she said, I need a shower – all this blood, look. Don't you find it disgusting?

Not a bit.

While she showered, he turned on the television. The football. Half-time. He ought to call Harry again, to tell him he would be later than planned. They were showing highlights, Argentina taking the lead with a penalty, England equalising with a penalty. Only penalties – perhaps he hadn't missed much.

I didn't know you were interested in football, Anthea called across. She was standing by the hob, in a bathrobe, smelling of lime and checking saucepans.

I'm not usually, he called back, but Argentina against England is epic.

Epic?

It's about war and empire and nationhood.

Not men kicking a bit of leather about?

It's what Marx said – history happens the first time as tragedy, the second time as a football match.

Did he say that?

More or less. Can I do anything?

No, she said, five minutes and it'll be ready. Just sit there while I get dressed.

The hairdryer went on in the bedroom. She'd be flicking the back of her hand under the tufts stuck to her neck, as women do. More highlights from the first half. The ball was with David Beckham, blond and blue-eyed, more German than the Germans, the role Bobby Moore filled when England won the World Cup in 1966. Nat was nine then. 30 July: the first anniversary of having no father. They spent the day with Uncle Jack and Aunt Nancy, who played croquet with his mother in the garden while he – having begged – was allowed to watch the match inside. At prep school football meant rugby football, a game he hated. He didn't much like soccer, either, but the sense of occasion seduced him, just as now. England v Germany was a replay of the war, goodies v baddies: it was like a film or comic strip, with Bobby Moore as the commanding officer, Alf Ramsey as the back-room brains, and Geoff Hurst as the squaddie who wins glory. Tonight's game had a war behind it, too, the Falklands. Another action replay. Beckham played the ball to Michael Owen, the boy wonder, who took it on with a flick of his right foot. Three men stood between him and the goalkeeper. He left the first one trailing, danced round the second, and was in on goal before the third could move across. Paul Scholes arrived alongside, ready to take over, but Owen wasn't going to share his moment. The ball finished in the top left corner – where Geoff Hurst had put the fourth goal in 1966. Owen ran to celebrate by the corner flag and was buried under his teammates. 'Is there nothing beyond this eighteen-year-old?' the commentator said. The coverage switched to three pundits in the studio.

Nat felt his heart racing, as it had in bed. A more communal kind of ecstasy – the grip of a country not a cunt. That Anthea could make him feel like this was wonderful; that football could, too, seemed faintly shameful, and yet it did.

Good match? Anthea shouted through.

It's half-time, but I think we're winning.

We?

England.

You're full of surprises, Dr Raven. I never took you for a patriot.

Who else would I support? I grew up here.

I don't believe in nationality, she said. It doesn't mean anything.

We all have to come from somewhere. It's integral to our identity . . .

Not to mine.

It was her birthday. He didn't want to argue. And they were showing another replay from the first half: a free kick just outside England's penalty area. Argentina must have equalised then; they had; they did, not with a bending shot but a feint, a ball laid out right, a swift piece of interpassing. 2–2. Earlier he had goosebumps. Now his heart sank. How could men he didn't know, playing a game he didn't play, have this effect? He wouldn't call himself a patriot, and yet.

I'm the least jingoistic person in the universe, he said, but it's OK to support your nation at sport.

Is it? she said, coming through with a glass of champagne. When that lot go on the rampage, is that OK too?

She pointed at the screen. The coverage was live now, the teams coming out for the second half and the camera panning through the crowd: row on row of Englishmen, striped with red battle paint. He thought of his own face, half an hour ago. The stripes of love and war.

Maybe you're right, he said.

I know I'm right, she said. I hate all those flags. There's something so small and mean about England. So hostile to foreigners.

That's what people always say, he said. But my mother's grandfather didn't have a penny when he came here from Poland and he ended up owning a clothing business in Manchester. *He* did all right.

A Polish refugee, she said – does that mean Jewish?

Yes, he said, but he married out and anglicised himself. So did his kids. There's not much Jewish blood left in me.

Knowing Anthea's simplistic views about Israel and Palestine, he needed to emphasise that. Otherwise she'd start arguing about Zionism.

You're lucky, she said. I've no foreign genes in me at all, only English and Welsh. I think that's why I want to get away.

You're young, he said, it's natural to want to travel.

It's not about travelling, she said, kissing him. I want to work and settle somewhere and never come back.

For a second he thought she might be serious but the kiss spared him from taking it to heart. Round her left arm was a spiral of metal bracelets, which cascaded down and chinked about her wrists, like hoopla. She was the prize he had won at the fair.

Hungry? she said.

Ravenous, he said.

A ravenous Raven, she said, I like that.

Prawn and saffron wafted from the oven. The ball was with Beckham, who went down. There was some sort of kerfuffle as he lay there.

Come and eat then, she said.

He turned the set off and joined her at the table.

## 13

# JACK

BEYOND THE bed, dark blue figures danced across the screen, trailing white shadows. The volume was turned right down, so he could hear the thrush's dusk call outside. How much was Nancy taking in? Television seemed to calm her, anyway. Some nights when he was feeding her she'd spit the mush out, as though in protest at the indignity. Tonight, eyes on the screen, she didn't register the spoon going in, just chewed. Not that mashed banana needed chewing. Often she just held it there, till it dissolved. It was Aileen who had suggested banana as a way of settling Nancy last thing – easy on the stomach, full of protein, simple to administer. There were the pills as well, washed down with milk. Milk from a glass, not a teat. But otherwise just like feeding a baby.

Why was the football so entrancing to her? She had never liked it in life. Put that another way: she had never liked it before the stroke. He'd read a piece in the *Telegraph* about that novelist woman with Alzheimer's whose favourite telly was the *Teletubbies*. Maybe Nancy ought to try them as well. Perhaps she had already tried them. Who was to say how she spent her mornings? You had to trust the nurses to know best, though he hadn't trusted Anna, the Germanic one, who looked the sort who might be rough. Easy to see the temptation. A great lump of flesh to look after all day. And if you had no connection, no sense of the person your charge had once been, the odd slap or hair-tug might not seem so wrong. Even for him there had been times – tucking Nancy up, say – when his movements were rougher than required. All that anger inside him. And the wish to shake her back to life. It wasn't her fault but who else could he take it out on? Only Marcus.

He set the mush aside and reached for his tumbler of Haig's. Bloody Marcus. What a world, when someone could be number two in a family engineering firm *without being family* and, worse, *without knowing a thing about engines*. But no one knew about engines these days. When Jack was small they had seemed glamorous. Ships, trains, cars, planes, motorbikes, even mowers were what had made the empire great. If only businesses had been allowed to get on and produce, instead of being taxed by the government and hammered by the unions. Mrs Thatcher had done her best to stop the rot, but it was too late and the floating exchange rate came as a death blow. Britain ought to be closer to Europe. The Tories had got that wrong.

Nancy sighed and turned her head towards him, as though his gloom had drawn her to him like a magnet. Should he switch channels? Since the Englishman was sent off half an hour ago, nothing much had happened. Despite the state she was in, maybe she grasped that the game was a stale-mate. Stale mate: hah. She rolled her head back towards the screen. Beckham: that was the name. Blond hair. Married to that dreadful Spice woman, Snooty, was it? Too pleased with himself by half. And now he'd let the team down. Not that he was the one who started it. But from the ground, face down, after being fouled, he raised his leg. A gentle flick. Didn't even touch the chap but the cunning blighter had collapsed in agony, as though from a snakebite. Snake himself. All the Argies were. General Galtieri – another snake. Spring 1982, the British fleet sailing from Portsmouth. Then the *Belgrano* and Goose Green. Three hundred Argies dead. Properly dead, too, not like the one on the football field shamming it. They had shown the replay several times and each time it looked more innocuous. Not that that made Beckham any less of an idiot. So-called professional earning more in a week than Jack did in a year. They should make an example, never pick him again.

Ah, 1982: the year of Michelle and the Paris Show. If he was ever going to sleep with her, that would have been the time. On the last night, they'd sat up together drinking cognac till three. He'd attributed his excitement to the business they were doing. Only later did he realise it was her.

Nearly full-time, and still level, 2–2. But we were a man short – the Argies were bound to win. Not a bad game, football, when you bothered to watch. Absorbing for Nancy, anyway. He should get a satellite dish. All the best sport was on Sky, so Harris said. They could spend every evening like this: the ascent in the Stannah, mashed banana and Sky. There were worse lives. He had no right to complain. Just because his wife wasn't the woman he married. No wives were, past the age of fifty. They changed, filled out, went off the rails or off their rocker. It was only a difference of degree. Lately, he'd had this terrible thought: that there had never been a time when Nancy wasn't comatose; that her present condition was the fulfilment of her previous. Unfair, untrue, but was thinking it any worse than grieving at how much the stroke had changed her? Every night, once she was off, he went down-stairs to sedate himself with Scotch, so that a certain sentence wouldn't appear. It was a disloyal sentence – ugly and ungrateful. He could feel its shape, smell its sickroom odour, taste its ashes, hear the silence of its roar.

Drink held it at bay but if he dropped his guard it crept up on him. *She'd be better off dead.*

He swigged from his tumbler. Empty already. Her eyes were open but when she stared at the set like this, or at him, there was nothing in them.

For a brief, glorious month in the nursing home, she had begun to recover speech. The words she came out with were mostly obscene – *fuck* and *shag* and *bollocks* and *arsehole* and *cunt* – but the nurses, unembarrassed, said stroke patients were often this way: at least she was talking. But then as suddenly as it started, the talking stopped, as though she had heard herself and the shock was too much. Hunter said she had probably suffered a further mini-stroke but that it needn't be a permanent setback – they must keep trying. They did keep trying, all except Nancy. Till then Jack thought she under-stood the questions he asked her, that the problem wasn't comprehension but coordination – hence her upset (and the expletives) when she failed. But the upset passed; she withdrew; the fire went out; her brain became a mashed banana, its kilo of soft tissue closed to the world. 'Unusual case,' Hunter said. But to Jack it made perfect sense. The sociability cells had burned out; she had lost interest in rejoining the world. Friends and carers tried to reel her back, to make her Nancy again. But to her it was all white noise. She had become defunct – like one of his unsold mowers rusting in the yard at work.

He looked outside. The sun had dragged the brightness with it, below the horizon, leaving the sky the colour of unripe tomatoes or terracotta pots. Was that what she was staring at on television, the reflection of orange windowpanes in one corner of the screen? He drew the curtain. Three plastic hooks came off, so it sagged at the centre. His fault for pulling too hard. Nancy used to tell him off. 'The place is falling apart,' she'd say. Untrue. In those days, given time, he fixed things. Now the curtain was missing three hooks, the laundry tap was dripping, a drawer handle had come off the kitchen dresser, it was weeks since he'd mown the grass and a dozen tiles had slipped on the roof. Easily fixed. But he'd lost the sense that things were worth fixing. People offered, like Elise today – 'If ever you need company . . .' But he felt too proud. He'd manage on his own, thanks.

There was still no light bulb in the living room. The empty socket had become a shrine. Why light the living room when no living went on in there? He wanted it gloomy.

A whistle from the television. End of the match. No, the players were still on the pitch, sitting down or swigging from water bottles. Extra time. Next goal wins. Would Nancy object if he tuned out? He leaned over to ask – 'Keep talking as if she's there,' the doctors said – but found that she had gone off. Out like a light. Not that the light seemed ever to be on, but this was different, a lower kind of consciousness. There was always that thought, when he despaired: it could be worse. Awake, she gave hints of attentiveness; asleep, she was temporarily unreachable; dead, she would be gone for good. They used to discuss euthanasia, in the abstract: what if . . . Parkinson's . . . terminal cancer . . . motor neurone disease . . . what if one of them, lacking the means, what then? The deal was that the other would do the necessary. When she made that racking noise in her throat, that 'Jack' gargle, she might be telling him 'I've had enough'. The pillow was there, behind her head, easy to use. He would not hesitate, if asked. But he needed clearer instructions. An unambiguous 'Do it for me'. The command of a fully conscious look.

He lifted her head, flattened the pillow, then eased her down. Soft oblivion. Like a baby. Her own babies had once looked like this: flushed cheeks and innocent sleep. Impossible not to love them. Did they love their mother, now she had lost all awareness of being one? In the early weeks they'd visited a lot, but Sasha was living in Paris, and Ischia in Edinburgh, and they had their boyfriends and careers. You couldn't blame them. Neither was ready to look after a baby yet, let alone a parent. Sasha flinched from the messiness – the incontinence pads, the drooling, her mother as a shell. Ischia shed tears and liked to sing – her mother's daughter, believing music could heal. Last time she visited he caught her singing 'My Darling Clementine': lost and gone for ever, dreadful sorry, etc. Role reversal: the daughter at the bedside, lullabying her mother to sleep. Maybe he should sing for Nancy too. But the only tune in his repertoire was 'Greensleeves'. And all 'Greensleeves' would mean to her was trouble at work.

When Tony Blair's father suffered a stroke, he didn't speak for three years. Yet he'd come back, and his son was all the tougher for it. No call to despair. The medics were always coming up with new treatments. Just hang in there.

He crept out, careful to avoid the loose floorboard. With luck she would be out till morning, but if she woke and was unhappy he'd soon know: on the nurses' advice, he had bought a baby monitor from Mothercare and stuck it next to the toaster. He could hear her sniffly intakes now, as he prepared a bite. The house had that hollow sound you get when the furniture has been cleared for the decorators – an emptiness beyond empty. Granary bread, liver pâté, mature English Cheddar, stick of celery, Branston pickle, Glenfiddich: it was no kind of meal, but more than enough – Widower's Supper. A hollow groan filled the room: not Nancy on the monitor but him, Jack Raven, an echo from within. He could remember his father groaning like that. It was an old man's habit. Now he, too, was an old man. He switched the portable television on for company. Still the football. Still 2–2. Must be nearly over now. Noises on the intercom: a sigh, a swish of sheets, Nancy rolling over in bed. Since the stroke, her bed sounds had changed. It was the sleep of plants she slept, not animals, but that was better than the sleep of stones. England moved upfield and won a corner. The cross came to the far post. A head rose above the Argie defence, and the ball flew in the net. Big black bloke. One of ours. Wonderful. Jack felt the hairs on his neck stand up, like that time Virginia Wade won at Wimbledon. But something was wrong. No one was celebrating. A disallowed goal. The replay showed what happened – another player, Shearer, climbing on one of theirs. Numbskull. Stupid as Beckham. Cheating was inevitable in any game, but you had to be subtle about it, like the Argies, who'd sneakily taken their free kick and were straight down our end. Six against three: a certain goal. Until an English tackle came in. Reprieved.

Still in with a shout. But England would lose in the end. Defeat was the English condition.

He switched the set off. Football wasn't his game. There were no games any more – only work, Nancy, hunting and Scotch.

Time for one last tumbler, then bed. He checked the monitor for breathing. Dead out. Silent as the grave.


## 14

## ANTHEA


SHE DIDN'T mean to cause a scene, but she had been drinking and it was her birthday and over dessert, the stupid mango-and-melon concoction that neither of them touched, her eyes filled. He put his arm round her but nothing could stop the tears, not even the thought of that stupid song her mother used to play. *It's my party and I'll cry if I want to.*

It was he who set her off, by calling her Ant. She ought to be used to it. He meant it as an endearment. She was his life, his love, his anagram, etc. But hearing him say it only brought home the scuttling life they led. The deceit. The secrecy. The lack of downtime to do ordinary things together.

If he left his wife, she wouldn't feel so marginal. But he mustn't leave his wife.

Crying couldn't be helped but, if it allowed you to say what had to be said, crying wasn't unhelpful.

'What's wrong?' he said. 'Tell me.'

Why not tell him? The speech was clear in her head. She would begin by saying how compromised she felt ('I don't approve of affairs'). Explain how she drifted into one with him by accident ('because I was lonely, because my job's demoralising, because of Jake'). Accuse him of having his cake and eating it ('whereas I get no cake at all, not even on my birthday'). Berate him for exploiting her ('I'm just a cosy fuck you can sneak home from to your wife'). And then hit him where it hurt ('You're too old for me'). After that, she would be gentler: say that she loved him deeply but doubted the relationship could ever work; that it was wrong to steal him from his family; that she had been serious when she mentioned leaving England to do some good in the world. That was the plan. But he was so attentive – holding her face, stroking her hair, wiping her tears – she held her tongue. The cat got it. It was like the time with Old Nod, when she failed to deliver her speech about trees. Scaredy-cat Anthea all over again.

'Please tell me what's wrong,' he said.

'It's nothing,' she said. 'I always get tearful on my birthday. My dad's death-day is just afterwards.'

She hadn't intended to say it. But it was true.

'I know how you feel,' he said.

'Do you?'

'I lost my dad round this time of the year too. Not just once, twice.'

'Twice?'

'He left home on the 30th of July. And died on the 21st, twenty-two years later.'

'Mine died on the 5th of July,' she said.

'Which year?'

'Nineteen eighty-seven?'

'Same here,' he said. 'Nineteen eighty-seven. That's when mine died, too.'

'Of what?'

'A heart attack.'

'Snap.'

Same month, same year, same cause.

She cried some more then. The coincidence was too much. Their mothers shared a middle name, Elspeth, their star signs were compatible, and now this thing with their fathers. How could she dump him after that?

They held each other for a long time.

'You've never talked about your father before,' she said.

'It makes me too angry. My mother was barely thirty when he left. She never found anyone else.'

'Mine, neither,' Anthea said, 'though it's not for lack of trying.'

'My friend Harry's dad left him as a child, too.'

'Losing your dad when you're little is devastating.'

'I know,' he said, though she could see he had missed the subtext, the risk of his kids losing him. 'My lovely, orphaned Ant.'

'You're only kissing me because you're sorry for me,' she said, coming up for air.

'It's me I'm sorry for. Why didn't I meet you years ago?'

'You did. At the class. I made no impression.'

'I was too afraid. Some part of me must have known what it would mean. What I'd have to do. What I will have to do soon.'

'Shh,' she said, 'don't talk like that. You are still being careful? If she suspects . . .'

'Yeh, yeh. I've hidden your postcards.'

'And deleted all my emails.'

'Yes.'

'Even the one I sent last night?'

'I think so.'

'You'd better have.'

'She wouldn't check up on me. She's not like that.'

'It's not just her. All sorts of people hack in. You could be blackmailed.'

'OK, OK.'

'And it's nearly ten. You should get going.'

'In a minute. Christ, I almost forgot. Your present.'

He fumbled in his pocket. It was a brooch. Antique silver. In the shape of a fox. Not something she would ever have chosen, yet entirely her.

'I trust it's a she,' she said. 'A vixen.'

'I couldn't swear to that.'

'I love it, anyway.'

'There's a catch,' he said.

'I know,' she said, fastening it to her blouse.

'Not that sort of catch. The brooch comes with two conditions.'

'Which are?'

'That you promise to send your stories to my friend Mike.'

'One day maybe. When they're finished. And the other?'

'That you let me make love to you before I go.'

'There isn't time.'

'I'm taking my present back, then.'

'Meanie. It's far too nice. I won't let you.'

When he mock-grabbed at the brooch, she pulled him to her.

She was almost at the summit when the phone rang. Leave it, she thought, keep hauling on the rope, and for a second or two the noise stopped and the trig point came in view. But then her voice spoke from the answering machine ('Sorry I'm not here'), and her mother spoke in reply, and she found herself descending peg by peg. When the room fell silent again, she tried to climb back to where she'd been: unlocking her legs, with him still inside, she rolled over and perched on top, usually the surest way, but not this time – she was stuck below the final rock face, yanking on him, harder and harder, till she felt him rush past, a movement she might have stopped by slowing down, but there was no point, she would never get there herself, let him go. He went. He'd gone. *Che sera.* There would be other times. Maybe the coil had inhibited her: you weren't supposed to be conscious of it, but she was. Or maybe it was the blood. Or the thought of their fathers. Same month, same year, same cause.

She made him wash himself again before he left. Blood, saliva, vaginal fluid, another woman's DNA: how could a wife not sniff them out? It would be so easy to trap him. To let his wife know. To get pregnant even. But she wouldn't stoop that low.

After he'd gone, she called her mother back. The phone was cordless and small enough to wedge under her chin.

'Hi, Mum,' she said, carrying plates through to the kitchen. 'Sorry I missed you.'

'You sound a bit flat.'

'Not really. Just tired.'

'So how did you celebrate?'

'You know – a meal, champagne and stuff.'

'With friends?'

'Just the one friend.'

'Male?'

'Yes.'

'Well, I hope he's taking care of you.'

'Um.'

'Not like that other young man.'

'Mum, please.'

'It's not your boss, is it?'

'We don't have bosses, only team leaders.'

'It can be a problem, falling in love with your superior.'

'My superior?'

'You know what I mean.'

'I'm not stupid, Mum.'

'So long as you're happy.'

'I am.'

She changed the subject – to her mother's gutter repairs, the relative costs of gas and electricity, Gordon Brown, when she'd next get up to the Lakes to visit. Her mother circled back.

'So where did you go to eat?'

'Not far,' Anthea said, silently stacking the dishwasher. 'Local place.'

'What sort of cuisine?'

'Spanish.'

'That's nice. They've opened a Peruvian in Keswick. Apparently . . .'

She put the knives in with the blades pointing downwards, to be safe. There'd been that story in the newspapers of a child falling against an open dishwasher and dying of a knife wound through his chest. Poor kid. The thought made her wince and became an image of Nat's daughters, killed by her fucking their father – a blade through innocent hearts.

'So what's he like?' her mother asked.

'What's who like?'

'Your boyfriend. You can tell me his name, can't you?'

She chinked the flutes she was holding and rapped the worktop.

'Oh God, Mum, sorry, that's someone at the door.'

'Your boyfriend again? At this hour?'

'Maybe. Anyway, call you tomorrow.'

The wine glasses were too fragile for the dishwasher, so she filled a bowl and added Fairy Liquid. Boiling hot. Should she scrub the clogged paella dish or let it soak? Too much Fairy. The sink brimmed over with suds like the magic porridge pot in that children's story.

*So what's he like?* She felt confused again. She didn't want him, she didn't not. There was Nat, living two lives, and there was her, living half of one. By ten o'clock he'd already gone – it was pathetic. Yet she had made him go – it was her choice. If she asked him to stay over one time, surely he would. In bed, she was his mentor, his enabler, the one in charge. Common sense told her to give him up, but her power over his body was disempowering. Jake had been cool, take-it-or-leave-it, take-or-leave her. Nat was hot and bothered, all puff and sweat, a steam train. She doubted she wanted him as badly as he wanted her. But it would do. No, she thought, scouring the pan, it's bad, it won't do at all, he's with someone else, and anyway he's too old. They were on a voyage aboard each other's bodies, he said. But was it a ghost ship drifting nowhere?

In the bedroom she undressed and stared in the mirror. Big stomach after that meal. Bruise on her right shoulder. Silver stain on her inside thigh. New streaks of blood. This is the body he loves, she thought. If his wife can't keep him, tough shit. But to dislodge him from his home, to dislodge him from his life – he wouldn't cope. Oh, he thinks he would. But I know him better than he knows himself.

Then again, there's a lot to be said for him. The ticks outnumber the crosses. Yes, he's carrying baggage, but he's kind, clever, devoted and he loves me. What more could I want?

A headlight beam crossed the ceiling. He's restored my confidence, she thought. But it's not like it was with Jake. Something's missing. Or is that too harsh? Maybe I could love him, if I allowed myself, and we could be together properly. Unless him being married is part of the allure. The forbiddenness. The thrill of the illicit. If we were together all the time, openly, would we desire each other less or more?

And if I were with him would that help me achieve all I want to achieve? Or would it hold me back, wrapping me up in domesticity and making me dribble my life away in boring old England?

I'm confused. That's why people warn young single women against getting involved with older married men – not because it's immoral but because you ending up getting hurt.

I'd be less hurt if I finished with him now. But then I'd be lonely. Something is better than nothing. Isn't it?

Oh, it's no good trying to reason this out. We're talking about love here. Love doesn't listen to reason.

I'm twenty-five today. Yet I've no more idea of who I am and what I believe than I had at fifteen.

The clock said 11.59. Happy birthday, she whispered, while it still was.

## 15

## HARRY

HARRY HEARD the bell go as Veron was walking to the spot. Nat's usual impeccable timing. He buzzed him in without taking his eyes off the screen. Veron hit it high above Seaman. 2–1 on penalties to the Argentinians. 4–3 overall. Harry opened the door.

'Shh,' he said. 'Penalty shoot-out. They're ahead.'

'I was listening on the car radio,' Nat said. 'I thought they'd missed one.'

'Ince missed, too.'

Ince had done the same as Crespo, popping it too close to the keeper. An easy save. Harry took it personally: one of his own team fucking up. But Ince had been a terrier for 120 minutes. And Sol Campbell had been even better, not only holding the defence together, which was his job, but making daring forays upfield. If there was a villain, apart from Beckham, it was the Ging-er, Scholes. At 2–1 he had the easiest of chances and fluffed it. 3–1 at half-time would have killed the game off. Instead they equalised and here we were. The lottery of penalties.

Berti and Veron for them, Shearer for us. Now Merson could level the scores. Roa, their keeper, tried to unnerve him, by leaving his goal. Was the ball precisely placed on the penalty spot? Roa thought not.

'Where've you been?' Harry asked.

'Work thing. Overran.'

'Come on, Merson.'

Merson was fine, just. In off the post. 2–2.

'If Libby asks, don't tell her I was late, OK?'

'She knows. She called.'

'Shit. Well, don't tell her I was this late.'

'She wants you to call her back.'

'I will. After this. Who's he?'

'Gallardo. One of their subs.'

The third of their subs to take a penalty, in fact. The ball flew low past Seaman's right hand. Ice-cool. 3–2.

'I thought Latins were supposed to be temperamental.'

'What's the problem with Libby knowing you're late?'

'It's not a problem exactly. That's Owen, isn't it? I saw his goal.'

'I thought you were at work.'

'Long story. Why Owen? He's too young. Let Beckham take it.'

'Beckham was sent off. Just after half-time. Didn't you know?'

'I've only seen highlights.'

'That was a highlight. I'm confused. *Yes.*'

The ball squeezed in high up, off the left-hand post. Owen turned away, a disbelieving jammy-bastard smile on his face, a kid nonplussed by the occasion, as though this were no more than a Sunday-morning kickaround.

'So if you weren't at work, where have you been?'

'It's hard to explain. Who's this?'

'Ayala.'

Ayala, the commentator was saying, had had a bad season with his club.

'He'll miss,' Nat said.

'He'll score. There – what did I tell you?'

A cheeky, wrong-footing shuffle, and the ball rolled in to Seaman's left. 4–3. If we missed the next penalty, the game was over.

'So?' Harry said.

'You're Libby's friend as well as mine. That's what makes it difficult.'

'You're making no sense. Have a beer. This isn't like you.'

'It's true. I feel different. I've changed.'

'Changed how?'

'Inside. How I feel about things.'

'Batty,' Harry groaned, 'not *Batty.*'

'How I feel about Libby.'

'Why not Sol Campbell? Why Batty?'

'I thought it'd be OK. That I could still love her regardless.'

'Compose yourself, man. Take your time.'

'But maybe you can't love two people at once.'

'Don't try to place it, belt it.'

'Or the love you feel for one person makes your love for the other person seem tepid.'

'He should take a longer run-up.'

'And it's not because of marriage or having children. They should strengthen love. But when a more intense love comes into your life . . .'

'NO!'

Batty dollied it up; Roa saved; England had lost.

'Just like 1990,' Harry said. 'Just like Euro '96. Will we ever learn to take penalties?'

'All I know is I love Anthea more.'

'If we'd just kept that lead until half-time.'

'More than I've loved anyone.'

'And Beckham hadn't got himself sent off.'

'More than even Libby and the girls.'

'And Sol Campbell's goal hadn't been disallowed. And they'd played Ian Wright instead of Shearer.'

'*That's* how much I love Anthea.'

'What did you say?'

'Anthea. That's her name.'

'Whose name?'

'The one I've been seeing.'

'You've been seeing a girl?'

'Woman. She's twenty-five. As of today. That's where I've been. Celebrating her birthday. And our fathers died of heart attacks in the same month. Isn't that amazing?'

'You've lost me,' Harry said, turning off the television. 'You've been cheating on Libby with some chick?'

'I'm going to come clean with Libby. I *will* tell her.'

'Hey, hey, hey, hey, I didn't say tell her. Wait a minute. This is serious.'

'I know, I've never felt so serious in my life.'

'Slow down here. How long have you been fucking this girl?'

'Woman. Anthea. Making love to. For two or three months.'

'And you've been married to Libby for . . . ?'

'Ten years this autumn.'

'And you've had two children together. Whereas this infant you've just met, this slag, this fuckette . . .'

'Harry.'

'I'm angry, Nat.'

'Because of losing the match.'

'Because of you. This could end your marriage.'

'Maybe it should end – that's the point.'

'How are your daughters going to feel if it does?'

'I'll still see them.'

'What, at weekends?'

'Why not? That's how it is these days. That's how it's always been. Your father left you. Mine left me. Anthea's died when she was fourteen. Fatherlessness is expected. It's routine. Feminists have been saying it for

186

years. We're redundant, Harry. Invisible. Absence defines us. I'm not reneging on my role, I'm fulfilling it.'

'Spare me the riff, Nat. I remember now. The other week. Davey's. You were late. Student thing, you said. You'd been with her, right?'

'Yes.'

'If she's a student, this could fuck up your job, too.'

'She *was* a student of mine – years ago. She isn't now.'

'Twenty-five, you said. She's still a baby.'

'She has a job, a flat of her own, she writes stories, I think it could work.'

'And what will it do to Libby?'

'Oh, she'll be angry to begin with. But she'll get the house. And she still has her work. She's very good at her work.'

'She's good at it because she feels secure.'

'She doesn't need me any more, Harry.'

'But you need her. In all sorts of ways. Not least financial. What are you going to live on?'

'I'll get by. Anthea has her job with the council –'

'The council! How much does that pay?'

'And once our writing careers take off . . . I'm working much better these days, Harry.'

'It's not just the buzz of fucking some bimbo?'

'I feel ten years younger.'

'She *must* be good in bed.'

'That's such a cliché.'

'*You're* such a cliché. Married man, single girl fifteen years his junior, woomph, euphoria, three months of fucking like rabbits, he leaves his wife, they set up together, then next thing she's off wrecking someone else's marriage or he gets bored with her and trades in his second family for a third. It's standard serial stuff. And there was I thinking you were a one-off.'

'I'm sorry to be a disappointment, Harry. I didn't know you'd so much invested in me. You should have sold up.'

'She's pregnant – is that it?'

'You would think that, of course.'

'Fuck you, Nat.'

He stood up to fetch two beers. By the fridge, inside a pink folder, was the typescript of his ancient screenplay, which he'd dug out from his desk at half-time: having decided there was no risk of Nat turning up, he wanted to see if it was as bad as he remembered. It was. Even the title embarrassed him: *A Fire in My Heart*, for God's sake. He had done right to shove it in a drawer. And that's what he did again now, slipping the folder under a sheaf of tea towels before Nat clapped eyes on it.

'Sorry,' Nat said, accepting the beer. 'Forget what I just said.'

'OK, we're even – I'm sorry I called her names. I'm sure she's perfectly nice, whatever she's called.'

'Anthea.'

'But Jesus – twenty-five years old.'

'It's not such an age gap,' Nat said. 'Look at Clinton and this Lewinsky woman.'

'You're not comparing yourself with Clinton?'

'No, but –'

'Anyway, Clinton says nothing happened.'

'He would, wouldn't he.'

'He's right to,' Harry said. 'Millions of husbands have affairs. Most have the sense to shut up about them.'

'If it was just an affair I would shut up about it.'

'If Libby asks, you should deny it.'

'And marginalise the woman I love?'

Harry took a swig. What planet was Nat living on?

'Look,' he said, 'maybe you do love her. But you mustn't be pressurised.'

'She's not pressurising me. It's what I want.'

'It's what you think you want. It might look different by tomorrow morning or next week. Slow down here.'

'It's not fair to go on pretending.'

'If you'd been fair, you'd not have got into this in the first place.'

'Still, I could atone now.'

'Just wait a little longer. Please.'

'I don't know, Harry.'

'Come on, promise me – not now.'

'OK, I promise, not yet.'


16

## LIBBY


I SHOULDN'T be doing this, thought Libby, as she sat in Nat's study. It was a rule she had made after Rose's birth: no bringing work home; a sixty-hour week at the office was enough. But the launch of Thin Libby was only a week away. Emails came all hours. Nat was out somewhere and the girls were asleep. She might as well take advantage of the peace.

She made a clearing and turned on his PC. It was slow to warm up, as though infected by the lassitude of its user. She riffled through his papers while she waited, still on the lookout for the nit comb. There was that postcard again, the Georgia O'Keeffe. She detached it from the typescript to which it was paper-clipped and turned it over. Pushy little number, thanking him for his help on the last story, asking for feedback on the new one, and hoping they'd meet as usual next week, xx. One of his protégées from the masterclass. Here was another card. Same handwriting. More trilling and gushing and hoping he had time to read the attached, then 'See you in Inca – will email if a prob, xxx'. Inca? Extra lessons, presumably, but there was no Inca near the college as far as she knew. Antonia, Annabel, Andrea – she couldn't make out the name. Some needy girl out to impress him. How voracious students were. Inappropriate, too. If a lecturer sent kisses to a student, he would be sacked. Yet a lecturer was expected not to notice when a student came on strong. The funny thing about Nat was he didn't notice – not even Claire, who'd been attending his class for years and was obviously besotted with him. Reassuring in a way, to find your husband of a decade attracting younger women. She too had been impressionable when she fell for him. Back then he had his hair and virility. It couldn't be his looks these days. But a good teacher always had charisma. Men who knew stuff turned women on.

She keyed in the password and checked her emails. Top of the pile was a belated thank-you from Rikky Falcon for supper last week. (There had already been a card from the wife.) He hoped things were all right at home, better than they seemed to be and better than they were *chez lui*. Was she by any chance free to join him for a drink next Monday evening, to exchange moans – and perhaps more? Hmm. Not a word about FizzCo. Or about coming to the launch party. 'Alas, Rikky,' she typed, 'next week's no good for me.' Little else. Josh had sent some background on Hothouse, whose decking account he thought they should pitch for – she would print out the attachments later, to read on the way to work. Damian was suggesting some dates for lunch or dinner, 'preferably the latter'. Mr Michaels had emailed, too, from his hotel – old-world courtesy at new-world speed. His 'agri-business' had turned out to be an engineering company making chainsaws, mowers and assorted garden machines; his plan was to break into the British market with a strimmer ad. Libby felt so bored listening to him that she had quoted an exorbitant sum, which he, to her amazement, was now accepting – he hoped they could discuss it further at her party, which he planned to attend. God preserve her. She one-sentenced him back and came offline, to work at her speech.

What to say at the launch? Spontaneous would sound best. But skeleton notes were needed, in case she panicked. How long should she speak for? The guests would have champagne flutes in their hands and be itching to get to the Almeida or The Ivy. Five minutes max. Why launch a new agency now? she could begin. Because she had always dreamed of running her own business. Too self-centred, that. Because she wanted to make a mint. Too avaricious. Because the industry needed more women at the top. Too feminist. Because we were living in a new country, the Cool Britannia of Tony Blair and the Spice Girls. Bullshit. Something wittier then. A client–agency relationship was like marriage, she would say. Over time it lost its edge. And you couldn't run a successful ad campaign, any more than you could have good sex, if you weren't excited by your partner (all this said with a wink at the more lucrative clients). Nah, cheap. Rikky would mis-construe and Mr Michaels think of whores in Amsterdam windows. Better to be honest. Say she founded Raven McCready because she saw a gap in the market which a dynamic young agency – and she had every confidence hers was that – could fill. Be tough, clear and upbeat, then thank people. Emote. Not cry, of course, but (did the verb exist?) *effuse*. Talk of the *wonderful* clients who had come rushing to see her the *very first moment* they heard about her plans. Say how *enormously grateful* she felt for her good fortune, which was chiefly down to the *amazing team* she had. Confess she had never realised that starting a business could be *such fun*. Golly-gosh-gushing like this didn't come naturally to Libby. People knew her as level-headed – and she mustn't let that reputation slip. But this wasn't a lecture at the Royal Geographical Society. This was a launch. And at launches you had to talk things up.

It was late, gone eleven thirty. Where the hell was Nat? At Harry's, presumably – he should have called long ago but she wasn't going to demean herself by checking up on him. They would be deep into post-match analysis and men talk now. Hard to imagine Harry going in for men talk. He wasn't unmacho – the shaved head, the runner's flat stomach – but his manner was gentle, and she sometimes wondered, as she did with Damian: was he gay? Impossible: there was Stephen. But Harry might have changed. Over the years, she'd had him round for supper with many an attractive woman. But nothing had come of her manoeuvrings. Did he and Nat ever discuss their sex lives? she wondered. Nat had none to discuss. She had been too tired to take the initiative lately and, to judge by his floppiness, he couldn't have performed even if he wanted to.

She yawned. The speech could wait till tomorrow. She ought to shut down and go to bed. But on impulse she signed on as Nat. It was easy to do – she had created his password for him – but harder to explain to herself later. Somewhere was the thought she would tidy up for him, and throw away his rubbish, just as she did around the house. She wasn't suspicious. She wasn't unhappy. But nor was it a habit of hers to open his post. A gut-feeling, then – her brain hadn't worked it out but her body had. The Georgia O'Keeffe postcard – was that it? The genitalia of those lilies. Another woman's cunt.

She thought nothing of it at first. There was so much junk in his inbox, she failed to pick up the common motif. He obviously never deletes anything, she thought; he probably doesn't even know *how* to delete; I must teach him. Then she noticed how many of the mails were pornmails. *Hi, I'm hot for you, wanna see me live on my webcam? Click here for cheating wives, Asian vixens and lezzy sluts.* There were offers of car insurance and septic tanks, too. But pornmails predominated. He must have been sent them because he was known to be a regular punter – then he'd kept them as a fast-track to sexsites. So this was how he spent his spare time – why no work got done. How easily it fell into place, how hard to believe. She had seen it yet not seen it: the distracted-ness, the buoyancy, the indifference in bed. Why keep this stuff, unless a user?

Of 209 items in his inbox, 127 were offers of porn. She counted, before deleting them all. Surely conclusive.

No, no, she thought, this is stupid, I'm tired and imagining it, he never throws anything away and keeping emails isn't the same as browsing websites.

But the thought, now she'd had it, couldn't be banished.

She signed off and looked through his folders. Among them was one called *Ant*.

It was a play, a two-hander, with a pair of characters called A and B. A was female and, it became clear, the reluctant mistress of B, reluctant because B – a sexually rampant middle-aged man – had a wife.

B for Barnaby, Nat's middle name. A for . . . ? And *Ant*, why *Ant*, what sort of title was that for a play about a man and woman?

B for Nat. But A was a fantasy of some kind. He had made her up. Those cyberspace whores had overheated him and *Ant* was the outcome: a solipsistic Internet romance.

It wasn't much of a play. No observation of the unities, no arc or trajectory, and – even allowing for its unfinishedness – no promise of resolution. Nor was it well written. She had never known his dialogue to be so lacking in wit.

*It feels wrong to be so happy. And it is of course. That's what I struggle with. Knowing it's wrong but wanting it so badly.*

That was A. As for B:

*When I'm inside you, really inside you, it's as though I've come to the place I've been searching for all my life.*

Yuk.

*Of course, I feel I'm inside you anyway, or that you're inside me. I carry you round in my head and heart all day long.*

Did people really talk like this? If she had read it in a book, she would have blushed.

It got worse. She didn't think it could get worse, but it got worse.

*When I rest my head on your breasts, or push my tongue between your thighs, and feel your body vibrate, as though to a tuning fork . . .*

It was the kind of writing Nat used to read aloud to her in mockery. 'Wilberforced', they called it, in homage to his old artist friend, with his erotic woodcuts. Yet in Ant there was no sense of irony. Nor the slightest hint of – wasn't this Nat's phrase for it? – 'authorial distance'.

*What we experienced last night the French call 'extase'. Or is it 'jouissance'? There's no equivalent in English. These are foreign delights. Foreign to me, anyway. I've never felt such sensations before.*

Not with his wife? The more Libby read of *Ant*, the more personally she took it. Though the wife figure remained offstage, she came over, in B's descriptions, as a harridan.

*You know how men complain their wives don't understand them? The problem with my wife is that she does understand me. She knows I'm easy-going and she takes advantage. I've only begun to see this since falling out of love with her.*

If Nat even remotely resembled B, if Libby even remotely resembled B's wife, this was terrible.

*When I'm inside your sweet little . . .*

It briefly occurred to her that Nat might be having an affair – that actual experience, rather than porn, had inspired him. She felt ashamed for having the thought. But an affair might almost be preferable to this. Pornographer or adulterer: which was worse?

*When I'm inside your sweet little cunt, or you take my cock between your red lips, like one of the daughters of Jerusalem feasting on a pomegranate . . .*

You had to laugh. But you couldn't. She couldn't. This went beyond laughter. The ground had gone from under her feet.

No question, she was married to a pervert. At least she knew now, and knowledge was power. She would take control, help Nat to get treatment, bring him to his senses. Her hand was shaking. She mustn't let it shake. He was having a midlife crisis, that was all. These things happened. Put it down to experience. *C'est la vie.* Lizzie Raven the Stoic. Another challenge faced, another problem solved . . . It was no good. She tried to imagine herself shrugging it off, and failed. This was Armageddon. Armageddon as a soap opera, maybe, but Armageddon. Her eyes filled thinking of her daughters, asleep in their beds, innocent of adult perversion. How would they cope if they ever understood?

First the acorn of those undeleted porn ads. Then the saplings of dialogue in Nat's crappy play. And now this forest of distress.

She read on. A dark new idea dawned. The real issue in *Ant* wasn't sex, she realised, it was age.

*A: When we're together, I forget the huge gap in our ages. But afterwards, alone . . .*

*B: You're so grown-up in many ways, but also an innocent, and I'd hate to despoil that innocence.*

A huge gap in age: how huge? And then this talk of innocence despoiled: was B's fantasy female a girl below the age of consent? The more Libby read of *Ant*, the more convinced she became. The man was an abuser, coercing an innocent. Nat wasn't just a pornographer, but a paedophile. The play was his way of imagining a sexual relationship with someone much younger – maybe even as young as Hannah and Rose.

What if it was Hannah and Rose he was fantasising about?

And who was to say it was just fantasy? Suppose it was based on *something that had already happened.*

That's ludicrous, she thought. Whatever his inadequacies as a parent, there's no doubt Nat loves the girls.

Unless he loves them too much.

*When I'm inside your sweet little cunt.*

This is madness, she thought, I'm exhausted, my worst fears have run away with me, the play's just a play. He tossed it off one day – yes, exactly that – when he was bored. Or one of his students wrote it: they send him stuff at home all the time, and he downloads and files it. I must stop reading, before my thoughts get crazier still.

Her thoughts got crazier still. Suppose Nat was part of a paedophile ring. And suppose he'd disseminated photos of Hannah and Rose. And suppose Harry was in on it too, and that instead of watching football they were, at this very moment, watching kiddie porn or having sex with children.

*When I'm inside* . . . I'm always telling clients that an image is worth a thousand words, she thought. But a single phrase has launched a thousand images in my head.

She would have to confront him. But confronting him would mean speaking to him and she didn't want to speak to him ever again. She wanted to kill him.

Wham-bang.

She heard the door slam downstairs and hastily exited from his file. The bastard was home at last. Straight from the scene of his latest depravity, with Harry primed to cover for him – Mr Alibi, the pervert's best friend.

'Beth?'

His old name for her, shouted from below. The screen blackened. Shutdown. He had reached the landing. She had a choice. Let it sink in, ask innocent questions, leave confrontation till later. Or hit him with it now. Literally might be best. No time like the present. That little electric fire looked solid enough to stove in a skull. Or there was his old cricket bat from school. Or there, look, it had been there all along, next to the fax machine, the nit comb. Long steel shaft you could penetrate a heart with. And teeth to flay the skin. After she had pierced his lungs and stabbed his eyes and ripped his face, she would work at his hairline and scalp him. *When I'm inside you, deep inside you* . . . She'd hang the scalp in place of a light bulb, and then chop his body to bits with the SteelCutt cleaver (that thank-you from Jimmy Adams, SteelCutt's Chief Exec, after their ad campaign won three awards), and deposit him in bagged portions in the Thames before the smell of rotting flesh set in. His footstep on the stair. She turned the light off. The girls need never know, she would tell them he had moved to Hollywood, to write a screenplay, that though Daddy loved them his literary ambitions always came first (which was no lie) and they must get used to the idea of not seeing him again for a very long time – perhaps never. The attic room would become a shrine to his depravity, till one day when they had almost forgotten him she would sell up and move away. And no one would be the wiser or wonder whatever happened to Nat Raven.

Except Harry. But it would be easy to silence Alibi Harry.

'Libby?'

He was there, in the doorway. She sat in his chair, the nit comb in her fist, waiting for the light to snap on.

# Draft of *A Fire in My Heart*:

a screenplay by Harry Creed

*EXTERIOR. A STREET IN SOUTH LONDON IN THE EARLY 1980S. NIGHT.*

*Shot of the front of a house, the camera slowly moving in to focus on its door, number 439. The door opens then closes again, as two youths in their late teens,* HARRY *and* WINSTON, *come out with two girls,* MARCIA *and* PAULETTE, *seemingly of the same age. As the four descend the front steps and move away, the camera lingers on the door again, number 439.*

HARRY *(voiceover)*: Funny thing is, I was only at that party for twenty minutes. Most of the kids were much younger than us, and when the two girls we met there told us about another party, just down the road, we split with them. But what happened that night changed my life forever. Two years later, the fire's still burning in my heart.

*EXTERIOR. A SOUTH LONDON STREET. NIGHT.*

*The four teenagers walk down the street.* WINSTON, *the more dominant of the boys, is walking with* MARCIA, *and laughing;* HARRY, *wearing glasses, lags behind in awkward silence with* PAULETTE.

HARRY *(voiceover)*: Winston had first pick, of course. But that was fine by me. It was Paulette I fancied at first, not Marcia. If I was tongue-tied, it was because I couldn't believe my luck.

*INTERIOR. A NOISY, SMOKY, CROWDED KITCHEN. NIGHT.*

*We see* WINSTON, PAULETTE, MARCIA *and* HARRY *push through into the kitchen, where there's drink – beer, wine boxes, bacardi bottles. Giggling, excited, but with* HARRY *still painfully awkward, they grab four beer bottles.*

*INTERIOR. A NOISY, SMOKY LIVING-ROOM. NIGHT.*

*Drinks in hand,* WINSTON, PAULETTE, MARCIA *and* HARRY *are standing watching as people dance. A joint goes round, and the four of them draw on it in turn.* WINSTON *grabs* MARCIA *for a dance.* PAULETTE *looks sulky. Rapid cuts and changes of music to establish a sense of time passing.* WINSTON *tries to touch* MARCIA; *she brushes him off.* HARRY *tries to talk to* PAULETTE, *above the noise, but she ignores him. Finally he summons up the courage.*

HARRY *(shouting above the noise)*: Wanna dance?

PAULETTE *(shouting back)*: I can't – I have to go.

HARRY: What?

PAULETTE *(pointing to the door)*: I have to go.

HARRY: Oh, right, yeh.

PAULETTE *pushes through the dancers, and grabs* MARCIA, *and they disappear together.* WINSTON *walks over to* HARRY.

WINSTON: Where've they gone?

HARRY: To the toilet . . . She seems OK, Marcia.

WINSTON: Nah, ass like ice, man. I'd rather have yours.

HARRY: You can fuck off.

WINSTON, *laughing, moves into the crowd and begins to dance with another girl.* HARRY *stands watching, awkward at being alone. Time passes. Finally* MARCIA *returns and stands with* HARRY.

HARRY: Where's Paulette?

MARCIA: She went.

HARRY *(dismayed)*: But I thought . . . Where?

MARCIA: Back to that other party. Her mum's collecting her. She ain't allowed out late, see. She's only fourteen.

HARRY *(shocked)*: Oh.

MARCIA: I know, all the guys think she's twenty . . . I see your mate's having fun. *(They watch* WINSTON, *in a clinch with another girl.)* She's welcome. I ain't getting horny wiv him. *(Pause.)* Come on, let's dance.

*She pulls him into the crowd of dancers.* HARRY *is noticeably awkward.*

HARRY *(making conversation as they dance)*: How come you know Paulette?

MARCIA: We're in the same class.

HARRY: So you're . . . ?

MARCIA: Fifteen. Last month. And you?

HARRY: Eighteen.

MARCIA: Same as my boyfriend.

HARRY: Oh.

MARCIA: Ex-. I ain't going wiv him now.

HARRY *smiles. Rapid cuts establish* HARRY *gradually loosening up and starting to enjoy himself with* MARCIA. *The fast music turns slow, and, awkwardly at first but then closely, they hold each other. Her hand is on his neck, and finally they kiss – deep and slow. The camera moves in on* HARRY*'s eyes, which have been closed, but which now open in a look of horror. Cut to . . .*

*INTERIOR. A POORLY FURNISHED KITCHEN IN 1960S STYLE. DAY.*

*A middle-aged* MAN *and* WOMAN *are standing by the kitchen sink in an embrace. He is kissing her so hard that his head forces hers back, one hand in her hair, the other clutching her buttocks. They continue to kiss, oblivious to the arrival in the kitchen of a small* BOY, *aged about five, who – disturbed – stares and stares. Cut to . . .*

*EXTERIOR. THE REAR PAVED YARD OF A HOUSE. NIGHT.*

HARRY *and* MARCIA *are sitting on the back wall, smoking. From inside comes the sound of loud music.*

MARCIA: You all right?

HARRY: Just felt funny. Needed some air.

MARCIA: Not used to kissing, uh?

HARRY: I had this memory. From being a kid. Of my mum and dad kissing. You know, *really* kissing.

MARCIA: Yeh, well, people do, even parents.

HARRY: The next day he walked out and we never saw him again. We'd been happy till then.

MARCIA: So he was kissing her goodbye?

HARRY: Maybe. I just know the two things went together. First the kiss then the catastrophe.

MARCIA *(putting her hand on his arm)*: You not kissing me no more then?

HARRY: I didn't say that.

*They smile, lean into each other and kiss.*

*EXTERIOR. A BUSY, LITTER-STREWN SOUTH LONDON STREET. NIGHT.*

HARRY *and* MARCIA *are walking hand in hand. They stop outside a house we recognise from earlier, 439. Loud music from inside.*

MARCIA: Sounds lively now. I wonder if Paulette's still there.

HARRY: You wanna go in?

MARCIA: My mum'll be waiting up. You go if you like.

HARRY: Me? Nah.

*Shots of them walking, holding hands.*

*EXTERIOR. A QUIET STREET OF SMALL TERRACED HOUSES. NIGHT.*

MARCIA: That's my house. I'll be all right now.

HARRY *(his old awkwardness returning)*: Yeh, well. See you around then.

MARCIA *(disappointed)*: Yeh. See you around.

*She puts the key in her front door. He walks away.*

*INTERIOR. A TEENAGE BEDROOM. DAY.*

*A head under the covers* – HARRY *asleep. His mother* GRACE *enters, worried.*

GRACE: Tank de Lord. You *are* here.

HARRY: What?

GRACE: I never hear you come in. My heart was drumming with dread.

HARRY: What you on about, Mum?

GRACE: The fire. At a party. I just hear on the radio. They say some kids bin killed.

HARRY: Which party?

GRACE: New Cross Road.

*EXTERIOR. THE HOUSE IN NEW CROSS, NUMBER 439. DAY.*

*Firemen rolling up their hoses, policemen directing traffic, people standing in the street, bunches of cellophaned flowers. And a smoking, badly blackened building.* HARRY *stands staring up at the house.*

HARRY *(voiceover)*: I caught the bus up from Peckham to see – like a ghoul, or a trainee journalist, or because I thought Paulette might be one of the victims. A broad black stripe ran up the front of the house, and there were wisps of smoke puffing from the brickwork. By then thirteen teenagers were dead or dying, their bodies suppurating in Greenwich hospital or stretched out in Ladywell morgue. The police said Paulette wasn't on the list but I didn't believe them – to them all blacks look the same.

*EXTERIOR. THE FRONT DOOR OF MARCIA'S HOUSE. DAY.*

HARRY *knocks. A woman answers.*

WOMAN: Yeh?

HARRY *(agitated)*: Is Marcia in?

WOMAN *(shouting)*: Marcia!

*She disappears,* MARCIA *takes her place in the door.*

MARCIA: Oh, it's you.

HARRY: I've been down to the fire. Paulette was in there, right? She's dead, isn't she?

MARCIA: What are you on about? I spoke to Paulette ten minutes since.

*Long pause.* HARRY *looks embarrassed by his previous hysteria.*

HARRY: Oh, well, that's all right.

MARCIA *(her eyes filling, upset)*: No it ain't. Two girls from our school died. People are saying a racist threw a firebomb or something. It's terrible.

HARRY *puts his arms round her. They stay locked in an embrace but don't kiss.*

WOMAN'S VOICE *(from inside)*: Marcia! It's freezing with that door open. Get inside, girl.

HARRY *(disentangling)*: I'd better be off.

MARCIA: Bye then.

HARRY: Bye.

*He seems reluctant to go and she remains standing on the step.*

MARCIA: You going to ask me out then?

*EXTERIOR AND INTERIOR. SOUTH LONDON STREETSCAPES. NIGHT AND DAY.*
*A series of shots accompany the following voiceover, including a funeral procession;* HARRY *handing out anti-racist leaflets to passing shoppers;* MARCIA *and* HARRY *out walking alone by the river; the two of them sitting in a café with* PAULETTE; *then the two of them alone again – queuing for the cinema, dancing.*

HARRY *(voiceover)*: The New Cross fire. The night the thirteen kids died. The night that politicised me. The night I ended up with the wrong girl. Except that Marcia wasn't so wrong: only fifteen, true, but smart, ambitious, top of her class. She was going to go to art school. Or train as a doctor. Or be the new Aretha Franklin. She had big plans.

*EXTERIOR. THE STREET OUTSIDE A CINEMA. NIGHT.*
*The sign above the entrance says 'Chariots of Fire'.* MARCIA *and* HARRY *emerge from the foyer into the street, holding hands.*

MARCIA: All them students was so posh.

HARRY: East London Poly won't be.

MARCIA: I bet you'll like it, though. You're studious.

HARRY: Is that how you see me? *Studious?*

MARCIA: Yeh, quiet and studious. Don't knock it, Harry. It's why I like you.

*They laugh and walk off down the street arm in arm.*

HARRY *(voiceover)*: *Studious?* Her saying that made me feel pathetic – by now any other boy would have had sex with her – or tried to. But she *was* only fifteen and I worried what might happen. It was only when I went to Poly, and had my own room, that we could be alone together. We were taking it slowly even then. But in December she had her birthday. And one night in January . . .

*INTERIOR. STUDENT HALL OF RESIDENCE. NIGHT.*

MARCIA *in corridor knocking on door.*

HARRY *opens door and smiles.*

HARRY *and* MARCIA *sitting on bed – awkward kiss.*

HARRY *and* MARCIA *lying on the bed, semi-clothed.*

MARCIA *(naked except for bra and panties)*: I should be going.

HARRY *(naked except for briefs)*: You know what today is?

MARCIA: What?

HARRY: Our anniversary. It was a year ago. January 18th. Remember – you and me and Winston and Paulette.

MARCIA *(sombre)*: The night of the fire. *(brightening).* It was Paulette you fancied – admit it.

HARRY: Yeh, well. *(kisses her)* My mistake.

MARCIA: I do love you, Harry.

HARRY: And I love you.

*They clutch at each other's clothes and begin to make love.*

HARRY *(voiceover)*: It was as if we thought we could wind the clock back, snuff out the flames, revive the victims in their urns. It didn't work. We were both too nervous. And I worried I didn't really love her. But we did what had to be done, and that was that. There were a few other times; it wasn't just that once. But I was getting into my studies, and as winter turned to spring we began to drift apart.

*INTERIOR. A SEMINAR ROOM. DAY,*

HARRY *sits reading from an essay, while other students (all white) listen, and the tutor, a trendy-looking sociologist type in leather, nods approvingly.*

HARRY: Mrs Thatcher once claimed that the people of Britain were (I quote) 'really rather afraid that this country might be rather swamped by people with a different culture'. Notice how our supposedly plain-speaking Prime Minister can only express herself there with two nervy, pusillanimous gulps (*'rather . . . rather'*), as if horrified by her own sentiments. Surely she's right to be horrified. In the subtextual slime of her *swamp*, immigrants are seen as creatures of the bog, monstrous, misshapen, and sheathed in primeval mud. Yet not a single newspaper picked her up on this. When people talk about a crisis in contemporary journalism, that's why. However liberal-minded the British press, all the journalists are white. They'll condemn apartheid in South Africa but when there's racism in their own country they fail to see it.

HARRY *folds his essay up and puts it on the table.*

TUTOR: Excellent. Thank you. Now any comments on – sorry, I've forgotten your name.

HARRY: Harry Creed.

TUTOR: Any comments on Harold's essay, anyone?

*INTERIOR. A ROOM IN A STUDENT HALL OF RESIDENCE. DAY.*

HARRY *is sitting writing at a small desk, loud music is playing in the background.*

HARRY *(voiceover):* OK, I wasn't setting the world alight. But I was making progress. Until . . . *(A knock on the door.)*

HARRY *(calling out):* It's open.

MARCIA *enters, looking tense.* HARRY *seems surprised to see her – and not altogether pleased. The music continues to play loudly.*

HARRY: Hey, how you doing?

MARCIA: What do you care?

HARRY: I've been busy. Essays and stuff.

MARCIA: Sure. Me too. Turn that off, will you.

HARRY *(standing up, belatedly aware she's on a serious mission, turning music off):* What is it?

MARCIA: I'm pregnant.

HARRY: Pregnant?

MARCIA: Yeh, *pregnant,* as in a man and woman have sex and his sperm fertilises her egg. I've done the test, I'm thirteen weeks.

HARRY: But I thought . . . we only . . .

MARCIA: Yeh, well.

MARCIA *sits on the bed and puts her head in her hands.* HARRY *puts his arms round her. We see from his face how appalled he is, though he is trying to hide it from her.*

HARRY: You haven't thought of . . .

MARCIA: I'm not getting rid of it.

HARRY: Of course not, I didn't mean . . . *(look of resolve)* I'll stand by you.

MARCIA *(angry):* I don't want you to stand by me, I want you to want the baby.

HARRY *(defensive):* You're sure it's me who...

MARCIA *(angrier still):* I knew you'd be like this. *(stands up, ready to leave)* I shouldn't have come.

HARRY *(grabbing):* Hey, hey, you've got me wrong.

MARCIA: No, I've got you spot-on, Harry. I thought you were different. But you're just a young buck, like all the others. So much for *studious.*

*They both seem shocked by the last remark. It dissipates the anger.* MARCIA *sits down again. There's a mood of resignation – even though* MARCIA *is bitter.*

HARRY: Does your mum know?

MARCIA: Course.

HARRY: And?

MARCIA: I told her it could be several boys. I'd rather she called me a slut than know it's you.

HARRY: But maybe in time...

MARCIA: Yes, when she's calmed down, maybe I'll tell her you're the dad.

HARRY: How you going to cope?

MARCIA: I'll be OK. I'm bored with school anyways.

HARRY: I've not much money but . . .

MARCIA: I didn't come here to ask for money. I wanted to see if you still loved me. And now I know.

HARRY: You don't have to be like this, it's just . . .

MARCIA *(standing up):* I mean it, Harry. I've the baby to think of. I don't want it having a dad who don't want it – and who don't love its mum, neither.

*INTERIOR. LIBRARY. DAY.*

*Shots of* HARRY *studying.*

HARRY *(voiceover)*: Stephen was born last October. Six pounds twelve ounces. With forceps. I worked the dates out later. Exactly thirty-nine weeks after the first time – she'd got pregnant that night, one year on from the fire. I wasn't there when Marcia had the baby. In fact, I've only ever seen him once, from a distance. Of course, my mum and sisters know. And my friend Nat knows. But I don't want other people knowing. They'd only stereotype me – 'Got a girl of sixteen pregnant, these young bucks are all the same' – and I want to prove I'm not a stereotype.

*EXTERIOR. DAY.*

HARRY *stands in the street outside number 439, looking up.*

HARRY *(voiceover)*: I walk past sometimes, to remind myself where it all started. People leave flowers outside. I can still smell the scorched brickwork. And feel the fire burning in my heart.

*Screen fades. End.*

# Part 3

## *I Can't Talk Now*

30 December 1999

## *HARRY*

HARRY NEARLY missed out on Errol Winthrop. He was away the weekend the story broke and had been scrambling to make up for it since. Every day – and this was Day 12 – brought a new twist. But last night had been the breakthrough. His face in the bathroom mirror looked tired. Deborah's call was what woke him. Skip the office, she said, and go straight there. It wasn't far. If he cut through Deptford Church Street, it would take him twenty minutes. Or he could take the scenic route, along the Thames. Either way, he had time to kill. Orange juice, coffee, slice of toast. He'd caught up at last. Errol was his now. He had earned the right.

December 18 had been the start. He had gone to Paris the previous day – a bargain mini-break, first class, departing Friday, returning late Monday, £99. On the Eurostar going over he felt conspicuous, a lonely Moor among Inuits, and took offence when the guard asked to check his ticket. Chill out, he told himself, they're checking everybody's, no one's accusing you of being a stowaway, the illegal immigrants come in the other direction. He stayed in a tiny double by the Sorbonne – skylight, Toulouse-Lautrec print, half-bottle of Moët in the minibar – and *did* Paris like no one ever had before, as you do. There was the pretext of buying Christmas presents. But he knew that he was running away from something. And (harder to admit) that the thing he was running away from was Stephen.

Six months ago he'd finally called Marcia. This couldn't go on, he said. He felt bad about never seeing his son. Stephen was sixteen now. For years he'd sent him Christmas and birthday presents, and received photos and thank-you letters in return, but that was all. It was time to rebuild their relationship. '*Re*-build?' Marcia protested. 'I think you mean build.' But she was pleased, he could tell, and promised to get Stephen used to the idea – then in due course, if he was agreeable, they could meet. Progress was slow. She didn't want Stephen being unsettled with GCSEs coming up. He'd grown used to having no father, or to having a father who took no interest – and now this. It was agreed Harry should phone a few times, to estab-lish contact; even phoning would be more than he'd offered before. The calls were difficult. Regular pattern, every Sunday evening, but when they spoke only Harry spoke – Stephen had nothing to say. He was sixteen now, would be taking eight GCSEs next month, played basketball for the Quaggy Allstars, hoped to study law at university, and co-DJ'd Sunday house-and-bass nights at the Albany. But confronted with Harry, on the phone, he couldn't speak. At his age, Harry hadn't had a father not to speak to. But he understood Stephen's reluctance. Civility even to a regular dad was uncool and Harry hadn't been around in sixteen years. Harry allowed for that. He persevered. But Stephen's silences crackled with such parricidal intent that it was a relief to be put back on to Marcia. He felt unhappy. This was never going to work.

Then they met. Unchaperoned. On 16 October, a Saturday, the day before Stephen's birthday, at the McDonald's on Evelyn Street. Harry walked there via the Pepys Estate (in which, two months later, little Errol would go missing), arriving ten minutes ahead of time. Unsure what a boy of seventeen would want as a present, he had spread the risk by buying several (a Charlton Athletic football shirt, HMV tokens worth £30, two videos, an Elmore Leonard novel and a mouse mat). Twenty minutes passed. He sat alone with his carrier bag of goodies. A bunch of teenage boys came in, right age, right colour, and he looked for Stephen among them, before realising Stephen would be too embarrassed to bring friends. It was after they'd gone that he ambled in: six foot two, Levi's hanging off him, baseball cap, size thirteen trainers, mobile phone. He hesitated, spotting his father (the only black man in the place) but pretending not to. Harry got up, and tried to shake hands, but even that seemed to discomfit Stephen, so he concentrated on ordering two burgers. They sat at a table with their polystyrene boxes and talked about school, or rather Harry asked questions and Stephen one-word-answered him back. This is OK, Harry thought, he's just nervous, once he trusts me he'll open up: better nerves than the parricidal smoulder of those phone calls. Their burgers finished, Harry suggested a walk. The choice was Southwark Park or the river, so they chose the river. I should have taken him to a football match or something, Harry thought, but it was all right, they were out together, not talking much but walking side by side, heads down, hands in pockets, the son (as is the way) two inches taller than the father, but the family resemblance plain to anyone who cared to see. Then Stephen's mobile went off, and the silent boy became a noisy player, yo-ing with whoever it was, a friend, a girlfriend, a whole gaggle by the sound of it. Not that Harry could hear the words being said to Stephen but he could hear Stephen's responses, and what he heard made him feel, as he hadn't during the earlier silences and had succeeded in denying to himself through the months leading up to this meeting, *I do not know my son at all.*

Not *We've been estranged and I would like to get to know him better* but *I haven't the faintest fucking clue who he is.*

It was the same or worse when Stephen finished the call. Less tense now, he began to talk, voluntarily and at alarming speed, chucking out names that meant so little to Harry that Stephen might have been speaking in tongues. Of the rush of friends, singers, record labels, television programmes, websites, sports teams, music venues and south London clubs, not one was familiar to Harry. Before we meet again, he joked to Marcia later, I'll have put in six months mugging up on his hobbies. ('Hobbies?' Marcia said, incredulous. '*Hobbies.* That shows how little you know.') They parted with a handshake – no embarrassment this time. It hadn't gone badly. Indeed, according to Marcia, judging it by Stephen's mood that night, it had gone well. But it wasn't what Harry had envisaged. Instead of finding his son, he'd spent two hours with a stranger. And the strangeness was so disturbing to him – so accusing – he wasn't sure he wanted to see Stephen again. So though the phone calls on Sunday evenings continued, no further outings had taken place. In fact Harry had twice cancelled Stephen, the second time the weekend he went to Paris, a city he had long intended to visit but might never have got round to but for an anxiety, bordering on panic, at the prospect of being stuck in London with no reason not to see his son.

It was in the Channel Tunnel, late at night, on his way home, that he first came across the story – fifty words in a discarded tabloid on the Eurostar: *growing concern for three-year-old Errol Winthrop last seen outside his home in Deptford on Saturday evening . . . discovery of a child's trainer . . . frogmen searching the Thames . . . mother and three siblings being cared for by relatives . . . the Met 'cautiously optimistic'.* Next morning, the Tuesday, up early, he flicked on the television, where the story ran as the second item on the regional news. A perkily pious reporter stood windswept on the Pepys Estate, brushing her hair from her eyes as she spoke: 'This south London community is in shock today [shot of woman standing on doorstep with arms folded]. But hopes remain that little Errol [photo of a grinning toddler] will be found safe and well. Fiona Billingham, *Newsroom South-East,* Deptford.'

Harry left for work at once, imagining a perfunctory editorial conference the day before at which Mills, with his innate lack of news sense, had persuaded Deborah to give the story a miss. 'This kid in Deptford . . .' 'Yeh, I saw.' 'Shall we send someone down?' 'Nah. Leave it till tomorrow.'

By the time Harry reached the office, he had convinced himself the story was his.

'Good break?' Deborah said, from her glass sanctuary. The lid was still on her cappuccino. She could only just have beaten him in.

'So-so. You've seen about this child?'

'Sure. Suzie's working on it.'

'Shit. I was afraid you'd say that.'

'What's wrong with Suzie?'

There was plenty wrong with Suzie: green as the acres of her father's agribusiness in Hampshire, half her pieces ended on the spike, the only good thing she had ever written was the New Cross Fire story – and that was thanks to him.

'Nothing's wrong with Suzie,' he said. 'The story's more me, that's all.'

'We had to get on with it. And Mills suggested Suzie.'

Mills would, of course. He treated Suzie as his special project, 'bringing her on' like a seed in his hothouse. The Protégé Syndrome (Nat suffered from it, too): a condition, afflicting middle-aged men, in which sexual attractiveness is confused with intellectual talent. Mills was always talking of *prioritising* Suzie, to the point where the word had become a joke among the staff ('Prioritise anyone last night?'). Now he had given her Errol.

'I should be writing it,' Harry said. 'It's my kind of thing.'

The young Brockley accountant last seen on Brighton beach. The twenty-four-year-old from New Cross whose body rotted in a faulty mortuary fridge before they could establish cause of death. The Eltham fireman (father of four) knocked off his bike by an unidentified transit van. Over the past year, he had begun to specialise in deaths and disappearances.

'A missing child: is that really you?'

'In this case, yes.'

'Why?'

'He's black, for one thing.'

She smiled.

'Am I hearing you right, Harry? Whenever I ask you to cover a story about race, you say I'm stereotyping you.'

'I don't know if it *is* about race. I've just a hunch.'

She licked the chocolate from her cappuccino lid, weighing him up.

'The nationals are already on to it. Will people want it in the *Gazette*?'

'Someone else's tragedy – readers always like that, especially at Christmas. And if the child turns up safe, it's good tidings and general merriment. Perfect story, either way.'

'And big doesn't put you off?' she said, not ready to concede. 'I mean, good if it doesn't, it's time you spread your wings a bit, that's why I got you off the subs' desk – but you seem happier with smaller stuff.'

'In the past. Not any more.'

She lit up her first fag – her first *office* fag anyway.

'OK. But I'm not taking Suzie off the story. You'll have to find a way to share it out.'

That's what he did, joined Suzie down on the Pepys Estate, where she filled him in. Not that there was much to tell. Errol was still missing. The family were too distressed to talk to the media. The police had arranged a press conference for midday. Otherwise zilch. To her credit, Suzie didn't mind him muscling in: she owed him one, after all, and there was more to the story than she could cope with. Harry gathered some quotes from neighbours ('He's a smashing kid, was Errol, always beautifully turned out and that', 'Sharon's a single mum, yeh, but she don't leave her kids alone when she goes out', 'Makes you worried for your own, innit'). A couple of film crews were standing round by the tape that sealed off Errol's house. Beyond, near the front door, a forensics man crouched on the pavement, scraping street-dreck into a plastic bag. When a detective inspector ducked under the tape, Harry grabbed a word, or tried to. No, there'd been no sightings of the boy. No, an arrest didn't look on the cards yet. No, he couldn't say where Sharon Winthrop was staying, and he'd no message for readers of the (piddling) *Gazette*. The DI's hair was double-striped with grey, like a badger. 'Shitface,' Harry muttered, as the squad car whisked away.

It was a sour blustery day. He walked to the river path, where the Thames was brimming with gulls and tied-up barges, then turned south with the current, downstream. If the child were alive still, trapped in a drain or sluice-gate, he might come upon him and play the rescuer – the hack turned hero, subject of his own front-page story, the ultimate scoop. But really he was looking for colour. When kids went missing, the culprit was usually the dad, or stepdad, or a paedophile uncle, or a bent stranger. But a black child going missing, in an area infamous for racial attacks – surely colour had to be a factor. Only a week ago several British black celebrities – sportsmen, entertainers, politicians – had received an anonymous letter. 'When the clock strikes midnight on 31/12/99,' it read, 'the White Wolves will begin to howl, and when the wolves begin to howl the wolves begin to hunt. You have been warned. HAIL BRITANNIA.' Loner-loser looniness – too crackpot even for the BNP. And yet, and yet. He had a hunch. Not that he could articulate it yet. But still.

The police held their daily press briefings at the leisure centre in Oxestalls Road. The leisure centre had an oast-house roof, as though hops not fitness were its business. Now news was its business – the badminton nets had been taken down in the main sports hall and plastic chairs set out for the press. Holding briefings here, 'in the heart of the community', was part of the Met's 'access and visibility strategy', after the Stephen Lawrence debacle. Harry took a seat by the trestle table where three policemen were sitting, one of them, he noticed, the DI with the badger stripe of grey. The news that lunchtime came from the forensics team, who had found bloodstains on Errol's yard wall, 'venous' and in the pattern of a fine spray, which indicated a sudden and brutal attack. And then more bloodstains, and a trail of twigs, along the pavement, suggesting the child had been abducted or dragged away. One journalist asked about reports of a gang of white teenagers seen bullying small children only minutes before Errol disappeared. That's news to us, the DI said, from his trestle-table dais, but I've fifty men down there knocking on doors, so if there's anything to it we'll soon know. There were more questions, and more syrupy reassurances in reply. *Major investigation . . . no effort spared . . . frogmen dredging the Thames . . . hundreds of officers sacrificing holiday leave to join the search . . . numerous leads being followed up . . . anyone who saw anything suspicious urged to call the helpline . . . important not to give up hope.* Harry let it all wash over him. As he emerged from the leisure centre, a flock of birds passed over, like an oily cloth swished across the sky.

He and Suzie filed their story later that day. By the time the *Gazette* came out, the nationals were giving Errol double spreads. WILL HE BE HOME FOR CHRISTMAS? one tabloid asked. With his grin and curls, Little Errol had become a seasonal icon, displacing reports of the millennium bug and the opening of the Dome. The story kept finding fresh legs – PEPYS BOY DROWNING THEORY, PAEDOPHILE LINK IN ERROL CASE, SCANDAL OF THE SINK ESTATE – till taking a darker turn on Christmas Eve. SECRET LIFE OF PEPYS MOTHER read the headline in the *Sun*: 'Fun-loving Sharon Winthrop spent *long hours away from home* working in a *Mayfair massage parlour* that offers *sex romps to Middle East businessmen*, we can reveal.' The story flushed Sharon out of hiding. She appeared at the daily press briefing that lunchtime, smartly dressed, in dark glasses, flanked by her partner Louis and a WPC from the Met. The tabloid hacks were raring to crucify her – as the slag who gave blow jobs to ragheads while leaving Errol home alone; as the slut who'd had kids by four different fathers (and only the last of those fathers, Louis, white). But her faltering voice disempowered them: 'You never think it can happen to you. But it can. It does. Errol's Christmas presents are sitting under the tree ready to be opened. So I'm appealing to whoever took him away – and he knows who he is – to bring him back.'

Sharon looked good on grief, Harry thought. The weave of her hair. The long fingernails gnawing at her palms. The high-cheekboned and faintly exotic face. He felt guilty for noticing how attractive she was. And how hard she was trying to look composed. The eyes under the glasses might be reddened by the *Sun*, but there were no tears.

Ms Winthrop would take a few questions, they were told. A copse of arms sprung up.

How had she spent the past few days?

'Praying for Errol to come home. And recording the *Teletubbies* for him.'

So she'd not given up hope?

'In my heart I feel sure he's still alive.'

When she said that Errol's abductor knew who he was, did that mean *she* knew who he was?

'I've pointed the police in certain directions.'

This job of hers, in a massage parlour . . .

'A health and beauty salon. The stuff in the paper's all lies.'

So these so-called sex romps . . .

'Like I said, them papers is lying.'

Final question, DI Fleming said. Unable to think of one, Harry stared down at his notebook and tried not to imagine Sharon as a masseuse. Suzie, next to him, raised her hand.

How did Sharon feel, as a mother?

Harry bowed his head, outshamed by Suzie. *How do you feel?* The burning question of the age. *How do you feel?* The only question left, now the planet had been mapped and emotions were the last terra incognita. *How do you feel?* If Suzie hadn't asked, someone else would have. Still, the indecency of the question struck him as never before.

'I feel dead inside,' Sharon said. 'I just want my baby back.'

Deborah called Harry at home after watching the press conference on television. The *Gazette* had packed up for Christmas. The next issue wouldn't be till January. But she knew Harry would still be on the case.

'The mother didn't cry,' she said. 'I find that eerie.'

'Eerie as in suspicious?' Harry said.

'Eerie as in unmaternal.'

'It's probably the sedatives she's taking,' he said.

'She should get off them, then.'

'And fall apart? She could barely hold herself together as it was.'

'You think because she's pretty she must be innocent.'

'You think because she didn't cry she must be guilty.'

'Twenty quid she did it.'

'Twenty quid she didn't.'

'Done. Happy Christmas, Harry. See you in 2000.'

That night, on the news, Sharon was described as 'impassive'. And hopes of finding Errol alive were said to be 'fading fast'.

Harry spent Christmas Day in Deptford, at his mother's, along with his two sisters and their sons – Darren was six now, and little Daniel three and a bit (the same age, Harry realised, as Errol). While dinner was cooking, Harry walked the boys to the park. Lovable uncle was a role he enjoyed, compensation for having been an unloving father. But this was Deptford, not far from where Errol went missing, and he felt uneasy in the early-falling dark. The boys had barely warmed up – swings, ropes, slides, climbing frame – before he was ushering them away again.

It wasn't just Harry. The streets were deserted. A pall hung over the Dome and the millennium celebrations. Two years ago, with the death of Diana, the British had been taught about grief. Now Little Errol was teaching them about terror.

They were by the park gates when Harry's mobile rang. 'Happy Christmas,' Marcia said. 'I have Stephen for you.' Spoken like a secretary, though these days she was working as a radiographer. He could hear whisperings and muttered protests in the background. 'Thanks, Dad,' Stephen's voice said at last. Tell him for what, Marcia was saying. 'Thanks for the £50, Dad.' It was gratitude under duress, but the *Dad* made up for that. And you couldn't blame the boy. Harry hadn't seen him for two months – not as bad as failing to see him between the ages of nought and sixteen, yet in some ways worse, since it violated their reconciliation agreement, according to which they would get together every couple of weeks. He could hear Marcia nagging in the background ('Tell him about your presents . . . Describe what we're having for dinner . . . Just say something!'). It was hard to talk to someone who didn't want to talk. But that might change, if Harry worked at it. 'So when are we going to meet?' he said, as he stood by the park gates, shepherding his nephews home through the ruined streets, mindful how he had never shepherded his son. Stephen's response was an *uh* followed by some whispering and a 'You'd better talk to Mum. Here she is.' Just a minute, Marcia said, and he heard the volume drop, and a door slam, as she entered another room. Listen, she hissed, you've not seen him for ten weeks, Harry, what happened to the regular contact? I made him call to thank you for the £50, but if you're going to fuck him around like this we might as well go back to nothing, at least with nothing there were no ambiguities. I'm sorry, he said, I'm out with my nephews, I can't really talk now, it's not a good time. It never is a good time with you, Harry, she said, that's my point, you make no room for him, you came back into his life and then you dropped him, if you can't do better than that, just stay away. Then she put the phone down.

What could he say? For sixteen years he had denied his son's existence. Now he wanted to acknowledge it. But faced with the reality – the man-size, incomprehensible reality – he had lost his nerve.

On Boxing Day Errol slipped off the front pages and Harry went back to the Pepys. Out on the water, eight rowers and a bobbing cox hauled against the current. Closer to, by the tide wall, a gang of teenage boys hung round on bikes. Their surliness wasn't encouraging but Harry began asking questions, which they answered with questions of their own. From the press, was he? The *Gazette* was rubbish, innit? They were all rubbish, why did none of them print the facts, the truth what everyone knows, how Errol got took by an animal? Came out at night, and snap. Big thing it was, a wolf or Dobermann. Lived in the drains, under the river. Been prowling the Pepys for months. They'd never seen it themselves, like. But mates of theirs had. The kid at number 36 were there when it happened – heard the roar and screams, and ran, but not before he saw the thing lock Errol in its jaws and drag him off. Ridiculous, Harry thought, the little buggers must have seen me coming. But next day, at the lunchtime press briefing in the leisure centre, the Met issued copies of an updated forensic report. The blood found on the pavement outside Errol's house matched that of the missing toddler, the report confirmed. But it also noted in passing – the words made the hairs on Harry's neck stand up – that saliva and urine 'of a canine species' had been present on the pavement nearby. None of the other hacks seemed to notice. Why should they? – many people on the Pepys kept dogs as pets. But the Deptford Beast had been born in Harry's head.

He slept badly that night, haunted by the image of a creature in a maze, half-man, half-wolf. In his worst dreams, the creature appeared to be him.

In a week of roaming the Pepys, he had heard many different theories about Errol's disappearance. None was remotely plausible, let alone print-able in the *Gazette*, but he had recorded them in his notebook nonetheless.

- Errol had been killed in a satanic sacrifice.
- Errol had been strangled with a skipping rope, after an argument over a bar of Toblerone.

- Errol had been tied to the railway tracks, by two Bermondsey teenagers obsessed with the Bulger case.
- Errol had been kidnapped by NASA, who were planning to launch a child in space in the year 2001. The boy's face was being remoulded, his brain washed and his family history rewritten, so that when he became a famous child astronaut no one would know it was him.

'It's an end-of-millennium thing,' Nat said, when they met by the Thames that afternoon. 'A year ago no one could even *spell* millennium. Now it's all they think about. It was the same in AD 999. Plagues, floods, earthquakes, comets, rumours of imminent catastrophe. People feel out of control and at the mercy of sinister forces, so science flies out the window and super-stition flies in.'

Nat had his daughters with him. It seemed he'd spent Christmas on his own, but whatever the problem was he didn't want to talk about it. They walked together from Deptford towards Tower Bridge, over iron-railed lock bridges and along slopping wooden piers marked 'Residents Only'. Near Surrey Docks Farm, ignoring the waft of cage shit, the girls sat on the concrete tide wall and began to paint – 'My Christmas present to them,' Nat said, nodding at their matching paint sets. He had a few of their earlier efforts in a holdall and produced them for Harry. Top of the pile was a figure with an enormous belly: 'My Dad' it said. And underneath a view of a garden, with the orange smudge of an animal crossing the lawn: 'My House'.

'Good, eh?' Nat said, stuffing the drawings back. 'I'm hoping they'll grow up to be artists.'

'Remember that story I once wrote about a fox attacking a child?' Harry said, not really listening.

'Course I remember. The dodgy dad. You sent the whole thing up.'

'Maybe I was wrong to. There are people on the Pepys who say that's what happened to Errol.'

'That he was killed by a fox?'

'A large animal of some kind.'

'Come on, Harry, that's bonkers. Whatever happened will turn out to be banal. He'll have fallen in the Thames or under a car or been killed by his mum.'

'Why his mum?'

'His father or stepfather then. Something involving sexual jealousy anyway – with the child ending up the victim.'

'The police think it could have been a paedophile.'

'They would,' Nat said. 'Priests, teachers, sports coaches, librarians, everyone's suspected of being a paedophile, these days – abusing children is the new holocaust. You should hear Libby on the subject.'

'Really? What does she say?'

But Nat was off on a riff ('Every age has its story and paedophilia is the story of ours') and didn't elaborate.

'I'd like to think the kid's still alive,' Harry said, 'but I've this sense of evil.'

'I don't believe in evil,' Nat said.

'Not even nameless evil?'

'Especially not nameless. I believe in finding words for things.'

'Me too. But some things can't be explained.'

'What do you think happened to Little Errol, Uncle Harry?' one of the girls asked, without looking up from her painting. They had been listening of course. He was touched by 'Uncle' but disturbed to think they'd heard the stuff about paedophilia. Abuse of children wasn't a subject for children.

'I don't really know,' he said.

'Is he dead?'

'I don't know that, either.'

'Enough of Little Errol,' Nat said. 'It's getting cold.'

They walked on to the end of Limehouse Reach, then took a bus back to Lewisham. From the upper deck Harry spotted a search party near Southwark Park – volunteers moving in line through waste ground, in what the evening news would call 'a systematic combing of the area'.

'Any plans for New Year?' he asked Nat, before they went their separate ways.

'The girls want to go the Dome.'

'Yes please, Daddy, yes please.'

'It's fifty-seven quid for a family ticket. Ridiculous price.'

Harry had been wondering about taking Stephen to the Dome. Or would Stephen, at seventeen, find that uncool?

'Say hi to your mum for me,' he said, kissing the girls goodbye.

Next day the search for Errol was scaled down. He had been gone ten days. He wasn't coming back. His mother and three sisters *did* come back, to a wall of flowers where their maisonette had been. The cameras were there for their return. 'I'll never give up hope till he's found,' Sharon said, a framed photograph of Errol in her hand. 'I've recorded the *Teletubbies* for him and I know in my heart he'll be home to watch.' It felt like closure. There was nowhere left for the story to go.

That was yesterday morning. Today was a day off and he'd been thinking about getting together with Stephen. Then late last night he'd seen the catchline on Teletext: PEPYS BOY: NEW TWIST. There were no details but 'a significant announcement' was expected – and this morning it had come. 'Don't be late, Harry,' Deborah said, when she rang him half an hour ago. 'Be there.'

Be there! As if he'd be anywhere else.

## 2

## *ANTHEA*

CLOUDS ENVELOPED the summit but in the valley there was no rain. Anthea left at first light, with boots, waterproofs, compass, Kendal mint cake, Wainwright guide and a one-inch map. Both Skiddaw or Blencathra were reachable from Applethwaite, but Skiddaw was the closer and she had promised to be back by lunch. The house lay tiny in the curve of the mountains, like a surfer under a giant wave. But for a handful of sheep, she was alone.

Her mother had moved to Applethwaite six years ago, to 'make a new start'. At the time Anthea had little expectation of it working. Applethwaite was a tiny village frequented only by fell-walkers. And Bella's previous experience of the outdoor life hadn't extended beyond cocktails on the patio. As it turned out, though, the solitude of Applethwaite was her redemption: no neighbours meant no socialising and no excuse to drink. Only one in seven alcoholics genuinely recover, Anthea read, but the people at the Grange had done the job, or fear of destitution had, and when she visited she could detect no relapse – no gin bottles hidden in cereal packets or wine boxes in the tumble dryer. These days Bella worked mornings at a Keswick travel agent; it was enough to live simply and get by on, and a widowed ex-alcoholic ex-actress living in Cumbria couldn't be choosy. The little things that used to irritate Anthea sometimes resurfaced – Bella's incapacity to listen, for instance, and her desperation to see her daughter married off. But after the traumas of the binge years, it was almost comforting to have the niggles back. Better a boring mother than a crazy one. Tomorrow she'd go back to London with an easy mind.

It was cold above the first fell, with a hint of drizzle. Sheep grazed on tussocks, below the shale. The clouds were plush and frilly-bottomed, like armchairs in an old people's home. A grey, easy day, but it would be different up on the peaks, where a breeze could become a gale and drizzle a stinging hailstorm. One murky evening, two or three years ago, she had missed the path on the way down, and been forced to retrace her steps, and spent an hour, soaked and torchless, descending through darkness guided by cairns. The experience had excited rather than scared her. The peaks drew you on. That's where truth lived, up with the trig points, set like altars among shale and snow. Not that Anthea believed in God. But mountains gave her a lift. She had come to depend on these visits.

Beyond the second col the wind got up, and she pulled her hat tighter over her ears. She was climbing to clear her head – as though the hills could tell her what to do. Remember those dreams of making the world a better place: how could helping Mr Fell eradicate germs from London restaurants ever fulfil them? She had no great estimate of her talents but there must be better ways to employ them or better places, abroad, to make herself useful. In recent months she had been haunted by a photograph of a Kurdish schoolgirl setting herself ablaze outside the Greek Embassy in London. Necla Kanpeper, just fifteen years old, with her head on fire and her fingers splayed for victory. A martyr in jeans and trainers. Haloed in gold like a quattrocento madonna. Police had snuffed the fire out with their jackets, but Necla's body would be scarred for life. Anthea pitied the scars but envied the conviction. To put your body on the line like that! To care that much! 'The Kurds have no friends but the mountains,' Necla had told reporters. Climbing Skiddaw, Anthea felt she understood.

It wasn't just the day job that had proved a dead end, it was the writing. At least the fantasy of being published was over now, thanks to Mike Thingy. Her cheeks under the bobble hat reddened at the memory. Mike was an old friend of Nat's and Nat had pushed and pushed her to exploit the contact. A month ago, she had finally sent the typescript to Mike at Hotline. *Foxed* she had retitled it. She was amazed to get a phone call three days later. The little she knew of publishing, you were lucky to hear back within a decade. Yet here was Mike Thingy – or here was his trilling personal assistant, on his behalf – inviting her to lunch the following week. Would he order champagne, drink to her brilliant debut and offer £250,000? She would have to take the day off but Mr Fell owed her masses of leave and surely Mike Thingy wouldn't have phoned unless he liked the book. 'Yes,' she told his assistant, 'that'll be great.'

She had planned to arrive a chic fifteen minutes late, but the train into

Charing Cross ran on schedule for once and she killed time inspecting jacket blurbs in Waterstone's. 'Formerly a feature writer for *Harper's & Queen* . . . now divides her time between London and Provence' seemed pretty typical. 'Formerly a tree officer . . . divides her time between Thamesmead and Woolwich' hadn't the same ring. The Strand milled with groups of office workers on early Christmas lunch outings. At 1.03 she walked down the stairs of Volpone's. It looked like a basement office: shiny steel, hard seats and overhead lighting. If there had been keyboards instead of cutlery, she would not have been surprised. Most of the diners were talking into mobiles or scratching their organisers rather than eating. Mike Thingy was an exception, but only because he hadn't shown up. Anthea was directed to a minuscule table next to Toilets This Way. People stared as she passed, until they recognised her unrecognisability and resumed not having lunch. It looked as if she too would not be having lunch. They were all going to not have lunch together, at separate tables of one. Slowly the other halves began to trickle in, apart from Mike. She ordered a tomato juice to calm her nerves. Waiting was something she was used to: waiting for Jake to call, or Old Nod to sack her, or Nat to come round, or her father to return from the dead and tell her it wasn't her fault – Mike Thingy was just another late-running male. Unless she had come to the wrong place. No, Volpone's, Hillingdon St, her diary said, and his secretary had taken her mobile number, just in case. At 1.39, as she was preparing to pay up and go, a twelve-year-old with spiky hair and pink cheeks came up to the table and said she must be Anthea. She took him for a courier bearing an apology, but he said he was Colin Someone, an associate of Michael Thingy, and would she please call him Col for short. He didn't look flustered and made no excuse for Mike Thingy's absence – nor for turning up forty minutes late.

He ordered two starters and she, not wishing to look greedy, followed suit. So she'd like to know more about publishing, he said, and began to talk. Despite his boyishness, he had been in the business for several years and had witnessed many a takeover and merger. The great challenge for the modern-day publisher was to find new talents you could invest in at an early stage of their career, he said, the business being so tough out there, the pressures so fierce. Not that having to compete meant publishing trash. But no editor could expect a free ride any more and he, Col, saw nothing wrong in aspiring to commercial success – best-sellers weren't *always* tacky and anyway their profits paid for the mid-list authors you believed in. She gazed at him dutifully between mouthfuls. There was no sign of her typescript, but presumably he had notes to consult or a photo-graphic memory. Over the second starter, he embarked on a run of gossipy anecdotes, which she might have enjoyed if she had known the people involved and hadn't been waiting for word of *Foxed*. It dawned on her that lunch was a pleasant preamble before they went back to his office and met Mike. She relaxed and ordered summer pudding: however many calories she had absorbed from the smoked salmon, mushroom risotto and two glasses of Chablis, her nerves would have burned off more. The writers Hotline took on weren't just quality writers, he said, but knew how to put themselves across, how to communicate, how to look good, how to [laugh] be an ornament to a dust jacket, which didn't mean looking *glamorous* neces-sarily but did mean having some kind of story: sex, humour, mystery, sagacity, the glow of having come through suffering, it didn't matter which but the face on the jacket should tell you what to expect inside – something bold, beautiful, accessible, inviting.

She couldn't help but notice how closely Colin was examining *her* face and jacket. The jacket was an embarrassment, since she had splattered walnut oil on it. And the face was doubtless etched with anxiety. Finally the conversation turned to her: where did she work, where did she live, was she married, how come she knew Mike Thingy? He didn't seem inter-ested in her answers and twice broke off from listening to send text messages. There was an undercurrent of sexual attentiveness all the same. He was young, and she was young, and after a couple of hours in the office looking at *Foxed*, what was to stop them buying champagne and going back to his place? All this was lurking over the double espressos, enough for her to panic back and forth between the boxes that said sleeping with him would/wouldn't help her career. And still he texted and stared. In the Ladies, she dabbed water on the jacket stain and asked her reflection what the odds against topping the best-seller charts were: 'Mirror, mirror on the wall . . .' She turned her profile to the glass, and imagined it gracing his autumn catalogue.

I must have been drunk, she thought, three weeks and two hundred-odd miles away from the fiasco. Opening the Ordnance Survey map, sheet 90, she held it up, as though to shut out the rest of the scene. But the map, knotty with contours, was no help: beyond Skiddaw it showed two peaks called Great Cockup and Little Cockup.

Back at the table, events had taken a turn for the worse. Colin settled the bill, and said he must get back to the office – it had been nice meeting her, and here was his business card, and if she'd like to call sometime perhaps they could meet up and get to know each other better. Oh, and Mike would in any case be in touch about *Foxy*. *Foxed*, she corrected him. Sorry, he said, of course – but didn't she think *Foxy* a more selling title? She wasn't sure it suited the content, she said. Perhaps she was right, he said – he had to admit he hadn't yet read the typescript. But certainly Mike would read it, once he had a moment, or ask one of his assistants to read it. With so many meetings to get to, Mike usually ended up delegating – and even then the slush pile grew higher by the day. But when the team at Hotline *loved* a book, and the sales department gave their backing, and terms were agreed with an agent, then everything swung into action, publicity, marketing, interviews, serialisation, the process was tremendously exciting, and he had his fingers crossed for *Foxy* – sorry, *Foxed*! – though they must be realistic and he did gather it was a book of short stories, which wasn't *necessarily* a disaster but she should realise the market for story collections was very limited these days and that a full-length novel would have a far greater chance of acceptance, say 1 in 1,000 rather than 1 in 100,000, and even if, speaking hypothetically, everyone in the team felt her stories were worth making an exception for, there would still be the problem of finding a niche. They weren't by any chance *children's* stories? No, she said. That was a pity, he said – the success of the Harry Potter books had made everyone aware of the enormous potential in the children's market, and if they could present hers as stories for *children of all ages from eight to eighty* that would make the marketing so much easier. They're a bit like fairy tales, Anthea said, but strictly for adults. Mmm, that sounded promising, he said, faintly erotic even, which was why *Foxy* seemed to him such a good title – but if she was really adamant against using it there was a young female author he knew whose work-in-progress the title *Foxy* would suit rather well and to whom, if Anthea didn't object, he might suggest it. He stood up. So good to meet, he said. Mike had told him she would appreciate the chance to learn about publishing.

They ascended together into day. Since he was running late, he trusted she wouldn't mind if he took the first cab. Which she didn't, and he did, and that was that.

She looked at his business card. *Colin Tosher, Associate Marketing Manager, Hotline Books*.

The wind blew down from Skiddaw to carry her shame away. 'Arsehole!' she had shouted on the train back to Woolwich, unsure at whom the word was directed – herself, Colin, Mike Thingy or Nat. Mike clearly took her for a starry-eyed bimbo, one so grateful to meet a publisher that she wouldn't object if he sent a marketing minion to teach her about profit margins – in return for which Mike need offer zilch, not even the courtesy of reading her typescript. Why had he formed that impression? Which arsehole was to blame? She consoled herself that it could have been worse. Colin might have left her to pay the bill. He might have asked her back to his flat. He might have been sent to tell her *Foxed* had been turned town. As to the last, taking no chances, she sent Mike Thingy a card next morning, asking him to bin the typescript because (lies) she wanted to revise it. *Foxed* turned up in the post just before Christmas, unbinned but also unread, with a note from Mike to say he hoped she would resubmit it, though not to him, since he was moving to another division, Reference. Excellent, she thought: I need never refer to you again.

Now, under her bobble hat, she could see the funny side. Thanks to Mike, she had avoided becoming a widget in a fiction factory – a package, a product, a consumer commodity. Yesterday's visit to the Keswick bookshop had completed the process of disillusion. It wasn't just the sight of all the books sitting on the shelves. It was the leaflet she had picked up, inviting aspirant writers to sign up for Wolverine Lodge, 'a horizon-broadening residential centre, uniquely situated on windswept moors, which offers up to 80 creative writing courses a year, with places for up to 20 students on each. Come blow the cobwebs from your mind!' What struck Anthea wasn't the blurb but the numbers. Many universities and colleges also offered creative writing programmes, full- and part-time. Say there were a hundred such programmes in the UK, each with thirty new students every year. Add those to the residential courses, and even allowing for overlaps and dropouts that meant 5,000 people doing creative writing courses in any one year – 50,000 over a decade, plus thousands of other hopefuls scribbling away in private on their own. When she had first joined Nat's class, she saw writing as the preserve of introverts and oddballs. But suddenly everyone she knew was working on a book. Rachel was. Mr Fell's wife was. The fitness coach at Arches was. And doubtless the postman, the electric-meter man, Old Nod, the waitresses at the Parakeet restaurant, and her mother's cat Suttee were all working on their books. It was great. Everyone had a book in them. But maybe in was better than out. Because who was going to buy all these books? Which wannabes could spare the time to read someone else's stuff when consumed by the drama of writing their own? If she'd been a literary genius, Anthea might have stuck at literature. But only Nat had told her she was a literary genius. And that was just to get her into bed.

At Broad End, the ground fell away before the last ascent. Crossing the boggy streambed, she watched the clouds pour off the summit, like steam from a kettle. She could see other walkers rising in her wake – bright dots of red and orange against the grey of Derwent Water. Her mother would be awake now and 'pottering', faintly resentful of being left alone when Anthea was leaving tomorrow. But they would have lunch together in the Applethwaite cottage, then drive to Keswick to see the solicitor, and tonight they had booked a table at the Cygnet for eight thirty. It wasn't easy being with her mother for as long as five days. But they had survived Christmas without a major falling-out, and shopped in Ambleside, and watched the hill-cupped lake water turn pink near Rydal Mount. And getting Daddy's photos out last night, laughing and crying over him, had been cathartic. She felt better for coming to the Lakes. And for this head-clearing walk. Through the gaps in the clouds, she caught glimpses of England laid out below – in miniature, as if from a plane – and hints of sea, to the west, stretching away to wider horizons.

The final path to the summit was a narrow zigzag up icy scree. Her tendons ached from the steepness, but it wasn't far now, and if the sky cleared the view would be spectacular – Blencathra close by, and Helvellyn to the south, and the light rippling to Glaramara and the Jaws of Borrowdale. That the clouds should lift a moment wasn't much to ask. She deserved a moment of clarity. For the world to open up and her place in it become apparent at last. The new millennium was nearly here.

### 3

### JACK

WHERE THE milk crates were stacked outside the village shop, a FOR SALE sign had gone up.

'So it's true,' Jack said. 'You're selling up.'

'We put it on the market last week,' Ramsden said, breathing hard. Funny time to choose, Jack thought – dead of winter, Siberian gusts across the Fens, the distraction of Christmas and the millennium. But Mona, Ramsden's wife, had had enough. And Ramsden was said to be ill in some way. Even the effort of handing Jack his *Telegraph* seemed to exhaust him.

'Sorry to hear that,' Jack said. Dust lay on the Heinz soup cans. In his black suit and tie, he felt overdressed.

'There's not the custom,' Ramsden said.

The lack of custom wasn't surprising. Ramsden had little talent for shop-work and even less for bonhomie.

'Any offers yet?' Jack said.

'Nope.'

'Sellers' market. They'll be queuing up.'

'For the house, maybe. Not the shop.'

At a parish council meeting three months before, the Ramsdens had launched an SOS campaign – Save Our Shop. 'If people buy their news-papers and a few basic groceries here,' Mona said, 'then we can keep going.' Mona's dress was the same speedwell blue as her eyes. She had never met Nancy but always asked after her health. 'It's not for our sake, it's for the village,' she pleaded to the rows of wooden seats. 'Let's keep the shop alive.' 'Hear, hear,' Jack said, as she sat down. Mr Wissell, the local historian, said there'd been a shop in Frixley since 1903, and that they ought to start planning a centenary. Then the mutterers took over. 'The Harchope super-market is cheaper', 'There's nothing on the shelves', 'All you get when you go in is tattle and gossip'. Gillian Isaacson, a cellist with the LSO, said the shop was the lifeblood of the village, but she was a weekender and her views didn't count. 'If the owners can't make a fist of it, that's *their* problem,' said Mr Blackwood, whose farm shop stood to benefit if the Ramsdens failed. Mona's eyes filled. Next day she let it be known that certain villagers – 'them as kicked us in the teeth' – were no longer welcome at her counter. She had since taken a job with a solicitor, leaving Ramsden to run things down. Opening hours had been reduced. The alcohol shelf, once merci-fully well stocked, had dwindled to quarter-bottles of Bell's.

'What about the post office?' Jack said.

'The licence runs out in March.'

The post-office section was separate. When people came in with parcels or pensions books, Ramsden – tutting and sighing – had to leave his counter to unlock the glass cubicle in the corner. Most villagers now drove to Harchope for their postage stamps rather than endure his gloom.

'So where will you live?' Jack asked.

'We're looking up Norwich way,' Ramsden said. 'We don't much care.'

At the end of their first year Mona had given Jack a coffee cake, as a thank-you for his custom. Now a second year had passed and the Ramsdens were going. The shop had had four owners in seven years.

The bell rang over the door and Felix blew in, formerly the village postman. In 1954 the top of his left ear had been bitten off by the GP's Alsatian – it looked like a half-eaten biscuit. He was ninety-odd now but walked the half-mile to the shop every morning.

'Sad day,' Felix said.

'Yes,' Jack said. 'Ramsden just told me.'

Felix looked confused.

'I'll be there,' he said.

'Ah, church, yes, sorry.'

'Mona sends her sympathies,' Ramsden said, softening. Jack assumed word would get round, but the shop had been closed over Christmas and the old village intimacy had gone. There were people who didn't know who Nancy was – who Nancy had been.

'Many family coming?' Felix asked.

'My daughters, anyway.'

'Sasha and Ischia,' Felix said, to show he remembered their names.

When he was postman, the girls used to tease Felix and he'd tickle them back. You didn't worry about abuse or abduction then – kids didn't go missing like this one in the papers.

'April 16th and October 23rd are their birthdays,' Felix said, showing off.

'Spot on.'

Memory like an elephant; innocence of a lamb. Perhaps the secret was having no children of his own.

'Morning, Jack, morning, Felix, is that my *Mail?*' Nelly said, pushing through the door.

Nelly worked night shifts at the young offenders institute (female section), and would be on her way home to bed. Three customers at once: if the shop stayed as busy as this all day, it would make a fortune, Jack thought.

'Whose pup is that outside?' Nelly said.

'Mine,' Jack said. 'Christmas present.' Thumper was a black Labrador, twenty weeks old. Sasha and Ischia had ordered him months ago, then worried about the timing. Not to worry, Jack said – a dog would give him something else to think about.

'He don't like being tied up, do he?' Nelly said.

Thumper was whining from the milk crates. Jack would have brought him in but for Ramsden's new notice, NO DOGS. Mrs Lee, from the big house, who used to bring her Pekinese in a shopping basket, had already taken her custom elsewhere.

'House-trained is he?' Nelly said.

'I'm working on it,' Jack said. Pissing all over the place, if the truth be known.

'You should have bought a beagle to go hunting with you.'

'No point, eh, Jack,' Felix said. 'Them MPs in London are going to ban it.'

Jack nodded grimly. An outright ban looked more and more likely. Luc, in his smarmy Christmas card, had expressed incredulity: 'If the worst happens you can move to France and hunt wild boar with me, old friend.' In Spain and Italy, buggers with guns happily shot down songbirds and no one stopped *them*.

'And how's Na—?', Nelly asked Jack before Felix nudged her and butted in.

'The funeral's at three – are you coming, Nelly?'

'I'm so sorry, Jack,' Nelly said. 'I didn't know. When did . . . ?'

'Before Christmas. But the vicar couldn't do it till today.'

A carol started up on Ramsden's CD player, despite it nearly being new year: *O the rising of the sun / And the running of the deer.*

On 20 December, early morning, in day-dark like this. The last stroke. Or mini-stroke. Less than a week after the one that put her back in hospital. There was a fold-up bed with a skinny mattress next to hers, and for five nights he lay on it, monitoring her breath, watching the dials, exhausting himself. 'Go home and get some sleep – there's no immediate danger,' the doctor said, and doctors are supposed to know. So on the sixth night he went home and slept. The phone rang at 4 a.m. He knew before they told him. No point rushing over, though he did. Peacefully, they said. But no one was with her at the vital moment, the end of vitality. He had failed her with the first stroke and then with the last.

'She'd suffered enough,' Jack said.

'She was a good woman,' Nelly said.

'The best,' Felix said.

Whether they meant it was beside the point. They were trying to show community still counted for something, that despite the closing of shops, and loss of jobs, and cutting of bus routes, and away-drift of children, and government plans to outlaw their pleasures and traditions, a village was the best place to live.

*The holly bears a prickle / As sharp as any thorn.*

He pretended to look for a packet of biscuits.

'You on tomorrow night?' Donal asked Nelly.

'For my sins,' she said. 'The guv'nor's organised a firework display. The girls will be racketing round till God knows when.'

Nelly paid for her paper and left. Jack lingered on in sympathy, elder to elder, while Felix emptied his basket on the counter: bread, can of beans, corned beef, custard, two bananas, packet of fig rolls, three Granny Smiths. He had been using the village shop for seventy years. Old Reg, with the harelip, was the same; and Ruth Kilbane, whose disabled son had died at thirteen – the last of their breed, the last of the indigenes, or indigents. However steep its prices, they would not give up the shop. But now the shop was giving up on them.

*The holly bears a bark, / As bitter as any gall.*

'That it, Felix?' Ramsden said.

'Bottle of sherry, too.'

'We don't stock sherry any more. When do you need it?'

'Tomorrow. To see the New Year in.'

'I can't promise for tomorrow,' Ramsden said. 'We close at midday.'

Mona would have helped out – driven to the off-licence, given Felix her own sherry bottle, anything to oblige. But even goodwill hadn't saved the shop. They were closing everywhere – Drayshot, Thedderton, Barsham.

On impulse, Jack bought a packet of bacon. He rarely bothered with cooked breakfast, but today was special. Today they would be burning Nancy.

The rashers damp against his heart, he yanked Thumper the half-mile home.

In the kitchen, on Radio 4, Tony Blair was talking. 'We will never be a run-of-the-mill people doing run-of-the-mill things,' he said. True enough, Jack thought, opening the bacon. What time did I order the hearse for again?

Odd how comforting it is to cook, he reflected, over the gas: the sizzle, the smell, the smooth black hollow of the pan. He had last seen Nancy on Christmas Eve, in the Chamber of Rest – a touch of his fingertips to her cold brow, before Chilton, the undertaker, closed the lid. The only smell was candlewax, though they must have used formaldehyde to preserve her. Like curing bacon. He sliced a tomato and tossed its red halves in the fat. He felt no horror at the thought of Nancy catching alight; it wouldn't be her. The bacon slid in the pan, easy-peasy. Whoever invented non-stick must have made a fortune. A Mr Teflon was he? The men whose gadgetry filled the household – the inventor of the grapefruit knife, the oven hood, the microwave, the coffee grinder – were rarely household names. Tomorrow's New Year's honours list would be the same as it always was, full of cack-handed artists and tone-deaf musicians and wastrels who couldn't *make* something to save their life.

Nothing much in the *Telegraph*. FTSE up to 6835. Another rise in house prices. Indian airliner hijack negotiations continue. And a list of newly popular children's names, culled from this year's christenings: Callum, Ryan, Ciaran, Liam, Brandon, Shannon, Niamh, Siobhan – Jesus, Mary and Joseph, why was everyone *Irish* these days?

He flipped the bacon over with his fingers. No need for the fish slice. That happened as you got older: you became less sensitised. Nancy's old metal frying pans gripped anything inside them – you used to have to scour them with Brillo pads after use. Brillo pads! Redundant now, but in their day they too had been a breakthrough. One invention displaced another. One generation gave way to the next. Would Raven & Son be prospering if he had fathered a son to bring in new ideas? There was Marcus but Marcus wasn't family and though less useless at his job than Jack had expected he hadn't turned the business round. A floorboard creaked upstairs – one of the girls waking. There were rashers enough for both of them, but you could be sure they would want only coffee.

He wasn't yet used to Nancy being gone. It was like a pair of reading glasses – long after you removed them, you could still feel their impress in your hair.

Britain, Blair was saying, in that insincerely sincere voice of his, must be a *beacon* to the world. Stupid bloody image. Since the Second World War the only beacon Britain had been was a Belisha beacon, a warning to the world what not to become. Who wrote these speeches? Some minder probably. Every word Blair spoke was carefully scripted for him. Still, he had found time to get his wife pregnant. Child number four. Another son, they said. You had to hand it to him. The man had balls.

Jack cracked an egg open and watched it whiten. Count your blessings. He had no son to boast of but Sasha and Ischia were lovely daughters. For sixty years he had been loved, tended to, *babied*. Hadn't Michelle once made some bitter remark about him having it all too easy? She should see him now, on his rock of grief, while the steamship *Life* voyaged on without him. It will get better, everyone said. It already was better: no more rushing to and from hospital, no more conversing with an empty shell. But feeling better also made you feel worse. There was the guilt at not being there when Nancy went, then the guilt at feeling relieved she had gone.

As a rule, he avoided wakes. To stand round more stiffly than a corpse, trying to think consoling thoughts, could be worse than your grief for the deceased. But this was Nancy. He couldn't not ask people back to the house. Her friends expected it. Her daughters insisted on it. It was his duty.

The morning walk had knackered Thumper, who lay sleeping in his basket, oblivious to the smell of Jack's cooking. Bacon, egg, tomato, mush-rooms, fried bread: in hotels they called it a full English.

The girls would soon be down to join him. But this time tomorrow they'd be gone again, off to their New Year parties. A meal for one, in an empty room: this was where life led you. He sat at the wooden table and ate his full English, while the wind sighed under the door.

## 4

## NAT

'DEAD?' HE asked.

'Dunno,' she said. 'Maybe just shock.'

They were heading north on the M11, Nat at the wheel, Libby beside him, the girls in the back listening to storytapes. Roadworks, he thought, when the traffic slowed, until he saw the old Rover. It was resting against the crash rail in the outside lane of the opposite carriageway; it seemed to have parked there. There was no damage, only a gently dented front wing. But police had stopped the southbound traffic, and the cars ahead of him, with their flashing hazard lights, had slowed to look. In the instant of passing, the driver's frozen eyes stared back at Nat's. His chin lay sideways on the dashboard, wedged under the slope of windscreen. He looked at peace, unbloodied, open-mouthed, mildly surprised. It was as though he had pulled up for a snooze.

'Dead, definitely,' Nat said.

'What?' Hannah said, her voice overloud not from excitement or a desperation to be heard but because she was wearing headphones.

'Nothing,' Libby said. 'Go back to your tape.'

'Probably a heart attack,' Nat said, sotto voce.

'Or a stroke.'

Nat tried to shut out the image. The Rover's windscreen had been an open coffin, the passing traffic a procession of mourners. Eighty years old, by the look of him. There should be a law against pensioners driving cars. The newspapers were always carrying stories: old chap caught speeding wrong way down dual carriageway; old lady circles M25 three times, unable to find exit. But sixty-five no longer seemed so far off. Uncle Jack must be there already and would hate not having a car to get about in. Nat could remember the exhilaration of being driven in Jack's MGB, in the days before seat belts – the wind through your hair, the smell of leather, the teeth-chattering rattle over cattle grids. Or was he thinking of his father, who had also briefly owned a sports car? Everyone said they looked like twins, though Ronnie was five years older. It had been several years since Nat last saw Uncle Jack. He used to be ruddy and youthful, but by now the shine must have worn off.

The wind buffeted from blank fields, forcing Nat to grip the wheel more tightly. The waxy face in the windscreen kept gusting back to him, in cold repose. The longer he drove, the more dead it became, till rigor mortis set in. And the more it looked like a Raven face, Uncle Jack's or even his father's. Ronald Raven: back in the eighties, when Reagan was US President, saying the name became a party piece – *My father's called Ronald Raven.* Ronnie, to everyone who knew him. Twelve years since he died, though as a father (meaning someone who talked to, played with or enjoyed contact with his offspring) he had been dead for over thirty. Nat hadn't gone to the funeral. They told him about it only afterwards. He knew as little about his father as he did about the face in the windscreen.

'Are we there yet?' Rose asked.

'Still a while, sweetie,' Libby said. 'We'll stop for lunch soon. How's your tape?'

'All right,' she said.

'Why are farmers so horrid to the foxes?' Hannah asked.

'Farmers think they're a pest.'

'Do you think that, Mummy?'

'They can do a lot of damage.'

*The Fantastic Mr Fox.* A favourite with the girls, if not with Nat. The eponymous hero made him feel guilty and accused. If it were *his* family under siege from the likes of Boggis, Bunce and Bean, would he be as brave and resourceful? He liked to think so. But why, then, had he been disloyal? Why hadn't he held things together, instead of (in Libby's parlance, the world's parlance) running off with a woman half his age? The accusation was unfair. He hadn't run off. And an occasion like today's proved they were still a family and he still a father, not a fantastic father but good enough. The atmosphere in the car was funereal, Libby silent except when spoken to, the girls gravely wired to their Walkmans, Nat haunted by that face in the windscreen. But they were together.

Near Stansted the traffic slowed to funnel between cones. Before the girls were born, when he and Libby sometimes drove this way to vist Jack and Nancy, the M11 had been a quiet motorway, little used. Leaving London had seemed a cleansing experience then – the rancid streets disappeared in the wing mirror and you reached cornfields, reedy broads, acres of light. A rural homecoming. For him at least. Libby found unsettled areas unsettling. Perhaps the girls, being London girls, felt the same away. When his parents first took him to London, at the age of six, he had felt besmirched – the noise, the crowds, the litter. But for Hannah and Rose cities were the norm. He had tried to detoxify them, with holidays in north Norfolk. But the city wasn't easily expelled, and the countryside of the 1990s – barns like aircraft hangars, polythene lakes, garish rape fields, pigs in Nissen huts, combine harvesters with computerised controls – looked like an industrial plant.

'What's that smell?' Libby said.

'Which?'

'Oil or petrol. Can't you smell it?'

He sniffed the air and checked his gauges – no problems as far as he could tell. A blaze of light filled his rear-view mirror, and he moved over. Motorways were like escalators in the Underground: the patient majority waited in line while a handful of maniacs pushed by on the outside. As the BMW swept past, Nat threw a fuck-you stare at the driver, who was talking on a mobile phone – one of life's self-appointed Mr Indispensables, indispensable till someone pushier replaced him. Libby had some of the traits – a driven woman, narrowly focused on work targets, whatever they were. She loved the girls but had lost all interest in him long before he strayed, if finding one's way could be called straying. He flashed his lights as the BMW sped away, a bit of afters. What kind of man would be in a hurry today, with the world shut down for the millennium? At least Libby had a life. And Nat, to use Relate jargon (though he had never been so undignified as to go to Relate), was still there for her.

North of Cambridge they left the M11 and veered east. They were off the motorway now, between long, flat fields, in racehorse-breeding country, green road signs instead of blue. The radio flashed news of a breakthrough in the case of the missing child. Libby turned it off.

'*Please* can we stop now?' the girls chorused from the back. It was twelve thirty. The funeral, an hour's drive away, wasn't till three. The choice was a Little Chef or Happy Eater, no choice at all. He saw a sign up ahead, and took the exit. As he braked, a cloud of blue-white smoke – the colour of ice – billowed up behind, and the van driver following him down the slip road made extravagant, hand-flipping movements across his face in protest.

'You're burning oil there, mate,' he said, as they parked together outside the diner.

'Yes, thanks, I know,' said Nat, hiding his ignorance. Burning oil – did that mean there was too little oil or too much? He remembered Uncle Jack teaching him about engines, with pencil diagrams of pistons and carburettors. He rather wished he had listened. But if he'd listened he wouldn't have been Nat.

'You go ahead,' he said to Libby, propping the bonnet open with the unclipped metal cane. Inside, a display of half-familiar engine parts faced him, like a tray of objects in a children's memory game. Where was the dipstick? He spotted the curly pigtail, pulled it up, wiped the sludge-black blade and poked it back in. This time when he drew it from its scabbard it was clean, except for a fingernail of black at the bottom. Lucky he'd spotted it. He'd buy a can or two of oil after they'd eaten. See, he *did* know about cars. Libby would be lost without me, he thought, remembering she was without him and that he ought to hurry up and join her. He wiped his hands on an old rag in the glove compartment, feeling restored, manly, resourceful, a fantastic Mr Fox.

Inside, Libby and the girls were waiting with other disgruntleds behind a rope. But by the time he'd washed the oil from his hands, they had graduated to a plastic-padded bench at a melamine table. The waitress had a pinch mark in her nose, the afterprint of a ring, not unsightly, just a staple dent – Anthea's was similar, since she'd removed her stud. How long before the skin closes up? he wondered. How long to heal the injuries we do ourselves? The menus sat in a white plastic rack and were themselves plastic, bendily resistant to wear and tear. There were few words on them but plenty of pictures, in case you had forgotten what bacon, sausage, egg and beans looked like. Libby ordered a Caesar salad, the girls chicken nuggets and chips. He chose Meal 6, tagliatelle with a side plate of coleslaw, and wondered whether to hope it turned out different from the photograph. 'Coleslaw's off,' said the waitress with the nose pinch, and asked was potato salad all right instead.

'The car's OK,' he said, when she left. 'Bit short of oil, that's all.'

'You did get it serviced?'

'It's OK, promise.'

Libby had a new Mercedes – the company car. She let him keep their old Renault for running the girls around, on condition he had it serviced. But he had been short of money and let it slide. They should have come in the Mercedes but Libby didn't fancy driving and he wasn't insured to drive it so the Renault would have to do.

To the girls, the appeal of the diner was the play area – Lego, soft toys and video games. Libby took them over, then disappeared – to the Ladies, she said, though he suspected she was calling her bloke. She could do it in front of him, for all he cared. Or was that empty bravado? He'd had a twinge of something when the bloke was first mentioned. He was going through a bad patch then. Now things were better, he could afford to be pleased on Libby's behalf. From the little he knew, the relationship wasn't deep; the bloke was more chaperone or confidant than sexual partner. Still, some balance had been restored. She, too, had another life now. He could stop feeling guilty.

The nose-pinched waitress brought the drinks over: Coke for the girls, tea for Libby, coffee for him. He peeled the top off his cream carton and settled in for the long haul. After ten minutes or so, Libby returned.

'No food yet?' she said, overwrought. She must be hungry. Or had rowed with her boyfriend, perhaps, and realised the hopelessness of the relationship. Or maybe the trouble was him, Nat, whose betrayal she couldn't forgive and whose body she still missed.

'How fucking long does it take?' she said. God, she was angry. You never heard Libby say 'fuck'.

'They haven't worked out how to microwave Caesar salad,' he said.

'Or they're defrosting your tagliatelle.'

'One thing's certain. When it comes, it'll be crap.'

She laughed and sipped her tea. When her brow wasn't furrowed with frustration, the ghost of what had first drawn him to her briefly reappeared. Which was what? Her energy? Her love of silly jokes? Her *unhamperedness* – that was it. It wasn't he who had killed that off, but motherhood, middle age, Mammon, the cares of the world. Perhaps she'd grown into the person she was always going to be. But the Beth he met at Wilberforce Jackson's exhibition, whose silk sleeve he held at supper, with whom he slept that first night, wasn't the woman sitting across from him now. He had gone on loving her till he met Anthea, and only then discovered his mistake. Mistake was too harsh. They had grown apart. Without Anthea they mightn't have noticed how wide the gulf was. But in time they would surely have found out. Better now than at fifty or sixty, when there wasn't time to meet new partners or make new lives. Even Libby seemed to accept that, though her pride was hurt, and, unlike him, she hadn't yet found love. He imagined it wouldn't take much for her to have him back – that her indifference was a mask. He too, just now, hearing her laugh, watching her sip tea (her little finger poking out at ninety degrees, inimitable), still felt affection for his wife, or the wife she had been.

'How's the teaching going?' she asked.

'OKish.'

What was OK was that there wasn't too much of it; what was less OK was that there'd soon be none at all. Already under threat, his contract was now endangered by a new Euro law, which prevented part-timers from being rehired for more than four years in succession. 'According to our records,' the Principal had written last week, 'you expire on 31 August 2000, and current legislation prevents us from renewing you.' Meanwhile, his evening class, Getting Started, was definitely to be axed after Easter, leaving him £100 a week worse off and deprived of the only teaching that gave him pleasure. A bad business. But one best kept from Libby. She'd only gloat.

'You *will* tell your mother today,' she said.

'I promise,' he said.

'You should have told her ages ago.'

'I didn't want to ruin her Christmas.'

'Why not? You ruined mine.'

This was how she was: they'd seem to be getting on, then bitterness would seep in. A pity she couldn't be more mature about it.

'My Christmas wasn't much fun, either,' he said.

'Poor baby. No Antsy-Pantsy to pull crackers with?'

'I told you, she —'

'Forget it Nat. I don't want to hear about your girlfriend.'

Funny, but he didn't think of Anthea as a girlfriend. Nor as a mistress, even when he was seeing her furtively. She was his lover, and he was hers – a mutual passion, nothing cosy. He wondered what she was doing now. Shopping? Eating? Walking? She was in the Lakes anyway, would be there for the duration. He had invited her to the funeral, but it didn't seem the right occasion to meet his mother. So they decided against. Which was just as well, since Libby, to his surprise, said she would like to come and that they might as well travel up together. Together though apart. Cordial for the children's sake but not so friendly as to raise false hopes.

'Looks like our food,' he said.

'If you can call it food,' she said.

The waitress with the nose dent was heading their way with an armful of plates. But she veered off to another table at the last moment.

'You've not forgotten about tomorrow night?'

'What?'

'Christ, you *have* forgotten. You agreed to babysit.'

'Yeh, yeh, it's under control.'

It wasn't. He had forgotten. She was going to that party at the Dome, the one to which he hadn't been invited. Not that he minded missing out. Not that he'd ever have gone. But they might at least have asked him. It was he who had made the bigger contribution to British culture, after all.

'You'll need to collect them by four at the latest,' she said. 'I need time to get ready.'

'Fine,' he said, 'no problem.'

He'd have to call Anthea. She would be furious.

'Are the girls going to be OK about the funeral?' he said, changing the subject.

'I've warned them about the coffin,' she said. 'That'll be the worst.'

'And people crying.'

'It might do them good to cry. They were fond of Nancy. They remember her talking to her tomatoes. Ah, here it comes at last. Chips with everything. I'll go and fetch the girls.'

They left the diner fifteen minutes later, anxious about time – it was 1.45 p.m., there wasn't much leeway. He worried even more when he pulled out from the service station and saw a cloud of exhaust behind. But at a steady 60mph on the A11 the smoke cleared – the new oil doing its job, he decided, easing, lubricating, replenishing. He feared the scorn of Uncle Jack, who would take it personally if they turned up with a knackered engine. But Jack had more important matters on his mind and now the engine was behaving. So he thought till he slowed at the next roundabout and smoke billowed up behind again, vast clouds of it, like a shot from the Gulf War, those burning oil wells in Kuwait. The engine clunked as he accelerated away. The red warning light came on. They were nowhere near town but he ground on for two miles to the next village, where he spotted a garage and pulled up. Two ancient green pumps, a corrugated shed, a workshop with a pit – he couldn't believe his luck. A mechanic wandered out, wearing white.

'Problem, sir?'

This time when he opened the bonnet oil was flooding all corners, indistinguishable bits poking through it like seabirds struggling in a slick. Nat felt ashamed, as though he had vomited this himself, or as though his inner life were laid out for inspection. He stepped back, letting the mechanic disappear in the car's black mouth, like Jonah swallowed by the whale. Libby stood with her arms folded, saying nothing, which said it all. *Cars go wrong if you don't look after them, Nat. Relationships, too.*

It's nonsense, he thought. I fell in love. People can't help falling in love.

That's true, her folded arms said, but they can avoid acting on some juvenile crush.

It wasn't a crush.

It was enough to crush our marriage.

This argument is going nowhere, he thought. It hasn't even made it into words.

'Twisted oil filter,' the mechanic said, removing a distended white canister, like a tumour. 'Safety release valve must have gone. Let's stick another one in and see how she ticks over.'

While Nat waited, Libby crossed the road to the village shop, returning with Liquorice Allsorts and a newspaper (LITTLE ERROL: NEW LEAD AS HUNT GOES ON). The fields stretched greyly away, to meet a grey sky. Under the bonnet, the mechanic was trunk and legs. Nat stamped his feet and looked at his watch. Two twenty. The church was still half an hour away, down country lanes. He couldn't afford to wait much longer. Were there taxis out here? He was preparing to ask when the mechanic emerged and started the engine. It sounded sickly, whiny, firing on three cylinders, but the clunking had stopped.

'Your piston rings are knackered. How far you going?'

'Fifteen miles. A family funeral.'

'Best carry on, then – the damage is done now, you can't do no more. Get the car to me tomorrow morning and I'll sort it for you. Biggish job, mind.'

'How much do I owe you for the oil filter?'

'You get to your funeral, we'll settle up later.'

That was the countryside for you, Nat reflected, pulling away: honesty, trust, attendance to the solemn rituals; 'What can I do for you?' not 'What can I do you for?' Two twenty-five: no time to stop off at Jack's house, but if they drove straight to the church they should beat the hearse. Beside him, wriggling in her seat, Libby swapped jeans and jumper for a black trouser suit. When was the last time he watched her undress? He wasn't watching now but, sensing her tightless legs beside him, her bare arms, her bra, he cast an instinctive, appraising glance – which she caught and, silent, hostile, outraged, coldly cast back. He fixed his eyes on the road and shrugged, as though to say come on, it's only habit, we were married once – it's not as if I tried to touch you. Unlike her, he wouldn't need to change clothes. He was wearing black already; even his fingers were gloved with oil. What would Uncle Jack be wearing? How was he coping? Whatever his grief, he'd notice the whine of a ruined engine. Harsh words would follow. But with luck he'd know someone who could mend it for next to nothing. Better that than driving fifteen miles back to that garage.

Nat recognised the spire two miles before they reached it. The church wasn't round-towered or thatched, like some in the area, but gargoyles framed its porch – open-mouthed, like that face in the windscreen. He parked behind the other cars and harried his family out into the cold. One of Jack's neighbours, by the church gate, caught sight of them and waved – hurry, it's starting. They took a pew near the back, as the vicar emerged from his vestry. *Dearly beloved.*

The mouths of half a dozen choirboys opened and closed. It was hard to hear them, from so far back, though the church wasn't crowded. 'Hear what the voice from heaven proclaims / For all the pious dead; / Sweet is the savour of their names, / And soft their sleeping bed.' Isaac Watts, was it? He looked around, sniffing stale whitewash, then knelt on the dusty hassock. 'The days of our age are threescore years and ten.' What had Aunt Nancy been – sixty? His father had been less than that. Not encouraging – if his genes were the same as his father's genes, he would be dead before the girls left university. And suppose he and Anthea were to have children. Not that they planned to just yet, but they'd considered the question in general: was this a world fit to bring kids into? Hannah reached for his hand, along the low heating pipe, down by the hassocks. 'Man that is born of woman hath but a short time to live, and is full of misery. He cometh up and is cut down.' Hannah's hand tightened. He was close to crying now, not for Nancy but for his girls, from whom his passion for Anthea had sundered him.

They sat up in the pew again, while a lesson was read. Christ stared from the stained-glass window, in pieces. He was feeding the five thousand – with a loaf the shape and colour of an oil filter. Christ the Saviour, wearing white and bringing comfort to the troubled, like that garage mechanic. Miraculous that such men still existed, Nat thought. Mustn't forget to drop in on the way home and settle up. Five pounds for the collection plate when it comes round and ten for fitting that oil filter. That seemed about right.

## 5

## *HARRY*

THE MAGISTRATES' court was opposite Kwik-Fit, the tyre and exhaust centre. In Harry's experience the two places worked the same way: in and out, £100, no messing. An hour before the court was due to be in session, there was already a solid police presence, with four vans parked discreetly in a side street and a dozen officers in riot gear sitting in each. Traffic was light, most businesses having closed till the next millennium. Patrolmen in lurid yellow signalled at drivers not to obstruct the flow. But there was no flow to obstruct, only odd cars trickling by to the New Year sales. The court's front door had been fenced off with metal barriers. This was infanticide, and feelings were running high. Yet Harry could see no members of the public, only reporters like him.

He was supposed to meet Malcolm, the *Gazette*'s John Lennon-lookalike photographer, whose plan was to get a close-up of the suspect as he was escorted from the armoured car. Harry said it wouldn't work – that the guy's face was bound to be buried under a blanket. They were still arguing about it, by mobile phone (neither having spotted the other), when the armoured car, under police escort, appeared from the direction of Blackheath Hill. A murmur ran through the press pack. Several snappers, necklaced with Nikons, ran towards it. But the armoured car was too quick for them, turning right into a side street then left into a yard at the rear of court, where two high metal gates closed behind it.

On the steps out front, Harry ran into Kendal Platt, his rival from the *South London Mercury* – they sometimes drank together in Yates's Wine Lodge. Kendal had a boil on his cheek and eyebrows that joined in the middle. He had already been knocking on doors.

'So, what's the story?' Harry said, as they moved indoors, towards the queue under the arch of the metal detector.

'They've charged the father.'

'Which father?'

'Errol's father. Ray Nuard.'

'Why him?'

'I don't know yet. The neighbours don't know, either.'

'What do they say about him?'

'Bit of a loner, that's all. No one can get their heads round it. They were told Errol might be a drowning, or a neglect case – and now it turns out Uncle Ray did it.'

'*Uncle* Ray?'

'That's what the girls call him. Errol's half-sisters.'

Harry's mobile went as he reached the arch of metal detector.

'All phones to be switched off,' the security man said.

Shit, Harry thought, it'll be Deborah. I can't not take the call.

'Sorry,' he said, retreating to the steps outside.

It wasn't Deborah but Marcia, apologising for her abruptness with him on Christmas Day. Things were difficult, she knew, and she could see he was making an effort, but Stephen needed careful handling, and before they met up again it might make sense for the two of *them*, as parents, to get together first, to find a way to move things forward that wouldn't destabilise Stephen, who was doing well at school but found it hard to talk about his feelings – like most men, she added. Is that a dig at me? Harry said, from the cold of the courtroom steps. I expect so, she said, you never discussed your feelings with me, it probably runs in the genes. It's a long time ago now, he said. Yes, she said, but it's an issue for Stephen, and that makes it an issue for you, too. *What's* an issue? he said. He wonders what you really felt about me, how casual our relationship was, why you ran out when I got pregnant, stuff like that – I've talked to him about it, but he needs to hear about it from you, it affects his self-esteem.

As he stood with the phone to his ear, Harry saw the DI with the badger stripe join the queue into the courtroom – he was chatting with the hacks, perhaps divulging things which Harry ought to hear. You're not listening to me, Marcia said. Of course I'm listening, he said, and he did listen, or try to listen, as she talked about Stephen. I know he's prickly, Marcia said, but he can see there are benefits to having a dad. Harry watched the queue dwindling by the metal detector. The case was due on any minute. You're still there, aren't you? Marcia said. Yes, he said, remembering how small the public seating area in Court 1 was – what if all the seats were taken? We were both very young, she said, but I did love you, you know, or I'd never have gone out with you as long as I did, and it's not an emotion I've often felt, except for Stephen, of course, and my mum, but that's a different kind of love – you do understand what I'm saying, Harry? Yes, he said, watching the last reporter enter the metal arch. *I did love you, you know.* The words lapped at Harry's ear, inviting reciprocation, but the last reporter had disappeared. How would he explain to Deborah that he wasn't in court to see the Errol killer? Marcia's silence lay hot and expectant against his cheek. It's hard for me to talk now, he said, heading towards the door, I'm at the magistrates' court, a big breakthrough in the Errol Winthrop case, there's this camera crew filming as I speak – turn on your television and you might see me. Can I call you back? No reply. Marcia? Silence. She must have hung up several sentences ago. He shoved his mobile, keys and coins in a plastic tray and passed through the metal arch.

The public gallery was packed, three short rows of wooden seats, but the usher recognised him and squeezed him in next to Kendal. The dock, so-called, was a glass screen to the left – the accused were brought up from cells in the basement. The case in progress was a car theft. Ray Nuard would be next.

'You know that Ray is estranged from Sharon,' Kendal whispered, resuming their conversation. 'The DI says that's his motive. Never got over her. Took his revenge by killing Errol.'

Harry remembered Sharon's face. It was easy to imagine not getting over her. But the motive seemed too obvious.

'And of course Ray's black,' Harry said. 'No surprises there.'

'Aren't two of the other dads black, too?'

'Mixed race. Like Sharon. There's a difference.'

'Forget the race card,' Kendal said. 'It's irrelevant.'

'Not to the police.'

'The police must know something or they wouldn't have charged Ray.'

'All they know is they have to charge someone. So as to get the whole thing over with.'

'You're a cynic, Harry.'

'I'm a realist, Kendal.'

The young black man in the dock was bailed, pending probation reports. Solicitors with briefcases came and went. Then another man was behind the glass screen, thirtyish, with a torn leather jacket, his hair hanging in catkins, his eyes shifty and raw, Securicor guards on either side of him. A remand hearing, Raymond Nuard, charges of abduction and murder, slipped in among the petty thieves and parking offenders. Would counsel for the defence be making an application for bail? No, m'lud, said a voice Harry recognised, what's-his-name, they met a few months ago, the solicitor representing the hit-and-run victim whose body had rotted in the mortuary fridge, an accident was how it looked, and the verdict was misadventure, but the victim had massive drug and gambling debts and they both thought it could have been murder – Luke Tilbey, that was it. His client would be pleading not guilty, he said. The stipendiary magistrate conferred with both lawyers. The two minutes this took was long enough for Ray Nuard to make a poor impression – manic eyes, jiggling shoulders, sweaty palms. When the guards took his arm to lead him off, he jerked his elbow away. Harry sneaked a look at Kendal's notebook. 'Aggression. Lack of remorse. Hint of psychopathy?' he had scribbled. Luke Tilbey nodded as he was leaving. OK-if-I-call-you? Harry mouthed, splaying his thumb and little finger. Luke nodded again.

'You know Ray's solicitor?' Kendal said.

'We've met a few times,' Harry said.

'What's his mobile number?'

'I forget.'

'Liar.'

'He won't want me to give it out.'

'You're a miserable bastard, Harry.'

In the downstairs hall by the drinks machine, the DI with the badger stripe was briefing journalists and narrating the lead-up to the arrest: 'You'll understand this is strictly *sub judice*.'

Ray was the father of Errol, he said, the third of Sharon's four children. Unlike Sharon's first two partners, the fathers of Mia (nine) and Emmalou (seven), Ray had been an active father and had lived with Sharon for over a year. But the relationship had ended acrimoniously eighteen months ago, when she became pregnant with baby Charmain. Louis, Charmain's dad, used to play snooker with Ray; Ray felt betrayed. There were threats of violence, and back in March, just days before Charmain's birth, Ray was arrested outside Sharon's house while in possession of offensive weapons – a machete, chains, an iron bar and a nine-inch knife. After that things calmed down. Louis and Ray made their peace. Ray and Sharon began speaking again. And Ray was allowed to collect Errol from the house on access days. But on the evening of 18 December Ray and Sharon had a violent row, immediately after which Errol disappeared.

'So why did you take so long to get him?' someone asked.

'We questioned him before Christmas. But he had alibis. We needed stronger evidence. Then we got it.'

When officers first searched Ray's flat, the DI said, they removed various items of clothing. Laboratory analysis showed nothing to link him to the crime. However, a second search disclosed an item they had missed, a jacket which Ray admitted to wearing on the day of Errol's disappearance. In its pocket was a small plastic toy from McDonald's, a freebie model of Disney's Pluto, on which were traces of Errol's skin and saliva. A McDonald's restaurant is located half a mile from the Pepys estate. An employee there believed she remembered a man and a small boy arriving 'in a dishevelled state' round 7.30 p.m. on the evening Errol disappeared. Receipts tallied with this: an order for one quarter-pound cheeseburger meal with chocolate milkshake and one chicken nuggets with Coke was logged at 7.33. Ray was known to like chocolate milkshakes. Errol was not known to like chicken nuggets but might, Sharon thought, have been forced to have them – 'that would be just like Ray'.

To the police, the evidence suggested that Ray had struck and injured Errol outside his house, and dragged him off in the bushes intending to kill him. But, disturbed by someone or something, he relented and took the child to McDonald's, as a treat or bribe or apology. Once there, his resolve hardened again. There was a car pound nearby, and a container depot, and a patch of wasteland, all places where he could have murdered Errol then disposed of the body. A corpse could be crushed under metal, hidden in a container bound for a distant country, or sunk with weights to the bottom of the Thames – and no one would be the wiser.

'You're suggesting he did it to get back at the mother?'

'It's an obvious motive.'

'But you haven't found a body?'

'Even without a body, the evidence is overwhelming. The accused has confessed.'

'His solicitor says he's pleading not guilty.'

'We have a confession. That's all I can tell you for the moment, gents. Happy New Year.'

Outside, the only traffic was heading south, out towards the channel ports.

'Sounds pretty conclusive,' Kendal said.

'Convenient, anyway,' Harry said. 'The new millennium's nearly on us and hey presto, they crack the case just in time. So we can all go away and forget about it. Just what the government ordered.'

'You never used to be a conspiracy theorist, Harry.'

'There never used to be so many conspiracies.'

'Remember to let me have that solicitor's mobile number.'

'Yeh, yeh.'

'Arsehole.'

They said goodbye and promised to read each other's pieces when they appeared.

'But mine'll be better,' Kendal said. 'Because I have an open mind.'

'For the police to fill with crap.'

'It's you that's full of crap, Harry.'

Only Kendal could say a sentence like that and convey affection.

So where does that leave me? Harry wondered. I told Deborah I had a hunch. I said race might be part of the story. Then I began to think an animal was. But if the police are right, then Nat is right, too: it's just a story about sexual jealousy. It wasn't worth my getting involved. Nor worth the upset I've caused Marcia.

He called her back from the forecourt of Kwik-Fit, but she was out and so was Stephen. *I did love you, you know*. For decency's sake, he ought to say the same. He had loved her, up to a point. But perhaps loving someone up to a point was a contradiction. The nature of love was excess. The nature of love was to exceed yourself. He had never done that. He was too cautious, too circumspect. But he wanted to do right by her now – and by Stephen.

He would speak to Marcia later. In the meantime, he must call Luke Tilbey. First things first.

6

*JACK*

WITH THE furniture pushed back to make more room, it felt like one of their old parties. Cold meats covered the dining-room table – sliced beef, sausages on sticks, cured ham from Emmett's, slices of leftover turkey. He hadn't bothered with a tree this year but there were sprigs of holly on the mantelpiece. And cards, of course, 'Happy Christmas' mingling with 'Deepest Sympathy'. He didn't want sympathy. He was doing perfectly well, thanks. Grief could drive you out of your wits, people said. But he noticed things he normally wouldn't, like the castored circles in the carpet where the sofa had stood and the wood pigeon calling from the wood.

After the church service, the crem had been bleak and perfunctory,

with a curtain snagging on the coffin as it slid past and the vicar referring to Nancy as Ann, her given name, which she detested. Still, the
worst was over now. And to judge by the past half-hour, hosting a wake
was less deadly than attending one – your job was to keep topping up
drinks, so when a guest became boring or maudlin you had an excuse
to move away. The drink Jack topped up most frequently was his own,
of course. He'd had a snifter or two before church, to calm the nerves.
The measures since the crem were for strength to field the condolences.
Later he would drink for oblivion.

'Another drop in that, Libby?'

'Go on then.'

'Girls all right?'

'They're watching cartoons next door.'

'Good idea,' he whispered. 'Keep them away from all us geriatrics.'

You were meant to be too traumatised to care but in church he had
counted heads. Family, of course. Then friends – Harris and Elise, Dom
and Jeannie, Tony and Greta. The villagers – Felix, Nelly, Donal, Greg,
plus Rilda from the dog kennels and Mona, Ramsden's wife. The carers
– Dr Bruin and the little Irish agency nurse Aileen. A handful from
work – Hook, Karen, the Bushey brothers, Robin Arleigh (whom they'd
made redundant, for Christ's sake) and even (give him his due, he had
driven down from his parents' home in Cheshire) young Marcus. No
sign of Bruno, despite Jack's weekly patronage of the George. Nor of
the bloody houseman who'd sent him home that night. And no one
from the tennis club committee or Women's Institute, despite all Nancy's
fund-raising. He mustn't judge. It was no skin off his nose. But he felt
angry at all the spare pews. The whole world should have turned out
for Nancy.

'More wine, Harris?'

'I won't, Jack. I'm driving.'

'Suit yourself.'

None of the others seemed to need replenishing, either, so he plonked
himself next to Eunice, his sister-in-law, Ronnie's widow, who went through
this herself twelve years ago, though by then she and Ronnie were long
divorced. She was still wearing her hat – black veil, silver feather, upended
bowl like a Christmas pudding – and she perched on her chair edge, as
though ready to fly off. It couldn't be easy for her, being reminded. Heart
attack. In Spain, in bed, at the hotel Ronnie ran in Los Alcazarez. Doubtless
brought on by bonking that fancy woman of his, Ramona, though by then

they had been together for a decade. Spain was Ronnie's 'spiritual home', Ramona said, over the phone, and he would be buried there. She wasn't expecting them to attend. It was Eunice who insisted. Catholic ceremony in a small stone church, to which the whole of the village came. They didn't linger afterwards but agreed, flying back to Heathrow, that it had 'helped'. Had today helped? Seeing Nancy's coffin was the thing he had dreaded, but what nearly made him lose it was the organist, Mrs Chadwick – not the fluting music but the words piped into his head as he watched her, organ stop, organ stop, organ stop. 'Let it out,' everyone said, since Princess Diana. (Ramsden and Mona had burned Di candles in the village shop, as though relations of the Spencer family.) But Jack refused to weep even for Nancy.

'So how are you keeping?' he asked.

'Mustn't grumble,' Eunice said, but then did, at length. He sat, Scotch in lap, pretending to listen, his right leg crossed over his left knee, his suspended black shoe gently ticking. Sixty beats a minute, regular as clockwork. Surely slower than his heartbeat. How could that be? Effect of alcohol maybe? Dr Bruin would know, but to ask would look like hypochondria. Worth bearing in mind, though: if ever he lost his watch, he could keep time by crossing his legs.

'Once everyone's gone, it's going to feel empty,' Eunice said, patting his hand to let him know she understood.

'It feels empty already,' he said, staring into his glass.

'It gets worse,' she said, reassuringly. 'At least you've Sasha and Ischia.'

'Both living away.'

'I've only Nathaniel and he's married.'

Was married, Jack thought. Sasha had heard rumours they'd split up. And their body language seemed to confirm it. That must have been why, when Jack rang with the news, Libby said she would pass on the message. Covering for her ex. Not wishing to add to Jack's woes by letting on that his nephew no longer lived there. Why should she think he gave a bugger? But it was true he approved of Libby and didn't like to think of her being hurt.

'At least Nancy had a good life,' Eunice said.

'Sixty years,' Jack said. 'I don't call that good.'

'Eight years longer than Ronnie. And he was so miserable.'

There was a pause, then a non sequitur. Or did Eunice – not famed for her logic – see a connection?

'Isn't it awful about the missing coloured child,' she said. 'Virtually on Nathaniel's doorstep. He has to watch the girls all the time.'

Libby, standing nearby, overheard.

'We *both* watch them,' she said.

'I'm sure you try, dear. But when you're working all hours . . .'

Had Eunice not been told about Nat moving out, then? She had never liked her daughter-in-law, Jack knew that much. Whereas he thought Libby terrific – bright, level-headed, good at business, and altogether wasted on his nephew. Was it true she had caught him screwing some student? He must ask Sasha for the details. Stupid bugger, just like his father, but with even less of an excuse to play away. Eunice was never a looker. But how could a man mislay a wife like Libby? Blue eyes, hint of auburn in her hair, Irish mouth and chin – a cracker.

'Bloody awful world when children can't trust grown-ups,' Jack said.

'That's if it was a grown-up,' Elise said. The conversation had become general now. The missing child was everyone's favourite news story and a safer topic than Nancy.

'I've a journalist friend working on the case,' Nat said, to impress the yokels. 'He thinks an animal could have taken the child.'

'Some sort of dog?'

'Or even a large fox,' Nat said.

'Rubbish,' Jack said, with irritation. The only merit in credulous Londoners thinking that foxes were dangerous would be if it made them less eager to ban hunting.

'In Los Angeles,' Sasha's American fiancé chipped in, 'we had this case of a three-year-old killed by a coyote. She was sitting on the kerb outside her house when it dragged her away by the neck.'

Jack had met Stadler only last night. These weren't the best circumstances for getting to know your daughter's intended.

'In Australia there was the dingo, remember.'

'Yes, baby Azaria, mother called Lindy something.'

'Chamberlain. The dingo took the baby from a tent and killed it.'

'Or the mother did.'

Libby broke in to stop the blabbing. 'I heard on the radio that a man has been charged,' she said. That seemed to shut people up, but just to make sure Jack added:

'Whatever happened, it was nothing to do with a fox.'

He made a tour with the wine bottles, to quell his irritation. There was a meet of the Harchope & Nelles today. Large outing, up to eighty riders, in splendid countryside. He'd been looking forward to it.

'Sorry, Jack, I have to be off,' Jeannie said, at his elbow. Dom needed her help at the garden centre: there was a rush on for millennial bouquets. Jack saw her to the front door, so no one would hear when she became embarrassing.

'You were a devoted husband, Jack,' she said, hugging him on the step. 'Everyone knows that.'

Was he? Did they? At this precise moment he hated Nancy for dying so inconveniently, at the peak of the hunting season. Would a devoted husband do that?

Dusk already, though it was only four fifteen. He watched Jeannie's headlights rake the drive, then slipped into the cloakroom for a piss. Hint of red: must be that beetroot from last night. Nancy thought beetroot was bad for him but – small mercies – he was free to eat what he liked now. December 20th, early morning. Peacefully, they said. But what did they know? A shadow passing over brain and heart; a painless shutting down; organ stop. Nothing could have saved her. But she might have cried out, or reached for his hand. Others forgave him. But he didn't forgive himself.

Zipping away his shrunk cock, he washed his hands at the basin. *Ruht wohl*. The words floated in his head. Where from? A Bach Passion, maybe, chorusing on Nancy's radio, between the pots and seed trays. *Ruht wohl, und bright auch mich zur Ruh*. She had slept for two years, but only now, turned to ash, would she rest. He too would like to rest: let the young have the next millennium to themselves. But there were guests to attend to, a business to run, two daughters to live for. You couldn't gatecrash death. Death was the ultimate nightclub. You stood behind the rope and waited your turn.

'There you are,' Elise said, as he came out of the cloakroom. 'I've been wanting a word with you, Jack Raven.'

She slipped her arm in his and drew him into the study. Over his desk were photos Nancy had put up, snapshots of family history. Great-grandfather Raven in goggles, at the wheel of the firm's first car; Jack's father riding a 750cc Viking Arrow; Jack himself, posing with Michelle at the Paris Trade Show (if Nancy had caught a whiff of *that* episode, the photo wouldn't have been there). There was a wedding photo, too, and Sasha and Ischia as toddlers, and a succession of Jacks: at Repton with Ronnie, in graduation robes, shaking hands with Niki Lauda in a Brands Hatch hospitality tent, and (several times over) riding out as MFH. A framed photo of Nancy stood apart from these, on top of Jack's desk. Taken at the Askews' silver wedding bash, in 1996 – the last photo of her before the stroke. Elise avoided looking at it, he noticed. She was trying to be upbeat.

'I like the riding ones,' she said. 'You're very dashing with your whip.'

'Crop.'

'Whatever.'

'You should come along to a meet, before they ban us. Bring Harris. Make a day of it.'

'He'd be bored. He only likes sports with balls.'

'Shame.'

'You come to us, instead. It's been ages. You're naughty, Jack. We can't go on not meeting like this.'

Graveside pity, disguised as flirtation. Black trouser suit, perfect waist, little cat mouth, marble-green eyes – funny how reluctant he'd been to recognise her attractiveness. Though his veins were furred with grief and whisky, he recognised it now.

'I'll call with some dates,' she said. 'If dinner's no good, then come and have tea with me. I'd love that.'

Would she? He scanned her green depths for a sign. There had been other offers – as his daughters kept saying, people were so kind – but none he felt like taking up.

'No excuses,' she said, and leaned her head on his shoulder as they stood together under the photos. The lemony whiff of her hair dispersed his gloom. Was there a touch of Chinese about her, as well as French? Must ask one day. No reason not to. While Nancy was alive, he had avoided being over-friendly with her friends. Now it didn't matter. Elise's flirtatiousness was merely good manners. He had never heard of her carrying on with someone, though if she did who could blame her. Harris was still dipping his pen in company ink, people said, but he had found a new inkwell – some twenty-five-year-old from his Relationship Team. Had Elise heard the rumours? Did she care? Jack's arm was round her (where else to put it, with her standing so close?) but flatly, neutrally, not as a lover's arm would be. What would Harris think if he came through from the dining room and saw them, her head on Jack's shoulder like a wreath? Deepest sympathy, that was all. But she stirred up feelings that a chap oughtn't to have for another chap's wife – least of all on a day like today.

It was time to resume his numbing duties in the living room. But Elise's head was on his shoulder, and – eyes watering – he inhaled her lemon balm while he could.

# 7

# *LIBBY*

'SORRY,' LIBBY said, walking in on Uncle Jack and the little Frenchwoman. They had been having a cry together, it seemed, in front of Nancy's photograph. Jack looked embarrassed, as though caught with his fingers in the till – typical male of his generation, afraid to show emotion, in thrall to the myth of imperturbability. Libby exchanged a look with the Frenchwoman – God, men – before blundering on.

'I need to make a phone call,' she said.

'Help yourself,' Jack said, blushing. 'Phone on the desk, look.'

'I have a mobile. It was the quiet I was after. Bit noisy next door.'

'Call from here – we're just going. Or there's Nancy's bedroom. Even quieter. First on the right, top of the stairs.'

'Thanks, perfect.'

She left them to it, reminscence, consolation, the wiping away of tears. It was good that Jack had close friends – especially women friends, who would understand what he was going through. Had Nat spoken to him about the car yet? The plan had been to drive back this evening. Now they would have to stay somewhere and wait till it was fixed – unless she caught a train back with the girls. Norwich was the nearest mainline station. But it was miles away and the last train to London had probably left: this was the countryside, remember, where nothing happened after dark. Thank God she didn't have to be at the office tomorrow. She should never have agreed to come in that clapped-out car.

Nancy's room felt cold, denuded of Nancy. A cylinder and oxygen mask sat, uncollected, by the bed. Libby stood in the window, trying to get a signal. Was Nancy dust and ashes yet? Where had her soul gone? SEARCHING, the mobile said. Where Nancy had fetched up couldn't be as depressing as this room: yellow chintz curtains, green velvet bedspread, white woodchip walls. Could poor colour coordination kill? Cheap joke. A signal at last. She pushed the keys eleven times. Damian's mobile. Damian's voice. But no Damian.

She left a message and called the office, but Angie was engaged. She ought to go downstairs again and be sociable. But that would mean listening to her mother-in-law, and she no longer felt obliged to make the effort. Nat thought it 'inevitable' that mothers- and daughters-in-law be at war. His peace solution had been to renege on his marriage, so Libby and Eunice need have no further contact. Libby ought to be grateful for that. In a way, she was grateful. But even when Eunice knew about the separation (so far Nat had failed to tell her), there would still be occasions when they couldn't avoid each other, such as this. Would Eunice be more accepting of an *ex*-daughter-in-law? Unlikely.

She sat on the bed, gently bouncing to test the mattress: some spring in it still, despite Nancy having been beached there for so long. Poor Nancy. In the two years since her stroke, they'd failed to visit. Libby felt bad about that. But Nancy had been Nat's aunt, not hers. And he was too busy destroying his immediate family to care about his extended. That was an overdramatic way of putting it. Neither she nor the girls had been destroyed. And separating was in everyone's interests, she saw that now. Still, it would have been better to have some choice in the matter, or to be the one whose infidelity had caused the break-up. At least Nat had had some fun.

What rankled was her gullibility. She should have ended it that night in the attic. (Eighteen months ago to the day. She had worked it out in the car travelling up here. Today was a kind of anniversary.) Of course he wasn't a porn-browser. Of course he wasn't a paedophile. But she had been on to his treachery. How dumb of her to have believed his innocence. When she asked him about *Ant*, his embarrassingly explicit play-in-progress about an older man and a younger woman, he said it was a 'Wilberforceish spoof', consisting of quotes – from Lawrence, de Sade, Henry Miller, Anaïs Nin, Kenneth Tynan – specially chosen for their porny awfulness. The nit comb slack in her hand, she had made him scroll through. 'So that's pure fiction, Nat?' 'Impure, maybe, but yes.' In her heart she knew there was more to this. But the time wasn't right for confrontation. That was the bargain she made with herself: in order to run the office, she would ignore the shit at home. Once her company was launched, she'd face the truth. Acknowledge it now – *believe what she knew* – and she and Raven McCready would collapse.

She continued not to believe what she knew even after she heard the message being left on his answering machine. It was some months later, a Tuesday, and he had left for his evening class earlier than usual. She happened to be in his room – not to check up on him, or look for evidence of a porn habit, but to find a copy of *Black Beauty* to read to the girls. The female voice came on while she searched between Salinger and Solzhenitsyn: *The entryphone system isn't working, sweets, so phone me when you arrive and I'll come down to let you in.*

She played it to him when he got back. What's *that* about? she said. The Tuesday masterclass, he said. The Tuesday masterclass is being held in someone's flat? Yes, he said, surely I told you, it's more relaxed that way than at college. And how many students come? Oh, a few. Who's the one with the entryphone, then? She's called Anthea, he said. Isn't 'sweets' an unusually intimate endearment between student and teacher? She calls everyone 'sweets'. A bit indiscriminate in her affections, is she? She's one of the brightest talents I've ever had. *Had,* Nat? Don't be stupid, he said.

She was stupid all right. But the desperation of Nat's denials swayed her. Even if he's lying, she thought, he regrets whatever minor misdemeanour there has been.

It was agreed, under the eaves, after extensive discussion and a drink or two, that he had been 'inappropriate' with Anthea, that his encouragement of her was 'open to misinterpretation', and that her not being officially enrolled as one of his students was no excuse: Christ, he wasn't even being *paid* to encourage her. He said he would back off, give up the masterclass, stop emailing her, reply perfunctorily to any stories she sent for comment, re-establish proper boundaries. And he apologised: Libby was his wife, the mother of his children, and he would never knowingly hurt her. They went to bed, and lay in each other's arms, and instead of staying awake with the truth she shut it off, closed her eyes, willed the left side of her brain to sleep so that the right side could do its worldly best.

At work she was Ms Dynamite, Thin Libby, prospective Businesswoman of the Year. At home she played Beth, the credulous housewife. Her powers of repression were such that she failed to make the connection: Anthea, *Ant,* the one who'd sent him Georgia O'Keeffe postcards, the one who'd got in touch with him hoping for 'feedback'. And yet she knew: here was their nemesis, Antsy-Pantsy, the Ant in his Pants.

He betrayed me for over a year, she later worked out. Without my knowledge. Or with the connivance of my repressed knowledge.

*Where've you been?* That's all she remembered from the months of denial. Standing quaking in the hallway whenever he came home: 'Where you've been?' He had been teaching. Or with his students in the pub. Or round at Harry's. Or being feted by a new agent. The answer didn't interest her. Putting the question dissolved her suspicions. It became a reflex. *Where've you been?* Did she expect him to tell the truth? He spared her, anyway. There must have been times when he didn't lie as well as the times he did, but the whole period was a black hole, with only one image – her quaking in the hallway – retrievable from the vortex. Any sane person could see he was having an affair. But his denial of it had driven her mad. That was what she couldn't forgive – not him fucking another woman but him fucking with her, Libby's mind. So it was all right for her to go nuts? So he was happy for her to become a contemptible, deluded woman, a pathetic housewife – a mousewife? What contempt for her he must have felt to behave as he did.

Finally, roused from her stupor, home early one day, she tailed him to Anthea's flat. Followed his car, parked, watched while he went in, waited ten minutes, walked across to the building, found the name on the name-plate – Hurt, Anthea, No. 43 – and pushed the buttons to several other flats till some duped fellow resident buzzed her in. Took the lift to the fourth. Stood outside the door and listened till she had no doubt: ah-ah-ah-ah, a high young voice, not smoky-husky like her own; and a male baritone, uh-uhing in accompaniment. She ought to have battered the door down. Instead she drove home in a daze and opened the wardrobe and threw his shoes out the window, his shirts, his jackets, his trousers, then climbed to the attic and threw out his books, his files, his typescripts, his dusty school cricket bat. It was ten at night, a soft June gust drifting in over the sill as his possessions tumbled out – a year of treachery, a June too late. The girls woke, and stood in the study doorway, with eyes like big white dinner plates, while she sweated out his poison. She sobbed as she worked, till the girls began crying. 'It's all right, it's all right,' she said, soothing, but she didn't stop. She wasn't as wild as she appeared – the next-door neighbours were away, the yard was dark, the only noise was the soft swoosh of him falling to earth. And though she would have sworn she had followed him on impulse, that till six that evening she utterly trusted him, the timing was meticulous – two major new clients had signed with the company that day, the nanny had agreed to stay on for six more months, the builders had finished the conservatory, she felt secure and could afford the disruption. His life and art, expelled, fetched up below. When he returned, the door was chained against him. His ringing and knocking ignored, he walked round the back and found the detritus of himself, then understood and went away again, back to his slut. She hoped a dog fox would come and spray the heap. Or that rain would fall and dissolve it. But his possessions were layered like an archaeological site: books and papers at the top, then clothes, then shoes, all open to retrieval at some future point – unlike his marriage, which had been obliterated.

That same night she moved her exercise bike into the attic. Thin Libby: she liked to work out.

From Nancy's window she gazed below, into the darkness, as she had that night. SEARCHING, the mobile said. Of the many options she had considered after chucking Nat out, moving to the country barely figured. Selling the business, retraining as a lawyer, going to New York, buying a small vineyard in New Zealand, even moving back to Northern Ireland – all came higher on the list. In the event she had done nothing, if cutting her office hours to give more time to Hannah and Rose could be called nothing. When the last of his things had settled below (whether from weariness or pity, she stopped short of chucking out his computer), she told the girls that Daddy was leaving because he loved someone else; that Mummy was upset and angry, because she loved Daddy and felt betrayed by him; that in future Daddy might not live with Mummy, but they, the girls, would see lots of him; and that though it would be strange for a while going to visit him in another house, he was still the same Daddy, *their* Daddy, the only Daddy they would ever have. They were lovely girls, no daughters could be more perfect (OK, sometimes they were naughty, but), and both Mummy and Daddy loved them. So they mustn't think this was their fault – grown-ups simply fell out of love sometimes. 'But won't you and Daddy get back?' Hannah asked, as the three of them cuddled up – *get back*, a phrase from the soaps and one which made Libby feel her speech had been superfluous, that the girls already knew the script from *Brookside* and *EastEnders* and that Mummy, to whom breaking up with Daddy was shocking and unprecedented, came across to them as a TV stereotype uttering platitudes. 'No, I don't think we'll get back,' she said, 'but maybe one day Daddy and I can be friends again.'

Today they had shared a car for a hundred miles without fighting. It wasn't exactly Truth and Reconciliation. But nor was it Gallipoli or the Somme. Friends had expected her to be hard on him. She was hard, in the first weeks. The contempt was for herself – so easily duped – but the anger for him. The greatest affront was that he took it like a lamb – no roars of indignation at being chucked out, just a quiet bleat about his workbooks being ruined. She had sunk the best years of her life into him. She had borne his children. Yet he was content to go with barely a whimper. Too proud to take it out on him in person, she took it out on his photographs instead. Late at night, half drunk, she retrieved the albums from the shelf behind the television, and censored and shredded like a Communist Party archivist, till all evidence of his existence was excised. The sense of justice was pleasing. He had ripped her life to bits. Ditto.

Then he turned up one night, asking – pleading – to come back. A trial rapprochement followed, with him in the spare bedroom. She didn't know what she felt or if they had a future; she would kill off the relationship with Anthea first, and *then* decide. Once she hurled a fork at him over supper; another time, as he slept, she stood over him with a large marble ashtray, daring herself to smash it over his head. She could see it ending like *The Wars of the Roses*, both of them crashing to their deaths. How long would you have gone on lying to me, she asked him, if I hadn't found out? Oh, I'd have told you eventually, he said. That made her even angrier – the sense of him biding his time, choosing the moment, suiting himself. Hadn't his bigamy made Anthea feel cheap, too? He had played them off against each other, strung them along, had the best of both worlds. That was another source of enragement. *Through the time of her delusion, Libby had gone on having sex with Nat.* Not every night, not every week, and not in a manner that satisfied her, but still they had sex. She found that revolting – not physically but emotionally. The contamination of another woman's body she could cope with, but not the duplicity of her man.

At half term, she escaped to the Canaries, where bougainvillea was in bloom, and the girls ate fresh pineapple for breakfast, and the sun burned off her misery. But after three days a storm blew in, thrashing the palms, and she came back even angrier than before.

The friends she talked to said she should meet Anthea – that talking to her would be cathartic, and that by seeing her (and seeing what Nat had seen in her) she would be able to see her off. But she was too proud. Anthea was a pathetic creature from the anthills. To meet her would be a form of victimhood. 'What was she like?' she asked Nat, with emphasis on the 'was', during the weeks of their trial rapprochement. An 'idealist', it seemed, much preoccupied with cruelty and injustice, and never mind her cruelty and injustice to Hannah and Rose. She also cared passionately about the environment, he said, especially trees. Trees! The little idiot thought of trees as victims, because of that double 'e'. Libby had no sympathy. Libby was with the trers.

The rapprochement was a trial all right. The office became Libby's refuge. She expected her work to suffer because she was suffering, but the company went from strength to strength. It must be hard for a woman to prosper in a male-dominated industry, people said. *Au contraire*, most of the men in advertising were lazy, mechanical, graceless and lacking in ideas. In this, Libby realised, they were just like Nat. The revelation came to her driving home through the Blackwall Tunnel in the new Mercedes, and was as cataclysmic – and liberating – as his infidelity. 'Nat's uncreative,' she thought, then said it aloud, laughing, 'Nat's uncreative,' then let it echo through the subterranean traffic-roar: 'Uncreative. Uncreative. Uncreative.'

The following week, at her insistence, he moved out, to a flat she helped find and fund the renting of. Life without him felt easier – one less dependent to worry about.

The only time she lost it was with Harry, when she bumped into him at the cinema. She was with Angie, on their way in to see *Shakespeare in Love*.

'How's tricks?' he said, seeing her. The casualness, the levity, was part of the affront.

'You've a nerve, Harry.'

Libby's voice was only a whisper but Angie must have heard the hiss. She moved away, to buy some popcorn.

'You knew all along,' she said.

'I'm not with you.'

'Exactly. And there was I thinking we were friends.'

'We *are* friends. What's this about?'

'Nat and I have split up.'

'*No.*'

'Don't pretend to be surprised.'

'I've not seen him for ages.'

'You knew he had a girlfriend.'

He paused then, lost for an answer, and reached for her arm, to take her aside. She shook him off, standing her ground. People were watching. Let them. Let the whole world know, for all she cared.

'You knew about her and I didn't. How do you think that feels?'

Silence. Then:

'I'm sorry, I –'

'It's too late to be sorry, Harry.' People in the queue were looking again. She raised her voice, to give them their money's worth. 'You're as big a shit as he is.'

She stomped off to join Angie. In the dark of the cinema she calmed down and felt vaguely ashamed. By the time he phoned, later that night, she was ready to forgive him – but first he would have to grovel.

'Of course I wanted to tell you,' Harry said, 'but I'd have felt I was betraying him.'

'So you betrayed me instead.'

'I hoped it would blow itself out. That you'd never get wind of it.'

'Oh, I got wind of it but he said I was being paranoid – and went on fucking her for another six months.'

'I told him to give her up.'

'Rubbish – the two of you were in cahoots. Lads sticking together. Wey-hey, good on yer, Nat, mum's the word. Whenever he came back late, he said he'd been with you.'

'He never told *me*.'

'Maybe you like her, Harry.'

'I've never met her. It would make no difference, even if I had. He's married to you.

'*Was* married.'

'He and I don't see each other any more.'

'He's too busy in bed, I expect.'

'Too ashamed to face me,' Harry said.

'I doubt that. He's entirely pleased with himself, as far as I can see.'

'He's a fucking fool.'

'So you didn't have a matey pact?'

'I told you, no.'

'And he never had sex with her round at your flat?'

'Jesus, of course not.'

'OK, I believe you. And I'm sorry about earlier, at the cinema. Angie told me off.'

'Forget it.'

'She thinks you're cute.'

'Uh.'

'Let's have supper sometime, to make up for it.'

'There's nothing to make up for.'

'Because I want to, then. OK?'

Talking to Harry was a turning point. Till then, she had seethed against Nat as a scheming Lothario. Now she saw him as Stan Laurel, buffoonish, an idiot-child out of his depth, one fine mess after another. She had spent a decade cleaning up his messes because she loved him. Now she was free. People had warned her breaking up would be terrible, and it was. But no more so than going through a car wash – after the thunder and waterspouts and your body rocking in grief, you came out cleansed. Most women would have given up on Nat years ago. Or avoided marrying him in the first place. She was in control now. Let him stew in remorse and self-vilification. It was a stew whose taste he seemed to like.

There were low points. But whenever she was down she thought of the enemy who had put her there and, rather than fantasise about killing herself, fantasised about killing Anthea instead.

And she wasn't vindictive about access. 'I think children need a father,' she told Deborah, over a drink. More to the point, she thought *her* children needed *their* father, since they were used to having him around. So the girls went to Nat one night a week and most weekends. The flat was a mile and a half away, in Lee – close but not too close. Without Libby's help he couldn't have afforded it, but if the girls were going to sleep there she didn't want him living in a dosshouse. The arrangement, she warned him, was strictly temporary: keeping an *ex*-husband stuck in the craw. He and the Ant were 'back together', it seemed, but not when the girls were there. Which was how Libby preferred it – no daughter of hers was going to mix with a lowlife no-hoper. How together two lovebirds could be when living in separate nests was a mystery to Libby. Perhaps the relationship wasn't the great passion Nat said it was. They hadn't even spent Christmas together. Was it for this he had sacrificed his marriage?

She pressed Redial again and this time Angie answered. The office was nominally closed for the duration, but Angie had suggested they operate a skeleton staff, namely her. At size 16, Angie was no skeleton, but she had shed her frumpishness and taken to wearing silky blouses. Just before Christmas a bouquet of white lilies came. Angie's eagerness to man the office must mean a man, people said: with no one around, she would be having love trysts. Whatever the truth, Libby was pleased for Angie. So long as the admirer didn't turn out to be a shit.

'All quiet?' Libby asked.

'As a grave,' Angie said. 'How's it with you?'

'Well, yes, exactly so.'

'Sorry,' Angie said. 'I forgot.'

'It was a mercy. She'd been a vegetable for two years.'

'Well, you've missed nothing here. Two calls all day, one a wrong number.'

'Don't bother about going in tomorrow then.'

'Oh I'll be here. I'm still sorting out your invite.'

'*What?*'

The letter had come weeks ago: Ms Elizabeth Raven and partner were being asked to a Millennium Eve Party, at the Dome, in the presence of HM the Queen, the Rt Hon. Tony Blair, the Archbishop of Canterbury and ten thousand others – a formal invitation would follow. Her first thought was to decline. The Dome had painful memories. While it was going up, she and Nat had often walked past and played a game of what-does-it-look-like with the girls. (A tent with guy ropes tied to the sky. A pincushion. A conker. A spiked helmet. A punk haircut. A birthday cake with skew-whiff candles.) Now she lacked a husband to take as her partner. Nor was she interested in being feted by New Labour – couldn't someone else go in her place? No way, Angie said: it was an honour to be asked, *of course* she had to attend. It'll be a circus, Libby said. But you can't not go to the circus, Angie said, all the papers have been on about it for weeks – there'll be music and fireworks and trapeze artists and ten thousand bottles of champagne. Who else will be there? Libby said. Oh, everyone who's anyone, Angie said. But I've no idea why they invited me, Libby said. Who cares why they invited you, Angie said, Willard White's going to be singing and Simply Red. All right, Libby said, tell them yes. The girls would resent her absence but she could take them to the Dome early in the new year.

'It's a shambles,' Angie said. 'They've still not sent out the invites. Now they're asking guests to collect them tomorrow night.'

'The Dome's easy from Brockley. I'll go by minicab.'

'You can't. The invites are being left at Stratford tube.'

'That's ridiculous.'

'I know. But I'm working on it.'

'Nothing else? Computers still OK?'

'*Libby*, for God's sake.'

They made a joke of it, but Libby's worries on that point weren't so easily laughed off. She had the image of an explosion, triggered in a second *by* a second, as 23.59.59.31.12.99 became 00.00.00.01.01.00. Computer screens would shatter, televisions catch fire, clocks melt like Dali watches, skyscrapers collapse, waterfalls freeze, mountains implode, children turn old, cats become dogs, flesh become grass. She was lucid, commonsensical, a good judge of people, but, in respect of science and logic, she might as well have been living in 1 BC. She blamed the reverend in Ballymena for filling her head with visions of Judgement Day. She blamed Nat for turning her world upside down. But really she blamed herself. An IT man had come at vast expense to install new software. But her mindset was less easy to adjust. The car engine going up in smoke today was an omen. At a nanosceond past midnight the horsemen of the Apocalypse would ride in. Just as well the invite to the Dome had failed to arrive. She ought to stay home with her children.

'Time you knocked off,' she told Angie.

'I'll hang on a bit. I'm off to see a film.'

'Not on your own, I hope.'

'No, not on my own.'

'Well, be good.'

She tried Damian again, before going back down. Still his voicemail. Not worth leaving a second message. He'd be at the gym or something. He would call.

<br>

8

*ANTHEA*

<br>

YELLOW CAGOULES lit Keswick's pavements like a host of daffodils. Early for the appointment, Anthea and Bella slipped into a café noisy with hikers. The glass counter steamed with fresh-baked scones and Anthea suggested they have one. But her mother wasn't remotely enticed. Scones meant crumbs on your clothes and extra calories. And Bella, even in Keswick, was *elegant*.

'Didn't Mr Coghlan say anything else?' Anthea asked.

'You have to be there when he reads it, that's all.'

'*Reads* it? Aloud, you mean?'

'That's what he said.'

'Just me?'

'Who else would there be?'

'It's so old-fashioned.'

Anthea had been fond of her grandmother – Granny, that is, rather than her mother's mother, who was, or had been, Nan. She used to visit her in Swansea twice a year and spend a week with her every summer in Pembrokeshire. Each visit would end with Granny fetching her purse – 'a little something to tide you over' – and Anthea guiltily accepting the largesse. They'd a lot in common, including the loss of the same man, son to one and father to the other. And Anthea had stayed in close touch even when Granny moved into a nursing home, Mellow Vista. The nursing costs weren't cheap and, as her one surviving blood relation, Anthea became involved in the finances, including the sale of Granny's terraced house to pay for her nursing care. 'There goes your nest egg,' Anthea's mother said, and sure enough they were down to the last £500 when Granny, on cue, died of pneumonia, in October – just short of the new millennium and her eighty-sixth birthday. The only heirlooms Anthea could think of were a wedding ring and silver necklace, but these had gone missing from the nursing home and she felt too upset to pursue them. Now Granny's will had come to light, and Mr Coghlan proposed to read it, but since she'd nothing left to bequeath the exercise seemed peculiarly pointless.

'Three fifteen,' Bella said. 'You'd better get going.'

Coghlan & Sunter were offically closed till 4 January, but Mr Coghlan was coming in specially from the golf course.

'It's rather unusual, Miss Hurt,' he said, as Anthea sat opposite. His pale broad head bore a single strand of hair, like a tress of weed in a wide white river. 'Your grandmother specifically requested the will be read aloud in your presence. Sorry if this seems like something out of a Trollope novel. But it won't take long.'

She sat in silence while he read, not paying full attention, distracted by that freak last hair. 'To the animal welfare charity Strays I give the sum of one thousand pounds,' she heard: well, Granny had always been a cat lover, nothing surprising there – except there was nothing left to give to the cats. As to the rest of the estate, 'comprising my house, garden and all contents, as well as all bank assets, I give to my granddaughter Anthea, provided that my executors are satisfied that she is putting the proceeds to proper use, namely for her personal edification.'

'The bit about your "personal edification" is certainly odd,' Mr Coghlan said. 'But you could always challenge the will if you object to it.'

'Of course not. She meant well. And it's not her fault there was nothing left to give.'

'I'm sorry?'

'Granny moved into a nursing home a few years before she died. We sold her house to pay for that, and the funds were almost used up.'

'That's not quite the case, it seems. There's a building society account in your name, in effect a trust fund – you knew about that?'

'No . . .'

'Your grandmother was obviously aware she could give away £3,000 a year without incurring inheritance tax, and she took full advantage.'

'But she never had much money. I don't see how she can have saved anything.'

'If she lived frugally and invested wisely, there's no great mystery about it. We're not talking about a vast fortune.'

'How much *are* we talking about, then?'

'It's a provisional calculation, until probate, but something in the region of £80,000.'

Driving back to Applethwaite through the drizzle, Anthea marvelled at the lights coming on in the country darkness – headlamps, security lights, Christmas lanterns, flashing Santas, the torches of men out walking their dogs through the dusk. When her mother enquired, she said only that she'd been left 'a little something'. She would tell her how much when she knew for sure. Maybe not even then. Bella would find the news difficult to deal with. It could even send her off the rails. If Granny had seen how Bella had triumphed over her drink problem – no relapse for six years – she might have left her something, too. On the other hand . . . Bella had never liked Granny. Even when Daddy was alive, there had been tension. And when he died prematurely, Bella – in Granny's hearing – blamed his 'weak Welsh genes'. There was nothing in the will to say that Anthea must keep its contents secret. But the money was intended strictly for her. Spend it wisely was the message. Use it to travel, or study, or help someone less fortunate. *But don't let your mother get her mitts on it.*

'Penny for them?' Bella said, from the steering wheel.

'I was thinking about Granny,' Anthea said, not untruthfully.

'Funny old bird. Spoiled your father rotten.'

'She was kind to me, too.'

'She was kind to everyone. One of life's do-gooders.'

Why was the term do-gooder always used pejoratively? Anthea wondered. Would the term a do-badder be preferable? A do-wickeder?

'Still, I'm glad if she left you something,' Bella said. 'You deserve it. You were very patient with her.'

'I liked her.'

More than I like you, Mummy, she was tempted to add. But that was mean and undaughterly. Bella was a good person now. Bella had conquered her addiction. Bella was a survivor.

But if she's a survivor, Anthea thought, she won't need a share of my pot of gold. In Pembrokeshire once, when Anthea was about six, there had been a rainbow, immaculately ROYGBIV, like something out of a colouring book. Granny said that where the arch met the sea, a few miles out, there was a pot of gold, like a lobster pot, and one day they would row a boat out and collect it. They never did, of course. But now Granny had magicked it to Keswick.

A *deus ex machina*, Nat would call it. Not so much Trollope as a fairy tale. It was the push she had been waiting for. No more excuses.

As the car pulled into the drive of the Applethwaite cottage, she could hear the phone ringing inside.

# 9

## *NAT*

SHIT, HE thought, getting no reply. He had pulled over in the country lane and gone behind a hedge, pretending to pee. There was no point leaving a message. He had already left half a dozen. Where was she? He climbed back in the car.

The lanes were dark and his mother sat grumbling beside him. How old did you have to be before your mother stopped driving you nuts? How old did she have to be? Eunice was in her sixties but looked older, worn down with acerbity and a sense of being hard done by – hard done by by Ronnie, hard done by by the world.

It was Uncle Jack who had upset her this time. 'You'd better stay here,' he'd told Nat, when he learned of the car crisis. 'It'll make a nice change for me, having a houseful.' A kind offer, gratefully accepted, but the 'you' didn't extend to Eunice. Why should it? She had a room booked at the Station Hotel. But in the ten minutes since they set out in Uncle Jack's Jaguar (its warm, leathered hush a reproach to the rattling, apple-core squalor of Nat's Renault), she had complained to Nat at length of the injustice of her exclusion – surely with a bit of goodwill and shuffling round, she could have been part of the houseful, too. She didn't blame Nat, she said – sleeping arrangements weren't the province of men – 'but I do think your wife might have said something'. Nat instinctively came to Libby's defence ('I expect she felt that Jack wasn't in a state to be argued with'), then reminded himself that 'wife' was no longer accurate and that half the point of driving his mother to Norwich was to tell her this.

The other half was to ask for money. Living apart from Libby was more than he could afford.

'There's something I've been meaning to tell you,' he said, steeling himself.

'That sounds ominous,' Eunice said, perking up.

Till six months ago, there had been nothing much to to tell. When Libby first accused him of having an affair, he denied it. 'You did the right thing,' Anthea said next day, at an urgent, miserable lunch to discuss the future.

'I'm not cut out to be someone's mistress. This has to stop.' It stopped. The sex stopped, anyway. He mourned the loss. 'I feel like a Saudi looter who's had his arms cut off,' he said. 'Me, too,' she said, 'but it's justice: we *were* looters.' No touching was the rule; platonic love only. No emails, either: emails had been their secret life, and she wanted to live openly. No more sneaking round.

White-dotted lines flew under the car like film on a spool. My life's my own, he thought. Mother doesn't even like Libby. So why's it so hard to tell her?

'When you've phoned lately and I've not been at the house,' he said, 'that's because I'm renting a flat.'

'Very sensible. It must be impossible writing with the girls around. How *is* the writing?'

'So-so.'

'Well, a flat makes sense. You're a busy man. And men need their independence.'

Anthea had used the same word, as they were walking by the Thames one evening after the clocks had gone back: 'It's no good. Meeting like this is too painful. You need your independence. And I need mine.' They were wandering through the dreary post-industrial waste below Charlton – old scrapyards and empty factories, with rusting cement hoppers and disused conveyor belts and ragwort blooming in the concrete cracks. 'You're seeing someone else,' he said. 'I've every right to, but no.' 'You've stopped loving me.' 'Not that, either.' 'What then?' 'You're still living with your wife.' 'I thought we agreed that was best.' 'It is. But you can't have both.' They stopped for a drink at the Anchor & Hope, a breaker's yard blocking their view upstream, and argued for an hour, like Creon with Antigone, no ground given either side, the stichomythia of longing and loss. Battered, forlorn, she asked would he mind dropping her home – 'I feel too shaky for the bus'. This will be my last kiss, he thought, leaning across, outside her flat, but then she kissed him back – 'weakened', as she put it later, in tears, in bed.

He began going to her flat again, more and more, three or four times a week, daring Libby to notice, which eventually she did.

A pair of headlights came towards them, angry and undipped. Nat flashed impatiently then saw his own were on full beam. The workings of Uncle Jack's car were hard enough to get the measure of without the distraction of failing to confess to his mother.

'Things have been difficult,' he said. 'That's why we didn't come to you at Christmas.'

266

'Because Hannah and Rose were ill, you said.'

'No, it was me.'

'You were ill?'

'No one was ill, but because of me we couldn't come.'

'If you were writing, you should have told me. I'd have understood.'

'The flat isn't just for writing.'

'Of course not, you work late, you probably sleep there sometimes. It's good to be out of Libby's shadow.'

'God, Mummy, just listen.'

For a month he had moved in with Anthea. But her Thamesmead flat was small and the continuous proximity seemed to irritate her. As a holding position, he went home again, to the spare bedroom. He felt adrift, batted back and forth between two homes, two notions of himself, two competing furies. Then he made his choice – and moved out, to a rented flat in Lee. Anthea brightened the place with stuff picked up at flea markets – medicine jars in coloured glass, enamelled boxes, Chinese fans, peacock feathers, hand-painted plates. Things were working again. She often stayed over there or he did at hers. But it hadn't been easy.

Nor was this.

'The point,' he said, 'is that I sleep at the flat *all* the time. I'm not living at home any more. The flat *is* home. Libby and I have separated.'

Fifty-four white-dotted lines flew past before she spoke again.

'Oh, Nat, just like your father.'

He should have guessed it was the first thing she would say.

'No, not like him at all,' he said. 'I live ten minutes away. The girls stay with me at least two nights a week. I'm a proper father to them.'

'He always regretted leaving me, you know.'

Nat kept his eyes on the road. The last photo of his father, taken three months before he died, showed him by a pool, beer in one hand, fag in the other, gold chain round his neck, a crop of chest hair sprouting from his Hawaiian shirt. All that was missing was a *Playboy* bunny or two. No man could have looked more pleased with life.

'If he'd stayed with me, he would still be alive,' Eunice went on.

'I'm not like him, Mummy.'

'Yes, but poor Elizabeth.'

He should have seen that one coming, too, the reinvention of Libby as a sweet, capable, altogether wonderful daughter-in-law, cruelly abandoned.

'Libby's doing fine,' he said. 'She has the house. She has her work. She isn't crushed by it.'

'Nor was I crushed. But most women can only ever love one man.'

That she had room in her heart only for Ronnie, the heartless cad, was a well-worn refrain.

'You never said you were unhappy with Elizabeth,' his mother said.

'I didn't think I was. Then I met someone.'

'Ah-*ha*, you had an affair.' He felt like a naughty schoolboy in front of the teacher. 'Who was she?'

'Is she. We're still together. Anthea she's called. You'd like her, Mummy. I'll bring her to Sussex one weekend.'

No girlfriend brought to Sussex had ever met with Eunice's approval. But he was heady from having unburdened himself.

'At the moment we're renting separate flats,' he said. 'It's not ideal.'

It was expensive, and Libby resented contributing to the rent, small, temporary and eventually-to-be-refunded though her contributions were. The arrangement also seemed to frustrate Anthea, who in recent weeks had been behaving oddly. Some nights, in bed at his place or hers, she'd suddenly get up and leave, returning an hour or two later. 'Out,' she'd say, like a surly teenager, when he asked where she'd been. 'Out where?' 'Just out.' She had become touchy, too – not just about where the relationship stood but about her appearance. The other night, for instance, in bed, he had complimented her on her hair, which she now wore long and brunette. 'My natural colour,' she said. 'I don't know what possessed me to dye it.' 'But here your hairs have a touch of red,' he said, touching the soft strands under her armpits and adding, 'Don't most women shave under their arms?' 'Why should they?' she said, bristling. 'Do men?' 'It wasn't a complaint,' he said. 'I love your body.' 'My body's just a shell,' she said. 'I'd rather you loved what's inside.'

She was difficult with him all that week. And by the time they were back on good terms, she had arranged to spend Christmas with her mother. We could have escaped to Goa or Thailand, he grumbled. Instead of which, with Anthea in the Lakes, Libby and the girls in Belfast, and his mother to be avoided in Sussex, he had spent Christmas alone in his flat.

'So long as you're happy,' Eunice said.

'I am. Or will be. Once we sort out somewhere to live together. It's so expensive renting. Now if I had the *capital* to buy somewhere . . .'

That his mother had the capital was indisputable. The family's wealth was why his father had married her. And despite Ronnie's valiant efforts to dispose of it before leaving her, she still had her 'investments' – and a house far too large for one person.

'I know you've talked of downsizing, Mummy.'

'One day perhaps.'

'You see, if you did, I . . .'

'Hopcroft Hall is such a lovely family home. I've always hoped you might want to live there.'

'Ideally, yes, but . . .'

'We could convert the east wing to make a granny flat. It would still leave you four bedrooms.'

'Libby and I used to talk about it. But now of course . . .'

'I'm tempted to go ahead with the conversion, anyway. Bricks and mortar are a sound investment. And it's you who'll inherit.'

'But you'll go on for a good few years yet, we hope, and meanwhile I . . .'

'Where on earth are we, by the way?'

They were in Norwich, following signs that said STATION, on the basis that such signs would also lead to the Station Hotel, though after three wrong turnings, two cul-de-sacs and a scenic tour of the city's principal buildings he began to wonder.

'That's it,' he said finally, 'we're here,' though he had got nowhere.

The hotel lobby reeked of cigarettes. Nat dreaded one of his mother's scenes. She was a great walker-out of places, taking any failure in standards (a duvet with a minuscule stain, a dinner plate with a hairline crack) as a personal insult. He could foresee having to smooth her down, like a trainer with a racehorse, or departing red-faced behind her, muttering apologies, in search of a less 'sordid' establishment. Luckily, the bedroom they were shown to had been freshly aerosolled. And though the carpet by the minibar was stained with red wine, she failed to notice.

She sat on the bed and patted the space beside her.

'Sit here a minute.'

He sat.

'Tell me: is she the first?'

'Is who?'

'This Anthea. Have there been others?'

'No, of course not.'

It was true. Though it was also true that he worried about tying himself down again too quickly. He had noticed a new flirtatiousness in himself – in his emails especially. Claire from Getting Started, Lucinda Vurt, his ex-agent Stefan's PA – it was exhilarating how much you could tell a woman when you weren't looking her in the face. He loved the intimacy of emails, the chance for candour, nothing crude or explicit but with a peck on the cheek – or x on the screen – at the end. He wasn't disloyal to Anthea. There was love and there was *lurve* and there was e-love – and this was merely e-flirting. His correspondents knew that he had left his wife and was seeing a younger woman called Anthea, though 'seeing' was deliberately vague and provisional, as though to suggest: I'm with her *now* but who can say what the future holds. Perhaps Anthea sensed this, the side of him detached from her. Something, anyway, had made her difficult of late, edgy, non-committal, cooler than the situation – a love affair – required.

'Eunice rested her hand on his.

'Your father made a fool of himself, chasing women.'

'I won't. This is serious.'

'That's what he always said. "This is serious." About every fling.'

'I don't have flings.'

'The problem was his incorrigible *appetite*. He exhausted himself in infidelity. That's why he died so young.'

'You mustn't worry,' he said. 'I'm not like him.'

But perhaps he was. What if restlessness ran in the genes, and Anthea was only the first of many? He imagined himself in an ivied quadrangle, with a bunch of doe-eyed girl students at his feet. Or on the stage of the Lyttelton, after the world premiere of *Wilderness Avenue*, as the front stalls rose to acclaim him. Anthea had seemed a one-off, a gift, an enormous stroke of luck. But perhaps she proved that young women, or certain kinds of young women, found him attractive. If so, he had failed to make the most of it. For two decades at SORU he had faithfully observed the sexual conduct codes; for a decade of marriage he had been a faithful husband. But now he was free – and mustn't imprison himself, even for Anthea.

'I should get going,' he said. 'Will you be all right?'

'Will *you* be all right?' his mother said.

'I'll be fine. Finances are my only problem.'

'Will you be all right driving back in the dark, I mean?'

'Yes. But if you could see your way to . . .'

'Don't worry about me. I have my ticket for the train and the station's just across the street. You will phone tomorrow night, won't you?'

'Tomorrow night?'

'Your father used to. Every new year, at midnight on the dot, from Spain. That's how I knew he wanted to come back. Only pride stopped him asking. Don't you make the same mistake.'

'With Libby?'

'With me. Don't let pride stop you asking if ever you need something from me.'

'I won't. In fact, I . . .'

'Good. Now drive carefully. And happy New Year, darling.'


*10*


*LIBBY*


'. . . SO THE loyal Dallybrand brought the golden-haired princess to the prince, and her hair matched the golden hair that had been left on the pillow, and the prince claimed her as his bride. Just as they were finishing their wedding-feast, the little jenny-wren who'd saved the princess from the witch flew chirping through the feasting-hall to complete a perfect day. Not only did the prince and princess live happily in the palace overlooking the deep-brown river, along with a dozen or more smiling golden-haired children, but peace and prosperity ruled the land for many years to come.'

Libby's mother used to tell the story when she and her sister Patsy were small and blonde-haired. And now her own blonde-haired daughters demanded to hear it most nights. It wasn't hard to dream up alternative endings. When they found the girl with the golden hair, she was ugly as a dog and the prince refused to marry her. Or: The girl was really the witch's daughter and, once married, turned the prince into a frog. Or: The loyal Dallybrand kept the girl for himself, never returning. Or: A girl with golden hair was never found so the prince married a short-haired brunette instead. But the girls would protest if she changed a single syllable. And she didn't like to disenchant them. It was only lately she'd become disenchanted herself.

Sasha and Ischia, Jack's daughters, were busy downstairs, clearing plates, washing glasses, rolling sofas and chairs back to their rightful positions. She felt guilty not helping. But her own daughters – Hyper and Fractious – needed her more. Not having planned to stay over, she had brought no pyjamas for them, and the room was too cold to sleep in vests. So they were wearing adult fleeces (hers and Nat's) and playing at gorillas – ooh-ooh-ooh-ooh – with their sleeves trailing on the ground. It had taken the story to quieten them. Luckily she reached the end before her mobile rang.

'Hey, babe,' Damian said. 'Good funeral?'

Libby shooed the girls down the corridor into the bathroom. Even then she found herself talking in a whisper. They had inklings of a man in her life but she wasn't ready to expose them to the reality.

'Are funerals ever good?' she said. 'It was bearable.'

'So where are you now?'

'At Uncle Jack's. We're staying the night.'

'I thought you were coming back.'

'Car problem. Long story. I'll be sleeping in Nancy's bed.'

'Alone, I trust.'

'It's OK,' she said, pretending not to hear, 'it doesn't feel creepy.'

Sleeping arrangements were a problem – and not a subject for discussion with Damian. Both the spare room (for the girls) and Nancy's room had double beds. Either Uncle Jack hadn't heard about the break-up or he was being mischievous. No matter. Nat would be sleeping on the floor.

'If ever I get like your aunt . . .' he said.

'Nat's aunt.'

'Whatever. Promise you'll put me out of my misery.'

'Same here,' she said. 'Let's make a pact.'

'Assisted mutual euthanasia.'

'Laid out hand in hand, like those lords and ladies on marble tombs in churches, but with a poison bottle instead of a dog under our feet.'

'Very romantic.'

'*Romeo and Juliet* for the terminally ill.'

She could hear voices in the background, *his* background, one or more of them possibly female.

'It sounds busy there,' she said. 'What's happening?'

'Not much. I'm just back from squash. Some mates have dropped round.'

He was always vague about his 'mates'. Even the few whose names she knew – Nicky, Gabs, Sam – remained a genderless abstraction. All men compartmentalised. But she resented being confined to Damian's bedroom while the mates had the run of the flat.

'Sounds like you're having a party,' she said.

'A gathering,' he said.

'Wish I were there.'

'Well, jump in a taxi *now*.'

'You're crazy.'

'I'll pay the fare. What would it take – two hours?'

'I've got the girls with me,' she said, as Hannah and Rose trailed their sleeves back from the bathroom. Nat had promised to buy toothbrushes in Norwich, if he could find a shop open. She lifted the duvet, and motioned them underneath. They sat with their hands clasped under their chins, shivering, staring, hunched against the cold.

'Let Nat look after them. He's there, isn't he?'

She felt awkward, with the girls there.

'Not at this precise moment.'

'That wanker's never around when he's needed.'

She held the phone tighter to her ear. His tone was jokey but she disliked it all the same. Perhaps he had learned it from her. But as an ex-wife she was allowed to call Nat a wanker. Whereas Damian saying it implied a judgement on her for having married Nat in the first place – a judgement on her lack of judgement. In Damian's version of their emotional history, Nat was the Fool and he the Hero. The Fool had screwed up by screwing a student, a lapse which some wives would have forgiven ('All men have lapses, Libby.' 'Do they, Damian?') but which turned Libby to stone (or glass, or ice), until the Hero, through ardent pursuit, melted her heart and restored her to life. The Sleeping Beauty myth. Libby saw it more pragmatically. After Nat had betrayed her, Damian made her feel wanted again. But this wasn't a tale for two nosy daughters.

'Come and spend the night.'

'You're breaking up,' she said.

'You know you want to.'

'Poor reception.'

The girls sat waiting for her to implicate herself. Her reluctance to come clean about Damian, not just to them but to most of her friends, was, in part, his age. On a good day, in his Armani suit, he looked about nineteen. Stuff what people think, Angie said: choosing someone younger makes good sense – in Britain the average man dies at seventy-five, the average woman at eighty, so stick with Damian and odds are you'll expire about the same time. The same law applies with sex, Angie added: older men wilt whereas young ones stay upright. Go for it, she said. So Libby had. But she couldn't go for it now, with her daughters scanning her like X-rays and the sound of Nat in the hallway downstairs.

'I have to go,' she said.

'Won't you come out to play, then, babe?'

Voices were laughing in the background. What was it he'd recently pointed out to her? That in the days when they both worked at Arran & Arran, his desk on the fifteenth floor (so he worked out from the floor plan) lay directly below hers, 'so if the floors were glass I could have seen right up your skirt, babe'. So vulgar of him, so demeaning of her. She deserved to be taken more seriously.

'Call me later,' she said, and pressed the red.

While Nat did the business with the toothbrushes, she stood at the window again, gazing into the dark. *Babe.* How could she sleep with a man who called her babe? She had known Damian for over two years now, but sometimes it seemed she didn't know him at all. What was there to know? His Bermondsey flat was a homage to blankness. Polished floorboards, black leather sofa, white cushions, smoky coffee table, empty shelves. No newspapers. No ornaments. *No books.* The simplicity – vacuousness – had been seductive at first. Where Nat was a Victorian novel with its pages falling out, Damian was a blank sheet – a white space in which she could inscribe herself, begin a new chapter, remake her life. It was only friendship at first. He was too young; it was too soon. But back at his flat one night, after dinner, months on from throwing out Nat, she saw the possibility. There would be this man in a low-lit room with a Philip Glass CD playing, and you would do it with him and then you'd go. No strings. A Mr Anyone. A sweet, meaningless fuck with Anon. Wasn't that how sex should be, when you were single? If Damian had leaned across and kissed her then, she might have responded. She was glad now that he hadn't; that she got promiscuity out of her system without being promiscuous; that she was able to go home, sober up, rethink, and realise how unseemly casual sex would have been. A lucky escape. Later she decided it wasn't just luck. Damian had protected her from the young-man-desperate-for-a-shag bit of him and the abandoned-wife-in-search-of-affirmation bit of her. He had looked after the relationship instead of rushing in. She began to take him seriously.

All the same, she would probably never have slept with him but for the shopping. The suggestion was his: a Saturday afternoon in the West End buying clothes. Men and shopping? After Nat, she had no great hopes. But far from wilting after five minutes, Damian led her up and down the King's Road, greedy, energetic, relentless. In Dressed to Kill, he was greeted like an old familiar. Obviously he had taken other women there, which might have knocked her back, but his enthusings won her over – she must try the mauve jacket, the little slate-grey suit would look perfect, the short, lacy nightdress was *so so her*. Actually, it (the nightdress) wasn't her: the hem barely reached her navel. But he enjoyed establishing this for himself, round the fitting-room curtain. Not that his enthusiasm extended to actually buying her anything.

By the fifth till, her credit card £1,900 lighter, she began to wonder about this. But perhaps he was afraid of looking ostentatious or of presuming to treat her like a mistress. Either way, she was enthralled by the novelty. A man who liked to go shopping. When all she knew was Nat.

'Are there lots of men like you?' she said, as they left Hot Couture.

'Nah,' he said.

'Him and him,' she said, as two young men went by with bags from Harrods. 'They like shopping too. Maybe I should play the field.'

'Aren't I good enough for you?'

'I don't know. It depends.'

'On what?'

'Whether you want me just for my clothes.'

'Oh, you don't have to wear clothes.'

'*Now* he tells me. When I've just spent two grand.'

'They're great clothes. But.'

'Are you saying you find me sexually attractive, Damian?'

'Silly question.'

'So it's just sex then? Sex and shopping?'

'No, it's love. I love you, babe.'

When she slept with him that night, she wasn't sleeping with just Anyone.

It wasn't easy. She needed to know he loved her in order to open up to him; but believing it sent her in a panic. She wasn't ready for love; but without love, what was the point? If he wasn't a friend, she would not have slept with him; but once she slept with him, he wasn't just a friend. Sex with a friend was a fine idea but also an oxymoron. He had to say 'I love you' before she kissed him, touched him, felt the wetness between her legs. What had first drawn her to him was the unintimacy, the baggagelessness, the promise this wouldn't matter. But it was an ideal she couldn't live up to. She needed to know she counted for something, despite the fear that this would tie them more closely than she wanted to be tied. It wasn't easy. She wasn't easy. You couldn't blame him for not understanding. No young man would.

The sex wasn't easy, either. She was too married and too scared. To be made love to, you have to love yourself, and Nat's betrayal had delibidinised her – finding confidence again took time. Slowly she learned to trust. The less he pushed, the more she gave; the more space he allowed her, the more intimate she felt. One night, on his balcony, standing in the open, still fully dressed, she had her first orgasm with him. It felt like the first orgasm she had ever had. There she was, her eyes half closed, his hand stroking her clitoris, the Thames and Tower Bridge beyond his shoulder, and – from nowhere, despite herself – she came. Afterwards, when the quaking stopped, she felt absurdly, pathetically grateful, assuming love had made it happen – and that love would make it happen again. In reality, in the months since, she hadn't experienced such intensity again. It didn't matter. To be overwhelmed like that had been scary. In some ways she felt relieved. But it was strange.

The summer warmth, the balcony, the self-transcendence: thinking of them now, in Nancy's cold bedroom, with her girls along the corridor brushing their teeth, she felt embarrassed.

As she stood redialling Damian's number, a floodlight came on in the garden. It was Jack, carrying bottles out and staring up at the house. She backed away, not wanting him to see her. Poor Jack, she thought, poor Nancy. But at least their marriage had been simple: they made their choice and stuck. The same with her own parents – no confusions of the heart. She had dreaded telling her mother about the break-up. 'Such a lovely boy,' she always said of Nat. But even in Ballymena there was divorce these days. 'So long as you can manage on your own for a bit,' her mother said, the weekend Libby flew over to tell her. Her mother assumed the separation was temporary – to someone of her generation, widowhood was the only socially acceptable way of being without a man. 'It's over, Mum, I might be on my own for ever,' Libby said, then, seeing her mother flinch, added, 'though it won't be for want of trying.' That didn't go down well, either. Women mustn't push themselves, her mother said. If they didn't push themselves, Libby said, they never got anywhere. The two of them sat by the ticking electric fire, becoming heated. 'To push yourself at work is one thing,' her mother said, 'but in relationships it's different.' 'If a woman doesn't push herself, she'll never have relationships.' 'If she only has relationships, she's a slut.' Libby had been on the verge of shouting, but let the fire carry the tensions away, up the chimney. Remembering it now, from Nancy's silent bed, she missed the angry closeness of that moment, the ticking fire, the hearth-beat.

Jack couldn't be a nicer host but she felt alien here, in the darkness of the English shires. Even in London, where she had spent half her lifetime, she didn't belong. Always the outsider – because of her accent, her complexion, her Ballymena blood. Clearly others didn't see it that way, though. The invitation to the Dome was proof of that. As was Damian's reaction when she told him about it.

'You're joking,' he said. 'The big gig? Wow. No one at Arran & Arran's been invited. Congratulations.'

'Elizabeth Raven and partner it says.'

'Who's the lucky guy?'

'The man who chooses the right frock for me.'

'You're on.'

His boyish pleasure didn't fade when they went shopping that same afternoon, though his influence on her choices was limited. 'Think silk and taffeta,' he said, 'think sleeveless with slits.' But the Dome was a glorified marquee: in the flimsy outfits he suggested she would die of hypothermia. In the end she settled for a press-crushed, metallic polyester hooded dress (from Issey Miyake at Liberty's), to be worn under a velvet coat with faux-Mongolian lamb trim and embroidered panels (from Karen Millen). She bought some scarily expensive jewellery as well. The Dome was a hot ticket and she had to look good.

She still worried about taking Damian as her escort. They had been seen together already, in restaurants and theatres. All the same. She could imagine people sneering at his lack of gravitas – and at her, for bringing a toy boy. *Babe.* He was too flippant, too easy-come-easy-go. *Can you come out to play?* What sort of question was that? And what sort of man would ask it in front of his friends – friends who always sounded so rowdy?

'Friends come and go,' he once said. 'My love for you does not.' It sounded like a motto from a valentine card. Did he mean it? When he asked her to join him tonight, did he mean *that?* Or would there be friends – women friends – who didn't know about her? She could call his bluff and phone for a taxi – there must be cab drivers who'd be glad of a £200 fare. But that was Faeryland. Clearing off would upset the girls, be discourteous to Uncle Jack, and give Damian the impression that she was a) putty in his hands, b) a creature of whimsy, and/or c) a jealous bitch checking up on him, none of which was true or none of which, if true, it would be tactful to admit. She just wished she could trust him more – shrug when he held parties in her absence and believe the things he whispered in bed.

Then again, if he meant the things he whispered in bed she would have to marry him. And she couldn't marry him till her divorce came through. And she might not want to marry him even then.

This is absurd, she thought, I'm a thirty-seven-year-old mother of two, solvent, successful, with my own company, and free to do whatever I please. If only I knew what that was.

The security light whitened the garden again: Jack with more bottles. She backed away, mobile in hand, still searching.

## *ANTHEA*

NAT WAS speaking to the answering machine as they walked in: 'It's only me.' There were eight previous messages, and the phone rang again as they were listening to the last. 'Yes, she's here,' her mother said, mouthing 'It's him' as she passed the handset. Anthea didn't share her mother's excitement. In the car she had been in dreamland, spending her legacy, and now reality was dragging her back.

'I've been trying to get you,' he said.

'So it seems.'

'Your mobile was switched off.'

'I've been busy.'

'How are things?'

'OK.'

Her mother mouthed 'I'll go and make tea' – whether a diplomatic withdrawal or a ruse to listen in on the kitchen extension Anthea wasn't sure.

'I've missed you,' he said.

'You're with your family.'

'That doesn't stop me missing you.'

'You should have thought of that.'

'I wanted you to come.'

'Let's not go over it again.'

It was true he had invited her to the funeral – but with so little grace and conviction, she felt she was expected to decline. And once she decided to go to the Lake District to see her mother, he arranged to take his wife instead. Not that she was jealous at missing the funeral of a stranger. But she did feel sidelined. How long did it take to be granted legitimacy? She felt like his dirty little secret.

'What's the weather like there?' he said.

'Is that all you called for – a weather report?'

'No.'

'What then?'

'The party tomorrow night . . .'

'I'm leaving early. I'll be back in good time.'

'Good, but . . . it turns out Libby has a party too.'

'So?'

'Apparently I agreed to babysit.'

'You can't have. We arranged to go out.'

'I know. But I forgot I'd promised to have the girls. So I was thinking . . .'

'I'm not sitting at home on Millennium Night.'

'I don't expect you to.'

'We can't take your children with us – you're not suggesting that?'

'It's only a supper party. They could watch television.'

'I don't know him well enough to ask.'

'He'd understand. He has children too, you said.'

'Grown-up children. Forget it, Nat. I'll go on my own.'

She should have said no to Mr Fell in the first place. An evening with a bunch of fifty-year-olds was a dismal prospect. But he seemed so nervous when he asked ('Just a modest repast, among friends, I expect you'll have more exciting engagements, but if you were able to honour us with your presence'), she couldn't bear to disappoint him. 'And do bring your partner,' he said. 'Thanks,' she said, 'I will,' failing to mention what kind of partner Nat was (older, married, a father of two). The first would be apparent on sight but she had been hoping to hide the rest. Now she *could* hide the rest. She would go without him.

'Cry off,' Nat said. 'Tell him you're sick.'

'It would be rude.'

'But I want to spend the evening with you.'

'Tell your wife to find a babysitter, then.'

'At this stage? For Millennium Night?'

'It's not my problem, Nat.'

'We could stay in. Drink champagne. I'll cook for you.'

'And your daughters can be horrible to me all evening.'

'They like you! They find the situation unsettling, that's all.'

'So do I. What about my feelings?'

'It's difficult to talk now, I'm at the wake, at Uncle Jack's house – can I call you back?'

'Don't bother,' she said, hanging up with a rhetorical flourish. 'You stick to the dead while I get on with life.'

She was surprised by how angry she felt. Not even Jake had provoked such rage. But Jake hadn't been weak. Nat let his wife walk all over him. All over Anthea too.

From the kitchen came the noise of pots being banged – Bella's attempt to suggest she had been busy throughout the call.

Anthea paced the living room, too furious to sit. Till now the contract with Nat had been simple: she gave him her body, he gave her his mind. But was his mind worth having? It had seemed so lively at first. Now she knew him better, she saw it ran along fixed tracks. Listening to him was like sitting on a train watching the same few landscapes rush past – not a journey into the unknown but a dull commute. She had been in thrall to the romance of writing, convinced that under his tutelage she would become someone else. It hadn't happened. She was disappointed with him and angry with herself. The minds of men as God's gift to women – how had she swallowed that patriarchal crap?

It was true he had sacrificed a lot to be with her. But that was his choice – she mustn't feel bullied by it or ruin her own life out of gratitude. The only issue to address was: *Am I happy with him?* The trivial annoyances she could forgive – him snoring, picking his teeth, and never thinking to clean or wash up. The intrusion of his past life was more of a problem. Certain television programmes made him cry, because they reminded him of his daughters. Or the phone would go, and Anthea would pick it up, to hear the woman at the other end – his wife – breathing hatred. (How can you tell it's a woman? he asked. Or Libby in particular? Or hatred? Dunno, she said, but trust me, I can, it's her.) She had wanted proof that she mattered enough for him to leave his home. But she hadn't bargained on the reality: the laziness and self-absorption at one extreme, and the doglike slobbering over her at the other. To escape him, she sometimes went walking at night. He grumbled about it, denying her even this space. She had begun to sympathise with his wife. And to wonder if she was relieved to be shot of him.

I have Granny's legacy now, she thought. Well, I don't have it, but I will, and once I do I'll have more freedom and I can go away and do something real and make a difference somewhere, like I've been saying I will. Or is it pathetic to wait? What's to stop me going at once?

'That was quick,' her mother said, setting the tray down on the coffee table, away from the fire. Anthea drank only herb tea and never touched biscuits. Hence the pot of Assam and plate of chocolate digestives. 'All well?'

'He was tied up at his aunt's funeral. Couldn't really speak.'

'At least he made the effort. Most men wouldn't have rung at all.'

'Nat rings all the time. That's not the problem.'

'Is there a problem?'

'You could say that.'

'What sort of problem.'

'Basic incompatibility, I think.'

'Incompatibility's something you can work at, sweetie. Even the most perfect men seem ill-suited at first.'

Anthea wondered what a man would have to do for her mother to deem him ill-suited. Commit murder? Genocide? If a convicted rapist had proposed marriage, her mother would have urged Anthea to think twice before rejecting him. It was as if losing her own husband had made Bella more desperate to find one for her daughter. Hence her present exasperation: how could Anthea not throw in her lot with a man who bothered to phone?

'This isn't a sudden thing, Mum. I've been seeing him for eighteen months.'

'Are you worried about having sex with him? Is that it? Even your father and I had sex before we married, you know.'

Anthea stood up and threw a log on the fire. Once, when she was twelve, she'd heard her mother, drunk, noisy, through the bedroom wall, begging her father to make love – 'Come on, why won't you?' It sounded as though he was fighting her off. In disgust presumably. Though the disgust was mostly Anthea's, at having to listen.

'For God's sake, Mum,' she said, with her face to the fire. 'Of course I've had sex with him. What do you think I am?'

'Good. Then the next thing is to live together.'

Anthea watched the flames catch. The issue was a sensitive one and had come up only the other night. She was feeling low and for once in her life she had let rip – about her crap job, her shitty flat, her lack of personality, the loss of her best friend (Rachel having gone to Canada for a year), her pathetic attempts at writing, her failure to attract any man her own age other than Jake, from whom she had rebounded into the arms of someone supremely unsuitable. '*Supremely* unsuitable?' he said. 'Yeh: married, a father, obsessed with his work, short of money and unwilling to commit himself.' 'I am committed,' he said. 'So why aren't we living together?' 'No reason. Let's do it. I'll move in tomorrow.' 'So you can save on rent?' 'Because I want you.' 'As your pet. Your plaything. To keep in a box.' 'If we move in together, we'll be living in the same box,' he said. 'You're right,' she said, 'it's a bad idea. Who wants to live in a box with an old man?' She regretted 'old' even as she said it. Rows were meant to be purging and elemental, but there were places they shouldn't go and age, with Nat, was an open sore.

'He's a lot older than me,' she told her mother, brushing bark dust from her hands.

'Maturity's a good thing in a man.'

'And he has two children.'

'That won't stop him wanting children with you.'

'I don't know if I want children.'

'Of course you want them.'

Somewhere there must be mothers who listen to their daughters, Anthea thought. If only in fairy tales.

'He has such a nice voice,' her mother continued. 'And he's been so encouraging with your literary thingies.'

Anthea poured herself more tea. It spluttered from the spout, over the edge of the cup, on to the walnut table, forcing her mother to fetch a tissue. Good.

'Anyway, we had a row,' Anthea said.

'I thought you were short with him.'

'Not just now, before Christmas.'

After being called 'old', he had stormed out. She felt bad and ready to apologise, but when he climbed in bed with her some hours later, smelling of beer, she lost all sympathy. He tried to turn her body towards him. She stiffened. He traced a finger across her spine. She pulled away. He ran his lips down her thigh and nosed into her buttocks, cunnilingually, analingually, any cleft would do. She tightened herself against him. Rebuffed, pissed off, he sat up. 'You've never loved me,' he slurred. 'At this precise moment I don't, no.' 'Whereas my love is constant.' 'So constant that you give me no space.' 'I love you too much for space.' 'It's not me you love,' she hissed, 'you're in love with a fantasy.' Later she softened and they made up. But her anger hadn't abated. It was part of why she'd come to the Lakes.

Things came too easily to him. He'd even left his wife easily. What was to prevent him leaving her? Only finishing with him first.

'Perhaps you need talk to someone,' her mother said.

'I've been talking to you, haven't I?'

It was true. For a good hour. As the logs burned in the grate and night drew harder round the fells.

'Not me,' her mother said. 'A therapist.'

'Um,' Anthea said.

'Someone like Dr Fisher.'

'No thanks.'

Why pay good money to be told that Nat was a surrogate father? She was a big girl now and would work things out on her own.

When the mantel clock chimed seven, they moved to the kitchen, to slice carrots and celery, to go with the dips and cocktails. The cocktails were fruit juice, mixed with fruit juice. Anthea would have loved a proper drink, and perhaps she'd have one later at the Cygnet, but bringing alcohol into the house was out of the question. Several times lately half-sensations had returned from infancy – the sour tang of her mother's breath or an image of her listing like a reef-wrecked liner. The trauma of widowhood hadn't started Bella drinking, just made the drinking worse. Thank God she was on the wagon these days, even if it made her a bore.

I'm right not to mention the legacy, Anthea thought. It will throw Mum into a tizz. It might even start her drinking again. It's something I must break to her slowly.

*12*

*HARRY*

LUKE TILBEY had suggested a pub in Catford, round the corner from his office. When Harry arrived he was already at a table in the far corner, the *Evening Standard* in front of him (ERROL DAD MURDER CHARGE), MTV on overhead. What would it be? Harry asked. A pint of Young's, Luke said, lighting up a Marlboro. He was stocky, sweating and short-haired, with a ring in his right ear and a scar on his left cheek. All the solicitors Harry knew were middle-class liberals; Luke looked like a member of the BNP.

'This is off the record, right,' Luke said.

'Right.'

'If not I might as well talk to the tabloids – they've been offering thousands. My client the psychopath, et cetera.'

'You can trust me.'

'A journalist you can trust – that's a good one.'

'You saw my piece about that mortuary case?'

'I liked it.'

'Well then.'

'How long have you got?'

'As long as it takes.'

'Fire away.'

'How come it's you representing Ray Nuard?'

'The firm's been representing him and his brothers since they were teenagers – the usual stuff, drug offences, shoplifting, fights, driving cars that don't belong to them, nothing spectacular. Duane, the oldest, was the biggest trouble. Ray was the least. The only serious charge against him was two years ago, for carrying offensive weapons. I got him off. So he asked for me again.'

'You think he's innocent?'

'He says he's innocent. That's good enough for me.'

'It doesn't sound as if he's innocent. From what the police say.'

'I'm surprised they were so cooperative. You're small fry.'

'I'm sure they gave the nationals more.'

'Have you seen the witness statements?'

'No.'

'Ray's statements?'

'No.'

'The transcript of his interviews?'

'No.'

He laughed.

'What *did* they fucking give you, then?'

'They said he confessed.'

'Rubbish. Does he look like a murderer?'

'What do murderers look like? – I don't know.'

'Ray is distraught, just like you would be – Errol's his son.'

'The police say he was the last person to be seen with Errol. In McDonald's. They found a plastic toy in his jacket pocket.'

'Don't jump to conclusions.'

'Errol's saliva was on the toy.'

'Ray took Errol to McDonald's the week before. Not that night.'

'If Ray didn't kill Errol, who did?'

'Was Errol killed at all? That'll be our first submission – to stop the trial, because there isn't a body.'

'Will that work?'

'Probably not. There are precedents for murder trials without a corpse. But we'll do our best.'

'So you think Errol might still be alive?'

'I didn't say that.'

'You've no idea who his killer is?'

'I didn't say that, either.'

'Go on then.'

'Could we have another drink first?'

At the bar, Harry checked his mobile again. Still no word from Marcia. He'd been leaving messages on her answering machine all day.

'Who do I think killed Errol?' Luke said, dragging on another Marlboro. 'Here are some options. The baby's dad, Louis. Things can get stressed with four kids in a house. And he's known to be volatile. Then there's Sharon herself: suppose *she* killed Errol.'

'I find that hard to believe,' Harry said. 'I saw her at the press conference before Christmas.'

'She's a good-looking woman, you mean. Or a good actress.'

'She obviously loved Errol.'

'So did Ray – why would Ray kill *his* own child?'

'Where is Ray now?' Harry said, changing tack.

'In Maidstone prison. Where he'll be for the next year. That's how long this will take to come to court.'

'How's he doing?'

'He's shit-scared. First Sharon dumps him, then she disses him, then she frames him.'

'Did Sharon tell the police it was him, then?'

'She told them he had been threatening her. Hell hath no fury like a partner scorned – that'll be the case for the Crown.'

For the next hour and two more pints, Luke described the Nuard family. Harry found his candour alarming. Was he always this leaky? Best keep his number from Kendal Platt. Later, as the pub filled up for last orders, they talked about safer subjects: Harry about the *Gazette* and Luke, in no particular order, about his impending marriage (his Scottish partner of a year being 'up the duff'), his 'wasted year' reading Philosophy before he switched to Law, fat-cat barristers, Millwall FC, the attractions of Tenerife as a holiday resort and his 'evil bastard of a dad'. He was no more discreet about his private life than his professional. Maybe drink had loosened his tongue. But even after five pints he seemed quite sober.

'Whisky?' Luke asked, after the barman rang the bell.

'We're too late.'

'I've a bottle in the office. Plus some stuff that might interest you.'

I ought to go home, Harry thought. I promised myself I'd call Stephen. But this is important. I'd never forgive myself. I can't not go with Luke.

Here was his insight for the day. His millennial epiphany. To be at the heart of things a man must ignore his own heart.

Not even that. Forget the pieties. The truth was less glib. He hadn't ignored his heart but listened to it. Forget Stephen, it said, Errol Winthrop matters more.

'So are you coming?' Luke said.

'Sure.'


## 13

### *LIBBY*


AS LIBBY came downstairs, Jack was pulling his coat on.

'Just taking Thumper out,' he said. 'Fancy a walk?'

Thumper drooled and slurried round her feet. She didn't like dogs, least of all young and untrained dogs, but a breath of air would do her good.

Outside was black – no street lights and the moon in hiding. Jack's torch beam went ahead of them like a search party, discovering walls, fences, gateways, gravel drives. Occasional cars broke like waves along the bypass. It wasn't a night for going out unless you had to.

'How's your business?' she asked, sticking to small talk – anything but Nancy.

'Could be worse,' he said, but to Libby, listening, that seemed unlikely: people weren't buying quality mowers, the floating exchange rate had buggered exports, a loan he had taken out was all but spent. The bank, meaning Harris ('tall chap, eye for the ladies, you met him today, married to Elise, small, French, you certainly met *her*'), had indicated a further loan might be forthcoming – but only on the basis of 'significant restructuring', which would mean him, Jack, being put out to grass while his deputy, Marcus ('doesn't know his arse from his elbow'), became managing director.

'In effect, they'd be subsidising Marcus to buy me out,' Jack said, standing by the village telephone kiosk while Thumper cocked his leg.

'Is that so bad, if you get a fair price?'

'I won't. Anyway, it's *my* company.'

'Isn't anyone interested in acquiring you?'

'A couple of our rivals in Europe.'

'So talk to them.'

'They'd strip our assets then close us down. Half a dozen lads would be offered jobs in Belgium. But there'd be nothing for the others. Or for me.'

'There are things you could do, Jack.'

'Probus? The Rotary Club? A little consultancy work? I might as well be dead.'

'But if the market's against you . . .'

'That's what's frustrating. It's starting to turn. And the new model is our best yet. The Greensleeves Nine: state of the art. A few months' grace and we'd be laughing.'

They paused at the T-junction, by the Fox & Feathers, while Jack lauded his Greensleeves and Thumper took a dump. The pub sign creaked in the wind, like a man swinging from the gallows. Libby pulled her coat tighter. She was cold, the night air tickling her throat.

'Couldn't you get a venture capitalist involved, rather than the bank?' she said, coughing.

'All they want to invest in are Internet companies. Downtheplug-holedotcom. Mowers aren't sexy enough.'

'They could be. If you rebrand.'

'*Rebrand*? You sound like Marcus.'

'Reposition yourself, then.'

'That's his kind of bullshit, too. He wants to turn us into a waste-management company. I want to remind people we exist.'

'Sounds like you need an advertising campaign,' she said, coughing again.

'Sounds like you need a drink.'

They left Thumper whining in the porch and sat in a corner, away from the regulars at the bar. Vodka and tonic for her, Glenfiddich for him.

'You on the other hand are thriving,' he said. 'Or so I'm told.'

'Beginner's luck.'

'Would I have seen any of your adverts?'

'We've had two big poster campaigns. And stuff on telly.'

She didn't specify, afraid he'd disapprove. Raven McCready's profit margins might be healthy but she worried about the press they were getting. 'Sassy' was the initial consensus: 'bright, streetwise, a company that puts women on top'. More recently the word 'raunchy' had come up – 'or should we say raanchy?' – on account of the Raanch ad, designed by Tarquin (late of Arran & Arran, now freelance). The poster showed a black man's torso, rear-on, naked from butt to shoulder, with a woman's white hand curling round his waist, her fingernails painted silver, and the slogan: 'For a cooler pull, try Raanch.' Here's a stylish, multi-ethnic, post-macho lager, the subtext went, a better bet for attracting women than your laddish swill. The Raanch people loved the roughs and green-lighted the shoot, but Libby had argued with Tarquin about the positioning of the woman's hand on the man's torso: how obvious did it have to be that she was reaching upwards; that her head (half hidden from view) was level with his groin; that she was giving him a blow job? Five years before they would have been arguing whether you could use a black model at all – wasn't that too minority for a mainstream product? Now black was known to sell, Libby's clients were keen on Afro-Caribbean models. But a blow job? A *transracial* blow job? Even if the Advertising Standards Board let it through, how was Libby going to feel when the girls saw the poster (booked for sixty prime sites in London) and asked, 'What's the lady doing, Mummy'? In the end, Tarquin won her over and the ASB didn't demur. All there'd been was a passing mention in the trade press of 'raunchy – or should we say raanchy? – post-feminist start-ups like Raven McCready, as typified by their ads for Raanch lager and Hersuit shampoo'. (The latter had been a *Psycho*-ish spoof about a woman taking a shower; when the stalking camera pulled back the shower curtain, she wasn't stabbed to death but handed a bottle of Hersuit – 'Some shampoos can save your life.') Raunchy? Me? Libby? She felt reproached, like the time the RE teacher caught her snogging behind the sports pavilion and called her 'a little tart'. Sex sells, everyone knew that. But was Libby overselling sex because of changes in her own life? Not that what she did with Damian was kinky. All the same. Sex was on her mind more than it used to be – and she shouldn't bring her private life to the office.

'Ever thought of advertising?' she asked Jack.

'We did once,' he said. But 'we' turned out to be his father, circa 1953, who had launched *his* state-of-the-art machine with adverts in *The Times* depicting 'the five implements necessary for maintaining a perfect lawn': rake, fork, roller, edging shears, Greensleeves mower.

'It looked like a Victorian print,' Jack laughed. 'Orders dropped 30 per cent in six months.'

'I'm not surprised,' Libby said.

'After that, we decided adverts were a waste of time.'

'Ah, but . . .'

'I know: they *can* make a difference. Marcus and I have talked about it.'

'What's he say?'

'Oh, he's against. Till we've refinanced. Then with me gone he'll move into waste management, and there'll be no mowers to advertise anyway.'

'Um, I employed a Marcus once,' she said.

'They're all over the shop. Fancy another?'

'I'll get them.'

Her Marcus had been Gavin, Raven McCready's ex-Head of Accounts, who within a month of the company being launched, before two big contracts made it secure, held secret meetings with a couple of potential investors – 'strictly contingency' he claimed when (by accident, through a stray email) she found out, but in her eyes a weasel-ploy towards a takeover bid. She had 'let him go', with a modest pay-off. Jack couldn't let Marcus go without the bank foreclosing, but if he came up with a new business plan, a better one than Marcus's, perhaps they would give him another shot.

To make Raven & Son a viable concern (and turn a man round, restore his sense of purpose, bring him back from the dead) – she could help with that.

When she put the drinks down, and suggested Raven McCready get involved, he, true to form, resisted.

'You'd only be doing it from charity.'

'Rubbish,' she said. 'I've a business to run.'

'You're in London, we're in the sticks.'

'Doesn't matter. I see opportunities.'

'What would your rake-off be?'

'Considerable.'

Minimal. Insufficient even to cover costs. But to a small country business, it would sound convincingly steep.

'There's no point in advertising unless we sell thousands,' he said.

'If it works, you will sell thousands.'

'Who knows what works?'

'We know what works. That's our job.'

She meant it as a favour but was drawn by the challenge. She would get her research team on to it – they already had stuff on mowers from that Dutch agribusiness guy last year, Mr Michaels, who had drunkenly misbehaved at the launch party and failed to get in touch again. Carly could come up to Frixley to do some groundwork: a spot of country living might benefit her. And they would bring in a Creative like Zach, whose Tikko ad had won a string of awards. Then a little judicious flirting with Harris, the Frenchwoman's husband, and the bank might approve a further loan.

'What kind of advert would work for us, then?' Jack said.

'You're asking me *now*? Off the top of my head?'

Zach's trick was inversion: urban and rural, child and adult, land and sea. What could be done with a mower? Hadn't some director made a movie about a man riding a sit-on mower across America? Jack's enthusiasm for his new model was real enough. A Rolls-Royce of mowers, he said. Suppose they changed the association to Ferrari, Formula One, Michael Schumacher. Or brought in Wimbledon in some way, to exploit the links between grass and tennis. Either way, Greensleeves would have to go: it was far too folksy and old hat.

'Greensleeves will have to go,' she said, bracing herself. 'It's far too folksy and old hat.'

'You're right,' he said, 'time we dropped it,' just like that.

'Has Marcus never suggested dropping it?' she asked.

'Not that I can recall,' he said, slightly shifty.

'Liar,' she said.

'Maybe he did, but that's different.'

Perhaps the difference was trust. Or Nancy dying. Or the old millennium. Whatever the reason, Jack seemed receptive to her ideas. By last orders, half drunk at the dented brass table, they had a deal.

'If you give me some bumf to take back to London,' she said.

'And you send a team up for the day, to see how we operate.'

'Then I'll have a proposal on your desk within two weeks.'

'And if I don't like it, that's that and no hard feelings.'

'If you don't like it, I'll eat my hat.'

'Agreed.'

'Agreed.'

'No special favours because I'm family,' he said.

'You know me – tough as old boots. Anyway,' she said, coughing again, since this was hard to get out, 'I'm not really family any more.'

'So the girls told me.'

'The *girls* told you?'

'Mine, I mean. Sasha heard it somewhere. These things get round.'

Sasha had been to Oxford, some years after Nat. There were acquaintances in common.

'I hear you're the innocent party,' he said.

'I don't know about innocent. The injured party.'

'What was he playing at, the daft bugger?'

'He got bored, I suppose. And she's younger than me.'

'But you're coping?'

'I'm fine.'

'You've met someone else?'

'It'd be fast work if I had.'

'I saw you talking on the mobile. Up in Nancy's window. I was letting the dog out.'

'Oh, that.'

'You be careful now. My flaming nephew might not deserve you. But nor do plenty others.'

'Nat's good about seeing the girls.'

'Better than his father was at seeing him, you mean. That wouldn't be hard.'

'No, genuinely. He spends more time with them now than when he was living at home.'

'He still deserves a kick up the arse. Too late to save the marriage but I'd feel better for administering it.'

'It *is* all for the best, Uncle Jack. It was my choice.'

'I thought he buggered off and left you.'

'Not exactly. I'd had enough. I asked him to go.'

'Best way. Eunice kept forgiving Ronnie but he left her all the same.'

'God, it's half eleven.'

'They don't worry about closing time here.'

'Shouldn't we get back?'

'We should. The damn dog's whining. And Sasha and Ischia are leaving in the morning.'

'Let's be off then.'

'Absolutely. One for the road?'


*14*


*ANTHEA*


SHE WAS in bed, reading, when Nat called again round eleven thirty. Her mother brought the handset and hovered in the door.

'Sorry about earlier,' he said. 'Bit tricky to talk.'

'Bit tricky here, too.'

'How was the solicitor? Did he really read the will aloud?'

'Yes.'

'God, just like something out of Trollope.'

'So everyone keeps telling me.'

291

'And?'

She grimaced at her mother: Sorry, the grimace said, I can't talk freely because he knows you're in the room and if I'm going to make up with him, which you clearly want me to, I need to have a private conversation, so please, I mean this in the nicest possible way, fuck off. Her mother nodded encouragingly and fucked off.

'Granny set up a sort of trust.'

'Left you some money, you mean?'

'I might be due a little, eventually.'

'When you say a little . . . ?'

'Peanuts,' she said, conscious of how alluring, how *life-saving*, £80,000 would sound to Nat. 'Peanuts,' she repeated, with a brusqueness implying the subject was closed.

The brusqueness seemed to work.

'So what about tomorrow night?' he said.

'If we can't go out, it's hardly worth me coming back,' she said, ready to get angry again.

'Don't be like that,' he said. 'We can still be together. Just tell me what you want to do.'

'I don't know what I want any more. Generally.'

'You're still brooding about the book.'

'I've hardly thought about it.'

'You blame me for your rejection.'

'I wasn't rejected. I withdrew the typescript. What I blame you for is making me send it in the first place.'

'You're upset, naturally.'

'I'm not upset, I'm relieved the whole fucking fairy tale is over.'

'Most writers are rejected, to begin with.'

'You're not listening to me.'

'I'm saying be patient – even if we aren't recognised in our own lifetime we should keep going.'

'I don't want to write books for the unborn. In fifty years people won't be reading books anyway.'

'You mustn't give up.'

'I *have* given up. Writing doesn't do it for me. I want to live.'

He fell silent. *He* wasn't doing it for her – that's what he had taken her to mean. She could correct herself, reassure him, hit a kindlier note. But the legacy had changed things. Or clearing her head on Skiddaw had. Or the rumble of the new millennium.

As rain beat against the window, she thought of the long journey south, six hours on the motorway (more if the weather was bad), then another hour crossing London. She felt weary at the prospect, and weary from arguing, and weary with the sense of an ending. But she knew it was important to be honest.

She nerved herself to say it.

'I think it would be better if —'

'Sorry,' he said, 'Uncle Jack's shouting for me. You can imagine how he's feeling tonight. Is it OK if I call back in a few minutes?'

She let it go. This wasn't the time or place. It couldn't be easy for Nat in the aftermath of a funeral.

'Don't worry,' she said. 'I'm making no sense. Let's talk tomorrow.'

'You're coming back then?'

'If that's what you want.'

'Of course it's what I want. I love you.'

'And I love you.'

She picked up her book again, a collection of folk tales. It was a book which Granny had given her as a child (the inscription was there on the flyleaf: 'To Anthea, on her tenth birthday'), but evidently her mother now considered it hers since here it was in the guest bedroom, along with Catherine Cookson and Jilly Cooper. Flicking through and smelling its pages set off memories in Anthea, of her father reading aloud to her and her mother (gin-scented) kissing her goodnight. But the strongest memory the book triggered came from later in childhood and, with the rain against the window keeping her awake, it seemed important to set it down. From habit, she had brought her notebook with her; tired though she was, there was no excuse.

My last will and testament, she thought, as the green Pentel moved across the page. My farewell letter to Nat. And the first honest thing I've ever written.

15

NAT

GOD, *WOMEN*, Nat thought, even a feminist like me could lose his patience. They had made peace in the end, but Anthea's restlessness was unsettling. What could he do to make her happy? He'd had thoughts lately of moving north to Islington or Hampstead, south of the river seeming so drab these days, a place for losers: relocation might give a boost to his literary career. But moving was impossible without a loan from his mother and might do nothing to improve Anthea's state of mind. He was tempted to confide in Uncle Jack, who could be relied on for brusque advice. But Jack was too bruised just now. Nat's problems would seem trivial to him. The failings of women: hah! None could compare with Nancy's, in dying so disobligingly young.

'Have a Scotch,' said Jack, who by the look of him had had a Scotch or two already.

'Go on, then,' Nat said, taking his punishment, the malt burning his throat.

Uncle Jack made him nervous. He felt disapproved of – the nephew who had not come up to scratch. As Jack saw it (or as Nat saw Jack seeing it), he had let the family down three times over: first, by showing no interest in Raven & Son; second, by failing to stay married; third, by siring no sons. That Uncle Jack had also failed in the last respect was beside the point. Nat was the last male Raven.

They were sitting in Jack's study, on a cracked brown leather chester-field, in front of the gas-fired imitation coals. He could remember being afraid of the room as a child. It was the sanctum, and when you passed you had to whisper. As a teenager he was allowed in, by special dispen-sation. Uncle Jack would sit doing accounts at the roll-top desk while Nat read Kerouac or Vonnegut. The desk was piled with balance sheets, bank statements, share prices, pension plans, the daily round at the factory supplemented by nightly paperwork. Once Nat was shown a company invoice dated 1891 – a vain attempt at induction, or seduction. It didn't work. Gross yields left Nat cold. He sat there in the sanctum writing poems while Jack jiggled his profit margins. There had been a radio in the corner, whose *raison d'être* was to remain switched off, while work got done. There it sat still, an ancient Philips. Above the mantelpiece were photographs – weddings, christenings and a wide-angled shot of Jack at prep school, which Nat used to scan to find his father (bottom row, fifth from the right).

'How's the hunting?' he asked, remembering a promise he'd made.

'Haven't had the time lately,' Jack said.

'No, of course. But you're still a whatsit?'

'An MFH. The other chap does all the work, but yes, I'm still a joint one. Why the sudden interest?'

'I promised someone I'd ask you a favour. Rufus Huish. Do you remember him? He came to our wedding.'

'Don't think so.'

'Dark-haired. We were at school together. Then Oxford. Now he's an MP – stood at the last election and got in.'

'Labour, I take it.'

'Yes,' Nat said, 'but he's nice, you'd like him. His seat's near Birmingham. Hunting's quite an issue there, apparently.'

'How can hunting affect Brummies?'

'He gets a lot mail about it.'

'If he's Labour, he'll be anti.'

'Seemingly not. He'd just like to be better informed.'

'Makes a change. Most MPs prefer to stay clueless.'

'Not Rufus. Rufus is OK.'

Was Rufus OK? In the old days he'd been interested in the arts, but far from promoting the cause of little-known playwrights, or helping an old mate to get an intro to Number Ten, Rufus had made no contact until last week, when – remembering that Uncle Jack was a huntsman – he'd asked Nat to sound him out. Being anti-hunting himself, Nat vaguely resented the favour: what if Rufus was won over and became pro-? But he couldn't not help. And anyway Jack might enjoy the distraction.

'So this chap of yours wants to hear my views?' Jack said.

'More than that. He wants you to take him hunting.'

'Can he ride, then?'

'He's been taking lessons.'

'You have to be able to ride well. *You* know that.'

As a child, Nat had never taken to riding, despite Jack's efforts. He ignored the dig.

'Can I give him your number at least?'

'No harm, I suppose. Top you up?'

Nat slid his glass over.

'If we're doing things properly, we ought to blood him,' Jack said. 'Remember when we blooded you?'

Not something you forget: the brush of fur across his cheek, the acrid aftersmell, his Luxing away of the blood stain. Hunting was a form of barbarism. Why did Rufus Huish need to 'experience' it to have an opinion?

'Of course I remember,' Nat said. 'It was the summer my father left.'

'Ronnie never enjoyed chasing foxes much, either. He preferred chasing floozies.'

Nat felt his throat blaze with malt. Uncle Jack was goading him: for having been a wimp then, for being an adulterer (like his father) now.

'Chased them in London, chased them in Sussex, chased them all the way to Spain.'

I ought to allow for a certain asperity, Nat thought. Jack has just lost his wife and thinking about his brother must be painful. Even so.

'I've always wondered why he chose Spain,' Nat said.

'He had some hare-brained scheme to buy a vineyard. So he took his fancy woman with him. That was Ronnie for you, always off on some new venture or shacking up with some new bint.'

*Shack up with*: how romantic – a beach, a weatherboard hut, and fresh fish drying outside. But not to Jack, clearly. *Bint, floozy, fancy woman*: Nat knew who those were aimed at.

'But he stuck it out with her, didn't he?'

'Who?'

'The woman he ran off to Spain with.'

'Lucretia? No, she was back home again within the month.'

'The one he married, I mean.'

'Ramona, you mean. Yes, but she came six dolly-birds later.'

Ramona. He had never heard her name before – his mother only spoke of 'that harridan'. Ronnie and Ramona. They sounded like some sixties pop duo.

'When did they meet?'

'Round the time he opened his hotel,' Jack said. 'He'd had a hard time of it till then. Catholic country, you see. Not so easy to sleep with women and then drop them. He had to keep moving. Angry fathers, vengeful husbands, gun-toting brothers combing the land for him. Lucky he met Ramona. She calmed him down.'

'Didn't he think of coming back to England?'

'He was afraid to.'

'Why?'

'Because of the lawsuit.'

'Which lawsuit?'

'Your mother never told you? You don't know about *Priapus*?'

'No.'

'Delicate subject. Better have another.'

## 16

## JACK

JACK COULD see the blooding as if it was yesterday. The boy had been a sissy, throwing up on the ride home then refusing to leave the bathroom till his mother turned up to collect him. Maybe Jack had expected too much. Would he have put a son of his own through that? No way of knowing. Nancy always planned to have three but then came that miscarriage. Twelve weeks. In Jack's mind a son, definitely. Nancy said it was nature telling them to stop. She took up gardening and talked to plants, breathing the soul of her lost son into their throats. She went off sex, too, as though desire was merely the urge to procreate. If the physical side had been stronger would he have encouraged Michelle, if that's what he did? It was all water under the bridge now: the non-affair, the miscarriage, the blooding, and Ronnie absconding to Spain. And now his nephew's marriage was history, too. And Nancy.

Long day, long bloody day.

He had offered Nat a Scotch with a view to knocking some sense into him. But what was the point? The boy – man – was a prat and Libby was better off without him. Though a bloody nose was the least he deserved, Jack would settle for giving him a hangover.

Southern Comfort, this time: mixing drinks would produce a stonker in the morning.

Had he really never heard about *Priapus*? How typical of Eunice not to have told him. As well to know, though. You couldn't blame the boy for asking questions. Everything came out in the end.

'Your father owned a bookshop in the Charing Cross Road, you knew that?'

'Vaguely.'

'Lost money on it hand over fist. Would have lost a lot more but for a business he ran in the back room. For special collectors, he said, meaning chaps in raincoats. All very discreet. The average customer wouldn't have known it was there. You had to ask to see the Bibliography

Section and Ronnie would unlock the door. Just the one windowless room with a thousand dirty books in it – all kinds, history, manuals, fiction, illustrated. Imports, mostly. He also ran a mail-order service and that's how he kept afloat – mucky books sent under plain covers to chaps paying over the odds. This was the early sixties, just after the *Chatterley* trial, and though the police must have been suspicious they turned a blind eye. Until *Priapus*. Chester Gould got him into that. Chester owned a Soho club and a string of dirty magazines. It turned out they vaguely knew each other from school – they'd both been members of Lit. Soc. and here they were, years later, both flogging porn. Chester's new magazine, *Priapus*, was more upmarket than his others. So Ronnie made a deal to distribute it through his mail-order business, with him and Chester splitting any profits. God knows why, but *Priapus* took off. Five thousand subscribers in next to no time. Within a year, Ronnie wasn't just distributing the magazine, he'd taken it over. I think he wrote half the pieces himself, under a pseudonym. "A Magazine of Arts, Literature and Erotica", it was subtitled, "MALE". Quite classy-looking – no photos, only line drawings. After a year of *Priapus*, Ronnie stopped coming to me for loans. He even talked of paying me back. Until issue number 7. That was the one the police seized. There had been a complaint. Probably one of Ronnie's discarded shagbags, out for revenge.'

Jack paused for another swig. Eunice had obviously played down Ronnie's philandering, too. Not that she knew the half, but she ought to have told Nat what she did know, if only to stop him making the same mistakes.

'Your father was never very faithful to your mother,' he said, more gently. 'Came home every weekend but in London he lived like a bachelor – new dolly-bird every few weeks. Anyway, discarded girlfriend or not, someone complained. By then the police were tightening up on porn. Ronnie withdrew the magazine, hoping that would save him from prosecution – there was talk of relaunching it as *Bacchus*, subtitled "MALT", "a Magazine of Arts, Liquor and Travel". But the Attorney General was determined to proceed: rumour had it a kinky tale in issue 7 had personally offended him. Ronnie was on the blower right away: "You're going to have an infamous brother, Jack." Though he tried to make light of it, he was rattled. Expected little brother to bail him out, as per usual: "I know this barrister willing to represent me. Best man in town, everyone says. It'll cost us, of course." "Us, Ronnie?" "Come on, Jack. After pulping five thousand issues, I'm skint. Surely it's worth ten grand to keep this out of the papers." We screamed at each other for an hour, then I said I'd see what I could do. Next week we took the lawyer to lunch at L'Escargot – he thought we'd be able to settle out of court. But that was to reckon without Chester Gould, who wanted a fight: nominally, he was still half-owner of *Priapus*, and proud of it. Ronnie was torn. Fight or settle? He couldn't decide so bunked off to Spain instead, knowing no one would bother him there. It wasn't as if he was one of the Great Train Robbers – though Ronnie Biggs later turned up in Spain, too, as it happened, and people joked they were in cahoots. The Two Ronnies.'

'So he ran away rather than risk facing a trial?'

'Things were bad with your mother, too – it was all right him having mistresses in London, but when he began sleeping with friends of hers in Sussex she kicked up. But yes, the prospect of a trial clinched it. Even if they won, Ronnie stood to lose financially. So he sold the shop and smuggled the proceeds out with him. Not a lot, but enough to get by – and eventually he opened his hotel.'

'So what happened at the trial?'

'It never took place. With Ronnie gone, and the magazine out of circulation, there was no point.'

Jack poured his nephew a final slug. Funny word, slug. American probably. Same as their word for a bullet. Same effect, too, next morning – like a shot (another drink word) through the head. Would he regret this tomorrow – not the drink, the talk? He wished he could *like* Nat more. The boy hadn't had it easy: first Ronnie fucked off, then he kicked the bucket. Hard on a brother, but even harder on a son. Maybe he, Jack, was too tough on Nat. He had loved Ronnie. Why couldn't he love Ronnie's son?

'Is the bookshop in Charing Cross Road still there?' Nat asked.

'Haven't a clue,' Jack said.

'I wonder which number it was.'

'Somewhere on the right going up, I think.'

'And you say my father *wrote* things?'

'The magazine couldn't afford to pay anyone at first. He probably had to.'

'I've always thought of him running a naff hotel in Spain. Now I feel . . . well, sort of proud.'

Jack examined Nat through his whisky glass. Was he pissed?

'I can't see what there is to be proud of,' he said.

'He was an iconoclast.'

'He was a porn merchant.'

'He ran a bookshop.'

'He sold dirty magazines.'

'Only dirty by the standards of the time.'

Jack drained his glass. He wasn't going to argue. If the boy thought better of Ronnie, leave it at that.

'You best kip down here tonight,' he said. 'From what I gather, you won't be welcome upstairs.'

'Oh that. I'd been meaning to tell you.'

'Your wife told me. Ex-wife, should I say.'

'We're not divorced yet.'

'You soon will be, I hear.'

'Even then we'll still attend activities together, like today.'

'I don't call a funeral an activity.'

'Parents' evenings and such.'

'Nasty business, separation. Not easy on the children.'

'Not easy on any of us.'

'You should have considered that before you fucked your bimbo,' Jack thought, but all he said was: 'The chesterfield's not bad for sleeping on.'

It was only a two-seater but you could drop one of the armrests to make it longer. In the old days of working late, he had sometimes used it as a bed – despite his feet hanging over the end, and the bumps and buttons poking into his ribs, he preferred it to disturbing Nancy.

'I don't want to put you to any bother,' Nat said.

'It's no bother,' Jack lied. 'I'll get you a sleeping bag.'

And a couple of pillows, he thought. Two pillows for a pillock.

It was silent on the landing. As he opened the airing cupboard, to pull down the bedding, warm scents with Nancy in them spilled out.

After handing Nat the sleeping bag, he unlocked the bottom drawer of his desk.

'Here,' he said, blowing the dust off the brown package, 'some bedtime reading for you. All seven issues of *Priapus*. Collector's item. Kept under lock and key since 1965. I wouldn't have wanted Nancy coming across them but you're welcome to have a look. They'll probably seem pretty tame.'

## ANTHEA

Dearest Nat,

Do you remember how you used to ask me was there a personal story behind my fox stories? How you said you knew there must be one. And how I told you to forget it, since they were all made up. I meant what I said. I wasn't lying. But you were right. There *is* a story. I've been hiding it from myself. Tonight I realised.

June 1987 – the weekend before my father died. (That's how I remember it, though if someone said 'No, I happen to know it was two years before', I'd not be altogether surprised.) Down our garden there were some trees, which he'd been cutting back. My mother and I helped him pile the branches up, in a bonfire. Let's leave the bonfire till later, he said. No, my mother said, we must have it now. We were standing under the holm oak, by the garden fence, on the dry earth. The dryness worried him. Suppose the fire took off, out of control. But this was England, not a tinder forest in the Pyrenees, and my mother complained that he was putting things off: tomorrow it might be raining. Grumbling, put upon, he fetched newspapers and matches. A fox leapt over the fence behind us. We knew there were cubs around – four of them, we'd counted – but we assumed they were safe in the earth. He began stuffing the base with bombings, *coup d'états*, film stars, share prices, cricket scores, arts sections. There was a neat, bitter-smelling hole among the sticks: a lair. Soil had been scooped out to make a lying place below the branches: it looked warm still, but was empty, foxless, and he crammed it with tapers of newsprint, ready for firing. He struck the first match, and held it under a rolled-up headline. Soon the heap began to catch – yellow, orange, red – and the branches of lopped fir whooshed and flared. Red-furred, growling, the flames grew tall, singeing the tresses of holm oak, the heat so near and fierce it seemed the whole garden would go up. But gradually the blaze abated, its roar more river than ocean, and we threw on a last few sticks.

It was then we saw the cub, tottering from the circle of grey ash. It looked more mineral than animal: charred wood and smelted ore. Even from ten feet away we could smell it – not burning wood but fricassee of fur and blood. Had it been lying in the woodpile, too afraid to move? Had it rushed in, crazed, driven, like a moth to a light bulb? Or had its earth, beneath the fire, become a furnace of falling cinders? The cub was Cinders, in ragged dress. I wanted to wave a wand and make it well again, but it stood and shivered, gently smoking, teetering on the brink. I couldn't see its eyes. Perhaps it had none.

'My God,' my mother said. 'Would water help?' 'Water to drink, or water to spray it with?' 'Either.' The cub wobbled forward a yard. We willed it to go further, for the burns on its fur to be superficial, a light sprinkle of soot. It's the runt of the litter, we said, and wrong in the head; we mustn't blame ourselves if it dies. A blow from a spade would spare it further suffering. But we willed it to live, not just for its sake but for ours.

We watched till it sank into the bushes, out of sight, and we went indoors. That night I couldn't sleep for wondering where it might be – whether its parents had found it and would they recognise it even if they did. I imagined dawn coming and its black prints across the lawn, its empty eyes staring at the window. Next morning I went out to search – gingerly, for fear of meeting its shivers or stepping on its corpse. It was nowhere.

I can't have been looking properly. My dad found it later that day, where we last saw it, flies circling its nose. The fur looked less frizzled than the day before, the body shorter, barely the width of a spade. He dug a three-foot hole under the wall (deep enough for other foxes not to disinter the corpse), then walked over and slid the spade under, careful not to nick the fur. Something sticky was glueing its body to the earth but he prised it free: a pound of cub, carried on a spade. The body was already stiff, the tail in a frozen swirl. He lowered it quickly into the hole, but not before I saw it had no eyes. He chucked the soil on quickly, and tamped it down, brown on black, and stamped it flat, hiding the evidence. He walked away, put the spade in the shed, and poured himself a stiff drink. Freak accident, runt of the litter, nobody's fault: that was the kind of thing we said that night.

I thought we'd got away with it, but we hadn't.

On the morning of sports day I woke with a line in my head: 'The foxes are on fire.' It wasn't just the burned cub that had put it there, but the sight of its three siblings playing in our garden – the red of their coats as they chased each other round and round. The athletes later that day wore red shorts and vests. In the 100 metres there was a fat girl with long swirling brown hair called Geraldine Fox. It was after the 100 metres that my father collapsed.

I came to believe the foxes were stalking me: they had killed my father, and wrecked my mother, and I would be next. Then I realised they *were* me, that I had inherited their violence and cunning. And that the world, the whole world, consisted of foxes. That was the beginning of my 'breakdown', as the school called it, my 'acting out'. I got over it. But not. The experience was still inside when I met you.

All those stories I wrote – well, I don't need a therapist to tell me why I wrote them. Remember that first story I showed you? Story? More a haiku. You said it was too oblique, and you were right. Still . . .

> The foxes are on fire.
> The ember of their eyes,
> the flame of their fur,
> the ash of their white-tipped tails
> will burn through all eternity.

That's all my writing ever was: an attempt to put things right. And the stories were never as original as you thought. I've just been reading a book of folk tales I used to have as a child. There are loads of fox stories in it – the best ones are Chinese. That's not to say I stole. The stories I wrote were *my* stories. But they were more to do with therapy than literature. And now they've done their work, it's time for me to try new things.

That's why this letter is a farewell. Not just to writing, Nat, but to you. I didn't have a voice when I met you – remember the stammer – but now I do, and I want to use it to make a difference. Maybe that sounds portentous or pretentious or whatever. But I do need to be somewhere else and live another way. It's been a year now, Nat. Nearly two years since that café in St Martin's Lane. You say you're happy with things as they are, and I don't blame you: you've your daughters, and your teaching, and an ex you still care about. But it's different for me. I'm young.

In time, perhaps, we'll both meet other people, but you're wrong to suspect there's someone else in my life. There isn't, I just want to be free.

I know this letter will hurt you. And that will make it hard for me to give it you. Perhaps I never *will* give it you, and twenty years from now, when we've made a life together, you'll come across it somewhere, and force me to read it, and we'll look back and laugh: 'Remember the time we almost packed it in?' Who knows what will happen after tomorrow. The idea of living in a year with three noughts in it is weird enough. But I know what I believe it's right to do.

I love you. But love's not enough. We must treasure what we had and move on.

*18*

*HARRY*

LUKE'S OFFICE was opposite the Broadway Theatre, above a bedding shop. Maxon & Son Solicitors, the nameplate said. The light fell thin and yellow and the chairs were lined in red leather. According to Luke, the decor hadn't changed since the firm was established half a century ago. The top drawer of his filing cabinet doubled as a bar: he slid out a bottle of Jameson's and filled two tumblers, then sat back with his feet up on the desk, like a Hollywood detective from the 1950s.

'Don't get too excited,' he said, as the whiny cassette recorder played. 'To begin with Ray just stonewalls.'

It was true. Whatever approach the two police interviewers took – matey, threatening, playful, earnest, man-to-man – the suspect refused to budge. Occasionally, and indistinctly, Harry could hear Luke's voice in the background, asking could his client have a drink of water or saying he needed a rest. It was only when they asked about his son that Ray opened up.

– What do you feel about Errol, Ray?
– I love that boy.
– So if anyone ever hurt him?
– I'd kill him, man.

– Does Sharon ever hurt him?

– She's his mother, why she wanna hurt him?

– What about Louis?

– Louis hits Sharon sometimes, but he ain't ever hurt Errol.

– How do you know?

– Cos he'd tell me. He ain't big but he tell his daddy everything.

– How about the time Sharon heard the baby crying, and found Errol teasing her, and slapped him for being naughty to his little sister?

– Yeh, Errol told me that.

– About Sharon slapping him?

– Yeh.

– And what was your reaction?

– I vexed with Sharon. It's not the slapping, right, it's the treating her other kids different.

– She favours Charmain over Errol?

– She favours them all over him, man.

– Did you hear what Mia said to Sharon after the slap? She said, 'Errol's not our *real* brother, is he, Mum?'

– Yeh, Errol asked me about that. He's too young to understand, see.

– And what did Sharon reply?

– How would I know? I wasn't there.

– According to Mia, she said, 'No, Errol's only a half, cos his dad's only half the man that most men are.' How do you feel about her saying that?

– I hate her, man, she's a filthy mouth on her.

– What would you like to do to her?

– Punish her.

– Haven't you done that?

– How do you mean?

– Errol's gone. Hasn't she been punished already?

– Yeh, she been punished.

– Is that a confession, Ray?

– What?

– Was that a confession just now?

– [Inaudible.]

– For the benefit of the interview tape, can I record you nodded your head just there? [Inaudible.] I confirm that the accused is nodding his head.

– [Inaudible, Luke Tilbey, solicitor.]

– Is that right?

– Yes.

– [Inaudible.]

[End of tape.]

'Want to hear that last bit again?' Luke asked, rewinding. Harry strained hard as the tape was replayed it but all he heard was hiss and mumble.

'They introduce background noise,' Luke said, 'then insert incriminating words in the transcript.'

'Come on, that's ridiculous,' Harry said.

'I always carry my own tape recorder, as a precaution. Or I take notes. Here, look. No way did he confess. "Can I confirm you just nodded your head?" Can they fuck confirm it. He wanted a leak.'

Luke passed his notepad for Harry to read:

| | |
|---|---|
| POLICE | Is that a confession, Ray? |
| RAY | What? |
| POLICE | Was that a confession just now? |
| RAY | Can you tell them I want a leak? [Interviewee to Luke Tilbey, solicitor] |
| POLICE | For the benefit of the interview tape, can I record you nodded your head just there? |
| TILBEY | You heard that. He wants a leak. |
| POLICE | I confirm that the accused is nodding his head. |
| TILBEY | My client would like to go to the lavatory. |
| POLICE | Is that right? |
| RAY | Yes. |
| POLICE | We just got the bastard. |

'"We just got the bastard?" Come on, that's ridiculous.'

Luke laughed. 'OK, maybe that was me embroidering.'

'But you're saying they fixed him up?'

'You just listened to it – was *that* a confession?'

'I couldn't hear anything clearly. But nor will the jury.'

'Juries hear what they want to hear. By the time they get to court, they'll have read so much crap about Ray they'll assume he's guilty. Then the prosecution will poison their minds some more.'

'But that's outrageous.'

'Don't be naive, Harry. We're not talking about justice here. It's a cat-and-mouse game between defence and prosecution. We outwit them. They outwit us. Winner walks off into the sunset. Loser goes down for life.'

He filled their glasses again. The office was high up, above the traffic, and they were sitting in the window, brightly lit. Harry wondered what they looked like to passers-by – the odd couple, solicitor-skinhead and black journo, John Bull and Jim Crow.

Twelve fifty. Marcia would be asleep now. Stephen, too. No point calling.

'Cheers,' Luke said, clinking glasses, then, out of nowhere, as though Harry were leaking thought bubbles, 'You married?'

He thought of opening up then, just a little, as Ray had done. Luke had been frank about *himself*: why not? But it would take too long to explain. And heady though he was from the Jameson's, he wasn't ready to share his feelings with Luke. He found it hard enough to share them with himself.

'Single,' he said.

'With someone?'

'I live on my own.'

'No angry partner waiting up – lucky man.'

Lucky man for having a son he couldn't acknowledge. Lucky man for blowing the chance to put that right.

'You read the piece in tonight's *Standard*?' Luke said. 'The Deptford Fox, they're calling Ray. Because of something a neighbour said: "He never went out much, except at night, like a fox." The Yorkshire Ripper, the Boston Strangler, the Deptford Fox – you journos go in for that stuff. Actually, if anyone's a fox, it's the police.'

'Or the lawyers.'

'We're paid to be foxes – low cunning is our job.'

He slopped more brown into Harry's tumbler and they sat on, under the window, while the last cars died away and the yellow light grew cold. Harry thought of Ray Nuard in his Maidstone cell, an innocent man wrongly accused, so Luke said, and to Harry, quietly drunk now, it seemed so too. Who was the guilty party then? Louis, Sharon, a paedophile stranger, someone else? Or some*thing* else? The Deptford Fox, the Deptford Beast, that nameless thing stalking children south of the river, a creature which might have no substance but which loped through all of Harry's dreams?

It was restful in Luke's office – only the occasional night bus braking for the traffic lights. A gust under the sash lifted the blind-pull, which tocked against the pane, tock, tock. The digits of the office clock read 01.27, which they would not do again this millennium. Every hour was a last hour now, every minute a last minute – they were seeing out the age, or Harry was, since Luke, tilting sideways in his chair, deaf to the night bus braking for the lights and the blind-pull tocking on the pane, had fallen asleep.

# 'The Knot'

by 'R.R.'

from *Priapus*, 7 (February 1965)

## 1

In the autumn of 1928, in St John's Wood, an alarming accident befell a young couple of slender acquaintance. The full details I will presently disclose. Suffice to say that the experience was both painful and embarrassing. Among the words they used in describing their dilemma were 'horribly uncomfortable', 'd—ed humiliating' and 'far and away the worst thing that has ever happened to me'.

To understand their physiological impasse it is necessary, first, to furnish a brief history of their relationship, and I make no apologies for including a number of psychological observations. The Hunnishly pompous Dr Freud is a dangerous influence, and his so-called 'discoveries' about the mind can surely never take root in our native land. But we do well to remember that strictly rational models of diagnosis are sometimes insufficient. The body is a law unto itself.

## 2

They met at a private dinner dance thrown by the Bar. He was a newly qualified barrister, she a lowly female secretary in a nearby chambers. The French have an expression, *coup de foudre*, to describe that lightning flash of desire to which the English, less succinctly, sometimes attest. I do not know if there is an equivalent expression for mutual, instantaneous dislike, but – perhaps surprisingly in view of subsequent developments – this was the feeling experienced by both parties when they found themselves making up the numbers for a quadrille. She took exception not only to his little moustache and furtive eyes but to his ironic, scoffing, 'rather vulgar' manner, distinctly not that which her widower father, an Oxford man and retired colonel, had advised his only daughter to look for in young men. For his part, he found her stiff and humourless, and wondered what had happened to 'the pair of cheery harlots with their breasts spilling out who I'd seen when I first walked in'. As soon as decently possible at the conclusion of the dance, they moved away from each other, in the hope of finding other partners. But this being a small function composed largely of the married and middle-aged, alternatives were in short supply. *Faute de mieux*, to adopt another Gallic expression, they found themselves paired for further dances.

Even an interval which he spent 'downing double whiskies' at the bar and she 'hiding in the Ladies' did not furnish a satisfactory means of escape. Under duress from colleagues, as 'the only two in the room without partners', they danced again, taking each other by the arm with a nod of mutual self-pity. Their conversation was desultory, though they melted a little upon seeing each other's discomfiture ('The funny part was feeling I'd drawn the short straw, then realising she obviously thought the same', 'I was affronted by his indifference, but consoled myself in thinking how much more badly I would have been placed had he had designs on me'). Once the last number had been played, they thanked each other for the pleasure, and disappeared in opposite directions, he to the bar and thence to the Gents, she to the cloakroom and thence to the Ladies. To avoid all risk of meeting, both tarried inside cubicle and in front of mirror until the lack of sounds outside indicated that everyone else had safely left the club. Thus it came about that, a full quarter-hour after the party's conclusion, the couple met again in the lobby. To employ their words:

'He looked very embarrassed, as I was too, of course. Undaunted, we exchanged pleasantries and found ourselves on the pavement. He asked me where I lived and when I said St John's Wood he suggested we might take a cab together, his home lying not far from mine, in Hampstead. I could think of no good reason to refuse, my antipathy to him having by this point somewhat abated. Besides, I could see he wanted to behave as a gentleman, and I did not wish to be discourteous.'

'I wanted to be shot of her, but it would have been caddish to leave her to the mercies of the street so I suggested we ride together, secretly hoping she would contribute to the fare (thus reducing mine) and knowing if she didn't I would be able to impress her with my generosity. As we stood trying to hail a cab, I felt in an oddly good mood, grateful to have some company and pleased that a beastly evening would soon be over.'

But the dinner dance had run on later than either realised, and nowhere in the brown fog could they locate a cab. They began walking: from Piccadilly up Regent Street, then left along Oxford Street before turning north parallel to the Edgware Road. They began to talk, at first as constrainedly as they had done while dancing, but in due course candidly, volubly, from the heart. It was a long walk, four miles at least, and at the slow pace they proceeded – this slowness due partly to one of her boots having a tottery heel, but partly also to their increasing absorption in the discourse – it took them nearly two hours. She spoke, on her side, of the loss of her mother when she was six, the straitened upbringing in a cold Twickenham villa, the nanny who beat her with a wooden spoon, the governess who inspired her to read Keats and excel at several piano pieces by Chopin, the secretarial position she attained 'because it's important these days that a single woman in her twenties have some independence. Some stimulus, too: I don't say I'm as clever as all the barristers in our chambers, but there are two at least whose closing perorations in important trials I more or less drafted myself.' He listened attentively before describing in equally extensive detail the key characters and events of his own life: the modest three-up three-down family home in Norwood; his father, who until his recent retirement had worked in an insurance firm in the City, 'I've never asked as what exactly, but I know it was lowlier than he liked to pretend'; his mother, who had trouble with her nerves and scarcely left her bed; his three older brothers, who variously bullied him, as boys do, but the middle one quite brutally, his belt and penknife inflicting numerous marks ('I bear the scars to this day'); his gradual withdrawal into books when his brothers left home ('study-texts mostly, but also the whole of Conan Doyle'); the exams he did remarkably well at for one of his station; the scholarship to Cambridge; the steady progress in his chambers, 'though I'm still on the bottom rung'. As he talked, the swagger and irony that had so galled her earlier seemed to evaporate. Even the red moustache became him: she was reminded of photographs of her father, who when young and in the army had worn one of a similar kind. Perhaps he sensed she was warming to him, because as time passed he talked more freely of his ideas: how the rigidities of the English class system appalled him; how he would vote for any politician who promised to change that; how in choosing the law as a career he hoped to be part of the creation of a more just society. Under the street lights, his eyes glowed green. He noticed the same of hers: 'They had seemed grey when we danced, but now there was this leaping emerald light to them.'

Near Marylebone station, they saw a standing cab.

'Having come this far, I would prefer to continue walking,' he said, as they hesitated. 'But if your heel is bothering you . . .'

'No, I'm nearly home now.'

The cab driver watched them go. Their conversation moved on. She listened to him describing his literary enthusiasms, which struck her as unusually modern for a barrister: G. K. Chesterton, Arnold Bennett, Thomas Hardy, David Garnett.

'What about Virginia Woolf?'

'I tried. But found her too queer.'

'D. H. Lawrence?'

'A queer fish, too. But he's right about our civilisation running out of steam. And about people having sex in the head.'

He felt bold coming out with this, since he had no clue what Lawrence meant by it and had never previously uttered the word 'sex' in the presence of a lady. But the lateness of the hour was invigorating and their prolonged intercourse a liberation. And she rewarded his courage by replying:

'My father caught me reading Lawrence once, and was outraged, and made me return the book to the library at once. But since then I've read nearly all his novels. I think he talks a lot of sense. There's too much moral hypocrisy around, too much cowardice. Even my father . . .'

She hesitated. It was a story she had told no one. But as she looked into his gentle, puzzled eyes, she found herself telling him about a day some years before when she had come home early, and – hanging her coat up – heard noises coming from the billiard room, and after listening at the door gently pushed it open, to see her father standing against the billiard table with his bare buttocks, while the housemaid lay on the edge of it in her petticoats, her head tipped back over the green felt. 'I was appalled by the animality of it but also curious, and would have lingered and watched but for the fear of them seeing me. I withdrew, closing the door silently behind me, then went upstairs to my bedroom and was violently sick. I'm sorry, I don't know why I told you this story, I feel ashamed, forgive me.'

He reassured her that she was right to have unburdened herself – surely such things were better spoken of than hidden away. He meant this sincerely, but was shocked nonetheless by the intimate detail and even more so by his excitement at reimagining the scene. A year or two before, he had gone drinking with a couple of work colleagues and had later returned to their rooms, where a collection of pornographic photographs was brought out, which the three of them had studied and laughed over while drinking whisky from tumblers. But those photos, mostly of prostitutes and their clients, had failed to stir him. Whereas this tale, told by an educated woman of his own (or a higher) station, and a virtual stranger . . .

They continued walking, more subdued and taciturn now. He wondered if he should reciprocate with a tale of his own, but he could think of nothing apt, except the incident of the pornographic photos, which was unsavoury, and various visits to brothels, which might make her think the worse of him, a consequence he would not have minded earlier but now, puzzlingly, did. She seemed broad-minded, and would surely understand that it was normal for a man of his age and situation to have experience of brothels. But she, after all, had not spoken of a sexual experience of her own, only the trauma of observing her father *in flagrante*, and he feared he would add to her discomposure by once again placing her in the position of an embarrassed observer. As a result he said nothing, which made the next few minutes uncomfortable for them both.

Fortunately, they had now reached the street where her lodgings were – a four-storey house owned by a cousin of her father, which she shared with two other legal secretaries of her own sex.

'I deeply regretted having told the story and though I thought more highly of him than when we'd set out I wanted nothing now but to be rid of his presence and to hasten inside.'

'Suddenly she tripped, falling into the gutter. Her knee was grazed, but not badly, and I helped her to her feet, confident that she could walk the remaining distance. Unluckily, the injury was worse than appeared.'

'My chief sensation wasn't pain but stupidity. I'd known the heel would go sooner or later. If only we'd taken that cab. My right ankle was badly twisted, and quite unable to support me. For a few yards I hopped along with my right arm on his left shoulder. Then . . .'

'I picked her up and carried her in my arms. I am not a tall man, but my build is sturdy. Besides, we had but a few yards to her door.'

'I'd not been carried in a man's arms since the gardener brought me back to the house after I'd fallen out of the apple tree when I was seven. It should have felt romantic, but I was conscious only of my helplessness and the unending strangeness of the evening. As we reached the doorstep I asked him to set me down. But when informed my rooms lay on the second floor, he insisted on carrying me up the stairs. Unusually, both my fellow lodgers were away for the weekend at their parents', so I was spared the embarrassment of explaining his presence at this late hour.'

'Though she was light and slender, by the time we reached the landing I was panting like a dog. The first room I saw was a bedroom, and without thinking I walked straight in and laid her on the bed, myself collapsing beside her in a chair. I began to laugh at the absurdity of the situation: a few hours previously I'd happily have pushed the woman under the nearest train, but here I was late at night in her bedroom. She began to laugh, too, whether infected by my laughter or moved by her own sense of absurdity I couldn't tell. As our laughter finally ebbed, I rose to leave, and she sat upright on the edge of the bed. With a boldness that surprised us both, we smiled and took each other's hands.'

'Quite unexpectedly, he bent to kiss me, and rather than turn my face away, which my whole upbringing told me was the action required, I closed my eyes and held my lips for him, then kissed him back. I felt his tongue between my teeth as he stooped, with his hands clutching my shoulders, and as he kissed me more deeply I ran my own hands along his neck and down to his hips. He moved closer, leaning in to brush his lips across the back of my neck.'

'I couldn't credit it. I kissed her and she responded. Next thing, as I stood there, she began to undo . . .'

'His waistband was level with my face, and for reasons I've gone over many times but am as yet unable to fathom I began to unbuckle his belt. Almost at once his fingers were busy with the buttons at my neck. I shall always remember – whether it's shame or some perverse pride that makes me remember – it was I who made the first move.'

### 3

A veil must now be drawn. To describe what passed next would bring a blush to the cheeks of lay readers, while members of my profession could not help but find the detail redundant or banal. I have heard it argued, in particular by those returning from exotic parts of the Empire, that the average British husband and wife are sorely unenterprising in the matter of sexual congress principally on account of absence of information about the range of possibilities open to them. The ideologues who hold this view would like to see books of sexual information – some even use the word 'instruction' – made available on the open market. But the dangers of this are plain to see: imagine a young schoolboy or, worse still, innocent schoolgirl entering a high street bookshop and, in the quest for some uplifting classic, lighting upon such a tome. In any case, and here I come to my point, what occurred between the said couple strongly suggests that nature is its own guide, and that 'instruction' in these matters is superfluous. Though comparatively limited in their previous experience, they were able to explore a range of conjugal activity. To put it crudely, they took to the business like ducks to water.

'I blush to think of all we did, and of how little inhibition I felt about touching his body, and of how much I initiated – purely by instinct – myself.'

'We went at it like rabbits. Of course, I assumed she was a virgin, and was therefore gentle with her. But once we were over the first hump, there was no stopping her. And though it was mostly me leading the way, she taught me quite a few tricks herself. What a woman! And yet a few hours earlier she'd been stiff as starch.'

As I say, I intend to omit all details of the intimacy. But both parties were painstaking in furnishing me with particulars, and these particulars I have faithfully recorded in a private notebook which, in the hope of gleaning some seed of understanding, it is sometimes my habit (indeed it has become a nightly ritual) to peruse – with my study door safely locked, and a glass of brandy, a snuffbox, and a handkerchief close to hand. From their accounts I conclude that our young friends were swept away on a crest of passion, and that no action they performed, however depraved it might seem to you if I were to divulge the details, struck them at the time as unseemly. But the humiliation which they later endured, and which I am presently coming to, will understandably be seen, by the less scientific-minded, as a punishment from on high. It was certainly, as far as the victims were concerned, the worst torture a malevolent deity could ever conceive.

## 4

To resume. Our couple had now completed their exertions and were lying on the floor (only the first portion of their congress having been confined to the bed), she with her face and breasts pressed against the boards, he lying on – and fully covering the length of – her shoulder blades, back, buttocks, thighs and feet. For this information, I rely chiefly on the gentleman's account. Having twice earlier ejaculated on her stomach, so that 'she'd not get knocked up', he had, at the end of the last bout, ejaculated inside her body: 'having been so controlled the last two times, I thought, What the hell. Anyway, I'd so little spunk left in me I reckoned I couldn't have put a mouse in the club. Besides which, I was coming into her backwards, which made it safe.' Fellow professionals will already have recognised the anatomical weakness of this rationale. And indeed by this point doubt had also struck the originator of the thesis: 'Having dozed off for a bit while lying on her, I woke in a cold sweat. Suppose she was now up the spout?'

It is a sad fact that many men, no matter how deeply attached to the woman they have just been intimate with, experience, upon the completion of congress, the onset of disenchantment and a desire to quit the seat of their desire as swiftly as possible. I cannot say whether this is the same

317

feeling also attested to by our good neighbours the French when they speak (once again I must fall back on their language) of post-coital *tristesse*. But when the male protagonist in this case now attempted to leave his lover's side, or backside, he found himself thwarted at every twist and turn.

His embarrassment was as nothing compared to that of his *inamorata*, who while he slept had lain all too uncomfortably awake. Small though her prior acquaintance was in this field, it seemed to her unnatural that her consort should lie spreadeagled at the back of her head, rather than enfolded in her arms. Having opened herself to him so generously, and he to her, and having derived such pleasure from this surrender, she now wished him *with* rather than behind her, and rather regretted having allowed him there in the first place. She expected this lack to be remedied upon his waking, but when she felt him stir, yet fail to move as freely as he wished, she realised that something was amiss. She lay with her left cheek to the wooden floor, the tassels of a particularly lush Persian carpet only inches from her nose. She watched his hand, which had lain idly for a good half-hour, flex against the boards, and the muscles in his wrists tighten, and his forearms, levered from the elbow, move from horizontal to vertical. But to no avail.

'I think, er . . . if you wouldn't mind . . . so that I could just . . .'

She was too embarrassed to reply, but indicated that she had heard him, and would willingly, if it lay in her power, comply with his request. This she did by moving her torso, at first slowly, then with a series of short, sharp jerks at the coccyx, in the hope of releasing or in effect shaking him out. But far from these manoeuvres having a beneficial effect, 'It hurt like hell. I felt like a rabbit in the teeth of a terrier, and had to beg her to stop.' She had still not spoken, but now took the initiative of plucking at his arms, and bringing them round her neck, at the same time rolling on her side and bringing him with her, so that they both lay sideways facing the bed, under which she could descry a chamber pot, 'not the floral one, with matching jug, which I made habitual use of and kept on the dresser, but an ugly purple one, dirty and cracked, which presumably had been left by a previous tenant and which our housemaid must have failed to notice or had never bothered to remove'. The sight of this pot reminded her that it was some several hours since her last ablutions, and it occurred to her that this might partly explain the present dilemma, for she was conscious not only of some swelling and soreness but of being – to use her own words – in spasm, the whole of her nether region braced and tightened; perhaps urination would ease her plight. But she also presently realised that even if this diagnosis was correct, there was little prospect of administering the necessary antidote. To put it plainly, there was no chance of her sitting on the pot with the man's organ still inside her.

Why it persisted in remaining inside her was causing him, for his part, no less concern. Never before had a situation like this arisen, or even mildly threatened to ('Once spent, I'm tiny as a winkle and soft as a rotten pear'). But he had noticed earlier that the usual flaccidity had not ensued upon ejaculation, which was perhaps why congress had been so prolonged. And he was also conscious of some remaining stiffness: 'Not that I was excited and wanted to diddle her again. But I felt held, as if she had caught me and frozen me there.'

They lay for a few more minutes, examining the dusty under-area of the brass bed, each with their separate thoughts and discomfort, until he broke the silence.

'I expect it's a thing that sometimes happens,' he said.

'Yes,' she replied.

'But I can assure you in my experience it's not normal,' he added.

'No,' she said. 'Nor in mine.'

## 5

Even when they have known each other for many years, the potential for mistrust between human beings is considerable. Many husbands and wives will happily admit to this, outside each other's company. And even in our own profession, where a premium is placed upon mutual respect, it is not unknown for colleagues to be suspicious of each other and, as a result, to cast aspersions on each other's judgements. Why, I have even heard the methods and findings of my own research called into question. And though that can be explained as mere envy – intellectual giants, if I can employ that immodest phrase for a moment, must always endure the jealous pinpricks of pygmies – nevertheless in most careers, and most marriages, the inevitability of doubt and suspicion is, unhappily, an inescapable fact.

How much more active is mutual suspicion in a case of slender acquaintance such as this! Notwithstanding the closeness which the unfortunate pair felt less than an hour previously, they now had cause to reflect that they knew each other not a whit.

She, on her side, felt dismay at his last remark. To venture comment on their quandary was crass enough. But to need to reassure her of its *abnormality* was far worse, implying as it did, first, a condescending view of her familiarity with sexual matters, and, second, a need to trumpet the ampleness of his. Unable to meet his eyes, even when turning her neck backwards and upwards as fully as feasible, she found her initial doubts about him flooding back. She felt taken advantage of – not that he had seduced her, but he was now behaving like a seducer, denying her equal complicity and treating her as a pathetic, duped object he wished to discard. She thought he had recognised her as an independent spirit, a woman who set passion above the grey conformities of the age. But she had been foolish. In her misery she couldn't help measuring him unfavourably against the man, in Vienna, to whom she had given herself two years previously – the tutor who, over a summer of improving her knowledge of German, had also taught her the joys of love. Her first and, until now, only lover, he believed that the body was something to celebrate, not be ashamed of. How he had loved her! How deeply he wanted to make her his bride! How much they both suffered on account of his intractable father, who threatened to cut him off should he ever 'marry out' with a Gentile! He had sworn to defy his father, and twice sent letters after she returned to England declaring his lasting love. Though he had not written now for over a year, not since she proposed a return visit to Vienna, she would always remember him as a gentleman. Whereas the man she lay with now was a jackal who had seen she was easy prey. Perhaps he had even planned the whole business, intercepting her as she left the club. Certainly he had exploited her vulnerability. What sort of man would carry an injured woman up to her bedroom and ravish her? Only the sort her father would classify as a bounder. Part of his being a bounder was the cavalier disregard he had shown for modern contraceptive methods. There were, she knew, more sophisticated means of avoiding pregnancy than the one he had adopted, which in any case (as she could tell by the trickle between her legs) he had failed to adopt on the last occasion. What was wrong with the device her German lover had favoured? If such had been used here, he would have slipped from her as easily as a snakeskin. To be got with child by this man she barely knew and now frankly detested was a thought almost beyond endurance. She felt his flesh cooling on her back, the hairs on his chest bristling between her shoulder blades. She wished his body would evaporate – or that her own could be buried like banknotes under the floor-boards.

She would have been little consoled to discern the pattern of his own thoughts. He, too, was brooding. Up to that point, it had never occurred to him she might not be a virgin. He had been gratified to find her such an enthusiastic coital companion, but he put this down to expertise on his part and beginner's luck on hers – as with a friend to whom you explain the rules of poker, who then proceeds to beat you hands down. His not being able to remove himself from this woman afterwards merely confirmed him in his belief she was a sexual *naïf*. True, tightness (especially in virgins) was supposed to be felt at the outset of congress, rather than at its conclusion. But he had heard of *vagina dentata*, and he assumed this was some virulent expression of it. Having miraculously transcended the expected first-time constraints, this woman's body had gone into a rictus of self-recrimination – which was unfortunate, but indicative of her innocent nature.

Thus had he reasoned to himself. But now he came to reflect, the mistake was obvious. She had been so adept, so whorishly nifty. She had even – shockingly, for one of her sex – made the first move. Had she planned it all along? It seemed an unhappy accident their leaving the club at the same time, but perhaps she had been waiting for him. Later, the story of her father must have been told to excite a prospective partner. Then she tripped over in the street, and needed to be carried home – a cunning ruse. The ankle had not appeared to give her any trouble during congress, despite it finding itself in positions which should surely have pained it further. What was her game? He had heard of women from respectable society who would entertain men in like fashion and not expect payment for it. But surely, however morally depraved, she was too young for that. More likely, and more worryingly, she was looking to trap an innocent partner in marriage. Having learned the art of sexual enticement, she was preying on decent, unthinking fellows such as him. He thought back to earlier that night, and how several port-faced colleagues had urged him to dance with the woman. Had he missed their knowing looks? Had they winked at each other as he fell into her trap? Perhaps the woman was well known round Lincoln's Inn. He reckoned to hear most gossip, but his ear was not as close to the circuit as it should be. Perhaps she had made several attempts already at barristers in her own chambers, and even in his. Perhaps fellows he knew, even married ones, had experienced and even played some part in nurturing her expertise.

He shifted his position a little, in the faint hope of being released, and was dismayed to find himself more tightly bound than ever. An even worse thought then struck him. The obvious means for such a woman to entrap a fellow of his calibre in marriage would be for her to fall pregnant. Being of respectable birth, and having a foothold in an honourable profession, her claims could not easily be brushed aside. Her father the colonel would leave his rural fastness to kick up a fuss in the capital, and there would be rumours at the Garrick or Athenaeum which a chap's senior partners might come to hear. It could even be that she was *already* pregnant, as the result of some unsavoury liaison, and had tonight been looking for someone on whom she could later lay paternity. He had heard such tales before, never imagining he might feature in the role of Dupe.

From convenience rather than desire, his right palm, throughout this train of thought, lay cupping the woman's right breast, while the fingers of his left hand (this arm being trapped underneath her body) were spread across the jut of her hip. Now he moved both hands away as far as he was able, to the cold neutrality of the floorboards. She, too, shifted position, hunching her arms and legs closer together, and thus away from the involuntary encroachment of his body.

Their minds and emotions were now divorced, absolutely. Only at the groin could no man put them asunder.

## 6

Despite their discomfort, both in due course slept. When they woke – at the same moment, joined even in this – light was falling from the sash window, beyond which an elm stood, its leaves fraying in the wind. It was Sunday morning, rapidly approaching midday, but silent as midnight in the street. For a brief, hopeful moment, as each came to consciousness, recalled the dilemma, and ventured to slide away from the other, it seemed they might be separated. But it was not to be. Wordlessly, they rolled over so that his chest once more lay on top of her back; then rolled a further ninety degrees, to face the opposite wall; then turned again, with the utmost awkwardness, so that his back rested against the wooden floor and her face and breasts pointed at the ceiling. Manfully he arranged himself in even stranger positions, at one point revolving so that his feet lay by her head and vice versa. But to no avail. They reverted to the posture of two cupped spoons in a cutlery canteen, once more surveying the airy chasm under the bed. She remembered a newspaper item about Siamese twins. He recalled a boyhood tale about the Dutch boy who, bravely preventing a flood, was forced to remain for ever standing with his finger in a dyke. Both struggled with the realisation that their bodies were at present, and their fates might for all eternity be, inextricably entwined.

Despite such dismay, their moods had lightened somewhat thanks to sleep. And both were freshly conscious that tension and recrimination could only make matters worse. In short, they made an effort to be pleasant to each other, if only in the hope this might effect an escape.

'It's indecent to admit, but I'm fearfully hungry,' she said.

'Me too,' he concurred. 'I could murder gammon and eggs.'

'In the circumstances, I'd find it hard to oblige you. But there is a low table just outside the door, with a bowlful of fruit on it. To eat might do us good.'

Taking the hint, he prepared himself for action. By raising their shoulders, paddling with their elbows, and pushing up their ankles, they were able to shunt themselves across the floor. It was painful, halting progress, difficult to coordinate and, so he thought, 'a bit like a boat race crew on choppy water without a cox. At one point, she took this great lurch forwards before I was ready. I don't know which hurt more: the splinters in my leg or my cock being torn from my balls.' By degrees, they attained the doorway and, beyond it, the table with its bowl of fruit, which they reached up to and plucked at greedily, as she put it 'stuffing our mouths with apples and pears, like naughty children raiding an orchard'. The fruit bowl duly emptied, its sustenance having passed to their stomachs, they were in high spirits, and laughed together, he venturing that here was something they would one day be able to tell their grandchildren, she pouring scorn on this notion ('For shame!') but suggesting they look on the bright side.

'Whatever that is. Can you offer even one consoling thought?'

'Well, had it not been Sunday my fellow tenants would have been here to see us.'

'And thereby rescue us.'

'Oh, but the indignity!'

'Bugger indignity. The sooner we're out of this pickle, the better.'

'But surely that will happen naturally, without the intervention of others.'

'I hope so, but how?'

'I thought food might help.'

'Alas, no.'

'Perhaps we should just lie still.'

'But we have slept, rested and eaten, to no effect. Surely there must be some other remedy?'

'None I'm aware of,' he said. 'By the way, what time is it?'

'It's . . . oh, God,' she said, 'I'd forgotten completely, oh no.'

## 7

Her fresh distress came from seeing the clock on the wall, which showed that it was now well past midday. It was the habit of her aunt – her dead mother's sister – to call for tea each Sunday between two and four. Pretending to be out would be of no use, since the said aunt, being 'family' and therefore trusted, had a key to let herself in. This unpleasant news she relayed to her companion, urging him to 'Think of something, quick'.

He thought, but not productively. He had friends living close by, but how to summon them without leaving the house? Certainly not by telephone, since this house, in common with most houses, did not possess one. Shouting for help from the window might alert any passer-by to call a constable, and the front door be broken down. But his consort was unready to bear the shame of discovery. Shame might not be the end of it. The laws pertaining to sexual relations were not his speciality, but he knew them to be draconian, and it might well be that some ancient statute outlawed the physical position they had adopted, in which case they would face prosecution and social ruin. Hiding under the bed, or in a wardrobe, might furnish a temporary refuge from the prying aunt or fellow tenants, but soon enough the girl's absence would become cause for alarm and a more strenuous search be carried out.

He racked his brain to think what else could be done. He had heard of smoke being used to flush out rats and ferrets, but even supposing there were tobacco in the house he doubted whether his own burrowing creature would be responsive to vigorous puffs from a pipe or cigar. Tomorrow he had an important case beginning, a client he had to defend from charges of gross embezzlement, and if he were to miss the . . .

It was the thought of himself standing enrobed and bewigged in court that led to what he later called 'my brainwave, the first decent idea I'd had in eighteen hours'. Six months previously he had been the junior barrister for the Crown prosecuting a man charged with the theft, from Lloyds Bank at 17 Cornhill, of £20,000 in foreign currency. The man had been apprehended at London Bridge station some fifteen minutes after the robbery. He had no foreign currency on his person, and pleaded innocence. But since the clothes he wore, and the briefcase he carried, bore an exact resemblance to those described by fifteen witnesses both in the bank and along the route (several of whom picked him out at an identity parade), it was clear he had simply passed the money to a waiting accomplice. Or should have been clear. All had been going well for the Crown until the man's defence team had called as expert witness a certain doctor of high repute, resident in Highgate, whose medical report drew attention to 'an upper thigh injury, sustained by the accused during the Great War', which had resulted in a 'severe limp' and would have made it impossible for the man to walk from 17 Cornhill to London Bridge in a mere fifteen minutes, as the Crown and their witnesses alleged. The doctor, the young man had thought as he stood up to cross-examine him, would be easy meat: a bit of gentle mockery, an irony or two at the expense of his impenetrable medical jargon, and they would be home and dry. But he had sorely under-estimated his opponent, who spoke with wit, authority and blinding expertise. The jury unanimously acquitted the accused. He thought of the doctor now, for ever engraved on the memory with his handsome face, lavish whiskers and monocle. Unsurprisingly, since they resided at nearby addresses, they had sometimes passed each other while out walking, and, despite the young man's bitterness at the outcome of the case, had exchanged pleas-antries. This doctor seemed to know more about the workings of the human body than any other doctor in London, indeed the world.

'Do you have pen and paper handy?' he asked her, as they lay discon-solate by the fruit bowl.

'Yes, just there, in the little desk, if you can reach it.'

'And an envelope?'

'In the second drawer down.'

'And the key to the front door?'

'Right here, on the table.'

'Good. I think I have an idea.'


## 8


It is now, not before time, that I myself make an entry into this tale. It is my custom, after Sunday lunch, to retire to the study in order to make notes for my *magnum opus* or sometimes, on winter days, merely to cogitate before a blazing fire. That Sunday I was preoccupied with a colleague's research paper, the conclusions of which I found most ques-tionable, not least since they struck at the core of my own research. I expect I must have been meditating on the implausibility of certain cali-brations of his when, from the depths of my armchair, I was suddenly aware of my wife.

'Alfred, you've nodded off again.'

'Not at all, my dear, I was merely . . .'

'There's a boy at the door with an urgent letter.'

The boy, a fellow of fifteen or so, was shown in. His was a strange mission. He had, he said, been in the area of St John's Wood, on course to pay a visit to his grandfather, when a loud 'hallooa' from an upper window stopped him. Looking up, he descried the fellow who had shouted: he was leaning 'sort of sideways-on', at the edge of an open window, with, it seemed, 'not a jot on his back or bum'. In polite tones, but clearly under strain, the gentleman offered the boy a guinea to carry a letter to my address, it being, he said, 'a medical matter of some urgency'. The boy at once agreed, upon which a white envelope was dropped from the window to the garden, from where he retrieved it, bidding farewell to the gentleman and promising to be speedy. Which indeed he had been.

I tore open the envelope and upon finding a guinea therein dismissed the boy, adding a few pence for him from my own pocket. The letter was succinct in regard to the urgency of the situation, but disclosed few details beyond an address, a key to which was supplied for me to gain access. With bag and stethoscope, and a cursory word to my wife, I at once left the house, and was fortunate to find a cab at the end of the street.

The spectacle awaiting me on the second floor of the house in St John's Wood was, I need hardly tell the reader, bizarre in the extreme. In truth I had never come across the like in thirty years at the coalface of medicine. The discomfiture of the two participants – or patients as I prefer to call them – was at least as much social as physical: in the case of the lady, because she was naked; in the case of the gentleman, because he had previously encountered me in a very different context, as his oppo-nent in court. (I confess that I quite failed to recognise him, but perhaps this was no great surprise, even to him.) Since manoeuvring themselves, courtesy of a chaise longue, into a vertical position in order to hail the boy from the window (she having stood just beyond the frame, out of sight, he showing as little of himself as possible), they had, in effect, remained upright – though were now at rest in a sitting position in an armchair in the drawing room, a blanket discreetly draped about them. They looked at first rather charming and homely, the image of a newly married couple, he clasping her about the waist as she sat in his lap. But as they stood up, at my behest, to undergo a full medical examination, and the blanket fell away, I understood quite how lacking in charm and homeliness their predicament was. Naturally I tried to hide my consternation. A doctor's task – so I have always felt, long before younger colleagues made the idea fashionable – is in large part simply to reassure the patient.

'Have you moved position at all?' I asked.

'Yes, every which way. But it doesn't help.'

'A period of rest might . . .'

'We've tried that.'

'Or some food . . .'

'No good, either.'

'It is most puzzling.'

'Come on, you're supposed to be the doctor.'

'Excuse me, I must first make a few notes.'

I confess that this was merely a ploy to allow me to think. The prognosis, I understood at once, was bleak. The lovers having been locked to each other for over twelve hours, there was now little prospect of them separating of their own volition. It would almost certainly require a surgical operation, and thus their removal to the more public venue of a hospital, a removal which they would certainly resist. Worse, and this was the news I felt least able to disclose, the operation, to succeed, might mean amputation. With luck, the woman's sexual parts would suffer no damage at all, or none of consequence (she might lose her clitoris but would still be able to bear children). But the dice had rolled less kindly for the gentleman: in all likelihood, his organ would have to be sawn off at the scrotum.

I continued to scribble in my notebook, wondering how best to broach these unpleasant matters, when the gentleman said:

'You know what they do with dogs, don't you?'

'I'm sorry,' I said, genuinely perplexed, but also wishing to spare the young lady, who had begun to blush.

'I once saw it happen to a pair of mongrels on the street,' he went on. 'An old lady came out with a bucket of water and threw it all over them. It seemed to do the trick.'

'You're not suggesting . . . ?' she began to protest.

'You *do* have a bath, I take it.'

There are times when a doctor must respect the privacy of his patients, and this was one such. The young lady having conceded it was 'worth a try', they struggled like some pantomime horse to the bathroom, behind the door of which I could hear running water, occasional heavier splashes from a jug and much intake of breath. Though cold water is famous for its capacity to induce detumescence, I doubted its likely efficacy in this instance. With good cause. Some ten minutes later they re-emerged, goose-pimpled and teeth-chattering, but no less commingled than before.

'No luck, doc,' said the young man, somewhat superfluously. I could see a shadow of doubt, or disillusion, passing through him. Rightly, he had looked to me as perhaps the one doctor in the world capable of relieving his ailment. I deeply wished not to let him down. Nor did I wish to disappoint his consort, now once again seated in his lap and thereby exhibiting, I could not help but notice, a striking tuft of tawny pubic hair. Seeing me seeing her, she cried out in fresh agony, lamenting that she was undone and wondering aloud, 'What's to stop this d—ed nightmare going on for ever?'

Fortunately, the young man's earlier reference to canine precedent had set me thinking. Though my expertise is in the human field, not the animal, I am an enthusiastic burrower into all known species, and my shelves at home contain a number of zoological textbooks. In one of these, I felt sure, might be a relevant paragraph on the ailment and word of a cure; I even had a dim memory of reading such a passage. It was, as the young lady would have put it, 'worth a try'. Since I'd had the foresight to ask the cab driver to wait outside, it wouldn't even be necessary to abandon my patients. Seizing paper and envelope, I jotted down the names of three likely textbooks, issued instructions to my wife as to their precise location, and descended to the street to dispatch the driver *tout de suite*.

I climbed the stairs and resumed interrogation of the hapless couple, establishing the remarkable fact that they had not known each other until the previous evening. Barely had I begun to press them about this, however, than the doorbell rang and a key could be heard in the front door.

'Oh Lord, I'd quite forgotten again. This will be the death of me,' the young lady expostulated, and explained in hushed tones, as a pair of heels could be heard crossing the entrance hall, that this must be her aunt come to visit. Unruffled, I propelled the couple as speedily as they could go towards the bedroom, and closed the door. I turned to face the aunt, who was just then, breathlessly, reaching the top stair. A small, grey-haired woman in a green coat and with a fur stole about her neck, she looked surprised to see me.

'And who the devil are you, sir?'

I gave my name, and qualifications, and shook her hand.

'My good woman, I'm afraid your niece has had an accident.'

'An accident!'

'No need for alarm. A fall in the street, that is all. She has injured her ankle.'

'Broken it, you mean?'

'Only strained, I think. But I took the precaution of sending her to hospital. Knowing you were coming, she asked me to wait and inform you.'

'Which hospital? I must go there right away.'

'No call for that, madam. By the time you arrive, she will be discharged.'

'Then I'll wait here.'

'Impossible, I'm afraid. Your niece was most explicit. She asked that you return tomorrow.'

'But she needs nursing. And I'm her only relation hereabouts.'

'I'm aware of that, madam. And she was most solicitous on your behalf. But she has spent a sleepless night, and the most useful nursemaid now is that of rest. If she had not asked herself, I would, as her physician, have insisted upon it.'

'Since I am here, let us share a pot of tea. I'll just hang my coat up.'

'I'm afraid not, madam. I have other urgent calls to attend. Shall we step down together?'

With extreme reluctance, half a mind still on the unforthcoming pot of tea, the aunt descended the stairs at my side. On the front step I made some pretence of having forgotten my notebooks and medical bag: I would have to ascend again, it would not be worth her waiting. She looked reluctant to depart still, and the fear that she might engage me in further conversation was quickened by the sight, over her shoulder, of my driver turning into the street. Briskly, I bid her *adieu* and watched her slowly walk away.

## 9

I am blessed in having a photographic memory, and felt certain that the entry I was looking for lay towards the bottom of a right-hand page. I rapidly perused all three volumes as my patients, supine on the bed though they were, watched in eager anticipation through the open bedroom door. The first two books were of no use at all. The third looked scarcely more promising, and I had begun to despair when suddenly I came across the passage in question, in an entry for *Canidae* and in particular *Vulpes vulpes*, the red fox.

'In the early stages of courtship, the vixen is hostile to the male and will rebuff him if he approaches. But as the reproductive period draws near, she becomes more receptive and will often, before mating, indulge in vigorous play. Penetration takes place with the female, standing, facing away and the male clasping her round the lumbar region with his paws. Once intromission has occurred, the *bulbus glandis* near the proximal end of the penis enlarges and makes withdrawal impossible. If the male *does* dismount he and the female will end up standing side by side or facing in opposite directions, "knotted" or "tied". They remain thus for a period of between ten and thirty minutes before detumescence of the *bulbus* permits the penis to be withdrawn. Any attempt to separate before the lapse of this period can be very painful, especially, to judge by his screams, for the male.

'While the tie lasts, both dog fox and vixen are vulnerable to attack by other predators. So what is the purpose of the tie? First, the continuing presence of the male effectively excludes other suitors. Second, and relatedly, the tie increases the chance of pregnancy – research shows that further mating by, or genital stimulation of, the female would inhibit transport of the sperm. Also worthy of note is that the penis of *Vulpes vulpes* consists of a bone not, as in the human male, blood vessels and muscle. The baculum, or *os* penis, is a rod-like structure, grooved below for the passage of the urethra and the corpus spongiosum. Its functional significance appears to be twofold: for more effective pentration of the vaginal orifice (the male organ being larger than its vessel); and to provide vaginal stimulation. The groove in the baculum may serve to prevent occlusion of the urethral canal during copulation, and to enable "twisting" to take place during the tie.

'The tie, or knot, has also been observed in other canine species. It has even been known to affect dogs kept as family pets. Some believe it to be a legacy of a more promiscuous phase of evolution. Whatever the case, it is in *Vulpes vulpes* that its symptoms are most acute.'

As I read and reread the tome in my lap, I commanded an excellent view of the bed on which the unfortunate couple lay back to front and front to back. Their future happiness rested in my hands. I had precious little to go on; a less experienced physician might have dispatched his patients straight to the surgeon's knife. But one phrase – 'a more promiscuous phase of evolution' – had leapt out at me and seemed to hold the key.

## 10

The couple, for the sake of modesty, were by this point lying under the covers, and though, when I entered the bedroom, they made as if to sit up together, I suggested they stay put.

'Have you finished your reading, doc?' the gentleman asked.

'Yes,' I replied.

'And have you found a remedy?'

'That remains to be seen.'

'Oh, please let us be quick,' cried the young woman. 'My fellow lodgers are sure to return at any moment.'

'If I am to extricate you from this predicament, I must first ask some questions,' I said. 'And for my treatment to have some chance of success, I must entreat you to answer honestly. To begin with you, young sir. Can you tell me with how many women you have enjoyed sexual relations?'

'When you say "enjoyed" . . . ?'

'I do not, of course, refer to the pleasure quotient. I mean: of how many women have you had carnal knowledge?'

'And when you say "women" . . . ?'

'Surely there can be no ambiguity there.'

'You mean women of all stations?'

'Yes.'

'Well then, I have had experience of some four gentlewomen.'

'Continue.'

'And of perhaps a dozen or so women of the street.'

'That's about fifteen or sixteen in all?'

'And, when I travelled abroad, of half a dozen or so alien women as well.'

'And that is the sum?'

'Yes.'

'And you, young woman? Forgive me for having to ask, but was this your first experience?'

'No, doctor. In Germany, a couple of summers ago, my tutor there . . . We had a love affair.'

'And you had carnal knowledge of him more than once?'

'Many times, yes.'

'And he is the only man?'

'A gamekeeper in my father's employ touched me immodestly once, against my will, when I was thirteen. But that is all.'

'And what is your view of the moral and social conventions pertaining to sexual congress?'

'I would sleep with any man I loved, if I felt he loved me. I might even sleep with a man I merely desired, if I felt he respected me and would not hold it against me. I believe mutual desire and respect are what counts.'

'You do not condemn premarital sex.'

'It would be hypocritical of me to do so.'

'And you, sir?'

'I think it important a chap learn the ropes a bit, before he ties the knot. It's in his future wife's interest, too, that he gets to know what's what.'

'So neither of you thinks it unnatural that men and women should have congress outside the marriage bed.'

'No.'

'No.'

'And you think of congress as having a purpose quite distinct from fertilisation?'

'Yes. I certainly had no desire for fertilisation last night.'

'Nor me.'

'And you hold these views on sexual congress while knowing them to be at variance with the conventions of our time.'

'Yes.'

'Yes.'

'Now, let me ask you in turn what you feel to be each other's most striking physical feature.'

'His tawny moustache.'

'Her auburn hair – you know, down there.'

'Indeed so. And let me ask you finally if either of you has heard of the work of Professor Charles Darwin.'

'Of course, his theory of evolution . . .'

'And his adventures in the – what was it called . . . ?'

'HMS *Beagle*.'

'Yes. But I don't understand what Darwin has to do with us, Doctor.'

'Darwin speaks somewhere of hybridisation, or cross-fertilisation, as it affects plants and animals. By this he means interbreeding between different species. Our knowledge in this field is very limited, but it seems possible that during an early stage of evolution there were really very few species, and that a relation existed not only between man and apes, which is by now widely accepted, but between man and other mammals, too. What I mean to suggest is that traces of other species may still exist in the human species of today, and that in certain rare individual cases this primitive legacy may manifest itself. The vulgar expression is, I believe, of someone or something being a "throwback".'

'But I still don't see . . .'

'The condition that presently inconveniences you is one that commonly affects members of the dog family, in particular the common British fox. I note that you each alluded to the reddish colour of the other's facial or pubic hair. I also note that you both exhibit an acceptance of and perhaps even an inclination towards a habit of promiscuity more common in the animal kingdom than in the human.'

'Now, steady on, doc . . .'

'In short, I'd suggest that there could well be a residual canine streak in both of you, which explains why you were first repelled by, then attracted to each other, and, more to the point, also explains why you have become what zoologists call "tied" or "knotted".'

The gentleman seemed too outraged by my thesis to speak. The young woman, by contrast, was composed enough not only to absorb the argument but to raise a perfectly sensible objection.

'But surely dogs and foxes don't remain tied for more than twelve hours, as we have done.'

'That is correct, young lady. A residual canine streak explains what has locked you together. But what prevents you from separating is ordinary human anxiety. Because you do not know each other well, because of mutual suspicion, because of social embarrassment, because of guilt, because you both fear that fertilisation may have taken place – for all these reasons, the muscles in your genital region have gone into violent spasm. The good news is that diagnosis, where intelligent patients are involved, is often halfway to a cure.'

'Forgive me, Doctor,' said the young woman, 'but we have been lying here for nearly eighteen hours now. You're not suggesting the remedy is simply more of the same.'

'Indeed, young lady, *les mots justes*.'

'Stop gabbling in French,' snapped the young man. 'Explain yourself.'

'The explanation is perfectly simple, but requires us to consider a second anatomical theory. Excuse me for a moment while I fetch my book.'

And with that, bowing like a magician after a trick, I left them awestruck in the room.

333

## 11

Naturally I am dismissive of 'alternative' or fanciful methods of healing. If two thousand years of civilisation have taught us anything, it is that the accumulated wisdom of history's faith healers, tribal gurus and Red Indian medicine men does not amount to a thimble – whereas the rudimentary knowledge possessed by a single modern GP would fill barrels. Away with all potions of ant's blood, snail juice and beetle pee! Enough, once and for all, of this creepy veneration of *Nature*! Good Lord, why should nature provide a cure, when it is nature that makes us sick in the first place? Let us not resort to the mystic mumbo-jumbo of inferior races.

Nonetheless, there are some less than fully rational methods of healing which I have learned to respect, if only because their efficacy seems indisputable. One such is the medical model credited to Samuel Hahnemann of Leipzig (1755–1843), commonly known as homeopathy. Those familiar with it will know that its guiding principle is of like being cured by like, of the malady being remedied by the administration, in small doses, of what has caused it. The potential for its application here had struck me like a thunderbolt. Tentatively and discreetly, I outlined the principles of homeopathy to the unhappy figures clamped together on the bed. The woman was quick to grasp their implications, the gentleman somewhat slower, though he got there in the end.

'So you're saying, as well be hanged for a sheep as a lamb.'

'No, the point, sir, *au contraire*, is that this time you would strictly ration congress. Assuming that, last night you were sexually active for how long . . . ?'

'Seemed about four hours,' he said.

'Two certainly,' she blushingly corrected.

'Well, let us say three,' I said, 'then the dosage this time, on a principle of one part to a hundred, would be, um, let's see, 180, that's 1.8, which means roughly one minute and fifty seconds. If your congress were timed to that duration or thereabouts, and were of an equivalent energy, then I think we might be in business.'

Saying this, I pulled my watch chain from my breast pocket.

'That's all very well in principle, Doctor,' he said, studying me, 'but I'm not sure I'm up to it. Am I supposed to shoot my bolt, in that time?'

'I'd have thought it would help. But I don't think it's essential,' I said.

'Even so,' he went on, 'I'm not at all confident about getting started.'

'Ah,' I said, 'there I think I can be of help.'

The magician once more, I plucked from the inside pocket of my overcoat a book wrapped in plain brown paper – a slim volume of verse, entitled *Femmes*, by the poet Paul Verlaine, published clandestinely, or as the French put it *sous le manteau*, some years ago. Though not strictly a medical text, I had used this book more than once before with patients who, as the result of upper thigh wounds or neurasthenia, suffered from the delusion that they were impotent. In my experience, this book – though other books might suffice equally well – has remarkable aphrodisiac powers. (When I say 'in my experience' I mean, of course, as a doctor. Happily, in my personal life, I have never needed artificial stimulants to boost my virility – and indeed have sometimes found it difficult to conceal my contempt when some cringing half-man comes to me in search of libido-enhancing elixirs.)

'Listen to this,' I said to the couple on the bed, or more especially to the male of the species. I had picked up the Verlaine in Paris some years before and, on the principle that doctors need to play as well as work, had passed several amusing evenings turning it into a vigorous English of my own devising. It was this I read aloud now:

> I'm done – you've won my heart.
> All I want is your lovely arse
> To kiss, sniff and lick,
> And your sweet cunt to stick
> my huge . . .

The lady seemed a little discomfited, but, gratifyingly, the gentleman's eyes lit up. Continuing to read aloud, I withdrew to the next room, fearing my presence might inhibit the success of the experiment. I had a score of poems at my disposal but even before I had finished the first the jingling of bedsprings told me that any more would be redundant. Watch chain in hand, with bated breath, I lurked behind the door, ducking down to ensure – by means of the keyhole – that nothing untoward was taking place. One minute passed. The noise of the couple grew louder, their movements more vigorous. 'That's it, stop now!' I shouted, as one minute fifty seconds was reached. A moment later came the shriek of two human voices in unison, a sound not unlike that which pornographers (so I am told) describe as a couple 'coming together' but which I knew was something infinitely more triumphant: the sound of a couple coming apart.

The next sight I had was of two beaming faces. In one fell swoop, my prisoners were free.


## 12

The average reader will be rightly shocked to learn that two educated young people, of decent birth, could permit themselves within a few hours of meeting one another to achieve full sexual congress. But he can take comfort from the fact that they were, in effect, penalised for their impulsiveness. Their exceptional physiology should also be noted: on close examination after the event, I detected along various points of their bodies – behind the neck, under their arms, on their toes – the presence of long stiff hairs called 'vibrissae', normally present only in canine species and highly sensitive to sensual pleasure.

Thanks to a stroke of good fortune, I am currently conducting further research into this phenomenon. It transpires that the house in which the aforesaid young woman had her lodgings is shortly to be sold, and I have therefore been able to offer her a room in my own. My wife occasionally grumbles about our having 'yet another flibbertigibbet lodger', but she appreciates the prior claims of science – as, I trust, does the young lady, who has been allowed the most generous of rental agreements. Her bedroom, it happens, lies next to my study, and as I write this, the lamp guttering, I can hear the pleasing sounds of a young woman's boudoir – the loosening of stays, the slither of silk stockings, the press of young limbs on cool white sheets. It is an opportune moment for me to examine those vibrissae of hers. Forgive me, then, for breaking off here. You will, I know, await my findings with interest.

# Part 4

## *Love? You Can Keep It*

20 February 2001

## *LIBBY*

IT WAS a shock seeing her name in Arrivals. No taxi had been booked but there she was, LIBBY RAVEN, on the handwritten sign. For a moment she thought her mother must have died and that she would have to fly straight back to Belfast. But then Damian stepped forward, the sign in one hand, white lilies in the other. After kissing, he held her at arm's length. His eyes were usually sparrows, darting away, but today he was neither manic nor furtive. For the last six weeks, she'd barely seen him. But here he was, with a bunch of lilies and her married name.

'How did you . . . ?'

'You said. When you texted. First flight out.'

'Hoped to, I said. If she got no worse.'

'I took a chance.'

'Shall we get a taxi?'

'I've brought the car.'

He dumped the sign in the nearest waste bin and they walked arm in arm through the terminal. A tide of families swept against them, full of ski gear and golf bags and half-term hysteria.

'How is she?' Damian said.

'No better, no worse.'

'So you're home for a while?'

'My sister's with her.'

'But if things deteriorate . . .'

'It may take weeks. No one can say.'

He squeezed her hand as they crossed to the concrete car park. People couldn't be blamed for getting ill – apart from Nat, who was regularly, wilfully, almost professionally ill – and there was no right time for someone to have cancer. But with work so intense, the girls demanding, and the relationship with Damian in the balance, Libby felt vaguely resentful. Why *now*, God? Yes, my mother's over seventy, she's not been happy since my father died, in some ways it would be a mercy – but why now? She felt like a ransacked chest of drawers, the work drawer, parent drawer, daughter drawer, wife drawer, lover drawer yanked out and spilling their contents.

Her mother had finally owned up about the stomach pains at Christmas. Stoic as she was, she might have said nothing even then but for Libby asking outright. (And Libby might never have noticed her loss of appetite but for the girls whingeing, 'Why do we have to eat all our dinner when Nan never eats hers?') Libby dragged her to the local GP, who referred her to a Dr Monk at the local hospital; they operated six days later. The speed of it was ominous. Having flown home Libby flew back, to find her mother lying coffin-still among drips and monitors. The nurses directed her to Dr Monk. Naturally, she had assumed a him: it was Dr Monk this, and Dr Monk that, and her imagination supplied the trousers and hairy wrists. Instead of which, this chit of a thing, with blonde hair, milky hands and a china-doll face, telling her that the tumour, now removed, had been less 'contained' than anticipated. 'You're saying what exactly?' Libby said. Dr Monk shone a pencil torch at the X-rays. With her torch and red lipstick, she might have passed for a cinema usherette. If the secondaries moved slowly, she said, Mavis would have six months – but the family should know the condition was terminal. 'Should my mother know too?' Libby asked, not caring to hear her called Mavis when she was Maeve. 'That's up to the family,' Dr Monk said, 'I can't advise.' Back on the ward, her mother's eyes were wide and interrogative. 'Let's get you some water,' Libby said, ducking them. Later she spoke to her sister Patsy in the States, who booked a flight for the following day.

'Does she still recognise you?' Damian said, as they left the car park.

'Oh yes. All her wits about her.'

'But she doesn't know.'

'No. Unless she thinks she's sparing *us* by not referring to it.'

'Surely she's suspicious. Being in a hospice.'

'No one says the word hospice. But of course.'

She and Patsy had found the hospice – a 'terminal care facility' just outside Belfast – after visiting every nursing home within fifty miles. In a private room, their mother perked up, a hint of rose back in her cheeks. 'She looks good for another year,' Libby said to Patsy. But when she tried the word 'remission' on the hospice director, he wasn't encouraging: 80 per cent of his patients died within four weeks of admission, he said. Maeve had now been there for three.

Ahead, down the M4, London rose palely through the mist. A traffic helicopter blat-blatted overhead, and Libby imagined the view as the pilot was seeing it, the city towers like oblong magnets standing on end and a million cars drawn towards them like iron filings. It made her feel small, useless, in the grip of forces beyond her control. Her face in the passenger mirror looked grey, from all the shuttling back and forth. She might be here in body but her head was circling uselessly in Baggage Reclaim.

'She's talking, then?' Damian said.

'Yes.'

'What about?'

'Anything and everything.'

'Does she know about me?'

'Kind of.'

The previous day Maeve had asked after Nat. Though they had not been together for eighteen months now, she continued to assume the rift was temporary, the sort of amicable trial separation she knew about from women's magazines. 'I expect you both need your own space for a while,' she said, from her pillows. Libby would have preferred a tirade. Had she and Dad ever needed their own space? For Maeve, Nat would always be the perfect gentleman – so clever, so posh, so English. You're wrong, Mum, he's feckless, a waste of space, I'll never have him back – somehow the moment was never right to say that. As for Damian, her lips were sealed. Errant husbands, difficult boyfriends: her mother had enough on, dying, without those.

'I've missed you, you know,' Damian said.

'I've missed you too.'

'If I'd known how ill she was, I'd never have had that fight with you.'

'It was me who started it.'

'Even so.'

Spending every weekend away would have put a strain on any relationship. She had done her best to reassure him there was nothing sinister in her absences, only – only! – the imminence of her mother's death. An older man, even Nat, would have understood. But Damian retaliated by going missing, too. Whenever she called, she got only his answering machine. Later he would call back, with some excuse – he had been with friends, down the pub, at the gym, out shopping – but she began to have her suspicions. Was he seeing someone else? And then one night, after supper in a restaurant called Merope, she found that golden hair.

The evening had begun badly enough. They hadn't seen each other for two weeks. Even so, he contrived to be late. Just like Nat always used to be. But the whole point of Damian was his being Not-Nat.

'Sorry,' he said, chucking down a briefcase. 'Important call just as I was leaving.'

It occurred to her he had brought the briefcase as an alibi.

'More important than me, clearly,' she said.

'Then the traffic was bad.'

'It usually is at rush hour.'

'I said I'm sorry.'

'Why didn't you call?'

'Battery's going flat on my mobile.'

'And you thought I'd nothing better to do than sit around.'

She hated the sound of herself – the put-upon woman whingeing at her man.

'Don't get so stressed,' he said, unmoved, as though he'd heard it all before, 'you know I'd never hurt you, babe.'

For a time, the evening improved. They ordered food and Damian listened, and though she spared him the catheters and colostomy bags he seemed to grasp that things with her mother were grim. But then his mobile went off, which was awkward enough after the flat battery story and made worse by his furtive 'Can I call you back?' He switched the phone off after that, but there were interruptions from other diners, mostly women, coming over to say hello. Evenings out with Damian were like this. They'd go to a place where friends and colleagues of his were also going, and though officially with her, *à deux*, at a separate table, he would also be with them or they with him – that's when he wasn't on his mobile. It had attracted her at first. His jacket would be off, his tie loose, his shirt tail hanging out of his trousers – and he'd be sniffing, prowling, networking, marking out his territory. She loved the energy. But that night she wanted his attention, and the hand-squeezing under the table wasn't enough. Why *under* anyway? They had been out and about together for over a year. Or was there a particular woman in the room who wasn't supposed to know? The redhead in the turqoise dress? The blonde in the pinstripe suit? They had talked about certain women from Damian's past but she assumed there were now none to discuss. Perhaps she was wrong. At moments like this, marriage to Nat seemed preferable. She didn't want mess.

Then his mobile rang again: he must have turned it back on in the Gents, while making a sneaky phone call to whomever. Decisive, she stood up, opened her handbag, and chucked £50 on the table: 'My share of the bill.' Rushing upstairs, a familiar cramp in her stomach, she hailed a cab. But before she could close the door Damian was in beside her. The driver gave a quizzical look in the mirror, but when Damian said Tower Bridge she didn't protest. Back at his flat, she maintained her stony silence. Arms folded, like a teacher waiting for a truant to explain himself, she sat on a stool at his breakfast bar until he convinced her of his unswerving devotion.

There was a kitchen knife close at hand. Had he once, in the most roundabout way, attributed her anger with him to stress or PMT, she would have plunged it through his heart.

After 127 minutes she was satisfied. Undivorced as she was, she could not accept his marriage proposal but decided it was sincerely meant.

They went to bed – her reward to them both. It felt wonderful. Until she found the golden hair – a single strand, eighteen inches long, lying on his pillow, which she carried off with her to examine under the striplight of the bathroom mirror.

Just as dreams that seem to go on for hours last only seconds, so the two minutes she spent in the bathroom contained an aeon of conflicting thoughts: that he had obviously fucked someone; that he'd done it because Libby was spending all her time in Belfast; that sex with a stranger had been a kind of a comfort blanket for him; that this only proved how much he loved and depended on Libby; that she could either choose to say nothing about it, or make him confess and then forgive him; that shit, no, this was indulgent and pathetic, she didn't feel forgiving in the least, the bastard snoring in bed had been callowly, carelessly unfaithful, if he was going to fuck other women he might at least make more effort to conceal it, the hair on the pillow was insulting in part because such a cliché (what next? lipstick on his collar?), she deserved better than someone so unoriginal, and had better wake him up and give him hell.

Which she did.

But first she examined the hair in detail. Long and blonde. But not knee-length, as in the tale she used to tell her daughters. Not so glitteringly golden, either. In fact, the image it provoked – a buxom, forty-something would-be blonde, whose roots needed redoing – didn't flatter anyone: not Damian (so lacking in taste), not Libby (betrayed for one so brassy) and certainly not the woman herself. Still, this was a serious matter. An infidelity. She shook Damian awake and shouted at him. Liar. Bastard. Fucking fuckface fucking a fucking slag. (And that from someone who prided herself on never swearing.)

It was embarrassing to recall this now, on the Chiswick flyover.

'You didn't *really* think that I'd slept with someone?' Damian said, from the driving seat.

'What else was I to think? What would *you* have thought?'

343

'I'd have trusted me.'

'Really?'

'Yes. You know I'll always be there for you, babe.'

What had he said at the time, in defence? Everything she had antici-pated he would say while she sat brooding in the bathroom, though not necessarily in the same order. It wasn't a hair. It wasn't a human hair. It wasn't a woman's hair. It wasn't the hair of a woman he had been to bed with. It wasn't the hair of a woman he had been to bed with since meeting Libby. It wasn't the hair of a woman he had been to bed with since meeting Libby for whom he had the slightest feeling – there had only been the one woman, the once, before they properly started going out together, Gemma, a legacy of his singledom, a guttering old flame, with whom he'd had a drink for old times' sake, before one thing led to another, an unplanned event he immediately regretted because Gemma was a *prawn* (nice body but head full of shit), but in the circumstances, since Libby was interrogating him and since he had intended to tell her sooner or later anyway, because there should be no secrets between them, yes he had lapsed once ages ago ('All men have lapses, Libby.' 'Do they, Damian?'), though the hair at issue could not possibly have come from the head of Gemma. So if it wasn't any of those hairs, Libby asked, whose hair was it? Could he identify it? And explain its presence in his bed? He could. He did. It was Libby's (impos-sible). It was his own (ditto). It was the next-door cat's (unlikely, being Siamese). It was a dog's – his friend Tariq had recently been round with his golden Labrador (would the house-proud Damian have allowed a *dog* on his bed?). It was the cleaner's, the lady-who-did, paid to come in once a week and vacuum the already fanatically vacuumed and shampooed Indian rug (no chance: Damian's lady-who-did was a bald, male ex-taxi driver). No, it was the substitute lady-who-did's hair: that was it – light from the end of the tunnel shone in his eyes – the bald ex-taxi driver had phoned in sick and offered his daughter, Della, to do instead, and this was only two days ago, and Damian had specifically left a note asking Della to change the sheets and pillowcases, and though he had not been present when she came he remembered from the last time she stood in and did (when he *was* present) that – phew – *Della had long blonde hair.* Damian lay back, resting his case. Libby considered demanding to see the note he had left asking Della to change the sheets but she knew what he would say – Della had put it in the rubbish bag and the binmen had taken the rubbish away. Excited by his own ingenuity, he pulled her to him: trust me, he said, there's only you, babe. She pushed him off and went to the bathroom, where she flushed away the evidence. Officially, there was nothing to forgive. And seeing how desperate he was to hang on to her, she let the matter drop.

If she felt much better by the time she left, that was mostly thanks to the sex. Over the past few months, he'd become obsessed with taking her from behind, as if other kinds of sex didn't interest him and this kind, doggy, was his *droit de seigneur*. In principle, she was fine with doggy. But for her sex meant being with someone completely. And sex from behind – or *only* from behind – was less wholehearted, because you didn't look your lover in the eyes. That night, after the golden hair, she wouldn't turn tail for him. She held him above or underneath her, eye to eye, as a kind of test. There was no escape for him. He had to show his feelings. And as she pinned him there, and scanned his pupils, she felt her own desire slowly returning, until he groaned her name aloud and she came. A simple matter: she was back in control – and he a fish thrashing about in her keepnet. If she chose to, she could throw him back.

It felt embarrassing to be thinking of this, in the morning traffic. But the night of the golden hair episode had been a crisis. And though he'd satisfied her afterwards, in more ways than one, she'd had few chances to see him since – and had been amazed to find him waiting for her this morning. *You know I'll always be there for you, babe.* Perhaps it was true. He'd been there for her today, anyway. They were together again. It was going to be OK.

'I've something to tell you,' he said, backed up along the Cromwell Road.

Oh God, a confession, she thought, something grubby and painful and ruinous, just when I was allowing myself to feel happy. No wonder he brought those flowers.

'What?'

'The Cavaliere account. I won it. I did the pitch yesterday, they brought half the management team over from Italy, they're going to confirm later in the week, but Mark says they've told him it's in the bag.'

'Congratulations.'

'I wanted to tell you weeks ago, when it all started, but Mark thought you'd be pitching, too.'

'I would have, but for my mother being ill.'

Cavaliere were the second biggest ice-cream retailer in Europe.

'Even when we knew you weren't in the frame, Mark insisted I keep it quiet. That's why I've been so distracted. I've been working on it sixteen hours a day.'

What a shit Mark was. But she felt pleased for Damian. Vindicated, too:

it was she who'd brought him on board in the first place. Under the gaze of lorry drivers either side, she put her hand on his thigh.

'We should celebrate,' he said. 'Go to the Bahamas or somewhere. It's been a horrible time for you.'

'It still is. I feel bad being away from the girls so much.'

'Just for a week. Since there's no immediate danger with your mum. I'll treat you.'

'It's impossible.'

'But when your mum . . . once she . . . and there's no reason for you to be around . . . can't we then?'

'Maybe.'

They were easing forward at 5mph, in the middle lane, plumes of exhaust rising.

'More immediately,' he said.

'Yes?'

'Have dinner with me tonight.'

'It's half-term. I need to spend some time with the girls. Later in the week maybe.'

'No, it has to be tonight. Alfredo will be there, Cavaliere's marketing chief. He's flying back to Milan tomorrow.'

'A business dinner?'

'Absolutely not. His wife will be with him. I had a drink with them on Sunday. Amazing couple. House in Milan, villa in Umbria, flat in New York, the lot. Very Anglophile, too. I told them all about you. They really want to meet.'

I should feel flattered, she thought. He wants to show me off.

She studied his face from the passenger seat. There was something different about his brow, a wrinkle or two, the first creases of maturity.

Maybe the girls would be all right about tonight. If she made it up to them for the rest of the week.

Then she remembered.

'Oh God, I forgot, I can't. It's Nat's lecture.'

'What?'

'This evening. Nat's giving a lecture.'

'So?'

'I promised to take the girls.'

'To a *lecture*?'

'They've never seen him function outside the house. It'll be good for them. And for him. He's very down.'

'Because his chick pissed off and left him?'

'Generally.'

'You don't owe him anything.'

'He's still their father. And they want to go.'

'Let the nanny take them.'

'Maya? It'd be unfair on her.'

'*Please*, Libby. I can tell you don't want to go. And we've not had an evening together for ages.'

She hesitated. In Poland Maya had been a drama student. Nat's lecture was about theatre.

'I doubt Maya will be free,' she said.

'Call her and see.'

'My mobile's flat.'

'Use mine.'

She resisted for another minute or two, then dialled home. Hannah and Rose were still asleep, but Maya said sure, no problem, she'd like to.

'Nat'll be disappointed,' Libby said.

'Fuck him,' Damian said. 'You're with me now.'

'Where will we go?'

'They're coming to the flat first – they want to buy a place here, on the river, so I invited them. In fact, we could order in. We'd be freer to talk. And they'll be fed up of eating out by now.'

'Order in? You mean a takeaway?'

'Or I could cook.'

'You?'

'Is my cooking so bad?'

'No, but . . .'

On the Hammersmith flyover, the sun came out.

'Tell you what,' she said, 'you buy the food and *I'll* cook.'

'That's unfair on you. You won't have time.'

'I'm taking the day off, to be with the girls. But I could come to you at five. So long as Alfredo doesn't mind simple.'

'You're brilliant.'

'I'm a mug.'

If they're Anglophile, they'll want something old-fashioned, she thought. Artichoke soup, maybe. Fillet steak. Stewed pears to follow.

'What's *she* called?' she asked.

'Who?'

'Signora Ice Cream. Alfredo's wife.'

'Maria.'

She thought of an olive-skinned beauty with long black hair. What would such a woman eat?

Langoustine, lemon chicken, fresh figs.

If Damian wanted just a cook, she thought, any woman would do. But he needs my love and endorsement. 'There's only you, babe,' he likes to tell me. And perhaps it's true.

'If you're not going to work,' he said, 'I'll turn off here and take you home along the Embankment.'

'Is that OK?'

'Sure it's OK.'

'It won't make you late for the office?'

'Doesn't matter. I'm a fucking hero, remember. The man who got Cavaliere.'

Rocket salad with Parmesan. Monkfish. Crème brûlée. She'd work it out, over breakfast, then phone him with a shopping list.

It was only after he dropped her, a judicious three doors up from the house, that she felt manipulated. How could she possibly have agreed to cook? But saucepans and skillets would be useful therapy. And getting to know the Cavaliere guy might be useful to her own company long-term.

Mozzarella with vine tomatoes, escalope Milanese, blue cheese and black grapes.

Half a second after her key turned in the lock, the girls rushed down the hall crying, 'Mummy, Mummy, Mummy.'

2

## HARRY

'THE MAN from the *Mail*'s organising a sweepstake,' Harry said.

'Jesus,' Luke said, 'you vultures.'

'Murder, 7–4 on; charge reduced to manslaughter 4–1; not guilty, 11–2.'

'Fucking carrion, the lot of you.'

They were having breakfast at Sid's, in Grope Lane, a couple of blocks from the Old Bailey. The area boasted a bagel shop, a Starbucks, an Italian deli, all more pleasant than Sid's, but Luke liked greasy spoons. Since the trial began, they'd been meeting for breakfast every day. And though they forced themselves to discuss other subjects (women, football, Russell Crowe in *Gladiator*, Brown v Blair), they couldn't keep away from it for long.

Outside, at eight fifteen, it was still dark.

'How's Ray feel about being in the witness box?' Harry asked.

'Relieved. He was afraid we wouldn't call him. He wants his say.'

'The tabloids will go for him whatever.'

'But the cons in prison might stop doing. He's been threatened with razor blades, dustbin lids, cutlery, all sorts.'

'They think he's a murderer?'

'They think he's a nonce.'

The Home Office had denied the media any access to Ray, and even Luke couldn't smuggle Harry into Maidstone. But he had met all the people closest to Ray: his mum Roberta, his brothers Duane and Darren, and Chiddi Hines, the friend at the bowling alley who had initially given evidence against Ray then withdrawn his statement ('The police hassled me into it, man'). There were personal connections, too: Duane's wife Josie used to work at the same hospital as Marcia, and Marcia – with whom Harry was finally back on speaking terms – said the Nuards were a 'lovely' family. Harry needed little persuading. Impartial reporter though he was meant to be, he identified with Ray. The more he knew about the case, the more he believed in Ray's innocence. In fact, he felt desperate for Ray to get off.

'I thought he did all right yesterday,' Harry said.

'Yes, but it'll be Jay cross-examining this morning,' Luke said. 'That's going to be tough.'

It was thanks to Deborah that Harry had spent the past month in court. Mills thought a morning's colour would be enough but Deborah overruled him. 'Errol's our story,' she said, at conference, and then to Harry, in private: 'Spend as much time there as you need.' It was a luxury not to rush off and file copy every day. His only task was a brief weekly update. When the trial was over, Deborah had promised a double spread.

It wasn't his job to crack the case but the lack of an obvious solution was frustrating. No body had ever been found, but assuming Errol was dead, and that Ray didn't kill him, who did? Harry had knocked on doors and buzzed entryphones. But the spyholes closed their eyes to him; the voice of the neighbourhood held its tongue. Two more children had gone

349

missing south of the river since Errol, and a third had washed up as a headless torso. There was no evidence to link the cases, the police said, but Harry's instincts told him there must be. Was this a race murder? Or something even more sinister? Harry's wild-animal theory was so crackpot that he didn't dare put it to Luke, but nor could he quite discard it. Giant foxes, white wolves, creatures cloned in a futuristic gene pool or re-emerging from a primal swamp – whichever, whatever, there was more to this than people were willing to acknowledge.

'Eeuukky warhhst gibbon toonnk,' a voice crackled from the breast of a leather-clad courier.

'The chronology still puzzles me,' Harry said, between mouthfuls. 'There are things that don't add up.'

He had scribbled out the time sequence while waiting for Luke to turn up, and now he slid it across to him, between the vinegar bottle and the ketchup. For an interested party to make use of: Christ, what had got into him? Where was his journalistic impartiality? He'd lost all distance.

17.40: Ray turns up at house; row with Sharon
18.00: Ray departs
19.00: Alleged sighting of Ray in neighbourhood
19.19: CCTV image of man carrying toddler along Evelyn St
19.33: McDonald's receipt for adult/child meal
20.15: Sharon begins searching neighbourhood
20.47: CCTV image of Ray in Lewisham bowling alley
21.30: Sharon's partner Louis joins her in search
22.15: Sharon calls police to report Errol missing

'Looks right,' Luke said, buttering his last piece of toast.

'So why didn't Ray abduct Errol when he left at six? Why wait another hour?'

'The girls were playing outside. He was afraid they'd see him. That's what the Crown say anyway.'

'Also: why did Sharon take five days to tell the police about the row with Ray?'

'Maybe blaming it on Ray was Louis' idea and he took that long to persuade her.'

Louis worked as a security guard at the Millennium Dome, and when Sharon called to say Errol was missing he had driven straight home to help her search. For that he lost his job, till the uproar in the media – another Dome cock-up, they called it – got him reinstated. He still worked at the Dome, despite its closure, one of the few. It was he who had found Errol's left shoe lying abandoned. He cried in the witness box when he recalled it.

'Louis made a solid Crown witness,' Luke said. 'As you saw.'

'There's still Sharon. Are you going to call her?'

'No way. If she's there in black weeds and streaked mascara sobbing that Ray did it, that will fuck things up for us for sure. As if they weren't fucked up enough already after Mia.'

Mia was the oldest of Sharon's four children and the only one to give evidence. With her little voice and ribboned bunches, she was deemed too 'vulnerable' to appear in court, even behind a screen. But her police interviews were played to the jury, several of whom, according to this morning's papers, had been 'moved to tears'. Harry hadn't noticed the tears. He'd been too busy writing her words down in his notebook.

'I have it verbatim,' he said, flipping open his laptop.

Luke scraped his chair closer, for a better view.

'You type this stuff up every day?' he said.

'Every night. So I've a record.'

'You must have good shorthand.'

'And a tape recorder as backup.'

'You'll be in trouble if they catch you.'

'It was you who taught me the trick.'

'Christ, you've even got Jay's opening address,' Luke said. 'Are you writing a book or something?'

Rodney Jay had opened for the Crown, after Ray's defence team failed to get the trial postponed on the grounds of prejudicial reporting. 'The defence will tell you,' Jay began, 'that because Errol Winthrop's body has never been found there is no case to answer. That, we submit, is arrant nonsense. We have the child's bloodstains, evidence that he didn't just harmlessly disappear. We have witnesses who put the accused at the scene. We have a motive, his well-advertised intention to punish Errol's mother for the breakdown of their relationship. And we have more than one confession by the accused.'

'More than one?' Luke said, as Harry scrolled forward. 'That's a laugh. He means Dickie Bearing. We soon saw him off.'

Bearing was a fellow inmate at Maidstone, who claimed Ray had told him, 'I done Errol after we been to McDonald's.' But the defence managed to suggest that Bearing had made the story up in order to get himself a remission for a twelve-year manslaughter sentence.

'Here's an interesting bit,' Harry said. As they peered together into the small black screen, he noticed the eczema on Luke's hands – the pinkish stipple round his wedding ring, and the angry rash between his fingers. Like the court reporters, with their sweepstakes and banter, Luke affected invulnerability: child murder? – all in a day's work. But his skin had rebelled. It wouldn't wear the nonchalance. It was, like fashionable wall decoration, distressed.

'Oh yeh, the old guy,' Luke said. 'Lionel made short work of him.'

Lionel was Lionel Martin, 'Britain's leading black lawyer' according to *The Times*, and principal barrister for the defence, which also included the Sri Lankan-born junior Ranjit Sen and Luke himself. The old guy was a resident of the Pepys, who had described hearing 'howls' in the vicinity of Errol's house around the time of his disappearance.

– What kind of howls? Martin asked him.
– Very loud shrieking.
– Like someone or something in pain, you said in your statement.
– Yes.
– Had you ever heard noises like this before?
– Yes, something like.
– Hadn't you in fact written to complain to the council about them?
– Yes. We get a lot of noise from foxes. But this was different.
– In what way different?
– Louder.
– The cry of a wolf, you said in your statement.
– It could have been someone screaming.
– Nonetheless, your first thought was an animal.
– I suppose so, yes.

'I enjoyed that,' Luke said. 'We made him look stupid.'

'You don't think there might be something in it?'

'An animal attacking Errol? Get real, Harry. Where's the Mia bit? Isn't that what you wanted to show me?'

They whipped through thousands of words, stopping occasionally for Luke to admire some nifty defence work. If the evidence from workers at McDonald's was a low point (two of them claimed to have 'definitely, maybe' seen Ray there with Errol), the high was Ranjit Sen's cross-examination of the police officers who had arrested Ray and who described Ray's words on opening the door to them – 'I knew you'd come. Sharon sent you, innit?' – as 'a clear admission of guilt'; 'Was it really that?' Sen responded. 'Wasn't Mr Nuard simply saying that because of his troubled relationship with Ms Winthrop it came as no great surprise to him to be arrested?' 'Could be, I suppose.'

'Sen did well,' Luke said.

'But then there was Mia,' Harry said, hitting the spot.

– Can you remember where you were round five o'clock that day, Mia? [WPC Jessica Robins]

– Em and me was playing with our bikes outside.

– That's your sister Emmalou, is it?

– Yeh.

– And Errol?

– He were locked in his room again but then he come out.

– What kind of mood was he in?

– He were crying, like he always does. Kid Runt, Mum calls him, she says he's got the devil in him. He was trying to ride on Em's bike but it's too big for him – the week before he fell off and cut his head open – so we said no and he started squawking. We was getting real fed up with him. Then Uncle Ray came, and picked him up and took him in the house to see Mum, and me and Em was happy cos we don't have Kid Runt to look after no more and we can ride our bikes.

– Did Uncle Ray speak to you?

– Yeh, he said it were freezing and we shouldn't be out with no jackets.

– Then what happened?

– There was shouts in the house. Em and me carried on playing. Then Uncle Ray come out.

– With Errol?

– Nah, Errol's in the house.

– And then?

– Uncle Ray goes off, and me and Em go in.

– He didn't take Errol with him?

– No.

– And he definitely walked away?

– Yeh, but he might of come back and hung about.

– What did you do next?

– Went in and watched telly in the bedroom with Em.

– Not the living room?

– Nah, cos Errol was in there having a tantrum.

– Why was Errol having a tantrum?

– Cos we was given crisps and he ain't allowed none cos he's a little beast. Anyway, then we go out again.

– With Errol?

– Nah, Mum's shut him in his room again, cos of his bawling.

– Did you see Uncle Ray when you were outside?

– We saw a man by the bins who could of been him.

– Which bins were these?

– Over the road. We ain't allowed to play there cos if the bin lorry comes it could squash us.

– But you weren't sure it was Uncle Ray.

– It were dark.

– And then what?

– Me and Em went in and watched telly again. In the lounge this time cos Mum weren't there.

– Where was she?

– Upstairs. Putting Charmain down and having a bath. But then later she comes down and says Where's Errol and goes mental cos he ain't with us and he ain't in his room and the front door's open. So she puts on her coat and goes out and then she comes back and Uncle Louis' home – that's Charmain's dad – and we hear a lot of shouting cos Mum's upset like.

– Where were you at this point?

– Watching telly cos we don't want to get into no more trouble. Then Mum and Uncle Louis go out looking together in the car and they're gone a long time but they don't find him so they come back and call the police and Mum tells 'em Errol must of got out. But it ain't my fault the door were open, it's not fair me getting the blame. [Cries.]

– No one's blaming you, Mia. Don't cry. I know it's upsetting losing your brother like this.

– That ain't it. It's . . . [Cries. Inaudible.]

– Your mum's just outside, Mia, in the corridor. We'll get her to come in and cuddle you. Let's stop the tape.

[End of tape 1.]

[Resumption after 30-minute break, tape 2.]

– Now, Mia, you've had a little rest and a drink of orange juice.

– And a biscuit.

– And a biscuit [laughs] and you say you want to tell us something else.

– Yeh, Mum says she know it's not me to blame for Errol.

– And we know that, too, Mia.

– Cos Em might of told you how we was bullying him but that were only cos he were wailing and being Kid Runt – we ain't hurt or killed him or nothing.

– Of course not.

– And what I wanted to tell was the man by the bins – that was Uncle Ray.

– You're sure?

– Yeh.

– But earlier you weren't so sure.

– I didn't like telling on him. Mum says he's sad cos of her and him splitting up and he ain't got Errol living with him, so we have to be nice. But it were him by the bins. For definite.

– What about Errol? Where was he?

– By the bins with Uncle Ray.

– What makes you say that?

– When we goes out on our bikes again after the crisps, me and Em left the front door open, innit. We thought Errol was shut in his room for being naughty, but he weren't, so he got out.

– Did you see Errol come out, then?

– Nah, cos we was playing. But I thought I heard him in the bushes. And then I sees a little kid over by the bins.

– And that was Errol?

– Must of been.

– Didn't you think of going over?

– No, cos he went quiet after that and I thought he gone inside again to Mum, so we forgot about him and put the bikes away and watched telly.

– Anything else you want to tell us?

– That's it. Oh yeh, and Uncle Ray were angry, that's the other thing.

– By the bins?

– Earlier, when he came out the house, he was cussing and using bad words.

– Why was that?

– Cos of fighting with Mum.

– Can you remember anything else he did or said?

– Nah. I've finished now.

'It's obvious,' Luke said, leaning back. 'After the first interview, Mia spends half an hour with her mum. And when she comes back it isn't Maybe Ray but Definitely Ray. Sharon manipulated her.'

'Unless Mia was too scared at first. And only told the truth after Sharon encouraged her to.'

'That's what the Crown says. But it's rubbish.'

'Rubbish or not, it looks bad for Ray.'

'Unless he performs well in the box,' Luke said. 'Shit, it's gone nine, I'm meant to be with Lionel.'

'I'll pay,' Harry said.

'OK. My turn tomorrow. See you in there.'

As the door banged shut, a gust of cold swept in, dispersing the steam. Hard hat wedged under his arm, a brickie was paying the waitress at the till. Harry queued behind him and ordered more coffee. With an hour to kill before the morning court session, he could reread the interviews with Mia – and play the detective in search of vital clues.

He thought of Luke's hands next to the keyboard, the red distress flare of his eczema, and wondered what the trial might be doing to his own body. Immunity to others' sufferings was more or less a requirement of being human these days, the only means to get by without screaming, but no one could sit through the evidence of the past month and not be pierced by it – the venous bloodstains, the plastic McDonald's toy fibred with pocket fluff, the cast-off minuscule shoe – and if the capacity to be pierced was in some measure reassuring (so, he wasn't a hardened cynic after all), the larger damage was unreckonable and might, long-term, become the virus stalling his heart or the cancer killing his cells, the penalty for having loitered in the halls of pain. But there was no choice. Instinct told him an injustice was being done. And he couldn't not trust his instinct.

His mobile rang as he sat there. It was Marcia.

3

*NAT*

1. How strange to live like this, with nothing to do but jot down occasional thoughts and no one to read them but myself.

13. The longer we live, the more shame we endure: physical, emotional, intellectual, moral.

30. Those who constantly examine themselves in the mirror are the ones most lacking in self-knowledge.

43. Things in poor taste:
   – too many chairs in a living room
   – too many gnomes in a garden
   – too many names on a petition
   – too many children in a graveyard.

69. A problem shared is gossip half the world knows by next morning.

81. Wealth: an abundance of heirlooms to oppress your heirs.

82. Status: arbitrarily conferred, and a source of endless backbiting.

83. Wisdom: something that dies when you die or which rots in unread books.

84. Art: for most people, a source of bewilderment rather than consolation.

Nat was still in bed when the doorbell rang. He'd been awake and fully clothed since eight, hunting for aphorisms to brighten his lecture. But on mornings like this, the duvet, not the desk, was his workstation. 'You Have to Laugh' the lecture was called, a disquisition on half a century of West End theatre. He had sat up writing past three, printed out the typescript and gone to bed convinced of its brilliance. But in the bitter dawn – ice flowers shuttering the window, his breath like an untethered air balloon – the text seemed irredeemably inane. *You have to laugh,* Libby used to say. Fuck that for a philosophy. No wonder their marriage had failed. The doorbell rang a second time. How was a man supposed to work? He thought of *Snow White and the Seven Dwarfs,* an allegory of the dangers of answering the door to strangers. But the bell was insistent. He sighed, climbed out of bed and traipsed upstairs.

Another day of waking as myself, he thought, in the dingy corridor. Another dawn of uncreation. If I had peaked and gone out of fashion, I could feel nostalgic. But I'm not even a Has-Been. I'm a Never-Was.

*You have to laugh.* No, you don't. And there'd been no call for Libby to laugh ten days ago, when he phoned to say he had a leak. He could remember seeing a plumber's card on the cork noticeboard at home. 'It's not there now,' she said, 'Try the Yellow Pages.' Harry had laughed too. 'A leak, Nat? Who from? MI5?' But the leak was no metaphor – not even

357

a metaphor for Nat's life, which after years of being watertight had seeped, gushed, overflowed and flooded its owner out of house and home. This was a real leak, under the kitchen sink, and he didn't know how to stop it. The lowlier aspects of domesticity were ones he had always delegated, and in any case he had no tools. 'Call your landlord,' Harry said. But the landlord, Mr Bristow, wasn't interested: 'It's youse got to sort it out, mate. And where's the cheque for last month's rent?' Mr Bristow's only concession was to recommend a plumber – who when Nat finally reached him had promised to come straight round. That was three days ago. The Sod's Law of modern life, Nat reflected as the bell rang impatiently in the communal hall, was that the people you needed didn't show up and the people you didn't did. He ransacked his mental notebook for witticisms with which to repel the intruder, but could think of nothing better than 'Fuck off'.

Grey mist rolled in off the street. The outside temperature matched that of the flat. 'Fuck . . .' he said, then stopped, seeing the tool bag.

'Problem with your waterworks, squire?'

Dazed with gratitude, Nat led the way downstairs. With barely a glance at the comfortless room, the plumber knelt by the kitchen sink, as though in prayer. The prayer seemed to work. 'I can see your problem right off, guv: a knackered thread.' After tightening off the mains tap, he moved fast, taking off the guilty nut and prompting a gush of grey-green slime. The slime didn't bother the plumber, but it bothered Nat, and he fetched an old *Observer* to absorb the gunge. Headless under the sink, the plumber reached blindly into his canvas bag for washers, sealing thread, adjustable spanners and Boss White Compound while Nat, boiling the kettle, conversed with his backside.

'Big job, is it?'

'Nah. Soon have you sorted.'

'Coffee?'

'Milk and two sugars. Whoever done your plumbing was a chump.'

'Really?'

'Shocking mess. Lucky you got me, guv'nor.'

A tool dropped on to the lino with a clatter.

'What's that?' Nat asked.

'A wrench.'

'Ah, a wrench.'

Nat missed his lover, he missed his wife, he missed his girls. Each night strange cries floated from the flats upstairs. Listless with insomnia, he had become unmoored. Two months ago he'd fallen down in the bedroom, quite a feat since there was barely space to stand up. The room spun round like a 78rpm record (he was just old enough to remember those), with him clinging to the middle, for fear of disappearing down the hole. The bucket under the kitchen sink became his sick bowl, and he lay with it for hours, wondering what was happening to him: heart attack? stroke? mental break-down? During a calm spell, he rang the emergency doctor, who appeared very promptly, next day. 'Labyrinthitis,' he said, handing a prescription over. Labyrinthitis? It sounded like something out of Homer. But the illness was real enough: a virus of the inner ear, destroying the sufferer's sense of balance. He stayed in bed for three days, the blood choppy in his veins. When he got up, his legs shook, like a passenger disembarking from an Atlantic voyage. Slowly he found his bearings again. But there was no more at-oneness-with-the-world. He'd become un-, non-, Not-Nat, a shadow of himself. Was it a midlife thing? The strain of separating from his family? The effect of reading that story in *Priapus*, which had overturned his previous image of his father? Or the loss of Anthea, who day by day became less tangible, like a character he had invented for a play?

'There's the coffee when you're ready,' he said to the torso.

'Ta, matey, just a mo.'

Nat sat at the kitchen table, running his hand along its sides. He hadn't noticed before but there were drawing pins underneath, with clumps of green felt clinging to them: the table must once have been been a card table. So, it had come to this: where others used to drink and gamble, he ate his lonely meals. It was a smallish table, picked up cheap in Greenwich Market, along with the bed, crockery and fourteen-inch television. Most of his books were still back at the house. Comfort didn't interest him. His life had become a punishment regime. He felt pure, like a monk in a whitewashed cell.

'Just moved in, old cock?' the plumber said, standing up.

Nat's nose was running, and wiping it with the back of his hand failed to stem the flow.

'More or less,' he said.

It was a year now but any homeliness had departed with Anthea. Seeing the place as the plumber saw it, he felt ashamed. The floor was a maze of wires running to inactive appliances (radio-alarm clock, video recorder, food mixer, answering machine). Shrunken apple cores lay in the dust like dead mice. The walls were measled with Blu-tack and patched with sunless rectangles. The flat had seemed ideal when they found it, decently sized (with room for the girls to stay) and nicely situated. Even the shortage of natural light was appealing, as if they were living in a burrow below the earth. It had been cosy, till he became sole tenant. Now it felt cold.

The descent of Nat. He had begun in an attic and ended underground.

'Looking forward to doing it up, I bet.'

'Absolutely,' Nat said.

Absolutely not. Maintenance, refurbishment and improvement were petit-bourgeois denials of man's inevitable decline. If the place was a shambles, so what? He was a shambles, too.

'What line of business you in?'

He fumbled for a reply. The what and why of his life had been lost somewhere. He no longer understood the point of being Nat.

'I teach,' he said, remembering the lecture, though SORU had terminated his contract and the lecture was not an inaugural but an envoi.

'Nippers, is it?'

'Students,' Nat said, offended. 'Postgraduates, mostly.'

Mostly? Exclusively. She had not been in touch for over a decade, but as far as he knew Gayle Orden, the PhD student assigned to him in 1987, was still plugging away at 'Subtextuality and Suprasexuality in Aphra Behn'.

'Interesting work.'

'I'm considering a change,' Nat said. Cab-driving was one option, plumbing another. 'I gather plumbers are always in demand.'

'Good ones are.' The plumber swigged the last of his coffee. 'We go round mopping up other buggers' mistakes.'

While the plumber resumed his place under the sink, Nat turned on the PC. His days used to begin with email but lately he had lost heart. The other week some virus had sent out spam under his username: 'Boobs not big enough? Then double your cup size in six weeks.' Apologising to everyone in his address book ('Actually I think your breasts are just fine') had only compounded the offence. His powers of flirtatiousness had deserted him. Why bother emailing, when the one sender he wanted to hear from didn't send? On a good day, he thought of Anthea once a minute; on a bad, every three seconds. He felt her hand in his; saw her neck stretched on the pillow; heard that whispery voice of hers. But this was only his own love, projected. Hers for him had been ephemeral as a screen saver.

'Nearly there now,' the plumber said, as if Nat – rereading the text of his lecture – would appreciate regular bulletins.

Having only just lost his job, he had been surprised when the invitation came from the Principal's office: 29th Frederick Reeves Sturgeon Annual Memorial Lecture, would be delighted if he, topic of his choosing, but given his expertise, modern theatre ideal, West End theatre particularly apt, and some thoughts on comedy all the better. Claire had doubtless pushed the Principal into asking him. It was a sop, a guilt offering. But he had accepted because he needed the money – and in the hope it would distract him from Anthea. Big mistake that was. The lecture, like its orator, was all over the place. He thumbed through his black-and-red A6 notebook in search of quips to rescue it. Most of the pages were blank; those that weren't consisted of fragments – *The Saws and Sorrows of an Abandoned Man*. He wrote for himself now, a solipsistic aphorist. No more characters. No dialogue. No audience other than him.

64. Any art you haven't mastered by the age of forty you should give up. After that, there's no prospect of acquiring mastery by mere hard work.

38. Books, buildings, paintings, pieces of music: it's their incompleteness that makes them interesting to others. The finished work is a dead work.

50. There are innumerable instances of things which attach themselves to other things so as to destroy them: the tree has ivy; the body has lice; the house has termites; the Bible has priests; celebrities have stalkers; teachers have students; playwrights have reviewers.

22. A white canvas is best to paint on. A blank page is best to write on. Emptiness is accommodating.

75. Is it because the truth is so boring that the world is composed of lies?

The phone rang, disturbing his search. It was Harry.
'You on for lunch today?'
'Dunno. I've my lecture to finish. You *are* coming to my lecture?'
'When is it?'
'This evening. Seven o'clock.'
'Should be OK. Unless there's some sensation here.'
'Here?'
'I'm at the Old Bailey. Plenty places for lunch close by.'
'It might be tricky.'
'Go on, a break will do you good. I only have an hour. One o'clock sharp. On the steps outside. OK?'
'I suppose.'

'Lovely job.'

The last wasn't Harry but the plumber, who having arrived less than half an hour ago offered to settle for the call-out fee, £82.50 plus VAT, £96.93 in total – strictly speaking, he should charge for another half-hour, plus materials, but 'what with the coffee and that, you've been a gent'. Seeing as the flat's a shithole and you a sad wanker, I'll take pity was how Nat translated it. He wasn't complaining. He'd rather be pitied than ripped off.

'Who shall I write the cheque to?' he asked, hoping it wouldn't bounce.

'Pipe Dreams,' the plumber said.

'Let's call it a hundred,' Nat said, an ancestral urge to tip overcoming the knowledge that he could ill afford to throw away £3.07.

'Ah, a married man,' the plumber said, seeing Mr N and Ms E Raven on the chequebook. 'Same as me. Where'd we be without the missus?'

The cheque might have two names on it but the joint account no longer existed. He was living on borrowed time.

'I *was* married. And then I was living with someone. But then, well . . .'

These days Nat gushed his troubles to anyone who'd listen. But plumbers were paid to discourage outpourings. And this one was moving towards the door.

'Give us a shout if you've any problems,' he said on the doorstep, then added, over his shoulder, 'with your pipework, I mean.'

Downstairs, Nat made himself more coffee. On the table stood the wooden bowl which Anthea used to fill with soft fruit – the furred gash of peaches, the saucy derrière of damsons, gold globs leaking from yellow plums. Empty now, all ripeness gone.

*Why, why, why, why?* his head went, like some weeping seabird. If only he'd committed himself earlier. If only he'd given Anthea more space. If only he'd acted more quickly when she went out that day. His self-chiding had become a prison. Rage would be more useful. Yet he had loved her. And still did.

7. A man may excel at everything else but if he hasn't experienced love he's useless – like a plastic cup with a crack in it.

24. Yes, I confess, I once had sex with a child. My only excuse: I was a child myself at the time.

176. You know those letters or emails that begin: 'It's been such a long time.' They are the best.

141. Death never comes expectedly. You know it's imminent, but

362

when the moment arrives it's sudden, like the tide over mudflats. The same with the end of love.

The end, when it came, had been noiseless: no warning splash. It was a Friday in June, four months after they'd moved in together. (Friday: his writing day! But every day was a writing day now he had no job.) At lunchtime, Wilma, his new agent, who had recently moved across from selling residential property to selling intellectual, called to say that the Almeida were 'definitely maybe interested' in Nat's new play, *Wit's End*, a redraft of *Wilderness Avenue*: 'They love the upbeat title.' Excited, self-deluding, suppressing the subtext (that they had been bullied into agreeing to read it and would not be interested once they did), he went out to buy a bottle of champagne. At six thirty Anthea came home from work, her arms weighed down with carrier bags – shopping, he assumed, though he would later discover that the bags contained the contents of her desk, cleared that after-noon. They kissed. 'Sit down,' she said. 'There's something I must tell you,' but he shushed her with his own news – 'It looks like the Almeida are going to take *Wit*.' She seemed preoccupied, less pleased for him than she ought to be, but he insisted they drink to celebrate. While he fetched the bottle from the fridge, he was writing the scene in his head: two lovers in a room at dusk could be the opening of his next play. He removed the trap of wire. A shot rang out. The mouth of the dark green bottle gasped. Two blue-tinted flutes (another of Anthea's junk-shop bargains) froth-filled at a tilt. Their toast was like an owl call, hooting softly in the dusk.

'To *Wit*,' he said.

'To you.'

'To this.'

'To you.'

'To us.'

'To you.'

A less elated Nat might have noticed her reluctance to toast the rela-tionship. They moved to the sofa.

'Like I said, there's something I need to tell you,' she said, while he snuf-fled at her nape.

'Go on, I'm listening.' Then before she could speak he added: 'Strange whiff.'

'What?'

'You're wearing perfume.'

'You know I never wear perfume.'

Maybe it wasn't perfume, but she smelled even muskier than usual.

'Whatever the smell,' he said, 'I like it.'

He should have known better. She was touchy about any reference to her body. Even compliments seemed to annoy her.

'You were saying,' he said, tipping the bottle towards her, but she whisked her glass away and disappeared to the bathroom. Later he heard pots banging in the kitchen, but when he offered to help she snapped at him. He drank the last of the champagne alone, watching the news. In protest against rising fuel prices, lorry drivers had formed blockades outside petrol stations and were disrupting motorways with tortoise-slow convoys. People power, the media were calling it. I could make a good play from this, he thought. Centre stage would be the cab of a juggernaut.

Eventually Anthea carried the plates through, in silent martyrdom: You tell me I smell strange, yet I do all this for you. The theme of the meal was Small and Round: lentils for starters, then chickpeas with flat-leaf parsley and Swiss chard, followed by blackberries, redcurrants and crème fraiche. The berries made him think of the sick-mounds you find on doorsteps, the regurgitations of foxes and cats. As they ate, they talked, or rather he did – about the plays he was going to write when his teaching officially came to end in the summer. Her anger with him seemed to have passed. But she was quiet.

'You seem a bit down,' he said.

'I'm fine.'

'What was it you wanted to tell me?'

'Doesn't matter. Let's go to bed.'

The lights were off in the bedroom, but the amber street lamp, through the unblinded windows, turned her body russet – except for the neck, arching long and white. Sighing under his touch, she lay on her stomach. As he stroked her rump, he was writing in his head again: *My Doppelgänger, with her lovely globes.* She purred in his hands on the darkened bed, then rolled him over and sat on top. Her eyes were closed. As she churned on him, her cries became unearthly. Does she care that it's me she's doing this with, he wondered, or could I be anyone? He could remember thinking how *female* the worry was, and how it stemmed (*le mot juste*) from the position he was in, not grinding but being ground. Did feelings of victimhood derive from lying underneath? Was the excitement of the one on top the excitement of domination? Such were his thoughts, till she changed her posture – climbing on to all fours – and sensation drove them out.

It was while they were lying exhausted that he caught the sharp, hot smell again. He took it for her breath at first, or sweat. But when he kissed her mouth and shoulder – 'God, that was wonderful' – there was no trace. What was it? Though subterranean, not shit; though acidic, not piss. What then? An ascertaining lick and sniff along the length of her left him no wiser. The smell wasn't unpleasant. But it was strong.

'You were fibbing,' he said, stroking her. 'You *are* wearing perfume.'

She stiffened, like a dog or cat, hairs on end.

'No I'm not.'

'It suits you,' he said, afraid she had taken offence again. 'It *is* you. There's a wildness about it.' She unbraced a little, under his touch. 'It drives me wild, anyway.'

'Shush, you're imagining it. Go to sleep.'

He did as told, nestling in the crook of her left arm.

When he woke, round ten, the sheets were still warm, like a lair freshly vacated. She's in the bathroom, he thought. But the flat was silent and she was nowhere to be found. It wasn't unusual for her to disappear at week-ends, to shop or walk somewhere, but he was surprised to find no note. He got on – a shave, work at his PC, a lonely sandwich – and tried not to think about it. The girls were away with Libby for the weekend so, free from childcare duties, he was rereading *Wit's End* and wondering what could be cut if the Almeida considered four hours too long even for a masterpiece. Eventually he called Anthea's mobile. It rang from the bedside table where she had left it. That reassured him: without it, she couldn't have gone far. It was dusk before he realised that her suitcase was missing from the wardrobe.

In the hours that followed, he lost track. Where had she gone? *Why* had she gone? Because she felt unloved? Because she felt *too* loved, and threat-ened by it? Because he'd upset her with those questions about the perfume? Suppose she had been sacked – by now he'd found the carrier bags with the contents of her desk, such as they were (marker pens, Post-its, paper clips) – and the shame of dismissal had driven her into hiding? It seemed unlikely: the job, she often said, 'wasn't worth having'. In the small hours, he began to imagine darker possibilities. What if she had been abducted? or murdered? or gone missing even to herself? He remembered reading a *TLS* review of a book about *fugueurs* – people who take off on impulse while suffering some kind of brainstorm and who when halted after travelling some vast distance (Paris to Moscow, say) will wake, astonished, as if from a dream. Was Anthea a *fugueur*? Would she snap out of it and return? Nat's father had been a runaway, too. His mother used to sit listening for the key in the door, just as Nat was doing. But his father hadn't come back in twenty years.

Nor, by the Sunday afternoon, had Anthea.

That night he called the police, to report a missing person. They sent two officers up from Rushey Green – one of each sex – who sat taking notes, uninterested. The fact that Anthea had lived with him for only four months, her habit of wandering off, the recency of her departure ('You did say this was only yesterday morning, sir?') – all this made them sceptical. He should wait another day or two, they said, then contact them again. As the WPC went ahead, up the stairs, the DC took him aside, man to man: 'Bet she's back tomorrow, sir. Tail between her legs. You'll see.'

He was wrong. Days went by, and still nothing. When Nat called her office in Woolwich, all they would tell him was that she no longer worked there. He had her Nokia. Most of the names in its address book were unknown to him (Curt, Slicker, Ashy, Strav, Shan) and they answered with varying degrees of suspicion. Once he got past that, which he did with everyone expect Jake (her churlish ex-boyfriend), people were more sympathetic, but none had heard from her in weeks. That left her mother, Bella, on whose answering machine he left a series of messages. Wasn't her house in the Lakes the obvious place of refuge? He was on the brink of catching a train there when finally he got Bella in person. Could he speak to Anthea? he asked. No, he couldn't, Anthea wasn't there. Could she tell him where Anthea was, then? No, that would be breaking her word. Could she say if and when she was coming back? Yes and no, look, sorry, she would like to tell him more but she had already said too much, all she could say was not to worry – Anthea was alive and well. Well, would she ask Anthea to call him from wherever? She'd try – but meanwhile he must promise not to pursue her. She, Bella, greatly regretted this turn of events because he, Nat, seemed a nice man, and as far as she could tell his influence on Anthea had been entirely positive. She hoped one day Anthea would see that too – but for now he must accept things as they were.

Accept them? When he had no idea where she was and why she'd gone? To sleep or work was impossible. He kept seeing her – not close up, in person, but behind a veil, through a mist, on the far side of a lens. He saw her in a newspaper, among a thousand refugees gathered in a field – the photo had the look of a flower painting, and the people in it were tiny poppies, but by using a magnifying glass he could pick her out under a headscarf. He saw her on television, in a mob of people hurling abuse at a circus owner who had been fined for beating a baby chimp with a riding whip. He saw her in the park, out on the river, at rock concerts, in Cecil B. de Mille crowd scenes, always at a distance but irresistibly, irrefutably her.

She had left a residue of herself at the flat. A pair of blue jeans. A pair of blue trainers. A blue-and-grey checked jacket. A white linen blouse. Two butterfly earrings and a mascara brush. A *Buena Vista Social Club* CD. And among her books, a copy of Arthur Golden's *Memoirs of a Geisha*, turned over at page 394. Had these remainders or reminders been left by accident, or because she couldn't accommodate them in the suitcase? There was a third possibility: that she had left them by design, and that together they made a pattern which, deciphered, would lead him to her. At the top of the turned-over page in *Memoirs of a Geisha*, there was a sentence which read: 'Of course, a geisha who expects understanding from her *danna* is like a mouse expecting sympathy from the snake.' Was this how Anthea saw herself, as a mistress or kept woman? Was this how she saw him, as a snake? He tried the names in her Nokia again, but one by one they stopped returning his calls and Jake was especially obnoxious. 'Piss off, you sad loser,' he said, 'you're fucking crazy.'

And he was crazy. When Wilma called him 'to hopefully set up a meeting with the Almeida', he told her not to bother. But they're considering work-shopping *Wit's End*, she said. When they've decided they *will* workshop it then call me, he said. Needless to say, there was no workshop.

'Love you to bits,' Anthea used to say. Which was exactly what she'd done. Look at him now, in pieces.

Hannah and Rose came to stay at weekends. They had met Anthea only twice, a brief smile and hello as they arrived and she went out. But they noticed her absence from the bathroom – no more girly unguents – and word got back to Libby.

'I hear your girlfriend's gone,' she said, when he returned Hannah and Rose one Sunday night. It was said casually, on the doorstep, in a tone of what-do-I-care.

He wouldn't be drawn. She was away on a 'work thing', he said. Libby raised her eyebrows: tell me another, they said.

The following week, upset, he did tell her.

'I can't pretend to be surprised,' she said. 'No offence, but once the excitement of wrecking other people's marriages is over, bitches like her don't stick around.'

'She's not like that,' he said, though he could remember her once saying how jealous she had felt, after her father died, of 'normal happy families'.

'No? Well, just don't expect me to have you back.'

This was why they didn't talk, except about the girls. Libby was still bitter. She would be friendly for half a second, then flare up.

Soon afterwards, feeling no better, he reread *The Book of Foxes*. Anthea had destroyed her own copies and made him promise to do the same. But there was a set of first drafts stashed in his filing cabinet at college, as he discovered when he came to clear it for the new incumbent. The excitement offset his anger at losing his office. The stories might be flawed but their sexiness brought Anthea back: *le style, c'est la femme*. How had Mike Tindicott failed to see her potential? He called Mike to berate him for turning her down.

Mike sounded bewildered.

'You do remember, Mike? Anthea Hurt.'

'We get a lot of typescripts,' he said.

'They were stories about foxes.'

'Right.'

'A colleague of yours had lunch with her to discuss them.'

'Oh, yes, *those*. I skimmed the first few. They were *terrible*, Nat. I couldn't see what you saw in them.'

'Oh.'

'I was also worried where she'd got them from. I caught echoes here and there.'

'Echoes of what?'

'Not sure. Next thing she wrote asking for the typescript back. I didn't have time to check it out.'

Nat did have time. He went to the London Library and haunted its stacks. Anthea a plagiarist? The possibility had never occurred to him. But now it became the key. If the stories were original, then she was, and he was right to love and believe in her; if they weren't, she wasn't, and he'd be free to hate her. Every day he commuted to the Folklore section. The journey was labyrinthine (flat, train, library, café, library, train, flat), but one day – so he told himself – he would emerge from the maze, and the truth about Anthea be settled for good.

While clearing his filing cabinet, he had come across class registers for Getting Started. No record of a Ms A. Hurt. His record-keeping was haphazard. But he began to wonder. When they met in Inca, he hadn't recognised her. Had she made that up about coming to the class? Had *he* made *her* up?

Aesop, Grimm, Perrault, Hans Christian Andersen, La Fontaine. The library floors were made of metal grating, through which you could see down to the floor below, which was also grating, through which you could see down further, ad infinitum. He dreamed of falling down a long dark chute, at the bottom of which (if there was a bottom) lay truth. Or lies. Or was it death? He began to feel like death. He'd lost weight, everyone said. He was pining.

*The History of Reynard, The Brownie of Blednock, Clever Manka, Brer Rabbit, Anansi Plays with Fire*: slowly the euphoria of research wore off. He was getting nowhere.

In the Zoology section he read about real foxes. A crash course on the *Vulpes* family. Bat-eared foxes, crab-eating foxes, Arctic foxes, Bengal foxes, Tibetan sand foxes, corsac foxes, Cape foxes, fennec foxes, kit foxes, Island grey foxes, as well as foxes – the flying fox (fruit bat) and Simien fox (jackal) – that weren't really foxes at all. The knowledge took him no further. He prepared to give up.

Then one morning he discovered fairy foxes. They were Chinese and very different from Western foxes – not Machiavellian and male, but ghostly and female. Typically, the fairy fox assumed the form of a beautiful woman, moved in with a man, loved and looked after him, and even gave him children. But sooner or later something would happen to make her leave. She would get drunk and blurt out the secret of her foxiness; the hairy coat she had cast off and concealed when taking human form would be found in its hiding place; a rule she had laid down (no questions about my past! no peeking at my nakedness!) would be broken; her husband would criticise or hit her *or comment on her smell* and she, offended, would take off – whatever the reason, the beautiful woman would resume the shape of a fox, scuttle away with the children (now changed to cubs) and never come back.

The first fairy fox he met had been misshelved in Occultism. The next appeared in Topography, on the China shelf. Another turned up in History, in a book about the Opium Wars. The rest – how had he missed them? – were dispersed through anthologies in Folklore. The Jinju mountain fox was his favourite.

### The Fairy Fox Of Jinju Mountain

There was once a fairy fox who disguised herself as a pretty young shepherdess. One day, a travelling poet fell into conversation with her and, enchanted by her wit and beauty, asked her to live with him. The young man was very clever and handsome. So she said yes and renounced her foxy life.

The couple married and lived happily together under Jinju Mountain and had three children. But over time, the husband began to come home late and drunk, and his lonely wife lost the will to keep the house clean or to care for the children. One night he came home later and drunker than usual, in a foul mood.

'The place is a tip,' he said to his wife, 'and you don't look after the kids.'

'That's not fair,' she said.

'Plus, there's a terrible smell,' he said.

'I can't smell it,' she said.

'You can't smell it because it's coming from you,' he said.

'Say any more and you'll regret it.'

'I'll say what I like,' he said, raising his fist.

'Lay a finger on me and –'

Too late. As his knuckles met her left cheekbone, her clothes fell from her body, her hairy red pelt was exposed, and she scurried out the door on all fours. Her husband stood open-mouthed as their three children turned into fox cubs and ran out with her.

For a year he searched the crags. But there was no sign of a shepherdess with three children or a vixen with three cubs. He came home, and sat in a chair, his ear cocked for the noise of her coming back. He sat so long that in the end he became a heap of white bone.

The house is now a museum. If you go to Jinju Mountain, you should visit it – the house where a fox once lived as a woman and where a man, when she left, became bone.


He haunted the stacks, cross-referring, catching glints, treading the grating. Another fairy-fox trick, he discovered, was to make the man come first, in bed – in that way she stole his vitality and became more human. Hadn't Anthea done that to him? Now he was sick, lonely, insomniac and bereft, he could believe almost anything of her.

He read up on lycanthropy – was she a werefox? All the symptoms were there – the night walks, the melancholia, the silky body hair. He had wanted to create her as a writer. Suppose he had created her as a human being. Did that mean, now she had reverted, she was dead? Or merely shamming dead?

This was madness. He told himself he ought to get out more. But where? Going to the theatre was a torment – all those plays undeservedly written by someone else. Even drink brought no comfort: all he'd touch was Guinness, its blackness a mirror of his soul.

He would have cracked entirely but for the girls. Their *please, Daddy*s at weekends gave him a sense of purpose. His other saviour was Kenko, a medieval Japanese philosopher whose *Essays in Idleness* he came across in the Orientalist stacks. Kenko's aphorisms got him writing again. He had to force himself at first; even a single sentence was a stretch. But the lessness of aphorism was comforting. He couldn't imagine writing plays again. All those pages. All that dialogue. And to no end.

Then he found the letter, inside a copy of Naomi Klein's *No Logo*. Dated 30.12.99. A farewell to him, written six months before she left. Had she meant him to find it? Or simply forgotten leaving it there? When she came back from the Lakes for Millennium Night, he had proposed they finally live together. Why? Not why did he propose it (reading that story in *Priapus* had shown him the dangers of becoming a sad old roué), but why did she agree? Was her hope that moving in together would make things better? Or was the relationship doomed to finish anyway? The letter explained the origin of her obsession with foxes – that trauma of burning a cub. Did that make him less crazy or more crazy for thinking she must be a fairy fox?

He was still puzzling it out when, a month or so later, her email came. It was as brief and elusive as a Kenko aphorism. But at least it solved the mystery of her whereabouts.

Dearest N
   I have been in Scotland. Sorry for leaving so suddenly. It must have hurt. But there was no other way. I once wrote you a letter explaining, but didn't dare give it you. I do love you, you know. But we can't be together any more. Tomorrow I am moving to Seattle, to work for a charity. Don't come looking. I will contact you again when I'm feeling stronger. Trust me. Must sigh off now.
   A xxx

Scotland – *where* in Scotland? It didn't matter. She was moving to Seattle. How many charities could there be in Seattle? Pop 530,000 (he looked it up): it wouldn't take long to track her down. But she had asked him not to. *Trust me*, she said. Oddly, despite everything, he did. *Must sigh off*: how typically Anthea that misprint was. No fairy fox then; she wasn't in Faeryland. Or did that follow? She would soon be in the New World. And he knew nothing of her circumstances. To hear from her was appeasing; it helped. But he felt no wiser. If anything, more confused.

152. In what can we put our trust? Lovers betray us. Possessions are lost. Good minds become senile. Promises are broken. Beauty fades. But lack of trust corrodes the spirit. Be wary – and beware of wariness.

173. Absence makes the art grow stronger.

174. A bird in the hand is creature abuse.

181. Whether blooming or shedding, the chestnut tree says not a word.

After her email, the aphorisms came more freely. Twenty a day was his normal output – his cigarette count before he gave up smoking. If only one a week were worth preserving, that would still come to fifty a year; and by the time he reached pension age there'd be a thousand. Writing the entries was like putting on a mask – Nat the stoic, Nat the worldly-wise, Nat the unmoved. Publication was irrelevant. Anthea had been right about that. What mattered was the discipline.

But the mask hadn't detached him from his madness. Nor had her email brought him peace. He was still commuting to the Folklore section. The more he read of fairy foxes, the better he understood Anthea's behaviour: the passion, the shyness, the struggle with words, the changeability, the absences, the smells and howls – then the abrupt departure. There was only one thing missing. In Oriental legends, fairy foxes mated with humans and had children. And when they left the human world they took those children with them, as their passport home. Anthea hadn't had a child. So she couldn't be a fairy fox. Unless.

Unless. He had a wild idea. So wild it seemed perfectly credible. At lunchtime he would test it on Harry.

More immediately he had his lecture to finish. Or rewrite from scratch. 'You Have to Laugh'. His plan had been to make his audience laugh, with a series of savage jokes exposing the overblown reputations of a dozen or more contemporary British playwrights. But Claire had discouraged him.

'You're free to say whatever you like,' she said. 'But be subtle about it. And avoid being merely negative.'

'Come on, Claire, you know what I think of West-End theatre. You've sat in my class for years.'

'I'd have thought you could poke gentle fun without going overboard.'

'Take the piss while pretending to pay homage, you mean?'

'Something like that. Surely there's been the odd good play in the past fifty years.'

'I can't think of any.'

'Well, try.'

He had tried. He had reread the texts and borrowed production videos from the library and striven to reach conclusions that wouldn't look bitter and twisted. Subtlety: as Claire said, that was the thing. But how to be subtle, when he felt so wrecked?

He had a few hours left to knock the lecture into shape. Otherwise tonight would be a disaster.

## 4

## *JACK*

*D'ye ken that bitch whose tongue was death?*
*D'ye ken her sons of peerless faith?*
*D'ye ken that a fox with his last breath*
*Cursed them all as he died in the morning?*

JACK WASN'T a larker like Obie but he liked to be up early for a meet. You got the best of the day then: uplit hills, cock-crowing farms, brass streams, misty dips, the countryside in waiting. Set him down blindfold anywhere in the world and he could tell if it was England. In February, after rain, it oozed up round your feet. A boot clagged in mud: that was Englishness.

'More tea?' he said.

'Love some.'

He stuck the kettle on the hotplate resentfully. They should have left half an hour ago. He had explained this to Huish – he couldn't bear to call him Rufus – over a pint at the Fox & Feathers last night. Dom Askew and Dr Bruin were there too, as planned, and the talk, as also planned, turned to hunting. Huish seemed attentive. He even made notes in his notebook. 'Who's the bloke in the suit?' the landlord whispered, when Jack, just before the bell, ordered four large Glenfiddichs. 'MP up from London, coming out with us tomorrow,' Jack said. 'Keep it under your hat.' Perhaps the malts had been a mistake. They sampled several more back at the house, before Huish woozled off to the spare bedroom.

This morning several bouts of vigorous knocking had failed to rouse him, and it was 9 a.m. before he made it downstairs. Silver-sweaty and lime-green about the gills, he sat picking at his bacon. Two cigarettes smouldered in the ashtray and now he lit a third. This New Labour bunch were meant to be lean and vulpine. But Huish's girth was fuller than Harkaway's.

Rain fell dark and heavy as roof slates. The forecast was for showers with sunny intervals.

'We ought to get going,' Jack said, topping up the teapot at the Aga. Drips of water sissed across the hotplate like ball bearings.

'Goodness, I thought rural life was supposed to be leisurely,' Huish said.

'We've the kennels to see.'

'They can't keep till later?'

'No, the meet's at eleven.'

'Point taken. If I can just have that tea, then I'm ready.'

Ready is not what Jack would have called it. Polo-neck sweater, nylon-stretch breeches, sports jacket and rubber boots: they might do for a half-hour lesson in Hyde Park but not for hunting with the Harchope & Nelles. Otto, as acting MFH, was a stickler about dress code – though since he had taken up with Angela Hambold he seemed more mellow. Today's meet, specially arranged, was small. If Huish had come on Saturday, when eighty-odd riders turned up, he would have seen the Harchope & Nelles in full regalia. But big meets brought out the Antis and no one wanted Antis spoiling the show. Hence today, a half-term Wednesday, with only thirty or so riders expected, all in the know about Huish.

Was that a daffodil coming, beyond the rockery wall? February used to be good for tobogganing. In '63, when he was courting Nancy, there were six-foot snowdrifts. Now every winter was a mild winter. The snowdrops had already turned brown.

Jack poured the tea and sat down. Cooking breakfast for a visitor ought to be a pleasure – when was the last time? – but he had slept badly and felt tense. 'Stressed,' Marcus would say. But for once the stress wasn't about work, Libby's adverts having helped them turn the corner. Changing the product name had made a huge difference: the Apache range was selling much better than the Greensleeves had ever done. But the key was direct sales, and that, to be fair, was Marcus's idea. Jack had worried about the dealers being cut out, but in the event, as Marcus predicted, they had bene-fited: not all customers trusted mail order; demand increased in DIY stores and garden centres; everyone made a profit. Everyone except Libby, that is. It was only at the Harrogate Horticultural Fair, after talking to a rival sales manager, that Jack realised what a bargain he'd had; the display space alone must have absorbed her fee. He must take her out one day – go down to London and treat her to lunch. For a time she'd become a kind of daughter to him, which wasn't to say that he thought any less of his *real* daughters, who were on the phone to him most nights. He wished Sasha and Ischia would make him a grandfather but at least they were settled. Nancy had settled, too – to a name on a stone, an ever-present absence, a vase to fill with flowers. No, any stress today was down to Huish, not work or family. So much rested on his visit. And playing host to a man you had no respect for was a strain.

It had taken six months of delicate negotiating to bring him here. As Jack saw it, having a Labour MP ride with the hunt would be useful propaganda. Traditionally, the local MP could be relied on for support, but Freddy Finch was gone and while anxious not to upset her rural constituents by siding with Antis, Julie Rusby, Finch's successor, wouldn't come out in favour, either. (Typical bloody woman, the only issues on which she had spoken in the House were nursery provision and maternity leave.) So Huish was the best hope. But Huish had refused to come unless his anonymity could be guaranteed. When the hunting bill came back from the Lords to be debated in the Commons, he would come off the fence, he said; in the meantime, while he 'researched' the issue, the press mustn't catch a whiff. Jack spoke to Otto and between them they set up a meet – midweek, gentle run, special invitation only. On the phone, finalising arrangements, Huish seemed amiable enough. But when Jack met him off the train last night, he took against him: the leather coat, the wiffly handshake, the superciliousness. 'Recognised you at once,' Huish said, in the car. 'We met at Nat's wedding.' Jack had no memory of that and doubted Huish did either. The man was a bullshitter. Discourteous, too: he spent the half-hour between the station and Frixley making phone calls, as though he were a company chairman in a chauffeured limo (not that the calls were business calls, to judge by Huish's *hons* and *sweethearts*). In the pub he kept his hand in his pocket, even after they stood him a meal. Now he sat smoking, having spurned the eggs Jack had scrambled by special request. It would be satisfying to tell Huish a home truth or two. But that would defeat the object of his visit.

'You've seen this?' Jack said, sliding the *Telegraph* across. In brief, on an inside page: FOOT-AND-MOUTH ALERT AT ESSEX ABATTOIR.

Huish exhaled smoke, then doused his palate with tea.

'I've had a couple of text messages about it,' he said. 'No need for concern. We're taking the necessary steps.'

*We?* Were they? If the government was as slow to get going as Huish, the whole of England would already be infected. Jack could remember the last foot-and-mouth epidemic, in the 1960s. And before that myxomatosis, the rictus of rabbits in lonely fields. So many blights. Sheep tic, swine fever, brucellosis, BSE – it would be plagues of locusts next. The weather was more wayward, too: floods, droughts, ground frosts in August, even hurricanes. Old Brock, down at Swallow Farm, had a diploma in whingeing. But you couldn't blame him for feeling hard done by: if foot-and-mouth came to Frixley, he would be ruined.

'How far will we be riding?' Huish asked.

It was a stupid question – like wanting the result of a football match before kick-off.

'Depends on the fox,' Jack said. 'If we see a fox.'

'What about jumps?'

'You get the odd tiger trap. But if you don't fancy jumping there's usually a field gate.'

'Nat warned me about you blooding novices.'

'We'll spare you that. Unless you insist.'

'And you're sure there'll be no saboteurs?'

'We've taken every precaution.'

'Good. Of course I respect their right to protest, as animal lovers, but –'

'*Animal lovers?*' Jack snorted. 'When they throw marbles under horses' hooves? Or terrorise them with rockets and car horns? Or steal hounds from kennels and mutilate their ears?'

'Point taken. So long as they stay away, we'll be both be happy.'

Huish drained his tea and stubbed his cigarette out, indicating his willingness to depart. He had his mobile phone with him, and slipped it in his jacket pocket. If Otto spotted the breach of etiquette, would he bollock Huish or let it go?

Spider-threads brushed Jack's face in the hallway. Dampness seemed to attract spiders – or vacancy did. Yet the house felt benign, post-Nancy. He had expected some sort of after-impression – like the image of a light lingering on the eye long after you have turned the switch off. But Nancy's light had dimmed slowly. There was no call to be haunted by her absence. She had been absent even before she went.

'Did you bring a stick with you?' Jack asked, in the porch.

'Stick?'

'A riding crop. A *whip*.'

'Was I meant to?'

'Here,' Jack said, unhooking one from the hatstand, 'Harkaway's dozy. You'll need this to wake her up.'

Huish took it wrong way up, then tapped it experimentally on his thigh – more a tickle than a thwack.

'So where have you ridden, apart from Hyde Park?' Jack said, as they climbed into the car. The rain had eased to drizzle. He switched the headlights on as well as the wipers.

'Richmond.'

'Ah, Yorkshire – lovely area.'

'No, Richmond-upon-Thames.'

'So you haven't hacked much?'

'I went riding in Gloucestershire once, with a friend.'

Huish sat quietly smoking, his hand shaking with nerves or nausea. There were tractor prints of flattened cattle shit in the lanes.

'You should be all right then,' Jack said.

'Hope so. I'm looking forward to it.'

The kennels were part of Brockett's Farm. Jack parked out front and they walked through, between cowpats, towards the music of the hounds. Flat-capped and overalled, Obie stood waiting for them by the half-door. He was in his sixties now, with an accent so local that people from the next village couldn't decipher it. Jack wasn't worried about Obie sounding intelligible, only that he look the part – wheaty sideburns, furrowed brow, earthenware cheeks; man of the soil.

Jack did the introductions. Obie, Rufus; local, London; huntsman, MP.

'Come and see my beauties,' Obie said.

The whining and crooning grew louder as they walked in. Thirty hounds surged towards them, over straw, a torrent of brown and white.

'Quite a noise they make,' Huish said, backing away.

'Aye, they do sing, sir. The choir, we call it. When one drops the tune another picks it up. Fair sends a shiver through me to hear them. And they've a higher pitch on hunt days. God knows how they know, but they do. Maybe they smell it on me. These in here have missed the cut today. Billy Button's got the lucky ones in the lorry. Thirteen and a half couple we're taking – we always say it's the half what gets the fox.'

Obie explained about the draw – how he selected hounds according to fitness and terrain, and left behind those in the hothouse.

'That's the hut where we put bitches on heat.'

'You only use male hounds, then?' Huish said.

'No, sir. I've twice as many bitches as dogs. Bitches use their heads, they listen as well as look, they're the best at picking up the scent. But I wouldn't want all bitches. They tire quicker and they're less patient in a fix – less dogged than dogs. A mixed pack is best.'

'How do you tell them apart? I wouldn't have a clue.'

'Happen not, sir, but it's easy. There look: that's Hacksaw, Hades, Haggis, Hailstorm, Hairpin, Haji, Hayley, Halfblood, Hamish, Hamlet, Handsome, Hannah, Ha'penny, Happy, Harebell, Harlem, Harpic, Harrier, Hattie, Hawk – all sired by Hazlitt. We keep the first initials of the sire, see.'

'What do you feed them?' Huish asked, seemingly worried they might want to eat him.

'Depends what I'm offered. Some huntsmen use cooked meat, but with me it's raw. Horsemeat's a favourite. He loved to hunt, the owner will say when his old nag dies, so let him have one final run – that's in the belly of my hounds. Lately, since BSE, it's been cow I get. When Mr Osbaldeston lost one of his herd, he was straight on the blower offering us the carcass. Part of me was cursing: the chopping up and packing for the freezer can take all day. Still, beggars can't be choosers. If it's right what they're saying about these pigs in Essex, I'll be offered *them* next.'

'How long have you been a huntsman?'

'I took over from my old man twenty year since. I still hear him sometimes. It'll be mealtime, and I'll be stood at the feed-yard door wondering who to let in first, and he'll say "Harrier – he's a shy feeder" or "Hattie – she's looking lean around the ribs", so Harrier and Hattie it is. Discipline, that's what I learned from him. Kennels have to be run like barracks. But I love my hounds and they love me: that's the short of it.'

'Obie's single,' Jack explained, teasing.

'Right enough. I was near being had once, but I took care never to run my head into that collar again. No wife would dote on me like my bitches do.'

'It sounds rewarding work,' Huish said, nerving himself to pat a hound on the head.

'I don't know about rewarding. I can barely make tongue and buckle meet as it is. When *my* dad was a huntsman, he had a new coat, new boots and two new pairs of breeches every season – I'm lucky to get new equipment once every five. You don't do it for the money, that's for sure.'

He's handling it well, Jack thought: the skills, the tradition, the contribution to the rural economy – any neutral would see the point.

'If drag-hunting replaces fox-hunting,' Huish said, 'how will that affect you?'

'I'll be out of a job. There won't be hounds like these, only mongrels trencher-fed by farmers. And they can't compare. It takes ten years to make a pack – a *crack* pack. Jabs for rabies, boils to be lanced, road tar on their pads, clogged ears, cuts gone septic from barbed wire – I sort all that myself. No vet ever comes near the place.'

A hound poked its snout in Huish's groin.

'I tell you, sir – and I ain't been primed to say this, it's my own belief – if fox-hunting goes, the country will go with it. Them as live here will have nothing to believe in no more.'

'The bill's only in its early stages,' Huish said. 'I wouldn't worry overmuch.'

'But who'll stick up for us?'

'Oh, there are plenty MPs with an open mind on the subject.'

'You'll get our views across, then?'

'I'll do my best.'

The hounds whined and shuffled through the straw, till a revving engine drowned their noise.

'Hear that?' Obie said. 'Young Billy's getting impatient.'

'We'd better make a move, too,' Jack said.

He imagined the scene ahead at Stormbrooke Hall: wild-eyed mares whinnying over the half-doors, their nostrils boiling like kettles; flustered grooms carrying feed buckets; shining saddles and chinking bridles being carried from the leather-aired saddle room; and Lolly in her jodhpurs grooming Maiden. *Grooming*: you never heard the word these days, except in relation to pimps and paedophiles. But it was shorthand for a lot of hard work – all that washing, brushing, oiling, plaiting and polishing. And then the tacking, once the horse was ready to go: saddle on; bridle over head, throatlash buckled, drop-noseband tightened, snaffle bit chinking against teeth, girth pulled up a couple of holes. All the practicalities. And the rituals. Unless you lived here you had no idea.

Huish walked ahead, towards the car, scribbling in his notebook. Jack, turning to Obie, put both thumbs up. Obie made the wanker gesture at Huish's back.

'A real countryman, your Obie,' Huish said, as they drove away.

'Yes.'

379

'Salt of the earth.'
'Absolutely.'
'Heart of oak.'

## 5

## NAT

'YOU LOOK tired,' Harry said, outside the café.

Nat thought of Hi-Me-Minh, the hero in a Chinese folk tale, drained of all energy by his vampy mistress, a fairy fox in disguise.

'I'm knackered from writing this lecture,' he said.

'It's done, though?'

'One more para when I get back, then I'll print it out.'

Neither of them felt like lunch. They ordered café lattes and brownies. Nat's saucer slopped with froth as he carried it over. It tasted insipid, a caffeine consommé, and dripped in his lap.

'So you're happy with it?' Harry said.

'I guess.'

Not happy at all, not happy with anything, but he wasn't going to get into that with Harry. Harry was judgemental and Nat didn't feel strong enough to be judged.

A copy of the *Independent* lay on the table between them.

'I see your friend Blair is flying off to meet Bush,' Harry said.

'My friend?'

'You voted for him, Nat.'

'We all voted for him.'

'No, some of us voted for his party. Or what we thought was his party. On the grounds that it wasn't the other party. *You* voted for him.'

'He seemed a pretty straight kind of guy.'

'Not to me,' Harry said.

'He was going to prioritise schools and hospitals. And stop arms sales. And make us more European. And put more money into the arts.'

'So you were wrong. Admit it.'

Nat sipped his latte, imagining his brain as the cup, drained of all but froth.

'I was misled,' he said. 'We all were. Who could have anticipated him sucking up to the US? It was bad enough with Clinton as his ally. And now it's Bush.'

'Not that it would be Bush,' Harry said, 'if they had counted the votes in Florida properly.'

'Bush was always going to win, whatever,' Nat said. 'He's Texan and America's in love with oil.'

'Don't talk crap, Nat, if the Democrats had . . .'

Modern men were less competitive these days, Nat had read somewhere. Really? Whenever he and Harry got together, they joshed and bantered, bragged and argued, ridiculed and provoked. Keep your end up. Always have the last word. Don't let the other guy get the better of you. Being lonely and miserable was no excuse.

'Have you seen the Wolfowitz stuff?' Nat said. 'The Project for the New American Century? The goal is global domination. And the hawks who wrote it are Bush's closest friends.'

'Doesn't sound like your kind of reading material, Nat.'

'I got it off the Internet.'

'Anthea put you on to it?'

'Yes.'

'You're still in touch, then?'

'She put me on to it before she left.'

'So you've not heard from her.'

'She emailed once.'

'What's she up to?'

'She's in Seattle.'

'Doing what?'

'Working for a charity.'

'Ah.'

'Charity for the world but none for me.'

'It takes time, Nat.'

'What does?'

'Getting over someone, when they leave you. You've never had to do it before.'

'Have you?'

'Yes. With Marcia.'

'Marcia didn't leave you. That was your choice. Anyway, I *have* had to do it. Thirty years ago. When my dad left.'

'And that took time, didn't it? That's my point.'

He nibbled a corner of his brownie. He could date it precisely. The moment he began to feel better about his father was on 30 December 1999, sitting in Jack's study, when he read that story in *Priapus*. Which he decided must have been written by his father. And showed more imagination, never mind how porny, than he had credited him with till then. But also reminded him that, after years of Soho sleaze, his father had found happiness with someone, sadly not the wife who'd borne him a child but a woman worthy of his love nevertheless – a kindred soul. In short, reading the story had convinced Nat that his destiny was with Anthea and that they must stop shallying and move in together at once. Unfortunately Anthea, to whom he had gone on about the story at some length ('And it has a fox theme, just like your stories – how weird is that?') had a different sense of destiny. Her destiny was to be somewhere else.

'I've only begun to get over my father in the last year,' he said. 'At that rate, I'd be dead before I got over Anthea.'

'It's early days,' Harry said.

'It's been six months.'

'It will get better, Nat, trust me. Take me and Stephen.'

'Stephen?'

'Jesus, Nat, a man could get offended. My *son*.'

'Sorry, yes, *that* Stephen, right.'

'There've been a lot of difficulties between us,' Harry said. 'There still are. Only last night, he . . .'

'What?'

'Doesn't matter. Minor setback. But the point is, I am getting on better with him. With Marcia, too. After a long time of not seeing either of them. It'll be like that for you with Anthea. You'll be fine.'

'Maybe.'

'And you've your work. We all need that. I know I need mine.'

'How is your work?' Nat said, grateful to get off the subject of himself for once. 'How's the trial?'

'Where've you been? It's all over the papers.'

Where had he been? At home, immersed in his own headlines – MIDDLE-AGED MAN LOSES EVERYTHING SHOCK. But details of the trial had filtered through, and as Harry filled him in on the latest he prepared to test out his theory.

'Wasn't some fox hair found at the scene?' he said.

'Fox hair, fox piss, fox shit – the lot.' Harry looked interested. 'Why?'

'I remember you saying you thought Errol could have been attacked by a fox. Like that other kid.'

'By some sort of animal. Yes.'

'And what date was it that Errol went missing?'

'December 18th. Why?'

'Ah, nothing.'

The 18th was the day before Anthea went north, to visit her mother in the Lakes. The trip had been sudden, unplanned. But suppose she had been out on one of her walks, by the river, near Errol's house . . .

'It doesn't look like nothing,' Harry said. 'Tell me.'

Harry's my friend, he thought, and he thinks I'm bonkers anyway. There's nothing to lose.

'These fox traces at the scene,' he said. 'Suppose someone deliberately left them there, to cover their tracks.'

'To throw the police off the scent, you mean?'

'Precisely. I'm suggesting the abduction was planned.'

'I get that. But what kind of person would carry fox piss around?'

'Ah, well,' Nat said. 'Ever heard of the Fox Project?'

'Nope.'

'It's an animal-welfare charity down in Kent. Their main work is looking after foxes that have been lamed or injured. Anthea had some leaflets about them.'

'They sound like her kind of organisation.'

'Most of their work's done by volunteers.'

'So – what's the connection?'

'A volunteer would have the necessary to hand. To plant the traces and make it look like a fox attack.'

'But these people you're talking about *like* foxes.'

'In theory. But you could get someone who's disturbed in some way, someone obsessed.'

'Who wanted it to look like a fox attacked Errol, but did it himself?'

'Or herself.'

'Herself? You're not seriously . . .' Harry looked at him. 'You don't think . . . ?'

'The dates fit. Anthea went out that night and then disappeared for ten days.'

'Disappeared?'

'To her mother's. Supposedly. But she'd still have had time.'

'To dispose of the body?'

'Not necessarily.'

'Sorry, I'm lost.'

'No one ever found a body, did they? Suppose whoever it was wanted a child and abducted Errol?'

'But you know Anthea didn't abduct him.'

'Do I?'

'You moved in together. You lived with her, for Christ's sake.'

'Only for a few months. She could have been keeping the child some-where else.'

'In the woods? To raise as a wild child? Come on.'

'Maybe she had a lover – male or female – and they were raising him together.'

'This is nuts, Nat.'

'She was always going out. For walks, she said. For hours on end. She could have been visiting Errol. Feeding him. Playing with him. Then when she left me she took him with her to Scotland. To somewhere remote. Where no one would recognise them or be suspicious.'

'Nat.'

'Taking a child would have been a way to make up for her own childhood. Her father died when she was young, remember. She was unhappy. I was the runt of the litter, she used to tell me – the only child my parents had yet I was still the runt. Maybe she saw Errol crying by his house, an unhappy child just like she had been, and thought that together they could have a better life. And then there's the fairy-fox element.'

'The what?'

'If she was one. Or thought she was one. When fairy foxes revert to type and go back to the old world, or new world in Anthea's case, they have to take a child with them.'

'Stop it, Nat. This is bonkers.'

'That's supposing she wasn't the *other* kind of fairy fox, the werewolves, who metamorphose and kill, and then the minute they *have* killed they're horrified at what they've done and take to the hills. Did you realise that one of her stories describes exactly what happened to Errol? A child playing outside at dusk is abducted by a vixen. But the vixen doesn't kill the child, she brings it up in secret. Suppose she left that story as a clue.'

'This really is all bollocks, Nat.'

'I know. I just miss her so much.'

He folded his head in his arms then, in the small café. He would have said his dry-sobbing was inaudible, but Harry looked embarrassed by it so he let himself be steered outside.

'Come on,' Harry said, 'the air will do you good.'

They trudged through the shadowed alleys beyond the café – Limeburner Lane, Amen Corner, Playhouse Yard – to come out by the river on to Blackfriars Bridge, where the corpse of Roberto Calvi had once hung in the iron beams. Purple light glazed the tide. Nat stared down into the water, like George Bailey in *It's a Wonderful Life* wondering whether it wouldn't be better to end it all.

'I'm sorry for the mad stuff,' Nat said. 'It's the antidepressants talking. Plus I don't sleep much.'

'I didn't realise things were this bad,' Harry said.

''Fraid so. All-time low. Like a stock-market crash. My entire value wiped out. Not worth a sou.'

'*She's* not worth it,' Harry said. 'People leave people. It doesn't mean she didn't love you. Something changed, that's all.'

'Yes, she changed. Fairy foxes do.'

'Fuck the fairy foxes, Nat.'

'They're a metaphor to explain her.'

'What's to explain? She left. End of story.'

'But what was the motivation? It doesn't hang together.'

'It's not a play, Nat. People don't always know why they do what they do.'

'Then it must have been motiveless malignity. Which makes her an evil person.'

'She's not evil. She just chose to be apart from you. And now you're apart, you need to get on with your life.'

'I don't have a life. Anthea, Libby, the girls, the teaching, the writing – I've fucked up the lot.'

'It's a blip. A test of character.'

'I was innocent till I met Anthea. And full of hope. Now I sit around all day doing nothing.'

'Ring some colleges – there must be work going. Write a radio play. Do a column for the *Gazette*.'

'A column?'

'You used to be funny, Nat.'

'Life was funny.'

'Write a serious column, then.'

'Journalism's not me.'

'How do you know? You've never tried.'

'I'm too old to start. And already weeks behind on the rent.'

'If it's money that's the problem, I'll help you out.'

'Nothing will help. I'm beyond rescuing.'

His mobile rang as they stood on the bridge. He walked away a few paces, not wanting Harry to hear, which was a kind of madness too: Nat Raven, the last man in England to consider phone calls private.

It was Libby, about the lecture.

'Something has come up,' she said. 'I'm really sorry. I did want to be there, you know.'

'It'll be *two* people and a dog now,' Nat said.

'Maya is bringing the girls.'

'Pretty boring for them.'

'They want to come. They've never heard you give a lecture before.'

'Few people have.'

'How are things otherwise?'

'OKish. I'm with Harry.'

'Tell him to call me sometime.'

'I will.'

'And I'm really sorry about tonight.'

I've chosen well, he thought, tucking his mobile away. Few men can be luckier in their ex-wives.

'Libby,' he explained, walking back along the bridge towards Harry, the dark tide swirling below. 'She can't come tonight.'

'Well, I'm coming,' Harry said. 'But now I've got to get back.'

'I'll walk up with you.'

6

## HARRY

THEIR WALK took them back over Blackfriars Bridge, then up towards Ludgate Hill. Harry had plenty to worry about on his own behalf but for now it was Nat's troubles that consumed him. He had been serious just now when he said that Anthea wasn't worth it. Not that he actively disliked her. But when they'd finally met about a year ago (Nat – despite assurances that Harry would 'love' her – having been slow to introduce them), he knew immediately that Nat had made a bad mistake.

He could remember little else about the evening. But he saw it as soon as she walked into the restaurant. Libby! Same height, same length of hair, same eyes, same skin, same shape of face. She was Libby circa 1987 rather than Libby today but Libby nonetheless. Nat obviously couldn't see it: to him Anthea's appeal lay in being different, when in reality he was re-wooing his young wife. Yes, her voice was quieter than Libby's, her manner more tentative, her gaze less focused. But several times over the evening the illusion returned – that Nat had cheated on Libby with another Libby, that his lover was a clone of his wife. The resemblance confirmed all Harry's doubts. It was as though Anthea was playing a part. Or – masquerading as someone else – had no attachment to her present existence. Either way, not a woman on whom to stake your life.

'I didn't dislike Anthea, you know,' he told Nat now, at the corner with Pilgrim Street. 'She just struck me as a bit of a chameleon.'

'You're right,' Nat said, 'she was. I don't think I ever knew her. I don't think *she* ever knew her. She was with me, then she went, as though we'd never existed. What was that all about?'

'I should have warned you.'

'It would have made no difference. I was in love.'

'All the same. I'm sorry I didn't say anything. I was too immersed in my own problems, I guess. With Stephen. Which continue.'

'You were saying. Something happened last night . . .'

'Long story. Too long for now. I don't know all the details yet. But I'm meeting Marcia after your lecture to discuss it. Stephen, too, I hope. In fact, I told her to get him there early. He's taking drama at A level, so he might find the lecture interesting.'

'If there is a lecture. I ought to get back and finish it.'

As he hugged Nat goodbye, Harry thought of all the things that divided them (age, race, temperament, social origins) and how their friendship had survived regardless. Maybe that's what defined friendship: an indifference to difference.

There were metal barriers outside the Old Bailey. He made his way past security and up the stairs.

Stephen. Long story. After Harry's failures of a year or more ago, it took weeks of phone calls before they met up again. And several more weeks before either felt easy in the other's presence. But Harry kept at it, and as well as them going out together – to Charlton Athletic, to movies, to restaurants, even (once) to Center Parcs – occasionally Stephen stayed over at the flat. There were times (in truth, most of the time) when Stephen seemed like an alien – idle, lippy, boorish. But his friends were the same or worse. And there seemed to be no malevolence in Stephen. Any aggression was only teenage hormones.

One unexpected bonus in the arrangement was that Harry's relationship with Marcia also improved. They had dinner a few times, as friends, with Marcia insisting on going halves – 'only fair,' she said, 'now we're going halves over Stephen'. A joke: she still did nine-tenths of the parenting. But she was upbeat about Harry's newly purposeful role. I think your studiousness is rubbing off on him, she said. Hah, he said, you once told me my studiousness was fake – that I was just a young buck like all the others. Yeh, well, can you blame me? Marcia was thirty-five now and had improved with age. We might have been happy together, Harry thought – made a go of it, anyway. After dinner, saying goodbye, they kissed – chastely, on the cheek. It was tempting to see what a deeper kiss felt like, but that would have broken the rules. Better friendship than sex. If he and Marcia became lovers again, it was bound to unsettle Stephen.

Or was it just Harry's old fear: first the kiss, then the catastrophe? Over the years he had tried to conquer it. There were always girls ready to sleep with him, not least white girls, who seemed to regard him as an interesting experiment. One, Ellen, a medical student, owned up to fantasies about black men – not just the obvious fantasy, but how she'd expected Harry's skin to feel roasted and brittle, like pork crackling. He didn't tell Ellen his fantasies. The fear that he'd be struck dead for the sin of entering her. That at the moment of orgasm their bodies would melt. That the history of Marcia would repeat itself: first sex, then conflagration. Ellen was auburn, sweet-tempered and might have lasted longer than three months. She was so open about everything – so overt. All those flushes and blushes, those rashes and scratches, as if she was were wearing her depths on the surface; her pale skin was like overexposed film. But she gave up on him in the end, saying he was too cerebral and detached. And his other lovers were no less disappointed. Not that there were many: he could count them on two hands. The only woman with whom he felt comfortable these days was Libby, and she was (or had been) the wife of a friend. Perhaps her being off-limits was precisely why he did feel comfortable; she and Nat had always come as a pair. But sometimes they met alone and once, last year, at her house, he had held her as she cried. Libby was special. He'd like to tell her that. He lacked the courage, that was all.

Meanwhile there was the Stephen problem. Things had been good until three months ago, when he began getting into trouble, over drugs, fights, truancy, suspected shoplifting, or what the school and the police called 'general antisocial behaviour'. It's just peer-group stuff, Harry told Marcia, at his age I was the same. But both of them knew it wasn't true. Nor did the pressure of sitting mock A levels explain it, since Stephen had made no effort to revise and, a solid student in the past, was now in danger of screwing up his chances of university. If only Harry been a proper father to Stephen, Marcia complained when they ate out. If only he hadn't vacillated when he resumed contact. If only the two of them were living together and offering Stephen *consistency*.

Both Marcia and Harry had given Stephen pep talks. Moody and resentful, he'd pretended not to listen but seemed to be buckling down. Until last night, that is, when – so Marcia had reported to Harry this morning – he was stopped by the police while driving a black BMW. The BMW belonged to the father of a friend, but the friend wasn't in the car and when the police pulled Stephen over – had he not seen the traffic light change to red? – he panicked and lied. They held him at the station till 2 a.m. 'It was my son who told him he could borrow it,' the friend's father said, meaning to be helpful but making things worse: Stephen was charged with driving a car without the owner's permission, and for failing to have a valid driving licence or insurance. It's just the police trying to scare him back on the straight and narrow, Harry said. But Marcia was badly upset: if only this, if only that, and damn Harry for being a useless father.

Was he wrong to have reintroduced himself into Stephen's life? He felt closer to Stephen than he'd ever done, close enough to hug him whenever they met or said goodbye. But maybe this belated rush of intimacy was part of the problem. Harry had been brooding about it since listening to the psychiatrist for the Crown, Ursula Wynne, who in her assessment of Ray Nuard's mental health had spoken of his 'obsessive, overdemonstrative attachment to Errol, due to his being an estranged father' – a phrase that had cut Harry to the quick, no less so when Lionel Martin picked her up on it.

– Isn't it perfectly inappropriate for a man to show affection to his son, Miss Wynne?
– It depends what kind of affection.
– And what in your view is the correct kind?
– In this case, where the father wasn't even living with the child's mother,

it's likely the child would feel ambivalent towards him – and might suffer trauma if the affection became overdemonstrative.

– If it took the form of kissing and hugging?

– Possibly.

– Surely such physical affection towards a child would strike most people as perfectly proper and even desirable, Miss Wynne. But irrespective of that, are you not simply confirming for us that Ray Nuard was very fond of Errol Winthrop – and would have been the last person to want to hurt him?

– Not necessarily. A seemingly innocent attachment to a love object, where it stems from the subject's own unresolved childhood experiences of inconsistent parental love, could have seriously damaging consequences.

– I'm not sure I follow you.

– I am saying that Mr Nuard's obsessive attachment to his son is compatible with him harbouring more negative feelings. Often, fixation of this kind is a prelude to fantasies of violence which in extreme cases are acted out – rather in the same way that fans occasionally murder their idols. By over-identifying with a child, an adult may be put in touch with buried childhood traumas of his own and then seek to punish or obliterate the child for having opened up such secret history.

This afternoon there would be no expert witnesses. This afternoon, there'd only be Ray. But as he took his seat in the courtroom, Harry felt a chill of apprehension, as though the man on trial were himself.

No wonder I find it hard to be here, he thought, when Ray – handcuffed to two security guards – was led into the witness box. No wonder I can't keep my distance. Perhaps the reason I'm so desperate to believe in Ray's innocence is because I need to believe in my own. Of course, Stephen hasn't been abducted or killed. And the trouble he's in is minor. Still, he'll have to appear in court, the same court where Ray appeared when he was remanded in custody and for the same offence that Ray committed when *he* was eighteen, driving a car without the owner's consent, and chances are someone from the *Gazette* will be there and make the connection with me, and instead of only Deborah knowing (it was such a relief when I finally told her about Stephen the other month) there'll be nasty gossip round the office. Irrespective of that, having a criminal record will be bad for Stephen, will harden him, alienate him, disenfranchise him even – the sort of fate I hoped my involvement would save him from when in reality I've made things worse and, in Marcia's mind, caused him to fuck up in his late teens just as I did, the sins of the father visited on the son.

Or is this all madness? I just spent the past hour listening to Nat's madness, but here I am with my own. I'll have to watch out that no one diagnoses it, because if you're black (I know, I've seen the statistics) you're more likely to be sectioned, more likely to be diagnosed as schizophrenic, more likely to be given ECT treatment or sedated. I'm far too canny and together to let them do that to me but I can't pretend to be *normal*. Even my reason for writing about Errol in the first place is mad – as mad as Nat's fairy foxes. Bestial forces unleashed from the Deptford swamp: what kind of craziness is that?

7

*JACK*

BY THE time they reached Lower Saxton, a dozen horseboxes were already in the lane. Finding no space, Jack parked round the corner, behind the Albion. While Huish considered his descent from the cab, having shinned himself on the hub casing clambering up, Jack unbolted the ramp. Out came Harkaway, gleaming like a conker popped from its shell. She was as docile a ride as could be, but to Huish – rearing backwards in alarm – her hooves on the ramp might have been Kalashnikovs. 'Put her bridle on while I get Maiden,' Jack said, handing over the rope. It didn't seem much to ask, but five minutes later the idiot was still fumbling with the bit. 'I suppose in Hyde Park you've grooms to do this for you,' Jack said, taking charge. If this Labour lot believed all men were equal, why did Huish treat him like a servant? 'All set, your lordship,' he said, when Harkaway was tacked up. Huish, a smear of horse-slobber on his sleeve, missed the sarcasm.

Getting Huish in the saddle delayed things further. He had to stand on the verge, with Jack holding one arm and the left stirrup lowered almost to the ground, before he could swing his leg over. Then he caught his glove in the buckle and couldn't extract it. The ladies who rode in Hyde Park had clearly taught him bugger all. It was now past eleven. Jack hadn't heard the horn but at this rate Otto would be gone and never mind the special visitor. They trotted down the lane, Harkaway following Maiden out of habit, not from the prompt of Huish, who used neither whip nor heel. Moving at all seemed a trial for him so Jack stuck to tipputting gently, up-down, up-down, trit-trot. When they turned the corner, on to the green, there was Otto, still waiting, thank goodness, his immaculate outfit – black hat, cream stock, swallow-tail red coat – a reproach to Huish.

'Excellent, Jack, perfect timing,' Otto said, then greeted Huish as warmly as his offended sense of dress code would allow. 'I know you're going to have a good time, Mr Huish.'

'Call me Rufus, please.'

'Just remember to give the hounds plenty of berth, Rufus. Being in at the death doesn't mean killing the bloody fox yourself.'

'And be careful not to override the Master,' Jack added, when Otto had moved away.

'Override?'

'Get in front of.'

'Ah. Point taken.'

Otto's stablegirl was handing round glasses of hot punch. 'Calms the nerves,' Jack said, 'hair of the dog.' Huish needed no prompting, despite the difficulty he had in bending down to take one. The normal etiquette was to coffee-house with the other riders ('How's the squash, Rodney?' 'Who's the blonde on Nutmeg? I wouldn't mind a gallop with her'). But the presence of a guest inhibited banter. Jack counted twenty-six riders, all on their best behaviour. There were a couple of lads on bikes, and a car with three foot followers inside, but no sabs.

'Not many have turned up, then,' Jack said to old Tickner, the retired solicitor with the hearing aid.

'Thank you, I had it last week.'

'Just thirty or so.'

'Eighty-two, old boy, if you must know, and still fit as a fiddle.'

The entrance to the big house stood opposite, its pillars topped by stone lions. The hounds milled on the driveway, snuffing at the gravel, emptying in the rose beds, till Obie called them over. It was a grand sight, thirty tail-high hounds pouring over each other to be first. Jack handed down his empty punch cup, ready for the off.

'Shall I start with Keston Copse, sir?' Obie asked Otto.

'It's often good for one.'

'And if we've no luck there, Burnholme Wood? Dunson ain't a bad copse to try neither.'

'Whatever you say, Obie. Good man.'

You could see that Obie didn't like to be good-manned, but Otto meant no harm by it. It was an MFH thing, a firm but polite assertion of seniority. Jack's predecessor, Sir Bellingham Graham, had been the same.

A cloud of hounds floated round Maiden's hooves. Jack checked Huish over: girth, stirrups, hat, whip, gloves – all fine (except for the mobile secreted in his pocket). Obie nodded at Otto, then raised his hat.

'Hounds, please!'

Obie led them off down the lane, then left through a five-barred gate into a beet field. The pace was insultingly gentle. Even so, Maiden and Harkaway were soon back with the gate shutters, fifty yards adrift. Normally Jack would have cantered to catch up, but anything brisker than a trot seemed to unsettle Huish, and the object was to keep him in his saddle.

They watched the field fan out ahead of them. Dr Bruin was riding Tanglewood, who looked frisky from being over-oated and needed a nobber to tamp him down. Next to him, on Bluebell, sat Angela Hambold, Otto's girlfriend of six months, not the strongest rider but with an elegant seat. Dom Askew, in defiance of dress code, was wearing his usual green jacket (hence his nickname, the Parakeet). Anna Alabaster, ever the actress, was riding side-saddle on a sprig-tailed strawberry mare. The plait-tailed pony supporting Jimmy Spode seemed to bow beneath his eighteen stone – like a cane holding a cooking pot over a fire. By contrast, the only child present – one of the Hamley boys – was mounted on a sixteen-hand hunter, like a frog on the back of a camel. Nick Naphe, the Bungay mortgage broker, was there too – Loanshark, his horse ought to have been called, since he had bought it on the back of the housing boom. Some of the other mounts were already half pumped out: a hog-maned black mare; a sleepy-looking bay gelding; a thistle-whipping grey; a milk-white Arab dragging its slow length along. In an hour most of them would have had enough.

'All right?' Jack shouted across to Huish.

'Absolutely,' Huish said, breathless. Jack stayed abreast and chatted. Once the chase for a fox was on, perhaps Huish would forget to be nervous. In the meantime he would have to be coaxed.

The drizzle had stopped.

'I can sense it,' Jack said. 'We're going to have a good day.'

'What's a good day?'

'Two long chases. A couple of kills.'

'It doesn't sound too good for the fox.'

'Oh, I don't know.'

'Being terrified then torn to pieces.'

'Better than traps or poison.'

'Point taken.'

'Most riders don't see the fox die, anyway. They're too far behind. But if you're game for it, we'll try to keep up.'

Beyond the set-aside lay a water meadow. It had flooded last autumn, and the ground was boggy enough to suck a horseshoe clean off, but they plodded uneventfully round the edge. Jack could remember cattle grazing here, and a water trough from which, on icy mornings, you could lift a windowpane. The pleasures of a country childhood: even country kids no longer knew them. Where was it Huish grew up? He had said last night. Tufnell Park, was it? Hackney Downs? London Fields? Parson's Green? Something rural-sounding but unforgivingly urban.

After skirting a kale field dirked with flint, they finally arrived at Keston Copse. The brambly hollow of long tussocks bordering the wood looked promising and Obie set the hounds straight to it. The two whippers-in had come by Land-Rover and were waiting, Billy Button urging stray hounds to rejoin the pack, while Rod Christian stood on the blind side, blocking any escape route. The riders stood on point around the hollow, silent with taut hope. 'We don't want the hounds chopping the fox without a good run,' Jack whispered, 'but we can't let it sneak off, either.'

For five minutes, the hounds snuffled aimlessly in the long grass, their sleek shoulders and heads rolling like dolphins. Not a whiff, it seemed, and Obie looked set to move on. Then suddenly two hounds were out of the hollow giving tongue, as a russet brush swept ahead of them. Obie had his horn out in an instant and blew a throbbing 'Gone Away'. The pack chased after the two lead hounds and the horses chased after the pack.

How far Huish felt the excitement wasn't clear. The fox scuttered over clods, fifty yards ahead. The ground was soft and gently rising. A three-bar fence arrived, and the fox was up and over it, with the hounds behind (up and through and under). Jack steered Huish the long way round, through a field gate, but they were still in touch when the hounds pulled up, then cast back, spreading to all corners, in case they had overrun. Any holes or field drains should have been stopped up, with thorn or diesel-soaked paper. But perhaps the fox had found an unblocked grate. Whichever, it was gone.

'Beats me,' Obie said. 'I had John Shafto stopping up holes here only yesterday.'

'You want to move on?' Otto said.

'Not worth the delay of looking, sir.'

'Good man, I'm with you. Let's make for Burnholme.'

With no quarry to pursue, the hounds headed slowly north and, after half a mile, left the ploughed-up wheat field for a set-aside. The ground was firmer here, and the pace picked up – no hint of a fox but the hounds rushed full spate down the hill. Jack and Huish fell behind again. Luckily, the field petered out at Deskie's Dyke, an airless ditch sunk between two hawthorn hedges, muddy at the best of times and muddier still from the wheels of Sunday scramblers. You had to bend low here, between whipping branch spindles and neck-high nooses of honeysuckle. With the horses taking it single file, Maiden and Harkaway caught up. Bluebell's rump was just ahead of them, or rather Angela Hambold's rump was, and Jack could see Huish's eyes bobbing in time to it, up-down, up-down.

'You a married man?' Jack asked. Huish, to his credit, flushed.

'Yes.'

'Children?'

'Three.'

'Taking riding lessons, are they?'

'Not yet.'

As he spoke, and they came out of the ditch, white light broke from the trees ahead, a freak flash of sunlight on stripped bark, perhaps, or the glare of snowberry blossom, though it seemed more sudden, like a saboteur setting off a flare. None of the riders reacted. Maybe Jack had imagined it. The hunt moved on.

Beyond, on the wide bridle path through the evergreen copse, Huish, gaining confidence, moved up to talk to Angela, and Jack, diplomatic, dropped back. Pinewoods made him think of church – the hush and arches and filtered light. But this wood held a different memory. Spring of 1952 and him a teenager, out with an air rifle. A mare stood untethered at the edge of the wood. He should have shouted, to announce himself, but the silence of the pines bred a silence in him. The deeper he went, the stealthier his tread, till he heard some noise inside the noiselessness – the slap of flesh. He crept on, avoiding twigs, the air rifle broken under his arm, till he saw them. They were lying on a tartan rug, next to an upended pushbike, twenty yards away. The man's braces flapped as he ground down; the front wheel of the bike spun in accompaniment. The bike and braces were Ronnie's; the bare bottom, too. Who was the woman underneath? Her jodhpurs were laid out beside her. Her boots, neatly piled on top, showed a muddy pair of heels – unlike her feet, milky white behind Ronnie's back. Jack felt excitement as well as shame, and pressed himself lower, behind a clump of ferns. The wood was in suspense, no wind in its sails, like a becalmed yacht. From fields away, a sheep called for its lamb, panic catching its throat. A few last swipes and Ronnie collapsed. Seconds later, the woman sat up. She couldn't see Jack, under his ferns, but he could see her: Hilly Alabaster, the captain's daughter, leading light of the local amateur theatre group, now married (beneath her, everyone said) to the chemist. Ronnie was nineteen, on weekend leave from national service; Hilly had two children and couldn't have been less than forty.

Jack crept away, unseen, self-sworn to secrecy. The next day Ronnie returned to barracks, but he came back most weekends and though Jack didn't catch them *in flagrante* again, rumours began in the village. They had been seen in Wapskill's Meadow. They had been spotted at a hotel in Bungay. They had been overheard planning to elope. Jack felt guilty, as if his entering that wood had let the secret out. But then one weekend Ronnie came home with a girl his own age in tow. If Hilly Alabaster felt abandoned, nothing in her posture on horseback suggested it. Jack later heard that she had performed in farces like this before. She must be a widow of eighty-something now; her daughter Anna had taken over the riding and amateur dramatics, if not (as far as Jack knew) the sexual liaisons. At fifteen, he had been too young to understand the nuances. But he understood there was a pattern here – Ronnie's fleshly compulsions; him at a safe distance, watching.

Huish had some of Ronnie's flirtatiousness. Perhaps that was why Jack found him difficult to deal with. There he trotted, next to Angela, all fear of the saddle forgotten. Funny, it was the Tories who were meant to be philanderers. Had the right policies but, like old Freddy Finch, couldn't keep their trousers on.

The track through the pines brought them out by a pig field, with huts like little air-raid shelters. The hounds were picking up pace. A false alarm, Jack thought: you didn't get foxes in pig fields. But then all hell broke loose, the hounds giving song, Obie *halloa*-ing, and Huish bobbing after Angela Hambold's rump. The fox was heading for Ickley Copse, several fields off, and if John Shafto had done his work right the hounds would have their kill before they got there. Each field had a handy gate, and Jack was hopeful of getting Huish in at the death. But he had reckoned without the loss of a stirrup as the muddy pig field gave way to a chalky meadow, a change of terrain that Huish might have coped with had his eyes not been rump-fixed ahead. By the time Jack got alongside, slowing Harkaway down and easing Huish's boot back in its stirrup, they had fallen way behind – and all Jack's coaxing failed to get them on terms. The fox was taken half a mile short of Ickley Copse. By the time they reached it, the hounds were swirling about the remnants, like water round a drain.

'See that?' Otto shouted at Huish. 'Beginner's luck. We sometimes go all day without a kill, but you've had one already.'

Huish looked bemused. He hadn't clocked the fox in the first place, let alone realised it was dead.

'Sorry,' Jack said, as though it was his fault. 'I'll make sure we catch the next one.'

And he would have done, but for Huish letting Harkaway get her head down in the tussocks, an equestrian solecism even a novice should have known about – a horse chomping, neck-deep in clover, when it should be prinked to attention. Jack shouted at Huish to correct the error, but he was still limply dabbing at the reins when one of the hounds gave tongue, Obie blew his horn, the field moved off, and Harkaway threw her head up and bolted. Even then Huish might have saved himself, had he been prepared. But he slooshed backwards off the saddle and landed arse-end-up in the grass.

'You all right?' Jack said, dismounting.

'No worries,' said Huish, brushing himself down, his face ash-pale.

'Damn bad luck. Sort of thing that happens to anyone,' Jack said, though it wasn't. At least Harkaway, munching clover again, hadn't galloped off.

'Bit of a shock, that's all.'

Huish picked up his mobile phone, which had fallen from his jacket on to the grass.

'Um, a message,' he said, clamping the mobile to his ear. He glanced at his watch as he listened.

'Come on, I'll help you back up,' Jack said, lowering Harkaway's left stirrup again.

But Huish was in no hurry to remount. Phone pressed to ear, he stood weighing his options while the field disappeared over the horizon.

'We'll soon catch them,' Jack said, without conviction.

'To tell you the truth,' Huish said, looking at his watch again, 'I think I'd better call it a day.'

Was it the humiliation of having fallen off? Or the message on the mobile?

'But we've barely started,' Jack said.

'Oh, I've got a flavour, I think.'

'The further we go, the more fun it gets.'

'Point taken. But I'll stop now. If that's all right by you.'

'Of course,' Jack said, through gritted teeth.

Jack helped him back up and they trotted back in silence to Lower Saxton, where Huish disappeared inside the Albion to make a 'call of nature' and Jack fed Maiden and Harkaway into the horsebox. As they drove away, the high cab gave a clear view across the fields, but there were no red jackets to be seen, even in the distance, and no foot followers in the lanes. All they did meet was a fire engine. It was coming the other way where the road narrowed by a dyke bridge. Jack wound the window down as it squeezed past.

'Trouble?' he said, recognising the driver, whose brother worked at Raven & Son.

'Some idiot's stuck up a tree.'

'I thought only cats got stuck up trees.'

'Photographer, apparently. Rang us from his mobile. Trying to get a close-up, he said. What of – a bloody acorn?'

Huish, paying no attention, was on his mobile again. His end of the dialogue consisted mostly of 'Oh' and 'I see', though Jack did hear the word 'livestock'.

'Trouble?' Jack said, when he came off.

'Fuss about nothing, I expect. But I need to catch the London train.'

'Today?'

'Soon as possible, yes.'

Jack had booked a table for six at the Bull. Huish seemed to have forgotten that or felt no need to apologise for leaving early. Might he change his mind if he knew Angela Hambold was one of the supper party? Sod it. Let him go.

'Your leader wants you back, does he?' Jack said.

'Blair? No, he's flying to Washington to see George Bush.'

'So Brown will have to sort it.'

'It's not really Gordon's department.'

'Nick, I mean. Your Agriculture fellow.'

'Yup, Nick, of course.'

'What's he like?'

'Pretty good. Safe pair of hands.'

A homo, Jack had read somewhere.

'And our Rural Affairs people are first-rate,' Huish said. 'They know it's terribly important to preserve the countryside.'

*Preserve*, Lord help us, like raspberry jam.

From Stormbrooke Hall, after dropping the horsebox, Jack took the B-road back to Frixley. Then, after a sandwich and glass of wine by the living-room window (a heron, pestered by crows, stalking the pond), he drove to the station. Now his ordeal was over, Huish became more genial, and enthused about the 'social inclusiveness' of hunting: 'Not at all the gentlemen's club I'd imagined.' The man was a bullshitter and had ruined Jack's day. But if he was pro-hunting thanks to the Harchope & Nelles, it had been worth it.

'Charming woman I spoke to. What was her name again?'

'Angela Hambold.'

Jack resisted adding 'Otto's girlfriend'.

'Meant to get her telephone number. Turns out her sister is a constituent of mine.'

'I'll send it you,' Jack said. Let her be bait to lure him back.

'Kind of you to arrange everything,' Huish said, bag in hand outside the station.

'You'll come again?'

'I'd love to.'

'And stay longer next time.'

'Point taken.'

'So long as you enjoyed yourself.'

'Oh, tremendously. Real eye-opener.'

'We can count on you then?'

'Absolutely. I'll call you.'

## 8

## *HARRY*

– You were unemployed, Mr Nuard?

– Yes.

– I imagine that must have left you with a lot of time on your hands. You lived alone, you had no work to go to, no family . . .

– There was television. And pool. And Errol.

– How often did you see Errol?

– On Sundays.

– Every Sunday?

– Nearly every Sunday.

– For how long?

– From lunch till evening. Sometimes longer.

– So, averaging it out, you spent roughly five hours a week with your son?

– About that.

– And is five hours a week long enough, in your view, to maintain a good relationship with one's young son?

– Longer would be better.

– Longer would make you feel a better father?

– Yes.

Harry's place was to the side, at the end of a pew. The seats were unreserved but after a month in the same spot he would have ejected any hack who dared sit there. By this time next week (so he had bet £20 with the man from the *Mail*), the trial would be over. He was going to miss it here: the wood panelling, the glass-screened dock, the red-backed chairs, the clerk's solemn 'All rise'. Greenwich Magistrates' Court was humdrum in comparison, a Travelodge after the Savoy.

In the stand, with four security guards round him, Ray looked a different man from the one Harry had first set eyes on fourteen months ago. The jive-twitch in the shoulder had gone. His dreadlocks had become bare scalp. The ash-grey suit chastened him. You could tell that Luke had told him to give no lip. When he spoke he bowed his head in respect to the jury, five-sixths of which was white. The previous day, he had been spoonfed for two hours by Lionel Martin – then had twenty minutes of gentle inquisition from Isobel ('Izzie') Grimley, the cross-eyed junior barrister for the Crown. He answered firmly, sounded polite and carried just the right weight of sorrow – a father's grief, not a murderer's remorse. Asked about Charmain, the baby, and how he felt about her, he said, 'Like she was my daughter,' then added, before Izzie Grimley could head him off: 'Cos Sharon had her, that makes her mine too. I used to cuddle her when I went round – if Errol was alive, he'd tell you.' A sharper-clawed barrister would have asked: was that a tacit admission he knew Errol was dead? A more cerebral one would have pressed Ray on his notion of telegony, the belief that as a previous sire he had left his stamp on Sharon's fourth child, even though Louis was the father. But Izzie Grimley, with her dormouse mildness, let this go.

Ray had done well. Perhaps too well. This morning he looked relaxed, almost complacent. When counsel for the Crown stood up to cross-examine him, it wasn't softly-softly Izzie but Rodney Jay, a genteel, Etonian mugger, a thug born with a silver razor in his fist.

– You were, in fact, quite angry about how little time you spent with your son, weren't you, Mr Nuard? And angry that Sharon had registered Errol's surname as Winthrop not Nuard. You told your friend Winston Hadlow you were, and I quote (m'lud will forgive the profanity), 'pissed off at Sharon. First she don't let him take my name. And now I ain't getting my access rights.'

– I don't remember.

– You don't remember. Well, let's try to refresh your memory. According to Winston Hadlow, you said this to him over a drink, after a game of pool. You do play pool with Mr Hadlow?

– Yeh.

– And you went on to say that you had still not got over what she and Louis, Sharon's lover and the father of her fourth child, had done to you.

– Sorry, I don't recall.

– There's no need to apologise, Mr Nuard. This court can well understand why you find this matter upsetting to discuss. You thought of Louis as a friend. But he and Sharon betrayed you. She became pregnant by him. You were ejected from her bed. You could longer see your son on a daily basis. Anyone would feel angry. It may not have been right, but it was only human that you should express that anger through violence.

– Yeh, but I got the bad stuff out of my system.

– Not according to Mr Hadlow. He said that you were still threatening to settle with Sharon and Louis at the beginning of December – just days before Errol disappeared.

– No.

– You're saying Mr Hadlow is lying?

– I'm saying what I said was just words.

– Well, perhaps you only meant it to be words. But then something else happened, didn't it? The week before Errol disappeared, you took him out for the day. It was a Sunday. And what did he tell you?

– I dunno.

– Well, I'm surprised you don't know because you told the police about it. I'll quote from your statement: 'When I took Errol down the park, he said Sharon was always losing her rag and slapping and locking him in his room.'

– Yeh, he said that.

– And how did you feel about it?

– I was going to talk to Sharon, let her know that ain't right.

– And did you talk to her?

– No.

– No. So instead you took revenge by other means, didn't you?

– No.

– Didn't you, Mr Nuard?

– No.

– You are under oath, you realise?

– M'lud, I really must object to this harassment of the witness. [Lionel Martin]

– I would ask you to temper your line of questioning, Mr Jay. [Rex Royston]

– I apologise, m'lud. Might I have a moment to consult with my learned colleague?

Jay, whispering to Izzie Grimley, looked momentarily discomfited. Harry thought the defence lucky to have Lionel, who was a big man, six foot three and broad-shouldered, forbidding too, with his booming voice and perfect enunciation. He was from Barbados but, like Rodney Jay, had been educated at an English public school. Harry wondered what it meant to Lionel to be defending a fellow black. 'Fuck all,' according to Luke. 'He's a true cab-ranker – takes on anything. He'd defend a white racist if they asked.' Until Luke arranged for the three of them to have a drink, Harry couldn't believe Lionel was so disengaged. He had prepared a series of questions. Did Lionel think that a black man charged with murder began at a disadvantage? What did he feel about the media stereotyping of male Afro-Caribbeans? What was his view of a recent report alleging a high incidence of gang rape among young blacks? Was he affronted by the exclusion of economic factors from such reports? Had *he* experienced prejudice over the course of his career? All this and more. But when they met in the pub on the Friday of Week 3, Lionel looked even haughtier than in his wig and robe. He wore a black blazer, an MCC tie, a gold pin through his collar, and cufflinks swirlily engraved 'LM'. He wasn't unfriendly but when Harry tried to switch the talk from cricket to race he pretended not to hear – then said he had a train to Chipping Campden to catch and was gone. Not a great one for company. Nor a torch-carrier for civil liberties. But a professional. And more than a match for Rodney Jay.

– Mr Nuard, can I ask you how you spent the day of Errol's disap-pearance?
– Got up late, round twelve. Went out. Then down the bowling alley. Then round to Sharon's.
– And what happened at Sharon's?
– Her and me had a set-to.
– About what?
– About Errol. I wanted to take him Christmas shopping. To Bluewater. To see Santa. There was late-night opening, see. But Sharon kicked up. Said it wasn't my day for Errol. Said he'd been misbehaving. Said I'd have to wait till the Sunday.
– Sharon was simply abiding by the agreement drawn up with the family liaison officer, wasn't she?
– Yes, but it was Christmas. If I can't give my own son a treat at Christmas . . .
– I think the court will understand your frustration, Mr Nuard. And why matters then turned violent.
– Not violent.
– Come, come, Mr Nuard. Mia spoke of hearing shouts. Sharon alleges you made a number of physical threats and used words I won't repeat in this room. You yourself admit things became heated.
– Heated but not violent.
– Let's not quibble over semantics. The fact is that you left the house in a temper, am I not right?
– I did have a temper, inside. But then I calmed down.

Harry watched Sharon watching Ray. She sat in court every day, in the row reserved for the close relatives. Any evidence concerning possible injuries to Errol and she would step outside. But when the heat – as now – was on Ray, she narrowed her eyes and smouldered at him, as if to fan the flames. Over the past year, she had become a celebrity, the figurehead of a new victim support group, MOMMOs – Mothers of Murdered or Missing Offspring. On the anniversary of Errol's disappearance, one of the glossies had run an interview with her, with emphasis on her 'anguished but beautiful cheekbones' and 'defiantly stunning figure'. At eighteen, she confessed, she had done some modelling sessions ('only tasteful – no full frontals'), and now they posed her in grey skirts and black evening wear, to reflect her 'tragic circumstances'. The article was embarrassing, not least when the interviewer confessed to having joined 'Sharon's sisterhood of bereavement' after a recent miscarriage. But any neutral would have been persuaded of Sharon's grief at losing Errol – and of her innocence.

Harry felt sure that Ray was innocent, too. But the more accusingly Sharon stared at him in the witness box, the harder it became to believe his version of events. What could the source of her hatred be, other than the conviction he had killed their son? Things had been tough for her, even before she lost Errol. For being a single mother with four children by different fathers, she was called a slag. And her 'stuck-up ways' annoyed her immediate neighbours. There was something hard-bitten about Sharon. But she dressed her children immaculately and refused to bad-mouth their fathers. Till the loss of Errol, she had even been protective of Ray. That's why – she claimed – she took so long to admit her suspicions to the police. Luke called her a liar and manipulator: 'From what the kids said, when Errol went missing she was upstairs, in the bath, tarting herself up for a night out.' Harry thought that too harsh: why blame poor Sharon? But he didn't think Ray was guilty, either. A man who had killed a child couldn't look as *eager* as Ray did – as bright, curious, hopeful, self-righteous. Even now, forced to recall the worst evening of his life, the eagerness was still there.

– What time did you leave Sharon's, Mr Nuard?
– About six.
– And then?
– I went back to the bowling alley.
– What time would that have been?
– Hard to say.
– Come, come, surely you've a rough idea.
– About seven.
– I fear you're mistaken about that, Mr Nuard. You may recall that on the second day of this trial, the jury were shown CCTV images from a security camera at Lewisham Bowl. We have a still of you at 5.07. Then nothing till 8.23.

– The traffic was bad.

– So you told the police. Yet there were no reports of congestion on the route you said you took. And even if there had been: two and a half hours to get from Deptford to Lewisham, Mr Nuard?

– [Long pause] I could've stopped off.

– Stopped off? Where?

– At a club. Off Deptford High Street. I sometimes do.

– In your statement to the police – I have it here in front of me – you say nothing about a club.

– I didn't like to mention it.

– The club isn't an especially wholesome sort of place, you mean?

– Uh?

– It's the kind of club where illegal substances are taken – is that it?

– It's just a club.

– How bewildering that you haven't mentioned it before. You were the last person to see Errol alive. Yet instead of assisting the police with their inquiries, you misled them about your movements.

– Not misled. Forgot. I was confused.

– So around six o'clock, after violently rowing with your ex-partner about access arrangements, you left the Pepys Estate and may then have visited a place of ill repute, before eventually returning to the bowling alley. But unfortunately you're not quite sure. Which is rather convenient. Or then again maybe not, because while your version of events is hazy to the point of insult several witnesses are quite clear in their recollection of seeing you with Errol, still on the Pepys Estate, at seven o'clock.

– That's not true.

– And if it had been less dark these witnesses would also have been able to confirm what the scientific witnesses have inferred, namely that little Errol was by then already injured, because you in your rage against Sharon had lashed out at him, and hurt him, and made him bleed, so profusely there was a spray of blood on the wall and pavement.

– I never.

– But Errol was making too much noise, wasn't he? Several witnesses have spoken of hearing howls, and you were worried the noise would make people run to investigate. So you said, There, there, Errol, your daddy's sorry, he didn't mean to hurt you, let's go to McDonald's. And when you couldn't find his left shoe, the one he'd lost while you

405

were assaulting him, you put him on your shoulders and walked to McDonald's.

– I wasn't at McDonald's.

– Where you could get your breath back and plan the next move, before you took Errol somewhere quiet, a place where he couldn't run away, and no one would see and hear you, and his body could be hidden from view.

– This is all lies. [Sobs]

– M'lud . . . [Lionel Martin, rising]

– And Errol went with you happily, because after all, you were his daddy, Daddy Ray, and he loved and trusted you. He was just a child, only three years old. Where did it happen, Mr Nuard? And how did you do it? Why don't you tell us?

– [Sobs] I didn't kill him, I didn't. [Cries]

– M'lud, I really . . . [Lionel Martin]

– No more questions.


'Fucking disaster,' Luke said, on the steps outside. 'We briefed Ray for over an hour. We warned him Jay would go for him. But that business about a club – completely unscripted, total news to us. What did he think he was doing? A club in Deptford suggests a ganja den or a brothel. It's not an alibi. It's an anti-alibi. It's worse than having no alibi at all.'

'What's he saying in private?'

'That he's sorry he didn't tell us before but he only came out with it because he was rattled. And the club isn't a dive, it's a youth club, run by the church, which he used to go to every week, but he couldn't say he'd been to a youth club or the jury would think he was a weirdo or a paedophile.'

'Can you turn things round?'

'Not a chance,' Luke said, shoulders drooping, eyes heavy as roof tiles. 'I was watching the jury's faces. We're fucked.'

'What about your other witnesses?'

'There's none who can put Ray at the bowling alley before eight thirty. Which means he would have had time to kill Errol, dump the body somewhere and get back.'

'But he didn't kill Errol.'

'He says he didn't.'

'Don't tell me you've lost faith in him.'

'It's not about faith, Harry. This is a game. A performance. A gladiatorial bout. And Ray's going to get the thumbs down.'

406

# 9

## *ANTHEA*

Hi Nat

I said I would write and tell you how I'm getting on, and I will, soon. This is just to wish you luck with your lecture. My mother called me about it last night. She saw it on the college website, which she doubtless accesses on a daily basis in order to keep tabs on you. I think she expected me to jump straight on a plane. Which I can't, of course. But I will be thinking of you.

Anthea

xx

# 10

## *LIBBY*

INSTEAD OF walking straight to the flat, Libby crossed the road to Borough Market. She had texted Damian with a list of ingredients, but the deli would be good for extras. The smell of herby, fresh-baked loaves wafted by the sour, brown Thames.

She was buying olives when he tapped her on the shoulder.

'Harry – what are you doing here?'

'Shopping, same as you.'

'Well, it's nice to see you. I hear you had lunch with Nat.'

'And now I'm with you – two Ravens in a day.'

'One Raven and one ex-Raven. Where did you go? Cantata?'

'Our Cantata days are over, I'm afraid. I hardly ever see him.'

He had said the same at supper last year, when she cooked him escalopes and opened an expensive Chablis to make up for having raged at him that time in Greenwich Cinema. He had looked good that evening, she thought. They had reminisced, and toasted the renewal of their friendship, and when she cried, which was inevitable (her hurt at Nat's treachery still so raw), he had got up from his chair and taken her in his arms and held her there till the sobbing stopped. She was somewhere else now, happier, stronger, more like her old self. Today it was Harry who looked frazzled.

'Coffee?' he said.

'It'll have to be quick. I've supper to cook.'

'For the girls?'

'For a friend.'

'The friend you mentioned when we last met?'

'Yes. Damian.'

'Ah.'

There was a Starbucks off the cobbles of Clink Street. She stowed her two shopping bags under the table.

'You OK?' she said.

'Ish,' he said. 'Listening to the detail gets to you after a while.'

She shook her head. *Which* detail? About *what*? Men were like this, it was an Asperger's thing, they seemed to think you had a hotline to their consciousness.

'The Ray Nuard trial,' he said. 'I've just come from there. I'm covering it for the paper.'

'Of course, you told me. It must be upsetting.'

'It is. More than I expected. Everything gets tainted by it. Seeing Nat, for instance. That was upsetting, too.'

'Did you have one of your arguments?'

'He wasn't up to arguing.'

'I can't imagine that.'

'It's true. He's in a bad way.'

'He sounded OK, on the phone.'

'He's finally realised how disastrously he screwed things up with you.'

'Big deal. What am I supposed to do?'

'I don't know. Talk to him. See what he has to say.'

'Come on, Harry. It's taken me till now to feel even half OK again. Anyway, I'm seeing someone else now.'

'I know, you said.'

He swigged his coffee to drown it, but she caught the begrudging tone. The idea of her not being with Nat still seemed to bother him.

'Why shouldn't I see someone? Do you expect me to spend my life on my own?'

'Of course not. I miss us doing things together, that's all.'

'You want us to be a jolly threesome again.'

'No, what I want is . . .' He paused, suddenly shy. 'This isn't about Nat.'

'What is it about?'

'It's . . . I . . .'

She waited for him to explain. For a man whose profession was words, he could be strangely inarticulate at times.

'Stephen's in trouble again,' he said. 'That's the other upset.'

Now we're getting there, she thought, but I don't have time for this, Damian will be waiting for me, in two hours I have to put supper on the table.

'What's he done?' she said.

Harry had talked about Stephen last time, when she gave him supper. About Marcia, too, and how close they were again. ('Not close in *that* way,' he had added, 'though I think she'd be prepared to give it another go.' 'But you wouldn't?' 'No.')

He explained about the arrest. And how the recent efforts he had put into Stephen seemed to have been counterproductive. And how, sitting in court, he felt to be on trial himself. His hand shook as he spoke and for a moment she took it in hers. She felt pleased that he could confide in her like this; he'd never been one to talk about his feelings. Even so, she felt she wasn't getting the full story, as though there were other things he'd like to say to her. With encouragement, he probably *would* say them. But she was running late.

'I wish we could talk more,' she said, 'but now I really have to go.'

'Of course. Yes. Me too.'

It's such a waste he doesn't have a girlfriend, she thought, as they walked along the cobbles. If I weren't with Damian, I'd certainly see more of Harry – go to the odd film and stuff. Perhaps I could invite him to supper again. But I know it wouldn't work with the three of us. He resents Damian. He's jealous of him on Nat's behalf.

'I'll leave you here then,' he said, outside London Bridge station. 'I'm off to Nat's lecture now. If he's up to giving it.'

'He'll be fine,' she said. 'I've never known him miss a class.'

'Let's hope so.'

'Have fun,' she said, kissing Harry on the cheek.

'You have fun, too,' he said, though she could tell he didn't mean it in the least.

## II

# JACK

JACK HAD booked a table for six: himself, Huish, Harris and Elise, Otto and
Angela. A pleasant night out was the idea – good country cooking, fine
wines, intelligent talk. But the guest of honour would now be absent. And
once Otto, his voice drawling down the phone, had established this ('So our
chap's gone back to London.' 'Yes.' 'Not from disappointment with us, I
trust.' 'No, he was *summoned*.' 'Damn shame.'), he too cried off: Angela had
a bad cold; would Jack mind awfully if they sat this one out? That left Harris
and Elise, and a night with them would only remind him of his singleness.

His shoulder hurt from yanking at Harkaway. The fur of dusk rubbed
against the panes. Life's pleasures had reduced to hunting. And unless men
like Huish could be persuaded otherwise, they would vote to banish hunting
for ever.

He was by the phone, whisky in hand, debating whether to call Harris
and cancel, when Elise beat him to it.

'Harris has flu,' she said.

'Poor Harris,' Jack said.

'But I'm coming.'

Jack explained about the depletions.

'Doesn't matter to me,' she said. 'Unless you want to forget it.'

'I'm eating at the Bull anyway – there's no food in the house.'

'I'll join you then.'

'Don't feel you have to. If Harris needs you.'

'Oh, he'll just go to bed.'

'You mustn't put yourself out.'

'I won't – but if you'd rather eat on your own, I understand.'

'All I meant was it's not compulsory.'

They dithered and hedged, till Elise said: 'Look. I'll be there at seven.'

And so she was, with her green eyes and a voice the texture of tar.

'I came by minicab,' she said, 'so I don't have to worry about drink.'

Jack wasn't worrying, either. He'd had two doubles before setting off
and was now on to a third. There were no police between the Bull and

Frixley. The solitary patrol car hovered hawklike on bridges over the bypass, ready to plunge on commuters speeding home. If you stuck to the back roads, you were safe.

'Vodka and tonic,' she said, and out of gallantry, or a wish for equivalence, he made it a large one.

The Bull used to have a fruit machine and a darts board. But since the gallery had become a restaurant, the lounge bar was more anteroom than pub. A couple of regulars stood drinking Adnams at the bar. Everyone else sat in easy chairs studying the menu.

'So,' she said, putting her menu down, 'how was it with the MP?'

'OK, I think.'

'Why did he leave early then?'

'He had to. This foot-and-mouth business.'

'I heard on the news. Three more farms under investigation.'

'But he seemed fairly positive about hunting.'

'You got on with him?'

'No. He was clueless.'

'No good at riding, you mean?'

'Not only that.'

'You dislike his politics?'

'Detest them. New Labour don't give a bugger for the countryside – and that's why the countryside is buggered. But that's not the reason I took against Huish. He just wasn't my type.'

She had almost finished her vodka, he noticed.

'What is your type, Jack?'

Rather than answer he went to the bar. By the time he got back, the waiter had arrived, to take their orders. 'You choose the wine,' she said. He switched the talk to Harris's clarets. They were still talking clarets when they moved upstairs to the gallery.

'Your type, Jack,' she said, over their starters. 'You were saying.'

'Was I?'

'The MP didn't meet with your approval.'

'He was too full of himself.'

'You like men who're modest?'

'Unless they've something to be proud about, which he hadn't.'

'And women?'

He glanced around. Candles, long-stemmed glasses, couples talking in undertones at every table. No one listening. No one he knew.

'I don't have a type,' he said, embarrassed.

'I know, you loved Nancy. We all did. She was a one-off. But you must have had girlfriends before her. What were they like?'

'It's so long ago I've forgotten.'

'No one forgets. You must have feelings about women.'

'None I can share.'

'Sorry, I'm being intrusive.'

'None *fit* to share, I mean.'

'There's nothing shameful about sexual desires,' Elise went on. 'We all have them.'

She's trying to unstiffen me, he thought, but if I unstiffen I'll say things better left unsaid. Odd, the different connotations of stiffness. Excessive formality. A tumescent penis. And death.

'Or do you think having sexual desires is a betrayal of Nancy?' she persisted.

'Maybe.'

The waiter brought their mains – a welcome interruption. Enjoy your meal, he said, as waiters do. Just serve the frigging food, Jack thought, whether I enjoy it is up to me.

Hers was Dover sole. She ate it in small, neat bites, like a cat.

'Pork,' she said, as he struggled with his escalope. 'Is that wise?'

'Humans can't catch foot-and-mouth. Only the cloven-hoofed.'

'I won't be serving pork to Harris, then.'

He laughed – but then worried he was colluding with something she hadn't intended and said, making heavy weather of it, 'He's a devil at golf, you mean.'

'In other ways too,' she said.

He poured more wine, not meeting her eye.

'Did they say on the news where these new outbreaks are?'

'I can't remember,' she said. 'All pig farms, though.'

'The last time it spread to cows and sheep,' he said. 'In 1968.'

'Nineteen sixty-eight!' she said. 'That's the year I married my first husband.'

'*First*? So you . . .'

'Yes, I was married before Harris. To another Englishman. Also a banker. He liked to mess about in boats. And, unfortunately, with women. Hence, three years later, divorce.'

'But I thought . . .'

He stopped, blushing at his foolishness. He'd been enjoying her company too much.

'What?' she said.

'Doesn't matter.'

'You thought: I tolerate Harris fooling round, why not my first husband?'

'It's none of my business.'

'Every other man seems to think it's his. Maybe that's why I like you, Jack.'

'What is?'

'Other men assume that if I know all about Harris and don't mind, then he and I must have some sort of arrangement. So they flirt. Grope. Make passes. "Try it on." But I don't know all about Harris, and what I do know I mind quite a lot. Besides, these men don't attract me. Most of them are friends of yours, incidentally. Every man but you, Jack. What's this wine again? It's nice. I should shut up.'

'A New Zealand Sauvignon,' he said, acknowledging he had heard that much. 'No offence, but I've given up on French.'

'Very sensible. Anyway, I'm not French. My parents moved there when I was nine, but I was born in Putney. Did Harris never tell you? Probably not. He thinks being French is classy.' She pushed her plate aside, the mashed potato untouched, the rest licked clean. 'I hope I don't sound disloyal,' she said, dabbing her lips.

'To France?'

'To Harris. I'm very fond of him. I'd hate you to think I wasn't.'

'Of course.'

'I used to love him terribly.' She sipped the Sauvignon and paused. 'That was a cue, Jack.'

'What was?'

'*Used* to. Anyone else would have asked me to elaborate. But you're afraid I'm going to weep over your dinner plate and cause a scene.'

'Not at all.'

'Is a bit of emotion now and then really so bad? You're too proper, Jack. When was the last time you . . . ?'

'What?'

'Never mind. I've drunk too much. Can we have coffee? I don't want dessert.'

The brandy was his idea: he was over the limit anyway, one more could do no harm. He was surprised when she said she'd join him, but it wasn't his job to stop her and nothing suggested she was drunk. Who were her gropers? he wondered. Dom Askew? Dr Bruin? Otto? He felt indignant at the thought of their hands on her. But you couldn't blame them. She invited intimacy – raised eyebrows, little laughs, tongue between teeth – drawing you forward. It was a game. If he responded, she would pull back – and (as she had with the others) hold it against him. He mustn't be a fool.

'Penny for them?' she said.

'I ought to be off. The damn dog will be weeing all over the carpet. I'll get the bill.'

'OK, but don't think you're paying. We'll go halves.'

It was only nine thirty, and her taxi wasn't booked till ten thirty. He offered to drive her home.

'It's too far, Jack. I'll wait here, it's OK.'

'Come back to the house at least. That's halfway. The cab can collect you from there.'

'Are you sure?'

'Then we can have another drink,' he said.

'Perfect.'

Outside, the stars were scattered like white flints. A cold wind blew hard through the sky, sharpening their far-off light.

Her head lay on his shoulder as he drove ('Sleepy. You don't mind?'): lemony hair and leather upholstery. Half pissed, he felt at ease behind the wheel. In town you had to react to others' idiocies. But the only danger along these lanes was when a deer crossed over. The world felt calm for once, duveted in darkness. There was Elise, Nancy's friend, asleep on his shoulder, borne safely under the flint-white stars.

The gravel brought her back to life. Then the yapping in the hall. 'Who's a good boy then?'

He left her in the kitchen, calling the cab firm. She was still on the phone when he returned with the brandies. The remains of Huish sat on the table: uneaten scrambled egg from breakfast, a quarter-empty wine glass from lunch. But for her presence he wouldn't have noticed, but now he felt embarrassed and began to tidy up. She'll assume I'm still not coping, he thought – that *I'm* a mess.

'That was Harris,' she said, hanging up. 'I told him to go to sleep.'

'The flu's not too bad then?' Jack said, piling the plates in the sink.

'He'll be at work tomorrow, whatever.'

'I'm due to see him, as it happens.'

He drew two chairs next to the Aga, and they sat half facing each other, right shoulders to the heat.

'About another loan?' she said.

'To get advice about my pension. The firm's doing all right at present. We don't need more loans.'

'Is that down to Marcus?'

'Hardly. Marcus has other interests these days.'

Namely his fiancée, Carly, the girl Libby sent up for background research last year. The plan was for her to stay three days but soon she was commuting and then the secret came out. Unlikely couple: Marcus with his Gucci suits and Carly with her punk hairdo. Unlikely country-dwellers, too. But having a girl had made Marcus easier to work with.

'Well, I'm glad it worked out,' she said. 'I told Harris to give you more time.'

'*You* told him? I thought head office decided these things.'

'That's just rubber-stamping. I don't usually get involved. But it wasn't right to pressurise you. Not just after Nancy died.'

'You felt sorry for me,' he said, accusingly, the brandy swirling in his glass.

'What right did the bank have to make you stand down?'

'Every right – they lent me money and I was going bust.'

'But you didn't go bust. You're flourishing.'

'I was saved by charity.'

'And you resent that.'

'Wouldn't you? Everyone's so damn *kind*. They bump into me in Sainsbury's and see how lonely I look and they think: poor old sod, we'd better have him round for dinner, cheer him up, do our bit by Nancy. It's like frigging social work.'

'So I'm just a do-gooder, too?'

'You feel sorry for me. I'm a miserable old sod.'

'No. Just very English and repressed.'

'There's nothing very repressed about the English any more. Go into Harchope any Saturday night and you'll see.'

'Old-style English, then. Olde worlde. You're how England used to be, Jack.'

'A dinosaur.'

'Were there ever dinosaurs in England?'

'A dodo, then. The dodo MFH. The great auk of Frixley.'

'Poor Jack, the last of his breed.'

'There you go,' he said, 'being sorry for me again.'

'That's not why I'm here.'

'Why *are* you here, then?' he said, hearing the sound of his own petulance but going on with it anyway, and never mind if he sounded aggressive, because here was this bloody woman – this deeply fanciable woman – pitying and patronising him. 'I don't need coddling.'

He tipped his head back in the chair, to drain the last of the brandy, the gold bowl above his nose, and the flaky grey ceiling beyond it, the ceiling Nancy had talked of repainting, even greyer and flakier now, seeing which made his eyes water, or maybe it was the brandy making them water, but either way, because of the wateriness, not wanting Elise to think he was tearful, he had to close them. When he opened them again, she was standing in front him.

'I'm the one who needs coddling,' she said. 'I think I've caught Harris's flu. Will you hold me?'

He stood up to put one arm round her shoulder. But when she rested her head on his chest, he had to use two.

'Do I *feel* hot?' she said.

'A bit, maybe.'

'I can hear your heart beating.'

'It does tend to,' he said.

'Can you hear mine? Give me your hand. There. Mm. That's nice.'

He closed his eyes, to shut himself inside the sensation.

'You're beginning to feel hot, too,' she said, a little later. 'Don't you think we'd better lie down?'


*12*


## NAT


'YOU DON'T have a text?' Claire said, under her breath.

Nat gulped his Muscadet. With their dark clothes and solemn faces, the people outside the lecture theatre looked like mourners at a wake – *in memoriam* Nat Raven. Thanks to Claire, there had been posters all over college and an announcement in the *Gazette*. But publicity for open lectures was rarely effective, and half an hour ago, when the techies, testing voice levels, made him say 'One-two' into the mike, that seemed a plausible assessment of audience numbers. Now the lobby was crowded. It was the lure of free drink, of course. But if only half those swigging wine went into the lecture, that would still make a largish audience. And meanwhile the door behind Claire's left shoulder kept swinging open, as more people pushed in from the cold. It had been his dream, once, to address a large crowd. But this was becoming a nightmare.

'I have an earlier draft,' he whispered.

'Can't you remember the changes?'

'I totally rewrote it.'

If only he had tried printing the text out earlier. By the time he realised the cartridge needed replacing, he had no time to buy another. Procrastination had caught up with him at last. The Late Nat Raven, RIP.

'If you had emailed me an attachment, I could have printed it out for you,' Claire said.

'I didn't think to go online. I hardly ever do these days.'

'I could still print it out, if you have the disk with you.'

'I don't.'

'Hi, Nat,' a voice said. 'Remember me?'

Suzanne Gleeson, from the 1989 Getting Started class. He could even remember a couple of her sonnets. He rarely thought about his students once they left. But if ever he ran into them again, it all came back.

Except with Anthea.

'I was afraid I'd miss you,' she said. 'I had to wait two hours at Frankfurt airport.'

'You've flown from Frankfurt? For this?'

'Claire said we had to. No excuses. Grand Reunion Cabal. I'm making a holiday of it.'

Claire had also roped in her brother Mark to collect the tickets. From the small table by the auditorium doors, he stuck up both thumbs and mouthed, 'Full house.'

'I'm not feeling too good,' Nat said.

'Nerves,' Claire said. 'Have another.'

Another would be his third, and since breakfast he had eaten only a chocolate brownie. But he made no protest when Claire refilled the glass. He was used to seeing her in jeans and sweaters, but tonight she had dressed up, 'made an effort' as Libby would have put it – red cocktail shoes, silver necklace and a black dress that only half contained her breasts. There must be someone she wanted to impress.

The noise levels rose behind them. He recognised other ex-students. Did they realise he too was now an ex-? Ex-teacher, ex-husband, ex-writer, ex-lover, ex-everything.

'They've come to pay their last respects,' he said.

'No,' Claire said, 'they've come because they want to hear you speak.'

'I'm like a footballer having his testimonial. Dutiful turnout. Night of nostalgia. Let's hear it for good old Nat.'

'They *want* to be here. They're interested in the topic.'

'Humour in contemporary British theatre? I don't think so.'

'Some of the family are here, too.'

'Family?'

'The Sturgeon family. The people who endow the lecture.'

'With a cheque for two hundred measly quid. Wow.'

'It's not actually two hundred quid.'

'Fuck, Claire, I thought you said . . .'

'Shh. The Principal's coming – I'll explain later.'

'Ah, our speaker, I believe,' the Principal broke in. Nat had met Keighley Steel only twice before, once at a reception she had given for the 'hugely valued part-timers' of ICE, and the second time in her office, three months later, after the letter which said that this particular hugely valued part-timer would not be having his contract renewed. On the first occasion he had merely been unimpressed by her; on the second, after failing to persuade her she was guilty of a terrible mistake, he felt more actively antagonistic. There was the further resentment that she was at least ten years his junior. And the suspicion that she had agreed to invite him to lecture only out of pity. But here she was, with frozen curls and glossed lips, trying to be nice.

'Dr Raven,' she said, 'this is Oscar Scutt, director of WEIA.'

'West End Initiatives in Academe,' the man with the grey bouffant explained, his hand resting limp in Nat's.

'And this is Gavin Lowell from the Arran & Arran advertising agency.'

'I used to work with your wife,' the second grey man said. 'I think you know a colleague of mine, Damian Colne.' Damian: yes, it did ring a bell.

'And lastly Chip Rylance from HSBC.'

Chip was easy to tell from the other two because he had no hair.

'We've spent the day discussing ways to pool our resources,' the Principal said, 'and now this lecture is going to put the seal on our efforts. We're all so looking forward to hearing your thoughts, Dr Raven.'

Thoughts? Which were those? Since Anthea, his only thoughts had been about Anthea. He sipped more wine.

'But I mustn't keep you,' she said, leaning her scented cheek towards him. 'So kind of you to step in like this, by the way. See you in a moment. I'll be introducing you.'

The three men nodded 'Good luck' and followed her, like dogs tracking a bitch on heat.

'Step in?' Nat hissed at Claire.

'There was vague talk of inviting a celebrity,' she said, embarrassed. 'Till your name came up.'

'I'm a last-minute stand-in.'

'Only to Sean Connery. Who we all knew would never accept.'

'And I thought *you* were introducing me.'

'The Principal paid for the reception. I couldn't say no.'

'And who were those guys? What's WEIA?'

'It's a scheme to forge closer links between the college and West End theatre. The Principal's very keen. They send directors and actors to us to liven up the drama department, and we send students to fill empty seats on Shaftesbury Avenue.'

'And HSBC?'

'They put money in. Along with the other sponsors.'

'Why? What's in it for them?'

'Kudos. Tax breaks. First-night seats and honorary professorships.'

'It stinks.'

'Come on, I know you don't like Keighley much. But the extra income will be good for the college.'

'Excuse me while I throw up.'

Once in the Gents, his nausea was real enough. His legs had felt shaky since the labyrinthitis, and now his hands were trembling too. He should have eaten something. Drunk less. Pulled out this morning. Never accepted in the first place. He had only agreed as a favour to Claire. And now the Principal had hijacked the occasion for some sponsorship scam. As he stood at the urinal failing to pee, he pulled the text from his pocket and tried to decipher the opening paragraph, with its spidery inserts and sideways marginalia and spiralling balloons of second (and third, and fifteenth) thoughts.

The day ends in the West, where the sun goes down, and though, *pace* Shakespeare [? QUOTE? or wd this slow up too much?], the movements of the heavenly planets can't always [invariably? infallibly?] be relied on as a cultural index [as indices of artistic health/well-being?], in the case of West End theatre the astrological symbolism [astronomical reality?] seems inescapable. In 1946, that famous failure of early promise, the author [critic/man of

419

letters/belletrist] Cyril Connolly announced that it 'was closing time in the gardens of the west'. A deadly accurate diagnosis [prognosis?]? Or a premature death knell? Every dog must have its day. But is there life in the old dog yet or should it be buried along with its bones? [confusing?] That is the question I wish to pose [impose on you?] tonight, in relation to West End theatre. Cynical pundits [jaundiced reviewers? even experienced professionals like me?] have spoken of a sad, slow, terminal decline. Or does the patient's [dog's?] pulse show signs of life? I think it does and that I owe my students over the years a *mea culpa*. [I fear it doesn't – and that even the negative judgements I have made over the years are too kindly.] Tonight, more than half a century after Connolly, I can say with some confidence [a neutral observer can safely venture/I don't feel irresponsible/overly patriotic/merely sentimental in asserting] that certain encouraging dawnlike flickers [that those illusory harbingers of a revival attested to by squalid hack reviewers] . . .

'*There* you are,' Harry said.

'Did Claire tell you? The Principal expects an encomium to commercial theatre. I'm a pawn in a sponsorship game.'

'Just say what you think.'

'I don't know what I think. I can't even *read* what I think. Look.'

He held out the top page.

'Wing it. Just be you.'

'Who's me?'

'You know this stuff inside out.'

'I used to. I'm different now. I've nothing left to say.'

'You can't not speak, Nat. It's an honour.'

'The 29th Frederick Reeves Sturgeon Annual Memorial Lecture? Anyway, I'm in no fit state.'

'OK. Let's make a deal. Do you have your mobile?'

'It's in my pocket.'

'Good, leave it on, and if I see you're making a fuck of things, I'll call your number, right?'

'What good will that do?'

'You can pretend there's a crisis – that your mother's died or something, and that you have to leave the stage at once.'

'But you'll be in the audience. How can you speak?'

'I won't have to. I'll have the phone in my pocket, I'll press Call, you'll answer and I'll ring off. Then you improvise.'

'I like it. But what if *I* think I'm fucking up?'

'Make some kind of signal and I'll call you. Rub your left eyebrow with your right hand like this, see, three times.'

Nat practised the manoeuvre, as shown.

'But only if it's desperate,' Harry said.

'OK, deal.'

They shook hands.

'Thanks,' Nat said. 'How did the trial go this afternoon?'

'Badly. For Ray, that is. They only let him speak because they were desperate. He'd have done better to keep his mouth shut.'

'I know how he feels.'

'His defence have more or less thrown in the towel.'

'I know how *they* feel, too. But don't be so down. Whatever happens, you'll write a great piece. This is your moment, Harry.'

'No, it's yours, Nat. Or was yours. Jesus, it's gone seven. You're already late.'

Harry rushed him back to the anteroom, which was empty, apart from two catering ladies collecting glasses, and Claire.

'Where you've been?' she said.

'Pissing his life away,' Harry said.

'Having a nervous breakdown,' Nat said.

She took his left arm, and Harry his right, and they eased him forward like nurses wheeling a patient into theatre.

'Play your cards right and you'll get a job out of this,' Claire whispered. 'I just spoke to the Principal.'

'What?'

'She's full of plans. I'll tell you later.'

Inside the lecture hall the Principal, looking crossly at her watch, showed no sign of having plans that included Nat. He followed her on to the platform, avoiding the tripwire of audio cable by the lectern. Applause or even booing would have settled him but a hush fell instead. He took a seat at the table, which was draped with blue. While the Principal declaimed from the lectern ('. . . the pleasurable task of saying a few words about our distinguished speaker, but first . . .'), he reached for the carafe, taking care not to spill water on the top sheet of his lecture, though blots could have it made no more illegible. Gulping over the rim of the glass, he surveyed his listeners, steeply banked in a semicircle, ascertaining that he personally knew at least a quarter of them, though that still left the other three hundred. Claire and Harry, in the front row, smiled encouragingly. The real encouragement was that the Principal was still speaking four minutes in, paying fulsome tribute to Frederick Reeves Sturgeon, the late professor whose family had endowed the lecture three decades ago and whose contributions to the college seemed hearteningly endless ('Not content to rest on his laurels as a wartime code-breaker at Bletchley Park, his friendships with Turing and Wittgenstein, and his growing reputation as the foremost classicist of the day, he then switched disciplines and . . .'). At this rate she would use up the full hour. Nat drank more water and began to relax, wondering was it true that no academic other than Sturgeon had been both a Sophocles specialist and a nuclear physicist in the same lifetime, and how many celebrities other than Sean Connery had been approached to give the lecture, and was his mobile switched on, and who was that nice-looking woman with the beret in the side aisle, and had Marcia and Stephen turned up, and how odd to be sitting there slightly woozy while the Principal offered her observations on the Two Cultures, odd but oddly pleasant and really nothing to fret about, till her meanderings took an ominous turn ('But now I come'), and some far-too-terse approximation of his CV could be heard, and all hopes of a reprieve were dashed by a resounding 'without further ado', followed by his name and a scatter of applause.

He walked to the lectern as unhurriedly as he could, then spread his text out and leaned towards the microphone. 'Madam Principal,' he said, 'students, ladies and gentlemen,' then, spotting Hannah and Rose with Maya in the third row, 'boys and girls.' There were titters from the back, and a back-echo from the mike. He took a sip before going on. That fourth glass of wine had been a mistake. The words on the page swam like tadpoles through the water. Even when he put the glass down, they wouldn't keep still.

'A word, first, about the title,' he said. '"You Have to Laugh" is a phrase my wife likes to use. Or did like to use. Actually, I expect she still likes to use it, but she's no longer my wife. That's not quite right, either: legally, she still *is* my wife but we're no longer living together as a married couple. Which is more than you need to know, but that's where the title originated, with my wife, or not-quite-ex-wife, who sends her apologies that she can't be here tonight.'

There were more titters. He brushed his hand across his face, to remove the bogey or whatever it was that was making him look comic, then quickly stopped, in case Harry thought he was giving the signal, though that might not be a bad idea. In the second row sat Brik Pedersson – the Norse loon – glaring like an ice field.

'As to the subtitle, you'll see it's officially "Humour in Contemporary British Theatre", which sounds terrifically grand and wide-ranging, but what I propose to offer you tonight is something more personal. Not that I think myself so richly exceptional a human being. Or that my story, qua story, is any more interesting than the next person's. But a narrative – even an academic narrative – cannot be constructed without the intrusion, or should I say incursion, of the self, and I shall be transparent about my role in the action, even if it's a bit part rather than the lead.'

Someone coughed. The prevarications and disclaimers were making the audience restless. Unsure where to go next, he picked up his fifty-page script, remembering that he had forgotten to time how long it took to read, not that reading it was possible anyway in its – and his – current disarray. As far as he could recall, its hour-long-or-probably-much-longer appraisal focused on half a dozen celebrated West-End plays, which, depending on which version he read (the typed, the tippexed, the overwritten, the inter-scrawled), he either scathingly satirised for their witlessness or bouncily celebrated for their hilarity. But since the words were illegible, he would have to ad-lib.

'This morning a plumber came to my flat. I won't bore you with the details of my kitchen-sink drama. But it struck me later: what a terrific scenario for a play. The setting: a rented flat. The characters: two men, one worldly and practical, the other bookish and useless with his hands. The context: something gone wrong needs to be repaired. The subtext: emotional damage; absent guests; the other people – women – in these men's lives. The opening scene: a ringing bell, a halting conversation, an atmosphere of mutual suspicion and awkwardness. Where will the action go? How will it end? With a handshake or a murder? Any of these are possible. But we can be sure if this is a British play that the central concern will be with class.'

Phew. He had found his place now. Class and comedy. Off he went. The kitchen-sink dramas of John Osborne and Arnold Wesker, and how they mirrored the drawing-room comedies of Noël Coward and Terence Rattigan. The brain of Frayn. The wise whimsy of Bennett. The politics of Hare, Brenton and Edgar. For his Getting Started students, there was nothing new here. He barely needed to consult the script. But he waved his arms about, and paced about the platform, and by accentuating the positive he avoided offending the man from WEIA. The clock at the back of the room showed 7.30. Halfway there. If he kept this up, he would be fine.

When Hannah and Rose were ushered out by Maya as arranged, he joked about losing heart now the VIPs had left. He moved on to Alan Ayckbourn. It was going well.

Then his mobile rang. He took an age to locate the thing and switch it off, before stammering an apology. Had he rubbed his left eyebrow without realising? Or was the lecture really much worse than he thought? He looked at Harry, who shrugged a 'Not me, guv'. But it was too late – the call had knocked him off his stride. Going well? Really? The eyes of the audience were too glazed to meet his. The man from WEIA he'd thought was nodding in agreement was nodding from sleep. Brik Pedersson yawned obtrusively. Even his ex-students looked catatonic. They had come to hear him out of sympathy but couldn't wait to get it over with. Poor old Nat, they would be thinking, he's lost his way, no wonder the college sacked him. Sad case. He used to have edge. Now he just meanders. Motiveless benignity. Where did it all go wrong?

'And so I come,' he said, not knowing where he had come or was going next, 'to humour in British theatre today, 2001. And rather than sticking to this formal written treatise,' he added, holding the wodge of typescript high in front of him then letting it drop, a gesture which proved more theatrical than intended as the pages missed the slope of the lectern and scattered across the dais, like propaganda leaflets hurled from a plane, 'I will now depart from the script.'

He had their attention now. But how to use it? He poured himself a drink. Water slopped over the glass. Ah, yes.

'Let me remind you of my plumber,' he said. 'How might a play with a plumber in it develop, I asked. If it's a West End play, only one way: as a comedy about class. Why is that? What if my plumber has just been diagnosed with terminal cancer? Or if the client, me, has recently been abandoned by his lover? Or what if the leak is coming from the upstairs flat, where the beautiful neighbour with everything to live for will be found dead – her wrists slit – in the bath? Ask yourself: might not a plumber coming to mend a leak uncover a situation of tragic potential? and might he not himself be someone of metaphysical depth?

Holding his head high, he picked a spot above the back row, a poly-styrene ceiling tile, and addressed it intensely.

'*You have to laugh*, my wife used to say. I disagree. Why should British playwrights feel compelled to avert their eyes from the darkness of the human condition? My wife's Northern Irish compatriots are famous for raising a glass among the ruins – the *craic*, they call it, the *craic* of doom.

That's forgivable, even necessary. They at least acknowledge the ruins are there. The pain, the futility, the endless struggle – Beckett acknowledged them, too. Vladimir and Estragon waiting for Godot are like the two tribes of Ulster, Protestant and Catholic, waiting for the deliverance that never comes. "I cried till I laughed" might be Beckett's epitaph. Whereas the complacent hacks of contemporary British theatre want us to laugh till we forget. Theirs is the laughter of oblivion.

'*You have to laugh*. Why do you, when the humour is so feeble, when the only reason to laugh is social pressure? Have you ever noticed how worried people become in the theatre, how disorientated, when the playwright isn't feeding them gags? Oh, and the relief on their faces, the shining eyes, once someone onstage cracks a joke. Under pressure to "entertain", even the best playwrights lose their nerve. Instead of leaving pauses for an audience to *think*, they fill them with pathetic gags. Silence has become the great fear. It used to be broken only by coughs and the rustle of sweet wrappers. Now we break it with fatuity. If there's a hush in the auditorium, the dramatist thinks he's lost the plot, the actors that they've fluffed the line, the punters that they've missed the joke. They haven't. There's no joke to get.'

A laugh from the floor. Why? He wasn't trying to be funny. But this was better. Attention was being paid.

'Of course, a good comic playwright *can* make us ask questions. But at certain points in history, and this is one, humour becomes a form of censorship. Today theatre in Britain is an excuse to indulge in lazy guffaws. Look at any listings page. Note the giggling mobs of exclamation marks: "Hilarious!!!" "Villainously funny!!" "The funniest show in town!!!" The West End is one long gag these days. Gag, meaning a wisecrack, but also a form of restraint. What wisecracks strangle is seriousness and truth.'

To his right, the Principal coughed and tilted her watch at him. But the clock at the back of the room said he still had five minutes.

'This is why our present government is laughing: because we are; because we're doubled up and therefore quiescent – helpless with laughter. Back in 1997, we hoped it would be different. A journalist friend of mine was reminding me only this lunchtime how enthusiastic I'd been when Blair got in. I don't apologise for that. It was a buoyant moment after decades of gloom. And I imagined Blair would be a friend of culture. But the only culture he's been a friend to is scarcely culture at all – second-rate pop musicians and schmaltzy films and giggling plays.

'Current British theatre is a tepid bath of soap and froth. For many years, I taught a writing class here and showed my students a more bracing ocean. "You won't find my name up in lights in the West End," I used to tell them. And thank God, none of them has "enjoyed" "success" of that kind, either. Sour grapes, you might say – Nat Raven's only down on the literary establishment because he and his protégés have been rejected by it. But if I've been bitter in the past, I can assure you I'm bitter no longer. My career as a playwright is over – that's official, and it's fine by me.'

The Principal coughed, more noisily this time. But he wasn't quite done.

'Life as we now live it isn't funny. We've become a nation of dumbos and zombies, faddies and fatties, workaholics and shopaholics, abusers and self-harmers. We kid ourselves we're emotionally literate – that we're truly communicating at last, thanks to mobile phones and emails. But it's an illusion: real intimacy doesn't exist; no one listens; we don't have time for each other – we're all too busy. Even academia, which used to offer a sanctuary for independent thought, has become part of the rat race. In short, life is a nightmare, from which comedy is no escape. Cheer up, people say, it might never happen. But it does happen, it has happened, and we're living with the consequences. *You have to laugh.* No, you don't. It's no laughing matter.'

As he stood down, he felt neither triumph nor failure, merely relief. It was over; he had got through his hour without drying up or falling over; if the applause was ironic, at least no one hissed. The Principal, rounding off, proposed a vote of thanks 'for Dr Raven's highly idiosyncratic account'. Many would want to challenge it, she felt sure, but suggested that questions to him might be better put in private, outside the lecture hall, beyond the college walls, or perhaps not at all. The man from WEIA tossed his bouffant; Brik Pedersson shot a contemptuous parting look; the putative sponsors slipped away. But old students nudged Nat's arm and patted his back, and though Claire couldn't hide her exasperation ('Christ, Nat, you sure know how to shoot yourself in the foot'), once that was off her chest, her chest stayed gratifyingly close. As for Harry, who said his mobile had been switched off all along ('So you lied about the deal, you bastard'), he was rushing off to find Marcia and Stephen – but he knew the restaurant where Claire had booked a large table and would join them later.

Before Nat left, the woman in the side aisle came up, the nice-looking one with the beret, who turned out to be Zillah Sturgeon, the granddaughter of Frederick Reeves Sturgeon and, more to the point, the holder of the cheque, which she handed over, discreetly, in a sealed envelope, adding: 'Thanks for that. It's the first of these memorial lectures I've remotely enjoyed, let alone understood. Will you call me? You'll find my card attached to the cheque. There's something I'd like to discuss.' Nice woman, he thought, but if she thinks that I can help her get her grandfather's essays published, she's barking up the wrong tree.

Outside, in the chill February night, he remembered his mobile going off halfway through the lecture and checked the Call Register for the number. 028-something. The code for Ballymena. Libby's mother Maeve. Was she home from hospital then? Libby must have told her about the lecture. That she had bothered to ring, doubtless to wish him luck, was immensely touching. She would be in bed now, but he'd call her in the morning.

Lucky in his ex-wives. Lucky in his ex-mothers-in-law, too.

'Sorry if I wasn't positive enough for everyone,' he said to Claire, at his elbow.

'Oh, the audience loved it. It's just a pity from your own point of view. With the WEIA deal, the Principal has the funding for a new lectureship in playwriting. MA students only, two days a week and with a decent salary. Right up your street.'

'She'd never have considered me.'

'She was going to invite you to apply. She just needed to know you didn't hate contemporary theatre.'

'Ah.'

Poor Claire. He had blown it for her as well. She had obviously dressed up in hopes of getting off with one of the sponsors.

'You don't hate me,' he said, 'after all the trouble you went to?'

'No, I don't hate you, Nat. I think you're solipsistic, self-destructive and a pain in the arse. But I don't hate you.'


*13*

## *LIBBY*


LIBBY WAS barely through the door before Damian had her wearing an apron. His usual welcome-mat etiquette was to *remove* her clothing, but she shrugged and let him tie the strings. So much could have gone wrong with her various dependents that it seemed a miracle to be there at all. But Nat hadn't kicked up about her missing the lecture. Mother was no worse, so

Patsy said when she called from the hospice. As for Hannah and Rose, they seemed almost pleased when she told them she would be out. How indifferent they had become to her mothering; how accustomed to her being elsewhere.

The meal required no effort and was very English: leek and potato soup; roast duck; fruit salad. She panicked over the bitterness of the orange sauce. But by seven, when the buzzer went, everything was set, even the table. The Cavaliere man – Alfredo – was large, effusive and spoke good English. His wife, Maria, was small, shy and spoke almost none: much of the evening consisted of him translating for her. She was friendly, though. Both of them were. In Libby's experience of Milan, doing deals there and visiting the obvious (the Duomo, La Scala, the big Armani store on Via Manzoni), the Milanese were icily formal. But Alfredo and Maria knew how to enjoy themselves – perhaps because they came from the south. Looking back, next day, she felt appalled at how much she had laughed. But after a month of sickbed duties, laughter was excusable. The champagne broke the ice and became a conversation filler – in Milan Alfredo could buy a decent bottle for twelve euros, whereas here in London . . . While the other three stood admiring the view over the river, Libby moved to the kitchen. The flat being open-plan, this didn't mean leaving the room, just moving to another part of it, up half a dozen stairs.

'Put some music on, darling,' she shouted down, not caring what he chose, so long as it wasn't house or garage. The 'darling' sounded strange on her tongue, but she was in a good mood – the chance meeting with Harry had set it off (she always felt better for seeing him), and the warmth had now rubbed off on Damian. As she stirred the soup to a piece by Bartók, she watched him perform, remembering times when he'd charmed her – the job interview, drinks after work, the night he had knelt and proposed. In recent weeks, away, bereft, she had grown distrustful. But she understood now. He'd been closing a deal. Tonight was part of that but strictly sociable – like a box at the opera or game of golf with a business partner. Not even Damian would be so thrusting as to talk shop.

The phone went while she was snipping chives into the soup. She was about to invite everyone to sit down, and expected Damian to leave it to the answering machine, but he picked up, perhaps worried one of his football friends might leave a raucous message. His back was turned, and the microwave and Bartók were too loud for her to hear what he was saying. 'PE' was all she picked up (one of his friends at the gym?) and 'I'll pass on the message'. When she looked at him interrogatively, he shook his head. The message wasn't significant, then. Or not for her. They sat down to eat. Had it been a girlfriend calling? She set the thought aside and let Alfredo's enthusiasms – for the soup, the ciabatta, the views, Tate Modern and Tony Blair – carry away her suspicions.

'Today we are at the sightseeings,' Alfredo said. 'And finally we are fed up of them. Maria prefers to go to the London theatre.'

'Isn't it hard for her, with no English?' Libby said.

'We go to musicals. Every musical here is foreign, like ourselves. *Les Misérables, Mamma Mia!, The Phantom of the Opera, Chicago, Fame, Bombay Dreams.* What is happened with British theatre?'

'You should ask my husband,' Libby said, and knew from the pause that Damian had told them less about her than he claimed. 'Ex-husband,' she added, to a longer, disapproving-Catholic pause. 'We separated two years ago. He's a teacher and playwright: he could tell you about London theatre. In fact, he's giving a lecture on it as we speak.'

'Ah, a *professore*,' Alfredo said, helping her out.

She felt newly guilty about not being there. But Nat would be saying things she had heard too many times before.

'And you have children?' Maria asked, or Alfredo asked for her.

'Two girls.'

Maria smiled and held up two fingers, then four fingers.

'Maria also has two girls by her first marriage. And with me two more. Always girls, girls. It is no world for men, eh, Damian?'

Damian laughed. They all laughed. Not so strict-Catholic, then. Second helpings of soup were offered and the tensions disappeared.

Even Libby would have conceded that the food made the evening. Not that she took more than odd bites. To her, the attraction of cooking was the freedom it granted her not to eat. But Alfredo found the duck *buonissimo, delizioso, veramente squisito*, and Maria said they must come to Milan very soon, where she would cook them *fettuccine all' Alfredo*. Or so Alfredo (translating) said she said, adding that her *fettuccine all' Alfredo* was famous throughout Italy.

When Damian went to fetch more wine from the fridge Alfredo whispered, 'Great guy, your Damian,' then asked Libby please to tell him about her business.

'Well, we're called Raven McCready. And we set up two and a half years ago. We're still small. But expanding rapidly. A couple of television campaigns got us noticed – Boot Chic, Raanch and FizzCo are among our clients.'

'Ah, FizzCo.'

Yes, FizzCo. Her biggest account, in fact. No thanks to Rikky Falcon. It was only after they fired him that she secured it.

'The London operation is fine. Now we're thinking of opening an office in Paris. And we're definitely setting up in New York.'

'New York – Cavaliere has an office there also.'

'I love New York: waking at five because you're still on English time, and doing a day's work before they're up, and then keeping going. I always come back exhausted.'

'You are having American clients then?'

'Only one or two as yet, but the feedback has been great. So from September we're going to set up a little office downtown. I expect I'll be toing and froing a lot. In fact, I'm quite tempted to go there myself for the first year.'

'I'm against it,' Damian said, resting his hand on hers. 'Libby's better off staying here.'

'As you can hear, I'm encountering some resistance,' she laughed. 'On strictly commercial grounds of course. Seriously, it *is* a hard decision, with me having two children. Plus as Damian may have told you, my mother's been very ill.'

Damian, filling the glasses, put his hand on her shoulder.

'I don't know how Libby does it,' he told the visitors. 'Running a business, keeping her family *and* looking after me. She's amazing.'

'Delegating,' she said, squeezing his hand as it rested there. 'Trusting people. That's the secret.'

By ten thirty, Maria was nodding – not that this made much difference to conversation. Libby was wilting, too, but it was eleven thirty before they called a cab – and after midnight when it arrived.

'So we look forward to catch with you in Milan,' Alfredo said. 'Come and pass a weekend with us soon.'

'We'd love to.'

'Here is my card,' Alfredo said, handing it to Libby. 'Home, work, mobile, all my numbers – you have no pardon.'

He squeezed her hand and kissed both cheeks – an old-world gallant. She felt happy for the first time in weeks and pleased for Damian. Above, the stars were out – a rare sight in Bermondsey. The taxi shivered in the street; Libby shivered too, and tucked her right arm into Damian's left. With their free arms they waved till the cab turned out of sight.

'Come and sit with me, babe,' he said, making for the sofa.

'Not *that* yet,' she said, from the dining table. 'Let's clear up first.'

'No, really. I need to talk.'

'Alfredo's lovely. The deal's in the bag. Relax.'

'It's something else.'

'Something so bad I have to sit down for it?'

'Yes.'

She turned then and saw he wasn't joking.

'Though not unexpected,' he said.

Not unexpected? Now she had finished skivvying for him, he was going to dump her, was that it? He had met someone. Or the someone was pregnant.

He pulled her to him, so her face was over his shoulder, looking at the fridge.

'Your mother passed away.'

So there wasn't someone. Her first sensation – shamefully – was relief.

'What?'

'Your mother passed away.'

'I don't . . .'

'She passed away.'

'When?'

'About seven this evening.'

'But . . .'

'Your sister called.'

'She was going to warn me. If Mum's condition changed.'

'It was very sudden. Some sort of heart attack or blood clot – PE or something, your sister said.'

'Pulmonary embolism.'

'A side effect of the treatment. There was nothing they could do.'

'But didn't she want to speak to me?'

'Your mum?'

'Patsy. When was it she called?'

'This evening. Seven thirtyish.'

'I was here.'

'I know but . . .'

'The phone went. I remember now. We were about to eat.'

'Yes.'

'How did she get your number?'

'From your nanny, I think. Or maybe Nat – she said something about trying his mobile. She couldn't get you on yours.'

'It's at home, recharging. So what did you tell Patsy?'

'I said I was sorry. And that I'd pass on the message.'

'You told her I wasn't here?'

'Implied it. Kind of.'

'Jesus, Damian.'

She yanked away from him and sat, numb, in a chair, fixated by the fridge. There were some magnets stuck on near the top. Child magnets: a cow, a sheep, several piggies. *Babe*. Did he want children? Or think of her as a child? Or was he the child? Baby Damian. Who had lied to her sister.

'So Patsy thought I was out?'

'I said I'd break it to you, rather than you hearing it from her over the phone. She's sleeping at your mother's.' Libby looked at her watch: 12.15 a.m. 'She said to call her any time,' he added.

Patsy was slow to answer, not from sleepiness but the choke of tears. Hearing her, Libby too began to cry, the fact of it – her mother dead – borne in at last because of where her sister was speaking from. She could see it all: the Axminster rug, the table with the watermark, the ancient television, the sideboard with jugs, vases, plates and family photos. The photos included three of Libby – as a baby, in school uniform and marrying Nat. One each of Hannah and Rose as well. The previous weekend they had clamoured to go to Belfast with her, but she put them off, imagining a next time. There would be no next time. She wouldn't see her mum again, though she did now, as her sister talked from the house – in the armchair, a rug over her knees, watching *Brookside*, with a chamois leather wiping windows; putting tea on the table, and Dad washing his hands at the sink, and a girl in pigtails who would grow moody and anorexic but who now – then – is happily eating sausage, bacon, fried egg and baked beans. For a good ten minutes Libby cried with her sister – for the past, for her mother, for herself.

She rang off. Damian pulled her into his arms. They went to bed.

What happened next? Did she weep, sleep, scream, sob, talk, fuck, lie awake to the bass line of Damian's snores? All she could remember, later, was sitting bolt upright at 2.38, the time glowing on Damian's digital radio/CD/alarm clock/address book/electric shaver/Teasmade. She shook him awake.

'Why didn't you tell me?'

'What?'

'About my mother.'

'I did.'

'At the time. When Patsy rang. Why didn't you let me speak to Patsy?'

'I knew it would upset you.'

'Upset! What kind of word is that?'

'I don't know. I haven't lost a parent. Distress, devastate, traumatise, whatever.'

'Yes, all those. But so what? You should have told me.'

'It seemed the wrong moment.'

'When someone dies, there's no right moment. Correction. The right moment is straight away.'

'If we'd been on our own . . .'

'Yes?'

'. . . then I'd have told you. Or passed the phone over.'

'But because we had guests, you decided not to.'

'Yes.'

'You didn't want to spoil the evening.'

'It wasn't that.'

'You knew we'd have to send them away.'

'I knew that with them there you'd be unable to express your grief.'

'Bullshit.'

'If the message had been to come quickly, that would have been different.'

'Would it?'

'Of course. But it was too late to do anything. I thought it could keep.'

'My mother's death could keep?'

'She'd already passed away.'

'Died, Damian.'

'There was no point you rushing over. Your sister said so.'

'That was for to me to decide.'

'Do you think I enjoyed not telling you?'

'I've no idea. I'm totally bewildered.'

'Knowing when you didn't know, having to hold it back and carry on as if nothing had happened – that was hard.'

'Poor baby.'

'What I mean is, I did it for you.'

'For five fucking hours you sit there knowing I've just been orphaned but you don't tell me. How's that serving *my* interests?'

'You were enjoying yourself. I'm sure that's what your mother would have wanted.'

'How do *you* know what she wanted? You're wrong anyway. She'd have wanted me to know.'

'It was pure chance Patsy reached us. We might have been out some-where.'

'But we weren't. You let me chit-chat away, and laugh, and serve dinner, and all the while you knew and I didn't. I'll never forgive you for that.'

'I meant it for the best, babe.'

'Oh, it was best for you, no question. You knew if you told me I'd be distraught and on the first plane home or else I'd collapse and Alfredo and Maria, in the circumstances, would feel obliged to leave. And even suppose they had carried on regardless, which I very much doubt, because they're human beings with ordinary feelings, unlike you, you bastard, the news would have put a bit of a damper on things, wouldn't it, because I'd not be able to dish out the green beans for you, I'd be wailing from the bathroom and in no state for conversation. And of course, you hadn't actually closed the deal yet, not officially, there were no signatures on the contract, and suddenly this woman you wanted to impress them with, because it reflected well on you that she was your lover or fiancée or however you described her to them, suddenly she's a liability, she's the kind of woman whose mother goes and dies at an inconvenient moment, and you don't know how she'll react, if she'll faint or weep buckets or jump out the window, all you do know is that it won't look pretty, that it might be unsettling and off-putting, because in your head Alfredo and Maria aren't nice, ordinary, understanding people, they're business machines, they're automatons, they're fucking cash dispensers, ATMs, and you were so close to milking them, you were almost there, you'd put your card in and were ready to push the buttons, the money was going to come pouring out, and you'd be made for life, but uh-uh, brr-brr, the phone goes and hang on a minute, there's this nightmare happening, you're about to have a hysterical woman on your hands, and once you do what's to stop the cash machine telling you, sorry, it doesn't recognise the code you tapped in and when you try again it still doesn't, three times in all it denies you, before swallowing the card and your future with it. But it's all right, there's a solution, say nothing about the madwoman's mother dying and she'll not seem mad at all – far from it, she'll be an asset, you'll seal the deal, and when your guests have gone at last, and it's quiet, at your own convenience, you can tell her. Phew, what a relief. More than a relief, it's enjoyable, a power game, the ultimate tease, not shamming dead but shamming alive, pretending all's tickety-boo when someone's heart has stopped. The woman you claim to love has just lost her mother. But never mind. No need to let her in on the secret. It can keep.'

'You're upset,' Damian said. 'I'll make you some tea.'

'Tea!' she said. 'You can keep it.'

Those were the last words she spoke to Damian. To be more precise:

though other words were exchanged before she left for home, in a cab, a few minutes later, the last words she spoke to him were 'You can keep it'. As she dressed, she put on her three-monkeys face: not hearing, not seeing, not speaking. The face was one she used when negotiating: in the face of her expressionlessness, clients sometimes panicked and upped the money, even adding a nought. That night, with Damian, as he gabbled and pleaded, the three-monkeys face had a similar function – to stop her weakening. It worked, just. If he had said something heartfelt, about regret and remorse and her being the only one for him, she would have caved in. But he was too busy defending himself. And by the time he did say something, it was too late.

'Don't go, babe,' he said, as she detached his door key from her key ring. 'I love you.'

'Love?' she said, 'You can keep it.'


## 14

## *HARRY*


HARRY FOUND Marcia in the lobby, looking fraught. She had arranged to meet Stephen at home, so as to drive him to the lecture. But he hadn't turned up and wasn't answering his mobile. She waited and waited but then decided, in a fit of self-delusion, that he must have gone ahead without her. It was late by then: she'd only caught the last few minutes of the talk. 'So that's your friend Nat? Bit of a wanker,' she said, as they left the building, adding that, to be fair, she'd been too busy scanning the room for Stephen to take in more than the odd word.

In the wine bar across the road from college, she and Harry took turns on their mobiles. But Stephen's was switched off and he wasn't answering the landline at home. Marcia was for going home anyway, just in case. But Harry persuaded her to stay and eat something: Stephen would be at the cinema or playing basketball; you could hardly blame him for giving the lecture a miss; they mustn't fret. Marcia's trouser suit was a shade of yellow that mirrored Harry's mood – sickly, tense, slightly hysterical. Between fretting with her about Stephen's whereabouts, he was having flashbacks from the trial: Ray breaking down under questioning, little Mia talking about rubbish bins, Luke's eczema, the ice in Sharon's stare. Food arrived: moussaka and salad. As they ate, Marcia asked Harry about the *Gazette*, saying she'd met someone who played golf with Deborah's husband Travis; and Harry asked Marcia about the hospital. But soon enough they circled back to Stephen, whose reaction to the arrest, so she said, had been worryingly indifferent: 'A joyride ain't such a big deal, Mum – the car didn't get damaged or nothing.' Harry said that Stephen had a point and that the police had overreacted – had the driver been white, would they have charged him at all? Marcia said it was nothing to do with race, that Harry was too hung up on that, and what Stephen needed was firmer parenting. She said it with a look at Harry, who made the mistake of taking the bait. You want me to get tough with him, he said. You should have got tough with him years ago, she said, you should have been there for him as a kid. And yet you claim it's since I've been seeing him that he's gone off the rails, Harry said, you can't have it both ways. But she could, or seemed to want to: he knows you were against me having him, she said. No I wasn't, he said. Liar, she said, you'd have liked me to get rid of him, like drowning kittens. Harry ate his moussaka and felt hard done by. They were barely speaking by the time the bill came. When he offered to go back to the house with her to check on Stephen, she declined.

On his way home, he dropped in at the pizza place, as promised. A dozen or so of Nat's ex-students were round the table and he squeezed in and tried to make the best of it. But Nat was holding court and getting drunk. And Harry still felt battered by the day he'd had – Stephen's arrest, the trial, the awkward teatime chat with Libby, and now Marcia's angry accusations.

He left after one drink, as quickly as he could, still brooding about what Marcia had said: *you'd have liked me to get rid of him, like drowning kittens.* It chimed with something said at the trial. In time perhaps it would clarify – like brown water from an unused bathtap running clean.

## 15

## *JACK*

'ARE YOU all right?' Elise said, sometime later.

'No,' Jack said. 'Not *all right*, bloody marvellous. It's funny how you forget.'

Had he forgotten? Or never known? With Nancy sex had been different. Pretty damn good, as it would have had to be for the marriage to last, but not like this, the blood singing in his ears and every cell dancing.

'Not disappointed, then?'

'Do I sound it?'

'Or guilty?'

He paused, thinking of Nancy mashed in her urn and Harris with his flu. 'No.'

'Good. Me neither.'

They threaded fingers, and he thought how odd this was, lying in bed with a woman he'd known for years but whose body he hadn't touched till half an hour ago. Her skirt and blouse were in the kitchen, her underwear lay at the foot of the bed. But it was dark under the duvet and though her skin was warm against him he had no idea what she looked like naked. When passing headlights lit the bedroom wall only her face showed.

'Christ,' he said, sitting up. 'What time is it? Your sodding taxi.'

'It's all right. I told them not to come till midnight.'

He slid down again and pulled her head on to his collarbone.

'How clever of you,' he said.

'It wasn't some cunning plan to seduce you. I just didn't feel like rushing back.'

'So long as Harris isn't suspicious.'

'Why would he be? I don't make a habit of this.'

'Of course not.'

'I wanted to talk, that's all.'

'Well, we are talking.'

'A nice way to talk.'

'The best.'

He kissed her eyes.

'Was it so obvious?' he said.

'That you fancied me? No, I wasn't sure. And vice versa?'

'Not in a million years. You could have your pick of lovers. What chance did old Jack have?'

'Less of the old.'

'But I am old,' he said. 'Older than you anyway.'

'It's a state of mind.'

'Bollocks. There's the body too.'

'Yours seems to work all right.'

'I can't do all the things I used to.'

'Such as?'

'Today, with the MP, I only rode for an hour, but now I'm aching.'

'Where?' she said, rubbing. 'Here?'

'Mmm.'

While she massaged his neck and shoulders, he recounted occasions they had been at, and what she had worn or said or done there. It surprised him how much came back. The Askews' Christmas party, two months before – she had been wearing a sapphire Chinese jacket and drinking Campari by the mantelpiece ('Not Campari, cranberry juice.' 'Oh sure.'). The Golf Club Family Day, the summer after Nancy's stroke – they were standing together outside the clubhouse when Harris overshot the 18th ('His ball bounced right past us into the car park.' 'Out of bounds – it lost him the competition.' 'You had check trousers and a grey zip jacket, and you turned and smiled at me, as though you enjoyed seeing him screw up.' 'I knew you were enjoying it too.'). Ischia's twenty-first, the night of the summer hailstorm – in the dozen yards between the marquee and the house they'd both been soaked ('Your hair was stuck to your brow and your silver dress was wet against your breasts and your eyes were bright and you were laughing'). The school quiz, the gymkhana, the harvest supper, old Ollie Alabaster the chemist's funeral, each occasion an occasion with their spouses around but now those spouses were being edited out. The beach at Southwold, the tennis fund-raiser, Jack's fiftieth – the longer Elise massaged him, the further back the memories went, far far before Nancy's stroke.

'I never realised till now,' he said. 'I was watching you but I didn't notice myself watching. Some part of me knew but the rest of me couldn't admit it. Does that make sense?'

'Perfect sense. I like it when you talk, Jack.'

'I like it when *you* talk.'

'Though we don't *just* have to talk,' she said, sliding below the duvet. Then, 'See. Told you. You're not old.'


*16*


*HARRY*


IN THE taxi on the way home, Harry scribbled in his notebook.

'Kid Runt' – Mia's phrase about Errol.

Lots of talk about him whining and crying and being punished. 'Got the devil in him.' 'He's a little beast.'

Ray and Sharon argue. Ray leaves in a temper. Errol miserable. Sharon – end of tether? – locks him in his room.

Mia reports seeing Errol outside, by the bins. Says he got out through the front door, which she and Emmalou left open. But *what if Errol never came out at all?*

He must have come out: bloodstains were found.

No, the bloodstains could have been from him falling off the bike the week before.

If he didn't come out, he would have been locked in his room.

Unless he was upstairs with Sharon. In the bath.

Panic. Errol lost. Louis comes home.

Search of area. Or disposal of body?

Marcia: 'like drowning kittens'.

Useless, he thought, I've drunk too much, I can't make sense of this at all.


## *17*

## *ANTHEA*


Hi again, Nat

You'll think me mad – two emails in a day when I've sent you only one in the past six months. But the office is empty this afternoon, because my boss, Marmalade-Sky (I know, I think it's ridiculous too, but she's Californian) is out running a training course, so it's a good time to write.

I know you must still be wondering why I left you like I did. That's simple. From cowardice. I wasn't trying to be cruel, I just wanted to get away. I tried to tell you, to give you notice, to explain that I was suffocating. But you never listened, and in the end all I could do was run away – hide out at my mother's for a few days before crashing at Rachel's sister's flat in Glasgow. If you'd known where I was, you'd have come to fetch me, and I'd have been weak enough to let you. But I knew I had to start a new life. And the only way was to disappear.

Now I'm here in Seattle, working for a charity called GoHelp. The volunteers who work for it are supposed to have skills that will 'offer succour' in the Third World. Skills? I've only goodwill to offer, in return for which a) I receive free bed and board but no pay, and b) after a 'short' induction programme I'm to be posted to wherever my talents are most needed. Seattle's a good place to work, and most of the people at GoHelp are OK, with lofty ideals and modest egos. But Marmalade-Sky is the exception: she's so far in flight from the values of her hippie parents that she's fanatical about her 'team' keeping 9–5 hours, despite us all being unpaid. And her regime is making us all increasingly snappish – with daily disputes over coffee rotas and paper-clip supplies, and the sense of victimhood that comes of helping victims.

I know I shouldn't complain. People say hi when I arrive each morning. And I do my best to rub along with GoHelp's Christian ethos, as typified by the poster which Marmalade-Sky has stuck above her workstation – 'He who goes weeping into the wilderness, carrying seed to sow, will return bearing sheaves of joy.' When I do finally go into the wilderness, I'm sure it will be worth it. Calcutta, Ramallah, Srebenica, Beirut, Baghdad, Freetown or Kabul? I don't know yet and I don't much care – so long as I can be useful.

It's just, it's just . . . the Marmalade-Sky problem. She now claims that the induction programme isn't always that 'short' after all. That 'some people' – i.e. me – take longer to train than others. ('Training', I should point out, means learning to make camomile tea to Ms M-S's liking.) And she says that visas and permits can sometimes take months to come through. So it seems I'm stuck here for some time yet – unless I take matters in my own hands. I've been wondering about joining the Red Cross or Medecins Sans Frontières – it seems you don't have to be a doctor or nurse to work for them. And I've also made contacts with people in the occupied territories, so I may yet get to Palestine, somewhere (as you know) that I've always wanted to go.

So that's my news. How are things with you? Not too bad, I trust, though I see that you've an outbreak of foot-and-mouth disease. I don't expect it will affect you in south London. But it will be devastating for the farms round my mum's village in the Lake District. It's the way we treat animals that's caused the disease, of course: penning them in and feeding them extracts of themselves, etc. Forgive me for banging on, but until people in the West learn to accept that other creatures on the planet have rights, not least human creatures in Iraq or Palestine or Afghanistan, then we're fucked. It's no coincidence that the methods the US and Israel use against 'terrorists' and other undesirables (i.e. non-whites) are the same ones commonly applied with animals: we hunt them, cage them, beat, bully and torture them, then destroy them by making them eat shit.

Sorry, I'll shut up now. It's nearly six here, two in the morning your time, and I ought to go. I'll write again when I've sorted out my future, maybe. Don't worry about me. I may seem all over the place but I know what I want to do, and I will get there in the end.

Yours ever, Anthea (Ant)

xx

## 18

### NAT

THE PIZZA place was in Rotherhithe, Nat knew that much. And he could remember the envelope burning a hole in his pocket and Claire saying, as he opened it, 'I was trying to tell you earlier – because it's an endowed lecture, the cheque's for £750,' and him thinking, wow, that will help pay off my rent arrears. Or had he imagined the whole thing? There were ten of his ex-students there, and his pizza was a Neapolitana, and later Harry turned up. But he lost track long before dessert, conscious only of Claire, full-brimmed and in touching distance at his side. Who drove him home he had no idea, but he could hear anxious voices on the car radio talking of pigs and exclusion zones and Essex abattoirs. Back at the flat he thought of checking his emails, which he hadn't done for weeks, but it was late and he felt tired and after taking all his clothes off (how?) he climbed into bed, where warm sensations of reparation overtook him. Later, in the darkness, he dreamed that Anthea had come back, and heard a tap running and a floorboard creak and the base of a tumbler going down on the bedside table, and then he rolled over and touched flesh and knew he was awake and not alone.

## 19

## *HARRY*

THE LIGHT was blinking on Harry's answering machine when he got in. Two blinks. Two messages.

The first was from was from Luke. Could Harry call him when he got in, no matter how late. Big development. If he was quick about it, he might have a scoop.

The other message was from Marcia. Stephen was fine – he'd been to the cinema, just as Harry said. She was sorry about earlier: put it down to stress. Stephen would like to talk to him. If he was back before midnight, could he give him a call.

He looked at his watch. One forty-five. Sod it.

He called Stephen.

## 20

## *LIBBY*

LIBBY HAD the idea indecently quickly, before she reached the pavement under Damian's flat. But it was too late to call him at 3 a.m. And next morning, between packing bags, getting the girls ready and organising transport, she'd no time to try the Savoy. In the end, she got him at Heathrow.

'Alfredo?'

'Yes.'

'It's Libby.'

'Libby! What a pleasing surprise. Where are you?'

'Getting on a plane.'

'We also.'

'That's what I thought.'

They were at the same airport but at different terminals, he and Maria checking in for Milan, she in the transit lounge for Belfast. Hannah and Rose sat reading Harry Potter.

'I'm calling to say how nice it was to meet you both,' she said. 'And to wish you a good flight. But also to say – I'm sure Damian will tell you this but I wanted to tell you myself – that unfortunately my mother died last night; that lovely idea of us getting together in Italy might have to wait a while, I'm afraid. It's a terrible shock, of course, but she had been diagnosed with cancer, so we were expecting it and at least she'd been spared any more agony. I'm sorry – I don't mean to unburden myself like this. But we got on so well last night that I thought you should know.'

Alfredo said how sorry he was. She explained the funeral customs in Northern Ireland, or her tribe of it.

'I also thought I'd better call you,' she said, 'in case you got the wrong idea about Damian. He might have seemed under strain last night.'

'He seemed fine.'

'Good. That's reassuring. It's just – if he was a little odd and distracted, I wouldn't like you to think he's normally that way.'

'He is a great guy.'

'He is. He is. And you see his motives were the very best: he didn't want to upset me – or you and Maria.'

'Sorry, I am not understanding, Libby.'

'No, it's me who should be sorry for not explaining properly. Do you remember when the phone rang, just after you arrived? That was my sister, to tell me the news about my mother. But Damian decided it would ruin the evening to tell me, so he saved it for after you'd gone.'

'I see. He knew but . . .'

'It was sweet of him to try to protect me like that.'

'Yes. Though if I am wearing Damian's shoes I think . . .'

'If it had been you, you'd have told me, of course, and I admit I'm also a little confused and hurt by Damian's behaviour. But as I say, I do realise deep down that he meant well. It's only because he's young he makes these kinds of misjudgements. Not in his work, of course – I'm sure he makes none there. Nothing matters more to Damian than his work. Me, I'm different, family has always come first. It's part of the reason I still have a very good relationship with my ex-husband. Because – I'm sure you understand this – our separation went against my whole faith, and, however hurt I felt, I knew it was crucial we stay close for the sake of the children. Forgive me, I'm rambling – it's just I don't want you to form a harsh impression of Damian

443

just because I, in my grief, feel angry and betrayed by him. If I can manage to forgive him, if our relationship survives this, I'm going to try to help him mature, to give him a sense of values beyond work. If he hadn't had such a disturbed and difficult upbringing, I'm sure he'd not have these problems. It's only the legacy of that. And the misplaced enthusiasm of youth.'

'You are very kind to him.'

'I've tried to be understanding. Whether I can still be, in future, I don't know. Something like this destroys all trust. And trust is important in *all* relationships, at work as well as home. Anyway, I had better get my flight now – my sister and I are going to sit with my mother's body tonight.'

'Thank you for your calling, Libby. Let us be talking again when you are stronger.'

'That's kind. It may take a while. And the way I'm feeling at present it may not be the four of us like last night. But you can always get my number from Damian.'

'It is named Raven McCready, your company?'

'Yes.'

'Well, I can find you. I will not need to concern Damian.'

'No, but I expect you'll be seeing a lot of him, once the deal goes through.'

'*If*, Libby. We have some conversations to make at head office. I cannot say the decision is certain.'

'No, of course. And I'm rather sorry I didn't make a pitch for your business, but with my mother being so ill I wasn't in a position to do so. Anyway, do call me sometime. That would cheer me up.'

'Maria and I offer our, how do you say in English?'

'Deepest sympathies, the English say.'

'Our deepest sympathies.'

'Sorry for your trouble, we say in Ireland.'

'Sorry for your trouble.'

Sorry for the loss of her mother. And sorry for being involved with a shit like Damian.

It was a gamble. But not much of one. By the time she got back to work, she was confident there'd be a handwritten letter reiterating Alfredo and Maria's 'profoundest sorrows' and adding, in a PS, that because of an 'unforesighted difficulty' the deal with Arran & Arran had fallen through and would she, when she had a moment, please give him a call.

# 'Riding with the Dogs of War'

a speech by Rufus Huish to his constituency

Friends, party members, gentlemen of the press, I'm delighted to see so many people here this evening. I'm told some of you are listening to this in an annexe, because the hall is full, a fact I attribute not to my own celebrity – or as my opponents would have it, notoriety [*laughter*] – but to the vibrancy of the party under Tony Blair's current leadership. At a time when the electorates of Western Europe are said to have lost interest in politics, it's good to know the democratic process is alive and kicking in my own constituency. And I'm sure that bodes well for the next election – though please don't ask me when that will be: even if I did know the date, I wouldn't dare to reveal it with the media here [*laughter*].

I am here tonight to talk about fox-hunting, a subject close to my heart. I dare say that many of you will have seen a recent photograph purporting to show me riding with the Harchope & Nelles hunt in East Anglia earlier this year. Those of you who did will also have read the accompanying headline: MP'S SECRET RIDE OF SHAME. Some of my opponents in Parliament have interpreted my silence on the matter until now as an admission of guilt. They accuse me of consorting with the pro-hunt lobby, an accusation which I find more than a touch ironic, coming as it does from the party which during its eighteen years in power granted country landowners and sportsmen every privilege imaginable to man. But never mind. I concede my opponents are in one respect perfectly correct. Let me say it loud and clear. I did indeed go riding with the Harchope & Nelles. [*Cry of 'Shame' from the floor.*] Quite so. I dare say in your place I would feel the same. But before you shout me down, and before the journalist there at the back of the room taking notes rushes off to file an exclusive – yes, you, sir – I should explain that this is no confession. My excursion with the horses and hounds was strictly a one-off. [*Cry of 'That's what they all say'. Laughter.*] I wasn't there for fun, but for the purposes of research. [*Groans and jeers.*] Scoff all you like. This is how I have always practised politics, by rolling up my sleeves, getting down to brass tacks, and finding things out for myself. When a constituent of mine complains of being paid less than the minimum wage, then I will make an impromptu visit to his employer to check it out. If a bill is being drafted to give working mothers here the same rights enjoyed by working mothers in Denmark, then I will visit Copenhagen to determine whether the Danish system really works. You can't leave it to other people to make up your mind for you. You go and see. At least I do. And I make no apologies for that. It's the least any MP owes the people who voted for him. [*Stirrings of approval.*]

Thus it was that I took up riding a year or so ago with the express purpose of finding out about hunting. (You can follow a fox hunt on foot, or in a car, but from that safe distance you can't experience what goes on at first hand.) Three times a week for over six months I rode in Hyde Park, escaping the pressure cooker of Westminster in order to master the essentials of horsemanship – and though I say it myself, I got pretty good at it. In due course, a friend of a friend secured me an invitation to ride with Harchope & Nelles. Repelled though I was by the thought of persecuting an innocent animal, I felt duty-bound not to forgo the opportunity.

So I admit it. That photo of me out hunting was perfectly genuine. (Indeed, it may amuse you to hear that, far from faking it, the hapless snapper responsible, a Mr Dan Dichio, was able to attain his shot only by clambering up and concealing himself in the branches of a large oak-tree, from which he later had to be rescued by the local fire brigade.) The camera didn't lie, then. But if you take a careful look at my features in the photo [*projection of offending tabloid's front page on overhead screen*], you will find no trace in them of the slightest pleasure or blood-lust. Truth to tell, I was unable to complete my day out with the hounds. A mere hour and I'd had enough. So sickened was I by the brutal killing of a fox (a vixen), I immediately turned for home. It was a long, lonely trek back, but I had seen as much as I could bear.

A fox which knows that it is beaten is the saddest sight in the world. In that moment it sees that all its strength, intelligence and courage aren't enough, and it turns towards the pack with an eye of dark despair, ready to be torn to pieces. The fox we had pursued that morning had outwitted the hounds for three miles or more. But after an hour or so, it – she – was utterly worn out, and, seeing there was no escape, succumbed with quiet dignity to her fate. As she did, she seemed to catch my eye and hold it. I have seen that look twice before: once, in the eyes of a prisoner on death row, a young black man in Oklahoma who had shot dead his abusive stepfather and for this faced the electric chair; the other time, on the face of Bambi, in the Disney film, when he thinks he hears his mother calling and joyously runs towards her – only to discover, with a look of horror, the hunter who has just shot his mother dead. [*Pause – lump in throat.*] I confess I cried when I saw that film in the cinema. And I was close to crying again when I looked upon that vixen and watched her meet my pitying stare. It was as if in that moment she was electing me as the one person in that bloodthirsty throng who might be her saviour. (*OTT?*) And though I couldn't save her life, I promised myself in that moment that I would speak for her in death. And so, this evening, I will do so – and thereby explain to you why I shall be supporting Michael Foster's bill to outlaw fox-hunting, when it is put before Parliament. [*Applause.*]

Most of us are dimly aware of the case for fox-hunting, but few have heard it put by hunters themselves. I hope it will not sound like boasting if I say that I have. Over supper with my elderly host, and in the pub, the Dog & Duck, to which we afterwards adjourned, I heard several 'good men and true' put forward, as articulately as a hefty intake of real ale and malt whisky allowed [*laughter*], their considered reasons for retaining the right to brutalise foxes. Some were a little red in the face, others (from being swathed in too many layers of tweed, perhaps) positively hot-headed. But from their lips there did issue arguments of a sort, and it's only fair that I address them.

*1 Death by hunting causes the fox less pain than do other methods*

In the Dog & Duck I heard one heather-faced squire seriously contend that a fox does not suffer *at all* when torn to bits. But anyone who has ever stood on the tail of a pet dog or cat, and heard it cry out, knows that animals feel pain just as humans do. Old Heather-face added that the fox enjoys the thrill of the chase, much as, I suppose, an Albanian Muslim flushed from a ruined outbuilding in Kosovo by the Serbian Army might do. [*Is ethnic detail correct?*] The idea is obscene. Yes, other methods of killing foxes are unpleasant, too. But nothing is as calcula-tedly cruel as hunting. It was William Blake who wrote: 'Each outcry of the hunted Hare / A fibre from the brain does tear.' To which I'd want to add, if an MP can wax poetical for once: 'Each whimper from a wounded fox / The pity in man's heart unlocks.'

## 2 Hunting builds character

Presumably when people say this – and plenty do, both down at the Dog & Duck and up at the Big House – they mean the character of the hunter, since the character of their prey isn't built but totally demolished, along with its body. But as far as I can see, the only human character traits nurtured by hunting are entirely negative ones: cruelty, aggression and arrogance. We have enough of these traits already without encouraging them through field sports. [*Applause*]

## 3 Hunting is fun: only spoilsports oppose it

'The thrill of the chase', a phrase I heard more than once from the lips of my squirearchical host, implies that hunting is exciting and unpredictable. In fact, foxes are murdered in cold blood, after a premeditated ritual of chasing, stalking and ambush. No fun for the fox, then, and it can only be fun for the hunter if he enjoys torturing and killing, which, sad to say, my bumptious host clearly did – I'm thinking not only of his pleasure in seeing that vixen die, but of his dismay when he saw that I lacked a riding whip and of the haste with which he then supplied one, urging me to thrash my poor horse half to death.

If those of us against hunting are killjoys, so be it. Rather a killjoy than a killer. [*Applause.*]

## 4 Hunting is an activity which brings together all the social classes

Coming from men and women who earn upwards of £100,000 a year, this is, as they say, a bit rich. To be fair, I heard the argument put forward at the Dog & Duck as fervently as at the Big House. But only brainwashed country bumpkins (*too strong?*) could seriously believe it. The cost of buying a good horse these days is at least £10,000; of stabling, feeding and equipping it, another £5,000 a year; of buying the appropriate riding gear and of belonging to the hunt, another £2,000. Do these sound like sums which the average man or woman in Britain can readily afford? As for the contribution which hunting makes to the rural economy, the kennelman I interviewed – the man whose job it is to keep the hounds fit for his Masters – said he was paid starvation wages and could barely afford the modest clothes he stood up in.

The hunt as a democratic institution? Tosh.

## 5 Fox-hunting is one of the last great English traditions

This is the ultimate justification for hunting, and at the Dog & Duck they argue it with passion. Look at the paintings of horsemen in red jackets, they say, and the hunting horns hanging in pubs, and the iconography (all right, they don't actually use the word 'iconography') of the fox pursued by hounds: here is a sport – more than a sport, a whole culture – which the English gave to the world. How tragic it would be if that culture were to disappear.

Personally, I find it odd that the birth of Jesus should be commemorated each year on Christmas cards adorned with men in scarlet coats riding their horses through snow. But in any case fox-hunting isn't quite so English as its advocates believe. The practice of riding with hounds began in ancient Greece. And the authentically English cry of 'Tally-ho' is French in origin. No, the best way to show the world that we are truly English – tolerant, enlightened, humane – would be to abolish this barbarous practice forthwith and consign fox-hunting to the annals of folklore. [*Applause.*]

To sum up. The men who defend fox-hunting are so horsy they might as well be centaurs [*laughter*], and not one of their arguments carries any weight. If they want to hunt, let them go drag-hunting, a method which ensures a good run for hounds and riders, and which eliminates both the dreary 'blank day' (when no fox is found) and the bloody conclusion (when it is). The kennelman I talked to could see no objection to drag-hunting; indeed he rather looked forward to its inception. Why waste one's time pursuing foxes on horseback when there are many more efficient ways of controlling their numbers?

Ladies and gentlemen, I have a dream tonight. A dream of trust between people and animals. A dream of the blood-sodden fields of England becoming a haven of peace. A dream of the lion lying down with the lamb and of men and women coexisting happily beside foxes. Only when that dream is realised, through a total ban on hunting, will I find the nerve to look that vixen in the eye.

Thank you. [*Finish. Applause. Quickly leave platform, but then, as standing ovation continues, return several times to take bow?*]


ANDREW: *Here's a draft of the speech for Tuesday – I know the tabloids have been baying for my blood but this riposte will soon bury the story, I'm sure you'll agree. I've indicated in brackets how the audience will probably be responding at various points, though of course you never* know with live audiences (would it be worth arranging for one or two 'plants' to respond as indicated?). If you think the tone needs adjusting here and there to get my point across (am I being oversubtle?), do let me know. There are also a couple of queries – I'd appreciate you checking these out for me. By all means suggest cuts: you know how feeble people's attention spans can be, especially in local constituencies outside London.

It's strong stuff, and has to be, in the circs, but as regards libel, etc., I don't see any problems. A distant school friend of mine helped set things up for me, but I don't think he needs to see this. And the chap at whose house I stayed looked on his last legs to me – I doubt he'll cause us any trouble.

Naturally, it's vital you keep the text to yourself: if it leaks out to the press beforehand, it may lose impact. But by all means run it past the chief. I don't want to be off-message.

# Part 5

## *Deborah's Party*

4 May 2002

## *ANTHEA*

THEY CAME for her shortly after six. Wear bright clothes, she had told them, that's what I'll be doing, and she was – blue jeans, white trainers, yellow sweater, green jacket, short hair tucked under a red baseball cap. The colours were a form of body armour, along with the armband. She sat next to Herman in the front seat, with a dozing Georgie in the back. An oatmeal dustscape stretched to a washed-out sky, making her get-up look even more lurid. If people back home could see her, they would take the piss: Anthea the saviour, in her technicolour dreamcoat. So what. She had a job to do.

At HQ they quickly filled four food sacks, with medical supplies as well as food. Beit Mila wasn't far, but the traffic would be slow through town and if they were stopped they'd have some explaining to do. Best move fast. The day was already hotting up. You load the jeep, she told Herman, while Georgie and I get the paperwork. She was surprised by her own bossiness. But Herman and Georgie were new to this, and Adam, their chief, wasn't around. Someone had to take charge.

Their task was to get food into Beit Mila. Since Jenin, and now the siege in Bethlehem, the hours of curfew had been extended and the people were short of supplies. Beit Mila might be no worse off than other villages. The difference was that Anthea knew the place. Her first posting, a year ago, had been at the school there, giving English lessons to children of five and six – not the kind of placement she had in mind when signing up but more useful and enjoyable than the current one, in Admin, logging 'incidents' on the database and sticking red flags in the office map. If Adam had his way, that's all she would be doing today. But she was through with being dutiful. Next year she would be his age, thirty. It was time she stood up for herself.

Straight on here, she told Herman. On the office map, the road to Nablus was packed with red flags. But there was a dirt track before the roadblock, which swung off right then circled back. They would be fine.

A convoy of tanks went by. Georgie, nervous, leaned forward and clutched

Anthea's arm. She was twenty-two, straight out of Melbourne University, and hadn't yet learned how things worked here. We'll be fine, Anthea said, playing mother and stroking Georgie's hand.

She didn't feel fine. Last night, they'd all been drinking at the American bar, and her head was still fuzzy. Before she arrived from Seattle, she had imagined a life of altruistic self-denial – no drink, no sex, no drugs, no parties, no fun of any kind. How naive was that. Drink and sex went with the territory. Some aid workers – Adam, for instance – seemed to think of nothing else. You couldn't blame them. At quiet times, there was boredom to relieve. And now, every day, there was a death or two, the only cure for which was booze or bed. Usually the first led to the second, with a bout of braggadocio in between. Adam was the worst. He liked to hold forth about his adventures, or his friends' adventures, in Bosnia, Cambodia and Rwanda. And always some girl would be sitting there as he talked, fresh off the plane, wide-eyed at the tales of flying bullets, machetes, mass graves, disembowellings and saline drips – and later this girl would go off with Adam, back to his room, as if the smell of carnage made him irresistible or as if she owed him this, the present of her body, because of the suffering that he (or his friends) had witnessed. Last night Anthea had dragged Georgie away, before she made the same mistake. Anthea had made it herself, when she first arrived: but for a call from her mother, in Keswick, to ask how she was, she would surely have ended up in bed with him. Perhaps if she *had* slept with Adam he would have given her more of a break. She had fought him, time and again, for the chance to do more interesting work. But as her boss and protector, he had slapped her down: too dangerous for a newcomer, too physically demanding for a woman, too diplomatically sensitive for an aid worker, etc. It was Marmalade-Sky all over again. Fuck Adam. He had been here only nine months longer than Anthea had. Sure, as team leader of the East Jerusalem division, he was one up on mere operatives like her. But he wasn't a doctor or lawyer. And his behaviour was getting wackier by the week. He was now consumed with envy of the ISM (International Solidarity Movement), for out-manoeuvring the IDF (Israeli Defence Force) by delivering food sacks to the Palestinians inside the Church of the Nativity in Bethlehem and thereby attracting the attention of the world's press. 'It should have been us, we'd have done it better,' he said. People were beginning to talk about Adam, to say he'd lost it. If he carried on like this much longer, the reputation of WAWWAW (Western Aid Workers Working for the Alleviation of War) would be destroyed.

456

WAWWAW, ISM, IDF, MSF, IRC, DCO, UPMRC, UNRWA, UDC, IWPS, PRCS. Not to mention AK-47s, M-16s, 4WDs and APCs. It's a war of initials, Anthea thought, as the jeep headed through the morning. I don't know what half of them stand for and Adam thinks only one of them counts.

Poor Adam. She mustn't be nasty about him, just because he had a goatee beard and felt competitive with other charities. He was a good man, a Mormon. Maybe that's what explained the womanising: if he had stayed home in Salt Lake City, he might have ten wives by now. Maybe it explained his jealousy of the ISM people, too: the Church of the Nativity was allegedly built on the site of Jesus's birthplace, which made it sacred to someone like Adam, the driving force in whose life, aside from women and beer and guilt trips, was his childhood fundamentalism. If only he weren't such a pompous prick. (Above his desk was the same poster that Marmalade-Sky used to have above *her* desk in Seattle: 'He who goes weeping into the wilderness, carrying seed to sow, will return bearing sheaves of joy.') If only he weren't so patronising and misogynistic. If only he would trust his staff more. Last night, at the bar, Anthea had tried to outline her plans for today; strictly speaking, she needed Adam's approval to go ahead. Perhaps it was as well he hadn't been listening ('Yeh, yeh, you're leaving at 6 a.m., whatever. As I was saying about the siege . . .'). If he had taken in what she was telling him, they wouldn't now be crackling along a dirt track to Beit Mila.

There was no danger. Otherwise, she would not have asked Georgie to come. Nor Herman, who was Swedish and ice cool and wore a head-band over his long blond hair, like that old tennis player, Björn Borg, but who had hardly spoken since they left and, for all Anthea knew, might be terrified.

A dust cloud marked their progress. As they passed the last fields before the village, she warned Herman and Georgie what to expect: soldiers, and more soldiers, some civil, others not; endless questions, some to elicit infor-mation, others merely insulting; gunfire, some of it genuine (but with luck not aimed at you), some of it faked, since the army often set up loud-speakers and played tapes as intimidation.

Georgie looked thoughtful and sipped a Diet Coke. The day was hot now, the last of the mist burned off, and the side of her can was moist with sweat beads.

At the edge of Beit Mila, two bulldozers sat silent in a meadow of rubble. An electricity pole listed at an angle, improbably intact. Hanin, at whose house Anthea was staying, had a cousin who lived here. It was through him that they had heard how bad things were, under the curfew. There's no way in and no way out, he'd told Hanin from a borrowed cellphone, kids are going hungry and there's no medicine for the old. Anthea thought of her infant class. She hadn't much liked teaching but she had loved her charges – Ali, Mahmud, Abu, Adhaf, Isa, Samar – who followed her around so doggedly she felt like Mary Poppins. They too were a reason she'd come today.

Where the dirt track ran out to become the main street, the road was blocked with a bank of red earth and coils of barbed wire. CLOSED: MILITARY AREA, the sign said. She was prepared for this – but not for the checkpoint not to be manned. Perhaps the army had called off the curfew. Or the soldiers were in the middle of changing sentry shifts. Whatever the reason, there was no one to stop them passing through.

Let's go for it, she said.

They went for it, unloading the sacks from the jeep, lifting the barbed wire for each other in turn, and stepping through its diamond.

There were three sacks, one each, like bulging Santa bags, roped to stop the contents spilling out and too heavy to carry for more than a few yards at a time. After a while, where the ground evened out, she put hers down and dragged it along the street, hoping the rubble wouldn't tear it open. She should have thought to bring gloves – the scratchy hessian cut into her hands and her scalp under the baseball hat felt itchy. Her left foot was hurting, too: a little stone must have got in there. While Herman and Georgie paused for breath, she unlaced the trainer and tried to shake it out.

Most of the houses had holes in them the size of melons – the fruit of stray tank shells. Was everyone dead? Or asleep? Or too afraid to come out?

A window opened above their heads. For a second she thought Sniper and prepared to duck. But then a woman's face appeared, frowning, and an arm, gesturing ahead, down the street and turn right. Down the street and turn right was the tiny health centre, as Anthea knew – it was there she planned to take the sacks. She nodded at the woman and made a thumbs-up sign, OK, I understand, with her free hand.

You'd hadn't the power to stop the army occupying villages. But nor had they the right to stop you bringing aid.

Well, they could stop you. Normally they did stop you. But today was different. The tanks and soldiers were gone. It was a breeze.

OK, Georgie? OK, Herman?

Sure, fine. How much further?

Just fifty yards or so. Round this corner and we're home and dry.

But round the corner they saw two soldiers, on patrol outside the health centre, and beyond them, at the far side of the square, a tank. Now she realised why the woman in the high window had been gesturing – not to tell her where to go, but to warn her what she would find.

It wasn't too late to abort the mission and head back to the jeep. She could tell Herman and Georgie it had become too risky – by the look of them, they would be glad of the excuse. But she had expected soldiers. This wasn't the moment to lose her nerve.

What helped her stay calm was the thought of Hanin, who had got up specially early today to make breakfast: figs, oranges, pitta bread, honey, coffee in gold-rimmed cups. Hanin had lost several relations in recent years, including her husband – 'a good man,' she said, 'not a terrorist'. His death had left a space in more ways than one: Anthea slept in what used to be the children's bed, while the children, Noor and Neta, slept with their mother. In exchange for a room, Anthea taught them English and offered support. That was the idea anyway. This morning it had been them supporting Anthea. Over breakfast, she'd sat watching *The Simpsons* with the girls. The coffee, the television, the kids having their hair brushed for school, while Hanin fussed around them in a flowery nightgown – the ordinariness had calmed her nerves.

She could do with something to calm them now.

From across the square, the loudspeakers started up, not with gunfire but music – Eric Clapton singing 'I Shot the Sheriff'. She felt like an actor in a cowboy Western, the good guy come to rescue the other good guys, whose wagon train was surrounded by bad guys. The dust, the heat, the beaten-up streets, the guns – it was just the same.

*Sheriff John Brown always hated me / Why I don't know.*

The last time she'd heard the song was at the council Christmas party, in Woolwich. There'd been a weird moment when she thought Mr Fell might ask her to dance. What would he think, seeing her now?

The two soldiers had spotted her and were walking over. The good thing was they weren't carrying machine guns. The bad thing was they did have smoke canisters. If they used them, the smoke would block the square off from the rest of the village and any tank could open fire, unwitnessed. But surely no tank would fire on aid workers.

Let's put the sacks down, she said, in case they think we're suicide bombers.

A stupid thing to say. If the soldiers thought that, they would be dead by now. Their clothes marked them out as Westerners, and their armbands as aid workers. The soldiers could be under no illusions.

Except the illusion of their generals, that peace could come through war.

If Hanin's cousin owned a cellphone, they could have avoided this – been told which backstreets to take, via which alleys. In modern conflict, cellphones were indispensable. You could text the press or give online interviews in the middle of a siege, as the ISM were doing from that church in Bethlehem. Anthea, Georgie and Herman were all carrying cellphones. But there was no one useful they could call except Adam. And if they called Adam, he would scream abuse and order them to withdraw.

The two soldiers were carrying guns. They were young, still teenagers by the look of them. The taller one had acne, the other eyes the colour of the figs. The eyes were on her, as the woman in charge.

What were they doing? he asked.

They were bringing aid, Anthea said.

Had they not seen the signs prohibiting entry to the village?

They had seen them but this was a humanitarian mission.

*Humanitarian?* Phaw. So what was in the sacks?

Food.

What kind of food?

Water, rice, lentils, biscuits, olives, bread, powdered milk.

Nothing else?

Only medicine.

Not guns or bombs?

Of course not. The soldiers were welcome to check.

The fig-eyed soldier nodded at the acned soldier, who ripped the top of one of the bags open. Grains of rice gushed into the dust.

The people in the village were starving, Anthea said. Without food they would die.

The soldier begged to differ. In Beit Mila there was food in abundance, he said – cheese, pitta bread, tins of halva, cans of hummus, kilos of coffee. What the army would give for such a feast.

It was untrue, Anthea said. The villagers had been barricaded in for over a fortnight. Many had run out of supplies.

There were lemon trees by the church, the soldier said. Let them eat lemons.

*Lemons?* How were men supposed to live off lemons?

The men deserved no better, the soldier said. They were bandits, militiamen, bombers.

No, they were innocent people caught up in war.

In war no one is innocent, the soldier said, smiling at his own wit.

The loudspeaker died away. But Anthea's ears were still thrumming. Noise was the norm here – percussion grenades, helicopter gunships, spotter planes, bulldozers, tanks. Even weddings had gunfire – bullets shot to heaven to toast the bride and groom.

The fig-eyed soldier offered Anthea a cigarette. She didn't smoke but took one all the same. Her foot hurt from the stone and her hairline ran with sweat. Down the street, the door of the health centre opened from inside. A head peered round it. The three sacks sat just feet away. There was sufficient rice and lentils in there to keep a small village going for a week.

What was her name? the fig-eyed soldier asked.

Anthea. And his?

He was Daniel, the youngest of three brothers. After one more year of military service he would be off to college. His girlfriend, Anya, was at college already. They went to the cinema a lot. He played basketball and liked Hemingway's novels. What about her: where was she from?

England, Britain, the UK.

Why come to Israel?

To help, she said.

Is that what you call it? he said. His eyes were flirtatious, as though this was a nightclub not a war zone. Helping the enemy, you mean.

I'm a neutral, she said, I don't take sides.

*I* would never interfere in another country's business, he said.

I'm not interfering, she said, I'm bringing aid.

You and your friends only make trouble, he said.

As he gestured towards Georgie and Herman, a man stepped out of the health centre, picked up one of the sacks and dragged it inside. Either the soldiers hadn't noticed or they didn't care.

You people, Daniel said. You activists.

*Activists.* If only he knew how passive Anthea was, or used to be, or had been until today.

My commander has a name for you, he said. Terror-tourists.

Over his shoulder, across the square, Anthea heard a jeep start up. Military reinforcements, perhaps. She wished the people outside the health centre would hurry up and take the other sacks inside.

Terror-tourists, she said, blowing her cigarette smoke at his. That's ridiculous.

Daniel shrugged. He has a whole list for you. Guilt trippers. War vultures. Bleeding hearts.

And what do you think? she said.

The second and third sacks disappeared behind his back, as the jeep approached across the square.

I think you should be careful, Daniel said, seeing the jeep. Then, more in appeal than as a threat: It's dangerous here.

She was tempted to make a run for the health centre. It would be dark and cool in there. There was still time before the jeep pulled up.

I'm sure you'll protect me, she said, looking Daniel in the eye.

But the cigarette was finished. He could see trouble coming and had lost his nerve.

This was a war fought by kids, she realised. The soldiers were kids. The suicide bombers were kids. The aid workers were kids. Kids did the killing and kids cleaned up the mess. All kids. Except her – she was twenty-nine now and almost grown-up.

The jeep pulled up in two dust clouds. Four soldiers leapt out, one with stripes.

It's OK, she said, joining Herman and Georgie. More questions, that's all. Nothing to worry about.

She remembered her first month here, by the end of which, half disappointed, she had begun to think the predicted crisis would never arise. One night she lay in bed listening to boys play football in the street below. She was reading David Grossman's *The Yellow Wind*, an old paperback Adam had lent her. Or trying to read it: each thud of the football against the house made the walls of her bedroom shake. She opened the window and looked out. There must have been thirty boys in the street, some as young as five, one with BECKHAM on his back. In the next house a woman was singing love songs. The score mounted and the love songs drifted through the wall long past curfew, but no mother appeared to call her son away, and the soldiers, if there were soldiers, kept their distance. A moon came up over the aerials on the flat roofs. The boys, the dust, the rising moon, the love songs, the thud of the ball made life seem almost normal – till three men were shot dead at a roadblock next morning, and a suicide bomber blew up twenty teenagers in a disco, and the tanks and bulldozers moved in. How she missed that moment now, the idyll before the killings. How foolish to have wished it away.

462

There were still times she couldn't believe that she was here – that it wasn't just a movie. But she was a stronger person now. She had learned stuff. Rachel would be proud of her. Mr Fell would be proud of her. Even Old Nod might be proud of her, now she was helping people not trees. But she didn't like the look of the soldiers jumping from the jeep.

Let them do their worst, she thought. I'm wearing my armband, they'll not dare harm me. But she wished they would put their rifles down.

She opened her arms and spread her palms in a Jesus gesture: I'm a woman of peace, I work for WAWWAW, I've come carrying seed to sow and will return bearing sheaves of joy. But the soldier with the stripes was angry, shouting at Daniel and his cohort, waving them away down the street. And the other three soldiers, far from putting their guns down, raised them to their shoulders, like a firing squad.

She spread her arms again to show she had no weapons. She was innocent. But in war no one is innocent.

Sweat dripped from her brow like blood. Jesus on the cross, she thought. Anthea in the cross hairs. Nice juxtaposition of images. Nat would go for that. But he wouldn't like the rest of it. Being one-sixteenth Jewish or whatever it was, he had always been defensive about Israel. A blundering naïf, he'd call her. You would have done better to stay in England with me, my love.

It's all right, she whispered to the others, who had copied her gesture of submission. They know we're aid workers.

The sun beat down as the three of them hung there, in surrender. It was so silent, you could hear a trigger move.

Then her cellphone went off. Maybe Adam, at the office, wondering where they were. But after his skinful last night, Adam would still be in bed. More likely her mother, with her usual immaculate timing. Hi, Mum, yes, I'm fine, oh the usual, bit tied up at present, I'm standing in the cross hairs of three rifles, but hey, don't let that stop you.

The soldiers stared, daring her to answer. If she did, they might suspect a trick, so she let it ring. It occurred to her that she was following Bella's vocation at last – Anthea the drama queen, performing on the world stage.

After eight rings, the phone fell silent. Her mother, it had to be. Remember the time she called in the middle of sex with Nat?

The soldier with stripes nodded at his underlings, who laid their rifles down and fumbled with the handles. All was OK, just as she had promised Herman and Georgie. They were going to be questioned, nothing more.

Three sets of handcuffs appeared from the hollow of the rifle handles. You are in breach of regulations, the striped one said as his men stepped forward with the handcuffs. Come with me.

2

*JACK*

'SLEEP WELL?' Libby said.

'Like a log.'

It wasn't true. Street shouts had woken him at two, car tyres at four, and ticking radiators at six. But this was London. Quiet wasn't what you came for.

The basement kitchen was a shade of marine. A tropical fish tank sat on a shelf above the microwave. He felt at sea, in unknown waters. The last time he'd been in London was, oh, what, a decade ago, to see *Cats*, more Nancy's kind of show than his but a damn sight more enjoyable than the other one, even earlier, about the boy who stabs horses in the eye, nasty twisted stuff, a refund would have been in order, the play had a Latin title, they'd been expecting a musical set in ancient Rome, like the Sondheim. Coming to London had been a pleasure till then. Ever since he associated it with random violence. Walking round yesterday, he had been wary of every passing kid, as though they might be carrying blades.

'Make room for Uncle Jack, girls,' Libby said, and he slipped between them, with his back to the window. Light slanted down from the garden, christening the cutlery, the cafetière, the silver top on the marmalade jar.

'Toast? Cereal? Yogurt?'

'Whatever's going,' he said, though the chocolatey balls the girls were eating (which turned the milk in their bowls the shade of squitters) didn't much appeal. Coco Puffs, Chocolate Weetos, chocolate Pop-Tarts: you saw them piled up in supermarkets. What a sweet-toothed nation the English had become. Feminine influence maybe. It wasn't John Bull now, but Jane Bee.

'I'll put more toast on,' Libby said, and while he waited he made conversation with the girls: what their hobbies were, who their friends, which subjects they liked at school. Blue eyes and blonde hair, not a trace of

Libby's green and auburn; their father must be the predominant gene. Yet they seemed polite, unpampered, robust. These days adults handled kids like ancient Ming vases, as though one tiny knock might shatter them. Libby didn't stand for such nonsense.

She brought his toast: two thick slices of cracked wheat, lightly singed, just the ticket.

Hannah had a textbook beside her.

'Homework?' he asked.

'She's in her first year at secondary school, aren't you, sweetie?' Libby said.

'Which school is that?'

The name meant nothing to him.

'A girls' grammar school,' Libby explained.

'I thought grammar schools had been abolished,' Jack said.

'There are a couple, not far away. She had to sit an entrance exam to get in.'

'That's well done, Hannah,' Jack said, then added, teasingly, 'I hope you enjoy being at an all-girls school.'

'I want to go there, too,' Rose said. 'Boys are messy.'

'No, they're not,' Hannah said.

'They are. *Daddy* is.'

'Isn't.'

'Is.'

'Enough of your silliness,' Libby said. 'Plates in the dishwasher and do your homework, while I talk to Uncle Jack.'

He caught the gleam of knife blades from the dishwasher, before the door banged shut and the girls clattered upstairs.

'How *is* Nat?' Jack asked.

'He's fine,' Libby said, rather tersely, he thought. 'You can talk to him later. When I drop off the girls.'

Talking to Nat wasn't part of Jack's plan. But nor, till Libby phoned, was staying in London. She had phoned to see how he was, a catch-up courtesy call, but then he admitted he was 'due down on some private business', on a Friday as it happened, which was why she invited him to stay the weekend, and he, under pressure, accepted. Now staying the weekend had turned out to involve going to a party on the Saturday, i.e. tonight, at which he was bound to feel a spare part.

'So how did it go?' she said. 'Your private business?'

She was wearing jeans and a tight black T-shirt. Last night, when he

465

arrived, it had been a trouser suit. He felt an old codger in his cords and lambswool jumper – the poor relation up from the country.

'Fine, he said, 'all things considered.'

'I don't mean to pry.'

'It's just rather boring.'

'Boring's fine,' she said. 'Rather boring than bad.'

Maybe the second thing *was* bad. He felt safer with the first.

'I had two bits of business, actually. One was my pension.'

'Ah.'

It took some explaining. Though a businesswoman, she wasn't very interested in pensions. Nor had he been, till recently. The whole point of a pension was to stick your money in each month and forget about it till you retired. And the Equitable, everyone knew, was safe as houses – as dependable as death itself. Only after Nancy's death did he notice the stories in the *Telegraph*. The problem was the Equitable's GARs – 'guaranteed annuity rates' he spelt out for Libby, whose eyes were already glazing over – which it could no longer afford to pay. If I were you, I'd get your money out while you can, Harris had told him over a year ago. Good advice. But Jack had hung on, in the hope his nest egg would somehow be restored. More fool him.

'Can't you still get out?' Libby asked.

'At a price. Stay or go, either way I lose out. I was conned. We all were. The chap I saw yesterday admitted as much.'

The chap had worked with the Equitable before setting up as an independent financial adviser. That was the point of going to see him – not for the hard sell but for an inside view of the cock-up. According to him – swivelling in his buttoned leather chair – the board had known they were in trouble years ago. But they'd hidden the truth from the regulators and told whoppers to ordinary members like Jack.

'The chap compared it to the South Sea Bubble,' Jack said.

Libby yawned and poured herself more coffee.

'See,' he said, 'I warned you you'd be bored.'

'How much have you lost, then?'

'Put it this way. I planned to retire this year. Now I can't afford to.'

Everyone he knew felt insecure these days – and it wasn't just because of 9/11. Lloyds, Barings, Equitable Life: the old dependables were no longer to be depended on. A lowly carnivore, strong on cunning, could bring down a giant. Or else the giants brought down themselves. He should have seen the disaster coming.

*Equus*; that was the name of that twisted play, the one about the boy blinding horses.

'I'll cut back my hours,' Jack said, 'but I can't stop working altogether.'

'Couldn't you sell the house?'

'It's already on the market.'

'Must be worth a bit.'

'Less than you'd think.'

He had noticed the prices in her local estate agent's. Modest semis were going for half a million. And this wasn't an affluent part of London.

'If I buy a small flat in Harchope, I can fund my old age. But I'd hoped to leave the girls something.'

'Sasha and Ischia have good jobs. They'll be fine.'

'Of course. But it's the principle.'

'Are you and Uncle Jack talking about money?' Rose said, from the doorway. Hannah was behind her, with a maths book in her hand.

'Homework problem?' Libby said. 'I'm sure Uncle Jack could help you.'

'Sums aren't my strong point,' he said, 'but let's see.'

Hannah put the book in front of him. It was long division, 128 into 2843418, something he could manage, but when he tried to show her ('times the first number till it's close to the first three digits of the second number and put what's left underneath and . . .') she said it was all right, she remembered now, and anyway Mr Brack, their maths teacher, did long division a different way.

Rose was watching from Libby's knee.

'Why is Daddy poor, Mummy?' she said.

'He isn't, sweetie – he has a car, a flat, food to eat, that's not poor.'

'He always takes us to Pizza Hut, not Pizza Express. And he won't buy large milk shakes, only medium.'

'It's not Daddy's fault, my hon. Society doesn't reward teachers.'

'What's society?'

'People like us.'

'But we *want* Daddy to have money,' Rose reasoned. 'Anyway, Miss Birch who teaches Year Six has a Saab convertible.'

'Maybe her boyfriend's rich.'

'Kiera Clifford says she's a lesbian.'

'How do you know about lesbians?' Libby said.

'Everyone does, Mummy. I'm not a baby.'

'I wish you were. Now shoo, both of you.'

'Sorry about that,' Libby said. 'They must seem very streetwise to you.'

'Oh, it's the same in Frixley,' he said. 'At least your girls don't carry knives with them.'

'Well, I assume they don't.'

'That's the latest thing, round our way. Ten-year-olds taking knives to school for "protection". Or to vandalise cars on the way home. It'll be toddlers with handguns next. But don't get me on to that subject. I'm becoming a crusty old sod.'

'You're not crusty, Jack. It's lovely to have you.'

She was trying to be nice. But he felt crusty, with broken veins on his nose and clumps of hair in his ears and 'It wasn't like this in the old days' on his lips. Yesterday afternoon, on the way to see the pension chap, he had been pleasantly surprised by the wholesomeness of Soho. There were tables on pavements, and ordinary, decent-looking people eating and drinking al fresco. But by evening, after he stopped for a drink at the Pillars of Hercules, the place was full of teenagers puking on pavements and pissing against walls and touching each other up in public, and this at seven thirty, before it was dark, and if you looked or commented you would be the one at fault for sticking your nose in and who could say what the affronted party might do.

It was homely here, in Libby's kitchen, yet he felt precarious still, in strange waters, netted by troubling obsessions. Equitable. *Equus*. Inequity. Iniquity.

'What was the other thing?' she said.

'Sorry?'

'Yesterday. Your second bit of business.'

'Oh, that. Do you mind if I just use your whatsit?'

'First on the left. I thought we'd go for a walk in a minute.'

'Sounds good to me.'

Business wasn't the word for the other business. He had come to see a man about his body, more specifically his penis, though the word he used to Libby, in Greenwich Park, was 'waterworks'. The sun was out and the chestnut in bloom; it felt wrong to be discussing his ailments. But they were on their own now, the girls having been dropped at Nat's. And Libby was a sympathetic listener.

'Your waterworks?'

'I've a prostate problem.'

'Um, I remember my dad did.'

'We old chaps do.'

An avenue of elms stretched ahead of them. The straightness seemed very un-English – perhaps the park had been laid out by a Frenchman. He remembered the plane trees, neat as cemeteries, in northern France, the year he had driven to Paris and back in the MGB. In 1968, that was. The year of the 'events', though for Nancy and him the only event was her pregnancy. She sat there next him, with her bump, humming tunes by Piaf and Chevalier.

'So when did you first notice?'

'Oh, a few months ago.'

Well over a year ago, if he was honest. The symptoms were unignorable: wanting to pee at frequent intervals (particularly at night) but always struggling to produce something and having produced (a drizzle, a dribble, a driplet) feeling the urge to try again almost at once. It was like milking a cow when you didn't know how, a straining at the udder of oneself to no effect. Over time he almost forgot how different things had once been, in his heyday of flow and slash. It was a hint of pink that finally prompted him to call his GP. Nothing to worry about, Dr Bruin said, enlarged prostates were common in men over sixty and usually benign. He was sent for a check at the hospital nonetheless. The check became a series of tests (PSA, DRE, ultrasound probe, biopsy, IVP), none conclusive but each more sinister than the last. It wasn't the needles Jack minded, or the anaesthetics, but the rush of abbreviations, only two of which he understood: was he BPH (benign prostatic hyperplasia) or PCa (prostate cancer)? It was the head of the urology department, Mr (would you believe it?) Flowell, who confirmed the latter.

'God, Jack,' Libby said, 'not cancer?'

From the asphalt courts came the sound of two Englishmen playing tennis. Pock, *sorry*. Pock, *sorry*. Pock, pock, pock, *sorry*.

She laid her hand on his arm. Her mother had died of cancer last year. He ought to have kept his mouth shut.

'It's not as bad as it sounds,' he said. 'Nothing too virulent. This Flowell chap doesn't see the point of surgery.'

*WW* was his abbreviation for it: *watchful waiting*. Rather than operate, or pump Jack with drugs, they'd keep an eye on him. And he on it.

'You haven't thought of getting a second opinion?'

'Damn right. That's why I came yesterday, to see the prostate specialist at Guy's, Dr Epstein. Top man in the country, apparently.'

'And?'

'And the good news,' he said, sparing her the Gleason score, lymph node test, Partin tables, ECE assessment and the rest, 'is that he sees no need to operate, either. Odds are something else will kill me before the prostate does.'

For men his age, Dr Epstein had said, 'with a life expectancy of ten to fifteen years', the treatment was often worse than the disease.

'They just leave it as it is?' Libby said.

'They give me pills, and have me in every six months, and with luck I'll live to be ninety.'

He was putting a positive spin on it, as the doctors had done, and omitting all mention of side effects. With luck he would be fine, Dr Epstein said, but 'libidinal dysfunction' was a risk: not wanting to, not being able to, and mind-boggling stuff such as backwards ejaculation. Oddly enough, it was after that night with Elise that he began to acknowledge the problem. Not that he failed to perform for her. Or attributed the discomfort afterwards to an infection passed on from Harris. Or regarded his pain as symbolic – a punishment for sleeping with another chap's wife. But his penis seemed less private suddenly. He needed to know it was in order.

'Must have been worrying all the same,' Libby said, making him sit on a bench, as though the matter were too serious to consider standing up. A coach party of girls walked by – bare midriffs, jewelled navels, jeans so low-waisted you half expected to see pubic hair. Below, in a loop of the Thames, lay the old naval college and, opposite, Canary Wharf.

'It concentrates the mind all right,' Jack said. 'Makes you realise you've only so long. *Carpe diem*.'

Seeing those planes fly into the Twin Towers – towers like the ones across the river – had had a similar effect.

'Nat's always saying *carpe diem*,' Libby said, 'though all he's done with his life is sit on his bum. Oh, and be unfaithful. But I don't call that seizing the day.'

'Bad business,' Jack said.

He had seen Nat when they dropped the girls off, looking indecently well. There was an invitation for Jack to go round later to watch the Cup Final with him, 'Arsenal v Chelsea, should be a good match', but Jack had decided to pass. Not only had he no interest in football, he had yet to forgive Nat for the business with Huish, that treacherous shit of an MP, whom he, Jack, had entertained so royally, only for Huish to come out against hunting (in his weaselly speech, reported in *The Times*, he even got the name of Frixley's pub wrong, though that was the least of his lies and distortions). Jack had moaned about it last night to Libby, who claimed, with unwarranted loyalty, that Nat was blameless – he might not approve of hunting, but he thought Huish 'out of order' and had written him a stiff letter. If that was true, Jack ought be civil to Nat. But it was difficult to be civil to a twerp.

All the women walking by wore small leather rucksacks, Jack noticed – backpacks had taken over from handbags. Oh, and half the people here drove 4x4s, and wore hiking boots, and ate outdoors, on wooden decking, under kerosene lamps. London had become a city of campers.

'We're getting on better since the divorce came through,' Libby said.

'No fun being a single mother, though.'

'I do OK.'

'No new chap on the horizon?'

'I was seeing someone. Not any more.'

'Pity.'

'I was mad to have got into it in the first place. How about you?'

'Me?'

'Yes, Jack, *you*. Why not?'

'I'll ask you to the wedding when it happens.'

How could he tell her about Elise? What was there to tell? After that night, at his house, all his instinct had been to see her again, right away. As the man, the onus was on him to call her, but what would he say if Harris answered? And if it mattered enough, surely she could have called him – he was the one who lived alone. Eventually, he did call and they met for a walk by the coast – his favourite walk, the one he had taken the day of Nancy's stroke. Perhaps the memory put a damper on things. She wasn't cold with him – away from onlookers, they held hands by the shushing sea, while the dog nosed the bladderwrack on the shingle. But to kiss her seemed a dangerous presumption – he imagined her pulling away with a 'Jack, dear, whatever are you thinking of?' and him, crushed, muttering apologies. He talked about work, steering clear of intimacy, intimate though they had been. She grumbled about Harris and his golf, but teasingly, as a long-suffering wife might, not as a would-be divorcee. Two hours passed. In the car park, saying goodbye, they kissed – with a tenderness that brought their night back, enough for him to say, 'You will come again? To the house?' She smiled – 'Of course. Soon. I'll call.' – and drove away. No drunken lapse, then; it had meant something to her, too. But it was weeks before she did call, and then only to ask him to supper with the Askews. In bitter moments, too many whiskies down him, he felt betrayed. Suppose she had slept with him that once out of pity. Or that, despite what she said at the time, the sex had left her cold. Or having learned the habit of infidelity, she had moved on: Harris's friends were always making passes, she'd said, and perhaps she no longer resisted them. He spent dark nights imagining that. But then he'd be out somewhere, at a Rotary function or idiot fete, and there she would be, smiling, touching his arm, pressing into him when no one was looking, to let him know she hadn't forgotten, that this was a secret they shared, unerasable, and who could say what the future held.

Who could say what the future held or if he had one.

A Japanese couple approached with a mobile phone and asked could Libby take a photo. The phone as camera: whatever next? He watched her struggling to work it out. Forty, Irish, his nephew's ex-wife – there was no reason to feel this fond of her. Still, fond though he was, he couldn't bring himself to talk about Elise. What if Libby, wronged spouse as she was, identified with Harris?

'All these lovey-dovey couples,' she said, rejoining him on the bench. 'Must be the spring air.'

'I can't imagine being half of a couple again,' Jack said. 'I'm too used to my own company. And too old to change.'

That's what he had learned from Elise. Neither could face the disruption. He was too comfortable with his life, and she too comfortable with hers.

'But you *are* changing,' Libby said. 'Thinking of moving house. Cutting back on work. Giving yourself more space.'

'It doesn't mean I'm looking for someone.'

'Maybe you'll meet them tonight. We might both get lucky.'

'If I go at all.'

'You are going, no argument. Deborah's lovely. You'll have fun.'

'OK. But only if you let me buy you lunch. There must be restaurants near here.'

'There are. Down by the river. Let's go.'

They rose from the bench, and she slipped her arm in his, as a wife or lover might. As they left the kissing gate below the Observatory, past the tourists waiting to be photographed (their bodies bisected by the meridian line), he imagined time, which began here, beginning for him, with his body clock at five past rather than five to, and all his achievements still to come. To the faces bobbing past him up the hill, he must look a shrunken and silvered old man. But for a few minutes, dropping towards the river, he forgot his prostate fears and pension worries and knife terrors, and dreamed of an undiminished Jack Raven, man of business and MFH, soul of the party and king of the chase, Nancy's stud and Elise's stallion, fire-breather and earth-pounder, ready for the off.

## 3

## *HARRY*

'LET'S GO to Gloria on line one: what's your issue, Gloria?'

'That last caller, Jerome I think his name was, says the Queen is a waste of space. That's plain disrespectful.'

'So what's the Queen ever done for you and me, Gloria?'

'I met her once at the opening of a hostel in Honiton. Saw her anyways: I was one of the catering staff, serving teas. Lovely smile she had. This Golden Jubilee should be a time to honour her, not gripe.'

'Fair enough, Gloria. Queen Liz gets off her bum occasionally. But what about the rest of the family? Why subsidise *them*?'

'Prince Charles – I served him tea once, too. Very polite. I remember he . . .'

'That's great, Gloria,' Kwame said, making slit-throats at the producer to phase her out. 'I'm going to bring in my studio guest here. Harry?'

'Yes. Hi, Gloria. Gloria?'

'I think we've lost her,' Kwame said. 'You go on.'

'Well, I'm sure Gloria's love of royalty is deep and genuine. But I notice she said she worked in the service industry. And that's true of most black people in Britain. We're the ones doing the low-grade jobs – as caterers, cleaners, security guards, and so forth. That's the legacy of slavery. And of course the monarchy is inextricably bound up with colonialism. I've nothing against the Queen, you understand, I wish her well with the Jubilee celebrations. But I see where our previous caller was coming from. I've met a lot of young guys like him, who feel completely disconnected from the institutions of this country – not just the monarchy, but the law, the teaching profession, the civil service, the media and, above all, the government.'

'OK,' Kwame said, 'keep those calls coming. After the break we'll be discussing the BNP victory up in Lancashire: could it happen in London? And from the world of showbiz: is J-Lo getting too big for her butt? You're listening to *Rapback*, on 103.9 FM, with me Kwame Agyebane and my regular Saturday guest Harry Creed.'

Harry took his headphones off. It was 4.29 and they would be off air for the next three minutes, for news, weather, travel and sport. On most radio stations, Saturday afternoon was a graveyard spot. But the listening figures for *Rapback* were impressive. And Kwame had made a name for himself as a presenter – chiefly by being rude to those who called in.

'Recognise Gloria?' said Kwame, who was wearing a yellow silk robe over his T-shirt, and whose beaded hair fell in neat locks, five to the right, six to the left. That he looked – and sometimes sounded – like a tribal leader was an image 103.9 FM had carefully cultivated: King Kwame, emperor of phone-ins. His face appeared on the back of London buses. *Rapback*, the Talk Show with a Difference – King Kwame Dares You to Call.

'Why would I recognise her?' Harry said.

'She was on last week. Called herself Hortense then. We were discussing Blair's foreign policy and you were saying, you know, shit, the guy's a bigger warmonger than Churchill, and she came on with that same phrase, *plain disrespectful*. I mean, fuck, who says *plain disrespectful* any more?'

The station had imposed a ban on the word *fuck*, outside of song lyrics – a five-second time-lapse meant any phoned-in expletive could be beeped out before transmission. But Kwame was off air. And even on air, *diss*, *butt* and *shit* were allowable. This was *Rapback*, after all.

'I'm no good with headphones on,' Harry said. 'If my best friend called in, I wouldn't know.'

'I tell you, man, it was her.'

No talk-show host had a better knowledge of his listeners. The *nutters*, Kwame called them, not without affection.

'It's 1–0 to Arsenal, by the way,' Kwame said. 'You interested in football?'

'I used to be.'

'Before I ruined your Saturdays.'

'Before you ruined my Saturdays, yeh.'

It had been several months now, ever since the big piece came out. Harry used to dismiss ethnic media outlets as ghettoising. But 103.9 FM boasted good listening figures – not far behind Capital and Heart. Kiss FM was ethnic, too, of course, but 103.9 FM was more than a music station. And *Rapback* was its flagship.

Kwame put his headphones back on and gestured for Harry to do the same: the producer, Diran, sitting behind the glass screen, alerted them to waiting calls.

'We've one about the Jenin refugee camp. Happy to take that?'

'How is the Israeli Army a black issue?' Kwame said.

'It's an issue for Muslims,' Diran said. 'The caller's a Mohammed.'

'OK, sure. If there's time after the BNP.'

'Then we'll do light for the last five, up to the hour. And let Harry go home.'

Harry didn't do light. He was there as the brain – the Saturday complement to Kwame's cheeky populism, which went unchecked through the rest of the week. 'The sage Harry Creed,' Kwame sometimes introduced him as, tongue-in-cheek, '*Rapback*'s secular vicar.' Before him there *had* been a vicar, a Reverend Kolu from the Church of Seventh-Day Adventists, whose views on crime and abortion made Kwame look a wishy-washy liberal. The vicar resented being dumped and sometimes called in to make trouble. The £100 weekly fee meant little to Harry but it had made a lot of difference to the Reverend.

'OK, we're going to Derek on line three,' Kwame said.

'It's about the National Front winning seats,' the voice said.

'British National Party, they call themselves these days, you'll find, Derek.'

'Whatever. If that means they got MPs, then they're in London already, innit. At Westminster.'

'These were local elections, Derek. All they have is a few local councillors in Burnley. But go on.'

'Well, it's spreading like a disease.'

'Racism, you mean?'

'Before Blair was in charge, when we had people like Barbara Castle, God rest her soul, we didn't have these problems. Not where I live in the East End.'

'Your point being, Derek?'

Derek didn't have a point, not one that could be put briefly or with anything even faintly resembling coherence, so after baiting him for a while Kwame cut Derek off and brought in Harry, who said, well, yes, Derek was right to be worried, East End, Oswald Mosley, stoked-up fear of Jews, blacks, refugees, asylum seekers, etc., the BNP was small but growing, and this week's local election results were a wake-up call, OK, it was mid-term, you couldn't read too much into it, but a 34 per cent turnout showed how apathetic the British electorate had become, and as Derek rightly said in the heyday of Barbara Castle, whose death yesterday he, Harry, was sad

475

to read about, too, there'd been much more passion in politics and it would be good to get some of that passion back.

I must be tired, Harry thought, I'm as rambly as Derek.

On line two, Dolcis said Derek was right, that the BNP were already in London in the sense that racism pervaded institutions like the Met, and black men were being criminalised.

'Harry knows this better than anyone,' she added. 'I read his long article about Ray Nuard.'

'But hey, Dolcis,' Kwame said, 'some of these black men *are* criminals. The Met have a job to do, right?'

'But kids like my teenage brother get hassled for doing nothing.'

'So,' Kwame said, 'are a minority of young Afro-Caribbean men ruining things for the rest of us? Or do we blame the Met? Stay with us, Dolcis, I'll be coming to Harry for his comments in a second. First to the Millennium Stadium, where there's been a second goal in the Cup Final. Luther?'

Kwame raised his eyes at Harry, as though to say: *You must be sick of this Ray Nuard shit.* Harry smiled back to confirm it: *You're right, man, I totally am.* But it was a lie. That the calls were still coming proved his piece had struck a chord. He was here as an authority, Kwame Agyebane's cerebral stooge.

'So – back to crime. Harry?'

He made a few obvious points, tiredly, tamely, before Dolcis broke in.

'Can I ask you something?' she said. 'You followed the case from the start. You believed Ray was innocent – you even thought, like we all did, little Errol might be still alive. So how upsetting was it to see him dead? You never wrote about that.'

There was so much he hadn't written about: his whereabouts when they found the body (in a lecture theatre listening to Nat); his delayed response to the message from Luke on his answering machine (he spent two hours talking to Stephen first); his irritation when he finally spoke to Luke (meet at the *Dome*? at four in the morning? why?); his wry pleasure on entering the building, which he'd never visited during the year when it was open as a theme park. Once inside, Luke had led him down a set of concrete steps, under sputtering fluorescent tubes. A subterranean corridor ran out in the direction of the Thames, and at the far end two policemen stood guarding a makeshift barrier. Behind them, men in white overalls were working with tape measures and paintbrushes. In the dim light, they looked like spacemen.

'The forensics,' Luke whispered. 'See that ventilation grille?'

The corridor opened out into an oblong pump room, along the outer wall of which, every few yards, were metal grilles. One of the grilles had been completely removed, exposing a square hole in the breeze blocks.

'That's where they found the body. Errol's. Or we assume Errol's. Less a body than maggots and bones.'

'So . . .'

'The remains are at the morgue, for DNA tests. But what was left of his clothes match the description.'

'So how did he . . . ?'

'We don't know yet. The drain behind the grilles runs out to a sluice gate – if the tide was high enough the body might have floated in, from the Thames. But more likely he was brought here and dumped.'

'In which case . . .'

'Exactly. Ray wouldn't have had access to the Dome. Whereas Louis worked here as a security guard.'

'So . . .'

'Louis's already being questioned. Sharon, too. The trial will be stopped, whatever, while they establish cause of death. And once we know, those fuckers for the Crown will have to eat shit.'

In the bowels of the Dome, watching white-overalled spacemen sift the dust of a lost child, Harry was still struggling to catch up.

'So how . . . ?'

'Pure chance. A health and safety check. The whole area was once toxic and there's a huge ventilation shaft coming up from the Blackwall Tunnel. No one had ever bothered removing the grilles. But some busybody from Greenwich Council insisted. And noticed what looked like a sack in one of the river hatches. And asked his assistant to pull it out. But for him Ray would be serving a life sentence.'

'He might still serve one.'

'Nah. Ray's innocent. Like I always said.'

None of this conversation was included in Harry's piece – though he told the story of the fussy bureaucrat, an environmental health officer called Mr Fell, and his assistant, Alison Halifax, and how their vigilance had altered the course of Ray Nuard's trial which, as Luke predicted, was halted – and then collapsed.

'I read your article several times,' Dolcis said, on line two.

'Which took some doing, eh, Dolcis,' Kwame said, 'that was one mother of a piece.'

'Yeh, well, I did,' Dolcis said, 'and it's good and all, but I still don't know who you think killed Errol.'

'That's *sub judice*,' Harry said, 'till the new trial.'

'But it had to be Louis done it, right?'

'Dolcis,' Kwame said, 'can't you hear the man? He's not allowed to say.'

'All my piece tried to do,' Harry said, 'was highlight the flaws in the original investigation. The things we all missed.'

He had missed them himself. And though the drunken scrawl in his notebook pointed the way towards a solution, without the discovery of Errol's body Ray would have surely been convicted. The body was badly decomposed, but tests established that the liquid inside what remained of the lungs wasn't river water but bathwater. Though it was still theoretically possible for Ray to have abducted Errol, taken him home, drowned him, then disposed of his body in the Thames, all the evidence pointed to Sharon and Louis.

'We have a new caller,' Kwame said. 'Mohammed on line four. You're angry about Israel's mistreatment of Palestinians, and you think it's to do with hatred of Islam, right?'

'That's right, Kwame. But first, can I just ask Harry, is it true what I've been reading in the papers that Louis and Sharon blame each other?'

Kwame raised his eyebrows again: why the fuck could people talk of nothing else? But he valued his ratings too much to pull the plug.

'We'll have to wait for the trial to know the full story,' Harry said, 'but yes, there's no secret about that, they do.'

At separate police stations, through three days of questioning, Sharon and Louis had slowly changed their version of events. Sharon said that Louis had strangled Errol, having always hated him as 'a devil child'. Louis said he had found Errol lying suffocated in Sharon's bed. Confronted with the evidence that Errol had drowned, possibly in the bath, Sharon said that Mia and Emmalou had done it by accident, and Louis said that Sharon had done it deliberately – but that to protect her he had smuggled the body into the Dome in his cricket bag (once a useful batsman, he still turned out for a Sunday pub team in Beckenham). Louis blamed Sharon, and Sharon blamed Louis, or possibly Mia and Emmalou. It was impossible to know who was lying most.

'So this stuff in your piece,' Mohammed went on, 'about how at first you thought a beast done it . . .'

'There are still beasts out there. The beast of poverty. The beast of neglect. The beast of violence. The beast of ignorance. Whoever is found guilty at the trial, I think we all bear some measure of responsibility.'

'But you think Errol was killed in his own home?'

'It looks that way. Even so, the beast analogy can help us understand the motives behind what happened. We know animals sometimes kill the litters of their rivals, for instance. Or that they sometimes reject one of their own litter – the so-called runt. We mustn't pre-empt the trial but something of this kind may have gone on with Errol. Because Louis wouldn't accept him. Or because Sharon thought of Errol as the product of her "bad" self, not a true offspring.'

'But there's no *real* beast?' Mohammed said.

'I'm not sure. There are still cases of children going missing south of the river. And rumours of a large animal. None of us who live there feel safe.'

'All those callers on the line wanting to talk about J-Lo, I'm coming to you next,' Kwame said. 'Your point about the Palestinians please, Mohammed. Very quickly.'

Kwame gestured to Harry to take his headphones off and go. 'See you next week,' he mouthed, and shrugged – all these questions about Errol, would they never stop? But Harry didn't find it surprising. The case was still fresh in people's minds. And with the trial of Sharon and Louis not far off, the frenzy of interest had only increased.

He nodded at the producer behind the glass screen and made his own way to the lift. Whatever the outcome of the trial, the story had changed Harry's life. THE TRIAL THAT SHAMED DEPTFORD AND THE WHOLE NATION, the headline in the *Gazette* read, when the piece appeared on the anniversary of Ray's reprieve. Mills would have resisted something so lavish but Mills had taken early retirement and been replaced by his protégée, Suzie. Harry's 8,000 words, the longest article in the history of the *Gazette*, was later excerpted by the *Observer* and the *Mail*. Lawyers softened Harry's allegations of government interference in the case, much to his disgust. The colour was diluted, too, along with his claim that Ray had been randomly set up – even Deborah thought that a flourish too far. Still, the message of the article got through and reached far beyond south London. Harry knew that from the mail he received, some of it hate mail, but most of it saying *thanks* or *great piece* or *would you come and talk to our school, library, community-relations group, etc.* The calls to *Rapback* confirmed it, too, and he enjoyed fielding the questions. Radio released something in him which writing never had – opened him up, socialised him, made him more articulate. Outside the studio as well as in. He had found his niche.

The doors of the lift opened with a ting. He pressed G. 'So long as you don't let it go to your head,' Deborah had said, as the invites poured in. 'We don't want you giving up the day job.' Till last week he'd had no wish to give it up: he felt lucky in his work and lucky in his boss. But now an offer had come his way which even he, a stalwart of the *Gazette* and of south London, would be mad not to consider. He was tempted to test it out on Deborah tonight, in her own house, in a relaxed, distancing, if-someone-you-knew-was-approached kind of way. But she would soon see through that. Perhaps Nat could advise him, or Libby, both of whom would be at the party.

Downstairs, in the lobby of 103.9 FM, Kwame's voice was booming out.

'OK, that's one caller says J-Lo's butt is too big, one says it's booty-ful, and one says we're sexist pigs for talking like this. Reverend Kolu, on line four – what do you say?'

# 4

## *NAT*

'WHY DIDN'T you tell her?' Claire asked, from the dressing table.

'I couldn't, with Uncle Jack there.'

'So when will you?'

'Not tonight, obviously. But soon.'

'If it were me, I'd feel peculiar.'

'You *are* feeling peculiar.'

'You know what I mean. If I were in her shoes. It's a sensitive business.'

'She'll be fine.'

'And the girls? What do we tell them?'

'Let me deal with Libby first. She might want to be the one to tell them.'

'They keep asking me,' Claire said, '"When are you and Daddy going to . . . ?"'

'At least it proves they like you.'

'I suppose.'

She was fastening the earrings he had bought that morning, first the left ear, then the right, though in the mirror the order was reversed. He kissed both lobes, as though to glue them on – this was her third pair of clip-ons in six months. If only she'd get her ears pierced. Their inviolacy was costing him a fortune.

*Blind Date* floated from below. The attic floor was Claire and Nat's, while Hannah and Rose slept in what had been the dining room, across from the kitchen. The only reception room was the lounge (the drawing room as Nat preferred to call it), which was just big enough for all four of them to watch television together, as they usually did when the girls stayed over on Saturday night. But tonight he and Claire were going out, and the only adult present at home, scarcely an adult, would be Daniel Toft from over the road, a boy whose trustworthiness was fiercely attested to by his mother Madge (who had promised to come across should any 'problem' arise – fire, flood, pillage or nuclear fallout – and would in any case take over at midnight). To Nat it seemed the perfect arrangement, though Libby would doubtless berate him for allowing a young male into the house, or *any* male, all such persons being suspect when it came to babysitting. The girls had been sworn to secrecy. If Mummy asked them, they were to say their sitter was Madge.

The bell rang two floors below.

'That'll be Daniel,' Nat said, as the girls rushed downstairs and a set of excited 'Hiyas' rose from the front door. Perhaps sixteen *was* too young for a babysitter. Or the gap between sixteen and twelve too small.

'Ready?' Nat said, stroking her bare shoulders.

'Nearly.'

She was putting on mascara, which clogged and left black blobs in her lashes (like spiders sitting in a web), so that he had to pass her a tissue. Her lashes were long and lustrous; if you didn't know, you would think they were false. At the school quiz last week, there had been a question about that: in which year, for which film, were false eyelashes invented? Someone at the table knew the answer. Probably Claire. She was good at quizzes. Good at a lot of things, in fact. Hidden depths.

'You're not wearing that old jumper?' she said. It was less a question than a command.

'We're only going to Deborah's,' he said. 'There's no need to dress up.'

'*I'm* dressing up.'

'That's different.'

'How's it different.'

'You're a woman.'

'Bollocks.'

He shrugged, removed the jumper and put on a corduroy jacket. It too was old but the cut, so Claire said, made him look dignified, 'less of a scruff anyway'. He stood behind her, brushing fluff from the lapels. In the mirror the room seemed bigger than it really was. The en suite bathroom reeked of mildew, there were draughts from the dormer, and under the roof slope, where the bed was, you couldn't stand up without banging your head. But he felt at home here. Till Claire took him in, he had been adrift. Now he felt grounded. And whereas Libby had refused to let the girls stay over when he was with Anthea, she didn't object to them staying at Claire's.

'How cold is it?' she said. 'Should I wear a cardy or a jacket?'

Did anyone else under forty say *cardy*? he wondered. He could imagine using the word in a play – as spoken by a widow, say, in front of her beach hut, with a sea fret rolling in and a late-August chill in the dusk-pink air: 'I should have brought my cardy.' But Nat didn't write plays any more. He had enough on his plate, without plays. And soon he would have more.

'A jacket,' he said. 'The blue jacket.'

'The Chinesy one?'

'Yes.'

Chinesy: that too was quintessential Claire. Y-words were. Cosy diminutives to offset the cold rigours of the lab. Her word for their home – the maisonette – was *maisy*, an abbreviation for a place which had itself been abbreviated, split up by some previous owner (the top half of the house was theirs, the bottom half two separate flats). In time they would have to look for somewhere bigger. For Claire, with her love of smallness, that would be hard.

'Could you reach it out for me?' she said.

*Reach it out for me.* You had to live with someone – and be in love with them – before you noticed their idiom.

He slid the hangers along the rail till he found it, secreted inside her Indian sari. (China cosying up to India.) He had never seen her in the sari. He had never seen her in most of these clothes. Till a year ago, even with those he had seen her in, he hadn't seen *her*.

'You look lovely,' he said, slipping the jacket over her shoulders. He had said the same to Libby often enough. And to Anthea. But there was no sense of déjà vu. This was Claire and he was in love with her, uniquely.

Downstairs, the girls picked up the refrain: Claire looked lovely, they said, and 'you don't look too bad yourself, Dad'. Hannah and Rose were sitting on one sofa while Daniel sat shyly opposite, his eyes fixed on the set.

'Nice to meet you, Daniel,' Nat said. They had met once before, in fact, at Daniel's mother Madge's fortieth the other week, when he was serving canapés. But tonight he seemed less confident – a nervous, acned adolescent, free to babysit because he lacked a social life. When Rose offered him the bowl of Pringles, he blushed, extricated two crisps and resumed watching *Blind Date*. Nat felt sorry for him. Was he up to the job? Yet the shyness was also reassuring.

'Anything good on tonight?' Nat said, to make conversation.

'The usual,' Hannah said.

'There are tape things as well. You get to choose, Dan.'

The *Dan* was meant to put him at ease.

'They're called videos, Dad,' Hannah said.

'Or games. We've those, too.'

'I've a PlayStation,' Rose said.

'Board games, I meant.'

'Don't be sad,' Rose said.

'What's wrong with board games?' he persisted. 'What about Cluedo?'

'*Dad.*'

He'd recently retrieved a stash of board games from the old house, most given as Christmas presents and never played with, and a few dating back to *his* childhood, their assorted counters, pieces and dice lying pristine in plastic bags: Monopoly, Lotto, Misfits, Scrabble, Uno, etc. The only one the girls had enjoyed was Cluedo. 'They obviously aspire to country-house weekends,' Claire said, though Nat thought the appeal was the replica weapons. Now even Cluedo had joined the other board games on a dusty shelf.

'Just leave us,' Hannah said. 'Go to your party. We'll be fine.'

'Bed by ten at the latest,' Nat said, kissing Rose. 'And no bugging Daniel. OK, girls?'

'OK, Dad,' Rose said.

Hannah said nothing and pulled away when he tried to kiss her, as though, at twelve, exempt from both hugs and house rules. In recent weeks she had been campaigning to babysit herself – to babysit Rose, that was, and be paid £5 an hour for it. But she didn't protest when Nat brought in Daniel.

'OK, Daniel?' Nat said. 'Just say if you need anything. The girls will put themselves to bed.'

Daniel blushed again. Simply being addressed seemed to discompose him. Or perhaps it was the mention of bed, to which Hannah reacted too, rolling her eyes in exasperation: Christ, Dad, *obviously*, I don't need tucking up, stop treating me like a kid. She had little breasts these days. Not so little, either, in that T-shirt. Where had those come from? Not her mother, anyway. A father wasn't supposed to notice. But you couldn't not. Daniel must have noticed, too. Perhaps that's what was making him jittery.

As he left, Nat thought he saw the girls exchange a look – a bright, excited, innocent-malevolent sort of look, the kind seen on children's faces in Paula Rego paintings. Poor Daniel. They could twist him round their little fingers. Maybe Libby had a point about male babysitters. It was unfair to leave them with girls.

'I hope it'll be all right,' he said, closing the front door.

'He seems a nice boy,' Claire said. 'Not that I know much about boys.'

'You will. You will.'

5

*LIBBY*

'WOULD YOU like me to bring something?'

'Just yourselves.'

'I could make a dessert.'

'I've got caterers in. Food Parcels.'

'Very posh.'

'I don't have the time. None of us has. And their prices are reasonable.'

'And you're sure about me bringing Jack, Debs?'

'Of course.'

It was a pity no one Jack's age would be there. But he didn't seem old – not old like her mother had been at his age. At lunch they had eaten well, at the most expensive place he could find: an *amuse-bouche* of codfish foam with sea-urchin mousse; white-onion risotto with Parmesan; Chinese duck; fresh raspberries and double espresso. She felt stuffed – even now, hours later, after a nap, a hundred sit-ups and a hot bath, completely *stuffed*. In the wardrobe hung a row of little black dresses, and she chose the newest of them, which clung more tightly than it ought. Earrings, amber bracelet, shawl for when the temperature dropped: there was no need to dress up for Deborah's. Jack was downstairs, making inroads on the bottle of malt he had bought for the party. He seemed faintly disap-pointed to learn that he would not be needing his dinner jacket – the silver-buttoned navy blazer would do fine, she told him, and whether he put a tie on was up to him. Dear Jack. If only he drank less. A family trait, it seemed. Before his afternoon nap, she had made him tea in a silver pot he recognised from childhood. 'Weak or strong?' she asked, reflecting how strange it was that she should own this heirloom – passed down from Jack's father (and his before that?), through Ronnie, Eunice and Nat, to end with her, an ex-Raven. She ought to offer to hand it back; Claire might like it, even if Nat didn't. 'Strong,' Jack said, which she ought to have known would be the answer. Nothing tepid about Jack. For all the damage Nancy's death had done, he seemed full of vigour still. *Vigour*: a euphemism for sexual potency. But as to that, she'd no idea. What she liked about men Jack's age was that sex didn't come into it – you could be friendly without them misinterpreting, and if they listened when you talked it wasn't just to get you into bed. She wouldn't want someone like Jack working for her: past fifty, men closed down to new ideas. But she enjoyed his company. After Damian, she was on the rebound from youth.

'How you doing up there?' Jack shouted. 'Fallen asleep?'

Cheeky sod. What was the rush? He sounded just like her mother, who used to stand at the bus stop half an hour early, 'just in case'.

'We're not missing anything,' she shouted downstairs.

'The invite on your mantelpiece says eight o'clock. That was half an hour ago.'

'I'll be right with you, promise.' And fifteen minutes later she was. 'How do I look?'


6

*ANTHEA*


IT WAS night when she reached Hanin's house again. They had been held in a compound high on a hill and were released at different points, with Anthea, as ringleader, last to go. The army provided no transport, need-less to say. She had to walk the three miles into town, past glassless glasshouses and ruined olive groves and on through the curfewed dusk. Luckily Herman and Georgie had the sense to wait. And though a taxi was hard to find, because no driver would run the gauntlet of check-points, they finally found one willing to take them back to the jeep, which stood, miraculously unvandalised, where they had left it. From there the journey home was trouble-free. Herman, in the driver's seat, was almost loquacious. Now I see what they are like, he said. Georgie agreed: how outrageous to be held for eight hours, in a small hot yard, without food, water or the courtesy of an explanation. Anthea said little. In her case it had been ten hours, and she had let the other two have the only shade while she sat baking under her cap. Since she was leader, that was only right; Mr Fell, back in Woolwich, would have done the same. But now her legs ached, her neck was sore from sunburn, and the only comfort was the thought of bed.

Was the commander who interviewed her Daniel's commander, the one who called aid workers terror-tourists? 'Interview' was to dignify it: the questions had been perfunctory, and their purpose more to humiliate her than yield replies. She couldn't complain. She hadn't been beaten or tortured. She was still in one piece. In fact, her biggest worry as she sat across the table from him, under the ceiling fan, was the loss of her passport. What was your real purpose in Beit Mila? he began. Taking supplies to the innocent, she said. Not supplying arms to the guilty? Of course not, she said, my only role is to relieve the suffering of women and children. To give them – the word surprised her, it sounded so biblical, she must have picked it up from Adam or Marmalade-Sky – to give them succour. The army interrogator had two fingers missing on his left hand: a war wound, she wondered, or a boyhood accident? Give succour, he sneered. You're the sucker. Do you realise how happy you make the terrorists? You're their excuse for every new atrocity. She kept her mouth shut while he ranted. Her cellphone and passport had been taken from her when she arrived at the compound, and though the phone was sitting on the table, within reach of the commander's missing fingers, and even went off at one point, allowing him to taunt her ('Your friend calls you. One of your troublemaker friends. You don't want to talk to your friend?'), there was no sign of the passport. She could see herself being driven to the airport and put on the first plane home. It had happened to other aid workers. Once they had you down as a troublemaker, you were finished.

The commander sat browsing through a file. So what shall we do with you? he said. Instinct told her not to plead. Why do anything with me? she said. I am no threat. You entered Israel a year ago, he said, examining her papers. Thereabouts, she said. The Big Commander, the soldier guarding them had called him. Waiting for him to speak was worse than standing in the cross hairs earlier. Back then, she knew she would be safe

– even the fantasy film playing in her head, the Middle East cowboy Western, reassured her there'd be a happy ending. Now she was less sure. If the commander was to confiscate her passport . . . Suddenly she wanted to stay here very badly.

You like it in this country? he said.

Yes, I like it.

You are crazy, he said. There are too many crazies already. I should deport you.

Not crazy. Idealistic, maybe, but not crazy.

Ideals, he said, I know about ideals, but they are too dangerous.

She smiled, not to smarm or plead but in the spirit of Well, at least we understand each other. He sat back with his cigarette and looked at her. How did she seem to him? Dumb or dangerous? If the former, he'd surely let her go. But it also depended on his mood – whether he'd lost at cards last night, or his wife had been nice to him at breakfast. Despite the pleasure he took in his own jokes, his mood didn't seem good.

This place was a desert when we came here, he said. Now they want to push us into the sea.

Not the people I talk to, she said.

We are so small a country, we have to be strong.

You have all the weapons and they have none.

You're wrong, he said. They have world opinion. We have Sharon.

He stubbed his cigarette out.

Think of Samson. Samson's strength was here, he said, tapping his head. The same with us. That's all we have. Up here.

He closed the file in front of him and stood up. Go home and read about Samson, he said.

You're letting me go?

Stay away from terrorist villages, he said. Next time I won't be so kind.

The door banged shut behind him. They held her for another two hours before handing back the passport.

Though it was dark when she finally reached home, Noor and Neta came running to greet her, and Hanin, having heard her story, insisted on cooking a meal. But first you rest, Hanin added, and sent her upstairs, where she lay on the bed and savoured the look of the room again – the china birds on the wall, the tiny glass animals on the bookshelf, the vase of artificial flowers on the windowsill.

The Bible lay in the suitcase, under her bed – she had been given it at GoHelp. It took her a while to find the Samson passage, but once she did she realised she already knew it – not because of Delilah and the hair (everyone knew *that* story), but because of the foxes: 'And Samson went and caught three hundred foxes, and took firebrands, and turned tail to tail, and put a firebrand in the midst between two tails. And when he had set the brands on fire, he let them go into the standing corn of the Philistines, and burnt up both the shocks, and also the standing corn, with the vineyards and olives.' *Of course.* She had once written a story about God tying fox and vixen's tails together, and called it. 'The Birth of Sex'. She might as well have called it 'The Birth of War'.

She read on past the burning foxes, through escalating violence in Gaza and Hebron, to the thousands of deaths Samson caused when he pulled the pillars of the temple down: 'So the dead which he slew at his death were more than they which he slew in his life.' In what way was Samson meant to be clever or inspiring? Surely the commander with two fingers missing had meant something else.

She put her Bible on the bedside table and listened to her messages again, all from Adam – first angry, then worried, then desperate. Herman and Georgie would have filled him in by now. But she called him anyway.

You heard the news? he said, before she could tell him hers. They shot a man in the church at Bethlehem.

He had been shot in the churchyard, by a sniper, while hanging out clothes to dry. They had patched him up and made him comfortable, until an ambulance came, and priests in robes carried him out, but he was dying even then, everyone could see. A shit business, Adam said, but she could hear *Schadenfreude* as well: if it had been WAWWAW organising the siege, no one would have died – that was the gist.

I think you're too hung up on the siege, she said. We should be getting food into some of the villages. That's just as important.

Of course, he said, and you did well today, but . . .

I didn't have your official approval, she said, and I apologise for that.

It would have been better to take a photographer with you, that's all.

OK, we didn't make the news on CNN. So what? We got the food in.

It's media coverage that brings in donations. Why is it always some other outfit that gets the plaudits?

You're fucking obsessed with the media, Adam. It's doing my head in.

The phone went silent.

Forget what I just said, she said.

No, he said, you're right. I've been in this job too long. In fact, I'm planning to go back to the States soon, to train as a journalist.

If you can't beat them, join them, eh?

I'm serious, he said. I already drafted the resignation letter. I was going to tell you. I am telling you. In confidence. So you can think it over.

Think what over? she said.

Running the office, if they ask you. Taking over from me.

You think I'm up to it? she said.

Sure you're up to it, he said. You know the ground. Who to liaise with. And you're good with people. You understand what drives them to be martyrs.

Did she? *Martyr* was a word she hated. *Istishhad*, as they called it. The martyrs here were teenage boys in Semtex vests, who blew themselves (and others) up so as to wake in heaven, with a thousand virgins in attendance. When a man like Adam talked casually, acceptingly, of martyrs, then it was true – he'd been here too long.

I don't know if I could cope, she said.

But you'll think about it?

If you do decide to go, yes, I'll think about it.

The operation needed a shake-up. Less admin, more groundwork. Fewer teaching assistants, more human rights lawyers. Less pimping for media coverage, more replanting of olive groves. And resistance to bulldozers: that would be a priority. There was no justification for destroying people's homes. If lying down in front of bulldozers was what it took to stop them, that's what she would do.

Hanin was calling from downstairs. Supper was ready.

I should go, she said to Adam. A weird thing, though, this will amuse you. The commander who interrogated me said the Israelis were like Samson – basically weak, but with one gift up top that made them strong.

Their hair? I don't think so.

I think he meant their brains.

The superiority of the Jewish mind: yes, it's an old idea.

But why Samson? I've just read that bit of the Bible and I don't get it – what's clever about him?

I didn't know you read the Bible, Adam said, full of enthusiasm.

I don't, she said.

I guess the guy set you a riddle, Adam said.

I'm no good at riddles, she said. I like things to be simple.

Nothing's simple, Adam said.

Maybe he was talking about mental strength, she said. The power to endure.

Maybe, Adam said. If he ever detains you again, you'll have to ask him.

Downstairs Hanin served chicken and rice. The call to Adam had buoyed Anthea up and the mood in the kitchen was festive. She felt like a child again: these simple meals, and the family, had become a sanctuary. That was delicious, she said, cleaning her plate, and made Noor and Neta say it too: *dee-lish-us.* They were excited – English lessons at eleven at night! – and demanded to be taught other new words, and then new songs, to which they danced on the kitchen table. It had been a strange day but for Anthea this was the strangest part of all, watching two exhausted children pirouette on the wooden table as she sang *Green grow the rushes-o* and *I know an old lady who swallowed a fly.*

Outside, between verses, she heard a tank go by, and then an APC slowed, and there was the sound of men knocking on doors across the street. *Yahoud,* Hanin said, shooing the girls up stairs. One night, in Anthea's first week here, four soldiers had come rampaging through the house: a routine search, they said, and made the family wait in the kitchen while they ripped the place apart, leaving holes in the partition wall and broken ornaments strewn across the floor. Maybe Hanin's husband *had* been a terrorist and they thought there were arms hidden; or maybe a colleague had died and they were angry. The only room not to be violated was Anthea's: the cellphone, the minidisc player and laptop marked it out as the Western visitor's room and they left it alone. She felt bad about that and angry at her failure to protect the family. Now she was stronger. Soldiers: no problem, bring them on.

She sat in the darkened room holding hands with Hanin. Perhaps the commander changed his mind and they've come to deport me, she thought. But slowly the shouts died away and silence floated in from the street.

In bed, she lay brooding under the flight of china birds. Life here was a constant battle. But living with someone could be a battle, too. Or could incarcerate you, as had happened when she was with Nat. She could go home any time. The money Granny had left her was safe in a British bank account, and if she went back she could use it to travel or rent somewhere or set up a charity. But even if she did go back, she'd live a different life now. Be free of all ties. Have sex, if she needed sex. Even have children, if she wanted children. But never confuse sex with love – or let loving someone deflect her from her purpose.

A strange cry carried through the night, a wild dog, a desert fox, a human in prayer or pain, she couldn't tell, the warm wind brought all manner of things, few of them identifiable. The sole of her foot hurt, from where that stone or thorn had lodged in her trainer and she had failed to shake it out. But her little mission had been a success, she had proved herself in some way, and if a slight wound to mind and body was all she had to complain of at the end of a long day, the longest of her life, she should thank God or – since there was no God – the stars that had kept her safe. She might have been shot, in panic or error or cold blood. But she had survived, she was here to tell the tale, not a tale to publish in a book (that was a vanity she'd outgrown) but one to tell friends about on the phone, or post on a website, or lie here thinking about until the excitement passed, the euphoria of survival, and she slept at last, recharging herself, then waking at dawn ready for more, which was why she had come, and why she would stay, because she felt needed here, and needed to be here, which – all said and done – was as much as anyone could hope for.

<br>

## 7

## *HARRY*

<br>

THERE WAS no excuse. He had been warned that Marcia would be at the party. Her new 'partner', Tim (partner as in boyfriend), played golf each weekend with Deborah's husband Travis. Small world, Deborah said, I hope you don't mind. Of course not, he told her, there'll be somebody other than Nat and Libby I know for once. And perhaps he ought to have been pleased. But surely there were better occasions to meet Tim for the first time. He hadn't seen Marcia for several weeks, and though Stephen had broken the news to him – not the news about her having a steady boyfriend but the bigger news – he wasn't prepared for the stab of envy when he saw her. From a distance, her white-haired consort looked twenty years older, though as Harry moved closer – not too close – he saw the face was cheerful and unlined, as well it might be. A heart consultant, apparently, trained to diagnose irregular bumps. Harry's own heart felt in need of attention, because of Marcia's bump. Five months. He watched as she rested her hand on her stomach and thought: *It could have been mine.*

'More Pimm's?' He held out his glass, which was empty but for slivers of fruit. There were waitresses in school blouses and short black skirts and, behind the trestle table, an aproned chef carving ham and turkey. Harry felt full already from the finger food – chilli prawns and bacon, stoned prunes wrapped with carpaccio, boats of blue Stilton and chicory. It would be him with the big stomach if he kept eating.

*It could have been mine.* Well, kind of. At times in the past year he had felt so close to Marcia that wanting to sleep with her again seemed perfectly natural. But the risk of disruption was too great, both for themselves and for the child they *had* had together years before. As it was, their (non-sexual) togetherness seemed to do Stephen good. Or the scare with the police did. Or his three Bs at A level, good enough to earn him a place to study Law at Sheffield. Something, anyway. Stephen had made new friends and taken a gap-year job in a solicitor's office in Bromley and gone back to playing basketball. He was fine.

Meanwhile Marcia had met her heart consultant. And now look.

Harry's look must have been too blatant. Glancing up suddenly, she spotted him.

'How you doing?' he said, stepping over.

'I'm good. This is Tim. Tim, Harry.'

'Hello there.'

'Hi.'

'And these are two of our colleagues from St Mary's,' Marcia said.

Distracted by that *our* (with its affronting longevity), he didn't catch their names. They were doctors, anyway, and resumed letting each other know it. Waiting lists, fees, the withered salads in the staff canteen, the stroppiness of modern-day nurses: they were stuck in the shallows of medical gossip, and Marcia seemed happy to stay there. Harry had no good reason for disliking Tim. But the new world in Marcia's lap was reason enough

Besides which, he noticed, she was wearing an engagement ring.

He looked outside, where Nat was standing on the patio, and went to join him.


8


*NAT*


ALONG WITH the teaching post, Nat had taken up pipe-smoking. Smoking was out of favour these days and pipes were considered obnoxious – hence the appeal. With his sideburns, cord trousers, leather-elbowed jacket and bowl of tobacco, he looked like a turn-of-the-century professor – turn of the last century, not this. Modern life had nearly ruined him. The fug of pipe smoke was restoring his health.

'*There* you are,' Harry said, coming out through the French windows. Nat had been feeling pleasantly isolated (another advantage of pipe-smoking) but he was always happy to see Harry. 'How's the teaching?'

'Fine,' Nat said, 'I'm enjoying it. More than I expected.'

'Not too knackering?'

'Last term was. But this one's easier. Two more weeks and they begin exams.'

Zillah Sturgeon had called a fortnight after the memorial lecture, encouraging him to apply for a job at Belmont College: their drama lecturer was moving on and she thought Nat would be perfect for the post. He couldn't afford not to apply. And though the interview went badly, Zillah was deputy head there and (so he found out later) swung the wavering panel of governors his way. He had worried that a sixth-form college would be a step down, after SORU. But at AS and A level, he found, you could study texts in close detail. And some of the kids were genuinely talented (one Chinese girl already had an offer from Bristol). Most surprising of all, he found he liked teenagers – not from some fantasy of recovering his youth (he'd been through that with Anthea), but because they were, or could be on the right day, inquisitive, challenging and open to new ideas.

'It'll feel good to be shot of them, I bet,' Harry said.

'Well, yes. But they're nice kids. We get on.'

Though a few were cruelly satirical about his pipe, which he smoked at distant corners of the college playing field, most treated him as a lovable old fogey. His only worry was whether that would change when they found out (as they were bound to) that he and his girlfriend were going to have a baby. So far he and Claire had told no one, but after last week's amnio it was time they did. What arrangements were there at college for paternity leave? he wondered. When Hannah and Rose were born he had been present under duress and slipped off as soon as decently possible to work on his latest play. This time he intended to do things properly. It wasn't a matter of obligation but self-interest. Nothing mattered more.

'And things are OK with you?' he asked Harry.

'With my work, yes. Lots happening since the big article came out. Only . . .' Harry paused.

493

'Go on,' Nat said.

'At this precise moment, I'm reeling.'

'Why?'

'The pregnancy. It's quite a shock to be confronted by it.'

Nat felt shocked as well. If Harry had noticed Claire was pregnant, might Libby notice, too? And why *confronted*, which seemed so aggressive a word?

'I didn't think it was so obvious,' Nat said.

'You're joking. It's blatant. Don't get me wrong, I'm pleased for her, but . . .'

'But?'

'It feels odd, naturally. There's her, with a baby. And here's me, out in the cold.'

'You're still a friend, Harry. Nothing need change.'

'Don't be stupid. A baby changes everything.'

'I didn't know you felt so strongly about babies.'

'I don't, as a rule. But this one's special.'

'It's touching you feel like that,' Nat said.

'*Touching?*' Harry said, with a strange look. 'It's painful, Nat, thinking I could have been the father.'

'I don't understand,' Nat said. 'How could you have been the father?'

'When you've been close to someone, when you've slept with them, when they were once pregnant by you . . .'

'What are you saying?' Nat said, now affronted as well as confused.

'Till recently she and I were seeing a lot of each other. OK, we didn't have sex again, not like back then. But there were times I felt close enough to.'

'Why didn't you?' Nat said, with bitter sarcasm. 'Why the heroic restraint?'

Now Harry looked affronted. 'I was afraid it would wreck our friendship,' he said.

'Yours and mine?'

'Of course not. My friendship with her.'

'I can't get my head round this,' Nat said. 'She never told me about sleeping with you.'

'Why would she? Anyway, now she's having someone else's baby. He'll be a good husband to her, I'm sure, but still.'

'*He?* I deserve better than that.'

'What's it to you?' Harry said.

'I slept with her too, in case you didn't notice.'

494

'Fuck you, Nat, this isn't funny, you're pissing me off.'

'I'm the one who should be pissed off. You're telling me you slept with her when I'm her lover?'

'You're her lover?'

'Yes, Harry. *Obviously*. Since she's having my child.'

'Marcia?'

'No, not Marcia, you arsehole, Claire.'

'Claire's pregnant?'

'What the fuck else are we talking about?'

'I'm talking about Marcia. Who, as you can see if you look over by the fireplace, is unmistakably pregnant.'

'I thought you . . . Aha.'

'Aha, so . . .'

'Yes, Claire, too. We just had the amnio.'

'Oh, shit. Congratulations.'

They hugged each other then, and laughed.

'Well,' Harry said, teasing, 'I'm doubly jealous now.'

'It's due in November. A boy.'

'How's Claire feeling?'

'Sick in the morning. Excited at night.'

'God, a father again at your age.'

'I'm only forty-five, Harry.'

'Still. What does Libby think?'

'Shh. Libby doesn't know.'

'What don't I know?' Libby said, walking over with Jack.


## 9

## *JACK*


LIBBY'S FRIEND wasn't a bad chap, for a darkie. They ran into him on the patio, while taking a breather. Deborah, the hostess, was pleasant enough, but most of her guests worked in local government, God help them, and Jack's last conversation, if you could call it a conversation, had been with some social worker chap, a 'guardian' he called himself, whose guarding evidently consisted of removing children from their

495

parents, on the grounds that they, the parents, lacked 'nurturing skills', whatever those were. The poor sods had probably done no more than bawl their kids out in the supermarket until some busybody sneaked on them. At any rate, the five-minute induction into Southwark's children-at-risk intervention policy was four and three-quarter minutes too long for Jack's liking, and when Libby tugged his arm ('Come and meet my friend Harry') Jack followed with relief.

'What don't I know?' Libby said.

'You – um – Hi, Uncle Jack. Enjoying yourself?'

'Trying to. Bit above my IQ level, most of the yakking.'

'Jack, this is Harry,' Libby said.

The man had ebony skin but as they shook hands Jack noticed his shocking-pink palms. Shocking to Jack, anyway, whose acquaintance with non-whites was restricted to the waiters at Khan's, Harchope's Indian restaurant. Were *black* and *coloured* acceptable words these days? Or had they gone the way of *nig-nog* and *coon*? He remembered Grandfather speaking of *niggers*. Quite right such unpleasantness had gone. So long as immigrants pulled their weight, and fitted in, and didn't start outnumbering the English, they should be ignored and left in peace.

'You were saying,' Libby said.

'I forget now,' Nat said, uncharacteristically slow to speak. 'We were discussing Blair, I think.'

'Oh, please,' Libby said. 'Could we discussing something *interesting*? Like shopping or sex.'

The word sex seemed to embarrass Harry. It wasn't that he blushed, exactly – could black people blush? – but he swirled the fruit in his Pimm's round. Nat, too, was untypically stuck for words.

'I'll say one thing for Blair,' Jack said, breaking the silence. 'He's tough on terrorism. Striking back in Afghanistan was right, after the Twin Towers. I hope we do the same in Iraq.'

'I never knew you supported Blair,' Nat said.

'On terrorism, yes.'

'I'm amazed – my Labour-voting uncle.'

'Don't be ridiculous – I'll never vote Labour. But at least Blair has guts. Says what he thinks. Stands up for what he believes. Doesn't mind being unpopular.'

'He's certainly strong on the fox-hunting issue,' Nat said.

A low blow, Jack thought, all the lower given the business with Huish.

There was a thing or two Jack could say about his nephew's choice of friends.

'Hunting's the exception,' he said, ignoring the taunt. 'Blair's weak on that. He doesn't want to ban it. But his backbenchers are calling the shots.'

'It's pragmatism,' Harry said. 'He uses hunting to get his way on more important issues.'

'Uncle Jack's an MFH,' Nat said, still goading. 'To him hunting *is* important.'

'If I lived in the country,' Harry said, 'it might be important to me too. But Blair knows it's a minority interest. So every time he wants to do something unpopular, like joining Bush on a crusade, he buys off his backbenchers by promising to ban fox-hunting.'

'I'm a libertarian,' Nat said. 'And incidentally, I thought Rufus Huish behaved very badly, Uncle Jack. On the other hand . . .'

If Nat was going to argue for a ban on hunting, Jack would let him have it between the eyes. Luckily his girlfriend Claire appeared, which knocked him off his stride. She was rather mousy and not in the same league as Libby. Still, Libby seemed to bear Claire no grudges and the black fellow – Harry – smiled and winked at her.

'Anyway, Blair will soon be history,' Nat said. 'He made a deal with Gordon Brown, remember. He'll not be around for a third term.'

'Rubbish,' Jack said. 'No man in power ever chooses to surrender it. I can see Blair going on for another ten years. Unless fox-hunting brings him down. You shouldn't underestimate the mood in the country.'

'Country*side*,' Nat said. 'The country and the countryside are different.'

'Maybe,' Jack said, draining his whisky so as to have the last word. 'But the heart blood of England is the countryside. Lose the heart blood and you die.'

'Uncle Jack taught me about blood when I was a boy,' Nat said, turning to Claire and stroking her hair. 'By rubbing my nose in it.'

'Will you be all right for a minute, Jack?' Libby said, and slipped away before he could answer. She was looking rather peaky, he thought. Perhaps the mention of blood had upset her. Or it could be the cuisine: though the ham had been splendid, some of the canapés tasted very peculiar.

'I'd rather be dead,' Jack said, having the last word again, 'than be told I can't hunt any more.'

## *LIBBY*

THERE WAS a bathroom on the first-floor landing but she kept on climbing, past the stairgate, to the children's floor, where there was another bathroom, and no one would think to come. Till the door was bolted, and she stood by the basin, she couldn't be certain what she was feeling. But she knew she needed time alone. Catching her face in the mirror (pale, ugly, frightened, in shock), she turned the light off, to spare herself. White moonglow and yellow fluorescence seeped through the blinds. The window was large, with clear glass. The room must have been a bedroom once: the bath sat in the middle of it, like a stranded liner. She felt less shaky sitting down, and ran her hand along the bathside to meet a bridge of kiddie things – plastic ducks, water pistols, novelty containers of shampoo. She wished she were home, with a whole house to herself. But leaving the party would mean awkward explanations, to Jack as well as Deborah. This little bathroom would have to do. Best to get it over with and (the equivalent of sticking her fingers down her throat) let self-pity overwhelm her.

*Libby doesn't know.* It was true. But the moment Nat said it, she did know. Or knew when he avoided answering her question. Knew *something*, anyway, though it wasn't until Claire came up, with that hooded expression, when usually, with Libby, she was so unguarded (which was why the two of them, in such difficult circumstances, got on so surprisingly well, because they could *share* stuff), that the truth dawned, and even then it was a slow-motion dawn, an oh-so-gradual brightening, less a light flicked on than a pair of dipped headlights emerging from a tunnel. Metaphors weren't her métier, but *dipped* was right (because Nat and Claire wanted to spare her the full beam) and *pair* was right, because two different thoughts were coming at her simultaneously. To begin with, as the talk swam round Blair and fox-hunting, she had opted for the first and relatively untroubling thought, that what she hadn't known, but now did, was that Nat and Claire were going to marry, which would take some getting used to but was hardly worth the effort of concealment. Marriage she could accept. Marriage she would have accepted (setting aside her pique at having it kept from her), but then she noticed

Claire, as she stood there, holding her hand flat against her stomach, and added to that was the fact that Claire (a two-glasses-of-red-wine-a-night girl if ever there was one) was drinking orange juice, and that her face seemed fuller, and that her skin looked more flushed, and that, despite the blobs of mascara, baggy ankle-length skirt and Asiatic jacket (all rather a mess), she looked so pleased with herself. The sum of which was that Libby did know, full on, full beam, and immediately felt nauseous. Pride and stoicism made her hang in there, and even contribute to the conversation, but in the end, five minutes after knowing what she wasn't meant to know, and having just watched Nat stroke his girlfriend's hair, in a tender, soppy, co-parental way, she excused herself, headed inside and climbed the stairs to the children's bathroom, where she was now huddling in a foetal curl, with her back to the heated towel rail and her head pressed hard into her knees.

It was ridiculous. Why shouldn't they have a baby? What right had she to care? If Nat was going to have children with anyone, who better than Claire, who had restored his sense of purpose and (to be blunt about it) stopped him being a drain on Libby? Nor was a half-sibling any threat to Hannah and Rose, who would enjoy having a baby to fuss over. Since Claire, Nat had become a better father to the girls. Took more interest in them than before. And, when the baby came, would make sure they didn't feel ousted. If the logic of his new zeal for fathering was to become a father again, so be it.

And yet, and yet . . . She couldn't deny that she felt barren and sidelined. Claire had so long been a fixture of Nat's writing class that Libby tended to think of her as a kindly aunt figure, beyond childbearing, in spectacles and frumpy clothes. She had patronised Claire as 'sad' and made jokes about her being Nat's sidekick. Now the sidekick had taken centre stage and it was Libby weeping in the wings. She felt vanquished, a sensation that grew as she hunched on the cold bathroom floor while below, from the patio where she had been standing, meaningless words rose like bubbles in fizzy water (niney levin . . . terry wrist . . . alkai yeader . . . tally-ban . . . bin lardin . . . aff can cave . . . un tim down) and the world went merrily on without her. It was as though Claire had planned this all along, biding her time till Nat self-destructed, then cunningly moving in to claim him.

Somewhere she could hear a woman singing. *Voulez-vouz coucher avec moi, ce soir?* 'I must find you a new man,' Deborah had said the other week, meaning well but offending Libby, whose appetite for novelty and maleness had disappeared with Damian. She was lucky; she had her own business; she was only forty. But even work seemed more of a grind than it used to: there were always younger rivals coming through. She had begun to envy the brightness of her daughters' eyes, the unbrokenness of their skin. How long before she was shunted off, like an old engine on a rusty siding while a gleaming express screamed through? Ten more years? Five?

*When this old world starts getting me down.* The music must be coming from the living room. She ought to go down and join her friends. But who were they? Nat and Claire had deceived her. And Deborah clearly saw her as a desperate loner. As for Harry, she had noticed him winking when Claire came out to join them in the garden – winking because he knew her little secret. That wink showed where Harry's loyalties lay. He and Nat were lads together, and always would be. As the Drifters drifted upward, she felt newly sorry for herself – abandoned by her husband, betrayed by her friends, outshone by her children, vanquished by a woman she'd thought a nonentity, dropped and left behind in the race of life. Five years ago, life had been good. But then something had ghosted in to blight it, something acrid and mangy, like a fox crossing the garden at first light.

*At night the stars put on a show for free.*

The night sky south of the river was usually starless, but tonight the winking lights out there were fixed, not planes moving down to Heathrow. She moved to the window for a better look, then reached down and slid the sash up and stood with her hands on the sill, peering out. Too much Pimm's, too many tears: she felt spaced out. A downward look to the guests in the garden added to her giddiness. How odd to feel *dropped* when she was way up here. Directly below her, unaware, Deborah, Harry, Jack and others stood talking. She imagined how it would feel to drop in on them. To stamp her authority on the concrete patio. To fly down in her little black dress and reinsert herself in their existence. The window frame was large, the sill conveniently low, if she just hitched up her dress and swung one leg over, then the other leg, then . . . What was to stop her? Who would care? She rested her hands on the sill, weighing her options.

*11*

## NAT

NAT HAD vaguely noticed Libby disappearing but it was Claire who drew him aside, between the potted palms.

'Something's wrong with Libby,' she whispered.

'What?'

'When you were talking. She was off with me. I think she knows.'

'What makes you say that?'

'Female intuition. Hers, I mean. I caught her looking. Take it from me: she's worked it out.'

'I was telling Harry. She might have heard.'

'Christ, Nat.'

'I didn't see her come up. Anyway, who's to say she's not happy for us? She's probably inside, busy telling people.'

'I've looked. I can't see her anywhere.'

'So what should I do?'

'Find her. Talk to her. She must be upstairs somewhere.'

On his way to the stairs, Nat ran into Jack.

'Seen Libby?'

'Probably upstairs making love to some chap who appreciates her,' Jack said. He had a whisky in his hand, clearly not his first of the night.

'Claire thought she looked upset,' Nat said.

'Bit late in the day for you to fret about that, isn't it?'

The old fucker. A few drinks inside him and he always turned nasty. He had been the same the night of Nancy's funeral.

Nat controlled himself. 'Libby and I get along fine. And she's fine with Claire, too. She knows it's serious.'

'Not like your last one, then?'

'We'll probably get married soon. Even if we don't, we're . . .'

'What?'

'In confidence. We're going to have a baby. A son.'

'Does Libby know?'

'No. Yes. I don't know. We're worried. That's why I was looking for her.'

'Then go and find her, for God's sake. Get a move on.'

Nat headed upstairs, even more worried, a feeling which Jack, calling after him, couldn't allay.

'And, Nat. Well done, son. Congratulations.'

## 12

## *JACK*

SON, HE had called Nat, *son*. It was a term he sometimes used with employees. But Nat being family gave it a different weight. And once the word slipped out, prompting a rueful, embarrassed shrug from Nat on the stairs, Jack realised that was how he had always regarded him – as a prodigal son, needing a stern Victorian father to keep him in check (a role in which Ronnie had failed and Jack had been less than successful), but a son for all that. It couldn't be said their relationship was close. And he wouldn't have said *son* but for being a little merry from the malt. But having said it, he didn't regret it. The lad might be a prick but he was a Raven.

And now – the real revelation – the Raven line had a future after all. It was a pity the family business didn't have a future, too. Now Marcus had caught on at last and could be trusted with the daily grind, Raven & Son was just about ticking over. But the long-term prospects were poor and by the time any Raven grandson grew up the firm would have gone bust or been sold off and Jack himself have kicked the bucket. But he felt heartened by the news. A quiet toast was called for. Time to pour himself another from the bottle he had hidden in the kitchen.

Grandson, he was thinking just there. Great-nephew, in reality. Sod it – since Nat was *son* now, grandson would do.

## 13

## *HARRY*

ON HIS way to the downstairs cloakroom, he saw Marcia again. She was in the hall, saying goodnight to Deborah, while Tim jangled his car keys on the doorstep. The music drowned what she was saying, but he could imagine: *Touch of backache . . . did you get that when you were pregnant . . . ? Tim says I'm sleeping for two now, lots of rest, blah blah . . . sorry to be a party-pooper.*

He thought he could sneak past without her spotting him or without her hailing him even if she did. But there was someone in the cloakroom already and nowhere to hide.

'Harry,' she called over, 'let's meet up. Give us a ring and we'll arrange a time.'

All these *we*s and *us*es were worse than the bump.

'Sure, sounds good.'

'And Stephen asked me to ask have you booked the flights yet?'

Japan. The World Cup. Starting next month. He had tickets for the three group games, including the crunch match, the revenge game, with Argentina – a treat for Stephen after his A-level success, a treat for himself, too, to have his son with him.

'I'll do it tomorrow. Tell him not to worry.'

'Because Tim has offered to take him, if you don't have time.'

The impregnating, son-snatching bastard with the car keys.

'It's under control, right. Do you think I'd let Stephen down?' Yes, her look said, for eighteen years you did. But over the past eighteen months not once, his look said back. 'I wouldn't miss Japan for the world.'

Tim held the car door open and Marcia climbed in. Harry and Deborah watched them drive off.

## 14

## LIBBY

*THERE'S A place where I can go and tell my secrets to . . .*

A creak of floorboards and a shuffle at the door brought her back. One of Deborah's kids wanting a pee, perhaps. She backed away from the sill, pulled the bottom window down and turned the light on. 'Is that you, Ella?' she called into the corridor. 'Arthur?' Silence, apart from the Beach Boys.

She hoped her sobs hadn't been audible. Pull yourself together, she thought, and stood at the washbasin, hating what she saw in the mirror –

red eyes, black tear-streaks, electric-shock hair. The cold water was bracing. She dabbed her face with the towel then began to redeem herself, with lipstick, foundation and mascara. Forty was still young. The company needed her. The girls needed her. There was plenty of time to meet the right man. And even if she didn't meet him, she could have a baby. In her heart of hearts she knew she didn't want one. But just for now, in front of the mirror, it helped to imagine herself as a mother again, not the Libby who had given birth to Hannah and Rose and gone back to work within weeks, but her stay-at-home alter ego, earthbound, hearthbound, dabbing at the snot-smeared faces of toddlers with a spat-on Kleenex. The minute she thought of that – the mess, the noise, the colic, the spoon-feeding, the sleeplessness, the sheer boredom – she no longer envied Nat and Claire.

Her eyes in the mirror were still red. If anyone asked she would blame a contact lens. The flayed skin was harder to hide. Should she have it out with Nat? Not rage at him, which would be humiliating, but let him know, with due chastisement, that she knew? Ach, no, leave it till tomorrow. Her first duty tonight was looking after Jack.

She unbolted the door and left the landing, via the stairgate. On the floor below, outside Deborah's bedroom, stood Nat.


## 15

## NAT


'DO YOU recognise this?' he said, as she came down the stairs.

'Should I?'

'Look closely.'

A woodcut hung on the wall outside Deborah's bedroom. It showed a bearded man lapping at a pubis. The woman's mouth was an ecstatic O.

'It looks like a Wilberforce Jackson,' she said.

'It *is* a Wilberforce Jackson,' he said.

'No! How would Deborah have come across his work?'

'She didn't. Travis bought it for her for her birthday.'

'How do you know?'

'I sold it to him last year. I needed the dosh.'

'I remember now. It was over the bed. In your flat.'

'You made me take it down. And when we moved to the house, you wouldn't let me put it back up.'

'Not with the girls around, certainly not . . . I hope you got a good price for it.'

'The same as I paid for it. Two hundred pounds. I knew you wouldn't want it.'

'All the same. I'm not sure I like Deborah having it, either. "Disarmingly candid" you once called it.'

'I only said it to disarm you.'

'In the gallery. Before the meal at Luigi's. And then the private viewing back at your flat.'

'You remember then?'

'Of course I remember.'

They fell silent, not knowing where to look, not knowing whether nostalgia counted for much when the relationship it belonged to was over.

A voice oozed from below. *You've lost that lovin' feelin', and now it's gone, gone, gone, wo-oh-oh-oh-oh.* Smooch music, not dance music. It must be getting late.

'I suppose I should be congratulating you,' she said. 'I overheard you telling Harry.'

'It was an accident.'

'I should keep that to yourself.'

'Not the pregnancy, telling Harry – I was planning to tell you first.'

'Doesn't matter.'

'It hasn't upset you?' he said, noticing the red eyes.

'It feels a bit odd, that's all. Like the end of something, when a baby should be the beginning.'

'It was a shock to me, too.'

'You used to say you wanted a third,' she said, lightening the tone.

'Did I?'

'As a distraction for Hannah and Rose. So you'd be free to get on with your writing.'

'I was always obsessive about my writing. Not that it got me anywhere.'

'There's still time.'

'No, it's over with. It was a form of Asperger's. All careerism is a form of Asperger's.'

'Is that a dig at me?'

'No, women are allowed to have careers. It's a new thing for them. Men need to learn to be less workaholic. I'm a pioneer in that. I've no ambitions any more.'

'Except as a father,' she said, teasing rather than bitter. 'A responsible parent.'

'A pity I wasn't one earlier.'

'True. But there's still time to make up for it, even with Hannah and Rose.'

'So you don't mind about the baby?'

'I'll get over it.'

'Claire was worried.'

'Talk of the devil.' She noticed the figure in blue before he did. 'I just heard the news, Claire. Congratulations.'

'Are you all right?' Claire asked, sheepishly.

'*God*, why does everyone keep asking me that? I'm fine. We were just examining this remarkable artwork.'

'Oh dear,' Claire said, when she saw what it was.

'I wonder whatever happened to Wilberforce,' Libby said.

'I expect he's in LA making porn movies,' Nat said.

'Or running a strip club.'

'Or sitting slavering in one.'

'Do you think he still has a beard?'

'I doubt it,' Nat said. 'No one does these days. No one serious. You never met Wilberforce, did you?' he added, to Claire, before Libby could point out that he, Nat, had also once had a beard, or the rough draft of one, a wispy outline being all he could manage, and which finally, after a month's ungrowth, he gloomily removed, ashamed he could do no better. Libby used to tease him about it, affectionately, and he could imagine her teasing him again now, bitchily, so that Claire would understand what kind of hairless wonder had fathered her child. But it was all right. The moment passed.

'How's Uncle Jack doing?' Libby asked, moving towards the stairs.

'He's well away,' Nat said.


## 16

## JACK


HE NEVER intended to boff the chap. To boff someone you have to be angry and Jack was feeling top-notch. Some of the music was music he knew – the Beatles, the Beach Boys, the Bee Gees. And the newer stuff wasn't all bad. Though he hadn't yet dared to venture on to the dance floor, he didn't rule it out.

It was whisky that began the trouble, as it often did. He could have sworn he'd hardly touched a drop but the bottle was half empty and only he, or so he thought, had been drinking from it. Tumbler in hand, he stood watching the dancers, wondering which woman might like to smooch to 'Sitting on the Dock of the Bay': the hennaed harpy in the short red dress? the big-bummed blonde in black slacks? Deborah? The heat made him feel giddy and the floorboards trembled through his soles. He steadied himself by leaning on the door frame, till a passer-through banged his elbow ('Sorry!'), spilling his drink. He eased himself further inside, to stop the room swaying. Pissed? Jack Raven? Never. His wits were so keenly about him he could pick out the sax under the refrain, and spot at once that the bottle in the hands of the fat chap across the room was the whisky he had carefully hidden behind the microwave, not carefully enough, obviously, because the fat chap was offering large measures to his mates, and, worse, topping them up with lemonade.

*Christ.* Glenmorangie with lemonade. Sacrilege.

He wandered over, threading through the dancers.

'Could I trouble you for a splash, old chap?'

'Sure thing, buddy,' the thief said and tipped the bottle towards Jack's glass.

'Mind if I pour it?' Jack said, strenuously polite.

'Suit yourself.' With a shrug and raising of eyebrows (as though to say, *Christ, there's no pleasing some people*), the fat chap released the bottle.

The convention at parties was to share. But now the bottle was back in Jack's possession he would not be relinquishing it again.

The fat chap, indifferent, was busy talking to someone else. The incident could have been over. The incident needn't have *been* an incident. But the bottle felt clammy and contaminated. And whether from irritation, or a need to explain himself, Jack said: 'Brought this myself. Fifteen-year-old malt.'

The fat chap's neck was wider than his head.

'Good thinking,' he said, enunciating the words as though to some old codger. 'It's nice stuff.'

'But not for general consumption. I hate to see it go to waste.'

'Who's wasting it?'

'Malt should be taken neat or with a splash of water.'

'This is a party, mate, not a doctor's surgery.'

'Just putting you straight. My little war on ignorance.'

'Who you calling ignorant, you old pisshead?'

Deborah was dancing nearby and looked across inquisitively. Perhaps she had heard something, despite the music. Jack lowered his voice.

'There's a right way to do things, that's all.'

'Why don't you piss off back to the geriatric ward before *I* do something,' the fat chap said.

Jack took a step forward. He had no intention of boffing anyone at all.


## 17


## *LIBBY*


HOPE I *die before I get old.*

Harry intercepted Libby at the foot of the stairs.

'Do you have a moment?' he shouted, above the Who.

Though she wasn't especially pleased to see him, she was glad of the excuse to get away from Nat, and followed him up the patio steps on to the small, damp lawn. Long, scented candles flickered in the shadows. At the end of the garden, set in gravel, was a wooden bench.

'Are you OK?' he said, sitting down.

'Of course I'm OK. What's the matter with everyone?'

The bench was damp and splintered. The night was turning cold. And Harry had been disloyal. She didn't intend to stay long.

'I heard you were upset,' he said.

'I saw you winking at Claire,' she said. 'That did piss me off.'

'I was being friendly, that's all.'

'*Wey-hey, I see my mate's got yer in the club* – that sort of friendly.'

'I felt pleased for her. But I didn't mean to piss you off. We're in the same boat, after all.'

'Uh?'

'You're upset because of Claire. And I'm upset about Marcia.'

'Why? Surely you're pleased she's pregnant.'

'Pleased for her, maybe. For me it brings back the last time. And how crap I was . . .'

She'd heard the story of him letting Marcia down too many times. She wasn't in the mood.

'Is that all you asked me out here for,' she said, 'to listen to you moaning?'

'No. I want your advice. I've been offered a job. With a radio station. In the States.'

'Sounds great. Where in the States?'

'Baltimore.' He must have noticed her scepticism. 'I know, it's hardly New York. But it's a well-paid job. Serious, too: they want someone to cover international news for them – not many US radio networks bother. A couple of their producers heard me on *Rapback*. They just loved my accent, apparently. I'm *so, so* English.'

'Harry Creed, the new Hugh Grant.'

'It's a good moment, with Stephen going to university in the autumn. He could come over and stay during the holidays.'

'Do it, then. Take the job. I'll come and see you, too.'

'Really?'

'I nearly moved to the States last year. That's part of what pissed me off earlier. Knowing what I gave up for Nat, when I didn't need to.'

She hadn't realised till she said it how much it rankled. Plans to open a New York office had been in place even before her break-up with Damian. And for a time she found herself flying back and forth twice a month. The obvious next step was to rent a flat, find the girls a school, and put her deputy Josh in charge in London. It was Nat who held her back. He had only recently recovered from his breakdown and she worried he would go under. In reality, thanks to Claire, he was already on the road to recovery, but when Hannah and Rose demurred as well, on the grounds that they would miss their friends too much, she dropped the idea. Just as well, maybe: she'd not have wanted to be in New York on 9/11. Still, in making the decision to stay in London, it was Nat's interests she had at heart, whereas he, in making a baby, had shown no regard for hers.

'It's not too late, is it?' Harry said.

'It's a bad time. The bottom's dropped out of the ad market. I've put the idea on hold.'

'Resuscitate it. Let's both go. We could spend weekends together with the girls.'

'You'll be too busy fighting off women. All those Baltimore babes drooling over your English accent. Why would you want to see me?'

'You're an old friend, that's why.'

'Less of the old, please.'

'A *good* friend, then. Someone I *like* to see.'

She felt chilly suddenly. And unnerved by the night sounds of south London, the sirens, the yowls, the animal scufflings in the beech hedge.

'It's getting cold out here,' she said. 'Let's go in.'


## 18

## NAT


TO BRING some atmosphere to the dance floor, Travis had rigged up a moving spotlight, its beam circling at random before settling on the face of a dancer and seeming to illuminate him or her from within, then racing off to find another face, first this man exposed, then that woman, faster and faster, till they almost merged. I could use that in a play, Nat thought, and call it *Schizo Disco*. But his playwriting days were over. Lack of time was no excuse. Nor lack of content. The problem was contentment. To write you had to be unhappy. And he had never felt less unhappy in his life.

*You sure make me feel like loving you* . . .

Love? Was that what he felt for Claire? Of course. Not the first-sight desire he'd had with Libby at the Wilberforce Jackson show. Nor the manic intensity aroused by Anthea. But love all the same. He wouldn't say that his sights were lower. But passion had nearly destroyed him. Now passion, in midlife, must know its place. Which would he rather be: the scarecrow in the field, stripped bare by the north wind, arms spread in useless yearning? or the farmer in his firelit chair, the pasture full of cattle and the hay all in? No contest.

If Hannah and Rose were watching, they would be embarrassed by his style of dancing. How were they getting on with Daniel? he wondered. He used to look forward to the day when they'd be off his hands. But now that Hannah was nearly a teenager and Rose not far behind, he knew that day would never come. Their getting older hadn't reduced his anxieties for them – on the contrary, he worried more and more. Suppose Daniel were a rapist or a psychopath. He seemed so shy and well behaved. But weren't the quiet ones always the worst? Young men were at the mercy of their hormones. Not a week went by without some horror tale. Even as he and Claire were dancing, there might be mayhem back at home.

The Stones came on, demanding he dance faster. But Claire was tired and rested her head on his chest. They mustn't stay late. He had his children to think of. All three of them.

*19*

*JACK*

*JUMPING JACK Flash, it's a gas, gas, gas.*

He never intended to boff anyone. But Libby – arriving in the room with that Harry fellow – must have thought he was about to.

'I've been wanting to dance with *you* all night,' she said, interposing herself between him and the fat chap. He put the bottle down on the piano, where he could keep an eye on it. Just let the blighter try.

His movements were clumsy, from shyness, inebriation and lack of practice. Libby, smiling encouragingly, didn't seem to mind. She was acting as though nothing had happened. But during the next number, which was slower and quieter, she said: 'Bit of trouble back there?'

'Some oaf behaving oafishly. Who is he?'

'He works for Travis, I think. Was he annoying you?'

'He didn't care for my notes on etiquette.'

'Funny that. People can be so unappreciative.'

She smiled again and let him hold her.

*Birthday greetings, bottle of wine . . .*

'They're playing my song,' he said.

'You don't look sixty-four,' she said.

'I'm sixty-five next month. Is that what tonight's about, incidentally – someone's birthday?'

'Deborah likes giving parties, that's all. Though she did say something about celebrating five years of New Labour.'

'Christ. If you'd told me that, I wouldn't have come. I'm just a gate-crasher anyway.'

'Rubbish. It's lovely to have you.'

For a minute or two, he was back where he'd been in Greenwich Park, with a healthy prostate and a woman in his arms and all life's challenges still to come. Then reality broke in again, with Libby's compliment:

511

'And you're so energetic, Jack, for a man your age.'

The next song was some woman shrieking and he couldn't get the rhythm at all. He excused himself and went back to his malt.


## 20


## *HARRY*


*FINALLY IT happened to me, right in front of my eyes, and I just cannot hide it.*

Back in the living room he found Libby, dancing on her own. She seemed perfectly together – together in her aloneness – so he bobbed across from her, at a distance, nothing intrusive. As she moved, her narrow hips swinging, her stockinged feet running on the spot, her wrists twirling like a cheerleader without the pompom, he thought how lovely she was, and how he had never seen her let go like this, though – on second thoughts – the letting go was overdetermined, the fervour too deliberately frantic, as though to say: Look at me, everyone, you thought I was upset back there, but I'm OK. Well, perhaps she wasn't OK. But vulnerability could be attractive too. He remembered the time she'd cooked supper for him, after the break-up with Nat, and how she'd cried, and he had held her.

The old guy with the birthmark on his forehead was watching them dance, Nat's Uncle Jack. Country gent, as remote from Harry as anyone could get, boozy, bigoted and probably racist to boot. But earlier, in the garden, they had hit it off. And seeing him now, across the room, Harry beckoned come-and-join-us. Jack raised his hands in mock exhaustion – God-no-I'm-knackered-let-me-be. Next time Harry looked over he had gone again, doubtless to grab another drink. Harry wasn't complaining. He felt quietly possessive about Libby.

Strange how sexy cheap music can be, he thought. Or perhaps the sexiness was the heat, the sweat, the heaving bodies, the soft May night. Whatever, dancing to Motown, on a spring night, with an old friend shaking her butt in self-parody, *was* erotic.

A crackle, a change of pace, a voice like a seed husk: *Lay, lady, lay* . . . He moved in closer, so Libby could hold him and he could hold her. His mind was made up now. He would take that job. Call the guys in Baltimore tomorrow. Tell Deborah first thing Monday. Work out a mutually agreeable period of notice. He must work on Libby, too. The idea of her moving to New York was oddly exciting. Not that Libby was someone he had designs on, but – in another life, a different story, a sequel to this story – he could see them being close like this more often, her body pressed against his.


## 21

## *LIBBY*


GOD, SHE thought, pressed against him, that's an erection. A range of emotions swept over her as they swayed together. Surprise; embarrassment; embarrassment that she should be surprised, since in the heat, and crush of bodies, having an erection might well be (how would she know?) perfectly natural; shyness, at the thought of anyone else seeing or knowing; pleasure, that a man could feel desire for her; displeasure, because the man, as a friend, wasn't supposed to feel desire for her; relief, that the desire was probably non-specific, or at any rate not directed at her; annoyance, at the thought of him desiring someone else – a woman dancing close by? which? – when his groin was pushing into hers; further annoyance, with herself, for entertaining feelings of possessiveness or jealousy; general confusion; more specific confusion about what to do next – move away from him, thereby acknowledging that she had noticed, or stay up close, which might make him suppose she was gagging for it (and all that stuff men liked to suppose) when what she actually felt was surprise, embarrassment, shyness, etc.

*Why wait any longer for the one you love . . .*

She couldn't remember having danced to Bob Dylan before. Nor with Harry. Nor in such confusion of awkwardness and desire.

He was an attractive man, yet she had never had sexual feelings for him. Or never allowed herself to have them. Had he, about her? There'd been that once, after the break-up with Nat, their reconciliation dinner and a certain look he gave, longer and more intense than was called for. And then the coffee that day in Borough Market, when he seemed to want to tell her something, and might have done but for her being involved with Damian and not having the patience to listen. It was hard to tell where you were with people, even when, especially when, you were with them like this. He pressed in hard again, to the chords of a new song. This thing between them might be just a blip. Better rephrase that: this violation of a strictly platonic friendship might be just a blip. But as she swayed with him in the darkness, her head against his collarbone, she began to hope that it was not.

## 22

## *JACK*


IN THE little room down the end of the hall, Jack stood trying to pee. Zip down, cock out, he had been waiting five minutes already and, if recent history was a guide, would have to wait several minutes more. The porcelain bowl was clogged with tissue, and when he yanked the flush handle for encouragement there was only a hollow croak. Music jangling through the walls, raucous guests rattling at the door, a shit-stained toilet: even someone with a healthy prostate would struggle to perform in conditions like this. When was it people stopped having manners? When they lost the basic skills of civilisation – how to hold a knife, write a letter, navigate with a map, lay a table, drink malt whisky, use a lavatory without messing it for the next person? Maybe my generation is to blame, he thought. What we were taught as children we failed to pass on. We were too busy and didn't want the burden. So the accumulated wisdom was pissed away.

What was it the fat chap said? 'Why don't you piss off back to the geriatric ward?' Charming. He ought to call him outside and settle it like gentlemen. Old-fashioned fisticuffs. With their sleeves rolled up. There was always a first time.

It was no use. Giving up on the pee, he left the room, turned left through the back door, and gave up on the party as well. Libby's house was only three streets away and she had handed him a door key, 'just in case'. The idea was that they leave together but since she was otherwise engaged on the dance floor he might as well go ahead.

*In the absence of security I made my way into the night.*

Away from the thrumming house, the streets were quiet, just traffic-mutter and distant yobbish yells. Libby's key was actually a set of keys, a wheel of spikes, useful protection should anyone try to mug him. Turn right at the top of the street, wasn't it? In the yellow light, the place looked rougher than he remembered. But he was too old and pissed to feel scared.

Time to depart. Death didn't frighten him. He had reached the point in the flight where the plane suddenly dips and decelerates, nothing drastic, no hint of turbulence, the downward angle is almost imperceptible, but the sign has come on to fasten your seat belt, and after descending through the clouds you eventually see your destination, a bright-lit runway among flat green fields, not frightening, not unfamiliar, and for a time, it seems, in the holding pattern, not even imminent, a place you could turn away from if you chose, until the wings level, the lights dim, the wheels clunk down in readiness, the crew take their seats for landing, and the seriousness – the gravity – finally hits you, till all that's left is one last flurry and lurch.

Nancy had landed already. His turn next.

*And I miss you, like the deserts miss the rain.*

How a once-heard song could lodge in one's fuddled brain was a mystery that passed all understanding.

The road looked wrong, too steep to be running parallel to Libby's street, too narrow to house her kind of house. Should he have turned left instead of right? It wasn't far. He could double back. Or ask someone. *Ask someone?* Who? It was two in the morning and though lights simmered behind upstairs blinds no one would be daft enough to answer a ringing doorbell. Gawd, London, what a dump. He should get to bed, grab some kip, and head off back to Frixley first thing. The fish needed feeding. The dog would be whining at the kennels. Why stay a moment longer? Yet somewhere up ahead was the yelling he had heard earlier, now overlaid with noise on a higher register, falsetto and distressed, like the cry of a child or a woman or a fox.

At least the night was warm and he could see where he was going. Losing your bearings now and then was a thing that happened after a certain age. Like that time in the reed beds, the day of Nancy's stroke. Five years ago, almost exactly. The day everything changed. If only he had gone home and joined her lunch party. If only he had made her visit the GP. If only he had loved her more. You could play the *if only* game for ever. But Nancy was gone, and he was here, lost and half drunk, no denying it.

He walked on. Near the bottom of the street was a block of flats. Those cries were coming from behind them, yowlier now, more terrified. He had a choice: investigate or go home to Libby's. But which way was Libby's? Which way, come to that, was back to Deborah's? He must have come too far downhill. His heels echoed on the pavement. He was lost

515

– a big old horse from the shires clopping through the streets of south London.

The cries were sharper now, like knives. He turned towards them, left along the side of the flats, out towards the darkness. The row with the fat chap had fired him up. If he were a dog, hairs would be standing up on the back of his neck. Was that waste ground up ahead? Or had he wandered down as far as the Thames? Tall figures rose in the mist, whether trees or men or snuffed-out street lamps was impossible to tell. He closed his fingers over Libby's keys, with their wheel of spikes.

The screams might be a fox. Libby said she had them in her garden. Their earths covered half the earth.

If it was a fox, he would know what to do.

If a child or woman, he would rescue them.

If a gang, he would take his chances.

He had the keys in his hand. Better to die well than to live in fear.

The mist was fuzzing his vision, fuzzed already from tiredness and drink. If those half-glimpsed figures were men rather than trees, they were immense. That was how it was these days. The young grew tall by treading on the old. The old were their compost.

Jack would be no man's compost.

He had reached the Thames, no question. He could hear the water rush away and caught his name in it, Raven, J., the kindly roll-call of the tide. It was somewhere near here that the child had gone missing. And maybe other children.

His geography was hazy but he knew this was south of the river. He moved ahead, into the mist, towards the tall figures, towards the cries, towards the secret of a soft spring night.

## ACKNOWLEDGEMENTS

Among the books I found useful during the writing of this novel were: Joan Anim-Addo, *Longest Journey: The History of Black Lewisham* (1995); Michael Arlen, *Thirty Seconds* (1980); Terence Carroll, *Diary of a Fox-Hunting Man* (1984); Brian Cathcart, *Were You Still Up for Portillo?* (1997); Stephen Harris, *Urban Foxes* (1986); Moss Roberts (ed), *A Treasury of Chinese Literature* (1965); Josie Sandercock et al (eds), *Peace Under Fire: Israel/Palestine and the International Solidarity Movement* (2004); Roger Scruton, *On Hunting* (1998); Jane Shilling, *The Fox in the Cupboard* (2004); and Les Stocker, *The Complete Fox* (1994).

With thanks also to the staff of the London Library and Saatchi & Saatchi; my agent Pat Kavanagh; my editor Alison Samuel; and, for reading the typescript or helping in other ways, Jane Rogers, Janet Smith, Wendy Cope, Kate Bucknell, Jonathan Davies, Kristien Hemmerechts and, above all, my wife Kathy.